For the very real Kat Ogden

Who threatened, at an early age, to grow up and be
a tap dancing,
fencing,
judoka,
movie-star,
archaeologist,
and
President of the United States.

And is getting frighteningly close to the end of her list.

Never mistake the movie for the book

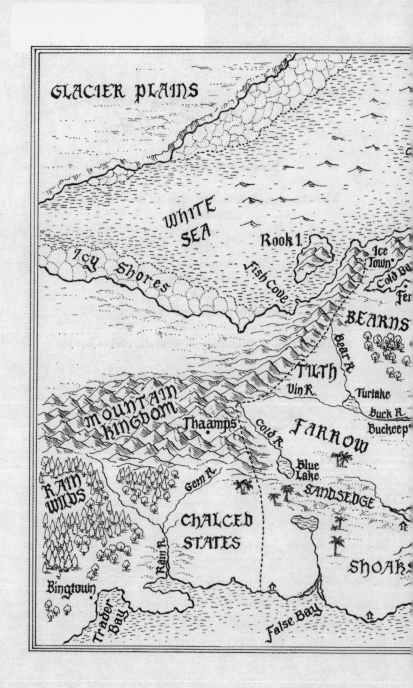

ROBIN HOBB

Book Three of The Farseer Trilogy

HARPER
Voyager

Harper*Voyager*
An imprint of HarperCollins*Publishers*
1 London Bridge Street,
London SE1 9GF

www.harpercollins.co.uk

This paperback edition 2014

7

First published in Great Britain by
HarperCollins*Publishers* 1997

A catalogue record for this book
is available from the British Library

ISBN: 978 0 00 756227 5

This novel is entirely a work of fiction.
The names, characters and incidents portrayed in it are
the work of the author's imagination. Any resemblance to
actual persons, living or dead, events or localities is
entirely coincidental.

Printed and bound by
CPI Group (UK) Ltd, Croydon, CR0 4YY

MIX
Paper from
responsible sources
FSC **FSC™ C007454**
www.fsc.org

FSC™ is a non-profit international organisation established to promote
the responsible management of the world's forests. Products carrying the
FSC label are independently certified to assure consumers that they come
from forests that are managed to meet the social, economic and
ecological needs of present and future generations,
and other controlled sources.

Find out more about HarperCollins and the environment at
www.harpercollins.co.uk/green

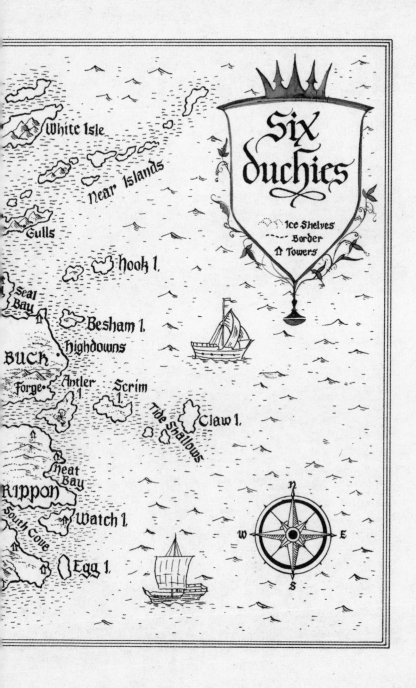

PROLOGUE

The Unremembered

I awake every morning with ink on my hands. Sometimes I am sprawled, face down, on my work table, amidst a welter of scrolls and papers. My boy, when he comes in with my tray, may dare to chide me for not taking myself off to bed the night before. But sometimes he looks at my face and ventures no word. I do not try to explain to him why I do as I do. It is not a secret one can give to a younger man; it is one he must earn and learn on his own.

A man has to have a purpose in life. I know this now, but it took me the first score years of my life to learn it. In that I scarcely think myself unique. Still, it is a lesson that, once learned, has remained with me. So, with little besides pain to occupy myself these days, I have sought out a purpose for myself. I have turned to a task that both Lady Patience and Scribe Fedwren had long ago advocated. I began these pages as an effort to write down a coherent history of the Six Duchies. But I found it difficult to keep my mind long fixed on a single topic, and so I distract myself with lesser treatises, on my theories of magic, on my observations of political structures, and my reflections on other cultures. When the discomfort is at its worst and I cannot sort my own thoughts well enough to write them down, I work on translations, or attempt to make a legible recording of older documents. I busy my hands in the hope of distracting my mind.

My writing serves me as Verity's map making once served him. The detail of the work and the concentration required is almost enough to make one forget both the longings of the addiction, and the residual pains of having once indulged it. One can become lost in such work, and forget oneself. Or one can go even deeper, and find many recollections of that self. All too often, I find I have wandered far from a history of the duchies into a history of FitzChivalry. Those recollections leave me face to face with who I once was, and who I have become.

I

When one is deeply absorbed in such a recounting, it is surprising how much detail one can recall. Not all the memories I summon up are painful. I have had more than a just share of good friends, and found them more loyal than I had any right to expect. I have known beauties and joys that tried my heart's strength as surely as the tragedies and uglinesses have. Yet I possess, perhaps, a greater share of dark memories than most men; few men have known death in a dungeon, or can recall the inside of a coffin buried beneath the snow. The mind shies away from the details of such things. It is one thing to recall that Regal killed me. It is another to focus on the details of the days and nights endured as he starved me and then had me beaten to death. When I do, there are moments that still can turn my bowels to ice, even after all these years. I can recall the eyes of the man and the sound of his fist breaking my nose. There still exists for me a place I visit in my dreams, where I fight to remain standing, trying not to let myself think of how I will make a final effort to kill Regal. I recall the blow from him that split my swollen skin and left the scar down my face that I still bear.

I have never forgiven myself the triumph I ceded to him when I took poison and died.

But more painful than the events I can recall are those that are lost to me. When Regal killed me, I died. I was never again commonly known as FitzChivalry, I never renewed bonds to the Buckkeep folk who had known me since I was a child of six. I never lived in Buckkeep Castle again, never more waited on the Lady Patience, never sat on the hearthstones at Chade's feet again. Lost to me were the rhythms of lives that had intertwined with mine. Friends died, others were wed, babes were born, children came of age, and I saw none of it. Though I no longer possess the body of a healthy young man, many still live who once called me friend. Sometimes, still, I long to rest eyes on them, to touch hands, to lay to peace the loneliness of years.

I cannot.

Those years are lost to me, and all the years of their lives to come. Lost too, is that period, no longer than a month, but seeming much longer, when I was confined to dungeon and then coffin. My king had died in my arms yet I did not see him buried. Nor was I present at the council after my death when I was found guilty of having used the Wit magic, and hence deserving of the death that had been dealt me.

Patience came to lay claim to my body. My father's wife, once so distressed to discover he had sired a bastard before they were wed, was the one who took me from that cell. Hers the hands that washed my body for burial, that straightened my limbs and wrapped me in a grave cloth. Awkward, eccentric Lady Patience, for whatever reason, cleansed my wounds and bound them as carefully as if I still lived. She alone ordered the digging of my grave and saw to the burying of my coffin. She and Lacey, her woman, mourned me, when all others, out of fear or disgust at my crime, abandoned me.

Yet she knew nothing of how Burrich and Chade, my assassin mentor, came nights later to that grave, and dug away the snow that had fallen and the frozen clumps of earth that had been tossed down on my coffin. Only those two were present as Burrich broke through the lid of the coffin and tugged out my body, and then summoned, by his own Wit magic, the wolf that had been entrusted with my soul. They wrested that soul from the wolf and sealed it back into the battered body it had fled. They raised me, to walk once more in a man's shape, to recall what it was to have a king and be bound by an oath. To this day, I do not know if I thank them for that. Perhaps, as the Fool insists, they had no choice. Perhaps there can be no thanks nor any blame, but only recognition of the forces that brought us and bound us to our inevitable fates.

ONE

Gravebirth

In the Chalced States, slaves are kept. They supply the drudge labour. They are the miners, the bellows workers, the galley rowers, the crews for the offal wagons, the field workers, and the whores. Oddly, slaves are also the nursemaids and children's tutors and cooks and scribers and skilled craftsfolk. All of Chalced's gleaming civilization, from the great libraries of Jep to the fabled fountains and baths at Sinjon's, are founded on the existence of a slave class.

The Bingtown Traders are the major source of the slave supply. At one time, most slaves were captives taken in war, and Chalced still officially claims this is true. In more recent years there have not been sufficient wars to keep up with the demand for educated slaves. The Bingtown Traders are very resourceful in finding other sources, and the rampant piracy in the Trade Islands is often mentioned in association with this. Those who are slave owners in Chalced show little curiosity about where the slaves come from, so long as they are healthy.

Slavery is a custom that has never taken root in the Six Duchies. A man convicted of a crime may be required to serve the one he has injured, but a limit of time is always placed, and he is never seen as less than a man making atonement. If a crime is too heinous to be redeemed by labour, then the criminal pays with his death. No one ever becomes a slave in the Six Duchies, nor do our laws support the idea that a household may bring slaves into the kingdom and have them remain so. For this reason, many Chalced slaves who do win free of their owners by one path or another often seek the Six Duchies as a new home.

These slaves bring with them the far-flung traditions and folklore of their own lands. One such tale I have preserved has to do with a girl who was Vecci, or what we would call Witted. She wished to leave her parents' home, to follow a man she loved and be his wife. Her *parents did not find him worthy and denied her permission. When they would not let her go, she was too dutiful a child to disobey them. But she was also too ardent a woman to live without her true love. She lay down on her bed and died of sorrow. Her parents buried her with great mourning and much self-reproach that they had not allowed her to follow her heart. But unbeknownst to them, she was Wit-bonded to a she-bear. And when the girl died, the she-bear took her spirit into her keeping, so it might not flee the world. Three nights after the girl had been buried, the she-bear dug up the grave, and restored the girl's spirit to her body. The girl's gravebirth made her a new person, no longer owing duty to her parents. So she left the shattered coffin and went seeking her one true love. The tale has a sad ending, for having been a she-bear for a time, she was never wholly human again, and her true love would not have her.*

This scrap of a tale was the basis for Burrich's decision to try to free me from Prince Regal's dungeon by poisoning me.

The room was too hot. And too small. Panting no longer cooled me. I got up from the table and went to the water barrel in the corner. I took the cover off it and drank deeply. Heart of the Pack looked up with an almost snarl. 'Use a cup, Fitz.'

Water ran from my chin. I looked up at him steadily, watching him.

'Wipe your face.' Heart of the Pack looked away from me, back to his own hands. He had grease on them and was rubbing it into some straps. I snuffed it. I licked my lips.

'I am hungry,' I told him.

'Sit down and finish your work. Then we will eat.'

I tried to remember what he wanted of me. He moved his hand toward the table and I recalled. More leather straps at my end of the table. I went back and sat in the hard chair.

'I am hungry now,' I explained to him. He looked at me again in the way that did not show his teeth but was still a snarl. Heart of the Pack could snarl with his eyes. I sighed. The grease he was using smelled very good. I swallowed. Then I looked down. Leather straps and bits of metal were on the table before me. I looked at them for a while. After a time, Heart of the Pack set down his straps and wiped his hands on a cloth. He came to stand beside me, and I had to turn to be able to see him. 'Here,' he said, touching the leather before me. 'You were mending it here.' He stood over me until I picked it up again. I bent to sniff it and he struck my shoulder. 'Don't do that!'

My lip twitched, but I did not snarl. Snarling at him made him very, very angry. For a time I held the straps. Then it seemed as if my hands remembered before my mind did. I watched my fingers work the leather. When it was done, I held it up before him and tugged it, hard, to show that it would hold even if the horse threw its head back. 'But there isn't a horse,' I remembered out loud. 'All the horses are gone.'

Brother?

I come. I rose from my chair. I went to the door.

'Come back and sit down,' Heart of the Pack said.

Nighteyes waits, I told him. Then I remembered he could not hear me. I thought he could if he would try, but he would not try. I knew that if I spoke to him that way again, he would push me. He would not let me speak to Nighteyes that way much. He would even push Nighteyes if the wolf spoke too much to me. It seemed a very strange thing. 'Nighteyes waits,' I told him with my mouth.

'I know.'

'It is a good time to hunt, now.'

'It is a better time for you to stay in. I have food here for you.'

'Nighteyes and I could find fresh meat.' My mouth ran at the thought of it. A rabbit torn open, still steaming in the winter night. That was what I wanted.

'Nighteyes will have to hunt alone this night,' Heart of the Pack told me. He went to the window and opened the shutters a little. The chill air rushed in. I could smell Nighteyes and further away, a snow cat. Nighteyes whined. 'Go away,' Heart of the Pack told him. 'Go on, now, go hunt, go feed yourself. I've not enough to feed you here.'

Nighteyes went away from the light that spilled from the window. But he did not go too far. He was waiting out there for me, but I knew he could not wait long. Like me, he was hungry now.

Heart of the Pack went to the fire that made the room too hot. There was a pot by it, and he poked it away from the fire and took the lid off. Steam came out, and with it smells. Grains and roots, and a tiny bit of meat smell, almost boiled away. But I was so hungry I snuffed after it. I started to whine, but Heart of the Pack made the eye-snarl again. So I went back to the hard chair. I sat. I waited.

He took a very long time. He took all the leather from the table and put it on a hook. Then he put the pot of grease away. Then he brought the hot pot to the table. Then he set out two bowls and two cups. He put water in the cups. He set out a knife and two spoons. From the cupboard he brought bread and a small pot of jam. He put the stew in the bowl before me, but I knew I could not touch it. I had to sit and not eat the food while he cut the bread and gave me a piece. I could hold the bread, but I could not eat it until he sat down too, with his plate and his stew and his bread.

'Pick up your spoon,' he reminded me. Then he slowly sat down in his chair right beside me. I was holding the spoon and the bread and waiting, waiting, waiting. I didn't take my eyes off him but I could not keep my mouth from moving. It made him angry. I shut my mouth again. Finally he said, 'We will eat now.'

But the waiting still had not stopped. One bite I was allowed to take. It must be chewed and swallowed before I took more, or he would cuff me. I could take only as much stew as would fit on the spoon. I picked up the cup and drank from it. He smiled at me. 'Good, Fitz. Good boy.'

I smiled back, but then I took too large a bite of the bread and he frowned at me. I tried to chew it slowly, but I was so hungry now, and the food was here, and I did not understand why he would not just let me eat it now. It took a long time to eat. He had made the stew too hot on purpose, so that I would burn my mouth if I took too big a bite. I thought about that for a bit. Then I said, 'You made the food too hot on purpose. So I will be burned if I eat too fast.'

His smile came more slowly. He nodded at me.

I still finished eating before he did. I had to sit on the chair until he had finished eating, too.

'Well, Fitz,' he said at last. 'Not too bad a day today. Hey boy?'

I looked at him.

'Say something back to me,' he told me.

'What?' I asked.

'Anything.'

'Anything.'

He frowned at me and I wanted to snarl, because I had done what he told me. After a time, he got up and got a bottle. He poured something into his cup. He held the bottle out to me. 'Do you want some?'

I pulled back from it. Even the smell of it stung in my nostrils.

'Answer,' he reminded me.

'No. No, it's bad water.'

'No. It's bad brandy. Blackberry brandy, very cheap. I used to hate it, you used to like it.'

I snorted out the smell. 'We have never liked it.'

He set the bottle and the cup down on the table. He got up and went to the window. He opened it again. 'Go hunting, I said!' I felt Nighteyes jump and then run away. Nighteyes is as afraid of Heart of the Pack as I am. Once I attacked Heart of the Pack. I had been sick for a long time, but then I was better. I wished to go out to hunt and he would not let me. He stood before the door and I sprang on him. He hit me with his fist, and then held me down. He is not bigger than I. But he is meaner, and more clever. He knows many ways to hold and most of them hurt. He held me on the floor, on my back, with my throat bared and waiting for his teeth, for a long, long time. Every time I moved, he cuffed me. Nighteyes had snarled outside the house, but not very close to the door, and he had not tried to come in. When I whined for mercy, he struck me again. 'Be quiet!' he said. When I was quiet, he told me, 'You are younger. I am older and I know more. I fight better than you do, I hunt better than you do. I am always above you. You will do everything I want you to do. You will do everything I tell you to do. Do you understand that?'

Yes, I had told him. *Yes, yes, that is pack, I understand, I understand.* But he had only struck me again and held me there, throat wide, until I told him with my mouth, 'Yes, I understand.'

9

When Heart of the Pack came back to the table, he put brandy in my cup. He set it in front of me, where I would have to smell it. I snorted.

'Try it,' he urged me. 'Just a little. You used to like it. You used to drink it in town, when you were younger and not supposed to go into taverns without me. And then you would chew mint, and think I would not know what you had done.'

I shook my head at him. 'I would not do what you told me not to do. I understood.'

He made his sound that is like choking and sneezing. 'Oh, you used to very often do what I had told you not to do. Very often.'

I shook my head again. 'I do not remember it.'

'Not yet. But you will.' He pointed at the brandy again. 'Go on. Taste it. Just a little bit. It might do you good.'

And because he had told me I must, I tasted it. It stung my mouth and nose, and I could not snort the taste away. I spilled what was left in the cup.

'Well. Wouldn't Patience be pleased,' was all he said. And then he made me get a cloth and clean what I had spilled. And clean the dishes in water and wipe them dry, too.

Sometimes I would shake and fall down. There was no reason. Heart of the Pack would try to hold me still. Sometimes the shaking made me fall asleep. When I awakened later, I ached. My chest hurt, my back hurt. Sometimes I bit my tongue. I did not like those times. They frightened Nighteyes.

And sometimes there was another with Nighteyes and me, another who thought with us. He was very small, but he was there. I did not want him there. I did not want anyone there, ever again, except Nighteyes and me. He knew that, and made himself so small that most of the time he was not there.

Later, a man came.

'A man is coming,' I told Heart of the Pack. It was dark and the fire was burning low. The good hunting time was past. Full dark was here. Soon he would make us sleep.

He did not answer me. He got up quickly and quietly and took up the big knife that was always on the table. He pointed at me to go to the corner, out of his way. He went softly to the door and waited. Outside, I heard the man stepping through the snow. Then I smelled him. 'It is the grey one,' I told him. 'Chade.'

He opened the door very quickly then, and the grey one came in. I sneezed with the scents he brought on him. Powders of dry leaves are what he always smelled like, and smokes of different kinds. He was thin and old, but Heart of the Pack always behaved as if he were pack higher. Heart of the Pack put more wood on the fire. The room got brighter, and hotter. The grey one pushed back his hood. He looked at me for a time with his light-coloured eyes, as if he were waiting. Then he spoke to Heart of the Pack.

'How is he? Any better?'

Heart of the Pack moved his shoulders. 'When he smelled you, he said your name. Hasn't had a seizure in a week. Three days ago, he mended a bit of harness for me. And did a good job, too.'

'He doesn't try to chew on the leather any more?'

'No. At least, not while I'm watching him. Besides, it's work he knows very well. It may touch something in him.' Heart of the Pack gave a short laugh. 'If nothing else, mended harness is a thing that can be sold.'

The grey one went and stood by the fire and held his hands out to it. There were spots on his hands. Heart of the Pack got out his brandy bottle. They had brandy in cups. He made me hold a cup with a little brandy in the bottom of it, but he did not make me taste it. They talked long, long, long, of things that had nothing to do with eating or sleeping or hunting. The grey one had heard something about a woman. It might be crucial, a rallying point for the Duchies. Heart of the Pack said, 'I won't talk about it in front of Fitz. I promised.' The grey one asked him if he thought I understood, and Heart of the Pack said that that didn't matter, he had given his word. I wanted to go to sleep, but they made me sit still in a chair. When the old one had to leave, Heart of the Pack said, 'It is very dangerous for you to come here. So far a walk for you. Will you be able to get back in?'

The grey one just smiled. 'I have my ways, Burrich,' he said. I smiled too, remembering that he had always been proud of his secrets.

One day, Heart of the Pack went out and left me alone. He did not tie me. He just said, 'There are some oats here. If you want to eat while I'm gone, you'll have to remember how to cook them. If you go out of the door or the window, if you even open the door or the window, I will know it. And I will beat you to death. Do you understand that?'

'I do,' I said. He seemed very angry at me, but I could not remember doing anything he had told me not to do. He opened a box and took things from it. Most were round metal. Coins. One thing I remembered. It was shiny and curved like a moon, and had smelled of blood when I first got it. I had fought another for it. I could not remember that I had wanted it, but I had fought and won it. I did not want it now. He held it up on its chain to look at it, then put it in a pouch. I did not care that he took it away.

I was very, very hungry before he came back. When he did there was a smell on him. A female's smell. Not strong, and mixed with the smells of a meadow. But it was a good smell that made me want something, something that was not food or water or hunting. I came close to him to smell it, but he did not notice that. He cooked the porridge and we ate. Then he just sat before the fire, looking very, very sad. I got up and got the brandy bottle. I brought it to him with a cup. He took them from me but he did not smile. 'Maybe tomorrow I shall teach you to fetch,' he told me. 'Maybe that's something you could master.' Then he drank all the brandy that was in the bottle, and opened another bottle after that. I sat and watched him. After he fell asleep, I took his coat that had the smell on it. I put it on the floor and lay on it, smelling it until I fell asleep.

I dreamed, but it made no sense. There had been a female who smelled like Burrich's coat, and I had not wanted her to go. She was my female, but when she left, I did not follow. That was all I could remember. Remembering it was not good, in the same way that being hungry or thirsty was not good.

*   *   *

He was making me stay in. He had made me stay in for a long, long time, when all I wanted to do was go out. But that time it was raining, very hard, so hard the snow was almost all melted. Suddenly it seemed good not to go out. 'Burrich,' I said, and he looked up very suddenly at me. I thought he was going to attack, he moved so quickly. I tried not to cower. Cowering made him angry sometimes.

'What is it, Fitz?' he asked, and his voice was kind.

'I am hungry,' I said. 'Now.'

He gave me a big piece of meat. It was cooked, but it was a big piece. I ate it too fast and he watched me, but he did not tell me not to, or cuff me. That time.

I kept scratching at my face. At my beard. Finally, I went and stood in front of Burrich. I scratched at it in front of him. 'I don't like this,' I told him. He looked surprised. But he gave me very hot water and soap, and a very sharp knife. He gave me a round glass with a man in it. I looked at it for a long time. It made me shiver. His eyes were like Burrich's, with white around them, but even darker. Not wolf eyes. His coat was dark like Burrich's, but the hair on his jaws was uneven and rough. I touched my beard, and saw fingers on the man's face. It was strange.

'Shave, but be careful,' Burrich told me.

I could almost remember how. The smell of the soap, the hot water on my face. But the sharp, sharp blade kept cutting me. Little cuts that stung. I looked at the man in the round glass afterward. Fitz, I thought. Almost like Fitz. I was bleeding. 'I'm bleeding everywhere,' I told Burrich.

He laughed at me. 'You always bleed after you shave. You always try to hurry too much.' He took the sharp, sharp blade. 'Sit still,' he told me. 'You've missed some spots.'

I sat very still and he did not cut me. It was hard to be still when he came so near to me and looked at me so closely. When he was done, he took my chin in his hand. He tipped my face up and looked at me. He looked at me hard. 'Fitz?' he said. He turned his head and smiled at me, but then the smile faded when I just looked at him. He gave me a brush.

'There is no horse to brush,' I told him.

He looked almost pleased. 'Brush this,' he told me, and roughed up my hair. He made me brush it until it would lie flat. There were sore places on my head. Burrich frowned when he saw me wince. He took the brush away and made me stand still while he looked and touched beneath my hair. 'Bastard!' he said harshly, and when I cowered, he said, 'Not you.' He shook his head slowly. He patted me on the shoulder. 'The pain will go away with time,' he told me. He showed me how to pull my hair back and tie it with leather. It was just long enough. 'That's better,' he said. 'You look like a man again.'

I woke up from a dream, twitching and yelping. I sat up and started to cry. He came to me from his bed. 'What's wrong, Fitz? Are you all right?'

'He took me from my mother!' I said. 'He took me away from her. I was much too young to be gone from her.'

'I know,' he said, 'I know. But it was a long time ago. You're here now, and safe.' He looked almost frightened.

'He smoked the den,' I told him. 'He made my mother and brothers into hides.'

His face changed and his voice was no longer kind. 'No, Fitz. That was not your mother. That was a wolf's dream. Nighteyes. It might have happened to Nighteyes. But not you.'

'Oh, yes, it did,' I told him, and I was suddenly angry. 'Oh, yes it did, and it felt just the same. Just the same.' I got up from my bed and walked around the room. I walked for a very long time, until I could stop feeling that feeling again. He sat and watched me. He drank a lot of brandy while I walked.

One day in spring I stood looking out of the window. The world smelled good, alive and new. I stretched and rolled my shoulders. I heard my bones crackle together. 'It would be a good morning to go out riding,' I said. I turned to look at Burrich. He was stirring porridge in a kettle over the fire. He came and stood beside me.

'It's still winter up in the Mountains,' he said softly. 'I wonder if Kettricken got home safely.'

'If she didn't, it wasn't Sooty's fault,' I said. Then something turned over and hurt inside me, so that for a moment I couldn't catch my breath. I tried to think of what it was, but it ran away from me. I didn't want to catch up with it, but I knew it was a thing I should hunt. It would be like hunting a bear. When I got up close to it, it would turn on me and try to hurt me. But something about it made me want to follow anyway. I took a deep breath and shuddered it out. I drew in another, with a sound that caught in my throat.

Beside me, Burrich was very still and silent. Waiting for me.

Brother, you are a wolf. Come back, come away from that, it will hurt you, Nighteyes warned me.

I leaped back from it.

Then Burrich went stamping about the room, cursing things, and letting the porridge burn. We had to eat it anyway, there was nothing else.

For a time, Burrich bothered me. 'Do you remember?' he was always saying. He wouldn't leave me alone. He would tell me names, and make me try to say who they were. Sometimes I would know, a little. 'A woman,' I told him when he said Patience. 'A woman in a room with plants.' I had tried, but he still got angry with me.

If I slept at night, I had dreams. Dreams of a trembling light, a dancing light on a stone wall. And eyes at a small window. The dreams would hold me down and keep me from breathing. If I could get enough breath to scream, I could wake up. Sometimes it took a long time to get enough breath. Burrich would wake up, too, and grab the big knife off the table. 'What is it, what is it?' he would ask me. But I could not tell him.

It was safer to sleep in the daylight, outside, smelling grass and earth. The dreams of stone walls did not come then. Instead, a woman came, to press herself sweetly against me. Her scent was the same as the meadow flowers, and her mouth tasted of honey. The pain of those dreams came when I awoke, and knew she was gone forever, taken by another. At night I sat and looked at the fire. I tried not to think of cold stone walls, nor of dark eyes weeping and a sweet mouth gone heavy with bitter words. I did not sleep. I dared not even lie down. Burrich did not make me.

Chade came back one day. He had grown his beard long and he wore a wide-brimmed hat like a pedlar, but I knew him all the same. Burrich wasn't at home when he arrived, but I let him in. I did not know why he had come. 'Do you want some brandy?' I asked, thinking perhaps that was why he had come. He looked closely at me and almost smiled.

'Fitz?' he said. He turned his head sideways to look into my face. 'So. How have you been?'

I didn't know the answer to that question, so I just looked at him. After a time, he put the kettle on. He took things out of his pack. He had brought spice tea, some cheese and smoked fish. He took out packets of herbs as well and set them out in a row on the table. Then he took out a leather pouch. Inside it was a fat yellow crystal, large enough to fill his hand. In the bottom of the pack was a large shallow bowl, glazed blue inside. He had set it on the table and filled it with clean water when Burrich returned. Burrich had gone fishing. He had a string with six small fish on it. They were creek fish, not ocean fish. They were slippery and shiny. He had already taken all the guts out.

'You leave him alone now?' Chade asked Burrich after they had greeted one another.

'I have to, to get food.'

'So you trust him now?'

Burrich looked aside from Chade. 'I've trained a lot of animals. Teaching one to do what you tell it is not the same as trusting a man.'

Burrich cooked the fish in a pan and then we ate. We had the cheese and the tea also. Then, while I was cleaning the pans and dishes, they sat down to talk.

'I want to try the herbs,' Chade said to Burrich. 'Or the water, or the crystal. Something. Anything. I begin to think that he's not really . . . in there.'

'He is,' Burrich asserted quietly. 'Give him time. I don't think the herbs are a good idea for him. Before he . . . changed, he was getting too fond of herbs. Toward the end, he was always either ill, or charged full of energy. If he was not in the depths of sorrow, he was exhausted from fighting or from being King's Man to Verity or Shrewd. Then he'd be into the elfbark instead of resting. He'd forgotten how to just rest and let his body recover. He'd never wait for it. That last night . . . you gave him carris seed, didn't you? Foxglove said she'd never seen anything like it. I think more folk might have come to his aid, if they hadn't been so frightened of him. Poor old Blade thought he had gone stark raving mad. He never forgave himself for taking him down. I wish he could know the boy hadn't actually died.'

'There was no time to pick and choose. I gave him what I had to hand. I didn't know he'd go mad on carris seed.'

'You could have refused him,' Burrich said quietly.

'It wouldn't have stopped him. He'd have gone as he was, exhausted, and been killed right there.'

I went and sat down on the hearth. Burrich was not watching me. I lay down, then rolled over on my back and stretched. It felt good. I closed my eyes and felt the warmth of the fire on my flank.

'Get up and sit on the stool, Fitz,' Burrich said.

I sighed, but I obeyed. Chade did not look at me. Burrich resumed talking.

'I'd like to keep him on an even keel. I think he just needs time, to do it on his own. He remembers. Sometimes. And then he fights it off. I don't think he wants to remember, Chade. I don't think he really wants to go back to being FitzChivalry. Maybe he liked being a wolf. Maybe he liked it so much he's never coming back.'

'He has to come back,' Chade said quietly. 'We need him.'

Burrich sat up. He'd had his feet up on the wood pile, but now he set them on the floor. He leaned toward Chade. 'You've had word?'

'Not I. But Patience has, I think. It's very frustrating, some-times, to be the rat behind the wall.'

'So what did you hear?'

'Only Patience and Lacey, talking about wool.'

'Why is that important?'

'They wanted wool to weave a very soft cloth. For a baby, or a small child. "It will be born at the end of our harvest, but that's the beginning of winter in the Mountains. So let us make it thick," Patience said. Perhaps for Kettricken's child.'

Burrich looked startled. 'Patience knows about Kettricken?'

Chade laughed. 'I don't know. Who knows what that woman knows? She has changed much of late. She gathers the Buckkeep guard into the palm of her hand, and Lord Bright does not even see it happening. I think now that we should have let her know our plan, included her from the beginning. But perhaps not.'

'It might have been easier for me if we had.' Burrich stared deep into the fire.

Chade shook his head. 'I am sorry. She had to believe you had abandoned Fitz, rejected him for his use of the Wit. If you had gone after his body, Regal might have been suspicious. We had to make Regal believe she was the only one who cared enough to bury him.'

'She hates me now. She told me I had no loyalty, nor courage.' Burrich looked at his hands and his voice tightened. 'I knew she had stopped loving me years ago. When she gave her heart to Chivalry. I could accept that. He was a man worthy of her. And I had walked away from her first. So I could live with her not loving me, because I felt she still respected me as a man. But now, she despises me. I . . .' He shook his head, then closed his eyes tightly. For a moment all was still. Then Burrich straightened himself slowly and turned to Chade. His voice was calm as he asked, 'So, you think Patience knows that Kettricken fled to the Mountains?'

'It wouldn't surprise me. There has been no official word, of course. Regal has sent messages to King Eyod, demanding to know if Kettricken fled there, but Eyod replied only that she was the Six Duchies Queen and what she did was not a Mountain concern. Regal was angered enough by that to cut off trade to the Mountains. But Patience seems to know much of what goes on outside the keep. Perhaps she knows what is happening in the Mountain Kingdom. For my part, I should dearly love to know how she intends to send the blanket to the Mountains. It's a long and weary way.'

For a long time, Burrich was silent. Then he said, 'I should have found a way to go with Kettricken and the Fool. But there were only the two horses, and only supplies enough for two. I hadn't been able to get more than that. And so they went alone.' He glared into the fire, then asked, 'I don't suppose anyone has heard anything of King-in-Waiting Verity?'

Chade shook his head slowly. 'King Verity,' he reminded Burrich softly. 'If he were here.' He looked far away. 'If he were coming back, I think he'd be here by now,' he said quietly. 'A few more soft days like this, and there will be Red Ship Raiders in every bay. I no longer believe Verity is coming back.'

'Then Regal truly is King,' Burrich said sourly. 'At least until Kettricken's child is born and comes of age. And then we can look forward to a civil war if the child tries to claim the crown. If there is still a Six Duchies left to be ruled. Verity. I wish now that he had not gone questing for the Elderlings. At least while he was alive, we had some protection from the Raiders. Now, with Verity gone and spring getting stronger, nothing stands between us and the Red Ships . . .'

Verity. I shivered with the cold. I pushed the cold away. It came back and I pushed it all away. I held it away. After a moment, I took a deep breath.

'Just the water, then?' Chade asked Burrich, and I knew they had been talking but I had not been hearing.

Burrich shrugged. 'Go ahead. What can it hurt? Did he use to scry things in water?'

'I never tried him. I always suspected he could if he tried. He has the Wit and the Skill. Why shouldn't he be able to scry as well?'

'Just because a man can do a thing does not mean he should do a thing.'

For a time, they looked at one another. Then Chade shrugged. 'Perhaps my trade does not allow me so many niceties of conscience as yours,' he suggested in a stiff voice.

After a moment, Burrich said gruffly, 'Your pardon, sir. We all served our king as our abilities dictated.'

Chade nodded to that. Then he smiled.

Chade cleared the table of everything but the dish of water and some candles. 'Come here,' he said to me softly, so I went back to the table. He sat me in his chair and put the dish in front of me. 'Look in the water,' he told me. 'Tell me what you see.'

I saw the water in the bowl. I saw the blue in the bottom of the bowl. Neither answer made him happy. He kept telling me to look again but I kept seeing the same things. He moved the candle several times, each time telling me to look again. Finally he said to Burrich, 'Well, at least he answers when you speak to him now.'

Burrich nodded, but he looked discouraged. 'Yes. Perhaps with time,' he said.

I knew they were finished with me then, and I relaxed.

Chade asked if he could stay the night with us. Burrich said of course. Then he went and fetched the brandy. He poured two cups. Chade drew my stool to the table and sat again. I sat and waited, but they began talking to one another again.

'What about me?' I asked at last.

They stopped talking and looked at me. 'What about you?' Burrich asked.

'Don't I get any brandy?'

They looked at me. Burrich asked carefully, 'Do you want some? I didn't think you liked it.'

'No, I don't like it. I never liked it.' I thought for a moment. 'But it was cheap.'

Burrich stared at me. Chade smiled a small smile, looking down at his hands. Then Burrich got another cup and poured some for me. For a time they sat watching me, but I didn't do anything. Eventually they began talking again. I took a sip of the brandy. It still stung my mouth and nose, but it made a warmth inside me. I knew I didn't want any more. Then I thought I did. I drank some more. It was just as unpleasant. Like something Patience would force on me for a cough. No. I pushed that memory aside as well. I set the cup down.

Burrich did not look at me. He went on talking to Chade. 'When you hunt a deer, you can often get much closer to it simply by pretending not to see it. They will hold position and watch you approach and not stir a hoof as long as you do not look directly at them.' He picked up the bottle and poured more brandy in my cup. I snorted at the rising scent of it. I thought I felt something stirring. A thought in my mind. I reached for my wolf.

Nighteyes?

My brother? I sleep, Changer. It is not yet a good time to hunt.

Burrich glared at me. I stopped.

I knew I did not want more brandy. But someone else thought that I did. Someone else urged me to pick up the cup, just to hold it. I swirled it in the cup. Verity used to swirl his wine in the cup and look into it. I looked into the dark cup.

Fitz.

I set the cup down. I got up and walked around the room. I wanted to go out, but Burrich never let me go out alone, and not at all at night. So I walked around the room until I came back to my chair. I sat down in it again. The cup of brandy was still there. After a time I picked it up, just to make the feeling of wanting to pick it up go away. But once I held it in my hand, he changed it. He made me think about drinking it. How warm it felt in my belly. Just drink it quick, and the taste wouldn't last long, just the warm, good feeling in my belly.

I knew what he was doing. I was beginning to get angry.

Just another small sip then. Soothingly. Whispery. *Just to help you relax, Fitz. The fire is so warm, you've had food. Burrich will protect you. Chade is right there. You needn't be on guard so much. Just another sip. One more sip.*

No.

A tiny sip, then, just getting your mouth wet.

I took another sip to make him stop making me want to. But he didn't stop, so I took another. I took a mouthful and swallowed it. It was getting harder and harder to resist. He was wearing me down. And Burrich kept putting more in my cup.

Fitz. Say, 'Verity's alive'. That's all. Say just that.

No.

Doesn't the brandy feel nice in your belly? So warm. Take a little more.

'I know what you're trying to do. You're trying to get me drunk. So I can't keep you out. I won't let you.' My face was wet.

Burrich and Chade were both looking at me. 'He was never a crying drunk before,' Burrich observed. 'At least, not around me.' They seemed to find that interesting.

Say it. Say, 'Verity's alive'. Then I'll let you go. I promise. Just say it. Just once. Even as a whisper. Say it. Say it.

I looked down at the table. Very softly, I said, 'Verity's alive.'

'Oh?' said Burrich. He was too casual. He leaned too quickly to tip more brandy into my cup. The bottle was empty. He gave to me from his own cup.

Suddenly I wanted it. I wanted it for myself. I picked it up and drank it all off. Then I stood up. 'Verity's alive,' I said. 'He's cold, but he's alive. And that's all I have to say.' I went to the door and worked the latch and went out into the night. They didn't try to stop me.

Burrich was right. All of it was there, like a song one has heard too often and cannot get out of one's mind. It ran behind all my thoughts and coloured all my dreams. It came pushing back at me and gave me no peace. Spring ventured into summer. Old memories began to overlay my new ones. My lives began stitching themselves together. There were gaps and puckers in the joining, but it was getting harder and harder to refuse to know things. Names took on meanings and faces again. Patience, Lacey, Celerity, and Sooty were no longer simple words but rang as rich as chiming bells with memories and emotions. 'Molly,' I finally said out loud to myself one day. Burrich looked up at me suddenly when I spoke that word, and nearly lost his grip on the fine plaited gut snare line he was making. I heard him catch his breath as if he would speak to me, but instead he kept silent, waiting for me to say more. I did not. Instead I closed my eyes and lowered my face into my hands and longed for oblivion.

I spent a lot of time standing at the window looking out over the meadow. There was nothing to see there. But Burrich did not stop me or make me go back to my chores as he once would have. One day, as I looked over the rich grass, I asked Burrich,

'What are we going to do when the shepherds get here? Where will we go to live then?'

'Think about it.' He had pegged a rabbit hide to the floor and was scraping it clean of flesh and fat. 'They won't be coming. There are no flocks to bring up to summer pasture. Most of the good stock went inland with Regal. He plundered Buckkeep of everything he could cart or drive off. I'm willing to bet that any sheep he left in Buckkeep turned into mutton over the winter.'

'Probably,' I agreed. And then something pressed into my mind, something more terrible than all the things I knew and did not want to remember. It was all the things I did not know, all the questions that had been left unanswered. I went out to walk on the meadow. I went past the meadow, to the edge of the stream, and then down it, to the boggy part where the cattails grew. I gathered the green cattail spikes to cook with the porridge. Once more, I knew all the names of the plants. I did not want to, but I knew which ones would kill a man, and how to prepare them. All the old knowledge was there, waiting to reclaim me whether I would or no.

When I came back in with the spikes, he was cooking the grain. I set them on the table and got a pot of water from the barrel. As I rinsed them off and picked them over, I finally asked, 'What happened? That night?'

He turned very slowly to look at me, as if I were game that might be spooked off by sudden movement. 'That night?'

'The night King Shrewd and Kettricken were to escape. Why didn't you have the scrub horses and the litter waiting?'

'Oh. That night.' He sighed out as if recalling old pain. He spoke very slowly and calmly, as if fearing to startle me. 'They were watching us, Fitz. All the time. Regal knew everything. I couldn't have smuggled an oat out of the stable that day, let alone three horses, a litter and a mule. There were Farrow guards everywhere, trying to look as if they had just come down to inspect the empty stalls. I dared not go to you to tell you. So, in the end, I waited until the feasting had begun, until Regal had crowned himself and thought he had won. Then I slipped out and went for the only two horses I could get. Sooty and Ruddy. I'd hidden them at the smith's, to make sure Regal couldn't sell them off as well. The only food I could get was what I could pilfer from the guard-room. It was the only thing I could think to do.'

'And Queen Kettricken and the Fool got away on them.' The names fell strangely off my tongue. I did not want to think of them, to recall them at all. When I had last seen the Fool, he had been weeping and accusing me of killing his king. I had insisted he flee in the King's place, to save his life. It was not the best parting memory to carry of one I had called my friend.

'Yes.' Burrich brought the pot of porridge to the table and set it there to thicken. 'Chade and the wolf guided them to me. I wanted to go with them, but I couldn't. I'd only have slowed them down. My leg . . . I knew I couldn't keep up with the horses for long, and riding double in that weather would have exhausted the horses. I had to just let them go.' A silence. Then he growled, lower than a wolf's growl, 'If ever I found out who betrayed us to Regal . . .'

'I did.'

His eyes locked on mine, a look of horror and incredulity on his face. I looked at my hands. They were starting to tremble.

'I was stupid. It was my fault. The Queen's little maid, Rosemary. Always about, always underfoot. She must have been Regal's spy. She heard me tell the Queen to be ready, that King Shrewd would be going with her. She heard me tell Kettricken to dress warmly. Regal would have to guess from that that she would be fleeing Buckkeep. He'd know she'd need horses. And perhaps she did more than spy. Perhaps she took a basket of poisoned treats to an old woman. Perhaps she greased a stair-tread she knew her Queen would soon descend.'

I forced myself to look up from the spikes, to meet Burrich's stricken gaze. 'And what Rosemary did not overhear, Justin and Serene did. They were leeched onto the King, sucking Skill-strength out of him, and privy to every thought he Skilled to Verity, or had from him. Once they knew what I was doing, serving as King's Man, they began to Skill-spy on me as well. I did not know such a thing could be done. But Galen had dis-covered how, and taught it to his students. You remember Will,

Hostler's son? The coterie member? He was the best at it. He could make you believe he wasn't even there when he was.'

I shook my head, tried to rattle from it my terrifying memories of Will. He brought back the shadows of the dungeon, the things I still refused to recall. I wondered if I had killed him. I didn't think so. I didn't think I'd got enough poison into him. I looked up to find Burrich watching me intently.

'That night, at the very last moment, the King refused to go,' I told him quietly. 'I had thought of Regal as a traitor so long, I had forgotten that Shrewd would still see him as a son. What Regal did, taking Verity's crown when he knew his brother was alive . . . King Shrewd didn't want to go on living, knowing Regal was capable of that. He asked me to be King's Man, to lend him the strength to Skill a farewell to Verity. But Serene and Justin were waiting.' I paused, new pieces of the puzzle falling into place. 'I should have known it was too easy. No guards on the King. Why? Because Regal didn't need them. Because Serene and Justin were leeched onto him. Regal was finished with his father. He had crowned himself King-in-Waiting; there was no more good to be had out of Shrewd for him. So they drained King Shrewd dry of Skill-strength. They killed him. Before he could even bid Verity farewell. Probably Regal had told them to be sure he did not Skill to Verity again. So then I killed Serene and Justin. I killed them the same way they had killed my king. Without a chance of fighting back, without a moment of mercy.'

'Easy. Easy now.' Burrich crossed swiftly to me, put his hands on my shoulders and pushed me down in a chair. 'You're shaking as if you're going into a seizure. Calm yourself.'

I could not speak.

'This is what Chade and I could not puzzle out,' Burrich told me. 'Who had betrayed our plan? We thought of everyone. Even the Fool. For a time we feared we had sent Kettricken off in the care of a traitor.'

'How could you think that? The Fool loved King Shrewd as no one else did.'

'We could think of no one else who knew all our plans,' Burrich said simply.

'It was not the Fool who was our downfall. It was I.' And that,

I think, was the moment when I came fully back to myself. I had said the most unsayable thing, faced my most unfaceable truth. I had betrayed them all. 'The Fool warned me. He said I would be the death of kings, if I did not learn to leave things alone. Chade warned me. He tried to make me promise I would set no more wheels in motion. But I would not. So my actions killed my king. If I had not been helping him to Skill, he would not have been so open to his killers. I opened him up, reaching for Verity. But those two leeches came in instead. The King's assassin. Oh, in so many, many ways, Shrewd. I am so sorry, my king. So sorry. But for me, Regal would have had no reason to kill you.'

'Fitz.' Burrich's voice was firm. 'Regal never needed a reason to kill his father. He needed only to run out of reasons to keep him alive. And you had no control over that.' A sudden frown creased his brow. 'Why did they kill him, right then? Why did they not wait until they had the Queen as well?'

I smiled at him. 'You saved her. Regal thought he had the Queen. They thought they'd stopped us when they kept you from getting horses out of the stables. Regal even bragged of it to me, when I was in my cell. That she'd had to leave with no horses. And with no warm winter things.'

Burrich grinned hard. 'She and the Fool took what had been packed for Shrewd. And they left on two of the best horses ever to come out of Buckkeep's stables. I'll wager they got to the Mountains safely, boy. Sooty and Rud are probably grazing in Mountain pastures now.'

It was too thin a comfort. That night I went out and ran with the wolf, and Burrich made no rebuke to me. But we could not run far enough, nor fast enough, and the blood we shed that night was not the blood I wished to see run, nor could the hot fresh meat fill the void inside me.

So I remembered my life and who I had been. As the days passed, Burrich and I began to speak openly, as friends again. He gave over his dominance of me, but not without mockingly expressing his regrets for that. We recalled our old ways with one another, old ways of laughing together, old ways of disagreeing. But as things steadied between us and became normal, we were both reminded, all the more sharply, of all we no longer had.

There was not enough work in a day to busy Burrich. This was a man who had had full authority over all of Buckkeep's stables and the horses, hounds and hawks that inhabited them. I watched him invent tasks to fill the hours, and knew how much he pined for the beasts he had overseen for so long. I missed the bustle and folk of court, but hungered most keenly for Molly. I invented conversations I would have had with her, gathered meadowsweet and daysedge flowers because they smelled like her, and lay down at night recalling the touch of her hand on my face. But these were not the things we spoke of. Instead, we put our pieces together to make a whole, of sorts. Burrich fished and I hunted, there were hides to scrape, shirts to wash and mend, water to haul. It was a life. He tried to speak to me, once, of how he had come to see me in the dungeon, to bring me the poison. His hands worked with small twitching motions as he spoke of how he had had to walk away, to leave me inside that cell. I could not let him go on. 'Let's go fishing,' I suddenly proposed. He took a deep breath and nodded. We went fishing and spoke no more that day.

But I had been caged, and starved, and beaten to death. From time to time, when he looked at me, I knew he saw the scars. I shaved around the seam down my cheek, and watched the hair grow in white above my brow where my scalp had been split. We never spoke about it. I refused to think about it. But no man could have come through that unchanged.

I began to dream at night. Short vivid dreams, frozen moments of fire, searing pain, hopeless fear. I awoke, cold sweat sleeking my hair, queasy with fear. Nothing remained of those dreams when I sat up in darkness, not the tiniest thread by which I could unravel them. Only the pain, the fear, the anger, the frustration. But above all, the fear. The overwhelming fear that left me shaking and gulping for air, my eyes tearing, sour bile up the back of my throat.

The first time it happened, the first time I sat bolt upright with a wordless cry, Burrich rolled from his bed and put his hand on my shoulder, to ask if I was all right. I shoved him away from me so savagely he crashed into the table and nearly overset it. Fear and anger crested into an instant of fury when I would have killed him simply because he was where I could reach him. At that moment I rejected and despised myself so completely that I desired only to destroy everything that was me, or bordered on myself. I *repelled* savagely at the entire world, almost displacing my own consciousness. *Brother, brother, brother*, Nighteyes yelped desperately within me, and Burrich staggered back with an inarticulate cry. After a moment I could swallow and mutter to Burrich, 'A nightmare, that was all. Sorry. I was still dreaming, just a nightmare.'

'I understand,' he said brusquely, and then, more thoughtfully, 'I understand.' He went back to his bed. But I knew what he understood was that he could not help me with this, and that was all.

The nightmares did not come every night, but often enough to leave me dreading my bed. Burrich pretended to sleep through them, but I was aware of him lying awake as I fought my night battles alone. I had no recollection of the dreams, only the wrenching terror they brought me. I had felt fear before. Often. Fear when I had fought Forged ones, fear when we had battled Red Ship warriors, fear when I had confronted Serene. Fear that warned, that spurred, that gave one the edge to stay alive. But the night fear was an unmanning terror, a hope that death would come and end it, because I was broken and knew I would give them anything rather than face more pain.

There is no answer to a fear like that or the shame that comes after it. I tried anger, I tried hatred. Neither tears nor brandy could drown it. It permeated me like an evil smell and coloured every remembrance I had, shading my perception of who I had been. No moment of joy, or passion, or courage that I could recall was ever quite what it had been, for my mind always traitorously added, 'yes, you had that, for a time, but after came this, and this is what you are now'. That debilitating fear was a cowering presence inside me. I knew, with a sick certainty, that if I were pressed I would become it. I was no longer FitzChivalry. I was what was left after fear had driven him from his body.

* * *

On the second day after Burrich had run out of brandy, I told him, 'I'll be fine here if you want to go into Buckkeep Town.'

'We've no money to buy more supplies, and nothing left to sell off.' He said it flatly, as if it were my fault. He was sitting by the fire. He folded his two hands together and clasped them between his knees. They had been shaking, just a little. 'We're going to have to manage on our own now. There's game in plenty to be had. If we can't feed ourselves up here, we deserve to starve.'

'Are you going to be all right?' I asked flatly.

He looked at me through narrowed eyes. 'Meaning what?' he asked.

'Meaning there's no more brandy,' I said as bluntly.

'And you think I can't get by without it?' His temper was rising already. It had become increasingly short since the brandy ran out.

I gave a very small shrug. 'I was asking. That's all.' I sat very still, not looking at him, hoping he wouldn't explode.

After a pause, he said, very quietly, 'Well, I suppose that's something we'll both have to find out.'

I let a long time pass. Finally I asked, 'What are we going to do?'

He looked at me with annoyance. 'I told you. Hunt to feed ourselves. That's something you should be able to grasp.'

I looked away from him, gave a bobbing nod. 'I understood. I mean . . . past that. Past tomorrow.'

'Well. We'll hunt for our meat. We can get by for a bit that way. But sooner or later, we'll want what we can't get nor make for ourselves. Some Chade will get for us, if he can. Buckkeep is as picked over as bare bones now. I'll have to go to Buckkeep Town, for a while, and hire out if I can. But for now . . .'

'No,' I said quietly. 'I meant . . . we can't always hide up here, Burrich. What comes after that?'

It was his turn to be quiet a while. 'I suppose I hadn't given it much thought. At first it was just a place to take you while you recovered. Then, for a time, it seemed as if you'd never . . .'

'But I'm here, now.' I hesitated. 'Patience,' I began.

'Believes you dead,' Burrich cut in, perhaps more harshly than he'd intended. 'Chade and I are the only ones who know different.

Before we pulled you from that coffin, we weren't sure. Had the dose been too strong, would you be really dead from it, or frozen from your days in the earth? I'd seen what they'd done to you.' He stopped, and for a moment stared at me. He looked haunted. He gave his head a tiny shake. 'I didn't think you could live through that, let alone the poison. So we offered no hope to anyone. And then, when we had you out . . .' He shook his head, more violently. 'At first, you were so battered. What they'd done to you – there was just so much damage . . . I don't know what possessed Patience to clean and bind a dead man's wounds, but if she hadn't . . . Then later . . . it was not you. After those first few weeks, I was sickened at what we had done. Put a wolf's soul in a man's body, it seemed to me.'

He looked at me again, his face going incredulous at the memory. 'You went for my throat. The first day you could stand on your own, you wanted to run away. I wouldn't let you and you went for my throat. I could not show Patience that snarling, snapping creature, let alone . . .'

'Do you think Molly . . . ?' I began.

Burrich looked away from me. 'Probably she heard you died.' After a time, he added, uncomfortably, 'Someone had burned a candle on your grave. The snow had been pushed away, and the wax stump was there still when I came to dig you up.'

'Like a dog after a bone.'

'I was fearful you would not understand it.'

'I did not. I just took Nighteyes' word for it.'

It was as much as I could handle, just then. I tried to let the conversation die. But Burrich was relentless. 'If you went back to Buckkeep, or Buckkeep Town, they would kill you. They'd hang you over water and burn your body. Or dismember it. But folk would be sure you stayed dead this time.'

'Did they hate me so?'

'Hate you? No. They liked you well enough, those that knew you. But if you came back, a man who had died and been buried, again walking among them, they'd fear you. It's not a thing you could explain away as a trick. The Wit is not a magic that is well thought of. When a man is accused of it and then dies and is buried, well, in order for them to remember you fondly, you'd have to stay dead. If they saw you walking about, they'd take it as proof that Regal was right; that you were practising Beast magic, and used it to kill the King. They'd have to kill you again. More thoroughly the second time.' Burrich stood suddenly, and paced the room twice. 'Damn me, but I could use a drink,' he said.

'Me, too,' I said quietly.

Ten days later, Chade came up the path. The old assassin walked slowly, with a staff, and he carried his pack up high on his shoulders. The day was warm, and he had thrown back the hood of his cloak. His long grey hair blew in the wind and he had let his beard grow to cover more of his face. At first glance, he looked to be an itinerant tinker. A scarred old man, perhaps, but no longer the Pocked Man. Wind and sun had weathered his face. Burrich had gone fishing, a thing he preferred to do alone. Night-eyes had come to sun himself on our doorstep in Burrich's absence, but had melted back into the woods behind the hut at the first waft of Chade's scent on the air. I stood alone.

For a time I watched him come. The winter had aged him, in the lines of his face and the grey of his hair. But he walked more strongly than I remembered, as if privation had toughened him. At last I went to meet him, feeling strangely shy and embarrassed. When he looked up and saw me, he halted and stood in the trail. I continued toward him. 'Boy?' he asked cautiously when I was near. I managed a nod and a smile. The answering smile that broke forth on his face humbled me. He dropped his staff to hug me, and then pressed his cheek to mine as if I were a child. 'Oh, Fitz, Fitz, my boy,' he said in a voice full of relief. 'I thought we had lost you. I thought we'd done something worse than let you die.' His old arms were tight and strong about me.

I was kind to the old man. I did not tell him that they had.

TWO

The Parting

After crowning himself King of the Six Duchies, Prince Regal Farseer essentially abandoned the Coastal Duchies to their own devices. He had stripped Buckkeep itself and a good part of Buck Duchy of as much coin as he could wring from it. From Buckkeep, horses and stock had been sold off, with the very best taken inland to Regal's new residence at Tradeford. The furnishings and library of the traditional royal seat had been plundered as well, some to feather the new nest, some divvied out to his Inland dukes and nobles as favours or sold outright to them. Grain warehouses, winecellars, the armouries, all had been plundered and the loot carried off inland.

His announced plan had been to move the ailing King Shrewd, and the widowed and pregnant Queen-in-Waiting Kettricken inland to Tradeford, that they might be safer from the Red Ship raids that plagued the Coastal Duchies. This, too, was the excuse for the looting of furnishings and valuables from Buckkeep. But with the death of Shrewd and the disappearance of Kettricken, even this flimsy reason vanished. Nonetheless he left Buckkeep as soon after his coronation as he could. The tale has been told that when his Council of Nobles questioned his decision, he told them that the Coastal Duchies represented only war and expense to him, that they had always been a leech upon the resources of the Inland Duchies and he wished the Outislanders the joy of taking such a rocky and cheerless place. Regal was later to deny having ever uttered such words.

When Kettricken vanished, King Regal was left in a position for which there was no historical precedent. The child Kettricken carried had obviously been next in line for the crown. But both Queen and unborn child had vanished, under very suspicious circumstances. Not all were certain that Regal himself had not engineered it. Even if the Queen had remained at Buckkeep, the child could not assume even the title of King-in-Waiting for at least seventeen years. Regal became very anxious to assume the title of King as swiftly as possible, but by law he needed the recognition of all Six Duchies to claim it. He bought the crown with a number of concessions to his Coastal Dukes. The major one was Regal's promise that Buckkeep would remain manned and ready to defend the coast.

The command of the ancient keep was foisted off on his eldest nephew, heir to the title Duke of Farrow. Lord Bright, at twenty-five, had grown restless waiting for his father to pass power to him. He was more than willing to assume authority over Buckkeep and Buck, but had little experience to draw on. Regal took himself inland to Tradeford Castle on the Vin River in Farrow, while young Lord Bright remained at Buckkeep with a picked guard of Farrow men. It is not reported that Regal left him any funds to operate from, so the young man endeavoured to wring what he needed from the merchants of Buckkeep Town, and the already embattled farmers and shepherds of surrounding Buck Duchy. While there is no indication that he felt any malice toward the folk of Buck or the other Coastal Duchies, neither did he have any loyalty toward them.

Also in residence at Buckkeep at this time were a handful of minor Buck nobility. Most landholders of Buck were at their own lesser keeps, doing what little they could to protect their local folk. The most notable to remain at Buckkeep was Lady Patience, she who had been Queen-in-Waiting until her husband Prince Chivalry abdicated the throne to his younger brother Verity. Manning Buckkeep were the Buck soldiers, as well as Queen Kettricken's personal guard, and the few men who remained of King Shrewd's guard. Morale was poor among the soldiers, for wages were intermittent and the rations poor. Lord Bright had brought his own personal guard with him to Buckkeep, and obviously preferred them to the Buck men. The situation was further complicated by a muddled chain of command. Ostensibly the Buck troops were to report to Captain Keffel of the Farrow men, the commander of Lord Bright's guard. In reality, Foxglove of the Queen's Guard, Kerf of the Buckkeep Guard, and old Red of King Shrewd's guard banded together and kept their own counsels. If they reported regularly to anyone, it was Lady Patience. In time the Buck soldiers came to speak of her as the Lady of Buckkeep.

Even after his coronation, Regal remained jealous of his title. He sent messengers far and wide, seeking word of where Queen Kettricken and the unborn heir might be. His suspicions that she might have sought shelter with her father, King Eyod of the Mountain Kingdom, led him to demand her return of him. When Eyod replied that the whereabouts of the Queen of the Six Duchies was no concern for the Mountain folk, Regal angrily severed ties with the Mountain Kingdom, cutting off trade and attempting to block even common travellers from crossing the boundaries. At the same time, rumours that almost certainly began at Regal's behest began to circulate that the child Kettricken carried was not of Verity's getting and hence had no legitimate claim to the Six Duchies throne.

It was a bitter time for the small folk of Buck. Abandoned by their king and defended only by a small force of poorly-provisioned soldiers, the common folk were left rudderless on a stormy sea. What the Raiders did not steal or destroy, Lord Bright's men seized for taxes. The roads became plagued with robbers, for when an honest man cannot make a living, folk will do what they must. Small crofters gave up any hope of making a living and fled the coast, to become beggars, thieves and whores in the inland cities. Trade died, for ships sent out seldom came back at all.

Chade and I sat on the bench in front of the hut and talked. We did not speak of portentous things, nor the significant events of the past. We did not discuss my return from the grave or the current political situation. Instead, he spoke of our small shared things as if I had been gone on a long journey. Slink the weasel was getting old; the past winter had stiffened him, and even the coming of spring had not enlivened him. Chade feared he would not last another year. Chade had finally managed to dry pennant plant leaves without them mildewing, but had found the dried herb to have little potency. We both missed Cook Sara's pastries. Chade asked if there was anything from my room that I wanted. Regal had had it searched, and had left it in disarray, but he did not think much had been taken, nor would be missed if I chose to have it now. I asked him if he recalled the tapestry of King Wisdom treating with the Elderlings. He replied that he did, but that it was far too bulky for him to drag up here. I gave him such a stricken look that he immediately relented and said he supposed he could find a way.

I grinned. 'It was a joke, Chade. That thing has never done anything save give me nightmares when I was small. No. There's nothing in my room that's important to me now.'

Chade looked at me, almost sadly. 'You leave behind a life, with what, the clothes on your back and an earring? And you say there's nothing there you'd wish brought to you. Does that not strike you as strange?'

I sat thinking for a moment. The sword Verity had given me. The silver ring King Eyod had given me, that had been Rurisk's. A pin from Lady Grace. Patience's sea-pipes had been in my room – I hoped she had got them back. My paints and papers. A little box I had carved to hold my poisons. Between Molly and me there had never been any tokens. She would never allow me to give her any gifts, and I had never thought to steal a ribbon from her hair. If I had . . .

'No. A clean break is best, perhaps. Though you've forgotten one item.' I turned the collar of my rough shirt to show him the tiny ruby nestled in silver. 'The stickpin Shrewd gave me, to mark me as his. I still have that.' Patience had used it to secure the gravecloth that had wrapped me. I set aside that thought.

'I'm still surprised that Regal's guard didn't rob your body. I suppose the Wit has such an evil reputation they feared you dead as well as alive.'

I reached to finger the bridge of my nose where it had been broken. 'They did not seem to fear me much at all, that I could tell.'

Chade smiled crookedly at me. 'The nose bothers you, does it? I think it gives your face more character.'

I squinted at him in the sunlight. 'Really?'

'No. But it's the polite thing to say. It's not so bad, really. It almost looks as if someone tried to set it.'

I shuddered at the jagged tip of a memory. 'I don't want to think about it,' I told him honestly.

Pain for me clouded his face suddenly. I looked away from it, unable to bear his pity. The recollections of the beatings I had endured were more bearable if I could pretend that no one else had known of them. I felt shamed at what Regal had done to me. I leaned my head back against the sun-soaked wood of the cabin wall and took a long breath. 'So. What is happening down there where people are still alive?'

Chade cleared his throat, accepting the change in topic. 'Well. How much do you know?'

'Not much. That Kettricken and the Fool got away. That Patience may have heard Kettricken got safely to the Mountains. That Regal is angry with King Eyod of the Mountains and has cut his trade routes. That Verity is still alive, but no one has heard from him.'

'Whoa! Whoa!' Chade sat up very straight. 'The rumour about Kettricken . . . you remember that from the night Burrich and I discussed it.'

I looked aside from him. 'In the way that you might remember a dream you once had. In underwater colours, and the events out of order. Only that I heard you say something about it.'

'And that about Verity?' The sudden tension in him put a chill of dread down my spine.

'He Skilled to me that night,' I said quietly. 'I told you then that he was alive.'

'DAMN!' Chade leaped to his feet and hopped about in rage. It was a performance I had never witnessed before and I stared at him, caught between amazement and fear. 'Burrich and I gave your words no credence! Oh, we were pleased to hear you utter them, and when you ran off, he said, "Let the boy go, that's as much as he can do tonight, he remembers his prince". That's all we thought it was. Damn and damn!' He halted suddenly and pointed a finger at me. 'Report. Tell me everything.'

I fumbled after what I recalled. It was as difficult to sort it out as if I had seen it through the wolf's eyes. 'He was cold. But alive. Either tired or hurt. Slowed, somehow. He was trying to get through and I was pushing him away so he kept suggesting I drink. To get my walls down, I suppose . . .'

'Where was he?'

'I don't know. Snow. A forest.' I groped after ghostly memories. 'I don't think he knew where he was.'

Chade's green eyes bored into me. 'Can you reach him at all, feel him at all? Can you tell me he still lives?'

I shook my head. My heart was starting to pound in my chest.

'Can you Skill to him now?'

I shook my head. Tension tightened my belly.

Chade's frustration grew with every shake of my head. 'Damn it, Fitz, you must!'

'I don't want to!' I cried out suddenly. I was on my feet.

Run away! Run away fast!

I did. It was suddenly that simple. I fled Chade and the hut as if all the devils of the Outislander hell-islands were after me. Chade called after me but I refused to hear his words. I ran, and as soon as I was in the shelter of the trees, Nighteyes was beside me.

Not that way, Heart of the Pack is that way, he warned me. So we bolted uphill, away from the creek, up to a big tangle of brambles that overhung a bank where Nighteyes sheltered on stormy nights. *What was it? What was the danger?* Nighteyes demanded.

He wanted me to go back, I admitted after a time. I tried to frame it in a way that Nighteyes would understand. *He wanted me to . . . be not a wolf any more.*

A sudden chill went up my back. In explaining to Nighteyes, I had brought myself face to face with the truth. The choice was simple. Be a wolf, with no past, no future, only today. Or a man, twisted by his past, whose heart pumped fear with his blood. I could walk on two legs, and know shame and cowering as a way of life. Or run on four, and forget until even Molly was just a pleasant scent I recalled. I sat still beneath the brambles, my hand resting lightly on Nighteyes' back, my eyes staring into a place only I could see. Slowly the light changed and evening deepened to dusk. My decision grew as slowly and inevitably as the creeping dark. My heart cried out against it, but the alternatives were unbearable. I steeled my will to it.

It was dark when I went back. I crept home with my tail between my legs. It was strange to come back to the cabin as a wolf again, to smell the rising wood smoke as a man's thing, and to blink at the fire's glow through the shutters. Reluctantly I peeled my mind free of Nighteyes'.

Would you not rather hunt with me?

I would much rather hunt with you. But I cannot this night.

Why?

I shook my head. The edge of decision was so thin and new, I dared not test it by speaking. I stopped at the edge of the woods to brush the leaves and dirt from my clothes and to smooth back my hair and retie it in a tail. I hoped my face was not dirty. I squared my shoulders and forced myself to walk back to the cabin, to open the door and enter and look at them. I felt horribly vulnerable. They'd been sharing information about me. Between the two of them they knew almost all of my secrets. My tattered dignity now dangled in shreds. How could I stand before them and expect to be treated as a man? Yet I could not fault them for it. They had been trying to save me. From myself, it was true, but save me all the same. Not their fault that what they had saved was scarcely worth having.

They were at table when I entered. If I had run off like this a few weeks ago, Burrich would have leapt up, to shake me and cuff me when I returned. I knew we were past that sort of thing now but the memory gave me a wariness I could not completely disguise. However, his face showed only relief, while Chade looked at me with shame and concern.

'I did not mean to press you that hard,' he said earnestly, before I could speak.

'You didn't,' I said quietly. 'You but put your finger on the spot where I had been pressing myself the most. Sometimes a man doesn't know how badly he's hurt until someone else probes the wound.'

I drew up my chair. After weeks of simple food to see cheese and honey and elderberry wine all set out on the table at once was almost shocking. There was a loaf of bread as well to supplement the trout Burrich had caught. For a time we just ate, without talk other than table requests. It seemed to ease the strangeness. But the moment the meal was finished and cleared away, the tension came back.

'I understand your question now,' Burrich said abruptly. Chade and I both looked at him in surprise. 'A few days ago, when you asked what we would do next. Understand that I had given Verity up as lost. Kettricken carried his heir, but she was safe now in the Mountains. There was no more I could do for her. If I intervened in any way, I might betray her to others. Best to let her stay hidden, safe with her father's people. By the time her child came to an age to reach for his throne . . . well, if I was not in my grave by then, I supposed I would do what I could. For now, I saw my service to my king as a thing of the past. So when you asked me I saw only the need to take care of ourselves.'

'And now?' I asked quietly.

'If Verity lives still, then a pretender has claimed his throne. I am sworn to come to my king's aid. As is Chade. As are you.' They were both looking at me very hard.

Run away again.

I can't.

Burrich flinched as if I had poked him with a pin. I wondered, if I moved for the door, would he fling himself upon me to stop me? But he did not speak or move, just waited.

'Not I. That Fitz died,' I said bluntly.

Burrich looked as if I had struck him. But Chade asked quietly, 'Then why does he still wear King Shrewd's pin?'

I reached up and drew it out of my collar. Here, I had intended to say, here, you take it and all that goes with it. I'm done with it. I haven't the spine for it. Instead I sat and looked at it.

'Elderberry wine?' Chade offered, but not to me.

'It's cool tonight. I'll make tea,' Burrich countered.

Chade nodded. Still I sat, holding the red-and-silver pin in my hand. I remembered my king's hands as he'd pushed the pin through the folds of a boy's shirt. 'There,' he had said. 'Now you are mine.' But he was dead now. Did that free me from my promise? And the last thing he had said to me? 'What have I made of you?' I pushed that question aside once more. More important, what was I now? Was I now what Regal had made of me? Or could I escape that?

'Regal told me,' I said consideringly, 'that I had but to scratch myself to find Nameless the dog-boy.' I looked up and forced myself to meet Burrich's eyes. 'It might be nice to be him.'

'Would it?' Burrich asked. 'There was a time when you did not think so. Who are you, Fitz, if you are not the King's Man? What are you? Where would you go?'

Where would I go, were I free? To Molly, cried my heart. I shook my head, thrusting aside the idea before it could sear me. No. Even before I had lost my life, I had lost her. I considered my empty, bitter freedom. There was only one place I could go, really. I set my will, looked up, and met Burrich's eyes with a firm gaze. 'I'm going away. Anywhere. To the Chalced States, to Bingtown. I'm good with animals, I'm a decent scribe, too. I could make a living.'

'No doubt of it. But a living is not a life,' Burrich pointed out.

'Well, what is?' I demanded, suddenly and truly angry. Why did they have to make this so hard? Words and thoughts suddenly gouted from me like poison from a festering wound. 'You'd have me devote myself to my king and sacrifice all else to it, as you did. Give up the woman I love to follow a king like a dog at his heels, as you did. And when that king abandoned you? You swallowed it, you raised his bastard for him. Then they took it all away from you, stable, horses, dogs, men to command. They left you nothing, not even a roof over your head, those kings you were sworn to. So what did you do? With nothing else left to you, you hung onto me, dragged the Bastard out of a coffin and forced him back to life. A life I hate, a life I don't want!' I glared at him accusingly.

He stared at me, bereft of words. I wanted to stop, but something drove me on. The anger felt good, like a cleansing fire. I clenched my hands into fists as I demanded, 'Why are you always there? Why do you always stand me up again, for them to knock down? For what? To make me owe you something? To give you a claim on my life because you don't have the spine to have a life of your own? All you want to do is make me just like you, a man with no life of my own, a man who gives it all up for my king. Can't you see there's more to being alive than giving it all up for someone else?'

I met his eyes and then looked away from the pained astonishment I saw there. 'No,' I said dully after a breath. 'You don't see, you can't know. You can't even imagine what you've taken away from me. I should be dead, but you wouldn't let me die. All with the best of intentions, always believing you were doing what was right, no matter how it hurt me. But who gave you that right over me? Who decreed you could do this to me?'

There was no sound but my own voice in the room. Chade was frozen, and the look on Burrich's face only made me angrier. I saw him gather himself up. He reached for his pride and dignity as he said quietly, 'Your father gave me that task, Fitz. I did my best by you, boy. The last thing my prince told me. Chivalry said to me, "Raise him well." And I . . .'

'Gave up the next decade of your life to raising someone else's bastard,' I cut in with savage sarcasm. 'Took care of me, because it was the only thing you really knew how to do. All your life, Burrich, you've been looking after someone else, putting someone else first, sacrificing any kind of a normal life for someone else's benefit. Loyal as a hound. Is that a life? Haven't you ever thought of being your own man, and making your own decisions? Or is a fear of that what pushes you down the neck of a bottle?' My voice had risen to a shout. When I ran out of words, I stared at him, my chest rising and falling as I panted out my fury.

As an angry boy, I'd often promised myself that someday he would pay for every cuff he had given me, for every stall I'd had to muck out when I thought I was too tired to stand. With those words, I kept that sulky little promise tenfold. His eyes were wide and he was speechless with pain. I saw his chest heave once, as if to catch a breath knocked out of him. The shock in his eyes was the same as if I had suddenly plunged a knife into him.

I stared at him. I wasn't sure where those words had come from, but it was too late to call them back. Saying 'I'm sorry' would not un-utter them, would not change them in the least. I suddenly hoped he would hit me, that he would give both of us at least that much.

He stood unevenly, the chair legs scraping back on the wooden floor. The chair itself teetered over and fell with a crash as he walked away from it. Burrich, who walked so steadily when full of brandy, wove like a drunk as he made it to the door and went out into the night. I just sat, feeling something inside me go very still. I hoped it was my heart.

For a moment all was silence. A long moment. Then Chade sighed. 'Why?' he asked quietly after a time.

'I don't know.' I lied so well. Chade himself had taught me. I looked into the fire. For a moment, I almost tried to explain it to him. I decided I could not. I found myself talking all around it. 'Maybe I needed to get free of him. Of all he'd done for me, even when I didn't want him to do it. He has to stop doing things I can never pay him back for. Things no man should do for another, sacrifices no man should make for another man. I don't want to owe him any more. I don't want to owe anyone anything.'

When Chade spoke, it was matter-of-factly. His long-fingered hands rested on his thighs, quietly, almost relaxed. But his green eyes had gone the colour of copper ore, and his anger lived in them. 'Ever since you came back from the Mountain Kingdom, it's been as if you were spoiling for a fight. With anyone. When you were a boy and you were sullen or sulky, I could put it down to your being a boy, with a boy's judgment and frustrations. But you came back with an . . . anger. Like a challenge to the world at large, to kill you if it could. It wasn't just that you threw yourself in Regal's path: whatever was most dangerous to you, you plunged yourself into. Burrich wasn't the only one to see it. Look back over the last year: every time I turned about, here was Fitz, railing at the world, in the middle of a fistfight, in the midst of a battle, wrapped up in bandaging, drunk as a fisherman, or limp as a string and mewling for elfbark. When were you calm and thoughtful, when were you merry with your friends, when were you ever simply at peace? If you weren't challenging your enemies, you were driving away your friends. What happened between you and the Fool? Where is Molly now? You've just sent Burrich packing. Who's next?'

'You, I suppose.' The words came out of me any way, inevitably. I did not want to speak them but I could not hold them back. It was time.

'You've moved a fair way toward that already, with the way you spoke to Burrich.'

'I know that,' I said bluntly. I met his eyes. 'For a long time now, nothing I've done has pleased you. Or Burrich. Or anyone. I can't seem to make a good decision lately.'

'I'd concur with that,' Chade agreed relentlessly.

And it was back, the ember of my anger billowing into flame. 'Perhaps because I've never been given the chance to make my own decisions. Perhaps because I've been everyone's "boy" too long. Burrich's stable-boy, your apprentice assassin, Verity's pet, Patience's page. When did I get to be mine, for me?' I asked the question fiercely.

'When did you not?' Chade demanded just as heatedly. 'That's all you've done since you came back from the Mountains. You went to Verity to say you'd had enough of being an assassin just when quiet work was needed. Patience tried to warn you clear of Molly, but you had your way there as well. It made her a target. You pulled Patience into plots that exposed her to danger. You bonded to the wolf, despite all Burrich said to you. You questioned my every decision about King Shrewd's health. And your next to last stupid act at Buckkeep was to volunteer to be part of an uprising against the crown. You brought us as close to a civil war as we've been in a hundred years.'

'And my last stupid act?' I asked with bitter curiosity.

'Killing Justin and Serene.' He spoke a flat accusation.

'They'd just drained my king, Chade,' I pointed out icily. 'Killed him in my arms as it were. What was I to do?'

He stood up and somehow managed to tower over me as he had used to. 'With all your years of training from me, all my schooling in quiet work, you went racing about in the keep with a drawn knife, cutting the throat of one, and stabbing the other to death in the Great Hall before all the assembled nobles ... My fine apprentice assassin! That was the only way you could think of to accomplish it?'

'I was angry!' I roared at him.

'Exactly!' he roared back. '*You* were angry. So *you* destroyed our power base at Buckkeep! You had the confidence of the Coastal Dukes, and you chose to show yourself to them as a madman! Shattered their last bit of faith in the Farseer line.'

'A few moments ago, you rebuked me for having the confidence of those dukes.'

'No. I rebuked you for putting yourself before them. You should never have let them offer you the rule of Buckkeep. Had you been doing your tasks properly, such a thought would never have occurred to them. Over and over and over again, you forget your place. You are not a prince, you are an assassin. You are not the player, you are the game-piece. And when you make your own moves, you set every other strategy awry and endanger every piece on the board!'

Not being able to think of a reply is not the same thing as accepting another's words. I glowered at him. He did not back down but simply continued to stand, looking down at me. Under the scrutiny of Chade's green stare the strength of my anger deserted me abruptly, leaving only bitterness. My secret undercurrent of fear welled once more to the surface. My resolve bled from me. I couldn't do this. I did not have the strength to defy them both. After a time, I heard myself saying sullenly, 'All right. Very well. You and Burrich are right, as always. I promise I shall no longer think, I shall simply obey. What do you want me to do?'

'No.' Succinct.

'No what?'

He shook his head slowly. 'What has come most clear to me tonight is that I must not base anything on you. You'll get no assignment from me, nor will you be privy to my plans any longer. Those days are over.' I could not grasp the finality in his voice. He turned aside from me, his eyes going afar. When he spoke again, it was not as my master, but as Chade. He looked at the wall as he spoke. 'I love you, boy. I don't withdraw that from you. But you're dangerous. And what we must attempt is dangerous enough without you going berserk in the middle of it.'

'What do you attempt?' I asked, despite myself.

His eyes met mine as he slowly shook his head. In the keeping of that secret, he sundered our ties. I felt suddenly adrift. I watched in a daze as he took up his pack and cloak.

'It's dark out,' I pointed out. 'And Buckkeep is a far, rough walk, even in daylight. At least stay the night, Chade.'

'I can't. You'd but pick at this quarrel like a scab until you got it bleeding afresh. Enough hard words have already been said. Best I leave now.'

And he did.

I sat and watched the fire burn low alone. I had gone too far with both of them, much farther than I had ever intended. I had wanted to part ways with them; instead I'd poisoned every memory of me they'd ever had. It was done. There'd be no mending this. I got up and began to gather my things. It took a very short time. I knotted them into a bundle made with my winter cloak. I wondered if I acted out of childish pique or sudden decisiveness. I wondered if there was a difference. I sat for a time before the hearth, clutching my bundle. I wanted Burrich to come back, so he would see I was sorry, would know I was sorry as I left. I forced myself to look carefully at that. Then I undid my bundle and put my blanket before the hearth and stretched out on it. Ever since Burrich had dragged me back from death, he had slept between me and the door. Perhaps it had been to keep me in. Some nights it had felt as if he were all that stood between me and the dark. Now he was not there. Despite the walls of the hut, I felt I curled alone on the bare, wild face of the world.

You always have me.

I know. And you have me. I tried, but could not put any real feeling in the words. I had poured out every emotion in me, and now I was empty. And so tired. With so much still to do.

The Grey One has words with Heart of the Pack. Shall I listen?

No. Their words belong to them. I felt jealous that they were together while I was alone. Yet I also took comfort in it. Perhaps Burrich could talk Chade into coming back until morning. Perhaps Chade could leech some of the poison I'd sprayed at Burrich. I stared into the fire. I did not think highly of myself.

There is a dead spot in the night, that coldest, blackest time when the world has forgotten evening and dawn is not yet a promise. A time when it is far too early to arise, but so late that going to bed makes small sense. That was when Burrich came in. I was not asleep, but I did not stir. He was not fooled.

'Chade's gone,' he said quietly. I heard him right the fallen chair. He sat on it and began taking his boots off. I felt no hostility from him, no animosity. It was as if my angry words had never been spoken. Or as if he'd been pushed past anger and hurt into numbness.

'It's too dark for him to be walking,' I said to the flames. I spoke carefully, fearing to break the spell of calm.

'I know. But he had a small lantern with him. He said he feared more to stay, feared he could not keep his resolve with you. To let you go.'

What I had been snarling for earlier now seemed like an abandonment. The fear surged up in me, undercutting my resolve. I sat up abruptly, panicky. I took a long shuddering breath. 'Burrich. What I said to you earlier, I was angry, I was . . .'

'Right on target.' The sound he made might have been a laugh, if not so freighted with bitterness.

'Only in the way that people who know one another best know how to hurt one another best,' I pleaded.

'No. It is so. Perhaps this dog does need a master.' The mockery in his voice as he spoke of himself was more poisonous than any venom I had spewed. I could not speak. He sat up, let his boots drop to the floor. He glanced at me. 'I did not set out to make you just like me, Fitz. That is not a thing I would wish on any man. I wished you to be like your father. But sometimes it seemed to me that no matter what I did, you persisted in patterning your life after mine.' He stared into the embers for a time. At last he began to speak again, softly, to the fire. He sounded as if he were telling an old tale to a sleepy child.

'I was born in the Chalced States. A little coast town, a fishing and shipping port. Lees. My mother did washing to support my grandmother and me. My father was dead before I was born, taken by the sea. My grandmother looked after me, but she was very old, and often ill.' I heard more than saw his bitter smile. 'A lifetime of being a slave does not leave a woman with sound health. She loved me, and did her best with me. But I was not a boy who would play in the cottage at quiet games. And there was no one at home strong enough to oppose my will.

'So I bonded, very young, to the only strong male in my world who was interested in me. A street cur. Mangy. Scarred. His only value was survival, his only loyalty to me. As my loyalty was to him. His world, his way was all I knew. Taking what you wanted, when you wanted it, and not worrying past getting it. I am sure you know what I mean. The neighbours thought I was a mute.

My mother thought I was a half-wit. My grandmother, I am sure, had her suspicions. She tried to drive the dog away, but like you, I had a will of my own in those matters. I suppose I was about eight when he ran between a horse and its cart and was kicked to death. He was stealing a slab of bacon at the time.' He got up from his chair, and went to his blankets.

Burrich had taken Nosy away from me when I was less than that age. I had believed him dead. But Burrich had experienced the actual, violent death of his bond companion. It was little different from dying oneself. 'What did you do?' I asked quietly.

I heard him making up his bed and lying down on it. 'I learned to talk,' he said after a bit. 'My grandmother forced me to survive Slash's death. In a sense, I transferred my bond to her. Not that I forgot Slash's lessons. I became a thief, a fairly good one. I made my mother and grandmother's life a bit better with my new trade, though they never suspected what I did. About a hand of years later, the blood plague went through Chalced. It was the first time I'd ever seen it. They both died, and I was alone. So I went for a soldier.'

I listened in amazement. All the years I had known him as a taciturn man. Drink had never loosened his tongue, but only made him more silent. Now the words were spilling out of him, washing away my years of wondering and suspecting. Why he suddenly spoke so openly, I did not know. His voice was the only sound in the firelit room.

'I first fought for some petty land chief in Chalced. Jecto. Not knowing or caring why we fought, if there was any right or wrong to it.' He snorted softly. 'As I told you, a living is not a life. But I did well enough at it. I earned a reputation for viciousness. No one expects a boy to fight with a beast's ferocity and guile. It was my only key to survival amongst the kind of men I soldiered with then. But one day we lost a campaign. I spent several months, no, almost a year, learning my grandmother's hatred of slavers. When I escaped, I did what she had always dreamed of doing. I went to the Six Duchies, where there are no slaves, nor slavers. Grizzle was Duke of Shoaks then. I soldiered for him for a bit. Somehow I ended up taking care of my troop's horses. I liked it well enough. Grizzle's troops were gentlemen compared with the dregs that soldiered for Jecto, but I still preferred the company of horses to them.

'When the Sandsedge war was done, Duke Grizzle took me home to his own stables. I bonded with a young stallion there. Neko. I had the care of him, but he was not mine. Grizzle rode him to hunt. Sometimes, they used him for stud. But Grizzle was not a gentle man. Sometimes he put Neko to fight other stallions, as some men fight dogs or cocks for amusement. A mare in season, and the better stallion to have her. And I . . . I was bonded to him. His life was mine as much as my own was. And so I grew to be a man. Or at least, to have the shape of one.' Burrich was silent a moment. He did not need to explain further to me. After a time, he sighed and went on.

'Duke Grizzle sold Neko and six mares, and I went with them. Up the coast, to Rippon.' He cleared his throat. 'Some kind of horse plague went through that man's stables. Neko died, just a day after he started to sicken. I was able to save two of his mares. Keeping them alive kept me from killing myself. But afterwards, I lost all spirit. I was good for nothing, save drinking. Besides, there were scarcely enough animals left in that stable to warrant calling it such. So I was let go. Eventually, to become a soldier again, this time for a young prince named Chivalry. He'd come to Rippon to settle a boundary dispute between the Shoaks and Rippon Duchies. I don't know why his sergeant took me on. These were crack troops, his personal guard. I had run out of money and been painfully sober for three days. I didn't meet their standards as a man, let alone as a soldier. In the first month I was with Chivalry, I was up before him for discipline twice. For fighting. Like a dog, or a stallion, I thought it was the only way to establish position with the others.

'The first time I was hauled before the Prince, bloody and struggling still, I was shocked to see we were of an age. Almost all his troops were older than I; I had expected to confront a middle-aged man. I stood there before him and I met his eyes. And something like recognition passed between us. As if we each saw . . . what we might have been in different circumstances. It did not make him go easy on me. I lost my pay and earned extra duties. Everyone expected Chivalry to discharge me the second time. I stood before him, ready to hate him, and he just looked at me. He cocked his head as a dog will when it hears something far off. He docked my pay and gave me more duties. But he kept me. Everyone had told me I'd be discharged. Now they all expected me to desert. I can't say why I didn't. Why soldier for no pay and extra duties?'

Burrich cleared his throat again. I heard him shoulder deeper into his bed. For a time he was silent. He went on again at last, almost unwillingly. 'The third time they dragged me in, it was for brawling in a tavern. The City Guard hauled me before him, still bloody, still drunk, still wanting to fight. By then my fellow guards wanted nothing more to do with me. My sergeant was disgusted, I'd made no friends among the common soldiers. So the City Guard had me in custody. And they told Chivalry I'd knocked two men out and held off five others with a stave until the Guard came to tip the odds their way.

'Chivalry dismissed the Guards, with a purse to pay for damages to the tavern-keeper. He sat behind his table, some half-finished writing before him, and looked me up and down. Then he stood up without a word and pushed his table back to a corner of the room. He took off his shirt and picked up a pike from the corner. I thought he intended to beat me to death. Instead, he threw me another pike. And he said, "All right, show me how you held off five men." And lit into me.' He cleared his throat. 'I was tired, and half drunk. But I wouldn't quit. Finally, he got in a lucky one. Laid me out cold.

'When I woke up, the dog had a master again. Of a different sort. I know you've heard people say Chivalry was cold and stiff and correct to a fault. He wasn't. He was what he believed a man should be. More than that. It was what he believed a man should want to be. He took a thieving, unkempt scoundrel and . . .' He faltered, sighed suddenly. 'He had me up before dawn the next day. Weapons practice till neither of us could stand. I'd never had any formal training at it before. They'd just handed me a pike and sent me out to fight. He drilled me, and taught me sword. He'd never liked the axe, but I did. So he taught me what he knew of it, and arranged for me to learn it from a man who knew its strategies. Then the rest of the day, he'd have me at his heels. Like a dog, as you say. I don't know why. Maybe he was lonely for someone his own age. Maybe he missed Verity. Maybe . . . I don't know.

'He taught me numbers first, then reading. He put me in charge of his horse. Then his hounds and hawk. Then in general charge of the pack beasts and wagon animals. But it wasn't just work he taught me. Cleanliness. Honesty. He put a value on what my mother and grandmother had tried to instil in me so long ago. He showed them to me as a man's values, not just manners for inside a woman's house. He taught me to be a man, not a beast in a man's shape. He made me see it was more than rules, it was a way of being. A life, rather than a living.'

He stopped talking. I heard him get up. He went to the table and picked up the bottle of elderberry wine that Chade had left. I watched him as he turned it several times in his hands. Then he set it down. He sat down on one of the chairs and stared into the fire.

'Chade said I should leave you tomorrow,' he said quietly. He looked down at me. 'I think he's right.'

I sat up and looked up at him. The dwindling light of the fire made a shadowy landscape of his face. I could not read his eyes.

'Chade says you have been my boy too long. Chade's boy, Verity's boy, even Patience's boy. That we kept you a boy and looked after you too much. He believes that when a man's decisions came to you, you made them as a boy. Impulsively. Intending to be right, intending to be good. But intentions are not good enough.'

'Sending me out to kill people was keeping me a boy?' I asked incredulously.

'Did you listen to me at all? I killed people as a boy. It didn't make me a man. Nor you.'

'So what am I to do?' I asked sarcastically. 'Go looking for a prince to educate me?'

'There. You see? A boy's reply. You don't understand, so you get angry. And venomous. You ask me that question but you already know you won't like my answer.'

'Which is?'

'It might be to tell you that you could do worse than to go

looking for a prince. But I'm not going to tell you what to do. Chade has advised me not to. And I think he is right. But not because I think you make your decisions as a boy would. No more than I did at your age. I think you decide as an animal would. Always in the now, with never a thought for tomorrow, or what you recall from yesterday. I know you know what I'm speaking of. You stopped living as a wolf because I forced you to. Now I must leave you alone, for you to find out if you want to live as a wolf or a man.'

He met my gaze. There was too much understanding in his eyes. It frightened me to think that he might actually know what I was facing. I denied that possibility, pushed it aside entirely. I turned a shoulder to him, almost hoping my anger would come back. But Burrich sat silently.

Finally I looked up at him. He was staring into the fire. It took me a long time to swallow my pride and ask, 'So, what are you going to do?'

'I told you. I'm leaving tomorrow.'

Harder still to ask the next question. 'Where will you go?'

He cleared his throat and looked uncomfortable. 'I've a friend. She's alone. She could use a man's strength about her place. Her roof needs mending, and there's planting to do. I'll go there, for a time.'

'She?' I dared to ask, raising an eyebrow.

His voice was flat. 'Nothing like that. A friend. You would probably say that I've found someone else to look after. Perhaps I have. Perhaps it's time to give that where it is truly needed.'

I looked into the fire, now. 'Burrich. I truly needed you. You brought me back from the edge, back to being a man.'

He snorted. 'If I'd done right by you in the first place, you'd never have gone to the edge.'

'No. I'd have gone to my grave instead.'

'Would you? Regal would have had no charges of Wit magic to bring against you.'

'He'd have found some excuse to kill me. Or just opportunity. He doesn't really need an excuse to do what he wants.'

'Perhaps. Perhaps not.'

We sat watching the fire die. I reached up to my ear, fumbled with the catch on the earring. 'I want to give this back to you.'

'I would prefer that you kept it. Wore it.' It was almost a request. It felt odd.

'I don't deserve whatever it is that this earring symbolizes to you. I haven't earned it, I have no right to it.'

'What it symbolizes to me is not something that is earned. It's something I gave to you, deserved or not. Whether or not you wear that, you still take it with you.'

I left the earring dangling from my ear. A tiny silver net with a blue gem trapped inside it. Once Burrich had given it to my father. Patience, all unknowing of its significance, had passed it on to me. I did not know if he wanted me to wear it for the same reason he had given it to my father. I sensed there was more about it, but he had not told me and I would not ask. Still, I waited, expecting a question from him. But he only rose and went back to his blankets. I heard him lie down.

I wished he had asked me the question. It hurt that he hadn't. I answered it anyway. 'I don't know what I'm going to do,' I said into the darkened room. 'All my life, I've always had tasks to do, masters to answer to. Now that I don't . . . it's a strange feeling.'

I thought for a time that he wasn't going to reply at all. Then he said abruptly, 'I've known that feeling.'

I looked up at the darkened ceiling. 'I've thought of Molly. Often. Do you know where she went?'

'Yes.'

When he said no more than that, I knew better than to ask. 'I know the wisest course is to let her go. She believes me dead. I hope that whoever she went to takes better care of her than I did. I hope he loves her as she deserves.'

There was a rustling of Burrich's blankets. 'What do you mean?' he asked guardedly.

It was harder to say than I had thought it would be. 'She told me when she left me that day that there was someone else. Someone that she cared for as I cared for my king, someone she put ahead of everything and everyone else in her life.' My throat closed up suddenly. I took a breath, willing the knot in my throat away. 'Patience was right,' I said.

'Yes, she was,' Burrich agreed.

'I can blame it on no one save myself. Once I knew Molly was safe, I should have let her go her own way. She deserves a man who can give her all his time, all his devotion . . .'

'Yes, she does,' Burrich agreed relentlessly. 'A shame you didn't realize that before you had been with her.'

It is quite one thing to admit a fault to yourself. It is another thing entirely to have a friend not only agree with you, but point out the full depth of the fault. I didn't deny it, or demand how he knew of it. If Molly had told him, I didn't want to know what else she had said. If he had deduced it on his own, I didn't want to know I had been that obvious. I felt a surge of something, a fierceness that made me want to snarl at him. I bit down on my tongue and forced myself to consider what I felt. Guilt and shame that it had ended in pain for her, and made her doubt her worth. And a certainty that no matter how wrong it had been, it had also been right. When I was sure of my voice, I said quietly, 'I will never regret loving her. Only that I could not make her my wife in all eyes as she was in my heart.'

He said nothing to that. But after a time, that separating silence became deafening. I could not sleep for it. Finally I spoke. 'So. Tomorrow we go our own ways, I suppose.'

'I suppose so,' Burrich said. After a time, he added, 'Good luck.' He actually sounded as if he meant it. As if he realized how much luck I would need.

I closed my eyes. I was so tired now. So tired. Tired of hurting people I loved. But it was done now. Tomorrow Burrich would leave and I would be free. Free to follow my heart's desire, with no intervention from anyone.

Free to go to Tradeford and kill Regal.

THREE

The Quest

The Skill is the traditional magic of the Farseer royalty. While it seems to run strongest in the royal bloodlines, it is not all that rare to discover it in a lesser strength in those distantly related to the Farseer line, or in those whose ancestry includes both Outislanders and Six Duchy folk. It is a magic of the mind, giving the practitioner the power to communicate silently with those at a distance from him. Its possibilities are many; at its simplest, it may be used to convey messages, to influence the thoughts of enemies (or friends) to sway them to one's purposes. Its drawbacks are twofold: it requires a great deal of energy to wield it on a daily basis, and it offers to its practitioners an attraction that has been misnamed as a pleasure. It is more of a euphoric, one that increases in power proportionately with the strength and duration of Skilling. It can lure the practitioner into an addiction to Skilling, one which eventually saps all mental and physical strength, to leave the mage a great, drooling babe.

Burrich left the next morning. When I awoke, he was up and dressed and moving about the hut, packing his things. It did not take him long. He took his personal effects, but left me the lion's share of our provisions. There had been no drink the night before, yet we both spoke as softly and moved as carefully as if pained by the morning. We deferred to one another until it seemed to me worse than if we had not been speaking to one another at all. I wanted to babble apologies, to beg him to reconsider, to do something, anything, to keep our friendship from ending this way. At the same time, I wished him gone, wished it over, wished it to be tomorrow, a new day dawning and I alone. I held to my resolution as if gripping the sharp blade of a knife. I suspect he felt something of the same, for sometimes he would stop and look up at me as if about to speak. Then our eyes would meet and hold for a bit, until one or the other of us looked aside. Too much hovered unspoken between us.

In a horribly short time he was ready to leave. He shouldered his pack and took up a stave from beside the door. I stood staring at him, thinking how odd he appeared thus: Burrich the horseman, afoot. The early summer sunlight spilling in the open door showed me a man at the end of his middle years, the white streak of hair that marked his scar foretelling the grey that had already begun to show in his beard. He was strong and fit, but his youth was unquestionably behind him. The days of his full strength he had spent watching over me.

'Well,' he said gruffly. 'Farewell, Fitz. And good luck to you.'

'Good luck to you, Burrich.' I crossed the room quickly, and embraced him before he could step back.

He hugged me back, a quick squeeze that nearly cracked my ribs, and then pushed my hair back from my face. 'Go comb your hair. You look like a wild man.' He almost managed a smile. He turned from me and strode away. I stood watching him go. I thought he would not look back, but on the far side of the pasture, he turned and lifted his hand. I raised mine in return. Then he was gone, swallowed into the woods. I sat for a time on the step, considering the place where I had last seen him. If I kept to my plan, it might be years before I saw him again. If I saw him again. Since I was six years old, he had always been a factor in my life. I had always been able to count on his strength, even when I didn't want it. Now he was gone. Like Chade, like Molly, like Verity, like Patience.

I thought of all I had said to him the night before and shuddered with shame. It had been necessary, I told myself. I had meant to drive him away. But far too much of it had erupted from ancient resentments that had festered long inside me. I had not meant to speak of such things. I had intended to drive him away, not cut him to the bone. Like Molly, he would carry off the doubts I had driven into him. And by savaging Burrich's pride, I had destroyed what little respect Chade had still held for me. I suppose some childish part of myself had been hoping that someday I could come back to them, that someday we would share our lives again. I knew now we would not. 'It's over,' I told myself quietly. 'That life is over, let it go.'

I was free of both of them now. Free of their limitations on me, free of their ideas of honour and duty. Freed of their expectations. I'd never again have to look either of them in the eyes and account for what I had done. Free to do the only thing I had the heart or the courage left to do, the only thing I could do to lay my old life to rest behind me.

I would kill Regal.

It only seemed fair. He had killed me first. The spectre of the promise I had made to King Shrewd, that I would never harm one of his own, rose briefly to haunt me. I laid it to rest by reminding myself that Regal had killed the man who had made that promise, as well as the man I had given it to. That Fitz no longer existed. I would never again stand before old King Shrewd and report the result of a mission, I would not stand as King's Man to loan strength to Verity. Lady Patience would never harry me with a dozen trivial errands that were of the utmost importance to her. She mourned me as dead. And Molly. Tears stung my eyes as I measured my pain. She had left me before Regal had killed me, but for that loss, too, I held him responsible. If I had nothing else out of this crust of life Burrich and Chade had salvaged for me, I would have revenge. I promised myself that Regal would look at me as he died, and know that I killed him. This would be no quiet assassination, no silent venture of anonymous poison. I would deliver death to Regal myself. I wished to strike like a single arrow, like a thrown knife, going straight to my target unhampered by fears for those around me. If I failed, well, I was already dead in every way that mattered to me. It would hurt no one that I had tried. If I died killing Regal, it would be worth it. I would guard my own life only until I had taken Regal's. Whatever happened after that did not matter.

Nighteyes stirred, disturbed by some inkling of my thoughts.

Have you ever considered what it would do to me if you died? Nighteyes asked me.

I shut my eyes tightly for an instant. But I had considered it. *What would it do to us if I lived as prey?*

Nighteyes understood. *We are hunters. Neither of us was born to be prey.*

I cannot be a hunter if I am always waiting to be prey. And so I must hunt him before he can hunt me.

He accepted my plans too calmly. I tried to make him understand all I intended to do. I did not wish him simply to follow me blindly.

I'm going to kill Regal. And his coterie. I'm going to kill all of them, for all they did to me, and all they took from me.

Regal? There is meat we cannot eat. I do not understand the hunting of men.

I took my image of Regal and combined it with his images of the animal trader who had caged him when he was a cub and beat him with a brass-bound club.

Nighteyes considered that. *Once I got away from him, I was smart enough to stay away from him. To hunt that one is as wise as to go hunting a porcupine.*

I cannot leave this alone, Nighteyes.

I understand. I am the same about porcupines.

And so he perceived my vendetta with Regal as equivalent to his weakness for porcupines. I found myself accepting my stated goals with less equanimity. Having stated them, I could not imagine turning aside for anything else. My words from the night before came back to rebuke me. What had happened to all my fine speeches to Burrich, about living a life for myself? Well, I hedged, and perhaps I would, if I survived tying up these loose ends. It was not that I could not live my own life. It was that I could not stomach the idea of Regal going about thinking he had defeated me, yes, and stolen the throne from Verity. Revenge, plain and simple, I told myself. If I was ever going to put the fear and shame behind me, I had to do this.

You can come in now, I offered.

Why would I want to?

I did not have to turn and see that Nighteyes had already come down to the hut. He came to sit beside me, then peered into the hut.

Phew! You fill your den with such stinks, no wonder your nose works so poorly.

He crept into the hut cautiously and began a prowling tour of the interior. I sat on the doorstep, watching him. It had been a time since I had looked at him as anything other than an extension of myself. He was full grown now, and at the peak of his strength. Another might say he was a grey wolf. To me, he was every colour a wolf could be, dark-eyed, dark-muzzled, buff at the base of his ears and throat, his coat peppered with stiff, black guard-hairs, especially on his shoulders and the flat of his rump. His feet were huge, and spread even wider when he ran over crusted snow. He had a tail that was more expressive than many a woman's face, and teeth and jaws that could easily crack a deer's leg bones. He moved with that economy of strength that perfectly healthy animals have. Just watching him salved my heart. When his curiosity was mostly satisfied, he came to sit beside me. After a few moments, he stretched out in the sun and closed his eyes. *Keep watch?*

'I'll watch over you,' I assured him. His ears twitched at my spoken words. Then he sank into a sun-soaked sleep.

I rose quietly and went inside the hut. It took a remarkably short time for me to take stock of my possessions. Two blankets and a cloak. I had a change of clothes, warm woolly things ill-suited to summer travel. A brush. A knife and whetstone. Flint firestone. A sling. Several small cured hides from game we had taken. Sinew thread. A hand-axe. A small kettle and several spoons. The last were the recent work of Burrich's whittling. There was a little sack of meal, and one of flour. The leftover honey. A bottle of elderberry wine.

Not much to begin this venture with. I was facing a long overland journey to Tradeford. I had to survive that before I could plan how to get past Regal's guards and Skill coterie and kill him. I considered carefully. It was not yet the height of summer. There was time to gather herbs and dry them, time to smoke fish and meat for travelling rations. I needn't go hungry. For now, I had clothing and the other basics. But eventually I'd need some coin. I had told Chade and Burrich that I could make my own way, on my skills with animals and scribing skills. Perhaps those abilities could get me as far as Tradeford.

It might have been easier if I could have remained FitzChivalry. I knew boatmen who plied the river trade, and I could have worked my passage to Tradeford. But that FitzChivalry had died. He couldn't very well go looking for work at the docks. I could not even visit the docks, for fear of being recognized. I lifted my hand to my face, recalling what Burrich's looking glass had shown me. A streak of white in my hair to remind me where Regal's soldiers had laid my scalp open. I fingered the new configuration of my nose. There was also a fine seam down my right cheek under my eye, where Regal's fist had split my face. No one would remember a Fitz that bore these scars. I would let my beard grow. And if I shaved my hair back from my brow as the scribes did, that might be enough change to put off the casual glance. But I would not deliberately venture among those who had known me.

I'd be afoot. I'd never made an extended journey on foot.

Why can't we just stay right here? A sleepy inquiry from Nighteyes. *Fish in the creek, game in the woods behind the hut. What more do we need? Why must we go?*

I must. I must do this to be a man again.

You truly believe you wish to be a man again? I sensed his disbelief but also his acceptance that I would try. He stretched lazily without getting up, spreading wide the toes of his forepaws. *Where are we going?*

Tradeford. Where Regal is. A far journey up the river.

Are there wolves there?

Not in the city itself, I am sure. But there are wolves in Farrow. There are wolves in Buck still, too. Just not around here.

Save we two, he pointed out. And added, *I should like to find wolves where we go.*

Then he sprawled over and went back to sleep. That was part of what it meant to be a wolf, I reflected. He would worry no more until we left. Then he would simply follow me and trust his survival to our abilities.

But I had become too much a man again to do as he did. I began to gather provisions the very next day. Despite Nighteyes' protest, I hunted for more than we needed to eat each day. And when we were successful, I did not let him gorge, but jerked some of the meat, and smoked some of it. I had enough leather skill from Burrich's perpetual harness mending to make myself soft boots for the summer. I greased my old boots well and set them aside for winter use.

During the days, while Nighteyes dozed in the sun, I gathered my herbs. Some were the common medicinal herbs I wished to have on hand: willowbark for fever, raspberry root for cough, plantain for infection, nettle for congestion, and the like. Others were not so wholesome. I made a small cedar box and filled it. I gathered and stored the poisons as Chade had taught me: water-hemlock, deathcap mushroom, nightshade, elderberry pith, bane-berry and heartseize. I chose as best I could, for ones that were tasteless and odourless, for ones that could be rendered as fine powders and clear liquids. Also I harvested elfbark, the powerful stimulant Chade had used to help Verity survive his sessions of Skilling.

Regal would be surrounded and protected by his coterie. Will was the one that I most feared, but I would underestimate none of them. I had known Burl as a big husky boy and Carrod had been something of a dandy with the girls. But those days were long past. I had seen what Skill use had made of Will. It had been long since I had made contact with either Carrod or Burl, and I would make no assumptions about them. They were all trained in the Skill, and though my natural talent had once seemed much stronger than theirs, I had found out the hard way that they knew ways of using the Skill that not even Verity had understood. If I were Skill attacked by them, and survived, I would need the elfbark to restore myself.

I made a second case, large enough to hold my poison box, but otherwise designed like a scribe's case, to thus create the guise of a wandering scribe. The case would proclaim me as that to the chance acquaintance. Quills for pens I obtained from a nesting goose we ambushed. Some of the powders for pigments I could make, and I fashioned bone tubes and stoppers to hold them. Nighteyes grudgingly furnished me hair for coarse brushes. Finer brushes I attempted with rabbit hair, but with only partial satisfaction. It was very discouraging. A proper scribe was expected by folk to have the inks, brushes and pens of his trade. I reluctantly concluded that Patience had been right when she told me I wrote a fine hand, but could not claim the skills of a full scribe. I hoped my supplies would suffice for any work I might pick up on the way to Tradeford.

There came a time when I knew I was as well provisioned as I could be and that I should leave soon, to have the summer weather for travelling. I was eager for revenge, and yet strangely reluctant to leave this cabin and life. For the first time that I could recall, I arose from sleep when I awoke naturally, and ate when I was hungry. I had no tasks save those I set myself. Surely it would not hurt if I took a bit of time to recover my physical health. Although the bruises of my dungeon time had long faded, and the only external signs of my injuries were scars, I still felt oddly stiff some mornings. Occasionally, my body would shock me with a twinge when I leaped after something, or turned my head too quickly. A particularly strenuous hunt would leave me trembling and dreading a seizure. It would be wiser, I decided, to be fully healed before I departed.

So we lingered a time. The days were warm, the hunting was good. As the days slipped by, I made peace with my body. I was not the physically hardened warrior I had been the summer before, but I could keep pace with Nighteyes through a night's hunting. When I sprang to make a kill, my actions were quick and sure. My body healed, and I set behind me the pains of the past, acknowledging them, but not dwelling on them. The nightmares that had plagued me were shed like the last remnants of Nighteyes' winter coat. I had never known a life so simple. I had finally made peace with myself.

No peace lasts long. A dream came to wake me. Nighteyes and I arose before dawn, hunted, and together killed a brace of fat rabbits. This particular hillside was riddled with their warrens, and catching enough to fill ourselves had degenerated quickly to a silly game of leaping and digging. It was past dawn before we left off our play. We flung ourselves down in dappling birch shade, fed again from our kills and drowsed off. Something, perhaps the uneven sunlight on my closed eyelids, had plunged me into a dream.

I was back in Buckkeep. In the old watchroom, I sprawled on a cold stone floor in the centre of a circle of hard-eyed men. The floor beneath my cheek was sticky-slick with cooling blood. As I panted open-mouthed, the smell and the taste of it combined to fill my senses. They were coming for me again, not just the man with the leather-gloved fists, but Will, elusive invisible Will, slipping silently past my walls to creep into my mind. 'Please, wait, please,' I begged them. 'Stop, I beg you. I am nothing you need fear or hate. I'm only a wolf. Just a wolf, no threat to you. I'll do you no harm, only let me be gone. I'm nothing to you. I'll never trouble you again. I'm only a wolf.' I lifted my muzzle to the sky and howled.

My own howling woke me.

I rolled to my hands and knees, shook myself all over and then came to my feet. A dream, I told myself. Only a dream. Fear and shame washed over me, dirtying me in their passage. In my dream I had pleaded for mercy as I had not in reality. I told myself I was no craven. Was I? It seemed I could still smell and taste the blood.

Where are you going? Nighteyes asked lazily. He lay deeper in the shade and his coat camouflaged him surprisingly well there.

Water.

I went to the steam, splashed sticky rabbit blood from my face and hands, and then drank deeply. I washed my face again, dragging my nails through my beard to get the blood out. Abruptly I decided I couldn't stand the beard. I didn't intend to go where I expected to be recognized anyway. I went back to the shepherd's hut to shave.

At the door, I wrinkled my nose at the musty smell. Nighteyes was right; sleeping inside had dampened my sense of smell. I could hardly believe I had abided in here. I padded in reluctantly, snorting out the man smells. It had rained a few nights ago. Damp had got into my dried meat and soured some of it. I sorted it out, wrinkling my nose at how far gone it was. Maggots were working in some of it. As I checked the rest of my meat supply carefully, I pushed aside a nagging sense of uneasiness. It was not until I took out the knife and had to clean a fine dusting of rust from it that I admitted it to myself.

It had been days since I had been here.

Possibly weeks.

I had no idea of time's passage. I looked at the spoiled meat, at the dust that overlay my scattered possessions. I felt my beard, shocked at how much it had grown. Burrich and Chade had not left me here days ago. It had been weeks. I went to the door of the hut and looked out. Grass stood tall where there had been pathways across the meadow to the stream and Burrich's fishing spot. The spring flowers were long gone, the berries green on the bushes. I looked at my hands, at dirt ingrained in the skin of my wrists, old blood caked and dried under my nails. At one time, eating raw flesh would have disgusted me. Now the notion of cooking meat seemed peculiar and foreign. My mind veered away and I did not want to confront myself. Later, I heard myself pleading, tomorrow, later, go find Nighteyes.

You are troubled, little brother?

Yes. I forced myself to add, *You cannot help me with this. It is man trouble, a thing I must solve for myself.*

Be a wolf instead, he advised lazily.

I did not have the strength to say either yes or no to that. I let it go by me. I looked down at myself, at my stained shirt and trousers. My clothing was caked with dirt and old blood, and my trousers tattered off into rags below my knees. With a shudder, I recalled the Forged ones and their ragged garments. What had I become? I tugged at the collar of my shirt and then averted my face from my own stink. Wolves were cleaner than this. Nighteyes groomed himself daily.

I spoke it aloud, and the rustiness of my voice only added to it. 'As soon as Burrich left me here, alone, I reverted to something less than an animal. No time, no cleanliness, no goals, no awareness of anything save eating and sleeping. This was what he was trying to warn me about, all those years. I did just what he had always feared I would do.'

Laboriously I kindled a fire in the hearth. I hauled water from the stream in many trips and heated as much as I could. The shepherds had left a heavy rendering kettle at the hut, and this held enough to half-fill a wooden trough outside. While the water heated, I gathered soapwort and horsetail grass. I could not remember that I had ever before been this dirty. The coarse horsetail grass scrubbed off layers of skin with the grime before I

was satisfied I was clean. There were more than a few fleas floating
in the water. I also discovered a tick on the back of my neck and
burned him off with an ember twig from my fire. When my hair
was clean, I combed it out and then bound it back once more in
a warrior's tail. I shaved in the glass Burrich had left me, and
then stared at the face there. Tanned brow and pale chin.

By the time I had heated more water and soaked and pounded
my clothes clean, I was starting to understand Burrich's fanatical
and constant cleanliness. The only way to save what was left of
my trousers would be to hem them up at the knee. Even then,
there was not much wear left in them. I extended my spree to
my bedding and winter clothing as well, washing the musty smell
out of them. I discovered that a mouse had borrowed from my
winter cloak to make a nest. That, too, I mended as well as I
could. I looked up from draping wet leggings on a bush to find
Nighteyes watching me.

You smell like a man again.

Is that good or bad?

*Better than smelling like last week's kill. Not so good as smelling like
a wolf.* He stood and stretched, bowing low to me and spreading his
toes wide against the earth. *So. You do wish to be a man after all.
Do we travel soon?*

Yes. We travel west, up the Buck River.

Oh. He sneezed suddenly, then abruptly fell over on his side,
to roll about on his back in the dust like a puppy. He wiggled
happily, working it well into his coat, and then came to his feet
to shake it all out again. His blithe acceptance of my sudden
decision was a burden. What was I taking him into?

Nightfall found me with every garment I owned and all my
bedding still damp. I had sent Nighteyes hunting alone. I knew
he would not soon return. The moon was full and the night sky
clear. Plenty of game would be moving about tonight. I went
inside the hut and built up the fire enough to make hearth cakes
from the last of the meal. Weevils had got into the flour and
spoiled it. Better to eat the meal now than to waste it similarly.
The simple cakes with the last of the grainy honey from the pot
tasted incredibly good. I knew I had best expand my diet to
include more than meat and a handful of greens each day. I made

an odd tea from the wild mint and the tips of the new nettle growth, and that, too, tasted good.

I brought in an almost-dry blanket and spread it out before the hearth. I lay on it, drowsing and staring into the fire. I quested for Nighteyes, but he disdained to join me, preferring his fresh kill and the soft earth under an oak at the edge of the meadow. I was as alone, and as human, as I had been in months. It felt a little strange, but good.

It was when I rolled over and stretched that I saw the packet left on the chair. I knew every item in the hut by heart. This had not been here when last I was. I picked it up and snuffed at it, and found Burrich's scent faintly upon it, and my own. A moment later I realized what I had done and rebuked myself for it. I had best start behaving as if there were always witnesses to my actions, unless I wished to be killed as a Witted one again.

It was not a large bundle. It was one of my shirts, somehow taken from my old clothes chest, a soft brown one I'd always favoured, and a pair of leggings. Bundled up inside the shirt was a small earthenware pot of Burrich's unguent that he used for cuts, burns and bruises. Four silver bits in a little leather pouch; he'd worked a buck in the stitching on the front. A good leather belt. I sat staring at the design he'd worked into that. There was a buck, antlers lowered to fight, similar to the crest Verity had suggested for me. On the belt, it was fending off a wolf. Difficult to miss that message.

I dressed before the fire, feeling wistful that I had missed his visit, and yet relieved that I had. Knowing Burrich, he'd probably felt much the same at hiking up here and then finding me gone. Had he brought me these presentable clothes because he wanted to persuade me to return with him? Or to wish me well on my way? I tried not to wonder what his intent had been, or his reaction to the abandoned hut. Clothed again, I felt much more human. I hung the pouch and my sheath knife from the belt and cinched it around my waist. I pulled a chair up before the fire and sat in it.

I stared into the fire. I finally allowed myself to think about my dream. I felt a strange tightening in my chest. Was I a coward? I was not sure. I was going to Tradeford to kill Regal. Would a coward do that? Perhaps, my traitor mind told me, perhaps a coward would, if it was easier than seeking out one's king. I pushed that thought from my mind.

It came right back. Was killing Regal the right thing to do, or merely what I wished to do? Why should that matter? Because it did. Maybe I should be going to find Verity instead.

Silly to think about any of it, until I knew if Verity were still alive. If I could Skill to Verity, I could find out. But I had never been able to Skill predictably. Galen had seen to that, with the abuse that had taken my strong natural talent for Skill and turned it into a fickle and frustrating thing. Could that be changed? I'd need to be able to Skill well, if I wanted to get past the coterie to Regal's throat. I'd have to learn to control it. Was the Skill something one could teach oneself to master? How could one learn a thing if one did not even know the full scope of it? All the ability that Galen had neither beaten into nor out of me, all the knowledge that Verity had never had time to teach me: how was I to learn all that on my own? It was impossible.

I did not want to think of Verity. That, as much as anything, told me that I should. Verity. My prince. My king now. Linked by blood and the Skill, I had grown to know him as I knew no other man. Being open to the Skill, he had told me, was as simple as not being closed to it. His Skill-warring with the Raiders had become his life, draining away his youth and vitality. He had never had the time to teach me to control my talent, but he had given me what lessons he could in the infrequent chances he had. His Skill-strength was such that he could impose a touch on me, and be one with me for days, sometimes weeks. And once, when I had sat in my prince's chair, in his study before his worktable, I had Skilled to him. Before me had been the tools of his map-making and the small personal clutter of the man who waited to be king. That one time, I had thought of him, longed for him to be home to guide his kingdom, and had simply reached out and Skilled to him. So easily, without preparation or even real intent. I tried to put myself in that same frame of mind. I had not Verity's desk nor clutter to put him in mind, but if I closed my eyes, I could see my prince. I took a breath and tried to call forth his image.

Verity was broader of shoulder than I but not quite of my height. My uncle shared with me the dark eyes and hair of the Farseer family, but his eyes were set more deeply than mine, and his unruly hair and beard were shot through with grey. When I was a boy, he had been well-muscled and hard, a stocky man who wielded a sword as easily as a pen. These later years had wasted him. He had been forced to spend too much time physically idle as he used his Skill-strength to defend our coastline from the Raiders. But even as his muscle had dwindled, his Skill-aura had increased, until to stand before him now was like standing before a blazing hearth. When I was in his presence, I was much more aware of his Skill now than his body. For his scent, I called to mind the piquancy of the coloured inks he used when he made his maps, the smell of fine vellum, and, too, the edge of elfbark that was often on his breath. 'Verity,' I said softly aloud, and felt the word echo within me, bouncing off my walls.

I opened my eyes. I could not reach out of myself until I lowered my walls. Visualizing Verity would do nothing for me until I opened a way for my Skill to go forth, and his to enter my mind. Very well. That was easy enough. Just relax. Stare into the fire and watch the tiny sparks that rode upward on the heat. Dancing floating sparks. Relax the vigilance. Forget how Will had slammed his Skill-strength against that wall and nearly made it give way. Forget that holding the wall was all that had kept my mind my own while they hammered away at my flesh. Forget that sickening sense of violation the time that Justin had forced his way into me. The way Galen had scarred and crippled my Skill ability the time he had abused his position as Skillmaster to force his control on my mind.

As clearly as if Verity were beside me, I heard again my prince's words. 'Galen has scarred you. You've walls I can't begin to penetrate, and I am strong. You'd have to learn to drop them. That's a hard thing.' And those words to me had been years ago, before Justin's invasion, before Will's attacks. I smiled bitterly. Did they know they had succeeded at un-Skilling me? They'd probably never even given it thought. Someone, somewhere, should make a record of that. Someday a Skilled king might find it handy, to know that if you hurt a Skilled one badly enough with the Skill, you could seal him up inside himself and render him powerless in that area.

Verity had never had the time to teach me how to drop those walls. Ironically, he had found a way to show me how to reinforce them, so I could seal my private thoughts from him when I did not wish to share them. Perhaps that was a thing I had learned too well. I wondered if I would ever have time to unlearn it.

Time, no time, Nighteyes interrupted wearily. *Time is a thing that men made up to bother themselves with. You think on it until I am dizzy. Why do you follow these old trails at all? Snuff out a new one that may have some meat at the end of it. If you want the game, you must stalk it. That is all. You cannot say, to stalk this takes too long, I wish to simply eat. It is all one. The stalking is the beginning of the eating.*

You do not understand, I told him wearily. *There are only so many hours in a day, and only so many days in which I can do this thing.*

Why do you chop your life into bits and give the bits names? Hours, days. It is like a rabbit. If I kill a rabbit, I eat a rabbit. A sleepy snort of disdain. *When you have a rabbit, you chop it up and call it bones and meat and fur and guts. And so you never have enough.*

So what should I do, oh wise master?

Stop whining about it and just do it. So I can sleep.

He gave me a slight mind-nudge, like an elbow in the ribs when a companion crowds too close to you on the tavern bench. I suddenly realized how closely I had been holding our contact these past few weeks. Had been a time when I had rebuked him for always being in my mind. I had not wanted his company when I was with Molly, and I had tried to explain to him then that such times must belong to me alone. Now his nudge made it plain to me that I had been clinging as close to him as he had to me when he was a cub. I firmly resisted my first impulse to clutch at him. Instead I settled back in my chair and looked at the fire.

I took the walls down. I sat for a time, with my mouth dry, waiting for an attack. When nothing came, I thought carefully, and again lowered my walls. They believe me dead, I reminded myself. They will not be lying in wait to ambush a dead man. It was still not easy to will my walls down. Far easier to unsquint my eyes on a day of bright sunlight on the water, or to stand unflinching before a coming blow. But when finally I did it, I could sense the Skill flowing all about me, parting around me as if I were a stone in the current of a river. I had but to plunge into it and I could find Verity. Or Will, or Burl, or Carrod. I shuddered and the river retreated. I steeled myself and returned to it. A long time I stood teetering on that bank, daring myself to plunge in. No such thing as testing the water with the Skill. In or out. In.

In, and I was spinning and tumbling, and I felt my self fraying apart like a piece of rotten hemp rope. Strands peeling and twisting away from me, all the overlays that made me myself, memories, emotions, the deep thoughts that mattered, the flashes of poetry that one experiences that strike deeper than understanding, the random memories of ordinary days, all of it tattering away. It felt so good. All I had to do was let go.

But that would have made Galen right about me.

Verity?

There was no reply. Nothing. He wasn't there.

I drew back into myself and pulled my entire self about my mind. I could do it, I found, I could hold myself in the Skill stream and yet maintain my identity. Why had it always been so hard before? I set that question aside and considered the worst. The worst was that Verity had been alive and spoken to me, a few short months ago. 'Tell them Verity's alive. That's all.' And I had, but they had not understood, and no one had taken any action. Yet what could that message have been, if not a plea for help? A call for help from my king had gone unanswered.

Suddenly that was not a thing to be borne, and the Skill cry that went out from me was something I felt, as if my very life sprang out of my chest in a questing reach.

VERITY!

. . . Chivalry?

No more than a whisper brushing against my consciousness, as slight as a moth battering at a window-curtain. It was my turn, this time, to reach and grasp and steady. I flung myself out toward him and found him. His presence flickered like a candle-flame guttering out in the pool of its own wax. I knew he would soon be gone. I had a thousand questions. I asked the only important one.

Verity. Can you take strength from me, without touching me?

Fitz? The question more feeble, more hesitant. *I thought Chivalry had come back . . .* He teetered on the edge of darkness . . . *to take this burden from me . . .*

Verity, pay attention. Think. Can you take strength from me? Can you do it now?

I don't . . . I can't reach. Fitz?

I remembered Shrewd, drawing strength from me to Skill a farewell to his son. And how Justin and Serene had attacked him and leeched all his strength away and killed him. How he had died, like a bubble popping. Like a spark winking out.

VERITY! I flung myself at him, wrapped myself around him, steadied him as he had so often steadied me in our Skill contacts. *Take from me*, I commanded him, and opened myself to him. I willed myself to believe in the reality of his hand on my shoulder, tried to recall what it had felt like the times when he or Shrewd had drawn strength from me. The flame that was Verity leapt up suddenly, and after a moment burned strong and clean again.

Enough, he cautioned me, and then more strongly, *Be careful, boy!*

No, I'm all right, I can do this, I assured him, and willed my strength to him.

Enough! he insisted, and drew back from me. It was almost as if we stepped slightly apart and considered one another. I could not see his body, but I could sense the terrible weariness in him. It was not the healthy weariness that comes at the end of a day's labour, but the bone weariness of one grinding day piled upon another, with never food enough nor rest enough in between them. I had given him strength, but not health, and he would quickly burn the vitality he had borrowed from me, for it was not true strength any more than elfbark tea was a sustaining meal.

Where are you? I demanded of him.

In the Mountains, he said unwillingly, and added, *it is not safe to say more. We should not Skill at all. There are those who would try to hear us.*

But he did not end the contact, and I knew he was as hungry to ask questions as I was. I tried to think what I could tell him. I could sense no one save ourselves but I was not certain I would know if we were spied upon. For long moments our contact held simply as an awareness of one another. Then Verity warned me sternly, *You must be more careful. You will draw down trouble on yourself. Yet I take heart from this. I have gone long without the touch of a friend.*

Then it is worth any risk to myself. I hesitated, then found I could not confine the thought within myself. *My king. There is something I must do. But when it is done, I will come to you.*

I sensed something from him them. A gratitude humbling in its intensity. *I hope I shall still be here if you arrive.* Then, more sternly, *Speak no names, Skill only if you must.* More softly, then, *Be careful of yourself, boy. Be very careful. They are ruthless.*

And then he was gone.

He had broken the Skill contact off cleanly. I hoped that wherever he was, he would use the strength I had loaned him to find some food or a safe place to rest. I had sensed him living as a hunted thing, always wary, ever hungry. Prey, much as I was. And something else. An injury, a fever? I leaned back in my chair, trembling lightly. I knew better than to try to stand. Simply Skilling took strength out of me, and I had opened myself to Verity and let him draw off even more. In a few moments, when the shaking lessened, I would make some elfbark tea and restore myself. For now I sat and stared into the fire and thought of Verity.

Verity had left Buckkeep last autumn. It seemed an eternity ago. When Verity had departed, King Shrewd had lived yet, and Verity's wife Kettricken had been pregnant. He had set himself a quest. The Red Ship Raiders from the Out Islands had assailed our shores for three full years, and all our efforts to drive them away had failed. So Verity, King-in-Waiting for the throne of the Six Duchies, had set out to go to the Mountains, there to find our near legendary allies, the Elderlings. Tradition had it that generations ago King Wisdom had sought them out and they had aided the Six Duchies against similar raiders. They had also promised to return if ever we needed them. And so Verity had left throne and wife and kingdom behind to seek them out and remind them of their promise. His aged father, King Shrewd, had remained behind, and also his younger brother, Prince Regal.

Almost the moment Verity was gone, Regal began to move against him. He courted the Inland Dukes and ignored the needs of the Coastal Duchies. I suspected he was the source of the whispered rumours that made mock of Verity's quest and painted him as an irresponsible fool if not a madman. The coterie of Skill users who should have been sworn to Verity had long been corrupted to Regal's service. He used them to announce that Verity had died while en route to the Mountains, and then proclaimed himself King-in-Waiting. His control over the ailing King Shrewd became absolute; Regal had declared he would move his court inland, abandoning Buckkeep in every way that mattered to the mercies of the Red Ships. When he announced that King Shrewd and Verity's Queen Kettricken must go with him, Chade had decided we must act. We knew Regal would suffer neither of them to stand between him and the throne. So we had made our plans to spirit them both away, on the very evening he declared himself King-in-Waiting.

Nothing went as planned. The Coastal Dukes had been close to rising up against Regal; they had tried to recruit me to their rebellion. I had agreed to aid their cause, in the hope of keeping Buckkeep as a position of power for Verity. Before we could spirit the King away, two coterie members had killed him. Only Kettricken had fled, and although I had killed those who had killed King Shrewd, I myself was captured, tortured, and found guilty of the Wit magic. Lady Patience, my father's wife, had interceded on my behalf to no avail. Had Burrich not managed to smuggle poison to me, I would have been hung over water and burned. But the poison had been enough to counterfeit death convincingly. While my soul rode with Nighteyes in his body, Patience had claimed my body from the prison cell and buried it. Unbeknownst to her, Burrich and Chade had disinterred me as soon as they safely could.

I blinked my eyes and looked away from the flames. The fire had burned low. My life was like that now, all in ashes behind me. There was no way to reclaim the woman I had loved. Molly believed me dead now, and doubtless viewed my use of Wit magic with disgust. And anyway she had left me days before the rest of my life had fallen apart. I had known her since we were children and had played together on the streets and docks of Buckkeep Town. She had called me Newboy, and assumed I was just one of the children from the keep, a stable-boy or a scribe's lad. She had fallen in love with me before she discovered that I was the Bastard, the illegitimate son that had forced Chivalry to abdicate the throne. When she found out, I very nearly lost her. But I had persuaded her to trust me, to believe in me, and for almost a year, we had clung to one another, despite every obstacle. Time and again, I had been forced to put my duty to the King ahead of what we wished to do. The King had refused me permission to marry; she had accepted that. He had pledged me to another woman. Even that, she had tolerated. She had been threatened and mocked, as the 'bastard's whore'. I had been unable to protect her. But she had been so steadfast through it all . . . until one day she simply told me there was someone else for her, someone she could love, and put above all else in her life, just as I did my king. And she had left me. I could not blame her. I could only miss her.

I closed my eyes. I was tired, nearly exhausted. And Verity had warned me to Skill no more unless I must. But surely it could not hurt to attempt a glimpse of Molly. Just to see her, for a moment, to see that she was well . . . I probably wouldn't even succeed at seeing her. But what could I hurt by trying, just for a moment?

It should have been easy. It was effortless to recall everything about her. I had so often breathed her scent, compounded of the herbs she used to scent her candles, and the warmth of her own sweet skin. I knew every nuance of her voice, and how it went deeper when she laughed. I could recall the precise line of her jaw, and how she set her chin when she was annoyed with me. I knew the glossy texture of her rich brown hair and the darting glance of her dark eyes. She had had a way of putting her hands to the sides of my face and holding me firmly while she kissed me . . . I lifted my own hand to my face, wishing I could find her hand there, that I could trap it and hold it forever. Instead I felt the seam of a scar. The foolish tears rose warm in my eyes. I blinked them away, seeing the flames of my fire swim for a moment before my vision steadied. I was tired, I told myself. Too tired to try and find Molly with my Skill. I should try to get some sleep. I tried to set myself apart from these too-human emotions. Yet this was what I chose when I chose to be a man again. Maybe it was wiser to be a wolf. Surely an animal never had to feel these things.

Out in the night, a single wolf lifted his nose and howled suddenly up to the sky, piercing the night with his loneliness and despair.

FOUR

The River Road

Buck, the oldest Duchy of the Six Duchies, has a coastline that stretches from just below the Highdowns southwards to include the mouth of the Buck River and Bay of Buck. Antler Island is included in the Duchy of Buck. Buck's wealth has two major sources: the rich fishing grounds that the coastal folk have always enjoyed, and the shipping trade created by supplying the Inland Duchies with all they lack via the Buck River. The Buck River is a wide river, meandering freely in its bed, and often flooding the lowlands of Buck during the spring. The current is such that an ice-free channel has always remained open in the river year round, save for the four severest winters in Buck's history. Not only Buck goods travel up the river to the Inland Duchies, but trade goods from Rippon and Shoaks Duchies, not to mention the more exotic items from the Chalced States and those of the Bingtown Traders. Down the river comes all that the Inland Duchies have to offer, as well as the fine furs and ambers from the Mountain Kingdom trade.

I awoke when Nighteyes nudged my cheek with a cold nose. Even then I did not startle awake, but became soddenly aware of my surroundings. My head pounded and my face felt stiff. The empty bottle from the elderberry wine rolled away from me as I pushed myself to a sitting position on the floor.

You sleep too soundly. Are you sick?

No. Just stupid.

I never before noticed that it made you sleep soundly.

He poked me with his nose again and I pushed him away. I squeezed my eyes shut for a moment, then opened them again. Nothing had improved. I tossed a few more sticks of wood onto the embers of last night's fire. 'Is it morning?' I asked sleepily, aloud.

The light is just starting to change. We should go back to the rabbit warren place.

You go ahead. I'm not hungry.

Very well. He started off, then paused in the open doorway. *I do not think that sleeping inside is good for you.* Then he was gone, a shifting of greyness from the threshold. Slowly I lay down again and closed my eyes. I would sleep for just a short time longer.

When I awoke again, full daylight was streaming in the open door. A brief Wit-quest found a satiated wolf drowsing in the dappling sunlight between two big roots of an oak tree. Nighteyes had small use for bright sunny days. Today I agreed with him, but forced myself back to yesterday's resolution. I began to set the hut to rights. Then it occurred to me that I would probably never see this place again. Habit made me finish sweeping it out anyway. I cleared the ashes from the hearth, and set a fresh armload of wood there. If anyone did pass this way and need shelter, they would find all ready for them. I gathered up my now-dry clothing and set everything I would be taking with me on the table. It was pathetically little if one were thinking of it as all I had. When I considered that I had to carry all of it on my own back, it seemed plentiful. I went down to the stream to drink and wash before trying to make it into a manageable pack.

As I walked back from the stream, I was wondering how disgruntled Nighteyes was going to be about travelling by day. I had dropped my extra leggings on the doorstep somehow. I stooped and picked them up as I entered, tossing them onto the table. I suddenly realized I wasn't alone.

The garment on the doorstep should have warned me, but I had become careless. It had been too long since I had been threatened. I had begun to rely too completely on my Wit-sense to let me know when others were around. Forged ones could not be perceived that way. Neither the Wit nor the Skill would avail me anything against them. There were two of them, both young men, and not long Forged by the look of them. Their clothing was mostly intact and while they were dirty, it was not the ground-in filth and matted hair that I had come to associate with the Forged.

Most of the times I had fought Forged ones it had been winter and they had been weakened by privation. One of my duties as King Shrewd's assassin had been to keep the area around Buckkeep free of them. We had never discovered what magic the Red Ships used on our folk, to snatch them from their families and return them but hours later as emotionless brutes. We knew only that the sole cure was a merciful death. The Forged ones were the worst of the horrors that the Raiders loosed on us. They left our own kin to prey on us long after their ships were gone. Which was worse: to face your brother, knowing that theft, murder or rape were perfectly acceptable to him now, as long as he got what he wished? Or to take up your knife and go out to hunt him down and kill him?

I had interrupted the two as they were pawing through my possessions. Hands full of dried meat, they were feeding, each keeping a wary eye on the other. Though Forged ones might travel together, they had absolutely no loyalty to anyone. Perhaps the company of other humans was merely a habit. I had seen them turn savagely upon one another to dispute ownership of some plunder, or merely when they had become hungry enough. But now they swung their gazes to me, considering. I froze where I was. For a moment, no one moved.

They had the food and all my possessions. There was no reason for them to attack me, as long as I didn't challenge them. I eased back toward the door, stepping slowly and carefully, keeping my hands down and still. Just as if I had come upon a bear on its kill, so I did not look directly at them as I gingerly eased back from their territory. I was nearly clear of the door when one lifted a dirty hand to point at me. 'Dreams too loud!' he declared angrily. They both dropped their plunder and sprang after me.

I whirled and fled, smashing solidly chest to chest with one who was just coming in the door. He was wearing my extra shirt and little else. His arms closed around me almost reflexively. I did not hesitate. I could reach my belt knife and did, and punched it into his belly a couple of times before he fell back from me. He curled over with a roar of pain as I shoved past him.

Brother! I sensed, and knew Nighteyes was coming, but he was too far away, up on the ridge. A man hit me solidly from behind and I went down. I rolled in his grip, screaming in hoarse terror as he suddenly awakened in me every searing memory of Regal's dungeon. Panic came over me like a sudden poison. I plunged back into nightmare. I was too terrified to move. My heart hammered, I could not take a breath, my hands were numb, I could not tell if I still gripped my knife. His hand touched my throat. Frantically I flailed at him, thinking only of escape, of evading that touch. His companion saved me, with a savage kick that grazed my side as I thrashed and connected solidly with the ribs of the man on top of me. I heard him gasp out his air, and with a wild shove I had him off me. I rolled clear, came to my feet and fled.

I ran powered by fear so intense I could not think. I heard one man close behind me, and thought I could hear the other behind him. But I knew these hills and pastures now as my wolf knew them. I took them up the steep hill behind the cottage and before they could crest it I changed direction and went to earth. An oak had fallen during the last of the winter's wild storms, rearing up a great wall of earth with its tangled roots, and taking lesser trees down with it. It had made a fine tangle of trunks and branches, and let a wide slice of sunlight into the forest. The blackberries had sprung up rejoicing and overwhelmed the fallen giant. I flung myself to the earth beside it. I squirmed on my belly through the thorniest part of the blackberry canes, into the darkness beneath the oak's trunk and then lay completely still.

I heard their angry shouting as they searched for me. In a panic I threw up my mental walls as well. 'Dreams too loud,' the Forged one had accused me. Well, Chade and Verity had both suspected that Skilling drew the Forged ones. Perhaps the keenness of feeling it demanded and the outreaching of that feeling in Skill touched something in them and reminded them of all they had lost.

And made them want to kill whomever could still feel? Maybe. *Brother?*

It was Nighteyes, muted somehow, or at a very great distance. I dared open to him a bit.

I'm all right. Where are you?

Right here. I heard a rustling and suddenly he was there, bellying through to me. He touched his nose to my cheek. *Are you hurt?*

No. I ran away.

Wise, he observed, and I could sense that he meant it.

But I could sense too that he was surprised. He had never seen me flee from Forged ones. Always before I had stood and fought, and he had stood and fought beside me. Well, those times I had usually been well armed and well fed, and they had been starved and suffering from the cold. Three against one when you've only a belt knife as a weapon are bad odds, even if you know a wolf is coming to help you. There was nothing of cowardice in it. Any man would have done so. I repeated the thought several times to myself.

It's all right, he soothed me. Then he added, *Don't you want to come out?*

In a while. When they've gone, I hushed him.

They've been gone a long time, now, he offered me. *They left while the sun was still high.*

I just want to be sure.

I am sure. I watched them go, I followed them. Come out, little brother.

I let him coax me out of the brambles. I found when I emerged that the sun was almost setting. How many hours had I spent in there, senses deadened, like a snail pulled into its shell? I brushed dirt from the front of my formerly clean clothes. There was blood there as well, the blood of the young man in the doorway. I'd have to wash my clothes again, I thought dumbly. For a moment I thought of hauling the water and heating it, of scrubbing out the blood, and then I knew I could not go into the hut and be trapped in there again.

Yet the few possessions I had were there. Or whatever the Forged ones had left of them. By moonrise I had found the courage to approach the hut. It was a good full moon, lighting up the wide meadow before the hut. For some time I crouched on the ridge, peering down and watching for any shadows that might move. One man was lying in the deep grass near the door of the hut. I stared at him for a long time, looking for movement.

He's dead. Use your nose, Nighteyes recommended.

That would be the one I had met coming out the door. My

knife must have found something vital; he had not gone far. Still, I stalked him through the darkness as carefully as if he were a wounded bear. But soon I smelled the sweetish stench of something dead left all day in the sun. He was sprawled face down in the grass. I did not turn him over, but made a wide circle around him.

I peered through the window of the hut, studying the still darkness of the interior for some minutes.

There's no one in there, Nighteyes reminded me impatiently.

You are sure?

As sure as I am that I have a wolf's nose and not a useless lump of flesh beneath my eyes. My brother . . .

He let the thought trail off, but I could feel his wordless anxiety for me. I almost shared it. A part of me knew there was little to fear, that the Forged ones had taken whatever they wanted and moved on. Another part could not forget the weight of the man upon me, and the brushing force of that kick. I had been pinned like that against the stone floor of a dungeon and pounded, fist and boot, and I had not been able to do anything. Now that I had that memory back, I wondered how I would live with it.

I did, finally, go into the hut. I even forced myself to kindle a light, once my groping hands had found my flint. My hands shook as I hastily gathered what they had left me and bundled it into my cloak. The open door behind me was a threatening black gap through which they might come at any moment. Yet if I closed it, I might be trapped inside. Not even Nighteyes keeping watch on the doorstep could reassure me.

They had taken only what they had immediate use for. Forged ones did not plan beyond each moment. All the dried meat had been eaten or flung aside. I wanted none of what they had touched. They had opened my scribe's case, but lost interest when they found nothing to eat in there. My smaller box of poisons and herbs they had probably assumed held my scribe's colour pots. It had not been tampered with. Of my clothes, only the one shirt had been taken, and I had no interest in reclaiming it. I'd punched its belly full of holes anyway. I took what was left and departed. I crossed the meadow and climbed to the top of the ridge, where I had a good view in all directions. There I sat down and with trembling hands packed what I had left for travelling. I used my winter cloak to wrap it, and tied the bundle tightly with leather thongs. A separate strapping allowed me to sling it over a shoulder. When I had more light, I could devise a better way to carry it.

'Ready?' I asked Nighteyes.

Do we hunt now?

No. We travel. I hesitated. *Are you very hungry?*

A bit. Are you in so much of a hurry to be away from here?

I didn't need to think about that. 'Yes. I am.'

Then do not be concerned. We can both travel and hunt.

I nodded, then glanced up at the night sky. I found the Tiller in the night sky, and took a bearing off it. 'That way,' I said, pointing down the far side of the ridge. The wolf made no reply, but simply rose and trotted purposefully off in the direction I had pointed. I followed, ears pricked and all senses keen for anything that might move in the night. I moved quietly and nothing followed us. Nothing followed me at all, save my fear.

The night travelling became our pattern. I had planned to travel by day and sleep by night. But after that first night of trotting through the woods behind Nighteyes, following whichever game trails led in a generally correct direction, I decided it was better. I could not have slept by night anyway. For the first few days I even had trouble sleeping by day. I would find a vantage point that still offered us concealment and lie down, certain of my exhaustion. I would curl up and close my eyes and then lie there, tormented by the keenness of my own senses. Every sound, every scent would jolt me back to alertness, and I could not relax again until I had arisen to assure myself there was no danger. After a time, even Nighteyes complained of my restlessness. When finally I did fall asleep, it was only to shudder awake at intervals, sweating and shaking. Lack of sleep by day made me miserable by night as I trotted along in Nighteyes' wake.

Yet those sleepless hours and the hours when I trotted after Nighteyes, head pounding with pain, those were not wasted hours. In those hours I nurtured my hatred of Regal and his coterie. I honed it to a fine edge. This was what he had made of me. Not enough that he had taken from me my life, my lover, not enough that I must avoid the people and places I cared about, not enough the scars I bore and the random tremblings that overtook me. No. He had made me this, this shaking, frightened rabbit of a man. I had not even the courage to recall all he had done to me, yet I knew that when push came to shove, those memories would rise up and reveal themselves to unman me. The memories I could not summon by day lurked as fragments of sounds and colours and textures that tormented me by night. The sensation of my cheek against cold stone slick with a thin layer of my warm blood. The flash of light that accompanied a man's fist striking the side of my head. The guttural sounds men make, the hooting and grunting that issues from them as they watch someone being beaten. Those were the jagged edges that sliced through my efforts at sleep. Sandy-eyed and trembling, I would lie awake beside the wolf and think of Regal. Once I had had a love that I had believed would carry me through anything. Regal had taken that from me. Now I nurtured a hatred fully as strong.

We hunted as we travelled. My resolution always to cook the meat soon proved futile. I managed a fire perhaps one night out of three, and only if I could find a hollow where it would not attract attention. I did not, however, allow myself to sink down to being less than a beast. I kept myself clean, and took as much care with my clothing as our rough life allowed me.

My plan for our journey was a simple one. We would travel cross country until we struck the Buck River. The river road paralleled it up to Turlake. A lot of people travelled the road; it might be difficult for the wolf to remain unseen, but it was the swiftest way. Once there, it was but a short distance to Tradeford on the Vin River. In Tradeford, I would kill Regal.

That was the total sum of my plan. I refused to consider how I would accomplish any of this. I refused to worry about all I did not know. I would simply move forward, one day at a time, until I had met my goals. That much I had learned from being a wolf.

I knew the coast from a summer of manning an oar on Verity's warship the *Rurisk*, but I was not personally familiar with the inlands of Buck Duchy. True, I had travelled through it once before, on the way to the Mountains for Kettricken's pledging ceremony. Then I had been part of the wedding caravan, well mounted and well provisioned. But now I travelled alone and on foot, with time to consider what I saw. We crossed some wild country, but much, too, had once been summer pasturage for flocks of sheep, goats and cattle. Time after time, we traversed meadows chest-high in ungrazed grasses, to find shepherds' huts cold and deserted since last autumn. The flocks we did see were small ones, not nearly the size of flocks I recalled from previous years. I saw few swineherds and goose-girls compared to my first journey through this area. As we drew closer to the Buck River, we passed grainfields substantially smaller than I recalled, with much good land given back to wild grasses, not even ploughed.

It made small sense to me. I had seen this happening along the coast, where farmers' flocks and crops had been repeatedly destroyed by the raids. In recent years, whatever did not go to the Red Ships in fire or plunder was taken by taxes to fund the warships and soldiers that scarcely protected them. But upriver, out of the Raiders' reach, I had thought to find Buck more prosperous. It disheartened me.

We soon struck the road that followed the Buck River. There was much less traffic than I recalled, both on the road and the river. Those we encountered on the road were brusque and unfriendly, even when Nighteyes was out of sight. I stopped once at a farmstead to ask if I might draw cold water from their well. It was allowed me, but no one called off the snarling dogs as I did so, and when my waterskin was full, the woman told me I'd best be on my way. Her attitude seemed to be the prevailing one.

And the further I went, the worse it became. The travellers I encountered on the roads were not merchants with wagons of goods or farmers taking produce to market. Instead they were ragged families, often with all they possessed in a pushcart or two. The eyes of the adults were hard and unfriendly, while those of the children were often stricken and empty. Any hopes I had had of finding day-work along this road were soon surrendered. Those who still possessed homes and farms guarded them jealously. Dogs barked in the yards and farmworkers guarded the young crops from thieves after dark. We passed several 'beggar-towns', clusters of makeshift huts and tents alongside the road. By night, bonfires burned brightly in them and cold-eyed adults stood guard with staffs and pikes. By day, children sat along the road and begged from passing travellers. I thought I understood why the merchant wagons I did see were so well guarded.

We had travelled on the road for several nights, ghosting silently through many small hamlets before we came to a town of any size. Dawn overtook us as we approached the outskirts. When some early merchants with a cart of caged chickens overtook us, we knew it was time to get out of sight. We settled for the daylight hours on a small rise that let us look down on a town built half out onto the river. When I could not sleep, I sat and watched the commerce on the road below us. Small boats and large were tied at the docks of the town. Occasionally the wind brought me the shouts of the crews unloading from the ships. Once I even heard a snatch of song. To my surprise, I found myself drawn to my own kind. I left Nighteyes sleeping, but only went as far as the creek at the foot of the hill. I set myself to washing out my shirt and leggings.

We should avoid this place. They will try to kill you if you go there, Nighteyes offered helpfully. He was sitting on a creek bank beside me, watching me wash myself as evening darkened the sky. My shirt and leggings were almost dry. I had been attempting to explain to him why I wished to have him wait for me while I went into the town to the inn there.

Why would they want to kill me?

We are strangers, coming into their hunting grounds. Why shouldn't they try to kill us?

Humans are not like that, I explained patiently.

No. You are right. They will probably just put you in a cage and beat you.

No they won't, I insisted firmly to cover my own fears that perhaps someone might recognize me.

They did before, he insisted. *Both of us. And that was your own pack.*

I could not deny that. So I promised, *I will be very, very careful. I shall not be long. I just want to go listen to them talk for a bit, to find out what is happening.*

Why should we care what is happening to them? What is happening to us is that we are neither hunting, nor sleeping, nor travelling. They are not pack with us.

It may tell us what to expect, further on our journey. I may find out if the roads are heavily travelled, if there is work I can take for a day or so to get a few coins. That sort of thing.

We could simply travel on and find out for ourselves, Nighteyes pointed out stubbornly.

I dragged on my shirt and leggings over my damp skin. I combed my hair back with my fingers, squeezed the moisture from it. Habit made me tie it back in a warrior's tail. Then I bit my lip, considering. I had planned to represent myself as a wandering scribe. I took it out of its tail and shook it loose. It came almost to my shoulders. A bit long for a scribe's hair. Most of them kept their hair short, and shaved it back from the brow line to keep it from their eyes when they worked. Well, with my untrimmed beard and shaggy hair, perhaps I could be taken for a scribe who had been long without work. Not a good recommendation for my skills, but given the poor supplies I had, perhaps that was best.

I tugged my shirt straight to make myself presentable. I fastened my belt, checked to be sure my knife sat securely in its sheath, and then hefted the paltry weight of my purse. The flint in it weighed more than the coins. I did have the four silver bits from Burrich. A few months ago it would not have seemed like much money. Now it was all I had, and I resolved not to spend it unless I must. The only other wealth I had was the earring Burrich had given me and the pin from Shrewd. Reflexively my hand went to the earring. As annoying as it could be when we were hunting through dense brush, the touch of it always reassured me. Likewise the pin in the collar of my shirt.

The pin that wasn't there.

I took the shirt off and checked the entire collar, and then the complete garment. I methodically kindled a small fire for light. Then I undid my bundle completely and went through everything in it, not once, but twice. This despite my almost certain knowledge of where the pin was. The small red ruby in its nest of silver was in the collar of a shirt worn by a dead man outside the shepherd's hut. I was all but certain, and yet I could not admit it to myself. All the while I searched, Nighteyes prowled in an uncertain circle around my fire, whining in soft agitation about an anxiety he sensed but could not comprehend. 'Shush!' I told him irritably and forced my mind to go back over the events as if I were going to report to Shrewd.

The last time I could remember having the pin was the night I had driven Burrich and Shrewd away. I had taken it out of the shirt's collar and showed it to them both, and then sat looking at it. Then I had put it back. I could not recall handling it since then. I could not recall taking it out of the shirt when I washed it. It seemed I should have jabbed myself with it when I washed it if it was still there. But I usually pushed the pin into a seam where it would hold tighter. It had seemed safer so. I had no way of knowing if I had lost it hunting with the wolf, or if it were still in the shirt the dead man wore. Perhaps it had been left on the table, and one of the Forged ones had picked up the bright thing when they pawed through my possessions.

It was just a pin, I reminded myself. With a sick longing I wished I would suddenly see it, caught in the lining of my cloak or tumbled inside my boot. In a sudden flash of hope, I checked inside both boots again. It still wasn't there. Just a pin, just a bit of worked metal and a gleaming stone. Just the token King Shrewd had given me when he claimed me, when he created a bond between us to replace the blood one that could never be legitimately recognized. Just a pin, and all I had left of my king and my grandfather. Nighteyes whined again, and I felt an irrational urge to snarl back at him. He must have known that, but still he came, flipping my elbow up with his nose and then burrowing his head under my arm until his great grey head was up against my chest and my arm around his shoulders. He tossed his nose up suddenly, clacking his muzzle painfully against my chin. I hugged him hard, and he turned to rub his throat against my face. The ultimate gesture of trust, wolf to wolf, that baring of the throat to another's possible snarl. After a moment I sighed, and the pain of loss I felt over the thing was less.

It was just a thing from a yesterday, Nighteyes wondered hesitantly. *A thing no longer here? It is not a thorn in your paw, or a pain in your belly?*

'Just a thing from yesterday,' I had to agree. A pin that had been given to a boy who no longer existed by a man who had died. Perhaps it was as well, I thought to myself. One less thing

that might connect me to FitzChivalry the Witted. I ruffled the
fur on the back of his neck, then scratched behind his ears. He
sat up beside me, then nudged me to get me to rub his ears again.
I did, thinking as I did so. Perhaps I should take off Burrich's
earring and keep it concealed in my pouch. But I knew I would
not. Let it be the one link I carried forward from that life to this
one. 'Let me up,' I told the wolf, and he reluctantly stopped
leaning on me. Methodically I repacked my possessions into a
bundle and fastened it, then trampled out the tiny fire.

'Shall I come back here or meet you on the other side of town?'

Other side?

*If you circle about the town and then come back toward the river,
you will find more of the road there,* I explained. *Shall we find one
another there?*

*That would be good. The less time we spend near this den of
humans, the better.*

Fine, then. I shall find you there before morning, I told him.

*More likely, I shall find you, numb nose. And I shall have a full
belly when I do.*

I had to concede that was likelier.

Watch out for dogs, I warned him as he faded into the brush.

You watch out for men, he rejoined, and then was lost to my
senses save for our Wit-bond.

I slung my pack over my shoulder and made my way down to
the road. It was full dark now. I had intended to reach town
before dark and stop at a tavern for the talk and perhaps a mug,
and then be on my way. I had wanted to walk through the market
square and listen in on the talk of the merchants. Instead I walked
into a town that was mostly abed. The market was deserted save
for a few dogs nosing in the empty stalls for scraps. I left the
square and turned my steps toward the river. Down there I would
find inns and taverns aplenty to accommodate the river trade. A
few torches burned here and there throughout the town, but most
of the light in the streets was what spilled from poorly-shuttered
windows. The roughly-cobbled streets were not well kept up.
Several times I mistook a hole for a shadow and nearly stumbled.
I stopped a town watchman before he could stop me, to ask him
to recommend a waterfront inn to me. The Scales, he told me,

was as fair and honest to travellers as its name implied, and was easily found as well. He warned me sternly that begging was not tolerated there, and that cutpurses would be lucky if a beating was all they got. I thanked him for his warnings and went on my way.

I found the Scales as easily as the watchman had said I would. Light spilled out from its open door, and with it the voices of two women singing a merry round. My heart cheered at the friendly sound of it, and I entered without hesitation. Within the stout walls of mud brick and heavy timbers was a great open room, low-ceilinged and rich with the smells of meat and smoke and riverfolk. A cooking hearth at one end of the room had a fine spit of meat in its maw, but most folk were gathered at the cooler end of the room on this fine summer evening. There the two minstrels had dragged chairs up on top of a table and were twining their voices together. A grey-haired fellow with a harp, evidently part of their group, was sweating at another table as he fastened a new string to his instrument. I judged them a master and two journey singers, possibly a family group. I stood watching them sing together, and my mind went back to Buckkeep and the last time I had heard music and seen folk gathered together. I did not realize I was staring until I saw one of the women surreptitiously elbow the other and make a minute gesture at me. The other woman rolled her eyes, then returned my look. I looked down, reddening. I surmised I had been rude and turned my eyes away.

I stood on the outskirts of the group, and joined in the applause when the song ended. The fellow with the harp was ready by then, and he coaxed them into a gentler tune, one with the steady rhythm of oars as its beat. The women sat on the edge of the table, back to back, their long black hair mingling as they sang. Folk sat down for that one, and some few moved to tables against the wall for quiet talk. I watched the man's fingers on the strings of the harp, marvelling at the swiftness of his fingers. In a moment a red-cheeked boy was at my elbow, asking what I would have. Just a mug of ale, I told him, and swiftly he was back with it and the handful of coppers that were the remains of my silver piece. I found a table not too far from the minstrels, and rather hoped someone would be curious enough to join me. But other than a few glances from obviously regular customers, no one seemed much interested in a stranger. The minstrels ended their song and began talking amongst themselves. A glance from the older of the two women made me realize I was staring again. I put my eyes on the table.

Halfway down the mug, I realized I was no longer accustomed to ale, especially not on an empty stomach. I waved the boy back to my table and asked for a plate of dinner. He brought me a fresh cut of meat from the spit with a serving of stewed root vegetables and broth spilled over it. That, and a refilling of my mug took away most of my copper pieces. When I raised my eyebrows over the prices, the boy looked surprised. 'It's half what they'd charge you at the Yardarm Knot, sir,' he told me indignantly. 'And the meat is good mutton, not someone's randy old goat come to a bad end.'

I tried to smooth things over, saying, 'Well, I suppose a silver bit just doesn't buy what it used to.'

'Perhaps not, but it's scarcely my fault,' he observed cheekily, and went back to his kitchens.

'Well, there's a silver bit gone faster than I expected,' I chided myself.

'Now that's a tune we all know,' observed the harper. He was sitting with his back to his own table, apparently watching me as his two partners discussed some problem they were having with a pipe. I nodded at him with a smile, and then spoke aloud when I noticed that his eyes were hazed over grey.

'I've been away from the river road for a while. A long while, actually, about two years. The last time I was through here, inns and food were less expensive.'

'Well, I'd wager you could say that about anywhere in the Six Duchies, at least the coastal ones. The saying now is that we get new taxes more often than we get a new moon.' He glanced about us as if he could see, and I guessed he had not been blind long. 'And the other new saying is that half the taxes go to feed the Farrowmen who collect them.'

'Josh!' one of his partners rebuked him, and he turned to her with a smile.

'You can't tell me there are any about just now, Honey. I've a nose that could smell a Farrowman at a hundred paces.'

'And can you smell who you are talking to, then?' she asked him wryly. Honey was the older of the two women, perhaps my age.

'A lad a bit down on his luck, I'd say. And therefore, not some fat Farrowman come to collect taxes. Besides, I knew he couldn't be one of Bright's collectors the moment he started snivelling over the price of dinner. When have you known one of them to pay for anything at an inn or tavern?'

I frowned to myself at that. When Shrewd had been on the throne, nothing was taken by his soldiers or tax-collectors without some recompense offered. Evidently it was a nicety Lord Bright did not observe, at least in Buck. But it did recall me to my own manners.

'May I offer to refill your mug, Harper Josh? And those of your companions as well?'

'What's this?' asked the old man, between a smile and a raised eyebrow. 'You growl about spending coin to fill your belly, but you'd put it down willingly to fill mugs for us?'

'Shame to the lord that takes minstrels' songs, and leaves their throats dry from the singing of it,' I replied with a smile.

The women exchanged glances behind Josh's back, and Honey asked me with gentle mockery, 'And when were you last a lord, young fellow?'

' 'Tis but a saying,' I said after a moment, awkwardly. 'But I wouldn't grudge the coin for the songs I've heard, especially if you've a bit of news to go with it. I'm headed up the river road; have you perchance just come down?'

'No, we're headed up that way ourselves,' put in the younger woman brightly. She was perhaps fourteen, with startlingly blue eyes. I saw the other woman make a hushing-motion at her. She introduced them. 'As you've heard, good sir, this is Harper Josh, and I am Honey. My cousin is Piper. And you are . . . ?'

Two blunders in one short conversation. One, to speak as if I still resided at Buckkeep and these were visiting minstrels, and the other, to have no name planned out. I searched my mind for a name, and then after a bit too much of a pause, blurted out,

'Cob'. And then wondered with a shiver why I had taken to myself the name of a man I'd known and killed.

'Well . . . Cob,' and Honey paused before saying the name just as I had, 'we might have a bit of news for you, and we'd welcome a mug of anything, whether you're lately a lord or not. Just who are you hoping we won't have seen on the road looking for you?'

'Beg pardon?' I asked quietly, and then lifted my own empty mug to signal the kitchen-boy.

'He's a runaway 'prentice, Father,' Honey told her father with great certainty. 'He carries a scribe's case strapped to his bundle, but his hair's grown out, and there's not even a dot of ink on his fingers.' She laughed at the chagrin on my face, little guessing the cause. 'Oh, come, . . . Cob, I'm a minstrel. When we aren't singing, we're witnessing anything we can to find a deed to base a song on. You can't expect us not to notice things.'

'I'm not a runaway apprentice,' I said quietly, but had no ready lie to follow the statement. How Chade would have rapped my knuckles over this blundering!

'We don't care if you are, lad,' Josh comforted me. 'In any case, we haven't heard any cry of angry scribers looking for lost apprentices. These days, most would be happy if their bound lads ran away . . . one less mouth to feed in hard times.'

'And a scriber's boy scarcely gets a broken nose, or a scarred face like that from a patient master,' Piper observed sympathetically. 'So small blame to you if you did run away.'

The kitchen-boy came at last, and they were merciful to my flat purse, ordering no more than mugs of beer for themselves. First Josh, and then the women came to share my table. The kitchen-boy must have thought better of me for treating the minstrels well, for when he brought their mugs, he refilled mine as well, and did not charge me for it. Still, it broke another silver bit to coppers to pay for their drinks. I tried to be philosophical about it, and reminded myself to leave a copper bit for the boy when I left.

'So, then,' I began when the boy had left, 'what news from downriver, then?'

'And have not you just come from there yourself?' Honey asked tartly.

'No, my lady, in truth I had come cross country, from visiting some shepherd friends,' I extemporized. Honey's manner was beginning to wear on me.

'My lady,' she said softly to Piper and rolled her eyes. Piper giggled. Josh ignored them.

'Downriver is much the same as up these days, only more so,' he told me. 'Hard times, and harder to come for those who farm. The food grain went to pay the taxes, so the seed grain went to feed the children. So only what was left went into the fields, and no man grows more by planting less. Same is true for the flocks and herds. And no signs that the taxes will be less this harvest. And even a goose-girl that can't cipher her own age knows that less take away more leaves naught but hunger on the table. It's worst along the salt water. If a person goes out fishing, who knows what will happen to home before he returns? A farmer plants a field, knowing it won't yield enough both for taxes and family, and that there will be less than half of it left standing if the Red Ships come to pay a call. There's been a clever song made about a farmer who tells the tax-collector that the Red Ships have already done his job for him.'

'Save that clever minstrels don't sing it,' Honey reminded him tartly.

'Red Ships raid Buck's coast as well, then,' I said quietly.

Josh gave a snort of bitter laughter. 'Buck, Bearns, Rippon or Shoaks . . . I doubt the Red Ships care where one duchy ends and another begins. If the sea brushes up against it, they'll raid there.'

'And our ships?' I asked softly.

'The ones that have been taken away from us by the Raiders are doing very well. Those left defending us, well, they are as successful as gnats at bothering cattle.'

'Does no one stand firm for Buck these days?' I asked, and heard the despair in my own voice.

'The Lady of Buckkeep does. Not only firmly, but loudly. There's some as say all she does is cry out and scold, but others know that she doesn't call on them to do what she hasn't already done herself.' Harper Josh spoke as if he knew this at first hand.

I was mystified, but did not wish to appear too ignorant. 'Such as?'

'Everything they can. She wears no jewellery at all any more. It's all been sold and put toward paying patrol ships. She sold off her own ancestral lands, and put the money to paying mercenaries to man the towers. It's said she sold the necklace given her by Prince Chivalry, his grandmother's rubies, to King Regal himself, to buy grain and timber for Buck villages that wanted to rebuild.'

'Patience,' I whispered. I had seen those rubies once, long ago, when we had first been getting to know one another. She had deemed them too precious a thing even to wear, but she had shown them to me and told me some day my bride might wear them. Long ago. I turned my head aside and struggled to control my face.

'Where have you been sleeping this past year . . . Cob, that you know none of this?' Honey demanded sarcastically.

'I have been away,' I said quietly. I turned back to the table and managed to meet her eyes. I hoped my face showed nothing.

She cocked her head and smiled at me. 'Where?' she countered brightly.

I did not like her much at all. 'I've been living by myself, in the forest,' I said at last.

'Why?' She smiled at me as she pressed me. I was certain she knew how uncomfortable she was making me.

'Obviously, because I wished to,' I said. I sounded so much like Burrich when I said it, I almost looked over my shoulder for him.

She made a small mouth at me, totally unrepentant, but Harper Josh set his mug down on the table a bit firmly. He said nothing, and the look he gave her from his blind eyes was no more than a flicker, but she subsided abruptly. She folded her hands at the edge of the table like a rebuked child, and for a moment I thought her quashed, until she looked up at me from under her lashes. Her eyes met mine directly, and the little smile she shot me was defiant. I looked away from her, totally mystified as to why she wished to peck at me like this. I glanced at Piper, only to find her face bright red with suppressed laughter. I looked down at my hands on the table, hating the blush that suddenly flooded my face.

In an effort to start the conversation again, I asked, 'Are there any other new tidings from Buckkeep?'

Harper Josh gave a short bark of laughter. 'Not much new misery to tell. The tales are all the same, with only the names of the villages and towns different. Oh, but there is one small bit, a rich one. Word is now that King Regal will hang the Pocked Man himself.'

I had been swallowing a sip of ale. I choked abruptly and demanded, 'What?'

'It's a stupid joke,' Honey declared. 'King Regal has had it cried about that he will give gold coin reward to any who can turn over to him a certain man, much scarred with the pox, or silver coin to any man who can give information as to where he may be found.'

'A pox-scarred man? Is that all the description?' I asked carefully.

'He is said to be skinny, and grey-haired, and to sometimes disguise himself as a woman.' Josh chuckled merrily, never guessing how his words turned my bowels to ice. 'And his crime is high treason. Rumour says the King blames him for the disappearance of Queen-in-Waiting Kettricken and her unborn child. Some say he is just a cracked old man who claims to have been an adviser to Shrewd, and as such he has written to the Dukes of the Coastal Duchies, bidding them be brave, that Verity shall return and his child inherit the Farseer throne. But rumour also says, with as much wit, that King Regal hopes to hang the Pocked Man and thus end all bad luck in the Six Duchies.' He chuckled again, and I plastered a sick smile on my face and nodded like a simpleton.

Chade, I thought to myself. Somehow Regal had picked up Chade's trail. If he knew he was pock-scarred, what else might he know? He had obviously connected him to his masquerade as Lady Thyme. I wondered where Chade was now, and if he was all right. I wished with sudden desperation that I knew what his plans had been, what plot he had excluded me from. With a sudden sinking of heart, my perception of my actions flopped over. Had I driven Chade away from me, to protect him from my plans, or had I abandoned him just when he needed his apprentice?

'Are you still there, Cob? I see your shadow still, but your place at the table's gone very quiet.'

'Oh, I'm here, Harper Josh!' I tried to put some life into my words. 'Just mulling over all you've told me, that's all.'

'Wondering what pocked old man he could sell to King Regal, by the look on his face,' Honey put in tartly. I suddenly perceived that she saw her constant belittlement and stings as a sort of flirtation. I quickly decided I had had enough companionship and talk for an evening. I was too much out of practice at dealing with folk. I would leave now. Better they thought me odd and rude than that I stayed longer and made them curious.

'Well, I thank you for your songs, and your conversation,' I said as gracefully as I could. I fingered out a copper to leave under my mug for the boy. 'And I had best take myself back to the road.'

'But it's full dark outside!' Piper objected in surprise. She set down her mug and glanced at Honey, who looked shocked.

'And cool, my lady,' I observed blithely. 'I prefer the night for walking. The moon's close to full, which should be light enough on a road as wide as the river road.'

'Have you no fear of the Forged ones?' Harper Josh asked in consternation.

Now it was my turn to be surprised. 'This far inland?'

'You *have* been living in a tree,' Honey exclaimed. 'All the roads have been plagued with them. Some travellers hire guards, archers and swordsmen. Others, such as we, travel in groups when we can, and only by day.'

'Cannot the patrols at least keep them from the roads?' I asked in astonishment.

'The patrols?' Honey sniffed disdainfully. 'Most of us would as soon meet Forged ones as a pack of Farrowmen with pikes. The Forged ones do not bother them, and so they do not bother the Forged ones.'

'What, then, do they patrol for?' I asked angrily.

'Smugglers, mainly.' Josh spoke before Honey could. 'Or so they would have you believe. Many an honest traveller do they stop to search his belongings and take whatever they fancy, calling it contraband, or claiming it was reported stolen in the last town. Methinks Lord Bright does not pay them as well as they think they deserve, so they take whatever pay they are able.'

'And Prince . . . King Regal, he does nothing?' How the title and the question choked me.

'Well, perhaps if you go so far as Tradeford, you might complain to him yourself,' Honey told me sarcastically. 'I am sure he would listen to you, as he has not the dozens of messengers who have gone before.' She paused, and looked thoughtful. 'Though I have heard that if any Forged ones do make it far enough inland to be a bother, he has ways of dealing with them.'

I felt sickened and wretched. It had always been a matter of pride to King Shrewd that there was little danger of highwaymen in Buck, so long as one kept to the main roads. Now, to hear that those who should guard the king's roads were little more than highwaymen themselves was like a small blade twisted in me. Not enough that Regal had claimed the throne to himself, and then deserted Buckkeep. He did not keep up even the pretence of ruling wisely. I wondered numbly if he were capable of punishing all Buck for the lacklustre way he had been welcomed to the throne. Foolish wonder; I knew he was. 'Well, Forged ones or Farrowmen, I still must be on my way, I fear,' I told them. I drank off the last of my mug and set it down.

'Why not wait at least until the morning, lad, and then travel with us?' Josh suddenly offered. 'The days are not too hot for walking, for there's always a breeze off the river. And four are safer than three, these days.'

'I thank you kindly for the offer,' I began, but Josh interrupted me.

'Don't thank me, for I wasn't making an offer, but a request. I'm blind, man, or close enough. Certainly you've noticed that. Noticed, too, that my companions are comely young women, though from the way Honey's nipped at you, I fancy you've smiled more at Piper than at her.'

'Father!' indignantly from Honey, but Josh ploughed on doggedly.

'I was not offering you the protection of our numbers, but asking you to consider offering your right arm to us. We're not rich folk; we've no coin to hire guards. And yet we must travel the roads, Forged ones or no.'

Josh's fogged eyes met mine unerringly. Honey looked aside,

lips folded tightly, while Piper openly watched me, a pleading look on her face. Forged ones. Pinned down, fists falling on me. I looked down at the table-top. 'I'm not much for fighting,' I told him bluntly.

'At least you would see what you were swinging at,' he replied stubbornly. 'And you'd certainly see them coming before I did. Look, you're going the same direction we are. Would it be that hard for you to walk by day for a few days rather than by night?'

'Father, don't beg him!' Honey rebuked him.

'I'd rather beg him to walk with us, than beg Forged ones to let you go unharmed!' he said harshly. He turned his face back to me as he added, 'We met some Forged ones, a couple of weeks back. The girls had the sense to run when I shouted at them to do so, when I could not keep up with them any longer. But we lost our food to them, and they damaged my harp, and . . .'

'And they beat him,' Honey said quietly. 'And so we have vowed, Piper and I, that the next time we will not run from them, no matter how many. Not if it means leaving Papa.' All the playful teasing and mockery had gone out of her voice. I knew she meant what she said.

I will be delayed, I sighed to Nighteyes. *Wait for me, watch for me, follow me unseen.*

'I will travel with you,' I conceded. I cannot say I made the offer willingly. 'Though I am not a man who does well at fighting.'

'As if we couldn't tell that from his face,' Honey observed in an aside to Piper. The mockery was back in her voice, but I doubted that she knew how deeply her words cut me.

'My thanks are all I have to pay you with, Cob.' Josh reached across the table for me, and I gripped hands with him in the ancient sign of a bargain settled. He grinned suddenly, his relief plain. 'So take my thanks, and a share of whatever we're offered as minstrels. We've not enough coin for a room, but the innkeeper has offered us shelter in his barn. Not like it used to be, when a minstrel got a room and a meal for the asking. But at least the barn has a door that shuts between us and the night. And the innkeeper here has a good heart; he won't begrudge extending shelter to you if I tell him you're travelling with us as a guard.'

'It will be more shelter than I've known for many a night,' I told him, attempting to be gracious. My heart had sunk into a cold place in the pit of my belly.

What have you got yourself into now? Nighteyes wondered. As did I.

FIVE

Confrontations

What is the Wit? Some would say it is a perversion, a twisted indulgence of spirit by which men gain knowledge of the lives and tongues of the beasts, eventually to become little more than beasts themselves. My study of it and its practitioners has led me to a different conclusion, however. The Wit seems to be a form of mind linking, usually with a particular animal, which opens a way for the understanding of that animal's thoughts and feelings. It does not, as some have claimed, give men the tongues of the birds and beasts. A Witted one does have an awareness of life all across its wide spectrum, including humans and even some of the mightier and more ancient of trees. But a Witted one cannot randomly engage a chance animal in 'conversation'. He can sense an animal's nearby presence, and perhaps know if the animal is wary or hostile or curious. But it does not give one command over the beasts of the land and the birds of the sky as some fanciful tales would have us believe. What the Wit may be is a man's acceptance of the beast nature within himself, and hence an awareness of the element of humanity that every animal carries within it as well. The legendary loyalty that a bonded animal feels for his Witted one is not at all the same as what a loyal beast gives its master. Rather it is a reflection of the loyalty that the Witted one has pledged to his animal companion, like for like.

I did not sleep well, and it was not just that I was no longer accustomed to sleeping at night. What they had told me about Forged ones had put the wind up my back. The musicians all climbed up into the loft to sleep on the heaped straw there, but I found myself a corner where I could put my back to a wall and yet still have a clear view of the door. It felt strange to be inside a barn again at night. This was a good tight barn, built of river-rock and mortar and timber. The inn kept a cow and a handful of chickens in addition to their hire-horses and the beasts of their guests. The homely sounds and smells of the hay and animals put me sharply in mind of Burrich's stables. I felt suddenly homesick for them as I never had for my own room up in the keep.

I wondered how Burrich was, and if he knew of Patience's sacrifices. I thought of the love that had once been between them, and how it had foundered on Burrich's sense of duty. Patience had gone on to marry my father, the very man to whom Burrich had pledged all that loyalty. Had he ever thought of going to her, attempting to reclaim her? No. I knew it instantly and without doubt. Chivalry's ghost would stand forever between them. And now mine as well.

It was not a far jump from pondering this to thinking of Molly. She had made the same decision for us that Burrich had made for Patience and himself. Molly had told me that my obsessive loyalty to my king meant we could never belong to one another. So she had found someone she could care about as much as I cared for Verity. I hated everything about her decision except that it had saved her life. She had left me. She had not been at Buckkeep to share my fall and my disgrace.

I reached vaguely toward her with the Skill, then abruptly rebuked myself. Did I really want to see her as she probably was this night, sleeping in another man's arms, his wife? I felt an almost physical pain in my chest at the thought. I did not have a right to spy on any happiness she had claimed for herself. Yet as I drowsed off, I thought of her, and longed hopelessly after what had been between us.

Some perverse fate brought me dreams of Burrich instead, a vivid dream that made no sense. I sat across from him. He was sitting at a table by a fire, mending harness as he often did of an evening. But a mug of tea had replaced his brandy cup, and the leather he worked at was a low soft shoe, much too small for him. He pushed the awl through the soft leather and it went through too easily, jabbing him in the hand. He swore at the blood, and then looked up abruptly, to awkwardly beg my pardon for using such language in my presence.

I woke up from the dream, disoriented and bemused. Burrich had often made shoes for me when I was small but I could not recall that he had ever apologized for swearing in my presence, though he had rapped me often enough when I was a boy if I had dared to use such language in his. Ridiculous. I pushed the dream aside, but sleep had fled with it.

Around me, when I quested out softly, were only the muzzy dreams of the sleeping animals. All were at peace save me. Thoughts of Chade came to niggle and worry at me. He was an old man in many ways. When King Shrewd had lived, he had seen to all Chade's needs, so that his assassin might live in security. Chade had seldom ventured forth from his concealed room, save to do his 'quiet work'. Now he was out on his own, doing El knew what, and with Regal's troops in pursuit of him. I rubbed vainly at my aching forehead. Worrying was useless, but I could not seem to stop.

I heard four light foot scuffs, followed by a thud, as someone climbed down from the loft and skipped the last step on the ladder. Probably one of the women headed for the backhouse. But a moment later I heard Honey's voice whisper, 'Cob?'

'What is it?' I asked unwillingly.

She turned toward my voice, and I heard her approach in the darkness. My time with the wolf had sharpened my senses. Some little moonlight leaked in at a badly-shuttered window. I picked out her shape in the darkness. 'Over here,' I told her when she hesitated, and saw her startle at how close my voice was. She groped her way to my corner, and then hesitantly sat down in the straw beside me.

'I daren't go back to sleep,' she explained. 'Nightmares.'

'I know how that is,' I told her, surprised at how much sympathy I felt. 'When, if you close your eyes, you tumble right back into them.'

'Exactly,' she said, and fell silent, waiting.

But I had nothing more to say, and so sat silent in the darkness.

'What kind of nightmares do you have?' she asked me quietly.

'Bad ones,' I said drily. I had no wish to summon them by speaking of them.

'I dream Forged ones are chasing me, but my legs have turned to water and I cannot run. But I keep trying and trying as they come closer and closer.'

'Uhm.' I agreed. Better than dreaming of being beaten and beaten and beaten . . . I reined my mind away from that.

'It's a lonely thing, to wake up in the night and be afraid.'

I think she wants to mate with you. Will they accept you into their pack so easily?

'What?' I asked, startled, but it was the girl who replied, not Nighteyes.

'I said, it's lonely to awake at night and be afraid. One longs for a way to feel safe. Protected.'

'I know of nothing that can stand between a person and the dreams that come at night,' I said stiffly. Abruptly I wanted her to go away.

'Sometimes a little gentleness can,' she said softly. She reached over and patted my hand. Without intending to, I snatched it away.

'Are you shy, prentice-boy?' she asked coyly.

'I lost someone I cared for,' I said bluntly. 'I've no heart to put another in her place.'

'I see.' She rose abruptly, shaking straw from her skirts. 'Well. I'm sorry to have disturbed you.' She sounded insulted, not sorry.

She turned and groped her way back to the loft ladder. I knew I had offended her. I did not feel it was my fault. She went up the steps slowly, and I thought she expected me to call her back. I didn't. I wished I had not come to town.

That makes two of us. The hunting is poor, this close to all these men. Will you be much longer?

I fear I must travel with them for a few days, at least as far as the next town.

You would not mate her, she is not pack. Why must you do these things?

I did not try to form it into words for him. All I could convey was a sense of duty, and he could not grasp how my loyalty to Verity bound me to help these travellers on the road. They were my people because they were my king's. Even I found the connection so tenuous as to be ridiculous, but there it was. I would see them safely to the next town.

I slept again that night, but not well. It was as if my words with Honey had opened the door to my nightmares. No sooner had I dipped down into sleep than I experienced a sense that I was being watched. I cowered low inside my cell, praying that I could not be seen, keeping as still as I possibly could. My own eyes were clenched tight shut, like a child who believes that if he cannot see, he cannot be seen. But the eyes that sought me had a gaze I could feel; I could sense Will looking for me as if I were hiding under a blanket and hands were patting at it. He was that close. The fear was so intense that it choked me. I could not breathe, I could not move. In a panic, I went out of myself, sideways, slipping into someone else's fear, someone else's nightmare.

I crouched behind a barrel of pickled fish in old man Hook's store. Outside, the darkness was splintered by the rising flames and shrieks of the captured or dying. I knew I should get out. The Red Ship Raiders were certain to loot and torch the store. It was not a good place to hide. But there was no good place to hide, and I was only eleven, and my legs were shaking beneath me so that I doubted I could stand, let alone run. Somewhere out there was Master Hook. When the first cries arose, he had grabbed his old sword down and rushed out the door. 'Watch the store, Chad!' he had called after him, as if he were just going next door to hobnob with the baker. At first I had been happy to obey him. The uproar was far down the town, downhill by the bay, and the store seemed safe and strong around me.

But that had been an hour ago. Now the wind from the harbour carried the taint of smoke, and the night was no longer dark, but a terrible torch-lit twilight. The flames and the screams were coming closer. Master Hook had not come back.

Get out, I told the boy in whose body I hid. *Get out, run away, run as far and as fast as you can. Save yourself.* He did not hear me.

I crawled toward the door that still swung open and wide as Master Hook had left it. I peered out of it. A man ran past in the street and I cowered back. But he was probably a townsman, not a Raider, for he ran without looking back, with no other thought than to get as far away as he could. Mouth dry, I forced myself to my feet, clinging to the door jamb. I looked down on the town and harbour. Half the town was aflame. The mild summer night was choked with smoke and ash rising on the hot wind off the flames. Ships were burning in the harbour. In the light from the flames, I could see figures darting, fleeing and hiding from the Raiders who strode almost unchallenged through the town.

Someone came about the corner of the potter's store at the end of the street. He was carrying a lantern and walking so casually I felt a sudden surge of relief. Surely if he could be so calm, then the tide of the battle must be turning. I half rose from my crouch, only to cringe back as he blithely swung the oil lantern against the wooden storefront. The splashing oil ignited as the lamp broke, and fire raced gaily up the tinder-dry wood. I shrank back from the light of the leaping flames. I knew with a sudden certainty that there was no safety to be gained by hiding, that my only hope was in fleeing, and that I should have done it as soon as the alarms sounded. The resolution gave me a small measure of courage, enough that I leaped to my feet and dashed out and around the corner of the store.

For an instant, I was aware of myself as Fitz. I do not think the boy could sense me. This was not my Skilling out but his reaching to me with some rudimentary Skill sense of his own. I could not control his body at all, but I was locked into his experience. I was riding this boy and hearing his thoughts and sharing his perceptions just as Verity had once ridden me. But I had no time to consider how I was doing it, nor why I had been so abruptly joined to this stranger. For as Chad darted into the safety of the shadows, he was snatched back suddenly by a rough hand on his collar. For a brief moment he was paralysed with fear, and we looked up into the bearded grinning face of the Raider who gripped us. Another Raider flanked him, sneering evilly. Chad went limp with terror in his grasp. He gazed up helplessly at the moving knife, at the wedge of shining light that slid down its blade as it came towards his face.

I shared, for an instant, the hot-cold pain of the knife across my throat, the anguished moment of recognition as my warm wet blood coursed down my chest that it was over, it was already too late, I was dead now. Then as Chad tumbled heedlessly from the Raider's grasp into the dusty street, my consciousness came free of him. I hovered there, sensing for one awful moment the thoughts of the Raider. I heard the harshly guttural tones of his companion who nudged the dead boy with his booted foot, and knew that he rebuked the killer for wasting one who could have been Forged instead. The killer gave a snort of disdain, and replied something to the effect that he had been too young, not enough of a life behind him to be worth the Masters' time. Knew too, with a queasy swirling of emotions, that the killer had desired two things: to be merciful to a lad, and to enjoy the pleasure of a personal kill.

I had looked into the heart of my enemy. I still could not comprehend him.

I drifted down the street behind them, bodiless and substanceless. I had felt an urgency the moment before. Now I could not recall it. Instead, I roiled like fog, witnessing the fall and the sacking of Grimsmire Town in Bearns Duchy. Time after time, I was drawn to one or another of the inhabitants, to witness a struggle, a death, a tiny victory of escape. Still I can close my eyes and know that night, recall a dozen horrendous moments in lives I briefly shared. I came finally to where one man stood, great sword in hand, before his blazing home. He held off three Raiders, while behind him his wife and daughter fought to lift a burning beam and free a trapped son, that they might all flee together. None of them would forsake the others, and yet I knew the man was weary, too weary and weakened by blood-loss to lift his sword, yet alone wield it. I sensed, too, how the Raiders toyed with him, baiting him to exhaust himself, that they might take and Forge the whole family. I could feel the creeping chill of death seeping through the man. For an instant his head nodded toward his chest.

Suddenly the beleaguered man lifted his head. An oddly familiar light came into his eyes. He gripped the sword in both hands and with a roar suddenly sprang at his attackers. Two went down before his first onslaught, dying with amazement still printed plain on their features. The third met his sword blade to blade, but could not overmatch his fury. Blood dripped from the townsman's elbow and sheened his chest, but his sword rang like bells against the Raider's, battering down his guard and then suddenly dancing in, light as a feather, to trace a line of red across the Raider's throat. As his assailant fell, the man turned and sprang swiftly to his wife's side. He seized the burning beam, heedless of the flames, and lifted it off his son's body. For one last time, his eyes met those of his wife. 'Run!' he told her. 'Take the children and flee.' Then he crumpled into the street. He was dead.

As the stony-faced woman seized her children's hands and raced off with them, I felt a wraith rise from the body of the man who had died. It's me, I thought to myself, and then knew it was not. It sensed me and turned, his face so like my own. Or it had been, when he had been my age. It jolted me to think this was how Verity still perceived himself.

You, here? He shook his head in rebuke. *This is dangerous, boy. Even I am a fool to attempt this. And yet what else can we do, when they call us to them?* He considered me, standing so mute before him. *When did you gain the strength and talent to Skill-walk?*

I made no reply. I had no answers, no thoughts of my own. I felt I was a wet sheet flapping in the night wind, no more substantial than a blowing leaf.

Fitz, this is a danger to both of us. Go back. Go back now.

Is there truly a magic in the naming of a man's name? So much of the old lore insists there is. I suddenly recalled who I was, and that I did not belong here. But I had no concept of how I had come here, let alone how to return to my body. I gazed at Verity helplessly, unable to even formulate a request for help.

He knew. He reached a ghostly hand toward me. I felt his push as if he had placed the heel of his hand on my forehead and given a gentle shove.

My head bounced off the wall of the barn, and I saw sudden sparks of light from the impact. I was sitting there, in the barn behind the Scales inn. About me was only peaceful darkness, sleeping beasts, tickling straw. Slowly I slid over onto my side as wave after wave of giddiness and nausea swept over me. The weakness that often possessed me after I had managed to use the Skill broke over me like a wave. I opened my mouth to call for help, but only a wordless caw escaped my lips. I closed my eyes and sank into oblivion.

I awoke before dawn. I crawled to my pack, pawed through it, and then managed to stagger to the back door of the inn, where I quite literally begged a mug of hot water from the cook there. She looked on in disbelief as I crumbled strips of elfbark into it.

''S not good for you, you know that,' she warned me, and then watched in awe as I drank the scalding, bitter brew. 'They give that to slaves, they do, down in Chalced. Mix it in their food and drink, to keep them on their feet. Makes them despair as much as it gives them staying power, or so I've heard. Saps their will to fight back.'

I scarcely heard her. I was waiting to feel the effect. I had harvested my bark from young trees and feared it would lack potency. It did. It was some time before I felt the steeling warmth spread through me, steadying my trembling hands and clearing my vision. I rose from my seat on the kitchen's back steps, to thank the cook and give her back her mug.

'It's a bad habit to take up, a young man like you,' she chided me, and went back to her cooking. I departed the inn to stroll the streets as dawn broke over the hills. For a time, I half expected to find burned storefronts and gutted cottages, and empty-eyed Forged ones roaming the streets. But the Skill nightmare was eroded by the summer morning and the river wind. By daylight, the shabbiness of the town was more apparent. It seemed to me there were more beggars than we had had in Buckkeep Town, but I did not know if that was normal for a river town. I considered briefly what had happened to me last night, then with a shudder I set it aside. I did not know how I had done it. Like as not, it would not happen to me again. It heartened me to know Verity was still alive, even as it chilled me to know how rashly still he expended his Skill-strength. I wondered where he was this morning, and if, like me, he faced the dawn with the bitterness of Elfbark all through his mouth. If only I had mastered the Skill, I would not have had to wonder. It was not a thought to cheer one.

When I returned to the inn, the minstrels were already up and inside the inn breakfasting on porridge. I joined them at table, and Josh bluntly told me he had feared I had left without them. Honey had no words at all for me, but several times I caught Piper looking at me appraisingly.

It was still early when we left the inn, and if we did not march like soldiers, Harper Josh still set a respectable pace for us. I had thought he would have to be led, but he made his walking staff his guide. Sometimes he did walk with a hand on Honey's or Piper's shoulder, but it seemed more companionship than necessity. Nor was our journey boring, for as we walked he lectured, mostly to Piper, on the history of this region, and surprised me with the depth of his knowledge. We stopped for a bit when the sun was high and they shared with me the simple food they had. I felt uncomfortable taking it, yet there was no way I could excuse myself to go hunt with the wolf. Once the town was well behind us, I had sensed Nighteyes shadowing us. It was comforting to have him near, but I wished it were just he and I travelling together. Several times that day we were passed by other travellers, on horses or mules. Through gaps in the trees we occasionally glimpsed boats beating their way upriver against the current. As the morning passed, well-guarded carts and wagons overtook us. Each time Josh called out to ask if we might ride on the wagons. Twice we were politely refused. The others answered not at all. They moved hurriedly, and one group had several surly-looking men in a common livery that I surmised were hired guards.

We walked the afternoon away to the reciting of 'Crossfire's Sacrifice', the long poem about Queen Vision's coterie and how they laid down their lives that she might win a crucial battle. I had heard it before, several times, in Buckkeep. But by the end of the day, I had heard it two score times, as Josh worked with infinite patience to be sure that Piper sang it perfectly. I was grateful for the endless recitations, for it prevented talk.

But despite our steady pace, the falling of evening still found us far short of the next river town. I saw them all become uneasy as the light began to fail. Finally, I took command of the situation and told them we must leave the road at the next stream we crossed, and find a place to settle for the evening. Honey and Piper fell back behind Josh and me, and I could hear them muttering worriedly to one another. I could not reassure them, as Night-eyes had me, that there was not even a sniff of another traveller about. Instead, at the next crossing I guided them upstream and found a sheltered bank beneath a cedar tree where we might rest for the night.

I left them on the pretence of relieving myself, to spend time with Nighteyes assuring him all was well. It was time well spent, for he had discovered a place where the swirling creek water undercut the bank. He watched me intently as I lay on my belly and eased my hands into the water, and then slowly through the curtain of weeds that overhung it. I got a fine fat fish on my first try. Several minutes later, another effort yielded me a smaller fish. When I gave up, it was almost full dark, but I had three fish to take back to camp, leaving two, against my better judgment, for Nighteyes.

Fishing and ear scratching. The two reasons men were given hands, he told me genially as he settled down with them. He had already gulped down the entrails from mine as fast as I had cleaned them.

Watch out for bones, I warned him yet again.

My mother raised me on a salmon run, he pointed out. *Fish bones don't bother me.*

I left him shearing through the fish with obvious relish and returned to camp. The minstrels had a small fire burning. At the sound of my footsteps, all three leaped to their feet brandishing their walking staffs. 'It's me!' I told them belatedly.

'Thank Eda,' Josh sighed as he sat down heavily, but Honey only glared at me.

'You were gone a long time,' Piper said by way of explanation. I held up the fish threaded through the gills onto a willow stick.

'I found dinner,' I told them. 'Fish,' I added, for Josh's benefit.

'Sounds wonderful,' he said.

Honey took out waybread and a small sack of salt as I found a large flat stone and wedged it into the embers of the fire. I wrapped the fish in leaves and set them on the stone to bake. The smell of the cooking fish tantalized me even as I hoped it would not draw any Forged ones to our campfire.

I'm keeping watch still, Nighteyes reminded me, and I thanked him.

As I watched over the cooking fish, Piper muttered 'Crossfire's Sacrifice' to herself at my elbow.

'Hist the halt, and Cleave the blind,' I corrected her distractedly as I tried to turn the fish over without breaking it.

'I had it right!' she contradicted me indignantly.

'I'm afraid you did not, my lass. Cob is correct. Hist was the clubfoot and Cleave was blind from birth. Can you name the other five, Cob?' He sounded just like Fedwren hearing a lesson.

I had burned my finger on a coal and I stuck it in my mouth before answering. 'Burnt Crossfire led, and those around – were like him, not of body sound, but strong of heart. And true of soul. And herein let me count their roll – for you. 'Twas Hist the halt, and Cleave the blind, and Kevin of the wandering mind, hare-lipped Joiner, Sever was deaf, and Porter, who the foe men left – for dead, without his hands or eyes. And if you think you would despise such ones as these, then let me say . . .'

'Whoa!' Josh exclaimed with pleasure, and then asked, 'Had you bard's training, Cob, when you were small? You've caught the phrasing as well as the words. Though you make your pauses a bit too plain.'

'I? No. I've always had a quick memory, though.' It was hard not to smile at his praise of me, even though Honey sneered and shook her head at it.

'Could you recite the whole thing, do you think?' Josh asked challengingly.

'Perhaps,' I hedged. I knew I could. Both Burrich and Chade had drilled my memory skills often. And I'd heard it so often today I could not drive it from my head.

'Try it then. But not spoken. Sing it.'

'I have no voice for singing.'

'If you can speak, you can sing. Try it. Indulge an old man.'

Perhaps obeying old men was simply too deep a habit with me for me to defy it. Perhaps it was the look on Honey's face that told me plainly she doubted I could do it.

I cleared my throat and began it, singing softly until he gestured at me to raise my voice. He nodded his head as I worked my way through it, wincing now and then when I soured a note. I was about halfway through when Honey observed drily, 'The fish is burning.'

I dropped the song and sprang to poke stone and wrapped fish from the fire. The tails were scorched, but the rest was fine, steaming and firm. We portioned it out and I ate too rapidly. Twice as much would not have filled me, and yet I must be content with what I had. The waybread tasted surprisingly good with the fish, and afterwards Piper made a kettle of tea for us. We settled on our blankets about the fire.

'Cob, do you do well as a scribe?' Josh suddenly asked me.

I made a deprecating sound. 'Not as well as I'd like. But I get by.'

'Not as well as he'd like,' Honey muttered to Piper in mocking imitation.

Harper Josh ignored her. 'You're old for it, but you could be taught to sing. Your voice is not so bad; you sing like a boy, not knowing you've a man's depth of voice and lungs to call on now. Your memory is excellent. Do you play any instruments?'

'The sea-pipes. But not well.'

'I could teach you to play them well. If you took up with us . . .'

'Father! We scarcely know him!' Honey objected.

'I could have said the same to you when you left the loft last night,' he observed to her mildly.

'Father, all we did was talk.' She flashed a look at me, as if I had betrayed her. My tongue had turned to leather in my mouth.

'I know,' Josh agreed. 'Blindness seems to have sharpened my hearing. But if you have judged him someone safe to talk to, alone, at night, then perhaps I have judged him someone safe to offer our company to as well. What say you, Cob?'

I shook my head slowly, then, 'No,' I said aloud. 'Thank you all the same. I appreciate what you are offering, and to a stranger. I will travel with you as far as the next town, and I wish you well in finding other companions to travel with you from there. But . . . I have no real wish for . . .'

'You lost someone dear to you. I understand that. But total solitude is not good for any man,' Josh said quietly.

'Who did you lose?' Piper asked in her open way.

I tried to think how to explain without leaving myself open for more questions. 'My grandfather,' I said at last. 'And my wife.' Saying those words was like tearing a wound open.

'What happened?' Piper asked.

'My grandfather died. My wife left me.' I spoke shortly, wishing they'd let it be.

'The old die in their time,' Josh began gently, but Honey cut in brusquely with, 'That was the love you lost? What can you owe to a woman who left you? Unless you gave her cause to leave you?'

'It was more that I did not give her cause to stay,' I admitted unwillingly. Then, 'Please,' I said bluntly. 'I do not wish to speak of these things. At all. I will see you to the next town, but then my way is my own.'

'Well. That's clearly spoken,' Josh said regretfully. Something in his tone made me feel I had been rude, but there were no words I wished to call back.

There was little talk the rest of that evening, for which I was grateful. Piper offered to take first watch and Honey second. I did not object, as I knew Nighteyes would prowl all about us this night. Little got past that one. I slept better out in the open air, and came awake quickly when Honey stooped over me to shake me. I sat up, stretched, then nodded to her that I was awake and she could get more sleep. I got up and poked at the fire, then took a seat by it. Honey came to sit beside me.

'You don't like me, do you?' she asked quietly. Her tone was gentle.

'I don't know you,' I said as tactfully as I could.

'Um. And you don't wish to,' she observed. She looked at me levelly. 'But I've wanted to know you since I saw you blush in the inn. Nothing challenges my curiosity quite as much as a man who blushes. I've known few men who turn scarlet like that, simply because they're caught looking at a woman.' Her voice went low and throaty, as she leaned forward confidentially. 'I would love to know what you were thinking that brought the blood to your face like that.'

'Only that I had been rude to stare,' I told her honestly.

She smiled at me. 'That was not what I was thinking as I was looking back at you.' She moistened her mouth and hitched closer.

I suddenly missed Molly so acutely it was painful. 'I have no heart for this game,' I told Honey plainly. I rose. 'I think I shall get a bit more wood for the fire.'

'I think I know why your wife left you,' Honey said nastily. 'No heart, you say? I think your problem was a bit lower.' She rose and went back to her blankets. All I felt was relief that she had given up on me. I kept my word and went to gather more dry wood.

The first thing I asked Josh the next morning when he arose was, 'How far is it to the next town?'

'If we keep the same pace we struck yesterday, we should be there by tomorrow noon,' he told me.

I turned aside from the disappointment in his voice. As we shouldered our packs and set off, I reflected bitterly that I had walked away from people I had known and cared about to avoid the very situation I was now in with comparative strangers. I wondered if there were any way to live amongst other people and refuse to be harnessed by their expectations and dependencies.

The day was warm, but not unpleasantly so. If I had been alone, I would have found it pleasant hiking along the road. In the woods to one side of us, birds called to one another. To the other side of the road, we could see the river through the scanty trees, with occasional barges moving downstream, or oared vessels moving slowly against the current. We spoke little, and after a time, Josh put Piper back to reciting 'Crossfire's Sacrifice'. When she stumbled, I kept silent.

My thoughts drifted. Everything had been so much easier when I had not had to worry about my next meal or a clean shirt. I had thought myself so clever in dealing with people, so skilled at my profession. But I had had Chade to plot with, and time to prepare what I would say and do. I did not do so well when my resources were limited to my own wits and what I could carry on my back. Stripped of everything I had once unthinkingly relied on, it was not just my courage I had come to doubt. I questioned all my abilities now. Assassin, King's Man, warrior, man . . . was I any of them any more? I tried to recall the brash youngster who had pulled an oar on Verity's warship *Rurisk*, who had flung himself unthinkingly into battle wielding an axe. I could not grasp he had been me.

At noon Honey distributed the last of their waybread. It was not much. The women walked ahead of us, talking quietly to one another as they munched the dry bread and sipped from their waterskins. I ventured to suggest to Josh that we might camp earlier tonight, to give me a chance to do a bit of hunting or fishing.

'It would mean we would not get to the next town by noon tomorrow,' he pointed out gravely.

'Tomorrow evening would be soon enough,' I assured him quietly. He turned his head toward me, perhaps to hear me better, but his hazed-over eyes seemed to look inside me. It was hard to bear the appeal I saw there, but I made no reply to it.

When the day finally began to cool, I began to look for likely stopping places. Nighteyes had ranged ahead of us to scout when I sensed a sudden prickling of his hackles. *There are men here, smelling of carrion and their own filth. I can smell them, I can see them, but I cannot sense them otherwise.* The distress he always felt in the presence of Forged ones drifted back to me. I shared it. I knew they had once been human, and shared that Wit spark that every living creature does. To me, it was passing strange to see them move and speak when I could not sense they were alive. To Nighteyes, it was as if stones walked and ate.

How many? Old, young?

More than us, and bigger than you. A wolf's perception of odds. *They hunt the road, just around the bend from you.*

'Let's stop here,' I suggested suddenly. Three heads swivelled to regard me in puzzlement.

Too late. They've scented you, they are coming.

No time to dissemble, no time to come up with a likely lie.

'There are Forged ones ahead. More than two of them. They've been watching the road, and they're headed toward us now.' Strategy? 'Get ready,' I told them.

'How do you know this?' Honey challenged me.

'Let's run!' suggested Piper. She didn't care how I knew. The wideness of her eyes told me how much she had feared this.

'No. They'll overtake us, and we'll be winded when they do. And even if we did outrun them, we'd still have to get past them tomorrow.' I dropped my bundle to the road, kicked it clear of me. Nothing in it was worth my life. If we won, I'd be able to pick it up again. If we didn't, I wouldn't care. But Honey and Piper and Josh were musicians. Their instruments were in their bundles. None of them moved to free themselves from their burdens. I didn't waste my breath suggesting they do so. Almost instinctively, Piper and Honey moved to flank the old man. They gripped their walking sticks too tightly. Mine settled in my hands and I held it balanced and at the ready, waiting. For an instant I stopped thinking entirely. My hands seemed to know what to do of their own accord.

'Cob, take care of Honey and Piper. Don't worry about me, just don't let them get hurt,' Josh ordered me tersely.

His words broke through to me, and suddenly terror flooded me. My body lost its easy ready stance, and all I could think of was the pain defeat would bring me. I felt sick and shaky and wanted more than anything to simply turn and run, with no thought for the minstrels. Wait, wait, I wanted to cry to the day. I am not ready for this, I do not know if I will fight or run or simply faint where I stand. But time knows no mercy. *They come through the brush*, Nighteyes told me. *Two come swiftly and one lags behind. I think he shall be mine.*

Be careful, I warned him. I heard them crackling through the brush and scented the foulness of them. A moment later, Piper cried out as she spotted them, and then they rushed out of the trees at us. If my strategy was stand and fight, theirs was simply run up and attack. They were both larger than I was, and seemed to have no doubts at all. Their clothing was filthy but mostly intact. I did not think they had been Forged long. Both carried clubs. I had little time to comprehend more than that.

Forging did not make folk stupid, nor slow. They could no longer sense or feel emotions from others, nor, it seemed, recall what those emotions might make an enemy do. That often made their actions almost incomprehensible. It did not make them any less intelligent than they had been when whole, or any less skilled with their weapons. They did, however, act with an immediacy in satisfying their wants that was wholly animal. The horse they stole one day they might eat the next, simply because hunger was a more immediate want than the convenience of riding. Nor did they co-operate in a battle. Within their own groups, there was no loyalty. They were as likely to turn on one another to gain plunder as to attack a common enemy. They would travel together, and attack together, but not as a concerted effort. Yet they remained brutally cunning, remorselessly clever in their efforts to get what they desired.

I knew all this. So I was not surprised when both of them tried to get past me to attack the smaller folk first. What surprised me was the cowardly relief I felt. It paralysed me like one of my dreams, and I let them rush past me.

Honey and Piper fought like angry and frightened minstrels with sticks. There was no skill, no training there, not even the experience to fight as a team and thus avoid clubbing each other or Josh in the process. They had been schooled to music, not battle. Josh was paralysed in the middle, gripping his staff, but unable to strike out without risking injury to Honey or Piper. Rage contorted his face.

I could have run then. I could have snatched up my bundle and fled down the road and never looked back. The Forged ones would not have chased me; they were content with whatever prey was easiest. But I did not. Some tatter of courage or pride survived in me still. I attacked the smaller of the two men, even though he seemed more skilled with his cudgel. I left Honey and Piper to whack away at the larger man, and forced the other to engage with me. My first blow caught him low on the legs. I sought to cripple him, or at least knock him down. He did roar out with pain as he turned to attack me, but seemed to move no slower for it.

It was another thing I had noticed about Forged ones: pain seemed to affect them less. I knew that when I had been so badly beaten, a great part of what unmanned me was distress at the destruction of my body. It was odd to realize I had an emotional attachment to my own flesh. My deep desire to keep it functioning well surpassed simple avoidance of pain. A man takes pride in his body. When it is damaged, it is more than a physical thing.

Regal had known that. He had known that every blow his guards-men dealt me inflicted a fear with its bruise. Would he send me back to what I had been, a sickly creature who trembled after exertion, and feared the seizures that stole both body and mind from him? That fear had crippled me as much as their blows. Forged ones seemed not to have that fear; perhaps when they lost their attachment to everything else, they lost all affection for their own bodies.

My opponent spun about and dealt me a blow with his cudgel that sent a shock up to my shoulders as I caught it on my staff. Small pain, my body whispered to me of the jolt, and listened for more. He struck at me again, and again I caught it. Once I had engaged him, there was no safe way to turn and flee. He used his cudgel well: probably a warrior once, and one trained with an axe. I recognized the moves and blocked, or caught, or deflected each one. I feared him too much to attack him, feared the surprise blow that might streak past my staff if I did not constantly guard myself. I gave ground so readily that he glanced back over his shoulder, perhaps thinking he could just turn away from me and go after the women. I managed a timid reply to one of his blows; he barely flinched. He did not weary, nor did he give me space to take advantage of my longer weapon. Unlike me, he was not distracted by the shouts of the minstrels as they strove to defend themselves. Back up in the trees, I could hear muffled curses and faint growls. Nighteyes had stalked the third man, and had rushed in to attempt to hamstring him. He had failed, but now he circled him, keeping well out of range of the sword he carried.

I do not know that I can get past his blade, brother. But I think I can delay him here. He dares not turn his back on me to come down and attack you.

Be careful! It was all I had time to say to him, for the man with the club demanded every bit of my attention. Blow after blow he rained on me, and I soon realized he had stepped up his efforts, putting more force into his blows. He no longer felt he had to guard against a possible attack from me; he put all his strength into battering down my defence. Every jolt I caught squarely with my staff sent an echoing shock up to my shoulders. The impacts awakened old pains, jouncing healed injuries I had almost forgotten. My endurance as a fighter was not what it had been. Hunting and walking did not toughen a body and build muscle the way pulling an oar all day had. A flood of doubt undercut my concentration. I suspected I was overmatched, and so feared the pain to come that I could not plot how to avoid it. Desperation to avoid injury is not the same as determination to win. I kept trying to work away from him, to gain space for my staff, but he pressed me relentlessly.

I caught a glimpse of the minstrels. Josh stood squarely in the middle of the road, staff ready, but the battle had moved away from him. Honey was limping backwards as the man pursued her. She was trying to ward off blows from the man's club while Piper followed, ineffectually thwacking him across the shoulders with her slender staff. He simply hunched to her blows and remained intent on the injured Honey. It woke something in me. 'Piper, take his legs out!' I yelled to her, and then put my attention to my own problems as a cudgel grazed my shoulder. I dealt back a couple of quick blows that lacked force and leaped away from him.

A sword sliced my shoulder and skimmed along my rib-cage.

I cried out in astonishment and nearly dropped my staff before I realized the injury wasn't mine. I felt as much as heard Nighteyes' surprised yelp of pain. And then the impact of a boot to my head.

Dazed, cornered. *Help me!*

There were other memories, deeper memories, buried beneath my recall of the beatings Regal's guards had inflicted on me. Years before then, I had felt the slash of a knife and the impact of a boot. But not on my own flesh. A terrier I had bonded with, Smithy, not even full grown, had fought in the dark against one who had attacked Burrich in my absence. Fought, and died later of his injuries, before I could even reach his side again. I discovered abruptly there was a threat more potent than my own death.

Fear for myself crumpled away before my terror of losing Nighteyes. I did what I knew I had to do. I shifted my stance, stepped in and accepted the blow on my shoulder to bring me in range. The shock of it jolted down my arm and for an instant I couldn't feel anything in that hand. I trusted it was still there. I had shortened my grip on my staff, and I brought that end up sharply, catching his chin. Nothing had prepared him for my abrupt change in tactics. His chin flew up, baring his throat, and I jabbed my staff sharply against the hollow at the base of his throat. I felt the small bones there give way. He gasped out blood in a sudden exhalation of pain and I danced back, shifted my grip, and brought the other end around to impact his skull. He went down, and I turned and raced up into the woods.

Snarls and grunts of effort led me to them. Nighteyes had been brought to bay, his left forepaw curled up to his chest. Blood slicked his left shoulder, and beaded like red jewels on the guardhairs all along his left side. He had backed deeply into a dense thicket of tangled blackberry canes. The savage thorns and snagging runners that he had sought as shelter now fenced him round and blocked his escape. He had pressed into them as deeply as he could to avoid the slashes of the sword, and I could feel the damage to his feet. The thorns that jabbed into Nighteyes likewise kept his attacker at a distance, and the yielding canes absorbed many of the sword's blows as the man strove to hack through them and get at the wolf.

At the sight of me Nighteyes gathered his courage and rounded suddenly to face his attacker with a savage outburst of snarls. The Forged one drew back his sword for a thrust that would impale my wolf. There was no point on the end of my staff, but with a wordless cry of fury I drove it into the man's back so brutally that it punched through flesh and into his lungs. He roared out a spattering of red drops and rage. He tried to turn to confront me, but I still had hold of my staff. I threw my weight against it, forcing him staggering into the blackberry tangle. His outstretched hands found nothing to catch him save tearing brambles. I pinned him into the yielding blackberry canes with my full weight on the staff and Nighteyes, emboldened, sprang onto his back. The wolf's jaws closed on the back of the man's thick neck and worried at him until blood spattered both of us. The Forged one's strangling cries gradually diminished to passive gurglings.

I had completely forgotten about the minstrels until a deep cry of anguish recalled them to me. Stooping, I seized the sword the Forged one had dropped and ran back to the road, leaving Nighteyes to flop down exhausted and begin licking at his shoulder.

As I burst out of the woods, a horrifying sight met my eyes. The Forged one had flung himself upon a struggling Honey and was tearing at her clothes. Piper knelt in the road dust, clutching at her arm and shrieking wordlessly. A dishevelled and dusty Josh had climbed to his feet and, staffless, was groping toward Piper's cries.

In a moment I was in their midst. I kicked the man to lift him off Honey, then plunged the sword into him in a downward two-handed thrust. He struggled wildly, kicking and clutching at me, but I leaned on the blade, forcing it down into his chest. As he fought against the metal that pinned him, he tore the wound wider. His mouth cursed me with wordless cries and then panting gasps that flung droplets of blood with the sounds. His hands seized my right calf and tried to jerk my leg from under me. I simply put more weight on the blade. I longed to pull the sword out and kill him quickly, but he was so strong I did not dare release him. Honey ended him finally, bringing the end of her staff down in a smashing drive to the centre of his face. The man's sudden stillness was as much a mercy to me as to him. I found the strength to pull the sword out of him, then staggered backwards to sit down suddenly in the road.

My vision dimmed and cleared and dimmed again. Piper's screams of pain might have been the distant crying of seabirds. Suddenly there was too much of everything and I was everywhere. Up in the woods, I licked at my shoulder, a laying aside of dense fur with my tongue, a careful probing of the slash as I coated it with saliva. And yet I sat in the sun on the road, smelling dust and blood and excrement as the slain man's bowels loosened. I felt every blow I had taken and dealt, the exertion as well as the jolting damage from the club's impact. The savage way I had killed suddenly had a different connotation to me. I knew what it was to feel the kind of pain that I had inflicted. I knew what they had felt, down and struggling without hope, with death as their only escape from more pain. My mind vibrated between the extremes of killer and victim. I was both.

And alone. More alone than I had ever been. Always before, at a time like this, there had been someone for me. Shipmates at the end of a battle, or Burrich coming to patch me up and drag me home, and a home waiting for me, with Patience to come and fuss over me, or Chade and Verity to remonstrate with me to be more careful of myself. Molly arriving with the quiet and the darkness to touch me softly. This time the battle was over, and I was alive, but no one save the wolf cared. I loved him, but suddenly I knew that I longed for a human touch as well. The separation from those who had cared about me was more than I could bear. Had I been truly a wolf, I would have lifted my nose to the sky and howled. As it was, I reached out, in a way I cannot describe. Not the Wit, not the Skill, but some unholy blending of the two, a terrible questing for someone, anywhere, who might care to know I was alive.

Almost, I felt something. Did Burrich, perhaps, somewhere lift up his head and look about the field he worked in, did he for an instant smell blood and dust instead of the rich earth he turned up to harvest the root crops? Did Molly straighten up from her laundering and set her hands to her aching back and look about, wondering at a sudden pang of desolation? Did I tug at Verity's weary consciousness, distract Patience for a moment or two from sorting her herbs on the drying trays, set Chade to frowning as he set a scroll aside? Like a moth battering against a window, I rattled myself against their consciousnesses. I longed to feel the affection I had taken for granted. Almost, I thought, I reached them, only to fall back exhausted into myself, sitting alone in the dust of the road, with the blood of three men spattered on me.

She kicked dirt on me.

I lifted my eyes. At first Honey was a dark silhouette against the westering sun. Then I blinked and saw the look of disgust and fury on her face. Her clothes were torn, her hair draggled about her face. 'You ran away!' she accused me. I felt how much she despised my cowardice. 'You ran away, and left him to break Piper's arm and club my father down and try to rape me. What kind of a man are you? What kind of a man can do a thing like that?'

There were a thousand answers to that, and none. The emptiness inside me assured me that nothing would be solved by speaking to her. Instead I pushed myself to my feet. She stared after me as I walked back down the road to where I had dropped my pack. It seemed like hours since I had kicked it clear of my feet. I picked it up and carried it back to where Josh sat in the dust beside Piper and tried to comfort her. Pragmatic Honey had opened their packs. Josh's harp was a tangle of wood bits and string. Piper would play no pipes until her arm healed weeks from now. It was as it was, and I did what I could do about it.

And that was nothing, save build a fire by the side of the road, and fetch water from the river and set it to boiling. I sorted out the herbs that would calm Piper and soften the pain of her arm. I found dry straight sticks and shaved them flat for splinting. And up on the hillside in the woods behind me? *It hurts, my brother, but it did not go deep. Still, it pulls open when I try to walk. And thorns, I am thick with thorns like flies on carrion.*

I shall come to you now and pick out every one.

No. I can take care of this myself. See to those others. He paused. *My brother. We should have run away.*

Why was it so hard to go to Honey and ask quietly if she had cloth we could tear to bind the splinting to Piper's arm? She did not deign to reply to me, but blind Josh mutely handed me the soft fabric that had once wrapped his harp. Honey despised me, Josh seemed numbed with shock, and Piper was so lost in her own pain she scarcely noticed me. But somehow I got them to move over beside the fire. I walked Piper over there, my arm around her and my free hand supporting her injured arm. I got her seated, and then gave her first the tea I had brewed. I spoke more to Harper Josh than to her when I said, 'I can draw the bone straight, and splint it. I've had to do as much before for men hurt in battle. But I do not claim to be a healer. When we get to the next town, it may have to be set again.'

He nodded slowly. We both knew there was no real alternative. So he knelt behind Piper and held her by the shoulders, and Honey gripped her upper arm firmly. I set my teeth against the pain she felt and firmly drew her forearm straight. She screamed, of course, for no mere tea could deaden that sort of pain completely. But she also forced herself not to struggle. Tears coursed down her cheeks and her breath came raggedly as I splinted and bound her arm. I showed her how to carry it partially inside her vest to support the weight and steady it against movement. Then I gave her another mug of the tea and turned to Josh.

He had taken a blow to the head, and it had dazed him for a moment, but not knocked him out. There was swelling, and he winced at my touch, but the flesh had not split. I washed it with cool water, and told him the tea might ease him as well. He thanked me, and somehow I felt shamed by it. Then I looked up to where Honey watched me with cat's eyes across the small fire.

'Were you hurt?' I asked her quietly.

'There's a knot on my shin the size of a plum where he hit me. And he left claw marks down my neck and breasts trying to get at me. But I can care for my hurts myself, thank you all the same . . . Cob. Small thanks to you I am alive at all.'

'Honey.' Josh spoke in a dangerously low voice. There was as much weariness in it as anger.

'He ran away, Father. He felled his man and then he turned and ran. If he had helped us then, none of this would have happened. Not Piper's broken arm, nor your smashed harp. He ran away.'

'But he came back. Let us not imagine what would have happened if he had not. Perhaps we took some injuries, but you can still thank him that you are alive.'

'I thank him for nothing,' she said bitterly. 'One moment of courage, and he could have saved our livelihood. What have we now? A harper with no harp, and a piper who cannot lift her arm to hold her instrument.'

I rose and walked away from them. I was suddenly too weary to hear her out, and much too discouraged to explain myself at all. Instead I dragged the two bodies from the road, and pulled them onto the sward on the river side. In the failing light, I re-entered the woods, and sought out Nighteyes. He had already cared for his own injuries better than I could. I dragged my fingers through his coat, dusting thorns and bits of blackberry tangle from it. For a short time I sat next to him. He lay down and put his head on my knee and I scratched his ears. It was all the communication we needed. Then I got up, found the third body, gripped him by the shoulders, and dragged him down out of the woods to join the other two. Without compunction, I went through their pockets and pouches. Two of them yielded but a handful of small coins, but the one with the sword had had twelve silver bits in his pouch. I took his pouch and added the other coins to it. I also took his battered sword belt and sheath, and picked up the sword from the road. Then I busied myself until the darkness was complete in picking up river stones and piling them around and finally on top of the bodies. When I had finished, I went down to the river's edge and laved my hands and arms and splashed water up onto my face. I took off my shirt and rinsed the blood from it, then put it back on cold and wet. For a moment it felt good on my bruises; then my muscles began to stiffen with the chill of it.

I went back to the small fire that now lit the faces of the folk around it. When I got there, I reached for Josh's hand, and then set the pouch into it. 'Perhaps it will be enough to help you along until you can replace your harp,' I told him.

'Dead men's money to ease your conscience?' Honey sneered.

The frayed ends of my temper parted. 'Pretend they survived, for by Buck law they would have had to pay you restitution at least,' I suggested. 'And if that still does not please you, throw the coins in the river for all I care.' I ignored her much more thoroughly than she had me. Despite my aches and twinges, I unbundled the sword belt. Nighteyes had been right: the swordsman had been a lot bigger than me. I set the leather against a piece of wood and bored a new hole into the strap with my knife. That done, I stood, and fastened it about me. There was comfort in the weight of a sword at my side again. I drew the blade and examined it by the firelight. It was not exceptional, but it was functional and sturdy.

'Where did you get that?' Piper asked. Her voice was a bit wavery.

'Took it off the third man, up in the woods,' I said shortly. I resheathed it.

'What is it?' Harper Josh asked.

'A sword,' Piper said.

Josh turned his hazy eyes to me. 'There was a third man up in the woods with a sword?'

'Yes.'

'And you took it away from him and killed him?'

'Yes.'

He snorted softly and shook his head at himself. 'When we shook hands, I knew well it was no scriber's hand I gripped. A pen does not leave calluses such as you bear, nor does it muscle a forearm that way. You see, Honey, he did not run away. He but went to . . .'

'If he had killed the man attacking us first, it would have been wiser,' she insisted stubbornly.

I undid my bundle and shook out my blanket. I lay down on it. I was hungry, but there was nothing to be done about that. I could do something about how tired I was.

'Are you going to sleep?' Piper asked. Her face reflected as much alarm as she could muster in her drugged state.

'Yes.'

'What if more Forged ones come?' she demanded.

'Then Honey can kill them in whatever order she deems wise,' I suggested sourly. I shifted on my blanket until my sword was clear and handy, and closed my eyes. I heard Honey rise slowly and begin to put out bedding for the rest of them.

'Cob?' Josh asked softly. 'Did you take any coin for yourself?'

'I do not expect to have need of coin again,' I told him as quietly. I did not explain that I no longer planned to have much to do with humans. I never wanted to explain myself again to anyone. I did not care if they understood me or not.

I closed my eyes and groped out, to touch briefly with Nighteyes. Like me, he was hungry but had chosen to rest instead. *By tomorrow evening, I shall be free to hunt with you again*, I promised him. He sighed in satisfaction. He was not that far away. My fire was a spark through the trees below him. He rested his muzzle on his forepaws.

I was wearier than I had realized. My thoughts drifted, blurred. I let it all go and floated free, away from the pains that niggled at my body. Molly, I thought wistfully. Molly. But I did not find her. Somewhere Burrich slept on a pallet made up before a hearth. I saw him, and it felt almost as if I Skilled him but I could not hold the vision. The firelight illuminated the planes of his face;

he was thinner, and burnt dark with hours of field work. I spun slowly away from him. The Skill lapped against me, but I could find no control of it.

When my dreams brushed up against Patience, I was shocked to find her in a private chamber with Lord Bright. He looked like a cornered animal. A young woman in a lovely gown was evidently as startled as he to have Patience intrude on them. She was armed with a map, and she was speaking as she pushed aside a tray of dainties and wine to unfurl it on the table. 'I have found you neither stupid nor craven, Lord Bright. So I must assume you are ignorant. I intend that your education shall no longer be neglected. As this map by the late Prince Verity will prove to you, if you do not take action soon, all the coast of Buck will be at the mercy of the Red Ships. And they have no mercy.' She lifted those piercing hazel eyes and stared at him as she had so often stared at me when she expected to be obeyed. I almost pitied him. I lost my feeble grip on the scene. Like a leaf borne by wind, I swirled away from them.

I did not know if I next went higher or deeper, only that I felt all that bound me to my body was a tenuous thread. I turned and spun in a current that tugged at me, encouraging me to let go. Somewhere a wolf whined in anxiety. Ghostly fingers plucked at me as if seeking my attention.

Fitz. Be careful. Get back.

Verity. But his Skilling had no more force than a puff of wind, despite the effort I knew it cost him. Something was between us, a cold fog, yielding yet resisting, entangling like brambles. I tried to care, tried to find enough fear to send me fleeing back to my body. But it was like being trapped inside a dream and trying to awaken. I could not find a way to struggle out of it. I could not find the will to try.

A whiff of dog-magic stench in the air, and look what I find. Will hooked into me like cat claws, drew me tight against him. *Hello, Bastard.* His deep satisfaction reawakened every nuance of my fear. I could feel his cynical smile. *Neither of them dead, not the Bastard with his perverted magic nor Verity the pretender. Tsk, tsk. Regal will be chagrined to find he was not as successful as he had thought. This time, though, I shall make sure of things for him. My way*. I felt an insidious probing of my defences, more intimate than a kiss. As if he kneaded a whore's flesh, he felt me over for weaknesses. I dangled like a rabbit in his grasp, waiting only for the twist and jerk that would end my life. I felt how he had grown in strength and cunning.

Verity, I whimpered, but my king could neither hear nor respond.

He weighed me in his grip. *What use to you this strength you have never learned to master? None at all. But to me, ah, to me it shall give wings and claws. You shall make me strong enough to seek out Verity no matter how he may hide himself.*

Suddenly I was leaking strength like a punctured waterskin. I had no idea how he had penetrated my defences, and knew of no way to ward him off. He clutched my mind greedily to his and leeched at me. This was how Justin and Serene had killed King Shrewd. He had gone swiftly, like a bubble popping. I could find neither will nor strength to struggle as Will forced down all walls between us. His foreign thoughts were a pressure inside my mind as he scrabbled at my secrets, all the while drawing off my substance.

But within me, a wolf was waiting for him. *My brother!* Night-eyes declared, and launched at him, tooth and nail. Somewhere in the vast distance, Will shrieked in horror and dismay. However strong he might be in the Skill, he had no knowledge at all of the Wit. He was as powerless before Nighteyes' attack as I had been before his. Once, when Justin had Skill-attacked me, Night-eyes had responded. I had watched as Justin had gone down just as if he were being physically savaged by a wolf. He had lost all concentration and control over his Skill and I had been able to break free of him. I could not see what was happening to Will, but I sensed Nighteyes' snapping jaws. I was buffeted by the strength of Will's horror. He fled, breaking the Skill-link between us so suddenly that for a moment I was unsure of my identity. Then I was back, wide awake, inside my own body.

I sat up on my blanket, sweat streaming down my back, and slammed up every wall about myself that I could remember how to erect.

'Cob?' Josh asked in some alarm, and I saw him sit up sleepily.

Honey was staring at me from her own blanket where she sat keeping watch. I choked back a panting sob.

'A nightmare,' I managed huskily. 'Just a nightmare.' I staggered to my feet, horrified at how weakened I was. The world spun around me. I could barely stand. Fear of my own weakness spurred me. I caught up my small kettle, and carried it off with me as I headed for the river. Elfbark tea, I promised myself, and hoped it would be potent enough. I veered wide of the heaped stones that covered the Forged ones' bodies. Before I reached the bank of the river, Nighteyes was beside me, hitching along on three legs. I dropped my kettle and sank down beside him. I threw my arms around him, mindful of the slash on his shoulder, and buried my face in his ruff.

I was so scared. I nearly died.

I understand now why we must kill them all, he said calmly. *If we do not, they will never let us be. We must hunt them down to their own lair and kill them all.*

It was the only comfort he could offer me.

SIX

The Wit and the Skill

Minstrels and wandering scribes hold special places in the society of the Six Duchies. They are repositories of knowledge, not only of their own crafts, but of so much more. The minstrels hold the histories of the Six Duchies, not just the general history that has shaped the kingdom, but the particular histories, of the small towns and even the families who make them up. Although it is the dream of every minstrel to be sole witness to some great event, and thus gain the authoring of a new saga, their true and lasting importance lies in their constant witnessing of the small events that make up life's fabric. When there is a question of a property line, or family lineage, or even of a long-term promise made, the minstrels are called upon, to supply the details that others may have forgotten. Supporting them, but not supplanting them, are the wandering scribes. For a fee, they will provide written record of a wedding, a birth, of land changing hands, of inheritances gained or dowries promised. Such records may be intricate things, for every party involved must be identified in a way that is unmistakable. Not just by name and profession, but by lineage and location and appearance. As often as not, a minstrel is then called to make his mark as witness to what the scribe has written, and for this reason, it is not unusual to find them travelling in company together, or for one person to profess both trades. Minstrels and scribes are by custom well treated in the noble houses, finding their winter quarters there and sustenance and comfort in old age. No lord wishes to be ill remembered in the tellings of minstrels and scribes, or worse yet, not remembered at all. Generosity to them is taught as simple courtesy. One knows one is in the presence of a miser when one sits at table in a keep that boasts no minstrels.

* * *

I bid the musicians farewell at the door of an inn in a shoddy little town called Crowsneck the next afternoon. Rather, I bid Josh farewell. Honey stalked into the inn without a backwards glance at me. Piper did look at me, but the look was so puzzled that it conveyed nothing to me. Then she followed Honey in. Josh and I were left standing in the street. We had been walking together and his hand was still on my shoulder. 'Bit of a step here at the inn door,' I warned Josh quietly.

He nodded his thanks. 'Well. Some hot food will be welcome,' he observed and pushed his chin toward the door.

I shook my head, then spoke my refusal. 'Thank you, but I won't be going in with you. I'm moving on.'

'Right now? Come, Cob, at least have a mug of beer and a bite to eat. I know that Honey is . . . difficult to tolerate sometimes. But you needn't assume she speaks for all of us.'

'It's not that. I simply have something that I must do. Something I have put off for a long, long time. Yesterday I realized that until I have done it, there will be no peace for me.'

Josh sighed heavily. 'Yesterday was an ugly day. I would not base any life decision on it.' He swung his head to look toward me. 'Whatever it is, Cob, I think time will make it better. It does most things, you know.'

'Some things,' I muttered distractedly. 'Other things don't get better until you . . . mend them. One way or another.'

'Well.' He held out his hand to me, and I took it. 'Good luck to you then. At least this fighter's hand has a sword to grip now. That can't be bad fortune for you.'

'Here's the door,' I said, and opened it for him. 'Good luck to you as well,' I told him as he passed me, and closed it behind him.

As I stepped out into the open street again, I felt as if I had tossed a burden aside. Free again. I would not soon weight myself down with anything like that again.

I'm coming, I told Nighteyes. *This evening, we hunt.*

I'll be watching for you.

I hitched my bundle a bit higher on my shoulder, took a fresh grip on my staff and strode down the street. I could think of nothing in Crowsneck that I could possibly desire. My path took me straight through the market square however, and the habits of a lifetime die hard. My ears pricked up to the grumbles and complaints of those who had come to bargain. Buyers demanded to know why prices were so high; sellers replied that the trade from downriver was scarce, and whatever goods came upriver as far as Crowsneck were dear. Prices were worse upriver, they assured them. For all those who complained about the high prices, there were as many who came looking for what was simply not there. It was not just the ocean fish and the thick wool of Buck that no longer came up the river. It was as Chade had predicted; there were no silks, no brandies, no fine Bingtown gemwork, nothing from the Coastal Duchies, nor from the lands beyond. Regal's attempt to strangle the Mountain Kingdom's trade routes had also deprived the Crowsneck merchants of Mountain amber and furs and other goods. Crowsneck had been a trading town. Now it was stagnant, choking on a surplus of its own goods and naught to trade them for.

At least one shambling drunk knew where to put the blame. He wove his way through the market, caroming off stalls and staggering through the wares lesser merchants had displayed on mats. His shaggy black hair hung to his shoulders and merged with his beard. He sang as he came, or growled, more truly, for his voice was louder than it was musical. There was little melody to fix the tune in my mind, and he botched whatever rhyme had once been to the song, but the sense of it was clear. When Shrewd had been King of the Six Duchies, the river had run with gold, but now that Regal wore the crown, the coasts all ran with blood. There was a second verse, saying it was better to pay taxes to fight the Red Ships than pay them to a king that hid, but that one was interrupted by the arrival of the City Guard. There were a pair of them, and I expected to see them halt the drunk and shake him down for coins to pay for whatever he'd broken. I should have been forewarned by the silence that came over the market when the guards appeared. Commerce ceased, folk melted out of the way or pressed back against the stalls to allow them passage. All eyes followed and fixed on them.

They closed on the drunk swiftly, and I was one of the silent crowd watching as they seized him. The drunk goggled at them in dismay, and the look of appeal he swept over the crowd was chilling in its intensity. Then one of the guards drew back a gauntleted fist and sank it into his belly. The drunk looked to be a tough old man, gone paunchy in the way that some thickly-set men do as they age. A soft man would have collapsed to that blow. He curled himself forward over the guard's fist, his breath whistling out, and then abruptly spewed out a gush of soured ale. The guards stepped back in distaste, one giving the drunk a shove that sent him tottering off balance. He crashed against a market-stall, sending two baskets of eggs splatting into the dirt. The egg merchant said nothing, only stepped back deeper into his stall as if he did not wish to be noticed at all.

The guards advanced on the unfortunate man. The first one there gripped him by the shirt front and dragged him to his feet. He struck him a short, straight blow to the face that sent him crashing into the other guard's arms. That one caught him, and held him up for his partner's fist to find his belly again. This time the drunk dropped to his knees and the guard behind him casually kicked him down.

I did not realize I had started forward until a hand caught at my shoulder. I looked back into the wizened face of the gaunt old woman who clutched at me. 'Don't make them mad,' she breathed. 'They'll let him off with a beating, if no one makes them angry. Make them angry, and they'll kill him. Or worse, take him off for the King's Circle.'

I locked eyes with her weary gaze, and she looked down as if ashamed. But she did not take her hand from my shoulder. Like her, then, I looked aside from what they did, and tried not to hear the impacts on flesh, the grunts and strangled cries of the beaten man.

The day was hot, and the guards wore more mail than I was accustomed to seeing on City Guards. Perhaps that was what saved the drunk. No one likes to sweat in armour. I looked back in time to see one stoop and cut loose the man's purse, heft it, and then pocket it. The other guard looked about at the crowd as he announced, 'Black Rolf has been fined and punished for the treasonous act of making mock of the King. Let it be an example to all.'

The guards left him lying in the dirt and litter of the market square and continued their rounds. One guard watched over his shoulder as they strode away, but no one moved until they turned a corner. Then gradually the market stirred back to life. The old woman lifted her hand from my shoulder and turned back to haggling for turnips. The egg merchant came around the front of his stall, to stoop and gather the few unbroken eggs and the yolky baskets. No one looked directly at the fallen man.

I stood still for a time, waiting for a shaky coldness inside me to fade. I wanted to ask why City Guards should care about a drunkard's song, but no one met my querying glance. I suddenly had even less use for anyone or anything in Crowsneck. I hitched my pack a notch higher and resumed my trek out of town. But as I drew near the groaning man, his pain lapped against me. The closer I came, the more distinct it was, almost like forcing my hand deeper and deeper into a fire. He lifted his face to stare at me. Dirt clung to the blood and vomit on it. I tried to keep walking.

Help him. My mind rendered thus the sudden mental urging I felt.

I halted as if knifed, nearly reeling. That plea was not from Nighteyes. The drunk got a hand under himself and levered himself higher. His eyes met mine in dumb appeal and misery. I had seen such eyes before; they were those of an animal in pain.

Maybe we should help him? Nighteyes asked uncertainly.

Hush, I warned him.

Please, help him. The plea had grown in urgency and strength. *Old Blood asks of Old Blood*, the voice in my mind spoke more clearly, not in words but images. I Witted the meaning behind it. It was a laying on of clan obligation.

Are they pack with us? Nighteyes asked wonderingly. I knew he could sense my confusion, and did not reply.

Black Rolf had managed to get his other hand under himself. He pushed himself up onto one knee, then mutely extended a hand to me. I clasped his forearm and drew him slowly to his feet. Once he was upright, he swayed slightly. I kept hold of his arm and let him catch his balance against me. As dumb as he, I offered him my walking staff. He took it, but did not relinquish my arm. Slowly we left the market place, the drunk leaning on me heavily. Entirely too many people stared after us curiously. As we walked through the streets, people glanced up at us, and then away. The man said nothing to me. I kept expecting him to point out some direction he wished to go, some house claimed as his, but he said nothing.

As we reached the outskirts of town, the road meandered down to the riverbank. The sun shone through an opening in the trees, glinting silver on the water. Here a shoal of the river swept up against a grassy bank framed by willow woods. Some folk carrying baskets of wet washing were just leaving. He gave me a slight tug on the arm to indicate he wished to get to the river's edge. Once there, Black Rolf sank to his knees, then leaned forward to plunge not just his face but his entire head and neck into the water. He came up, rubbed at his face with his hands, and then ducked himself again. The second time he came up, he shook his head vigorously as a wet dog, sending water spraying in all directions. He sat back on his heels, and looked up at me blearily.

'I drink too much when I come to town,' he said hollowly.

I nodded to that. 'Will you be all right now?'

He nodded back. I could see his tongue move inside his mouth, checking for cuts and loose teeth. The memory of old pain rolled over restlessly inside me. I wanted to be away from any reminders of that.

'Good luck, then,' I told him. I stooped, upstream of him, and drank and refilled my waterskin. Then I rose, hefted my pack again, and turned to leave. A prickling of the Wit swivelled my head suddenly toward the woods. A stump shifted, then suddenly reared up as a brown bear. She snuffed the air, then dropped to all fours again and shambled toward us. 'Rolf,' I said quietly as I started to slowly back up. 'Rolf, there's a bear.'

'She's mine,' he said as quietly. 'You've nothing to fear from her.'

I stood stock-still as she shuffled out of the woods and down the grassy bank. As she drew close to Rolf, she gave a low cry, oddly like a cow's bawl for her calf. Then she nudged her big head against him. He stood up, leaning a hand on her sloping front shoulders to do so. I could sense them communicating with one another, but had no notion of their messages. Then she lifted her head to look directly at me. *Old Blood*, she acknowledged me. Her little eyes were deep set above her muzzle. As she walked, the sunlight sleeked her glossy, rolling hide. They both came toward me. I did not move.

When they were very close, she lifted her nose and pressed her snout firmly against me and began to take long snuffs.

My brother? Nighteyes queried in some alarm.

I think it is all right. I scarcely dared to breathe. I had never been this close to a live bear.

Her head was the size of a bushel basket. Her hot breath against my chest reeked of river fish. After a moment she stepped away from me, huffing an *uh, uh, uh* sound in her throat as if considering all she had scented on me. She sat back on her haunches, taking air in through her open mouth as if tasting my scent on it. She wagged her head slowly from side to side, then seemed to reach a decision. She dropped to all fours again and trundled off. 'Come,' Rolf said briefly, and motioned me to follow. They set off towards the woods. Over his shoulder, he added, 'We have food to share. The wolf is welcome, too.'

After a moment, I set out after them.

Is this wise? I could sense that Nighteyes was not far away and was moving toward me as swiftly as he could, eeling between trees as he came down a hillside.

I need to understand what they are. Are they like us? I have never spoken to any like us.

A derisive snort from Nighteyes. *You were raised by Heart of the Pack. He is more like us than these. I am not certain I wish to come close to a bear, or to the man who thinks with the bear.*

I want to know more, I insisted. *How did she sense me, how did she reach out to me?* Despite my curiosity, I stayed well back from the strange twosome. Man and bear shambled along ahead of me. They wended their way through the willow woods beside the river, avoiding the road. At a place where the forest drew densely down to the opposite side of the road, they crossed hastily. I followed. In the deeper shadow of these larger trees, we soon struck a game trail that cut across the face of a hill. I sensed Nighteyes before he materialized beside me. He was panting from his haste. My heart smote me at how he moved on three legs. Too often he had taken injuries on my behalf. What right did I have to ask that of him?

It is not as bad as all that.

He did not like to walk behind me, but the trail was too narrow for both of us. I ceded him the path and walked alongside, dodging branches and trunks, closely watching our guides. Neither of us were easy about that bear. A single swipe from one of her paws could cripple or kill, and my small experience of bears did not indicate they had even temperaments. Walking in the flow of her scent kept Nighteyes' hackles erect and my skin aprickle.

In time we came to a small cabin set snug against the side of the hill. It was made of stone and log, chinked with moss and earth. The logs that roofed it were overlain with turf. Grasses and even small bushes sprouted from the roof of the cabin. The door was unusually wide and gaped open. Both man and bear preceded us inside. After a moment of hesitation, I ventured near to peer inside. Nighteyes hung back, hackles half-raised, ears pricked forward.

Black Rolf stepped back to the door to look out at us. 'Come in and be welcome,' he offered. When he saw that I hesitated, he added, 'Old Blood does not turn on Old Blood.'

Slowly I entered. There was a low slab table in the centre of the room with a bench to either side of it, and a river rock hearth in a corner between two large comfortable chairs. Another door led to a smaller sleeping room. The cabin smelt like a bear's den, rank and earthy. In one corner was a scattering of bones and the walls there bore the marks of claws.

A woman was just setting aside a broom after sweeping the dirt floor. She was dressed in brown, and her short hair was sleeked to her head like an acorn's cap. She turned her head quickly toward me and fixed me with an unblinking stare from brown eyes. Rolf gestured toward me. 'Here are the guests I was telling you about, Holly,' he announced.

'Thank you for your hospitality,' I ventured.

She looked almost startled. 'Old Blood always welcomes Old Blood.'

I brought my eyes back to confront the glittering blackness of

Rolf's gaze. 'I have never heard of this "Old Blood" before.'

'But you know what it is.' He smiled at me, and it seemed a bear's smile. He had the bear's posture: his lumbering walk, a way of slowly wagging his head from side to side, of tucking his chin and looking down as if a muzzle divided his eyes. Behind him, his woman slowly nodded. She lifted her eyes and exchanged a glance with someone. I followed her gaze to a small hawk perched on a cross rafter. His eyes bored into me. The beams were streaked white with his droppings.

'You mean the Wit?' I asked.

'No. So it is named by those who have no knowing of it. That is the name it is despised by. Those of us who are of the Old Blood do not name it so.' He turned away to a cupboard set against the stout wall and began to take food from it. Long thick slabs of smoked salmon. A loaf of bread heavy with nuts and fruit baked into it. The bear rose on her hind legs, then dropped again to all fours, snuffing appreciatively. She turned her head sideways to take a side of fish from the table; it looked small in her jaws. She lumbered off to her corner with it and turned her back as she began on it. The woman had silently positioned herself on a chair from which she could watch the whole room. When I glanced at her she smiled and motioned her own invitation to the table. Then she resumed her stillness and her watching.

I found my own mouth watering at the sight of the food. It had been days since I had eaten to repletion and I'd had almost nothing in the last two days. A light whine from outside the cottage reminded me that Nighteyes was in the same condition. 'No cheese, no butter,' Black Rolf warned me solemnly. 'The City Guard took all the coin I'd traded for before I got around to buying butter and cheese. But we've fish and bread in plenty, and honeycomb for the bread. Take what you wish.'

Almost inadvertently, my eyes flickered toward the door.

'Both of you,' he clarified for me. 'Among the Old Blood, two are treated as one. Always.'

Nighteyes? Will you come in?

I will come to the door.

A moment later a grey shadow slunk past the door opening. I sensed him prowling about outside the cabin, taking up the scents of the place, registering bear, over and over. He passed the door again, peered in briefly, then made another circuit of the cabin. He discovered a partially-devoured carcass of a deer, with leaves and dirt scuffed over it not too far from the cabin. It was a typical bear's cache. I did not need to warn him to leave it alone. Finally he came back to the door and settled before it, sitting alertly, ears pricked.

'Take food to him if he does not wish to come inside,' Rolf urged me. He added, 'None of us believe in forcing a fellow against his natural instincts.'

'Thank you,' I said, a bit stiffly, but I did not know what manners were called for here. I took a slab of the salmon from the table. I tossed it to Nighteyes and he caught it deftly. For a moment he sat with it in his jaws. He could not both eat and remain totally wary. Long strings of saliva began to trail from his mouth as he sat there gripping the fish. *Eat*, I urged him. *I do not think they wish us any harm.*

He needed no more urging than that. He dropped the fish, pinned it to the ground with his forepaw and then tore off a large hunk of it. He wolfed it down, scarcely chewing. His eating awoke my hunger with an intensity I had been suppressing. I looked away from him to find that Black Rolf had cut me a thick slab of the bread and slathered it with honey. He was pouring a large mug of mead for himself. Mine was already beside my plate.

'Eat, don't wait on me,' he invited me, and when I looked askance at the woman, she smiled.

'Be welcome,' she said quietly. She came to the table and took a platter for herself, but put only a small portion of fish and a fragment of bread on it. I sensed she did so to put me at ease rather than for her own hunger. 'Eat well,' she bade me, and added, 'we can sense your hunger, you know.' She did not join us at table, but carried her food off to her chair by the hearth.

I was only too glad to obey her. I ate with much the same manners as Nighteyes. He was on his third slab of salmon, and I had finished as many pieces of bread and was eating a second piece of salmon before I recalled myself to my host. Rolf refilled my mug with mead and observed, 'I once tried to keep a goat. For milk and cheese and such. But she never could become accustomed to Hilda. Poor thing was always too nervous to let down her milk. So. We have mead. With Hilda's nose for honey, that's a drink we can supply ourselves with.'

'It's wonderful,' I sighed. I set down my mug, a quarter drained already, and breathed out. I hadn't finished eating, but the urgent edge of my hunger was gone now. Black Rolf picked up another slab of fish from the table and tossed it casually to Hilda. She caught it, paws and jaws, then turned aside from us to resume eating. He sent another slab winging to Nighteyes, who had lost all wariness. He leaped for it, then lay down, the salmon between his front paws, and turned his head to scissor off chunks and gulp them down. Holly picked at her food, tearing off small strips of dried fish and ducking her head as she ate them. Every time I glanced her way, I found her looking at me with her sharp black eyes. I looked back at Hilda.

'How did you ever come to bond with a she-bear?' I asked, and then added, 'if it isn't a rude question. I've never spoken to anyone else who was bonded to an animal, at least, no one who admitted it openly.'

He leaned back in his chair and rested his hands upon his belly. 'I don't "admit it openly" to just anyone. I supposed that you knew of me, right away, as Hilda and I are always aware when there are others of the Old Blood near by. But, as to your question . . . my mother was Old Blood, and two of her children inherited it. She sensed it in us, of course, and raised us in the ways. And when I was of an age, as a man, I made my quest.'

I looked at him blankly. He shook his head, a pitying smile touching his lips.

'I went alone, out into the world, seeking my companion beast. Some look in the towns, some look in the forest, a few, I have heard tell, even go out to sea. But I was drawn to the woods. So I went out alone, senses wide, fasting save for cold water and the herbs that quicken the Old Blood. I found a place, here, and I sat down among the roots of an old tree and I waited. And in time, Hilda came to me, seeking just as I had been seeking. We tested one another and found the trust and, well, here we are, seven years later.' He glanced at Hilda as fondly as if he spoke of a wife and children.

'A deliberate search for one to bond with,' I mused.

I believe that you sought me that day, and that I called out for you. Though neither of us knew at the time what we were seeking, Nighteyes mused, putting my rescuing him from the animal trader in a new light.

I do not think so, I told him regretfully. *I had bonded twice before, with dogs, and had learned too well the pain of losing such a companion. I had resolved never to bond again.*

Rolf was looking at me with disbelief. Almost horror. 'You had bonded twice before the wolf? And lost both companions?' He shook his head, denying it could be so. 'You are very young even for a first bonding.'

I shrugged at him. 'I was just a child when Nosy and I joined. He was taken away from me, by one who knew something of bonding and did not think it was good for either of us. Later, I did encounter him again, but it was at the end of his days. And the other pup I bonded to . . .'

Rolf was regarding me with a distaste as fervent as Burrich's was for the Wit while Holly silently shook her head. 'You bonded as a child? Forgive me, but that is perversion. As well allow a little girl to be wed off to a grown man. A child is not ready to share the full life of a beast; all Old Blood parents I know most carefully shelter their children from such contacts.' Sympathy touched his face. 'Still, it must have been excruciating for your bond-friend to be taken from you. But whoever did it, did the right thing, whatever his reason.' He looked at me more closely. 'I am surprised you survived, knowing nothing of the Old Blood ways.'

'Where I come from, it is seldom spoken of. And when it is, it is called the Wit, and is deemed a shameful thing to do.'

'Even your parents told you this? For while I well know how the Old Blood is regarded and all the lies that are told about it, one usually does not hear them from one's own parents. Our parents cherish our lines, and help us to find proper mates when the time comes, so that our blood may not be thinned.'

I glanced from his frank gaze to Holly's open stare. 'I did not know my parents.' Even anonymously, the words did not come easily to me. 'My mother gave me over to my father's family when

I was six years old. And my father chose not to . . . be near me. Still, I suspect the Old Blood came from my mother's side. I recall nothing of her or her family.'

'Six years old? And you recall nothing? Surely she taught you something before she let you go, gave you some knowledge to protect yourself . . . ?'

I sighed. 'I recall nothing of her.' I had long ago grown weary of folk telling me that I must remember something of her, that most people have memories that go back to when they were three or even younger.

Black Rolf made a low noise in his throat, between a growl and a sigh. 'Well, someone taught you something.'

'No.' I said it flatly, tired of the argument. I wished an end to it, and so resorted to the oldest tactic I knew for diverting people when they asked too many questions about me. 'Tell me about yourself,' I urged him. 'What did your mother teach you, and how?'

He smiled, his cheeks wrinkling fatly about his black eyes and making them smaller. 'It took her twenty years to teach it to me. Have you that long to hear about it?' At my look he added, 'No, I know you asked but to make conversation. But I offer what I see you needing. Stay with us a bit. We'll teach you what you both need to know. But you won't learn it in an hour or a day. It's going to take months. Perhaps years.'

Holly spoke suddenly from the corner in a quiet voice. 'We could find him a mate as well. He might do for Ollie's girl. She's older, but she might steady him down.'

Rolf grinned widely. 'Isn't that like a woman! Knows you for five minutes, and already matching you up for marriage.'

Holly spoke directly to me. Her smile was small but warm. 'Vita is bonded to a crow. All of you would hunt well together. Stay with us. You will meet her, and like her. Old Blood should join to Old Blood.'

Refuse politely, Nighteyes suggested immediately. *Bad enough to den among men. If you start sleeping near bears, you shall stink so that we can never hunt well again. Nor do I desire to share our kills with a teasing crow.* He paused. *Unless they know of a woman who is bonded with a bitch-wolf?*

A smile twitched at the corner of Black Rolf's mouth. I suspected he was more aware of what we said than he let on, and I told Nighteyes as much.

'It is one of the things that I could teach you, should you choose to stay,' Rolf offered. 'When you two speak, to one of the Old Blood it is as if you were shouting to one another over the rattle of a tinker's cart. There is no need to be so . . . wide open with it. It is only one wolf you address, not all of the wolf kindred. No. It is even more than that. I doubt if anything that eats meat is unaware of you two. Tell me. When was the last time you encountered a large carnivore?'

Dogs chased me some nights ago, Nighteyes said.

'Dogs will stand and bark from their territory,' Rolf observed. 'I meant a wild carnivore.'

'I don't think I've seen any since we bonded,' I admitted unwillingly.

'They will avoid you as surely as Forged ones will follow you,' Black Rolf said calmly.

A chill went down my spine. 'Forged ones? But Forged ones seem to have no Wit at all. I do not sense them with my Wit-sense at all, only with eyes or nose or . . .'

'To your Old Blood senses, all creatures give off a kinship warmth. All save the Forged ones. This is true?'

I nodded uneasily.

'They have lost it. I do not know how it is stolen from them, but that is what Forging does. And it leaves an emptiness in them. This much is well known among those of the Old Blood, and we know, too, that we are more likely to be followed and attacked by Forged ones. Especially if we use those talents carelessly. Why this is so, no one can say with certainty. Perhaps only the Forged ones know, if they truly "know" anything any more. But it gives us one more reason to be cautious of ourselves and our talents.'

'Are you suggesting that Nighteyes and I should refrain from using the Wit?'

'I am suggesting that perhaps you should stay here for a while, and take the time to learn to master the talents of the Old Blood. Or you may find yourself in more battles such as the one you fought yesterday.' He permitted himself a small smile.

'I said nothing to you of that attack,' I said quietly.

'You did not need to,' he pointed out. 'I am sure that everyone of Old Blood for leagues around heard you when you fought them. Until you both learn to control how you speak to one another, nothing between you is truly private.' He paused then added, 'Did you never think it strange that Forged ones would spend time attacking a wolf when there is apparently nothing to gain from such an attack? They only focus on him because he is bonded to you.'

I gave Nighteyes a brief apologetic glance. 'I thank you for your offer. But we have a thing we must do and it will not wait. I think that we shall encounter fewer Forged ones as we move inland. We should be fine.'

'That is likely. The ones that go so far inland are gathered up by the King. Still, any that may be left will be drawn to you. But even if you encounter no more Forged ones, you are likely to encounter the King's Guards. They take a special interest in "witted" folk these days. Of late, many of the Old Blood have been sold to the King, by neighbours, and even family. His gold is good, and he does not even ask much proof that they are truly Old Blood. Not for years has the vendetta against us burned so hot.'

I looked away uncomfortably, well aware of why Regal hated those with the Wit. His coterie would support him in that hate. I felt sickened as I thought of innocent folk sold to Regal that he might revenge himself on them in my stead. I tried to keep the rage I felt masked.

Hilda came back to the table, looked it over consideringly, then seized the pot that held the honeycombs in both her paws. She waddled carefully away from the table, to seat herself in the corner and begin a careful licking out of the pot. Holly continued to watch me. I could read nothing from her eyes.

Black Rolf scratched at his beard, then winced as his fingers found a sore spot. He smiled a careful, rueful smile at me. 'I can sympathize with your desire to kill King Regal. But I do not think you shall find it as easy as you suppose.'

I just looked at him, but Nighteyes rolled a light snarl in the back of his throat. Hilda looked up at that and thumped down on all fours, the honey jar rolling away from her across the floor. Black Rolf sent her a glance and she sat back, but fixed both Nighteyes and me with a glare. I don't think there is anything as gut-tightening as an angry glare from a brown bear. I did not move. Holly sat up straight in her chair but remained calm. Above us in the rafters Sleet rattled his plumage.

'If you bay out all your plans and grievances to the night moon, you cannot be astonished that others know of them. I do not think you shall encounter many of the Old Blood who are sympathetic to King Regal ... or any, perhaps. In fact, many would be willing to aid you if you asked them. Still, silence is wisest, for a plan such as that.'

'From your song earlier, I would suspect you share my sentiments,' I said quietly. 'And I thank you for your warning. But Nighteyes and I have had to be circumspect before about what we shared with one another. Now we know there is a danger of being overheard, I think we can compensate for it. One question I will ask of you. What care the City Guards of Crowsneck if a man has a few drinks and sings a mocking song about the ... King?' I had to force the word from my throat.

'None at all, when they are Crowsneck men. But that is no longer the case in Crowsneck, nor in any of the river road towns. Those are King's Guards, in the livery of the Crowsneck Guard, and paid from the town purse, but King's Men all the same. Regal had not been king two months before he decreed that change. He claimed the law would be enforced more equitably if city guards were all sworn King's Men, carrying out the law of the Six Duchies above any other. Well. You have seen how they carry it out ... mostly by carrying off whatever they can from any poor sot who treads upon the King's toes. Still those two in Crowsneck are not so bad as some I've heard of. Word is that down in Sandbend, a cutpurse or thief can make an easy living, so long as the guard gets a share. The town masters are powerless to dismiss the guards the King has appointed. Nor are they allowed to supplement them with their own men.'

It sounded only too much like Regal. I wondered how obsessed he would become with power and control. Would he set spies upon his spies? Or had he already done so? None of it boded well for the Six Duchies as a whole.

Black Rolf broke me from my musings. 'Now, I've a question I would ask of you.'

'Be free to ask,' I invited him, but held to myself how freely I should answer.

'Late last night . . . after you had finished with the Forged ones. Another attacked you. I could not sense who, only that your wolf defended you, and that he somehow went . . . somewhere. That he threw his strength into a channel I did not understand, nor could follow. I know no more than that he, and you, were victorious. What was that thing?'

'A servant of the King,' I hedged. I did not wish to entirely refuse him an answer, and this seemed harmless, as he seemed to already know it.

'You fought what they call the Skill. Didn't you?' His eyes locked with mine. When I did not answer, he went on anyway. 'There are many of us who would like to know how it was done. In our past, Skilled ones have hunted us down as if we were vermin. No one of the Old Blood can say that his family has not suffered at their hands. Now those days have come again. If there is a way to use the talents of the Old Blood against those who wield the Farseer's Skill, it is knowledge worth much to us.'

Holly sidled from the corner, then came to grip the back of Rolf's chair and peer over his shoulder at me. I sensed the importance of my answer to them.

'I cannot teach you that,' I said honestly.

His eyes held mine, his disbelief plain. 'Twice tonight, I have offered to teach you all I know of the Old Blood, to open to you all the doors that only your ignorance keeps closed. You have refused me, but by Eda, I have offered, and freely. But this one thing I ask, this one thing that might save so many lives of our own kind, you say you cannot teach me?'

My eyes flickered to Hilda. Her eyes had gone beady and bright again. Black Rolf was probably unaware of how his posture mimicked that of his bear. They both had me measuring the distance to the door, while Nighteyes was already on his feet and ready to flee. Behind Rolf, Holly cocked her head and stared at me.

Above us, the hawk turned his head to watch us. I forced myself to loosen my muscles, to behave much more calmly than I felt. It was a tactic learned from Burrich when confronting any distressed animal.

'I speak truth to you,' I said carefully. 'I cannot teach you what I do not fully understand myself.' I refrained from mentioning that I myself carried that despised Farseer blood. I was sure now of what I had only suspected before. The Wit could be used to attack a Skilled one only if a Skill channel had been opened between them. Even if I had been able to describe what Nighteyes and I had done, no one else would have been able to copy it. To fight the Skill with the Wit, one had to possess both the Skill and the Wit. I met Black Rolf's eyes calmly, knowing I had spoken the truth to him.

Slowly he relaxed his hunched shoulders, and Hilda dropped back to all fours and went snuffling after the trailing honey. 'Perhaps,' he said, quietly stubborn, 'perhaps if you stayed with us, and learned what I have to teach you, you would begin to understand what you do. Then you could teach it to me. Do you think so?'

I kept my voice calm and even. 'You witnessed the King's servants attack me last night. Do you think they will suffer me to remain here and learn more to use against them? No. My only chance is to beard them in their den before they come seeking me out.' I hesitated, then offered, 'Although I cannot teach you to do as I do, you may be assured that it will be used against the enemies of the Old Blood.'

This, finally, was a reasoning he could accept. He snuffed several times thoughtfully. I wondered uncomfortably if I had as many wolf mannerisms as he had bear and Holly had hawk.

'Will you stay the night at least?' he asked abruptly.

'We do better when we travel by night,' I said regretfully. 'It is more comfortable for both of us.'

He nodded sagely to that. 'Well. I wish you well, and every good fortune in achieving your end. You are welcome to rest safely here until the moon rises, if you wish.'

I conferred with Nighteyes, and we accepted gratefully. I checked the slash on Nighteyes' shoulder and found it to be no better than I had suspected. I treated it with some of Burrich's salve, and then we sprawled outside in the shade and napped the afternoon away. It was good for both of us to be able to relax completely, knowing that others stood guard over us. It was the best sleep either of us had had since we had begun our journey. When we awoke, I found that Black Rolf had put up fish, honey and bread for us to carry with us. There was no sign of the hawk. I imagined he had gone to roost for the night. Holly stood in the shadows near the house, regarding us sleepily.

'Go carefully, go gently,' Rolf counselled us after we had thanked him and packed his gifts. 'Walk in the ways Eda has opened for you.'

He paused, as if waiting for a response. I sensed a custom I was not familiar with. I wished him simply, 'Good luck,' and he nodded to that.

'You will be back, you know,' he added.

I shook my head slowly. 'I doubt that. But I thank you for what you have given me.'

'No. I know you will be back. It is not a matter of your wanting what I can teach you. You will find you need it. You are not a man as ordinary men are. They think they have a right to all beasts; to hunt them and eat them, or to subjugate them and rule their lives. You know you have no such right to mastery. The horse that carries you will do so because he wishes to, as does the wolf that hunts beside you. You have a deeper sense of yourself in the world. You believe you have a right, not to rule it, but to be part of it. Predator or prey; there is no shame to being either one. As time goes on, you will find you have urgent questions. What must you do when your friend wishes to run with a pack of true wolves? I promise you, that time will come. What must he do if you marry and have a child? When the time comes for one of you to die, as it must, how does the other make room for what is left, and carry on alone? In time you will hunger for others of your kind. You will need to know how to sense them and how to seek them out. There are answers to these questions, Old Blood answers, ones I cannot tell you in a day, ones you cannot understand in a week. You need those answers. And you will come back for them.'

I looked down at the trodden soil of the forest path. I had lost all certainty that I would not return to Rolf.

Holly spoke softly but clearly from the shadows. 'I believe in what you go to do. I wish you success, and would aid you if I could.' Her eyes darted to Rolf, as if this were a thing they had discussed, but had not agreed upon. 'If you are in need, cry out, as you do to Nighteyes, asking that any of Old Blood who hear you pass word back to Holly and Sleet of Crowsneck. Those who hear may come to help you. Even if they do not, they will send word to me, and I will do what I can.'

Rolf let out a sudden huff of breath. 'We will do what we can,' he amended her words. 'But you would be wiser to stay here and learn first how to better protect yourself.'

I nodded to his words, but resolved privately that I would not involve any of them in my revenge against Regal. When I glanced up at Rolf, he smiled at me wryly, and shrugged his shoulders. 'Go then. But be wary, both of you. Before the moon goes down you'll leave Buck behind and be in Farrow. If you think King Regal has a grip on us here, wait until you get to where folk believe he has a right to it.'

I nodded grimly to that, and once more Nighteyes and I were on our way.

SEVEN

Farrow

Lady Patience, the Lady of Buckkeep as she came to be called, rose to power in a unique fashion. She had been born into a noble family and was by birth a lady. She was raised to the loftier status of Queen-in-Waiting by her precipitous marriage to King-in-Waiting Chivalry. She never asserted herself in either position to take the power that birth and marriage had brought her. It was only when she was alone, almost abandoned, as eccentric Lady Patience at Buckkeep that she gathered to herself the reins of influence. She did it, as she had done everything else in her life, in a haphazard, quaint way that would have availed any other woman not at all.

She did not call on noble family connections, nor exert influential connections based on her deceased husband's status. Instead she began with that lowest tier of power, the so-called men-at-arms, who were just as frequently women. Those few remaining of King Shrewd's personal guard, and Queen Kettricken's guard had been left in the peculiar position of guardians with nothing left to guard. The Buckkeep Guard had been supplanted in their duties by the personal troops that Lord Bright brought with him from Farrow, and delegated to lesser tasks that involved the cleaning and maintenance of the keep. The former guards were erratically paid, had lost respect among and for themselves, and were too often idle or occupied with degrading tasks. The Lady Patience, ostensibly because they were not otherwise busied, began to solicit their services. She began by requesting a guard when she abruptly began to ride out on her ancient palfrey, Silk. Afternoon rides gradually lengthened to all-day forays, and then to overnight visits to villages that had either been raided or feared raids. In the raided villages, she and her maid Lacey did what they could for the injured, logged down a tally of those slain or Forged, and provided, in the form of her guard, strong backs to aid in the clearing of rubble from the main streets and the raising of temporary shelter for folks left homeless. This, while not true work for fighters, was a sharp reminder of what they had been trained to fight against, and of what happened when there were no defenders. The gratitude of the folk they aided restored to the guard their pride and inner cohesiveness. In the unraided villages, the guard were a small show of force that Buckkeep and the Farseer pride still existed. In several villages and towns, makeshift stockades were raised where the folk could retreat from the Raiders and have a small chance of defending themselves.

There is no record of Lord Bright's feelings regarding Lady Patience's forays. She never declared these expeditions in any official way. They were her pleasure rides, the guards that accompanied her had volunteered to do so, and likewise for the duties she put them to in the villages. Some, as she came to trust them, ran 'errands' for her. Such errands might involve the distance carrying of messages to keeps in Rippon, Bearns and even Shoaks, requesting news of how the coastal towns fared, and giving news of Buck; they took her runners into and through occupied territories and were fraught with danger. Her messengers often were given a sprig of the ivy she grew year round in her rooms as a token to present to the recipients of her messages and support. Several ballads have been written about the so-called Ivy Runners, telling of the bravery and resourcefulness they showed, and reminding us that even the greatest walls must, in time, yield to the over-climbing ivy. Perhaps the most famous exploit was that of Pansy, the youngest runner. At the age of eleven, she travelled all the way to where the Duchess of Bearns was in hiding in the Ice Caves of Bearns, to bring her tidings of when and where a supply boat would beach. For part of that journey, Pansy travelled undiscovered amidst the sacks of grain in a wagon commandeered by the Raiders. From the very heart of a Raiders' camp, she escaped to continue her mission, but only after she had set fire to the tent in which their leader slept in revenge for her Forged parents. Pansy did not live to be thirteen, but her deeds will be long remembered.

Others aided Patience in disposing of her jewellery and ancestral lands for coin, which she then employed 'as she pleased, as was her right' as she once informed Lord Bright. She bought grain and sheep from inland, and again her 'volunteers' saw to its transport and distribution. Small supply boats brought hope to embattled defenders. She made token payments to stonemasons and carpenters who helped to rebuild ravaged villages. And she gave coin, not much but accompanied by her sincerest thanks, to those guards who volunteered to assist her.

By the time the Ivy badge came into common usage among the Buckkeep guard, it was only to acknowledge what was already a fact. These men and women were Lady Patience's guard, paid by her when they were paid at all, but more important to them, valued and used by her, doctored by her when they were injured, and sharply defended by her acid tongue against any who spoke disparagingly of them. These were the foundation of her influence, and the basis of the strength she came to wield. 'A tower seldom crumbles from the bottom up,' she told more than one, and claimed to have the saying from Prince Chivalry.

We had slept well and our bellies were full. Without the need to hunt, we travelled the whole night. We stayed off the road, and were far more cautious than we had previously been, but no Forged ones did we encounter. A large white moon silvered us a path through the trees. We moved as one creature, scarcely even thinking, save to catalogue the scents we encountered and the sounds we heard. The icy determination that had seized me infected Nighteyes as well. I would not carelessly trumpet to him my intention, but we could think of it without focusing on it. It was a different sort of hunting urge, driven by a different sort of hunger. Each night we walked the miles away beneath the moon's peering stare.

There was a soldier's logic to it, a strategy Verity would have approved. Will knew I lived. I did not know if he would reveal that to the others of the coterie, or even Regal. I suspected he hungered to drain off my Skill-strength as Justin and Serene had drained King Shrewd's. I suspected there would be an obscene ecstasy to such a theft of power, and that Will would wish to savour it alone. I was also fairly certain that he would search for me, determined to ferret me out no matter where I hid. He knew also that I was terrified of him. He would not expect me to come straight for him, determined to kill not only him and the coterie, but also Regal. My swift march toward Tradeford might be my best strategy for remaining hidden from him.

Farrow's reputation is for being as open as Buck is craggy and wooded. That first dawn found us in an unfamiliar type of forest, more open and deciduous. We bedded down for the day in a birch copse on a gentle hill overlooking open pasture. For the first time since the fight I took off my shirt and by daylight examined my shoulder where the club had connected. It was black and blue, and painful if I tried to lift my arm above my head. But that was all. Minor. Three years ago, I would have thought it a serious injury. I would have bathed it in cold water and poulticed it with herbs to hasten its healing. Now, although it purpled my whole shoulder and twinged whenever I moved it, it was only a bruise, and I left it to heal on its own. I smiled wryly to myself as I put my shirt back on.

Nighteyes was not patient as I looked at the slice in his shoulder. It was starting to close. As I pushed the hair back from the edges of the cut, he reached back suddenly and seized my wrist in his teeth. Not roughly, but firmly.

Let it alone. It will heal.

There's dirt in it.

He gave it a sniff and a thoughtful lick. *Not that much.*

Let me look at it.

You never just look. You poke.

Then sit still and let me poke at it.

He conceded, but not graciously. There were bits of grass stuck in it and these had to be plucked loose. More than once he grabbed at my wrist. Finally he rumbled at me in a way that let me know he'd had enough. I wasn't satisfied. He was barely tolerant of me putting some of Burrich's salve on it.

You worry about these things too much, he informed me irritably.

I hate that you are injured because of me. It's not right. This isn't the sort of life a wolf should lead. You should not be alone, wandering from place to place. You should be with a pack, hunting your territory, perhaps taking a mate someday.

Someday is someday, and maybe it will be or maybe it won't. This is a human thing, to worry about things that may or may not come to be. You can't eat the meat until you've killed it. Besides, I am not alone. We are together.

That is true. We are together. I lay down beside Nighteyes to sleep.

I thought of Molly. I resolutely put her out of my mind and tried to sleep. It was no good. I shifted about restlessly until Nighteyes growled, got up, stalked away from me and lay down again. I sat up for a bit, staring down into a wooded valley. I knew I was close to a foolish decision. I refused to consider how completely foolish and reckless it was. I drew a breath, closed my eyes and reached for Molly.

I had dreaded I might find her in another man's arms. I had feared I would hear her speak of me with loathing. Instead, I could not find her at all. Time and again, I centred my thoughts, summoned all my energies and reached out for her. I was finally rewarded with a Skill-image of Burrich thatching the roof of a cottage. He was shirtless and the summer sun had darkened him to the colour of polished wood. Sweat ran down the back of his neck. He glanced down at someone below him and annoyance crossed his features. 'I know, my lady. You could do it yourself, thank you very much. I also know I have enough worries without fearing that both of you will tumble off here.'

Somewhere I panted with effort, and became aware of my own body again. I pushed myself away and reached for Burrich. I would at least let him know that I lived. I managed to find him, but I saw him through a fog. 'Burrich!' I called to him. 'Burrich, it's Fitz!' But his mind was closed and locked to me; I could not catch even a glimmer of his thoughts. I damned my erratic Skill ability, and reached again into the swirling clouds.

Verity stood before me, his arms crossed on his chest, shaking his head. His voice was no louder than a whisper of wind, and he stood so still I could scarcely see him. Yet I sensed he used great force to reach me. 'Don't do this, boy,' he warned me softly. 'It will only hurt you.' I was suddenly in a different place. He leaned with his back against a great slab of black stone and his face was lined with weariness. Verity rubbed at his temples as if pained. 'I should not be doing this, either. But sometimes I so long for . . . Ah, well. Pay no mind. Know this, though. Some things are better not known, and the risks of Skilling right now are too great. If I can feel you and find you, so can another. He'll attack you any way he can. Don't bring them to his attention. He would not scruple to use them against you. Give them up, to protect them.' He suddenly seemed a bit stronger. He smiled bitterly. 'I know what it means to do that; to give them up to keep them safe. So did your father. You've the strength for it. Give it all up, boy. Just come to me. If you've still a mind to. Come to me, and I'll show you what can be done.'

I awoke at midday. The full sunlight falling on my face had given me a headache, and I felt slightly shaky with it. I made a tiny fire, intending to brew some some elfbark tea to steady myself. I forced myself to be sparing of my supply, using only one small piece of bark and the rest nettles. I had not expected to need it so often. I suspected I should conserve it; I might need it after I faced Regal's coterie. Now there was an optimistic thought. Nighteyes opened his eyes to watch me for a bit, then dozed off again. I sat sipping my bitter tea and staring out over the countryside. The bizarre dream had made me homesick for a place and time when people had cared for me. I had left all that behind me. Well, not entirely. I sat beside Nighteyes and rested a hand on the wolf's shoulder. He shuddered his coat at the touch. *Go to sleep*, he told me grumpily.

You are all I have, I told him, full of melancholy.

He yawned lazily. *And I am all you need. Now go to sleep. Sleeping is serious*, he told me gravely. I smiled and stretched out again beside my wolf, one hand resting on his coat. He radiated the simple contentment of a full belly and sleeping in the warm sun. He was right. It was worth taking seriously. I closed my eyes and slept dreamlessly the rest of the day.

In the days and nights that followed, the nature of the countryside changed to open forests interspersed with wide grassland. Orchards and grainfields surrounded the towns. Once, long ago, I had travelled through Farrow. Then I had been with a caravan, and we had gone cross country rather than following the river. I had been a confident young assassin on my way to an important murder. That trip had ended in my first real experience of Regal's treachery. I had barely survived it. Now once more I travelled across Farrow, looking forward to a murder at my journey's end. But this time I went alone and upriver, the man I would kill was my own uncle and the killing was at my own behest. Sometimes I found that deeply satisfying. At other times, I found it frightening.

I kept my promise to myself, and avoided human company assiduously. We shadowed the road and the river, but when we came to towns, we skirted wide around them. This was more difficult than might be imagined in such open country. It had been one thing to circle about some Buck hamlet tucked into a bend in the river and surrounded by deep woods. It is another to cross grainfields, or slip through orchards and not rouse anyone's dogs or interest. To some extent, I could reassure dogs that we meant no harm. If the dogs were gullible. Most farm dogs have a suspicion of wolves that no amount of reassurances could calm. And older dogs were apt to look askance at any human travelling in a wolf's company. We were chased more than once. The Wit might give me the ability to communicate with some animals, but it did not guarantee that I would be listened to, nor believed. Dogs are not stupid.

Hunting in these open areas was different, too. Most of the small game was of the burrowing sort that lived in groups, and the larger animals simply outran us over the long flat stretches of land. Time spent in hunting was time not spent travelling. Occasionally I found unguarded hen-houses and slipped in quietly to steal eggs from the sleeping birds. I did not scruple to raid plums and cherries from the orchards we passed through. Our most fortuitous kill was an ignorant young haragar, one of the rangy swine that some of the nomadic folk herded as a food beast. Where this one had strayed from, we did not question. Fang and sword, we brought it down. I let Nighteyes gorge to his content that night, and then annoyed him by cutting the rest of the meat into strips and sheets which I dried in the sun over a low fire. It took the better part of a day before I was satisfied the fatty meat was dried enough to keep well, but in the days to follow, we travelled more swiftly for it. When game presented itself, we hunted and killed, but when it did not, we had the smoked haragar to fall back on.

In this manner we followed the Buck River northeast. When we drew close to the substantial trading town of Turlake, we veered wide of it, and for a time steered only by the stars. This was far more to Nighteyes' liking, taking us over plains carpeted with dry sedgy grasses at this time of year. We frequently saw herds in the distance, of cattle and sheep or goats, and infrequently, haragar. My contact with the nomadic folk who followed those herds was limited to glimpses of them on horseback, or the sight of their fires outlining the conical tents they favoured when they settled for a night or so.

We were wolves again for these long trotting days. I had reverted once more, but I was aware of it and told myself that as long as I was it would do me little harm. In truth, I believe it did me good. Had I been travelling with another human, life would have been complicated. We would have discussed route and supplies and tactics once we arrived in Tradeford. But the wolf and I simply trotted along, night after night, and our existence was as simple as life could be. The comradeship between us grew deeper and deeper.

The words of Black Rolf had sunk deep into me and given me much to think about. In some ways, I had taken Nighteyes and the bond between us for granted. Once he had been a cub, but now he was my equal. And my friend. Some say 'a dog' or 'a horse' as if every one of them is like every other. I've heard a man call a mare he had owned for seven years 'it' as if he were speaking of a chair. I've never understood that. One does not have to be Witted to know the companionship of a beast, and to know that the friendship of an animal is every bit as rich and complicated as that of a man or woman. Nosy had been a friendly, inquisitive, boyish dog when he was mine. Smithy had been tough and aggressive, inclined to bully anyone who would give way to him, and his sense of humour had had a rough edge to it. Nighteyes was as unlike them as he was unlike Burrich or Chade. It is no disrespect to any of them to say I was closest to him.

He could not count. But, I could not read deer scent on the air and tell if it were a buck or doe. If he could not plan ahead to the day after tomorrow, neither was I capable of the fierce concentration he could bring to a stalk. There were differences between us, neither of us claimed superiority. No one issued a command to the other, or expected unquestioning obedience of the other. My hands were useful things for removing porcupine quills and ticks and thorns and for scratching especially itchy and unreachable spots on his back. My height gave me a certain advantage in spotting game and spying out terrain. So even when he pitied me for my 'cow's teeth' and poor vision at night, and a nose he referred to as a numb lump between my eyes, he did not look down on me. We both knew his hunting prowess accounted for most of the meat that we ate. Yet he never begrudged me an equal share. Find that in a man, if you can.

'Sit, hound!' I told him once, jokingly. I was gingerly skinning out a porcupine that I had killed with a club after Nighteyes had insisted on pursuing it. In his eagerness to get at the meat, he was about to get us both full of quills. He settled back with an impatient quivering of haunches.

Why do men speak so? he asked me as I tugged carefully at the skin's edge of the prickling hide.

'How?'

Commanding. What gives a man a right to command a dog, if they are not pack?

'Some are pack, or almost,' I said aloud, consideringly. I pulled the hide tight, holding it by a flap of belly fur where there were no quills, and slicing along the exposed integument. The skin made a ripping sound as it peeled back from the fat meat. 'Some men think they have the right,' I went on after a moment.

Why? Nighteyes pressed.

It surprised me that I had never pondered this before. 'Some men think they are better than beasts,' I said slowly. 'That they have the right to use them or command them in any way they please.'

Do you think this way?

I didn't answer right away. I worked my blade along the line between the skin and the fat, keeping a constant pull on the hide as I worked up around the shoulder of the animal. I rode a horse, didn't I, when I had one? Was it because I was better than the horse that I bent it to my will? I'd used dogs to hunt for me, and hawks on occasion. What right had I to command them? There I sat, stripping the hide off a porcupine to eat it. I spoke slowly. 'Are we better than this porcupine that we are about to eat? Or is it only that we have bested it today?'

Nighteyes cocked his head, watching my knife and hands bare meat for him. *I think I am always smarter than a porcupine. But not better. Perhaps we kill it and eat it because we can. Just as,* and here he stretched his front paws out before him languorously, *just as I have a well-trained human to skin these prickly things for me, that I may enjoy eating them the better.* He lolled his tongue at me, and we both knew it was only part of the answer to the puzzle. I ran my knife down the porcupine's spine, and the whole hide was finally free of it.

'I should build a fire and cook off some of this fat before I eat it,' I said consideringly. 'Otherwise I shall be ill.'

Just give me mine, and do as you wish with your share, Nighteyes instructed me grandly. I cut around the hind legs and then popped the joints free and cut them loose. It was more than enough meat for me. I left them on the skin side of the hide as Nighteyes dragged his share away. I kindled a small fire as he was crunching through bones and skewered the legs to cook them. 'I don't think I am better than you,' I said quietly. 'I don't think, truly, that I am better than any beast. Though, as you say, I am smarter than some.'

Porcupines, perhaps, he observed benignly. *But a wolf? I think not.*

We grew to know every nuance of the other's behaviour. Sometimes we were fiercely competent at our hunting, finding our keenest joy in a stalk and kill, moving purposefully and dangerously through the world. At other times, we tussled like puppies, nudging one another off the beaten trail into bushes, pinching and nipping at each other as we strode along, scaring off the game before we even saw it. Some days we lay drowsing in the late afternoon hours before we roused to hunt and then travel, the sun warm on our bellies or backs, the insects buzzing a sound like sleep itself. Then the big wolf might roll over on his back like a puppy, begging me to scratch his belly and check his ears for ticks and fleas, or simply scratch thoroughly all around his throat and neck. On chill foggy mornings we curled up close beside one another to find warmth before sleep. Sometimes I would be awakened by a rough poke of a cold nose against mine; when I tried to sit up, I would discover he was deliberately standing on my hair, pinning my head to the earth. At other times I might awaken alone, to see Nighteyes sitting at some distance, looking out over the surrounding countryside. I recall seeing him so, silhouetted against a sunset. The light evening breeze ruffled his coat. His ears were pricked forward and his gaze went far into the distance. I sensed a loneliness in him then that nothing from me could ever remedy. It humbled me, and I let him be, not even questing toward him. In some ways, for him, I was not better than a wolf.

Once we had avoided Turlake and the surrounding towns we swung north again to strike the Vin River. It was as different from the Buck River as a cow is from a stallion. Grey and placid, it slid along between open fields, wallowing back and forth in its wide gravelly channel. On our side of the river, there was a trail that more or less paralleled the water, but most of the traffic on it were goats and cattle. We could always hear when a herd or flock was being moved, and we easily avoided them. The Vin was not as navigable a river as the Buck, being shallower and given to shifting sandbars, but there was some boat trade on it. On the Tilth side of the Vin, there was a well-used road, and frequent villages and even towns. We saw barges being drawn upstream by mule teams along some stretches; I surmised that such cargo would have to be portaged past the shallows. Settlements on our side of the river seemed limited to ferry landings and infrequent trading posts for the nomadic herders. These might offer an inn, a few shops and a handful of houses clinging to the outskirts, but not much more than that. Nighteyes and I avoided them. The few villages we encountered on our side of the river were deserted at this time of year.

The nomadic herders, tent dwellers during the hotter months, pastured their herds on the central plains now, moving sedately from waterhole to waterhole across the rich grazing lands. Grass grew in the village streets and up the sides of the sod houses. There was a peace to these abandoned towns, and yet the emptiness still reminded me of a raided village. We never lingered close to one.

We both grew leaner and stronger. I wore through my shoes and had to patch them with rawhide. I wore my trousers off at the cuff and hemmed them up about my calves. I grew tired of washing my shirt so often; the blood of the Forged ones and our kills had left the front and the cuffs of it mottled brown. It was as mended and tattered as a beggar's shirt, and the uneven colour made it only more pathetic. I bundled it into my pack one day and went shirtless. The days were mild enough that I did not miss it, and during the cooler nights we were on the move and my body made its own warmth. The sun baked me almost as dark as my wolf. Physically, I felt good. I was not as strong as I had been when I was pulling an oar and fighting, nor as muscled. But I felt healthy and limber and lean. I could trot all night beside a wolf and not be wearied. I was a quick and stealthy animal, and I proved over and over to myself my ability to survive. I regained a great deal of the confidence that Regal had destroyed. Not that my body had forgiven and forgotten all that Regal had done to it, but I had adapted to its twinges and scars. Almost, I had put the dungeon behind me. I did not let my dark goal overshadow those golden days. Nighteyes and I travelled, hunted, slept and travelled again. It was all so simple and good that I forgot to value it. Until I lost it.

We had come down to the river as evening darkened, intending to drink well before beginning our night's travel. But as we drew near, Nighteyes had suddenly frozen, dropping his belly to the earth while canting his ears forward. I followed his example, and then even my dull nose caught an unfamiliar scent. *What and where?* I asked him.

I saw them before he could reply. Tiny deer, stepping daintily along on their way down to water. They were not much taller than Nighteyes, and instead of antlers, they had goat-like spiralling horns that shone glossy black in the full moon's light. I knew of such creatures only from an old bestiary that Chade had, and I could not remember what they were properly called.

Food? Nighteyes suggested succinctly, and I immediately concurred. The trail they were following would bring them within a leap and a spring of us. Nighteyes and I held our positions, waiting. The deer came closer, a dozen of them, hurrying and careless now as they scented the cool water. We let the one in the lead pass, waiting to spring on the main body of the herd where they were most closely bunched. But just as Nighteyes gathered himself with a quiver to jump, a long wavering howl slid down the night.

Nighteyes sat up, an anxious whine bursting from him. The deer scattered in an explosion of hooves and horns, fleeing us even though we were both too distracted to pursue them. Our meal became suddenly a distant light thunder. I looked after them in dismay, but Nighteyes did not even seem to notice.

Mouth open, Nighteyes made sounds between a howl and a keen, his jaws quivering and working as if he strove to remember how to speak. The jolt I had felt from him at the wolf's distant howl had made my heart leap in my chest. If my own mother had suddenly called out to me from the night, the shock could not have been greater. Answering howls and barks erupted from a gentle rise to the north of us. The first wolf joined in with them. Nighteyes' head swivelled back and forth as he whined low in his throat. Abruptly he threw back his head and let out a jagged howl of his own. Sudden stillness followed his declaration, then the pack on the rise gave tongue again, not a hunting cry, but an announcement of themselves.

Nighteyes gave me a quick apologetic look, and left. In disbelief I watched him race off toward the ridge. After an instant of astonishment, I leaped to my feet and followed. He was already a substantial distance ahead of me, but when he became aware of me, he slowed, and then rounded to face me.

I must go alone, he told me earnestly. *Wait for me here.* He whirled about to resume his journey.

Panic struck me. *Wait! You can't go alone. They are not pack. We're intruders, they'll attack you. Better not to go at all.*

I must! he repeated. There was no mistaking his determination. He trotted off.

I ran after him. *Nighteyes, please!* I was suddenly terrified for him, for what he was charging into so obsessedly.

He paused and looked back at me, his eyes meeting mine in what was a very long stare for a wolf. *You understand. You know you do. Now is the time for you to trust as I have trusted. This is something I must do. And I must do it alone.*

And if you do not come back? I asked in sudden desperation.

You came back from your visit into that town. And I shall come back to you. Continue to travel along the river. I shall find you. Go on, now. Go back.

I stopped trotting after him. He kept going. *Be careful!* I flung the plea after him, my own form of howling into the night. Then I stood and watched him trot away from me, the powerful muscles rippling under his deep fur, his tail held out straight in determination. It took every bit of strength I had to refrain from crying out to him to come back, to plead with him not to leave me alone. I stood alone, breathing hard from running, and watched him dwindle in the distance. He was so intent on his seeking that I felt closed out and set aside. For the first time I experienced the resentment and jealousy that he had felt during my sessions with Verity, or when I had been with Molly and had commanded him to stay away from my thoughts.

This was his first adult contact with his own kind. I understood his need to seek them out and see what they were, even if they attacked him and drove him away. It was right. But all the fears I had for him whined at me to run after him, to be by his side in case he were attacked, to be at least within striking distance if he should need me.

But he had asked me not to.

No. He had told me not to. Told me, exerting the same privilege of self that I had exerted with him. I felt it wrenched my heart sideways in my chest to turn away from him and walk back toward the river. I felt suddenly half blind. He was not trotting beside and ahead of me, relaying his information to supplement what my own duller senses delivered to me. Instead, I could sense him in the distance. I felt the thrilling of anticipation, fear and curiosity that trembled through him. He was too intent on his own life at the moment to share with me. Suddenly I wondered if this was akin to what Verity had felt, when I was out on the *Rurisk*, harrying the Raiders while he had to sit in his tower and be content with whatever information he could glean from me. I had reported much more fully to him, had made a conscious effort to keep up a stream of information to him. Still, he must have felt something of this wrenching exclusion that now sickened me.

I reached the riverbank. I halted there, to sit down and wait for him. He had said he would come back. I stared out over the darkness of the moving water. My life felt small inside me. Slowly

I turned to look upstream. All inclination to hunt had fled with Nighteyes.

I sat and waited for a long time. Finally I got up and moved on through the night, paying scant attention to myself and my surroundings. I walked silently on the sandy riverbank, accompanied by the hushing of the waters.

Somewhere, Nighteyes scented other wolves, scented them clean and strong, well enough to know how many and what sexes they were. Somewhere he showed himself to them, not threatening, not entering their company, but simply announcing to them that he was there. For a time they watched him. The big male of the pack advanced and urinated on a tussock of grass. He then scratched deep furrows with the claws on his hind feet as he kicked dirt at it. A female stood and stretched and yawned, and then sat, staring green-eyed up at him. Two half-grown cubs stopped chewing one another long enough to consider him. One started toward him, but a low rumble from his mother brought him hastening back. He went back to chewing at his littermate. And Nighteyes sat down, a settling on the haunches that showed he meant no harm and let them look at him. A skinny young female gave half a hesitant whine, then broke it off with a sneeze.

After a time, most of the wolves got up and set out purposefully together. Hunting. The skinny female stayed with the cubs, watching over them as the others left. Nighteyes hesitated, then followed the pack at a discreet distance. From time to time, one of the wolves would glance back at him. The lead male stopped frequently to urinate and then scuff at the ground with his back legs.

As for me, I walked on by the river, watching the night age around me. The moon performed her slow passage of the night sky. I took dry meat from my pack and chewed it as I walked, stopping once to drink the chalky water. The river had swung toward me in its gravelly bed. I was forced to forsake the shore and walk on a tussocky bank above it. As dawn created a horizon, I cast about for a place to sleep. I settled for a slightly higher rise on the bank and curled up small amidst the coarse grasses. I would be invisible unless someone almost stepped on me. It was as safe a spot as any.

I felt very alone.

I did not sleep well. A part of me sat watching other wolves, still from a distance. They were as aware of me as I was of them. They had not accepted me, but neither had they driven me off. I had not gone so close as to force them to decide about me. I had watched them kill a buck, of a kind of deer I did not know. It seemed small to feed all of them. I was hungry, but not so hungry that I needed to hunt yet. My curiosity about this pack was a more pressing hunger. I sat and watched them as they sprawled in sleep.

My dreams moved away from Nighteyes. Again I felt the dis-jointed knowledge that I was dreaming, but was powerless to awaken. Something summoned me, tugging at me with a terrible urgency. I answered that summons, reluctant but unable to refuse. I found another day somewhere, and the sickeningly familiar smoke and screams rising together into the blue sky by the ocean. Another town in Bearns was fighting and falling to the Raiders. Once more I was claimed as witness. On that night, and almost every night to follow, the war with the Red Ships was forced back on me.

That battle, and each of the ones that followed are etched somewhere on my heart, in relentless detail. Scent and sound and touch, I lived them all. Something in me listened, and each time I slept, it dragged me mercilessly to where Six Duchies folk fought and died for their homes. I was to experience more of the fall of Bearns than any one who actually lived in that Duchy. For from day to day, whenever I tried to sleep, I might at any time find myself called to witness. I knew no logic for it. Perhaps the penchant for the Skill slept in many folk of the Six Duchies and faced with death and pain they cried out to Verity and me with voices they did not know they possessed. More than once, I sensed my king likewise stalking the nightmare-wracked towns, though never again did I see him so plainly as I had that first time. Later, I would recall that once I had dream-shared a time with King Shrewd when he was similarly called to witness the fall of Siltbay. I have wondered since how often he was tormented by witnessing the raids on towns he was powerless to protect.

Some part of me knew that I slept by the Vin River, far from this rampaging battle, surrounded by tall river grass and swept by a clean wind. It did not seem important. What mattered was the sudden reality of the ongoing battles the Six Duchies faced against the Raiders. This nameless little village in Bearns was probably not of great strategic importance, but it was falling as I watched, one more brick crumbling out of a wall. Once the Raiders possessed the Bearns coast, the Six Duchies would never be freed of them. And they were taking that coast, town by town, hamlet by hamlet, while the erstwhile King sheltered in Tradeford. The reality of our struggle against the Red Ships had been imminent and pressing when I had pulled an oar on the *Rurisk*. Over the past few months, insulated and isolated from the war, I had allowed myself to forget the folk who lived that conflict every day. I had been as unfeeling as Regal.

I finally awoke as evening began to steal the colours from the river and plain. I did not feel I had rested, and yet it was a relief to awaken. I sat up, looked about myself. Nighteyes had not returned to me. I quested briefly toward him. *My brother*, he acknowledged me, but I sensed he was annoyed at my intrusion. He was watching the two cubs tumble each other about. I pulled my mind back to myself wearily. The contrast between our two lives was suddenly too great even to consider. The Red Ship Raiders, the Forgings and Regal's treacheries, even my plan to kill Regal were suddenly nasty human things I had foisted off on the wolf. What right was there in letting such ugliness shape his life? He was where he was supposed to be.

As little as I liked it, the task I had set myself was mine alone. I tried to let go of him. Still, the stubborn spark remained. He had said he would come back to me. I resolved that if he did, it must be his own decision. I would not summon him to me. I arose, and pressed on. I told myself that if Nighteyes decided to rejoin me, he could overtake me easily. There is nothing like a wolf's trot for devouring the miles. And it was not as if I were travelling swiftly without him. I very much missed his night vision. I came to a place where the riverbank dropped down to become little better than a swamp. I could not decide at first whether to press through it or to try to go around it. I knew it could stretch for miles. At length I decided to stay as close to the open river as I could. I spent a miserable night, swishing through bulrushes and cattails, stumbling over their tangled roots, my feet wet more often than not, and bedevilled by enthusiastic midges.

What kind of a moron, I asked myself, tried to walk through an unfamiliar swamp in the dark? Serve me right if I found a bog-hole and drowned in it. Above me were only the stars, around me the unchanging walls of cattails. To my right I caught glimpses of the wide, dark river. I kept moving upstream. Dawn found me still slogging along. Tiny single-leaved plants with trailing roots coated my leggings and shoes and my chest was welted with insect bites. I ate dried meat as I walked. There was no place to rest, so I walked on. Resolving to take some good from this place, I gathered some cattail root-stocks as I trudged. It was past midday before the river began to have a real bank again, and I pushed myself on for another hour beyond that to get away from the midges and mosquitoes. Then I washed the greenish swamp slime and mud off my leggings, shoes and skin before flinging myself down to sleep.

Somewhere, Nighteyes stood still and unthreatening as the skinny female came closer to him. As she came closer, he dropped to his belly, rolled over on his side, then curled onto his back and exposed his throat. She came closer, a single step at a time. Then she stopped suddenly, sat down and considered him. He whined lightly. She put her ears back suddenly, bared all her teeth in a snarl, then whirled and dashed away. After a time Nighteyes got up, and went to hunt for meadow mice. He seemed pleased.

Again, as his presence drifted away from me, I was summoned back to Bearns. Another village was burning.

I awoke discouraged. Instead of pushing on, I kindled a small fire of driftwood. I boiled water in my kettle to cook the root-stocks while I cut some of my dried meat into chunks. I stewed the dried meat with the starchy root-stocks and added a bit of my precious store of salt and some wild greens. Unfortunately the chalky taste of the river predominated. Belly full, I shook out my winter cloak, rolled up in it as protection against the night insects and drowsed off again.

Nighteyes and the lead wolf stood looking at one another. They were far enough apart that there was no challenge in it, but Nighteyes kept his tail down. The lead wolf was rangier than Nighteyes and his coat was black. Not so well fed, he bore the scars of both fights and hunts. He carried himself confidently. Nighteyes did not move. After a time the other wolf walked a short way, cocked his leg on a tuft of grass and urinated. He scuffed his front feet in the grass, then walked off without a backward glance. Nighteyes sat down and was still, considering.

The next morning I arose and continued on my way. Nighteyes had left me two days ago. Only two days. Yet it seemed very long to me that I had been alone. And how, I wondered, did Nighteyes measure our separation? Not by days and nights. He had gone to find out a thing, and when he had found it out, then his time to be away from me would be over and he would come back to me. But what, really, had he gone to find out? What it was like to be a wolf among wolves, a member of a pack? If they accepted him, what then? Would he run with them for a day, a week, a season? How long would it take for me to fade from his mind into one of his endless yesterdays?

Why should he want to return to me, if this pack would accept him?

After a time, I allowed myself to realize I was as heartsore and hurt as if a human friend had snubbed me for the company of others. I wanted to howl, to quest out to Nighteyes with my loneliness for him. By an effort of will, I did not. He was not a pet dog, to be whistled to heel. He was a friend and we had travelled together for a time. What right did I have to ask him to give up a chance at a mate, at a true pack of his own, simply that he might be at my side? None at all, I told myself. None at all.

At noon I struck a trail that followed the bank. By late afternoon I had passed several small farmsteads. Melons and grain predominated. A network of ditches carried river-water inland to the crops. The sod houses were set well back from the river's edge, probably to avoid flooding. I had been barked at by dogs, and honked at by flocks of fat white geese, but had seen no folk close enough to hail. The trail had widened to a road, with cart-tracks.

The sun was beating on my back and head from a clear blue sky. High above me, I heard the shrill *ki* of a hawk. I glanced up at him, wings open and still as he rode the sky. He gave cry again, folded his wings and plummeted toward me. Doubtless, he dived on some small rodent in one of the fields. I watched him come at me, and only at the last moment realized I was truly his target. I flung up an arm to shield my face just as he opened his wings. I felt the wind of his braking. For a bird his size, he landed quite lightly on my upflung arm. His talons clenched painfully in my flesh.

My first thought was that he was a trained bird gone feral, who had seen me and somehow decided to return to man. A scrap of leather dangling from one of his legs might be the remainder of jesses. He sat blinking on my arm, a magnificent bird in every way. I held him out from me to have a better look at him. The leather on his leg secured a tiny scroll of parchment. 'Can I have a look at that?' I asked him aloud. He turned his head to my voice and one gleaming eye stared at me. It was Sleet.

Old Blood.

I could make no more of his thoughts than that, but it was enough.

I had never been much good with the birds at Buckkeep. Burrich had finally bid me leave them alone, for my presence always agitated them. Nevertheless, I quested gently toward his flame-bright mind. He seemed quiet. I managed to tug the tiny scroll loose. The hawk shifted on my arm, digging his talons into fresh flesh. Then, without warning, he lifted his wings and launched away from me into the air. He spiralled up, beating heavily to gain altitude, cried once more his high *ki, ki,* and went sliding off down the sky. I was left with blood trickling down my arm where his talons had scored my flesh, and one ringing ear from the beating of his wings as he launched. I glanced at the punctures in my arm. Then curiosity made me turn to the tiny scroll. Pigeons carried messages, not hawks.

The handwriting was in an old style, tiny, thin and spidery. The brightness of the sun made it even harder to read. I sat down at the edge of the road and shaded it with my hand to study it. The first words almost stilled my heart. 'Old Blood greets Old Blood.'

The rest was harder to puzzle out. The scroll was tattered, the spellings quaint, the words as few as would suffice. The warning was from Holly, though I suspected Rolf had penned it. King Regal actively hunted down Old Blood now. To those he captured, he offered coins if they would help find a wolf–man pair. They suspected Nighteyes and I were the ones he wanted. Regal threatened death to those who refused. There was a little more, something about giving my scent to others of Old Blood and asking that they aid me as they could. The rest of the scroll was too tattered to read. I tucked the scroll into my belt. The bright day seemed edged with darkness now. So Will had told Regal I yet lived. And Regal feared me enough to set these wheels in motion. Perhaps it was as well that Nighteyes and I had parted company for a time.

As twilight fell, I ascended a small rise on the riverbank. Ahead of me, tucked into a bend of the river, were a few lights. Probably another trading post or a ferry dock to allow farmers and herders easy passage across the river. I watched the lights as I walked toward them. Ahead there would be hot food, and people, and shelter for the night. I could stop and have a word with the folk there if I wished. I still had a few coins to call my own. No wolf at my heels to excite questions, no Nighteyes lurking outside hoping no dogs would pick up his scent. No one to worry about except myself. Well, maybe I would. Maybe I'd stop and have a glass and a bit of talk. Maybe I'd learn how much farther it was to Tradeford, and hear some gossip of what went on there. It was time I began formulating a real plan as to how I would deal with Regal.

It was time I began depending only on myself.

EIGHT

Tradeford

As summer mellowed to an end, the Raiders redoubled their efforts to secure as much of the coast of Bearns Duchy as they could before the storms of winter set in. Once they had secured the major ports, they knew they could strike along the rest of the Six Duchies coastline at their pleasure. So although they had made raids as far as Shoaks Duchy that summer, as the pleasant days dwindled they concentrated their efforts on making the coast of Bearns their own.

Their tactics were peculiar. They made no effort to seize towns or conquer the folk. They were solely intent on destruction. Towns they captured were burned entirely, the folk slain, Forged or fled. A few were kept as workers, treated as less than beasts, Forged when they became useless to their captors, or for amusement. They set up their own rough shelters, disdaining to use the buildings they could simply have seized rather than destroyed. They made no effort to establish permanent settlements but instead simply garrisoned the best ports to be sure they could not be taken back.

Although Shoaks and Rippon Duchies gave aid to Bearns Duchy where they could, they had coasts of their own to protect and scant resources to employ. Buck Duchy wallowed along as best it could. Lord Bright had belatedly seen how Buck relied on its outlying holdings for protection, but he judged it too late to salvage that line of defence. He devoted his men and money to fortifying Buckkeep itself. That left the rest of Buck Duchy with but its own folk and the irregular troops that had devoted themselves to Lady Patience as a bulwark against the Raiders. Bearns expected no succour from that quarter, but gratefully accepted all that came to them under the Ivy badge.

Duke Brawndy of Bearns, long past his prime as a fighter, met the challenge of the Raiders with steel as grey as his hair and beard. His resolution knew no bounds. He did not scruple to beggar himself of *personal treasure, nor to risk the lives of his kin in his final efforts to defend his duchy. He met his end trying to defend his home castle, Ripplekeep. But neither his death nor the fall of Ripplekeep stopped his daughters from carrying on the resistance against the Raiders.*

My shirt had acquired a peculiar new shape from being rolled in my pack so long. I pulled it on anyway, grimacing slightly at its musty odour. It smelled faintly of wood smoke, and more strongly of mildew. Damp had got into it. I persuaded myself that the open air would disperse the smell. I did what I could with my hair and beard. That is, I brushed my hair and bound it back into a tail, and combed my beard smooth with my fingers. I detested the beard, but hated taking the time each day to shave. I left the riverbank where I had made my brief ablutions and headed toward the town lights. This time, I had resolved to be better prepared. My name, I had decided, was Jory. I had been a soldier, and had a few skills with horses and a pen, but had lost my home to Raiders. I was presently intent on making my way to Tradeford to start life anew. It was a role I could play convincingly.

As the last of the day's light faded, more lamps were kindled in the riverside town and I saw I had been much mistaken as to the size of it. The sprawl of the town extended far up the bank. I felt some trepidation, but convinced myself that walking through the town would be much shorter than going around it. With no Nighteyes at my heels I had no reason to add those extra miles and hours to my path. I put my head up and affected a confident stride.

The town was a lot livelier after dark than most places I had been. I sensed a holiday air in those strolling the streets. Most were headed toward the centre of town, and as I drew closer, there were torches, folk in bright dress, laughter, and the sound of music. The lintels of the inn doors were adorned with flowers. I came to a brightly lit plaza. Here was the music, and merrymakers were dancing. There were casks of drink set out, and tables with bread and fruit piled upon them. My mouth watered at the sight of the food, and the bread smelled especially wonderful to one so long deprived of it.

I lingered at the edges of the crowd, listening, and discovered that the Capaman of the town was celebrating his wedding: hence the feasting and dancing. I surmised that the Capaman was some sort of Farrow title for a noble, and that this particular one was well regarded by his folk for his generosity. One elderly woman, noticing me, approached me and pushed three coppers into my hand. 'Go to the tables, and eat, young fellow,' she told me kindly. 'Capaman Logis has decreed that on his wedding night all are to celebrate with him. The food is for the sharing. Go on, now, don't be shy.' She patted me reassuringly on the shoulder, standing on tiptoe to do so. I blushed to be mistaken for a beggar, but thought better of dissuading her. If so she thought me, so I appeared, and better to act as one. Still, as I slipped the three coppers into my pouch, I felt oddly guilty, as if I had tricked them away from her. I did as she had bid me, going to the table to join the line of those receiving bread and fruit and meat.

There were several young women managing the tables, and one piled up a trencher for me, handing it across the table hastily, as if reluctant to have any contact with me at all. I thanked her, which caused some giggling among her friends. She looked as affronted as if I had mistaken her for a whore, and I quickly took myself away from there. I found a corner of a table to sit at, and marked that no one sat near to me. A young boy setting out mugs and filling them with ale gave me one, and was curious enough to ask me where I had come from. I told him only that I had been travelling upriver, looking for work, and asked if he had heard of anyone hiring.

'Oh, you want the hiring fair, up the water in Tradeford,' he told me familiarly. 'It's less than another day's walk. You might get harvest work this time of year. And if not, there's always the King's Great Circle being built. They'll hire anyone for that as can lift a stone or use a shovel.'

'The King's Great Circle?' I asked him.

He cocked his head at me. 'So that all may witness the King's justice being served.'

Then he was called away by someone waving a mug and I was left alone to eat and muse. *They'll hire anyone.* So I appeared that wayward and strange. Well, it could not be helped. The food tasted incredibly good. I had all but forgotten the texture and fragrance of good wheaten bread. The savoury way it mingled with the meat juices on my trencher suddenly recalled Cook Sara and her generous kitchen to me. Somewhere up the river, in Tradeford, she would be making pastry dough now, or perhaps pricking a roast full of spices before putting it in one of her heavy black kettles and covering it well, to let it slow cook in the coals all night. Yes, and in Regal's stables, Hands would be making his final rounds for the night as Burrich used to do in the stables at Buckkeep, checking to see that every beast had fresh clean water and that every stall was securely fastened. A dozen other stable-hands from Buckkeep would be there as well, faces and hearts well known to me from years spent together in Burrich's domain and under his tutelage. House servants, too, Regal had taken with him from Buck. Mistress Hasty was probably there, and Brant and Lowden and . . .

Loneliness suddenly engulfed me. It would be so good to see them, to lean on a table and listen to Cook Sara's endless gossip, or lie on my back in the hayloft with Hands and pretend I believed his outrageous tales of the women he had bedded since last I had seen him. I tried to imagine Mistress Hasty's reaction to my present garb, and found myself smiling at her outrage and scandalized offence.

My reverie was broken by a man shouting a string of obscenities. Not even the drunkest sailor I had ever known would so profane a wedding feast. Mine was not the only head that turned and for a moment all normal conversation lapsed. I stared at what I had not noticed before.

Off one side of the square, at the edge of the torches' reach, was a cart and team. A great barred cage sat upon it and three Forged ones were in it. I could make out no more than that, that there were three of them and that they registered not at all upon my Wit. A teamster woman strode up to the cage, cudgel in hand. She banged it loudly on the slats of the cage, commanding those within to be still, and then spun about to two young men lounging against the tail of her cart. 'And you'll leave them be as well, you great louts!' she scolded them. 'They're for the King's Circle, and whatever justice or mercy they find there. But until then, you'll leave them be, you understand me? Lily! Lily, bring those bones from the roast over here and give them to these creatures. And you, I told you, get away from them! Don't stir them up!'

The two young men stepped back from her threatening cudgel, laughing with upraised hands as they did so. 'Don't see why we shouldn't have our fun with them first,' objected the taller of the lads. 'I heard that down at Rundsford, their town's building their own justice circle.'

The second boy made a great show of rolling the muscles in his shoulders. 'Me, I'm for the King's Circle myself.'

'As Champion or prisoner?' someone hooted mockingly, and both the young men laughed, and the taller one gave his companion a rough push by way of jest.

I remained standing in my place. A sick suspicion was rising in me. The King's Circle. Forged ones and Champions. I recalled the avaricious way Regal had watched his men beat me as I stood encircled by them. A dull numbness spread through me as the woman called Lily made her way to the cart and then flung a plateful of meat bones at the prisoners there. They fell upon them avidly, striking and snapping at one another as each strove to claim as much of the bounty as he could. Not a few folk stood around the cart pointing and laughing. I stared, sickened. Didn't they understand those men had been Forged? They were not criminals. They were husbands and sons, fishers and farmers of the Six Duchies, whose only crime had been to be captured by the Red Ships.

I had no count of the number of Forged ones I had slain. I felt a revulsion for them, that was true, but it was the same revulsion I felt at seeing a leg that had gone to gangrene, or a dog so taken with mange that there was no cure for him. Killing Forged ones had nothing to do with hatred, or punishment, or justice. Death was the only solution to their condition and it should have been meted out as swiftly as possible, in mercy to the families that had loved them. Those young men had spoken as if there would be some sort of sport in killing them. I stared at the cage queasily.

I sat down slowly at my place again. There was still food on my platter but my appetite for it had faded. Common sense told me that I should eat while I had the chance. For a moment I just looked at the food. I made myself eat.

When I lifted my eyes, I caught two young men staring at me. For an instant I met their looks; then I recalled who I was supposed to be and cast my glance down. They evidently were amused by me, for they came swaggering over to sit down, one across the table from me and one uncomfortably close beside me. That one made a great show of wrinkling his nose and covering his nose and mouth for his comrade's amusement. I gave them both good evening.

'Good evening for you, perhaps. Haven't had a feed like this in a while, eh, beggar?' This from the one across from me, a tow-headed lout with a mask of freckles across his face.

'That's true, and my thanks to your Capaman for his generosity,' I said mildly. I was already looking for a way to extricate myself.

'So. What brings you to Pome?' the other asked. He was taller than his indolent friend, and more muscled.

'Looking for work.' I met his pale eyes squarely. 'I've been told there's a hiring fair in Tradeford.'

'And what kind of work would you be good at, beggar? Scarecrow? Or do you perhaps draw the rats out of a man's house with your smell?' He set an elbow on the table, too close to me, and then leaned forward on it, as if to show me the bunching of muscle in his arm.

I took a breath, then two. I felt something I had not felt in a while. There was the edge of fear, and that invisible quivering that ran over me when I was challenged. I knew, too, that at times it became the trembling that presaged a fit. But something else built inside me as well, and I had almost forgotten the feel of it. Anger. No. Fury. The mindless, violent fury that gave me the strength to lift an axe and sever a man's shoulder and arm from his body, or fling myself at him and choke the life out of his body regardless of how he pummelled at me as I did so.

In a sort of awe I welcomed it back and wondered what had summoned it. Had it been recalling friends taken from me for ever, or the battle scenes I had Skill-dreamed so often recently? It didn't matter. I had the weight of a sword at my hip and I doubted that the dolts were aware of it, or aware of how I could use it. Probably they'd never swung any blade but a scythe, probably never seen any blood other than that of a chicken or cow. They'd never awakened at night to a dog's barking and wondered if it were Raiders coming, never come in from a day's fishing praying that when the cape was rounded, the town would still be standing. Blissfully ignorant farm-boys, living fat in soft river country far from the embattled coast, with no better way to prove themselves than to bait a stranger or taunt caged men.

Would that all Six Duchies boys were so ignorant.

I started as if Verity had laid his hand on my shoulder. Almost I looked behind me. Instead, I sat motionless, groping inside me to find him, but found nothing. Nothing.

I could not say for certain the thought had come from him. Perhaps it was my own wish. And yet it was so like him, I could not doubt its source. My anger was gone as suddenly as they had roused it, and I looked at them in a sort of surprise, startled to find they were still there. Boys, yes, no more than big boys, restless and aching to prove themselves. Ignorant and callous as young men often were. Well, I would neither be a proving ground for their manhood, nor would I spill their blood in the dust on their Capaman's wedding feast.

'I think perhaps I have overstayed my welcome,' I said gravely, and rose from the table. I had eaten enough, and I knew I did not need the half-mug of ale that sat beside it. I saw them measure me as I stood and saw one startle plainly when he saw the sword that hung at my side. The other stood, as if to challenge my leaving, but I saw his friend give his head a minuscule shake. With the odds evened, the brawny farm-boy stepped away from me with a sneer, drawing back as if to keep my presence from soiling him. It was strangely easy to ignore the insult. I did not back away from them, but turned and walked off into the darkness, away from the merrymaking and dancing and music. No one followed me.

I sought the waterfront, purpose growing in me as I strode along. So I was not far from Tradeford, not far from Regal. I felt a sudden desire to prepare myself for him. I would get a room at an inn tonight, one with a bathhouse, and I would bathe and shave. Let him look at me, at the scars he had put upon me, and know who killed him. And afterwards? If I lived for there to be an afterwards, and if any who saw me knew me, so be it. Let it be known that the Fitz had come back from his grave to work a true King's Justice on this would-be king.

Thus fortified, I passed by the first two inns I came to. From one came shouts that were either a brawl or an excess of good fellowship; in either case, I was not likely to get much sleep there. The second had a sagging porch and a door hung crooked on its hinges. I decided that did not bode well for the upkeep of the beds. I chose instead one that displayed an inn board of a kettle, and kept a night torch burning outside to guide travellers to its door.

Like most of the larger buildings in Pome, the inn was built of riverstone and mortar and floored with the same. There was a big hearth at the end of the room, but only a summer fire in it, just enough to keep the promised kettle of stew simmering. Despite my recent meal, it smelled good to me. The tap-room was quiet, much of the trade drawn off to the Capaman's wedding celebration. The innkeeper looked as if he were ordinarily a friendly sort, but a frown creased his brow at the sight of me. I set a silver piece on the table before him to reassure him. 'I'd like a room for the night, and a bath.'

He looked me up and down doubtfully. 'If ye take the bath first,' he specified firmly.

I grinned at him. 'I've no problems with that, good sir. I'll be washing out my clothes as well; no fear I'll bring vermin to the bedding.'

He nodded reluctantly and sent a lad to the kitchens for hot water. 'You've come a long way, then?' he offered as a pleasantry as he showed me the way to the bathhouse behind the inn.

'A long way and a bit beside. But there's a job waiting for me in Tradeford, and I'd like to look my best when I go to do it.' I smiled as I said it, pleased with the truth of it.

'Oh, a job waiting. I see, then, I see. Yes, best to show up clean and rested, and there's the pot of soap in the corner, and don't be shy about using it.'

Before he left, I begged the use of a razor, for the washroom boasted a looking-glass, and he was glad to furnish me one. The boy brought it with the first bucket of hot water. By the time he had finished filling the tub, I had taken off the length of my beard to make it shavable. He offered to wash my clothes out for me for an extra copper, and I was only too happy to let him. He took them from me with a wrinkling of his nose that showed me I smelled far worse than I had suspected. Evidently my trek through the swamps had left more evidence than I had thought.

I took my time, soaking in the hot water, slathering myself with the soft soap from the pot, then scrubbing vigorously before rinsing off. I washed my hair twice before the lather ran white instead of grey. The water that I left in the tub was thicker than the chalky river water. For once I went slowly enough with my shaving that I only cut myself twice. When I sleeked my hair back and bound it in a warrior's tail I looked up to find a face in the mirror that I scarcely recognized.

It had been months since I'd last seen myself, and then it had been in Burrich's small looking-glass. The face that looked back at me now was thinner than I had expected, showing me cheekbones reminiscent of those in Chivalry's portrait. The white streak of hair that grew above my brow aged me, and reminded me of a wolverine's markings. My forehead and the tops of my cheeks were tanned dark from my summer outside, but my face was paler where the beard had been, so that the lower half of the scar down my cheek seemed much more livid than the rest. What I could see of my chest showed a lot more ribs than it ever had before. There was muscle there, true, but not enough fat to grease a pan, as Cook Sara would have said. The constant travelling and mostly meat diet had left their marks on me.

I turned aside from the looking-glass smiling wryly. My fears of being instantly recognized by any who had known me were laid to rest completely. I scarcely knew myself.

I changed into my winter clothes to make the trip up to my room. The boy assured me he would hang my other clothes by the hearth and have them to me dry by morning. He saw me to my room and left me with a good night and a candle.

I found the room to be sparsely furnished but clean. There were four beds in it, but I was the only customer for the night, for which I was grateful. There was a single window, unshuttered and uncurtained for summer. Cool night air off the river blew into the room. I stood for a time, looking out through the darkness. Upriver, I could see the lights of Tradeford. It was a substantial settlement. Lights dotted the road between Pome and Tradeford. I was plainly into well-settled country now. Just as well I was travelling alone, I told myself firmly, and pushed aside the pang of loss I felt whenever I thought of Nighteyes. I tossed my bundle under my bed. The bed's blankets were rough but smelled clean, as did the straw-stuffed mattress. After months of sleeping on the ground, it seemed almost as soft as my old feather bed in Buckkeep. I blew out my candle and lay down expecting to fall asleep at once.

Instead I found myself staring up at the darkened ceiling. In the distance, I could hear the faint sounds of the merrymaking. Closer to hand were the now-unfamiliar creakings and settling of a building, the sounds of folk moving in other rooms of the inn. They made me nervous, as the wind through the branches of a forest, or the gurgling of the river close by my sleeping spot had not. I feared my own kind more than anything the natural world could ever threaten me with.

My mind wandered to Nighteyes, to wondering what he was doing and if he were safe this evening. I started to quest out toward him, then stopped myself. Tomorrow I would be in Tradeford, to do a thing he could not help me with. More than that, I was in an area now where he could not safely come to me. If I succeeded tomorrow, and lived to go on to the Mountains to seek Verity, then I could hope that he would remember me and join me. But if I died tomorrow, then he was better off where he was, attempting to join his own kind and have his own life.

Arriving at the conclusion and recognizing my decision as correct were easy. Remaining firm in it was the difficult part. I should not have paid for that bed, but have spent the night in walking, for I would have got more rest. I felt more alone than I ever had in my life. Even in Regal's dungeon, facing death, I had been able to reach out to my wolf. Now on this night I was alone, contemplating a murder I was unable to plan, fearing Regal would be guarded by a coterie of Skill-adepts whose talents I could only guess at. Despite the warmth of the late summer night,

I felt chilled and sickened whenever I considered it. My resolution to kill Regal never wavered; only my confidence that I would succeed. I had not done so well on my own but tomorrow I resolved to perform in a way that would make Chade proud.

When I considered the coterie, I felt a queasy certainty that I had deceived myself regarding my strategy. Had I come here of my own will, or was this some subtle tweaking that Will had wrought on my thoughts, to convince me that to run toward him was the safest thing to do? Will was subtle with the Skill. So insidiously gentle a touch he had that one could scarcely feel when he was using it. I longed suddenly to attempt to Skill out, to see if I could feel him watching me. Then I became sure that my impulse to Skill out was actually Will's influence on me, tempting me to open my mind to him. And so my thoughts went, chasing themselves in tighter and tighter circles until I almost felt his amusement as he watched me.

Past midnight I finally felt myself drawn down into sleep. I surrendered my tormenting thoughts without a qualm, flinging myself down into sleep as if I were a diver intent on plumbing the depths. Too late I recognized the imperatives of that sinking. I would have struggled if I could have recalled how. Instead I recognized about me the hangings and trophies that decorated the great hall of Ripplekeep, the main castle of Bearns Duchy.

The great wooden doors sagged open on their hinges, victims of the ram that lay halfway inside them, its terrible work done. Smoke hung in the air of the hall, twining about the banners of past victories. There were bodies piled thickly there, where fighters had tried to hold back the torrent of Raiders that the heavy oaken planks had yielded to. A few strides past that wall of carnage a line of Bearns' warriors still held, but raggedly. In the midst of a small knot of battle was Duke Brawndy, flanked by his younger daughters, Celerity and Faith. They wielded swords, trying vainly to shield their father from the press of the foe. Both fought with a skill and ferocity I would not have suspected in them. Like matched hawks they seemed, their faces framed by short, sleek black hair, their dark blue eyes narrowed with hatred. But Brawndy was refusing to be shielded, refusing to yield to the murderous surge of Raiders. He stood splay-legged, spattered with blood, and wielded a battle axe in a two-handed grip.

Before and below him, in the shelter of his axe's swing, lay the body of his eldest daughter and heir. A sword blow had cloven deep between her shoulder and neck, splintering her collar-bones before the weapon wedged in the ruin of her chest. She was dead, hopelessly dead, but Brawndy would not step back from her body. Tears runnelled with blood on his cheeks. His chest heaved like a bellows with every breath he took, and the ropy old muscles of his torso were revealed beneath his rent shirt. He held off two swordsmen, one an earnest young man whose whole heart was intent on defeating this duke, and the other an adder of a man who held back from the press of the fighting, his longsword ready to take advantage of any opening the young man might create.

In a fraction of a second, I knew all this, and knew that Brawndy would not last much longer. Already the slickness of blood was battling with his failing grip on his axe, while every gasp of air he drew down his dry throat was a torment in itself. He was an old man, and his heart was broken and he knew that even if he survived this battle, Bearns had been lost to the Red Ships. My soul cried out at his misery, but still he took that one impossible step forward, and brought his axe down to end the life of the earnest young man who had fought him. In the moment that his axe sank into the Raider's chest, the other man stepped forward, into the half-second gap and danced his blade in and out of Brawndy's chest. The old man followed his dying opponent down to the bloodied stones of his keep.

Celerity, occupied with her own opponent, turned fractionally to her sister's scream of anguish. The Raider she had been fighting seized his opportunity. His heavier weapon wrapped her lighter blade and tore it from her grip. She stepped back from his fiercely delighted grin, turned her head away from her death, in time to see her father's killer grip Brawndy's hair preparatory to taking his head as a trophy.

I could not stand it.

I lunged for the axe Brawndy had dropped, seized its blood-slick handle as if I were gripping the hand of an old friend. It felt oddly heavy, but I swung it up, blocked the sword of my assailant, and then, in a combination that would have made Burrich proud, doubled it back to take the path of the blade across his face. I gave a small shudder as I felt his facial bones cave away from that stroke. I had no time to consider it. I sprang forward and brought my axe down hard, severing the hand of the man who had sought to take my father's head. The axe rang on the stone flags of the floor, sending a shock up my arms. Sudden blood splashed me as Faith's sword ploughed up her opponent's forearm. He was towering above me, and so I tucked my shoulder and rolled, coming to my feet as I brought the blade of my axe up across his belly. He dropped his blade and clutched at his spilling guts as he fell.

There was an insane moment of total stillness in the tiny bubble of battle we occupied. Faith stared down at me with an amazed expression that briefly changed to a look of triumph before being supplanted with one of purest anguish. 'We can't let them have their bodies!' she declared abruptly. She lifted her head suddenly, her short hair flying like the mane of a battle stallion. 'Bearns! To me!' she cried, and there was no mistaking the note of command in her voice.

For one instant I looked up at Faith. My vision faded, doubled for an instant. A dizzy Celerity wished her sister, 'Long life to the Duchess of Bearns'. I witnessed a look between them, a look that said neither of them expected to live out the day. Then a knot of Bearns warriors broke free of battle to join them. 'My father and my sister. Bear their bodies away,' Faith commanded two of the men. 'You others, to me!' Celerity rolled to her feet, looked at the heavy axe with puzzlement and stooped to regain the familiarity of her sword.

'There, we are needed there,' Faith declared, pointing, and Celerity followed her, to reinforce the battle line long enough to allow their folk to retreat.

I watched Celerity go, a woman I had not loved but would always admire. With all my heart I wished to go after her, but my grip on the scene was failing, all was becoming smoke and shadows. Someone seized me.

That was stupid.

The voice in my mind sounded so pleased. *Will!* I thought desperately as my heart surged in my chest.

No. But it could as easily have been so. You are getting sloppy about your walls, Fitz. You cannot afford to. No matter how they call to us, you must be cautious. Verity gave me a push that propelled me away, and I felt the flesh of my own body receive me again.

'But you do it,' I protested, but heard only the wan sound of my own voice in the inn room. I opened my eyes. All was darkness outside the single window in the room. I could not tell if moments had passed or hours. I only knew I was grateful that there was still some darkness left for sleeping, for the terrible weariness that pulled at me now would let me think of nothing else.

When I awoke the next morning, I was disoriented. It had been too long since I had awakened in a real bed, let alone awakened feeling clean. I forced my eyes to focus, then looked at the knots in the ceiling beam above me. After a time, I recalled the inn, and that I was not too far from Tradeford and Regal. At almost the same instant, I remembered that Duke Brawndy was dead. My heart plummeted inside me. I squeezed my eyes shut against the Skill-memory of that battle and felt the hammer and anvil of my headache begin. For one irrational instant I blamed it all on Regal. He had orchestrated this tragedy that took the heart out of me and left my body trembling with weakness. On the very morning when I had hoped to arise strong and refreshed and ready to kill, I could barely find the strength to roll over.

After a time, the inn-boy arrived with my clothes. I gave him another two coppers and he returned a short time later with a tray. The look and smell of the bowl of porridge revolted me. I suddenly understood the aversion to food that Verity had always manifested during the summers when his Skilling had kept the Raiders from our coast. The only item on the tray that interested me was the mug and the pot of hot water. I clambered out of bed and crouched to pull my pack from under my bed. Sparks danced and floated before my eyes. By the time I got the pack open and located the elfbark, I was breathing as hard as if I had run a race.

It took all my concentration to focus my thoughts past the pain in my head. Emboldened by my headache's throbbing, I increased the amount of elfbark I crumbled into the mug. I was nearly up to the dose that Chade had been using on Verity. Ever since the wolf had left me, I had suffered from these Skill-dreams. No matter how I set my walls, I could not keep them out. But last night's had been the worst in a long time. I suspected it was because I had stepped into the dream, and through Celerity, acted. The dreams had been a terrible drain both on my strength and my supply of elfbark. I watched impatiently as the bark leached its darkness into the steaming water. As soon as I could no longer see the bottom of the mug, I lifted it and drank it off. The bitterness nearly gagged me, but it didn't stop me from pouring more hot water over the bark in the bottom of the mug.

I drank this second, weaker dose more slowly, sitting on the edge of my bed and looking off into the distance outside the window. I had quite a view of the flat river country. There were cultivated fields, and milk cows in fenced pastures just outside Pome, and beyond I could glimpse the rising smoke of small farmsteads along the road. No more swamps to cross, no more open wild country between Regal and me. From hence forward, I would have to travel as a man.

My headache had subsided. I forced myself to eat the cold porridge, ignoring my stomach's threats. I'd paid for it and I'd need its sustenance before this day was over. I dressed in the clean clothes the boy had returned to me. They were clean, but that was as much as I could say for them. The shirt was misshapen and discoloured various shades of brown. The leggings were worn to thinness in the knees and seat and too short. As I pushed my feet into my self-made shoes, I became newly aware of how pathetic they were. It had been so long since I had stopped to consider how I must appear to others that I was surprised to find myself dressed more poorly than any Buckkeep beggar I could recall. No wonder I had excited both pity and disgust last night. I'd have felt the same for any fellow dressed as I was.

The thought of going downstairs dressed as I was made me cringe. The alternative however was to don my warm, woolly winter clothes, and swelter and sweat all day. It was only common sense to descend as I was, and yet I now felt myself such a laughing stock, I wished I could slink out unseen.

As I briskly repacked my bundle, I felt a moment of alarm when I realized how much elfbark I had consumed in one draught. I felt alert; no more than that. A year ago, that much elfbark would have had me swinging from the rafters. I told myself firmly it was like my ragged clothes. I had no choice in the matter. The Skill-dreams would not leave me alone, and I had no time to lie about and let my body recover on its own, let alone the coin to pay for an inn room and food while I did so. Yet as I slung my bundle over my shoulder and went down the stairs, I reflected that it was a poor way to begin the day. Brawndy's death and Bearns Duchy falling to the Raiders and my scarecrow clothing and elfbark crutch. It had all put me in a fine state of the doldrums.

What real chance did I have of getting past Regal's walls and guards and making an end of him?

A bleak spirit, Burrich had once told me, was one of the after-effects of elfbark. So that was all I was feeling. That was all.

I bade the innkeeper farewell and he wished me good luck. Outside the sun was already high. It bid to be another fine day. I set myself a steady pace as I headed out of Pome and toward Tradeford.

As I reached the outskirts, I saw an unsettling sight. There were two gallows, and a body dangled from each. This was unnerving enough, but there were other structures as well: a whipping post, and two stocks. Their wood had not silvered out in the sun yet; these were recent structures and yet by the look of them they had already seen a bit of use. I strode swiftly past them but could not help recalling how close I had come to gracing such a structure. All that had saved me was my bastard royal blood and the ancient decree that such a one could not be hung. I recalled, too, Regal's evident pleasure at watching me beaten.

With a second chill I wondered where Chade was. If Regal's soldiery did manage to capture him, I had no doubt that Regal would put a quick end to him. I tried not to imagine how he would stand, tall and thin and grey under bright sunlight on a scaffold.

Or would his end be quick?

I shook my head to rattle loose such thoughts and continued past the poor scarecrow bodies that tattered in the sun like forgotten laundry. Some black humour in my soul pointed out that even they were dressed better than I was.

As I hiked along the road I often had to give way to carts and cattle. Trade prospered between the two towns. I left Pome behind me and walked for a time past well-tended farmhouses that fronted the road with their grainfields and orchards behind them. A bit further and I was passing country estates, comfortable stone houses with shade trees and plantings about their sturdy barns and with riding and hunting horses in the pastures. More than once I was sure I recognized Buckkeep stock there. These gave way for a time to great fields, mostly of flax or hemp. Eventually I began to see more modest holdings and then the outskirts of a town.

So I thought. Late afternoon found me in the heart of a city, streets paved with cobbles and folk coming and going on every sort of business imaginable. I found myself looking around in wonder. I had never seen the like of Tradeford. There was shop after shop, taverns and inns and stables for every weight of purse, and all sprawled out across this flat land as no Buck town ever could. I came to one area of gardens and fountains, temples and theatres and schooling places. There were gardens laid out with pebbled walkways and cobbled drives that wound between plantings and statuary and trees. The people strolling down the walks or driving their carriages were dressed in finery that would have been at home at any of Buckkeep's most formal occasions. Some of them wore the Farrow livery of gold and brown, yet even the dress of these servants was more sumptuous than any clothing I had ever owned.

This was where Regal had spent the summers of his childhood. Always he had disdained Buckkeep Town as little better than a backward village. I tried to imagine a boy leaving all this in fall, to return to a draughty castle on a rainswept and storm-battered sea-cliff above a grubby little port town. No wonder he had removed himself and his court here as soon as he could. I suddenly felt an inkling of understanding for Regal. It made me angry. It is good to know well a man you are going to kill; it is not good to understand him. I recalled how he had killed his own father, my king, and steeled myself to my purpose.

As I wandered through these thriving quarters, I drew more than one pitying glance. Had I been determined to make my living as a beggar, I could have prospered. Instead, I sought humbler abodes and folk where I might hear some talk of Regal and how his keep at Tradeford was organized and manned. I made my way down to the waterfront, expecting to feel more at home.

There I found the real reason for Tradeford's existence. True to its name, the river flattened out here into immense rippling shallows over gravel and bedrock. It sprawled so wide that the opposite shore was obscured in mist, and the river seemed to reach to the horizon. I saw whole herds of cattle and sheep being forded across the Vin River, while downstream a series of shallow-draught cable barges took advantage of the deeper water to transport an endless shuttling of goods across the river. This was where Tilth met Farrow in trade, where orchards and fields and cattle came together, and where goods shipped upriver from Buck or Bearns or the far lands beyond were unloaded at last and sent on their way to the nobles who could afford them. To Tradeford, in better days, had come the trade-goods of the Mountain Kingdom and the lands beyond: amber, rich furs, carved ivory and the rare incense barks of the Rain Wilds. Here too was flax brought to be manufactured into fine Farrow linen, and hemp worked into fibre for rope and sailcloth.

I was offered a few hours' work unloading grain sacks from a small barge to a wagon. I took it, more for the conversation than the coppers. I learned little. No one spoke of Red Ships or the war being fought along the coast, other than to complain of the poor quality of goods that came from the coast and how much was charged for the little that was sent. Little was said of King Regal, and what few words I did hear took pride in his ability to attract women and to drink well. I was startled to hear him spoken of as a Mountwell king, the name of his mother's royal line. Then I decided it suited me just as well that he did not name himself a Farseer. It was one less thing I had to share with him.

I heard much of the King's Circle however, and what I heard soured my guts.

The concept of a duel to defend the truth of one's words was an old one in the Six Duchies. At Buckkeep there were the great standing pillars of the Witness Stones. It is said that when two men meet there to resolve a question with their fists, El and Eda themselves witness it and see that justice does not go awry. The stones and the custom are very ancient. When we spoke of the King's Justice at Buckkeep, often enough it referred to the quiet work that Chade and I did for King Shrewd. Some came to make public petition to King Shrewd himself and to abide by whatever he might see as right. But there were times when other injustices came to be known by the King, and then he might send forth Chade or me to work his will quietly upon the wrongdoer. In the name of the King's Justice I had meted out fates both mercifully swift and punitively slow. I should have been hardened to death.

But Regal's King's Circle had more of entertainment than justice to it. The premise was simple. Those judged by the King as deserving of punishment or death were sent to his Circle. There they might face animals starved and taunted to madness, or a fighter, a King's Champion. Some occasional criminal who put up a very good show might be granted royal clemency, or even become a Champion for the King. Forged ones had no such chance. Forged ones were put out for the beasts to maul, or starved and turned loose on other offenders. Such trials had become quite popular of late, so popular that the crowds were outgrowing the market circle at Tradeford where the 'justice' was currently administered. Now Regal was having a special circle built. It would be conveniently closer to his manorhouse, with holding cells and secure walls that would confine both beasts and prisoners more strongly, with seats for those who came to observe the spectacle of the King's Justice being meted out. The construction of the King's Circle was providing new commerce and jobs for the city of Tradeford. All welcomed it as a very good idea in the wake of the shutdown of trade with the Mountain Kingdom. I heard not one word spoken against it.

When the wagon was loaded, I took my pay and followed the other stevedores to a nearby tavern. Here, in addition to ale and beer, one could buy a handful of herbs and a smoke censer for the table. The atmosphere inside the tavern was heavy with the fumes, and my eyes soon felt gummy and my throat raw from it. No one else seemed to pay it any mind, or even to be greatly affected by it. The use of burning herbs as an intoxicant had never been common at Buckkeep and I had never developed a head for it. My coins bought me a serving of meal pudding with honey and a mug of very bitter beer that tasted to me of river water.

I asked several folk if it were true that they were hiring stable-hands for the King's own stable, and if so, where a man might go to ask for the work. That one such as I might seek to work for the King himself afforded most of them some amusement, but as I had affected to be slightly simple the whole time I was working with them, I was able to accept their rough humour and suggestions with a bland smile. One rake at last told me that I should go ask the King himself, and gave me directions to Tradeford Hall. I thanked him and drank off the last of my beer and set out.

I suppose I had expected some stone edifice with walls and fortifications. This was what I watched for as I followed my directions inland and up away from the river. Instead, I eventually reached a low hill, if one could give that name to so modest an upswelling. The extra height was enough to afford a clear view of the river in both directions, and the fine stone structures upon it had taken every advantage of it. I stood on the busy road below, all but gawking up at it. It had none of Buckkeep's forbidding martial aspects. Instead, the white-pebbled drive and gardens and trees surrounded a dwelling at once palatial and welcoming. Tradeford Hall and its surrounding buildings had never seen use as fortress or keep. It had been built as an elegant and pensive residence. Patterns had been worked into the stone walls and there were graceful arches to the entryways. Towers there were, but there were no arrow-slits in them. One knew they had been constructed to afford the dweller a wider view of his surroundings, more for pleasure than for any wariness.

There were walls, too, between the busy public road and the mansion, but they were low, fat stone walls, mossy or ivied, with nooks and crannies where statues were framed by flowering vines. One broad carriageway led straight up to the great house. Other narrower walks and drives invited one to investigate lily ponds and cleverly-pruned fruit trees or quiet, shady walks. For some visionary gardener had planted here oaks and willows, at least one hundred years ago, and now they towered and shaded and whispered in the wind off the river. All of this beauty was spread over more acreage than a good-sized farm. I tried to imagine a ruler who had both the time and resources to create all this.

Was this what one could have, if one did not need warships and standing armies? Had Patience ever known this sort of beauty in her parents' home? Was this what the Fool echoed in the delicate vases of flowers and bowls of silver fish in his room? I felt grubby and uncouth, and it was not because of my clothes. This, indeed, I suddenly felt, was how a king should live. Amid art and music and graciousness, elevating the lives of his people by providing a place for such things to flourish. I glimpsed my own ignorance, and worse, the ugliness of a man trained only to kill others. I felt a sudden anger, too, at all I had never been taught, never even glimpsed. Had not Regal and his mother had a hand in that as well, in keeping the Bastard in his place? I had been honed as an ugly, functional tool, just as craggy, barren Buckkeep was a fort, not a palace.

But how much beauty would survive here, did not Buckkeep stand like a snarling dog at the mouth of the Buck River?

It was like a dash of cold water in my face. It was true. Was not that why Buckkeep had been built in the first place, to gain control of the river trade? If Buckkeep ever fell to the Raiders, these broad rivers would become highroads for their shallow-draught vessels. They would plunge like a dagger into this soft underbelly of the Six Duchies. These indolent nobles and cocky farm-lads would waken to screams and smoke in the night, with no castle to run to, no guards to stand and fight for them. Before they died, they might come to know what others had endured to keep them safe. Before they died, they might rail against a king who had fled those ramparts to come inland and hide himself in pleasures.

But I intended that king would die first.

I began a careful walk of the perimeter of Tradeford Keep. The easiest way in must be weighed against the least-noticed one, and the best ways out must be planned as well. Before nightfall, I would find out all I could about Tradeford Hall.

NINE

Assassin

The last true Skillmaster to preside over royal pupils at Buckkeep was not Galen, as is often recorded, but his predecessor, Solicity. She had waited, perhaps overlong, to select an apprentice. When she chose Galen, she had already developed the cough that was to end her life. Some say she took him on in desperation, knowing she was dying. Others, that he was forced on her by Queen Desire's wish to see her favourite advanced at court. Whatever the case, he had been her apprentice for scarcely two years before Solicity succumbed to her cough and died. As previous Skillmasters had served apprenticeships as long as seven years before achieving journey status, it was rather precipitate that he declared himself Skillmaster immediately following Solicity's death. It scarcely seems possible that she could have imparted her full knowledge of the Skill and all its possibilities in such a brief time. No one challenged his claim, however. Although he had been assisting Solicity in the training of the two princes Verity and Chivalry, he pronounced their training complete following Solicity's death. Thereafter, he resisted suggestions that he train any others until the years of the Red Ship wars, when he finally gave in to King Shrewd's demand and produced his first and only coterie.

Unlike traditional coteries that selected their own membership and leader, Galen created his from hand-picked students and during his life retained a tremendous amount of control over them. August, the nominal head of the coterie, had his talent blasted from him in a Skill mishap while on a mission to the Mountain Kingdom. Serene, who next assumed leadership following Galen's death, perished along with another member, Justin, during the riot that followed the discovery of King Shrewd's murder. Will was next to assume the leadership of what has come to be known as Galen's Coterie. At that time but three members remained: Will himself, Burl and Carrod. It seems likely that

Galen had imprinted all three with an unswerving loyalty to Regal, but this did not prevent rivalry among them for Regal's favour.

By the time dusk fell, I had explored the outer grounds of the royal estate rather thoroughly. I had discovered that anyone might stroll the lower walks freely, enjoying the fountains and gardens, the yew hedges and the chestnut trees, and there were a number of folk in fine clothes doing just that. Most looked at me with stern disapproval, a few with pity and the one liveried guard I encountered reminded me firmly that no begging was allowed within the King's Gardens. I assured him that I had come only to see the wonders I had so often heard of in tales. In turn, he suggested that tales of the gardens were more than sufficient for my ilk, and pointed out to me the most direct path for leaving the gardens. I thanked him most humbly and walked off. He stood watching me leave until the path carried me around the end of a hedge and out of his sight.

My next foray was more discreet. I had briefly considered way-laying one of the young nobles strolling amongst the flowers and herbaceous borders and availing myself of his clothes, but had decided against it. I was unlikely to find one lean enough for his clothes to fit me properly, and the fashionable apparel they were wearing seemed to require a lot of lacing up with gaily-coloured ribbons. I doubted I could get myself into any of the shirts without the assistance of a valet, let alone get an unconscious man out of one. The tinkling silver charms stitched onto the dangling lace at the cuffs were not conducive to an assassin's quiet work anyway. Instead, I relied on the thick plantings along the low walls for shelter and made my way gradually up the hill.

Eventually I encountered a wall of smooth, worked stone that encircled the crown of the hill. It was only slightly higher than a tall man could reach at a jump. I did not think it had been intended as a serious barrier. There were no plantings along it, but stubs of old trunks and roots showed that once it had been graced with vines and bushes. I wondered if Regal had ordered it cleared. Over the wall I could see the tops of numerous trees, and so dared to count on their shelter.

It took me most of the afternoon to make a full circuit of the wall without coming out into the open. There were several gates in it. One fine main one had guards in livery greeting carriages of folk as they came and went. From the number of carriages arriving some sort of festivity was scheduled for the evening. One guard turned, and laughed harshly. The hair stood up on my neck. For a time I stood frozen, staring from my place of concealment. Had I seen his face before? It was difficult to tell at my distance, but the thought roused a strange mixture of fear and anger in me. Regal, I reminded myself. Regal was my target. I moved on.

Several lesser gates for delivery folk and servants had guards lacking in lace, but making up for it in their militant questioning of every man or woman who went in and out. If my clothes had been better I would have risked impersonating a serving-man but I dared not attempt it in my beggar's rags. Instead, I positioned myself out of sight of the guards on the gate and began to beg of the tradefolk coming and going. I did so mutely, simply approaching them with cupped hands and a pleading expression. Most of them did what folk do when confronted with a beggar. They ignored me and continued their conversations. And so I learned that tonight was the night of the Scarlet Ball, that extra servants, musicians and conjurers had been brought in for the festivity, that merrybud had replaced mirthweed as the King's favourite smoke, and that the King had been very angry with the quality of the yellow silk one Festro had brought him, and had threatened to flog the merchant for even bringing him such poor stuff. The ball was also a farewell to the King, before he embarked on the morrow for a trip to visit his dear friend Lady Celestra at Amber Hall on the Vin River. I heard a great deal more, besides, but little that related to my purpose. I ended up with a handful of coppers for my time as well.

I returned to Tradeford. I found a whole street devoted to the tailoring of clothes. At the back door of Festro's shop, I found an apprentice sweeping out. I gave him several coppers for some scraps of yellow silk in various shades. I then sought out the humblest shop on the street, where every coin I possessed was just sufficient to purchase loose trousers, a smock and a head kerchief such as the apprentice had been wearing. I changed my clothes in the shop, braided my warrior's tail up and concealed it under the kerchief, donned my boots and emerged from the shop a different person. My sword now hung down my leg inside the trousers. It was uncomfortable, but not overly noticeable if I affected a loping stride. I left my worn clothes and the rest of my bundle, save for my poisons and other pertinent tools, in a patch of nettles behind a very smelly backhouse in a tavern yard. I made my way back to Tradeford's keep.

I did not permit myself to hesitate. I went directly to the tradefolks' gate and stood in line with the others seeking admittance. My heart hammered inside my ribs but I affected a calm demeanour. I spent my time studying what I could see of the house through the trees. It was immense. Earlier I had been amazed that so much arable land had been given over to decorative gardens and walks. Now I saw that the gardens were simply the setting for a dwelling that both sprawled and towered in a style of house completely foreign to me. Nothing about it spoke of fortress or castle; all was comfort and elegance. When it came my turn, I showed my swatches of silk and said I came bearing Festro's apologies and some samples that he hoped would be more to the King's liking. When one surly guard pointed out that Festro usually came himself, I replied, somewhat sulkily, that my master thought stripes would better become my back than his, if the samples did not please the King. The guards exchanged grins and admitted me.

I hastened up the path until I was on the heels of a group of musicians who had come in before me. I followed them around to the back of the manorhouse. I knelt to refasten my boot as they asked directions and then straightened up just in time to follow them inside. I found myself in a small entry hall, cool and almost dark after the heat and light of the afternoon sun. I trailed them down a corridor. The minstrels talked and laughed among themselves as they hastened on. I slowed my steps and dropped back. When I passed a door that was ajar on an empty room, I stepped into it and shut the door quietly behind me. I drew a deep breath and looked around.

I was in a small sitting room. The furniture was shabby and ill-matched, so I surmised it was for servants or visiting craftsmen.

I could not count on being alone there for long. There were, however, several large cupboards along the wall. I chose one that was not in direct view of the door should it open suddenly, and quickly rearranged its contents in order to sit inside it. I ensconced myself with the door slightly ajar for some light and went to work. I inspected and organized my vials and packets of poisons. I treated both my belt knife and my sword's edge with poison, then re-sheathed them carefully. I arranged my sword to hang outside my trousers. Then I made myself comfortable and settled down to wait.

Days seemed to pass before dusk gave way to full dark. Twice folk briefly entered the room, but from their gossip I gathered that every servant was busy preparing for the gathering tonight. I passed the time by imagining how Regal would kill me if he caught me. Several times I almost lost my courage. Each time I reminded myself that if I walked away from this, I would have to live with the fear forever. Instead, I tried to prepare myself. If Regal were here, then his coterie would surely be close by. I put myself carefully through the exercises Verity had taught me to shield my mind from other Skilled ones. I was horribly tempted to venture out with a tiny touch of the Skill, to see if I could sense them. I refrained. I doubted I could sense them without betraying myself. And even if I could so detect them, what would it tell me that I did not already know? Better to concentrate on guarding myself from them. I refused to allow myself to think specifically of what I would do, lest they pick up traces of my thoughts. When finally the sky outside the window was full black and pricked with stars, I slipped out from my hiding place and ventured out into the hallway.

Music drifted on the night. Regal and his guests were at their festivities. I listened for a moment to the faint notes of a familiar song about two sisters, one of whom drowned the other. To me, the wonder of the song was not a harp that would play by itself, but a minstrel who would find a woman's body, and be inspired to make a harp of her breastbone. Then I put it out of my mind and concentrated on business.

I was in a simple corridor, stone-floored and panelled with wood, lit with torches set at wide intervals. Servants' area, I surmised; it was not fine enough for Regal or his friends. That did not make it safe for me, however. I needed to find a servants' stair and get myself to the second floor. I crept along the hall. I went from door to door, pausing to listen outside each one. Twice I heard folk within, women talking together in one, the clack of a weaving frame being used in another. The quiet doors that were not locked, I opened briefly. They were workrooms for the most part, with several given over to weaving and sewing. In one, a suit of fine blue fabric was pieced out on a table, ready for sewing. Regal apparently still indulged his fondness for fine clothing.

I came to the end of the corridor and peered around the corner. Another hallway, much finer and wider. The plastered ceiling overhead had been imprinted with fern shapes. Again I crept down a corridor, listening outside doors, cautiously peeping into some of them. Getting closer, I told myself. I found a library, with more vellum books and scrolls than I had ever known existed. I paused in one room where brightly-plumed birds in extravagant cages dozed on their perches. Slabs of white marble had been set to hold ponds of darting fishes and water lilies. There were benches and cushioned chairs set about gaming tables there. Small cherrywood tables scattered about held Smoke censers. I had never even imagined such a room.

I eventually came to a proper hall with framed portraits along the walls and a floor of gleaming black slate. I drew back when I spotted the guard and stood silent in an alcove until his bored pacing carried him past me. Then I slipped out to flit past all those mounted nobles and simpering ladies in their sumptuous frames.

I blundered out into an antechamber. There were hangings on the wall and small tables supporting statuary and vases of flowers. Even the torch sconces here were more ornate. There were small portraits in gilt frames to either side of a fireplace with an elaborate mantel. Chairs were set close together for intimate talk. The music was louder here, and I could hear laughter and voices as well. Despite the lateness of the hour, the merriment went on. On the opposite wall were two tall carved doors. They led to the gathering hall where Regal and his nobles danced and laughed. I pulled myself back around the corner as I saw two servants in livery enter from a door to my far left. They bore trays carrying an assortment of incense pots. I surmised they were to replace ones that had burned out. I stood frozen, listening to their footsteps and conversation. They opened the tall doors and the music of harps spilled out more loudly and the narcotic scent of Smoke. Both were quenched by the closing doors. I ventured to peep out again. All was clear before me, but behind me –

'What do you here?'

My heart fell into my boots, but I forced a sheepish smile to my face as I turned to face the guard who had entered the room behind me. 'Sir, I've lost my way in this great maze of a house,' I said guilelessly.

'Have you? That doesn't explain why you wear a sword within the King's walls. All know weapons are forbidden save to the King's own guard. I saw you sneaking about just then. Did you think with the merrymaking going on, you could just slip about and fill your pockets with whatever you found, thief?'

I stood frozen with terror, watching the man approach me. I am sure he believed he had discovered my purpose from the stricken look on my face. Verde would never have smiled so if he thought he advanced on a man he had helped beat to death in a dungeon. His hand rested carelessly on the hilt of his own blade and he grinned confidently. He was a handsome man, very tall and fair as many of the Farrow folk were. The badge he wore was Mountwell of Farrow's golden oak, with the Farseer buck overleaping it. So Regal had modified his coat of arms as well. I but wished he'd left the buck off it.

A part of me noticed all these things as another part relived the nightmare of being dragged to my feet by my shirt front and stood up, so that this man could strike me and drive me once more to the floor. He was not Bolt, the one who had broken my nose. No, Verde had followed him, beating me insensible a second time, after Bolt had left me too battered to stand on my own. He had towered over me then and I had cowered and flinched away from him, tried vainly to scrabble away from him over the cold stone floor that was already spattered with my blood. I remembered the oaths he had laughingly uttered each time he had had to haul me to my feet so he could hit me again. 'By

Eda's tits,' I muttered to myself, and with the words, fear died in me.

'Let's see what you have in that pouch,' he demanded, and came closer.

I could not show him the poisons in my pouch. No way to explain those away. No amount of smooth lying would let me escape this man. I would have to kill him.

Suddenly it was all so simple.

We were much too close to the gathering hall. I wished no sound to alarm or alert anyone. So I retreated from him, a slow step at a time, backing in a wide circle that took me into the chamber I had just left. The portraits looked down at us as I backed hesitantly away from the tall guardsman.

'Stand still!' he ordered, but I shook my head wildly in what I hoped was a convincing display of terror. 'I said, stand still, you scrawny little thief!' I glanced quickly over my shoulder, then back at him, desperate, as if I were trying to find the courage to turn and run from him. The third time I did so, he leaped for me.

I'd been hoping for that.

I sidestepped him and then drove my elbow savagely into the small of his back, adding just enough momentum to his charge that he went to his knees. I heard them smack bonily against the stone floor. He gave a wordless roar of both anger and pain. I could see how suddenly furious it made him for the scrawny thief to dare strike him. I silenced him sharply when I kicked him under the chin, clacking his mouth shut. I was grateful that I'd switched back to my boots. Before he could make another sound I had my knife out and across his throat. He gurgled his amazement and lifted both hands in a vain attempt to contain that warm gushing of blood. I stood over him, looking down into his eyes. 'FitzChivalry,' I told him quietly. 'FitzChivalry.' His eyes widened in sudden understanding and terror, then lost all expression as life left him. Abruptly he was stillness and nothingness, as devoid of life as a stone. To my Wit sense, he had disappeared.

So quickly it was done. Vengeance. I stood looking down at him, waiting to feel triumph or relief, or satisfaction. Instead I felt nothing, felt as lost to all life as he was. He was not even meat I could eat. I wondered belatedly if there was somewhere a woman who had loved this handsome man, blonde children who depended on his wages for food. It is not good for an assassin to have such thoughts; they had never plagued me when I had carried out the King's Justice for King Shrewd. I shook them from my head.

He was making a very large puddle of blood on the floor. I had silenced him quickly but this was just the sort of mess I hadn't wished to make. He was a large man, and he'd had a lot of blood in him. My mind raced as I debated whether to take time to conceal the body, or to accept that he would be quickly missed by his fellow guards and use that discovery as a diversion.

In the end I took off my shirt and sopped up as much of the blood as I could with it. Then I dumped it on his chest and wiped my bloody hands on his shirt. I seized him by the shoulders and dragged him out of the portrait hall, all the time almost shuddering with the effort of straining my senses to be aware of anyone coming. My boots kept slipping on the polished floors and the sound of my panting breath was a roar to my ears. Despite my efforts at mopping up the blood, we left a sheen of red on the floors behind us. At the door to the room of birds and fish, I forced myself to listen well before entering. I held my breath and tried to ignore the pounding of my heart in my ears. The room was clear of humans, however. I shouldered the door open and dragged Verde in. Then I caught him up and tumbled him into one of the stone fish pools. The fish darted frantically as his blood trailed and swirled out into the clear water. I hastily rinsed my hands and chest clean of blood in another pond, and then left by a different door. They'd follow the blood trail here. I hoped they'd take some time puzzling as to why the killer had dragged him here and dumped him in a pond.

I found myself in an unfamiliar room. I glanced quickly about at the vaulted ceiling and panelled walls. There was a grandiose chair on a dais at the far end. Some kind of an audience chamber then. I glanced about to get my bearings, then froze where I was. The carved doors to my far right swung suddenly open. I heard laughter, a muttered question and a giggling response. There was no time to hide and nothing to shelter behind. I flattened myself

against a wall hanging and was still. The group entered on a wave
of laughter. There was a note of helplessness in the laughter that
told me they were either drunk or giddy with Smoke. They walked
right past me, two men vying for the attention of a woman who
simpered and tittered behind a tasselled fan. All three of them
were dressed entirely in shades of red, and one of the men had
tinkling silver charms not just at the lace of his cuffs, but all
along his loose sleeves to his elbows. The other man carried a
small censer of Smoke on an ornamented rod, almost like a sceptre. He swung it back and forth before them as they walked so
that they were always wreathed in the sweetish fumes. I doubted
that they would have noticed me even if I had leaped out before
them turning cartwheels. Regal seemed to have inherited his
mother's fondness for intoxicants, and to be turning it into a
court fashion. I stood motionless until they had passed. They
went into the fish-and-bird room. I wondered if they would notice
Verde in the pond. I doubted it.

I flitted to the doorway from which the courtiers had entered,
and slipped through it. I found myself suddenly in a great entry
hall. It was floored with marble and my mind boggled at the
expense of hauling such an expanse of stone to Tradeford. The
ceiling was high and plastered white, with designs of immense
flowers and leaves pressed into the plaster. There were arched
windows of stained glass, dark now against the night, but between
them hung tapestries glowing with such rich colours as to seem
windows on some other world and time. All was illuminated with
ornate candelabra hung with sparkling crystals and suspended
from gilded chains. Hundreds of candles burned in them. Statues
were displayed on pedestals at intervals about the room and from
the look of them, most were of Regal's Mountwell ancestors from
his mother's side. Despite the danger I was in, the grandness of
the room captured me for a moment. Then I lifted my eyes and
saw the wide staircase ascending. This was the main staircase,
not the back servants' stairs I had sought. Ten men abreast could
have gone up it easily. The woodwork of the balustrades was dark
and full of twirling knots, but shone with a deep lustre. A thick
rug spilled down the centre of the steps like a blue cascade.

The hall was empty, as was the staircase. I did not give myself time to hesitate, but slipped silently across the room and up the stairs. I was halfway up when I heard the scream. Evidently they *had* noticed Verde. At the top of the first landing, I heard voices and running footsteps coming from the right. I fled to the left. I came to a door, pressed my ear against it, heard nothing, and slipped inside, all in less time than it takes to tell it. I stood in darkness, heart thundering, thanking Eda and El and any other gods that might exist that the door had not been fastened.

I stood in the darkness, my ear pressed to the thick door, trying to hear more than my own pounding heart. I heard shouts from below, and boots running down the staircase. A moment or so passed, then I heard an authoritative voice shouting orders. I slipped to where the opening door would at least temporarily conceal me, and waited, breath stilled, hands trembling. Fear welled up in me like a sudden blackness, threatening to overwhelm me. I felt the floor rock under me and I crouched down quickly to keep from falling in a faint. The world spun about me. I made myself small, hugging myself tight and squeezing my eyes shut, as if somehow that would better conceal me. A second wave of fear washed over me. I sank the rest of the way to the floor and fell over on my side, all but whimpering. I curled in a ball, enduring a terrible squeezing pain in my chest. I was going to die. I was going to die and I'd never see them again, not Molly, not Burrich, not my king. I should have gone to Verity. I knew that now. I should have gone to Verity. I wanted to scream and weep, for I was suddenly certain I could never escape, that I would be found and tortured. They would find me and kill me very, very slowly. I experienced an almost overwhelming drive simply to leap up and run out of the room, to draw sword against the guards and force them to end me quickly.

Steady now. They try to trick you into betraying yourself. Verity's Skilling was finer than a cobweb. I caught my breath, but had the wisdom to keep still.

After what seemed a long time, my blind terror lifted. I took a long shuddering breath and seemed to come to myself again. When I heard the footsteps and voices outside the door, my fear surged up again, but I forced myself to lie still and listen.

'I was sure of it,' said a man.

'No. He's long gone. If they find him at all, they'll find him out on the grounds. No one could have stood up to both of us. If he were still in the house, we would have flushed him out.'

'I tell you, there was something.'

'Nothing,' insisted the other voice with some annoyance. 'I sensed nothing.'

'Check again,' insisted the other.

'No. It's a waste of time. I think you were mistaken.' The first man's anger was becoming obvious despite their subdued voices.

'I hope I was, but I fear I am not. If I am correct, we've given Will the excuse he's been looking for.' There was anger in the second man's voice too, but also a whining self-pity.

'Looking for an excuse? Not that one. He speaks ill of us to the King at every turn. To hear him talk, you would think he was the only one who had made any sacrifices in King Regal's service. A maidservant told me yesterday that he makes no niceties at all about it any more. You, he says, are fat, and me he accuses of every weakness of the flesh a man can have.'

'If I am not as lean as a soldier, it is because I am not a soldier. It is not my body that serves the King, but my mind. As well look to himself before he faults us, him with his one good eye.' The whine was unmistakable now. Burl, I suddenly realized. Burl speaking to Carrod.

'Well. I am satisfied that tonight at least he cannot fault us. There is nothing amiss here that I can find. He has you jumping at shadows and seeing danger in every corner. Calm yourself. This is a matter for the guards now, not us. They'll probably find it was done by a jealous husband or another guardsman. I've heard it said that Verde won a little too often at dice. Perhaps that is why he was left in the gaming room. So if you will excuse me, I will return to the fairer company from which you distracted me.'

'Go, then, if that is all you can think of,' the whiner said sulkily. 'But when you've a moment to spare, I think we might be wise to take counsel together.' After a moment, Burl added, 'I've more than half a mind to go to him right now. Make it his problem.'

'You'd only end up looking like a fool. When you worry so much, you are but giving in to his influence. Let him mouth his warnings and dire predictions and spend every moment of his life on guard. To hear him tell it, his watchfulness is all the King needs. He seeks to instil that fear in us. Your quaking probably gives him much satisfaction. Guard such thoughts carefully.'

I heard one set of footsteps walking briskly away. The roaring in my ears softened a little. After a time, I heard the other man leave, walking more ponderously and muttering to himself. When I could no longer hear his footfalls, I felt as if a great weight had been lifted off me. I swallowed drily and debated my next move.

Dim light filtered in through tall windows. I could make out a bedstead, with the blankets turned back to expose the white linens. It was unoccupied. There was the dark shape of a wardrobe in the corner, and by the bed a stand held a bowl and ewer.

I forced myself to calmness. I took long steadying breaths, then rose silently to my feet. I needed to find Regal's bedchamber, I reminded myself. I suspected it would be on this floor, with servants' quarters in the higher levels of the house. Stealth had got me this far, but perhaps now it was time to be bolder. I crossed to the wardrobe in the corner and opened it quietly. Luck had favoured me again; this was a man's chamber. I went through the garments by touch, feeling for a fabric that felt serviceable. I had to work hastily, for I assumed the rightful owner was at the festivities below and might return at any time. I found a light-coloured shirt, much more fussy about the sleeves and collar than I could wish, but almost long enough in the arms. I managed to get into it, and a darker coloured pair of leggings that felt too loose on me. I belted them up and hoped they did not hang too strangely. There was a pot of scented pomade. I finger-brushed my hair back from my face with it and secured it afresh in a tail, discarding the tradesman's kerchief. Most of the courtiers I had seen earlier wore theirs in oiled curls much as Regal did, but a few of the younger ones kept their hair tied back. I felt about in several drawers. I found some sort of medallion on a chain and put it on. There was a ring, too large for my finger, but that scarcely mattered. I would pass a casual glance and hoped to attract no more than that. They would be looking for a shirtless man in coarse trousers to match the bloodied shirt I had left. I dared to hope they would be seeking him outside. At the threshold

I paused, took a deep breath, and then slowly opened the door. The hall was empty and I stepped out.

Once out in the light, I was not pleased to find the leggings were a dark green and the shirt a buttery yellow. Well it was no more garish than what I had seen folk wearing earlier, though I could scarcely blend with the guests at his Scarlet Ball. I resolutely set the worry aside and struck off down the hall, walking casually yet purposefully to seek a door that was larger and more ornate than the others.

I boldly tried the first one I came to, and found it unlocked. I entered, only to find myself in a room with an immense harp and several other musical instruments set out as if awaiting minstrels. A variety of cushioned chairs and couches filled the rest of the room. The paintings were all of songbirds. I shook my head, baffled at the endless riches of this one house. I continued my search.

Nervousness made the hall stretch out endlessly before me. I forced myself to walk in an unhurried and confident manner. I passed door after door, cautiously sampling a few. Those on my left seemed to be bedchambers, while those on my right were larger rooms, libraries and dining rooms and the like. Instead of wall sconces, the hall was lit with shielded candles. The wall hangings were richly-coloured, and at intervals niches held vases of flowers or small statuary. I could not help but contrast it to the stark stone walls of Buckkeep. I wondered how many warships could have been built and manned with the coin that instead went to ornament this finely-feathered nest. My anger fed my competence. I would find Regal's chamber.

I passed three more doors, then came to one that looked promising. It was a double door, of golden oak, and the oak tree that was the symbol of Farrow was inlaid upon it. I set my ear briefly to the door and heard nothing. Cautiously I tried the burnished handle; the door was latched. My sheath knife was a crude tool for this type of work. Sweat soaked the yellow shirt to my back before the catch yielded to my efforts. I eased the door open and slipped inside, quickly locking it behind me.

This was certainly Regal's chamber. Not his bedchamber, no, but his nonetheless. I went through it swiftly. There were no less than four tall wardrobes, two on each side wall with a tall looking-glass between each set. The ornately-carved door of one wardrobe was ajar; or possibly the press of the clothing from within would not allow it to be fully closed. Other garments hung on hooks and racks about the room or were draped on chairs. A set of locked drawers in a small chest probably held jewellery. The looking-glass between the wardrobes was framed by two branches of candles, now burned low in their holders. Two small censers for Smoke were set to either side of one chair that faced yet another mirror. Behind and to one side of the chair, a table held brushes, combs, pots of pomade and vials of perfume. A narrow twining of grey fumes still rose from one of the censers. I wrinkled my nose against the sweet odour of it, and went to work.

Fitz. What do you do? The faintest query from Verity.

Justice. I put no more than a breath of Skill onto the thought. I was not sure if it were my own or Verity's apprehension that I suddenly felt. I brushed it aside and turned to my task.

It was frustrating. There was little here that was a sure vehicle for my poisons. I could treat the pomade, but I was more likely to kill whoever dressed his hair for him than Regal. The censers held mostly ash. Anything I placed there would probably be dumped with the ash. The corner hearth was swept clean for the summer and there was no supply of wood. Patience, I told myself. His bedchamber could not be far, and opportunities would be better there. For now, I treated the bristles of his hairbrush with one of my more potent concoctions and used what was left to dip as many of his earrings as I could. The last drops I added to his vials of scent but with small hope that he would apply enough to kill himself. For the scented handkerchiefs folded in his drawer, I had the white spore of the death angel mushroom to beguile his hours until death with hallucinations. I took greater pleasure in dusting the insides of four sets of gloves with deadroot powder. This was the poison Regal had used on me in the Mountains, and the most likely source of the seizures that had plagued me intermittently since then. I hoped he would find his own falling fits as amusing as he had mine. I selected three of his shirts that I thought he would favour, and treated their collars and cuffs as well. There was no wood in the hearth, but I had a poison that blended well with the traces of ash and soot left on the brick. I sprinkled it generously and hoped that when they set a fire upon it, the burning fumes might reach Regal's nose. I had just returned my poison to my pouch when I heard a key turn the door latch.

I stepped silently around the corner of a wardrobe and stood there. My knife was already in my hand, waiting. A deadly calm had settled on me. I breathed silently, waiting, hoping fortune had brought Regal to me. Instead, it was another guardsman in Regal's colours. The man pushed into the room and cast a quick glance about. His irritation showed in his face as he impatiently said, 'It was locked. There's no one in here.' I waited for his partner to reply, but he was alone. He stood still a moment, then sighed and walked over to the open wardrobe. 'Foolishness. I'm wasting time up here while he's going to get away,' he muttered to himself, but he drew his sword and carefully prodded about the interior behind the clothes.

As he leaned to reach deeper into the wardrobe's interior, I caught a glimpse of his face in the mirror opposite me. My guts turned to water, and then hatred blazed up in me. I had no name for this one, but his mocking face had been forever etched into my memory. He had been part of Regal's personal guard, and had stood by to witness my death.

I think he saw my reflection at the same time I saw his. I did not give him time to react, but sprang on him from behind. The blade of his sword was still tangled inside Regal's wardrobe when my knife punched low into his belly. I clamped my forearm across his throat to give me leverage as I dragged up on the knife, gutting him like a fish. His mouth gaped open to scream, and I let go of my knife to slap my hand over his mouth. I held him a moment as his entrails bulged out of the gash I'd made. When I let him go, he went down, his unvoiced bellow turned to a groan. He'd not let go of his sword, so I stamped on his hand, breaking his fingers around its hilt. He rolled slightly to one side, to stare up at me in agony and shock. I went down on one knee beside him, put my face close to his.

'FitzChivalry,' I said quietly, meeting his eyes, making sure he knew. 'FitzChivalry.' For the second time that night, I cut a throat. It scarcely needed doing. I wiped my knife on his sleeve as he died. As I stood, I felt two things. Disappointment that he had died so swiftly. And a sensation as if a harp string had been plucked, letting out a sound I felt rather than heard.

In the next instant, I felt a wave of Skill inundate me. It was laden with terror, but this time I recognized it for what it was and knew its source. I stood firm before it, my defences strong. I almost felt it part and go around me. Yet I sensed that even that act was read by someone, somewhere. I did not wonder who. Will felt the shape of my resistance. I felt the echo of his surge of triumph. For a moment it froze me with panic. Then I was moving, sheathing my knife, rising to slip out the door and into the still-empty hallway. I had but a short time to find a new hiding place. Will had been riding with the guardsman's mind, had seen that chamber and me just as clearly as the dying man had. Like the sounding of horns, I could sense him Skilling out, setting the guards in motion as if he were setting dogs to a fox's trail.

As I fled, a part of me knew with undeniable certainty that I was dead. I might be able to hide myself for a time, but Will knew I was within the mansion. All he had to do was block off every exit and begin a systematic search. I raced down a hall, turned a corner and went up a staircase there. I held my Skill walls firm and clutched my tiny plan to myself as if it were a precious gem. I would find Regal's chambers and poison everything there. Then I would go seeking Regal himself. If the guards discovered me first, well, I'd lead them a merry chase. They couldn't kill me. Not with all the poison I was carrying. I'd take my own life first. It wasn't much of a plan, but the only alternative was surrendering.

So I raced on, past more doors, more statuary and flowers, more hangings. Every door I tried was locked. I turned another corner and was suddenly back at the top of the staircase. I felt a moment of dizzy disorientation. I attempted to brush it off but panic rose like a black tide inside my mind. It appeared to be the same staircase. I knew I had not turned enough corners to have come back to it. I hurried past the staircase, past the doors again, hearing the shouts of guardsmen below me as knowledge grew and squirmed queasily inside me.

Will leaned on my mind.

Dizziness and pressure inside my eyes. Grimly I set my mental walls yet again. I turned my head quickly and my vision doubled for a moment. Smoke, I wondered? I had no head for any of the fume intoxicants that Regal favoured. Yet this felt like more to me than the giddiness of Smoke or the mellowness of merrybud.

The Skill is a powerful tool in the hand of a master. I had been with Verity when he had used it against the Red Ships, to so muddle a helmsman that he turned his own ships onto the rocks, to convince a navigator that he had not yet passed a point of land when it was far behind him, to raise fears and doubts in a captain's heart before he went into battle, or to bolster the courage of a ship's crew so that they foolhardily set sail into the very teeth of a storm.

How long had Will been working on me? Had he lured me here, for this encounter, by subtly convincing me that he would never expect me to come?

I forced myself to halt at the next door. I held myself firm, focused myself on the latch of the door as I worked it. It was not locked. I slipped into it, closing the door behind me. Blue fabric was set out on a table before me, ready for sewing. I'd been in this room before. I knew a moment of relief, then checked it. No. This room had been on the ground floor. I was upstairs. Wasn't I? I crossed quickly to the window, stood to one side of it as I peered out. Far below me were the torchlit grounds of the King's Gardens. I could see the white of the great drive gleaming in the night. Carriages were coming up it and liveried servants darted here and there, opening doors. Ladies and gentlemen in extravagant red evening clothes were leaving in droves. I gathered that Verde's end had rather spoiled Regal's ball. There were liveried guards on the doors, regulating who might leave and who must wait. All this I took in at a glance, and realized also that I was up a lot higher than I had thought.

Yet I had been sure that this table and the blue garments waiting to be sewn had been down in the servants' wing of the ground floor.

Well, it was not all that unlikely that Regal would be having two different sets of blue clothes sewn. No time to puzzle about it; I had to find his bedchamber. I felt a strange elation as I slipped out of the room and fled once more down the hallway, a thrill not unlike that of a good hunt. Let them catch me if they could.

I came suddenly to a T in the corridor and stood a moment, puzzled. It did not seem to fit in with what I had seen of the building from outside. I glanced left, then right. Right was noticeably grander, and the tall double doors at the end of the hall were emblazoned with the golden oak of Farrow. As if to put spurs to me, I heard a mutter of angry voices from a room somewhere off to my left. I went right, drawing my knife as I ran. When I came to the great double doors, I put my hand to the latch quietly, expecting to find it locked tight. Instead the door gave easily and swung forward silently. It was almost too easy. I set those apprehensions aside and slipped in, knife drawn.

The room before me was dark, save for two candles burning in silver holders on the mantelpiece. I slipped inside what was obviously Regal's sitting room. A second door stood ajar, revealing the corner of a magnificently-curtained bed and beyond it a hearth with a rack of firewood laid ready in it. I pulled the door gently closed behind me and advanced into the room. On a low table a carafe of wine and two glasses awaited Regal's return, as did a platter of sweets. The censer beside it was heaped with powdered Smoke waiting to be ignited on his return. It was an assassin's fantasy. I could scarcely decide where to begin.

'That, you see, is how it is done.'

I spun about, then experienced a distortion of my senses that dizzied me. I stood in the middle of a well-lit but rather bare room. Will sat, negligently relaxed, in a cushioned chair. A glass of white wine waited on a table beside him. Carrod and Burl flanked him, wearing expressions of irritation and discomfiture. Despite my longing, I dared not take my eyes off them.

'Go ahead, Bastard, look behind you. I shan't attack you. It would be a shame to spring such a trap as this on one such as you, and have you die before you appreciated the fullness of your failure. Go on. Look behind you.'

I turned my whole body slowly, to allow me to glance back with a mere shifting of my eyes. Gone, it was all gone. No royal sitting room, no curtained bed or carafe of wine, nothing. A plain, simple room, probably for several lady's maids to share. Six liveried guards stood silent but attentive. All had drawn swords.

'My companions seem to feel that a drenching of fear will ferret out any man. But they, of course, have not experienced your strength of will as completely as I have. I do hope you appreciate the finesse I used, in simply assuring you that you were seeing exactly what you most wished to see.' He gave a glance each to Carrod and Burl. 'He has walls the like of which you have never experienced. But a wall that will not yield to a battering ram can still be breached by the gentle twining of ivy.' He swung his attention back to me. 'You would have been a worthy opponent, save that in your conceit you always underestimated me.'

I still had not said a word. I stared at them all, letting the hatred that filled me strengthen my Skill walls. All three had changed since I had last seen them. Burl, once a well-muscled carpenter, showed the effects of a good appetite and lack of exercise. Carrod's attire outshone the man within it. Ribbons and charms festooned his garments like blossoms on a spring-time apple tree. But Will, seated between them in his chair, showed the greatest change of all. He was dressed entirely in dark blue in garments whose precise tailoring made them seem richer than Carrod's costume. A single chain of silver, a silver ring on his hand, silver earrings; these were his only ornaments. Of his dark eyes, once so terrifyingly piercing, only one remained. The other was sunken deep in its socket, showing cloudy in the depths like a dead fish in a dirty pool. He smiled at me as he saw me looking at it. He gestured at his eye.

'A memento of our last encounter. Whatever it was that you threw into my face.'

'A pity,' I said, quite sincerely. 'I had meant those poisons to kill Regal, not half-blind you.'

Will sighed lackadaisically. 'Another admission of treason. As if we needed one. Ah, well. We shall be more thorough this time. First, of course, we will spend a bit of time ferreting out just how you escaped death. A bit of time for that, and however much longer King Regal finds you amusing. He will have no need for either haste or discretion this time.' He gave a minuscule nod to the guards behind me.

I smiled at him as I set the poisoned blade of my own knife to my left arm. I clenched my teeth against the pain as I dragged it down the length of my arm, not deeply, but enough to open my skin and let the poison from the blade into my blood. Will leapt to his feet in shock, while Carrod and Burl looked horrified and disgusted. I passed my knife to my left hand, drew my sword with my right.

'I'm dying now,' I told them, smiling. 'Probably very soon. I've no time to waste, and nothing to lose.'

But he had been correct. I had always underestimated him. Somehow I found myself facing, not the coterie members, but six guards with drawn blades. Killing myself was one thing. Being hacked to death while those I desired vengeance on watched was another. I spun about, and felt a wave of dizziness as I did so, as if the room moved rather than I myself. I lifted my eyes to find the swordsmen still confronting me. I turned again and again experienced a sensation of swinging. The thin line of blood along my arm had begun to burn. My chance to do anything about Will and Burl and Carrod was leaking away as the poison seeped through my blood.

The guards were advancing on me, unhurriedly, fanning out in a half circle and driving me before them as if I were an errant sheep. I backed up, glanced once over my shoulder and caught the most fleeting glimpse of the coterie members. Will stood, a step or so in front of the others, an annoyed look on his face. I had come here in the hope of killing Regal. I had barely succeeded in annoying his henchman with my suicide.

Suicide? Somewhere deep within me, Verity was horrorstruck.

Better than torture. Less than a whisper of Skill on that thought, but I swear I felt Will go groping after it.

Boy, stop this insanity. Get out of there. Come to me.

I cannot. It's too late. There's no escape. Let go of me, you only reveal yourself to them.

Reveal myself? Verity's Skill boomed suddenly in my mind, like thunder on a summer night, like storm waves shaking a shale cliff. I had seen him do this before. Angered, he would expend all of his Skill-strength in one effort, with no thought to what might befall him afterwards. I felt Will hesitate, then plunge into that Skilling, reaching after Verity and trying to leech onto him.

Study this revelation, you nest of adders! My king let forth his wrath.

Verity's Skilling was a blast, of a strength I had never encountered anywhere. It was not directed at me, but still I went to my knees. I heard Carrod and Burl cry out, guttural cries of terror. For a moment my head and perceptions cleared, and I saw the room as it had always been, with the guardsmen arrayed between me and the coterie. Will was stretched senseless on the floor. Perhaps I alone felt the great surge of strength it cost Verity to save me. The guards were staggering, wilting like candles in the sun. I spun, saw the door at my back as it opened to admit more guards. Three strides would carry me to the window.

COME TO ME!

There was no choice left for me in that command. It was impregnated with the Skill it rode on, and it burned into my brain, becoming one with my breathing and the beating of my heart. I had to go to Verity. It was a cry both of command, and now, of need. My king had sacrificed his reserves to save me.

There were heavy curtains over the window, and thick whorled glass behind them. Neither stopped me as I launched myself out into the air beyond, hoping there would at least be bushes below me to break some of my fall. Instead I slammed to the earth amid the shards of glass a fraction of a moment later. I had leaped, expecting to fall at least one storey, from a ground-floor window. For a split second I appreciated the completeness of how Will had deceived me. Then I staggered to my feet, still clutching my knife and my sword, and ran.

The grounds were not well lit outside the servants' wing. I blessed the darkness and fled. Behind me I heard cries, and then Burl shouting orders. They'd be on my trail in moments. I'd not escape here on foot. I veered off to the more solid darkness of the stables.

The departure of the ball's guests had stirred the stable to activity. Most of the hands on duty were probably around in front of the mansion, holding horses. The doors of the stable were opened wide to the soft night air, and lanterns were lit within it. I charged in, very nearly bowling over a stable-hand. She could not have been more than ten, a skinny, freckled girl, and she staggered back, then shrieked at the sight of my drawn weapons.

'I'm just taking a horse,' I told her reassuringly. 'I won't hurt you.' She was backing away as I sheathed my sword and then my knife. She spun suddenly. 'Hands! Hands!' She raced off shrieking his name. I had no time to give any thought to it. Three stalls down from me, I saw Regal's own black regarding me curiously over his manger. I approached him calmly, reached to rub his nose and recall myself to him. Perhaps it had been eight months since he'd smelled me, but I'd known him since he was foaled. He nibbled at my collar, his whiskers tickling my neck. 'Come on, Arrow. We're going for some night exercise. Just like old times, huh, fellow?' I eased his stall open, took his halter and walked him out. I didn't know where the girl had gone, but I could no longer hear her.

Arrow was tall, and not accustomed to being ridden bareback. He crow-hopped a bit as I scrabbled up onto his sleek back. Even in the midst of all the danger, I felt a keen pleasure at being on horseback again. I gripped his mane, kneed him forward. He took three steps, then halted at the man blocking his way. I looked down at Hands' incredulous face. I had to grin at his shocked expression.

'Just me, Hands. Got to borrow a horse, or they'll kill me. Again.'

I think perhaps I expected him to laugh and wave me through. Instead he just stared up at me, going whiter and whiter until I thought he'd faint.

'It's me, Fitz. I'm not dead! Let me out, Hands!'

He stepped back. 'Sweet Eda!' he exclaimed, and I thought surely he would throw back his head and laugh. Instead, he hissed, 'Beast magic!' Then he spun and fled off into the night, bawling, 'Guards! Guards!'

I lost perhaps two seconds gawking after him. I felt a wrench inside me such as I had not felt since Molly had left me. The years of friendship, the long day-in, day-out routine of stable-work together, all washed away in a moment of his superstitious terror. It was unfair, but I felt sickened by his betrayal. Coldness welled up in me, but I set heels to Arrow and plunged out into darkness.

He trusted me, did that good horse so well trained by Burrich. I took him away from the torchlit carriage path and the cleared walkways, fleeing through flowerbeds and plantings, before racing out past a huddle of guards at one of the tradefolks' gates. They had been watching up the path, but Arrow and I came thundering across the turf and were out the gate before they knew what we were about. They'd wear stripes for that tomorrow, if I knew Regal at all.

Beyond the gate, we once more cut across the gardens. Behind us, I could hear shouts of pursuit. Arrow answered my knees and weight very well for a horse that was used to a rein. I convinced him to push through a hedge and out onto a side road. We left the King's Garden behind us, and kept our gallop up through the better section of town over cobbled streets where torches still burned. But soon we left the fine houses behind as well. We thundered along past inns still lit for travellers, past shops dark and shuttered for the night, Arrow's hooves thudding on the clay roads. As late as it was, there was little movement on the streets. We raced through them as unchecked as the wind.

I let him slow as we reached the commoner section of town. Here street torches were more widely spaced and some had already burned out for the night. Still, Arrow sensed my urgency and kept up a respectable pace. Once I heard another horse, ridden hard, and for a moment I thought the pursuit had found us. Then a messenger passed us by, heading in the opposite direction, without even checking his horse's pace. I rode on and on, always fearing to hear horses behind us, waiting for the sounds of horns.

Just when I began to think we had eluded pursuit, I discovered that Tradeford held one more horror for me. I entered what had once been the Great Circle Market of Tradeford. In the earliest days of the city, it had been the heart of it, a wonderful great open market where a man might stroll and find goods from every corner of the known world on display.

How it had degenerated from that to Regal's King Circle I have never exactly been able to discover. I only knew that as I rode through the great open circle of the market, Arrow snorted at the smell of old blood on the cobbles under his hooves. The old gallows and the whipping posts were still there, elevated now for the benefit of the crowd, along with other mechanical devices whose uses I had no wish to understand. No doubt those in the new King's Circle would be even more imaginatively cruel. I kneed Arrow and passed them all with a chill shudder and a prayer to Eda that I be preserved from them.

Then a twist of feeling writhed through the air, wrapped itself around my thoughts and bent them. For a heart-thudding moment, I thought that Will reached after me with the Skill and sought to drive me mad. But my Skill walls were as stout as I knew how to raise, and I doubted that Will or anyone else would be soon able to Skill after Verity's blast. No. This was worse. This came from a deeper, more primal source, as insidious as clear water that was poisoned. It flowed into me, hatred and pain and stifling claustrophobia and hunger all rolled into one dreadful longing for freedom and revenge. It reawakened everything I had ever felt in Regal's dungeons.

It came from the cages. A great stench came from the row of them at the edge of the circle, a stench of infected wounds and urine and rotted meat. Yet even that affront to my nose was not as great as the press of hell-tinged Wit that emanated from them. They held but insane beasts, the creatures kept to savage the human criminals and Forged ones that Regal threw to them. There was a bear, heavily muzzled despite the bars he paced behind. There were two great cats of a kind I had never seen, in agony from the broken fangs and torn claws they had wasted on the bars, and yet stubbornly battling their prisons still. There was an immense black bull with a great sweep of horns. This last animal's flesh was studded with ribboned darts sunken in wounds that festered and oozed pus down his hide. Their misery dinned at me, clamouring for relief, yet I did not need to stop to see the heavy chains and locks that secured each cage. Had I had a pick, I might have tried to cheat the locks. Had I had meat or grain, I might have freed them with poison. But I had neither of those things, and even less time. So I rode past them, until the wave of their madness and agony crested over and drenched me. I pulled in on the reins. I could not leave them behind. But, *come to me*, the command surged through me, Skill-graven. It was not endurable to disobey it. I set my heels to jittering Arrow and left them behind, tallying up to Regal's account yet another debt that some day I would settle.

True light found us finally on the outskirts of town. I had never imagined that Tradeford was so large. We came to a slow stream feeding into the river. I pulled Arrow in, then dismounted and led him down to the waterside. I let him drink a bit, then walked him for a while, then let him drink some more. The whole time my mind seethed with a thousand thoughts. They were probably searching the roads that led south, expecting me to head back to Buck. I had a good lead on them now; as long as I kept moving, I had a good chance of escape. I recalled my cleverly-stashed bundle that would never be reclaimed. My winter clothes, my blanket, my cloak, all lost to me. I wondered suddenly if Regal would blame Hands for my stealing the horse. I kept recalling the look in Hands' eyes before he fled me. I found myself being glad I had not yielded to the temptation to track Molly down. It was hard enough to see that horror and disgust in the face of a friend. I never wanted to see it in her eyes. I recalled again the dumb agony of the beasts that my Wit made me witness. Such thoughts were pushed aside by my frustration that my attempt on Regal had been thwarted, and the wondering if they would detect the poisons I had used on his clothes, or if I might yet succeed at killing him. Over all, thundering through me, was Verity's command. *Come to me*, he had said, and I could not quite stop hearing those words. A small part of my mind was obsessed with them, nagged me even now not to waste my time in thinking or drinking, but merely to get back on the horse and go, go to Verity, that he needed me, commanded me.

Yet stoop to drink I did, and it was while I was on my knees at the water's edge that I noticed I wasn't dead.

I wet the sleeve of the yellow shirt in the stream, then gently peeled the blood-caked fabric loose. The cut I had inflicted on myself was shallow, not much more than a long slice up my arm. It was sore, and angry to look at, but it did not appear poisoned. I recalled belatedly that I had used my knife to kill twice that night, and wiped it off at least once. There had probably been no more than a trace of poison left on it when I cut myself.

Like a morning dawning, hope suddenly gleamed for me. They'd be looking for a body by the road, or searching for a poisoned man hiding somewhere in the city, too ill by now to bestride a horse. The whole coterie had watched me poison myself, and must have sensed my complete belief in my imminent death. Could they convince Regal I was dying? I wouldn't trust to that, but I could hope for it. I remounted and pushed swiftly on. We passed farmsteads, grainfields, and orchards. We passed farmers on carts, too, taking their crops to town. I rode clutching my arm to my chest, staring straight ahead. It would only be a matter of time before someone thought to question folk coming into town. Best to play my part.

Eventually we began to see stretches of unworked land, with sheep or haragar scattered across them in open pasturage. Shortly after noon, I did what I knew I had to do. I dismounted by a brushy creekside, let Arrow water again, and then turned his head back to Tradeford. 'Back to the stables, boy,' I told him, and when he did not move, I clapped him soundly on the flank. 'Go on, go back to Hands. Tell them all I'm dead somewhere.' I pictured his manger for him, brimming with the oats I knew he loved. 'Go on, Arrow. Go.'

He snorted at me curiously, but then paced off. He paused once to look back at me, expecting me to come after him and catch him. 'Go on!' I shouted at him, and stamped my foot. He startled at that, and then took off at his high-kneed trot, tossing his head. Scarcely even tired, that one. When he came back riderless to the stable, perhaps they'd believe I was dead. Perhaps they'd waste more time searching for a body instead of pursuing me. It was the best I could do to mislead them, and certainly better than riding the king's own horse for all to see. Arrow's hoofbeats were fading. I wondered if I'd ever again ride an animal that fine, let alone own one. It didn't seem likely.

Come to me. The command still echoed through my mind.

'I am, I am,' I muttered to myself. 'After I hunt for something to eat and get some sleep. But I'm coming.' I left the road and followed the creek up into deeper brush. I had a long and weary way to go, with little more than the clothes on my back.

TEN

Hiring Fair

Slavery is a tradition in the Chalced States, and is at the heart of much of its economy. They claim prisoners taken in war are the major source of its slaves. However, a great portion of the slaves who escape to the Six Duchies tell tales of being taken in pirate raids against their native lands. Chalced's official stance is that such raids do not occur, but Chalced also officially denies that they turn a blind eye to pirates operating from the Trade Islands. The two go hand in hand.

Slavery has never been commonly accepted in the Six Duchies. Many of the early border conflicts between Shoaks and the Chalced States had more to do with the slavery issue than actual boundary lines. Shoaks families refused to accept that soldiers wounded or captured in war would be kept the rest of their lives as slaves. Any battle that Shoaks lost was almost immediately followed by a second savage attack against the Chalced States to regain those lost in the first battle. In this way, Shoaks came to hold much land originally claimed by the Chalced States. The peace between the two regions is always uneasy. Chalced constantly brings complaint that the folk of Shoaks not only shelter runaway slaves, but encourage others to escape. No Six Duchies monarch has ever denied the truth of this.

My whole drive now was to reach Verity, somewhere beyond the Mountain Kingdom. To do it, I would have to cross all of Farrow first. It would not be an easy task. While the region along the Vin River is pleasant enough, the farther one travels from the Vin, the more arid the countryside becomes. The arable stretches are given over to great fields of flax and hemp, but beyond these are vast stretches of open, uninhabited land. The interior of Farrow Duchy, while not a desert, is flat, dry country, used only by the nomadic tribes who move their herds across it, following the forage. Even they forsake it after the 'green times' of the year are past, to congregate in temporary villages along rivers or near water places. In the days that followed my escape from Tradeford Hall, I came to wonder why King Wielder had ever bothered to subjugate Farrow, let alone make it one of the Six Duchies. I knew that I had to strike away from the Vin, to head southwest toward Blue Lake, to cross vast Blue Lake, and then follow the Cold River to the hems of the Mountains. Yet it was not a journey for a lone man. And without Nighteyes, that was what I was.

There are no sizeable cities in the interior, though there are rudimentary towns that subsist year round near some of the springs that randomly dot the interior. Most of these survive by virtue of the trade caravans that pass near them. Trade does flow, albeit slowly, between the folk of Blue Lake and the Vin River, and by this same path do the goods of the Mountain folk come into Six Duchies hands. The obvious course was to somehow attach myself to one of those caravans. Yet what is obvious is not always easy.

When I had entered Tradeford town, I had looked to be the poorest type of beggar imaginable. I left it finely dressed, on one of the best animals ever bred at Buckkeep. But the moment after I had parted with Arrow, the gravity of my situation began to dawn on me. I had the clothing I had stolen and my leather boots, my belt and pouch, a knife and a sword, plus a ring and a medallion on a chain. In my pouch there were no coins left at all, though it did contain implements for fire making, a sharpening stone for my knife and a good selection of poisons.

Wolves are not meant to hunt alone. So Nighteyes had once told me, and before the day was out, I came to appreciate the wisdom of that statement. My meal that day consisted of rice-lily roots and some nuts a squirrel had hoarded in too obvious a hiding place. I would gladly have eaten the squirrel, who sat overhead scolding at me as I raided his cache, but I had not the means to make that wish a reality. Instead, as I pounded the nuts with a stone to open them, I reflected that one by one, my illusions about myself had been stripped away.

I had believed myself a self-sufficient and clever fellow. I had taken pride in my skills as an assassin, had even, deep down, believed that although I could not competently master my Skill ability, my strength at it was easily the equal of any in Galen's Coterie. But take away both King Shrewd's largesse and my wolf companion's hunting ability, subtract from me Chade's secret information and plotting skill and Verity's Skill-guidance, and what I saw left was a starving man in stolen clothes, halfway between Buckkeep and the Mountains, with small prospect of getting any closer to either one.

Satisfyingly bleak as such thoughts were, they did nothing to assuage the nagging of Verity's Skill-suggestion.. *Come to me.* Had he intended for those words to burn into my mind with such command? I doubted it. I think he had sought only to keep me from killing both Regal and myself. And yet now the compulsion was there, festering like an arrowhead. It even infected my sleep with anxiety, so that I dreamed often of going to Verity. It was not that I had given up my ambition of killing Regal; a dozen times a day, I constructed plots in my mind, ways in which I might return to Tradeford and come at him from an unexpected angle. But all such plots began with the reservation, 'after I have gone to Verity'. It had simply become unthinkable to me that there was anything else that had a higher priority.

Several hungry days upriver of Tradeford is a town called Landing. While not nearly as large as Tradeford, it is a healthy settlement. Much good leather is made here, not just from cowhide, but from the tough pigskin of the haragar herds as well. The other main industry of the town seemed to be a fine pottery made from the banks of white clay that front the river. Much that one would expect to be made from wood or glass or metal elsewhere is made from leather or pottery in Landing. Not just shoes and gloves, but hats and other garments are of leather there, as are chair seats and even the roofs and walls of the stalls in the markets. In the shop windows I saw trenchers and candlesticks and even buckets made of finely-glazed pottery, all inscribed or painted in a hundred styles and colours.

I also found, eventually, a small bazaar where one might sell whatever one had to sell and not be asked too many questions. I traded away my fine clothes for the loose trousers and tunic of a working man, plus one pair of stockings. I should have got a better trade, but the man pointed out several brownish stains on the cuffs of the shirt that he believed would not come out. And the leggings were stretched from fitting me so poorly. He could launder them, but he was not sure he could get them back into their proper shape . . . I gave it up and was content with the bargain I'd made. At least these clothes had not been worn by a murderer escaping from King Regal's mansion.

In a shop further down the street I parted with the ring, the medallion and the chain for seven silver bits and seven coppers. It was not near the passage fare to join a caravan to the Mountains, but it was the best offer of the six I'd had. The chubby little woman who bought them from me reached out timidly to touch my sleeve as I turned away.

'I'd not ask this, sir, save I can see you're in a desperate way,' she began hesitantly. 'So I pray you, take no offence at my offer.'

'Which is?' I asked. I suspected she would offer to buy the sword. I had already decided I would not part with it. I would not get enough money for it to make it worth my while to go unarmed.

She gestured shyly toward my ear. 'Your freeman's earring. I've a patron who collects such rarities. I believe that one is from the Butran Clan. Am I correct?' She asked it so hesitantly, as if expecting that at any moment I might fly into a rage.

'I do not know,' I told her honestly. 'It was a gift from a friend. It's not a thing I'd part with for silver.'

She smiled knowingly, suddenly more confident. 'Oh, I know we are speaking of golds for such a thing. I would not insult you with an offer of silvers.'

'Golds?' I asked incredulously. I reached to touch the small bauble at my ear. 'For this?'

'Of course,' she assented easily, thinking I was feeling for a bid. 'I can see the workmanship is superior. Such is the reputation of the Butran Clan. There is also the rarity of it. The Butran Clan grants freedom to a slave but rarely. Even this far from Chalced, that is known. Once a man or woman wears the Butran tattoos, well . . .'

It took very little to draw her into a learned conversation about Chalced's slave trade and slave tattoos and freedom rings. It soon became apparent that she desired Burrich's earring, not for any patron, but for herself. She'd had an ancestor who had won his way out of slavery. She still possessed the freedom ring he'd been granted by his owners as the visible sign that he was no longer a slave. The possession of such an earring, correctly matching the last clan symbol tattooed on a slave's cheek, was the only way a former slave might move freely in Chalced, let alone leave that country. If a slave was troublesome, it was easily seen from the number of tattoos across the face, tracking the history of owner-ship. So that a 'mapface' was a byword for a slave that had been sold all over Chalced, a troublemaker fit for nothing but galley or mine work. She bade me take the earring off and truly look at it, at the fineness of the linked silver that made up the mesh that entrapped what was definitely a sapphire. 'You see,' she explained, 'a slave had not only to win himself free, but to then earn from his master the cost of such an earring. For without it, his freedom was little more than an extended leash. He could go nowhere without being stopped at the checkpoints, could accept no freeman's work without the written consent of his former owner. The former master was no longer liable for his food or shelter, but the former slave had no such freedom from his old owner.'

She offered me three golds without hesitation. That was more than caravan fare; I could have bought a horse, a good horse, and not only joined a caravan but travelled in comfort on that. Instead I left her shop before she could try to dissuade me with a higher offer. With a copper I bought a loaf of coarse bread and sat down to eat it near the docks. I wondered a great many things. The earring had probably been Burrich's grandmother's. He had men-tioned she had been a slave but had won free of that life. I wondered what the earring had come to mean to him, that he had given it to my father, and what it had meant to my father that he had kept it. Had Patience known any of this when she had passed it on to me?

I am human. I tempted myself with her offer of golds. I reflected that if Burrich knew of my situation, he would tell me to go ahead and sell it, that my life and safety were worth more to him than an earring of silver and sapphire. I could get a horse and go to the Mountains and find Verity and put an end to the constant nagging of his Skill-order that was like an itch I could not scratch.

I stared out over the river and finally confronted the enormous journey before me. From here I must journey through near desert to get to Blue Lake. I had no idea how I would cross Blue Lake itself. On the other side, forest trails wound through the foothills up into the rugged lands of the Mountain Kingdom. To Jhaampe the capital city I must go, to somehow obtain a copy of the map Verity had used. It had been based on old writings in the Jhaampe library; perhaps the original was still there. Only that map could lead me to Verity somewhere in the unknown territory beyond the Mountain Kingdom. I would need every coin, every resource I could command.

But despite all that, I decided to keep the earring. Not for what it meant to Burrich, but what it had come to mean to me. It was my last physical link to my past, to who I had been, to the man who had raised me, even to the father who had once worn it. It was oddly difficult to bring myself to do what I knew was wise. I reached up and undid the tiny catch that secured the earring to my ear. I still had the scraps of silk from my masquerade, and I used the smallest one to wrap the earring well and put it inside my belt pouch. The trader woman had been too interested in it and marked its appearance too well. If Regal did decide to send seekers after me, that earring would be one of the ways I'd be described.

Afterwards I walked about the city, listening to folk talk and trying to learn what I needed to know without asking questions. I loitered in the marketplace, wandering from stall to stall idly. I allotted myself the lavish sum of four coppers, and spent them on what seemed exotic luxuries: a small bag of tea herbs, dried fruit, a piece of looking glass, a small cooking pot and a cup. I asked at several herb stalls for elfbark, but either they did not know it or they knew it by another name in Farrow. I told myself it was all right, for I did not expect to have any need for its restorative powers. I hoped I was right. Instead I dubiously purchased something called sunskirt seeds, which I was assured would revive a man to wakefulness no matter how weary he might be.

I found a rag woman who let me go through her cart for two more coppers. I found a smelly but serviceable cloak and some leggings that promised to be as itchy as they were warm. I traded her my remaining scraps of yellow silk for a head kerchief, and with many leering remarks she showed me how to tie it about my head. I did as I had done before, making the cloak into a bundle to carry my things, and then went down to the slaughteryards east of town.

I had never encountered such a stench as I found there. There was pen after pen after pen of animals, veritable mountains of manure, the smell of blood and offal from the slaughtersheds and the harsh stinks of the tannery pits. As if the assault on my nose was not enough, the air was likewise filled with the bawling of cattle, the squealing of haragars, the buzzing of the blowflies and the shouts of the folk moving the animals from pen to pen or dragging them off to slaughter. Steel myself as I would, I could not insulate myself from the blind misery and panic of the waiting animals. They had no clear knowledge of what awaited them, but the smell of the fresh blood and the cries of the other beasts awoke in some of them a terror equivalent to what I had felt as I sprawled on the dungeon floor. Yet here I must be, for this was where the caravans ended, and also where some began. Folk who had driven animals here to sell would most likely be returning. Most would be buying other trade goods to take back with them, so as not to waste a trip. I had hopes of finding some sort of work with one of them that would gain me the companionship of a caravan at least as far as Blue Lake.

I soon found I was not the only one with such hopes. There was a rag-tag hiring fair in a space between two taverns that fronted on the holding pens. Some of the folk there were herders who had come from Blue Lake with one herd, stayed in Landing to spend their earnings, and now, out of coin and far from home, were looking for passage back. For some of them, that was the pattern of their lives as drovers. There were a few youngsters there, obviously looking for adventure and travel and a chance to strike out on their own. And there were those who were obviously the dregs of the town, folk who could get no steady work, or had not the character to live in one place for long. I did not blend very well with any group, but I ended up standing with the drovers.

My tale was that my mother had recently died and turned over her estates to my older sister, who had little use for me. And so I had set out to travel to my uncle, who lived past Blue Lake, but my coin had run out before I had reached there. No, I'd not been a drover before, but we'd been wealthy enough to have horses, cattle and sheep, and I knew the basic care of them and, so some said, 'had a way' with dumb beasts.

I was not hired that day. Few were, and night found most of us bedding down right where we had stood all day. A baker's apprentice came among us with a tray of left-over wares, and I parted with another copper for a long loaf of dark bread studded with seeds. I shared it with a stout fellow whose pale hair kept creeping out of his kerchief and over his face. In return, Creece offered me some dried meat, a drink of the most appalling wine I'd ever tasted, and a great deal of gossip. He was a talker, one of those men who take the most extreme stance on any topic and have, not conversations, but arguments with their fellows. As I had little to say, Creece soon needled the other folk about us into a contentious discussion of the current politics in Farrow. Someone kindled a small fire, more for light than any need for warmth, and several bottles were passed about. I lay back, my head pillowed on my bundle and pretended to be dozing as I listened.

There was no mention of the Red Ships, no talk at all of the war that raged along the coast. I understood abruptly how much these folk would resent being taxed for troops to protect a coast they'd never even seen, for warships to sail an ocean they could not even imagine. The arid plains between Landing and Blue Lake were their ocean, and these drovers the sailors who travelled on it. The Six Duchies were not by nature six regions of land bound into a whole, but were a kingdom only because a strong line of rulers had fenced them together with a common boundary and decreed them to be one. Should all of the Coastal Duchies fall to the Red Ships, it would mean little for these folk here. There would still be cattle to herd, and loathsome wine to drink, there would still be grass and the river and the dusty streets.

Inevitably I must wonder what right we had to force these folk to pay for a war so far from their homes. Tilth and Farrow had been conquered and added to the duchies; they had not come to us asking for military protection or the benefits of trade. Not that they hadn't prospered, freed of all their petty inland herdlords and given an eager market for their beef and leather and rope. How much sailcloth, how many coils of good hemp rope had they sold before they were part of the Six Duchies? But it still seemed a minor return.

I grew weary of such thoughts. The only constant to their conversation was complaint about the trade embargo with the Mountains. I had begun to doze off when my ears pricked up to the words, 'Pocked Man'. I opened my eyes and lifted my head slightly.

Someone had mentioned him in the traditional way, as the harbinger of disaster, laughingly saying that Hencil's sheep had all seen him, for they were dying in their pen before the poor man could even sell them. I frowned to myself at the thought of disease in such close quarters, but another man laughed and said that King Regal had decreed it was no longer bad luck to see the Pocked Man, but the greatest good that could befall one. 'If I saw that old beggar, I'd not blanch and flee, but tackle him and take him to the King himself. He's offered one hundred golds to any man can bring him the Pocked Man from Buck.'

'Was fifty, only fifty golds, not a hundred,' Creece interrupted jeeringly. He took another drink from his bottle. 'What a story, a hundred golds for a grey old man!'

'No, it's a hundred, for him alone, and another hundred for the man-wolf that dogs his heels. I heard it cried anew just this afternoon. They crept into the King's Mansion at Tradeford, and slew some of his guard with Beast magic. Throats torn right out that the wolf might drink the blood. He's the one they want bad now. Dresses like a gentleman, they said, with a ring and a neck-lace and a silver dangle at his ear. Streak of white in his hair from an old battle with our king, and a scar down his face and a broken nose from the same. Yes, and a nice new sword-slash up his arm is what the King gave him this time.'

There was a low mutter of admiration from several of them at this. Even I had to admire Regal's audacity at claiming that, even as I turned my face back into my bundle and burrowed down as if to sleep. The gossip continued.

'Supposed to be Wit-bred, he is, and able to turn himself into a wolf whenever the moon is on him. They sleep by day and prowl by night, they do. It's said it's a curse put on the King by that foreigner queen he chased out of Buck for trying to steal the crown. The Pocked Man, it's told, is a half-spirit, charmed from the body of old King Shrewd by her Mountain magic, and he travels all the roads and streets, anywhere in the Six Duchies, bringing ill wherever he goes, and wearing the face of the old King himself.'

'Dung and rot,' Creece said disgustedly. He took another swig himself. But some of the others liked this wild tale and leaned closer, whispering for him to go on, go on.

'Well, that's what I heard,' the storyteller said huffily. 'That the Pocked Man is Shrewd's half-spirit, and he can't know any rest until the Mountain queen that poisoned him is in her grave as well.'

'So, if the Pocked Man is Shrewd's ghost, why is King Regal offering a hundred golds reward for him?' Creece asked sourly.

'Not his ghost. His half-spirit. He stole part of the King's spirit as he was dying, and King Shrewd can know no rest until the Pocked Man is dead so the King's spirit can be rejoined. And some say,' and he dropped his voice lower, 'that the Bastard was not killed well enough, that he walks again as a man-wolf. He and the Pocked Man seek vengeance against King Regal, to destroy the throne he could not steal. For he was in league to be king to the Vixen's queen once they'd done away with Shrewd.'

It was the right sort of night for such a tale. The moon was swollen and orange and riding low in the sky, while the wind brought us the mournful lowing and shifting of the cattle in their pens mixed with the stench of rotting blood and tanning hides. High tattered clouds drifted from time to time across the face of the moon. The storyteller's words put a shiver up my back, probably for a different reason than he thought. I kept waiting for someone to nudge me with a foot, or cry out, 'Hey, let's have a better look at him.' No one did. The tone of the man's tale had

them looking for wolf eyes in the shadows, not for a weary workman sleeping in their midst. Nonetheless, my heart was thudding
in my chest as I looked back down my trail. The tailor where I'd
traded clothes would recognize that description. Possibly the earring woman. Even the old rag woman who had helped me tie the
kerchief over my hair. Some might not want to come forward,
some might want to avoid dealing with the King's guards. Some
would, though. I should behave as if they all would.

The speaker was going on, embroidering his tale of Kettricken's
evil ambitions and how she had lain with me to conceive a child
we could use to claim the throne. There was loathing in the
storyteller's voice as he spoke of Kettricken, and no one scoffed
at his words. Even Creece at my side was acquiescent, as if these
bizarre plots were common knowledge. Confirming my worst fears,
Creece spoke up suddenly.

'You tell it like it's all new, but all knew her big belly came
not from Verity but from the Wit-Bastard. Had Regal not driven
off the Mountain whore, we would eventually have had one like
the Piebald Prince in line for the throne.'

There was a low murmur of assent to this. I closed my eyes
and lay back as if bored, hoping that my stillness and lowered
lids could conceal the rage that threatened to consume me. I
reached up to tug my kerchief more snugly about my hair. What
could be Regal's purpose in letting such evil gossip be noised
about? For I knew this kind of poison must come from him. I did
not trust my voice to ask any questions, nor did I wish to appear
ignorant of what was evidently common knowledge. So I lay
still and listened with savage interest. I gathered that all knew
Kettricken had returned to the Mountains. The freshness of the
contempt they had for her suggested to me that this was recent
news. There was muttering too that it was the fault of the Mountain witch that the passes were closed to honest Tilth and Farrow
traders. One man even ventured to say that now that trade with
the coast was shut down, the Mountains saw a chance to fence
Farrow and Tilth in and force them to come to terms or lose all
trade routes. One man recounted that even a simple caravan
escorted by Six Duchies men in Regal's own colours had been
turned back from the Mountain border.

To me, such talk was obviously stupid. The Mountains needed the trade with Farrow and Tilth. Grain was more important to the Mountain folk than the lumber and furs of the Mountains to these lowlanders. Such free trade had been openly admitted as a reason for wedding Kettricken to Verity. Even if Kettricken had fled back to the Mountains, I knew her well enough to be sure she would not support any cutting off of trade between her folk and the Six Duchies. She was too bonded to both groups, so intent on being Sacrifice for all of them. If there were a trade embargo as I had heard, I was sure it had begun with Regal. But the men about me grumbled on about the Mountain witch and her vendetta against the King.

Was Regal fomenting a war with the Mountains? Had he been attempting to send armed troops there under the guise of escorts for traders? It was a foolish idea. Long ago my father had been sent to the Mountains to formalize boundaries and trade agreements with them, marking the end of long years of border skirmishes and raids. Those years of battle had taught King Shrewd that no one was going to take and hold the Mountain Kingdom passes and trails by force. Unwillingly I followed that thought. Regal had been the one to suggest Kettricken as a bride for Verity. He had done all the courtier's work of wooing her for his brother. Then, as the time for the wedding drew near, he had attempted to kill Verity, with the aim of securing the princess as his own bride. He had failed, and his plots and plans had been revealed to only a few. The chance for him to claim Princess Kettricken as his own, and all that went with her, such as her eventual inheritance of the Mountain crown, had slipped through his fingers. I recalled some talk I had once heard between Regal and the traitorous Galen. They had seemed to think that Tilth and Farrow would be best secured if they could control the Mountain ranges and passes that backed them. Did Regal now think to take by force what he had once hoped to claim by marriage? Did he think he could rally enough ill will against Kettricken to make his followers believe they were waging a just war, one of vengeance against a Mountain witch, one to keep open key trade routes?

Regal, I reflected, was capable of believing anything he wished to believe. In the depths of his cups, head wreathed with his smokes, I did not doubt that he now believed his own wild tales. A hundred golds for Chade, and another hundred for me. I knew well enough what I had done lately to merit such a head-price, but I wondered keenly just what Chade had been up to. In all my years with Chade, he had always worked unnamed and unseen. He still had no name, but his pocked skin and resemblance to his half-brother were known now. That meant he had been seen somewhere, by someone. I hoped he was well and safe this night wherever he was. A part of me yearned to turn back, to return to Buck and track him down. As if somehow I could keep him safe.

Come to me.

No matter what I longed to do, no matter what I felt, I knew that first I would go to Verity. I promised myself that over and over and was finally able to drop off into a wary doze. I dreamed, but they were pale dreams, barely touched by the Skill, shifting and turning as if blown by the autumn winds. My mind seemed to have caught up and jumbled together thoughts of every person I missed. I dreamed of Chade taking tea with Patience and Lacey. He wore a robe of red silk patterned over with stars, cut in a very old style, and he smiled charmingly at the women over his cup and brought laughter even to Patience's eyes, although she looked strangely worn and weary. I then dreamed of Molly peeping out of a cottage door while Burrich stood outside it, pulling his cloak tight against the wind and telling her not to worry, he'd not be gone that long and any heavy chores could keep until he returned, that she should stay within doors and have only a care for herself. Even of Celerity did I dream, that she had taken shelter in the fabled ice caves of the Hungry Glacier in Bearns, and hid there with what troops she could still rally and many of her folk made homeless by the Raider wars. I dreamed she tended Faith, who lay suffering with a fever and a festering arrow wound in her belly. I dreamed finally of the Fool, his white face turned to ivory as he sat before a hearth and stared into the flames. There was no hope left in his face, and I felt that I was within the flames, looking deeply into his eyes. Somewhere nearby and yet not very near, Kettricken was weeping inconsolably. My dreams withered in my mind, and then I dreamed of wolves hunting, hunting, running down a buck, but they were wild wolves, and if my wolf was among them, he was theirs and mine no longer.

I awoke with a headache and a crick in my back from a stone I'd slept on. The sun had only begun to crack the sky, but I rose anyway, to go to a well and draw water for washing, and to drink as much as I could hold. Burrich had once told me that drinking a lot of water was a good way to stave off hunger. It was a theory I'd have to test today. I put an edge on my knife, considered shaving, then decided against it. Better to let my beard grow over the scar as swiftly as possible. I rubbed reluctantly at the coarse growth that already irritated me. I went back to where the others still slept.

They were just beginning to stir when a bulky little man appeared, to call shrilly that he would hire a man to help move his sheep from one pen to another. It was only a morning's work, if that, and most of the men shook their heads, wishing to remain where they might be hired for a drover's trip to Blue Lake. He almost pleaded, saying he must move the sheep through the city streets, hence he needed to get it done before the day's common traffic began. Finally, he offered to include breakfast, and I really think that was why I nodded to him and followed him. His name was Damon and he talked the whole time we walked, fluttering his hands about, explaining needlessly to me just how he wanted these sheep handled. They were good stock, very good stock, and he didn't want them injured or even flustered. Calmly, slowly, that was the best way to move sheep. I nodded wordlessly to his worrying and followed him to a pen far down the slaughter street.

It soon became apparent why he was so anxious to move his sheep. The next pen must have belonged to the luckless Hencil. A few sheep still baahed in that pen, but most of them were down, dead or dying of flux. The stench of their sickness added a new foul note to the other smells in the air. Some men were there, taking the skins off the dead animals to salvage what they could from the flock. They were making bloody, messy work of it, leaving the skinned dead animals right there in the pen with the dying ones. It reminded me in some gruesome way of a battle-field, with looters moving among the fallen. I turned my eyes from the sight and helped Damon bunch up his sheep.

Trying to use the Wit on sheep is almost a waste of time. They are flighty of thought. Even those ones who appear most placid are so because they have forgotten what they were thinking about. The worst of them are capable of an inordinate amount of wariness, becoming suspicious of the simplest act. The only way to deal with them is much as herd dogs do. Convince them they have had a good idea about where they wish to go, and encourage them in it. I amused myself briefly by considering how Nighteyes would have bunched up and moved these woolly fools, but my even thinking of a wolf caused a few of them to halt in their tracks suddenly and glance about wildly. I suggested to them they should follow the others before they were lost, and they started as if surprised at the notion, then crowded in amongst the rest of the sheep.

Damon had given me a general idea of where we were going, and a long stick. I worked the back and sides of the flock, running and soon panting like a dog, while he led the way and kept the flock from scattering at every intersection. He took us to an area on the outskirts of town, and we put the sheep into one of the ramshackle pens there. Another pen held a very fine red bull, while there were six horses in yet another. After we had caught our breath, he explained that tomorrow a caravan would be forming up here to travel to Blue Lake. He had bought these sheep just yesterday, and intended to take them to his home there to add to his flocks. I asked him if he might want another hand to herd the sheep to Blue Lake, and he gave me a considering look but no answer.

He was as good as his word about breakfast. We had porridge and milk, plain fare that tasted wonderfully good to me. It was served to us by a woman who lived in a house near the holding pens and made her living keeping watch over the animals penned there and providing meals and sometimes beds for those in charge of them. After we had eaten, Damon laboriously explained to me that yes, he was in need of an extra hand, possibly two, for the trip, but that he judged by the cut of my clothes that I knew little of the type of work I was seeking. He'd taken me on this morning because I was the only one who looked really awake and eager for the work. I told him my story of my heartless sister, and assured him that I was familiar with handling sheep, horses or cattle. After much dithering and druthering, he hired me. His terms were that he would provide my food for the journey, and at the end of it would pay me ten silver bits. He told me to run and fetch my things and say my goodbyes, but to be certain to be back here by the evening, or he would hire another to take my place.

'I have nothing to fetch, and no one to bid goodbye to,' I told him. It would not be wise to go back to town, not after what I'd heard last night. I wished the caravan were leaving right now.

For an instant he looked shocked, but then decided he was well pleased. 'Well, I have both to attend to, so I shall leave you here to watch over the sheep. They'll need water hauled to them; that was one reason I was leaving them in the town pens, they've a pump there. But I didn't like to have them so near sick sheep. You haul them water, and I'll send a man out with a cart of hay for them. See you give them a good feed. Now, mind, I'll judge how we are to go on together by how you begin with me . . .' And so on and so on he went, telling me to the last detail how he wished the animals watered, and how many separate piles of feed to make to be sure each animal got a share. I suppose it was to be expected; I did not look like a shepherd. It made me miss Burrich, and his calm assumption that I would know my business and do it. As he was turning to go, he suddenly turned back. 'And your name, lad?' he called to me.

'Tom,' I said after an instant's hesitation. Patience had thought once to call me that, before I had accepted the name FitzChivalry. The reflection called to mind something Regal had once flung at me. 'You have to but scratch yourself to find Nameless the dog-boy,' he'd sneered. I doubted he would think Tom the shepherd much above that.

There was a dug well, not very near the pens, with a very long rope to its bucket. By working constantly, I finally managed to get the water-trough filled. Actually, I filled it several times before the sheep allowed it to remain filled. About then, a cart with hay arrived, and I carefully created four separate piles of feed in the corners of the pen. It was another exercise in frustration, as the sheep bunched and fed off each pile as I created it. It was only after all but the weakest were satiated that I could finally establish a pile in each corner.

I whiled away the afternoon with drawing more water. The woman gave me the use of a large kettle to heat it, and a private place where I could wash the worst of the road from my body. My arm was healing well. Not bad for a deadly injury, I told myself, and hoped Chade would never hear of my blundering. How he would laugh at me. When I was clean, I fetched more water to heat, this for washing out the clothes I'd bought from the rag woman. I discovered the cloak was actually a much lighter grey than I had thought it. I could not get all the smell out of it, but by the time I hung it to dry, it smelled more of wet wool and less of its previous owner.

Damon had left me no provision for food, but the woman offered to feed me if I would haul the water for the bull and the horses, as it was a chore she'd grown much weary of doing for the last four days. So I did, and earned myself a dinner of stew and biscuits and a mug of ale to wash it all down. Afterwards I checked on my sheep. Finding them all placid, habit made me turn to the bull and the horses. I stood leaning on the fence, watching the animals, wondering how it would be if this were all there was to my life. It made me realize that it would not have been bad, not if there'd been a woman like Molly waiting for me to come home at night. A rangy white mare came over to rub her nose up my shirt and beg to be scratched. I petted her and found her missing a freckled farm-girl who had brought her carrots and called her Princess.

I wondered if anyone, anywhere, got to live the life he'd wanted. Perhaps Nighteyes finally had. I truly hoped so. I wished him well, but was selfish enough to hope that sometimes he'd miss me. Sullenly I wondered if perhaps that was why Verity had not come back. Maybe he'd just got sick of the whole business of crowns and thrones and kicked over all his traces. But even as I thought it, I knew it was not so. Not that one. He'd gone to the Mountains to rally the Elderlings to our aid. And if he'd failed at that task, then he'd think of another way. And whatever it was, he'd called me to help him do it.

ELEVEN

Shepherd

Chade Fallstar, adviser to King Shrewd, was a loyal servant of the Farseer throne. Few knew of his services during the years he served King Shrewd. This did not displease him for he was not a man who sought glory. Rather he was devoted to the Farseer reign with a loyalty that surpassed his loyalty to himself or any other consideration most men have. He took most seriously his vow to the royal family. With the passing of King Shrewd, he pursued his vow to see that the crown followed the true line of succession. For this reason alone, he was sought after as an outlaw, for he openly challenged Regal's claim to be King of the Six Duchies. In missives he sent to each of the dukes as well as to Prince Regal, he revealed himself after years of silence, declaring himself a loyal follower of King Verity and vowing he would follow no other until he was shown proof of the King's death. Prince Regal declared him a rebel and a traitor and offered reward for his capture and death. Chade Fallstar evaded him by many clever artifices and continued to rally the Coastal dukes to the belief that their king was not dead and would return to lead them to victory over the Red Ships. Bereft of any hope of aid from 'King' Regal, many of the lesser nobles clung to these rumours. Songs began to be sung, and even the common folk spoke with hope that their Skilled King would return to save them, with the legendary Elderlings riding at his back.

By late afternoon, folk began to gather for the caravan. One woman owned the bull and horses. She and her husband arrived in a wagon drawn by a brace of oxen. They built their own fire, cooked their own food and seemed content with their own company. My new master returned later, a bit tipsy, and goggled at the sheep to be sure I'd fed and watered them. He arrived in a high-wheeled cart drawn by a sturdy pony, one he immediately entrusted to my care. He'd hired another man, he told me, one Creece. I should watch for him to come and show him where the sheep were. He then disappeared into a room to sleep. I sighed to myself to think of a long journey with Creece's tongue and abrasive way to speed it, but did not complain. Instead I busied myself caring for the pony, a willing little mare named Drum.

Next to arrive was company of a merrier sort. They were a troupe of puppeteers with a gaily-painted wagon drawn by a team of dappled horses. There was a window in one side of the wagon that could be let down for puppet-shows, and an awning that could be unrolled from the side to roof a stage when they were using the larger marionettes. The master puppeteer was named Dell. He had three apprentices and one journey puppeteer, as well as a minstrel who had joined them for the trip. They did not make their own fire, but proceeded to liven up the woman's little house with song and the clacking of marionettes and a number of mugs of ale.

Two teamsters came next, with two wagons full of carefully-packed crockery, and then finally the caravan master and his four helpers. These were the ones who would do more than guide us. The very look of their leader inspired confidence. Madge was a stoutly-built woman, her slate-grey hair constrained from her face by a band of beaded leather. Two of her help seemed to be a daughter and a son. They knew the waterholes, clean and foul, would defend us from bandits, carried extra food and water, and had agreements with nomads whose pasturing territory we'd be passing through. That last was as important as any of the rest, for the nomads did not welcome folk who passed through their lands with grazing animals to eat the feed their own flocks needed. Madge called us together that evening, to inform us of this, and to remind us that they would keep order within our group as well. No theft or trouble-making would be tolerated, the pace set would be one all could sustain, the caravan master would handle all dealings at the watering places and with the nomads and all must agree to abide by the decisions of the caravan master as law. I murmured my assent along with the others. Madge and her help then checked the wagons to be sure each was fit for travel, that the teams were sound and that there were adequate water and food supplies for emergencies. We would travel a zig-zag course from watering place to watering place. Madge's wagon carried several oak casks for water, but she insisted every private wagon and team carry some for their own needs.

Creece arrived with the setting sun, after Damon had already gone back to his room and bed. I dutifully showed him the sheep, and then listened to his grumbling that Damon had not provided us with a room to sleep in. It was a clear, warm night with only a bit of wind, so I saw little to complain about. I did not say so, but let him mutter and complain until he was weary of it. I slept just outside the sheep pen, on guard lest any predators come near, but Creece wandered off to annoy the puppeteers with his dour nature and extensive opinions.

I don't know how long I truly slept. My dreams parted like curtains blown by a wind. I came alert to a voice whispering my name. It seemed to come from far away, but as I listened, I was compelled inexorably to it as if summoned by a charm. Like an errant moth, I became aware of candle flames and was drawn toward them. Four candles burned brightly on a rough wooden table and their mingling scents sweetened the air. The two tall tapers gave off the scent of bayberry. Two smaller ones burned before them giving off a sweet spring scent. Violets, I thought, and something else. A woman leaned forward over them, breathing deeply of the rising perfume. Her eyes were closed, her face misted with sweat. Molly. She spoke my name again.

'Fitz, Fitz. How could you die and leave me like this? It wasn't supposed to be this way, you were supposed to come after me, you were supposed to find me so I could forgive you. You should have lit these candles for me. I wasn't supposed to be alone for this.'

The words were interrupted by a great gasp, as of a wrenching pain, and with it a wave of fear, frantically fought down. 'It's going to be all right,' Molly whispered to herself. 'It's going to be all right. It's supposed to be like this. I think.'

Even within the Skill dream, my heart stood still. I looked down at Molly as she stood near the hearth in a small hut. Outside, an autumn storm was raging. She grasped the edge of a table and half crouched, half leaned over it. She wore only a nightrobe, and her hair was slick with sweat. As I watched aghast, she took another great gulping breath, and then cried out, not a scream, but a thin caw of a sound as if that were all she had strength for. After a minute she straightened a bit and put her hands softly on the top of her belly. I felt dizzied at the size of it. It was so distended, she looked pregnant.

She was pregnant.

If it were possible to lose consciousness when one is asleep, I think I would have done so. Instead my mind reeled suddenly, reordering every word she had said to me when we had parted, recalling the day when she had asked me what I would do, if she had been carrying my child. The baby was the one she had spoken of, the one she had left me for, the one she would put ahead of every other in her life. Not another man. Our child. She'd left to protect our child. And she hadn't told me because she was afraid I wouldn't go with her. Better not to ask than to ask and be refused.

And she had been right. I wouldn't have gone. There had been too much happening at Buckkeep, too pressing the duties to my king. She'd been right to abandon me. It was so like Molly to make the leaving and the facing this alone her own choice. Stupid, but so like her I wanted to hug her. I wanted to shake her.

She clutched the table again suddenly, her eyes going wide, voiceless now with the force that moved through her.

She was alone. She believed I was dead. And she was having the child alone, in that tiny windswept hut somewhere.

I reached for her, crying, Molly, Molly, but she was focused inwards on herself now, listening only to her own body. I suddenly knew Verity's frustration those times when he could not make me hear him and most desperately needed to reach me.

The door gusted open suddenly, admitting blowing storm winds into the hut and a blast of cold rain with it. She lifted her eyes, panting, to stare at it. 'Burrich?' she called breathlessly. Her voice was full of hope.

Again I felt a wave of astonishment, but it was drowned by her gratitude and relief when his dark face peered suddenly around the door frame. 'It's only me, soaked through. I couldn't get you any dried apples, no matter what I offered. The town stores are bare. I hope the flour didn't get wet. I'd have been back sooner, but this storm . . .' He was coming in as he spoke, a man coming home from town, a carry-sack over his shoulder. Water streamed down his face and dripped from his cloak.

'It's time, it's now,' Molly told him frantically.

Burrich dropped his sack as he dragged the door shut and latched it. 'What?' he asked her as he wiped rain from his eyes and pushed the wet hair back from his face.

'The baby's coming.' She sounded oddly calm now.

He looked at her blankly for an instant. Then he spoke firmly. 'No. We counted, you counted. It can't be coming now.' Abruptly he sounded almost angry, he was so desperate to be right. 'Another fifteen days, maybe longer. The midwife, I talked to her today and arranged everything, she said she'd come to see you in a few days . . .'

His words died away as Molly gripped the table's edge again. Her lips drew back from her teeth as she strained. Burrich stood like a man transfixed. He went as pale as I'd ever seen him. 'Shall I go back to the village and get her?' he asked in a small voice.

There was the sound of water pattering on the rough floorboards. After an eternity, Molly caught a breath. 'I don't think there's time.'

Still he stood as if frozen, his cloak dripping water onto the floor. He came no further into the room, stood still as if she were an unpredictable animal. 'Shouldn't you be lying down?' he asked uncertainly.

'I tried that. It really hurts if I'm lying down and a pain comes. It made me scream.'

He was nodding like a puppet. 'Then you should stand up, I suppose. Of course.' He didn't move.

She looked up at him pleadingly. 'It can't be that different,' she panted, 'from a foal or a calf . . .'

His eyes went so wide I could see the whites all round them. He shook his head fiercely, mutely.

'But Burrich . . . there's no one else to help me. And I'm . . .' Her words were suddenly torn away from her in a sort of cry. She leaned forward on the table, her legs folding so her forehead rested on the edge of it. She made a low sound, full of fear as well as pain.

Her fear broke through to him. He gave his head a tiny quick shake, a man awakening. 'No. You're right, it can't be that different. Can't be. I've done this hundreds of times. Just the same, I'm sure of it. All right. Now. Let's see. It's going to be all right, let me just ... uh.' He tore off his cloak and let it drop to the floor. He hastily pushed his wet hair back from his face, then came to kneel beside her. 'I'm going to touch you,' he warned her, and I saw her bowed head give a small bob of agreement.

Then his sure hands were on her belly, stroking down gently but firmly as I'd seen him do when a mare was having a bad time and he wished to hasten things for her. 'Not long now, not much more,' he told her. 'It's really dropped.' He was suddenly confident, and I felt Molly take heart from his tone. He kept his hands on her as another contraction took her. 'That's good, that's right.' I'd heard him say those same comforting words a hundred times in the stalls of Buckkeep. Between pains, he steadied her with his hands, talking all the while softly, calling her his good girl, his steady girl, his fine girl that was going to drop a fine baby. I doubt either of them heard the sense of what he said. It was all the tone of his voice. He rose once to get a blanket and folded it on the floor beside him. He said no awkward words as he lifted Molly's nightdress out of the way, but only spoke softly, encouragingly, as Molly clenched the table's edge. I could see the ripple of muscle, and then she cried out suddenly and Burrich was saying, 'Keep going, keep going, here we are, here we are, keep going, that's fine, and what do we have here, who's this?'

Then the child was in his grasp, head in one cupped, callused hand, his other supporting the tiny, curled body and Burrich sat down suddenly on the floor, looking as amazed as if he had never seen anything born before. The women's talk I had overheard had made me expect hours of screaming and pools of blood. But there was little blood on the babe that looked up at Burrich with calm blue eyes. The greyish cord coiling from the belly looked large and thick compared to the tiny hands and feet. All was silence save for Molly's panting.

Then, 'Is he all right?' Molly demanded. Her voice shook. 'Is something wrong? Why doesn't he cry?'

'She's fine,' Burrich said softly. 'She's fine. And as beautiful as she is, what would she have to cry about?' He was silent for a long time, a man transfixed. Finally he reluctantly set her gently aside on the blanket, turned a corner of it up to cover her. 'You've a bit more work to do here, girl, before we're done,' he told Molly gruffly.

But it was not long before he had Molly seated in a chair by the fire, a blanket about her to keep her from taking a chill. He hesitated a moment, then cut the cord with his belt knife before wrapping the child in a clean cloth and taking her to Molly. Molly immediately unwrapped her. While Burrich was tidying the room, Molly examined every inch of her, exclaiming over her sleek black hair, the tiny fingers and toes with their perfect nails, the delicacy of her ears. Then Burrich did the same while he held the baby and turned his back so that Molly might change into a nightgown that wasn't soaked through with sweat. He studied her with an intentness I'd never seen him give to a foal or a pup. 'You're going to have Chivalry's brow,' he told the babe softly. He smiled at her and touched her cheek with one finger. She turned her head toward the touch.

When Molly returned to her seat by the fire, he handed the child back to her, but crouched on the floor beside the chair as Molly put the babe to her breast. It took the baby a few tries to find and hold the nipple, but when she finally suckled, Burrich heaved such a sigh that I knew he had been holding his breath for fear she would not nurse. Molly had eyes only for the child, but I marked how Burrich lifted his hands to rub at his face and eyes, and that those hands trembled. He smiled as I had never seen him do before.

Molly lifted her gaze to him, her face like a sunrise. 'Would you make me a cup of tea, please?' she softly asked him, and Burrich nodded, grinning like a simpleton.

I came out of my dream hours before dawn, not knowing at first when I passed from thoughtfulness to wakefulness. I became aware my eyes were open and I was staring at the moon. It would be impossible to describe my feelings at that time. But slowly my thoughts took shape, and I understood the previous Skill dreams I'd had of Burrich. It explained much. I'd been seeing him through Molly's eyes. He'd been there, all this time, with Molly, taking care of her. She was the friend he'd gone to help, the woman who could use a man's strength for a bit. He'd been there with her, while I had been alone. I felt a sudden rising of anger that he had not come to me and told me that she carried my child. It was quickly quenched as I suddenly realized that perhaps he'd tried. Something had brought him back to the cabin that day. I wondered again what he had thought when he'd found it abandoned. That all his worst fears for me had come true? That I'd gone feral, never to return?

But I would return. Like a door swinging open, I suddenly understood that I could do that. Nothing truly stood between Molly and me. There was no other man in her life, only our child. I grinned suddenly to myself. I would not let so small a thing as my death come between us. What was death, compared to a child's life shared? I would go to her, and explain, I'd tell her everything this time, and this time she would understand, and she'd forgive me, because there would never be any other secrets between us.

I didn't hesitate. I sat up in the darkness, picked up my bundle that I'd been using as a pillow, and set out. Downriver was so much easier than up. I had a few silvers, I'd get onto a boat somehow, and when they ran out, I'd work my passage. The Vin was a slow river, but once I was past Turlake, the Buck River would rush me along in its strong current. I was going back. Home, to Molly and our daughter.

Come to me.

I halted. It was not Verity Skilling to me. I knew that. This came from within me, the mark left by that sudden and powerful Skilling. I was certain that if he knew why I had to go home, he'd tell me to hurry, not to worry about him, that he'd be fine. It would be all right. All I had to do was keep walking.

One step after another down a moonlit road. With each footfall, with each beat of my heart, I heard words in my mind. *Come to me. Come to me.* I can't, I pleaded. I won't, I defied them. I kept walking. I tried to think only of Molly, only of my tiny daughter. She would need a name. Would Molly have named her before I got there?

Come to me.

We'd need to get married right away. Find some local Witnesser in some small village. Burrich would vouch that I was a foundling, with no parentage for the Witnesser to memorize. I'd say my name was Newboy. An odd name, but I'd heard odder, and I could live with it the rest of my life. Names, once so important to me, no longer mattered. They could call me Horsedung, as long as I could live with Molly and my daughter.

Come to me.

I'd need to get work of some kind, any kind. I abruptly decided that the silvers in my pouch were far too important to spend, that I'd have to work for my entire passage home. And once I was there, what could I do to earn a living? What was I fit for? I pushed the thought aside angrily. I'd find something, I'd find a way. I'd be a good husband, a good father. They would want for nothing.

Come to me.

My steps had gradually slowed. Now I stood upon a small rise, looking down the road before me. Lights still burned in the river-town below. I had to go down there and find a barge heading downriver, willing to take on an unproven hand. That was all. Just keep moving.

I did not then understand why I could not. I took a step, I stumbled, the world swung around me dizzily, and I went to my knees. I could not go back. I had to go on, to Verity. I still do not understand it, so I cannot explain it. I knelt on the rise, looking down at the town, knowing clearly what I wished with all my heart to do. And I could not do it. Nothing held me back, no man lifted a hand or sword to me and bid me turn aside. Only the small insistent voice in my mind, battering at me. *Come to me, come to me, come to me.*

And I could not do otherwise.

I could not tell my heart to stop beating, I could not cease breathing and die. And I could not ignore that summoning. I stood alone in the night, trapped and suffocating in another man's will for me. A cool-headed portion of myself, said, there, well, you see, that is how it is for them. For Will and the rest of the coterie, Skill-imprinted by Galen to be loyal to Regal. It did not make them forget they had had another king, it did not make them believe what they did was right. They simply had no choice about it any more. And to take it back a generation, that was how it had been for Galen, forced to be so fanatically loyal to my father. Verity had told me that his loyalty was a Skill-imprinting, done by Chivalry when they were all little more than boys. Done in anger against some cruelty Galen had wrought against Verity. The act of an older brother taking revenge on someone who had been mean to his little brother. It had been done to Galen in anger and ignorance, not even knowing fully that such a thing was possible. Verity said Chivalry had regretted it, would have undone it if he had known how. Had Galen ever awakened to what had been done to him? Did that account for his fanatical hatred of me, had it been a passing down to the son of the anger he could not allow himself to feel toward Chivalry, my father?

I tried to get to my feet and failed. I sank slowly to the dirt in the centre of the moonlit road, then sat there hopelessly. It didn't matter. None of it mattered, save that there were my lady and my child, and I could not go to them. Could no more go to them than I could climb the night sky and take down the moon. I gazed afar to the river, shining blackly in the moonlight, rippled like black slate. A river that could carry me home, but would not. Because the fierceness of my will was still not enough to break past that command in my mind. I looked up to the moon. 'Burrich,' I pleaded aloud, as if he could hear me. 'Oh, take care of them, see they come to no harm, guard them as if they were your own. Until I can come to them.'

I do not recall going back to the holding pens, or lying down to sleep. But morning came and when I opened my eyes, that was where I was. I lay, looking up at the blue arch of the sky, hating my life. Creece came to stand between me and the heavens and look down on me.

'You'd better get up,' he told me, and then, peering closer, he observed, 'Your eyes are red. You got a bottle you didn't share?'

'I've got nothing to share with anybody,' I told him succinctly. I rolled to my feet. My head was pounding.

I wondered what Molly would name her. A flower name, probably. Lilac, or something like that. Rose. Marigold. What would I have named her? It didn't matter.

I stopped thinking. For the next few days, I did what I was told. I did it well and thoroughly, distracted by no thoughts of my own. Somewhere inside me, a madman raged in his cell, but I chose not to know of that. Instead I herded sheep. I ate in the morning, I ate in the evening. I lay down at night and I rose in the morning. And I herded sheep. I followed them, in the dust of the wagons and the horses and the sheep themselves, dust that clotted thick on my eyelashes and skin, dust that coated my throat with dryness, and I thought of nothing. I did not need to think to know that every step carried me closer to Verity. I spoke so little that even Creece wearied of my company, for he could not provoke me to argument. I herded the sheep as single-mindedly as the best sheep-dog that ever lived. When I lay down to sleep at night, I did not even dream.

Life went on for the rest of them. The caravan master guided us well and the trip was blessedly uneventful. Our misfortunes were limited to dust, little water, and sparse grazing, and those misfortunes were ones we accepted as part of the road. In the evenings, after the sheep were settled and the meal cooked and eaten, the puppeteers rehearsed. They had three plays and they seemed bent on perfecting all of them before we reached Blue Lake. Some nights it was merely the motions of the puppets and their dialogue, but several times they set up completely, torches, stage and backdrops, the puppeteers dressed in the pure white drapings that signified their invisibility, and went through the entire repertoire of plays. The master was a strict one, very ready with his strap, and he did not spare even his journeyman a lash or two if he thought he deserved it. A single line intoned incorrectly, one flip of a marionette's hand that was not as Master Dell dictated it, and he was amongst his cast, flaying about with the strap. Even if I had been in the mood for amusements, that would have spoiled it for me. So more often I went and sat looking out over the sheep, while the others watched the performances.

The minstrel, a handsome woman named Starling, was often my companion. I doubted that it was from any desire for my company. Rather it was that we were far enough from the camp that she could sit and practise her own songs and harpings, away from the endless rehearsals and the weeping of the corrected apprentices. Perhaps it was that I was from Buck, and could understand what she missed when she spoke quietly of the gulls crying and the blue sky over a sea after a storm. She was a typical Buck woman, dark-haired and dark-eyed, and no taller than my shoulder. She dressed simply, blue leggings and tunic. There were holes in her ears for earrings, but she wore none, nor were there any rings to her fingers. She would sit not far from me, and run her fingers over her harp-strings and sing. It was good to hear a Buck accent again, and the familiar songs of the Coastal Duchies. Sometimes she talked to me. It was not a conversation. She spoke to herself in the night and I just happened to be within earshot, as some men talk to a favourite dog. So it was that I knew she had been one of the minstrels in a small keep in Buck, one I'd never been to, held by a minor noble whose name I didn't even recognize. Too late to worry about visiting or knowing; the keep and the noble were no more, swept through and burned out by the Red Ships. Starling had survived, but without a place to rest her head or a master to sing for. So she had struck out on her own, resolved to head so far inland that she'd never again see a ship of any colour. I could understand that drive. By walking away she saved Buck for herself, as a memory of how it had been once.

Death had come close enough to her to brush her with its wingtips, and she wasn't going to die as she was, a minor minstrel for a lesser noble. No, somehow she was going to make her name, was going to witness some great event and make a song about it that would be sung down the years. Then she'd be immortal, remembered as long as her song was sung. It seemed to me she would have had a better chance of witnessing such an event if she'd stayed on the coast where the war was, but as if in answer to my unspoken thought, Starling assured me that she was going to witness something that left its witnesses alive. Besides, if you've seen one battle, you've seen them all. She saw nothing especially musical about blood. To that I nodded mutely.

'Ah. I thought you looked more like a man-at-arms than a shepherd. Sheep don't break one's nose, or leave a scar like that down your face.'

'They do if you tumble down a cliff looking for some in a mist,' I told her dourly, and turned my face aside from her.

For a long time, that was as close as I came to having a conversation with anyone.

We journeyed on, moving only as fast as laden wagons and a herd of sheep would permit. The days were remarkably similar. The countryside we passed was remarkably similar. There were a few novelties. Sometimes there were other folk camped at the watering places we came to. At one, there was a tavern of sorts, and here the caravan master delivered some small kegs of brandy. Once we were followed for half a day by folk on horseback who might have been bandits. But they veered off and left our trail in the afternoon, either bound to a destination of their own, or deciding what we possessed wasn't worth the effort of a raid. Sometimes other folk passed us, messengers and folk travelling on horseback, unslowed by sheep and wagons. Once it was a troop of guards in the Farrow colours, pushing their horses hard as they passed us. I felt an uneasiness as I watched them pass our caravan, as if an animal scrabbled briefly against the walls that shielded my mind. Did a Skilled one ride amongst them, Burl or Carrod, or even Will? I tried to persuade myself it was merely the sight of the gold and brown livery that unnerved me.

On another day we were intercepted by three of the nomadic folk whose grazing territory we were in. They came to us on tough little ponies that wore no more harness than a hackamore. The two grown women and the boy were all blonde with faces baked brown by the sun. The boy's face was tattooed with stripes like a cat. Their arrival occasioned a complete halting of the caravan, while Madge set up a table and cloth and brewed a special tea, which she served to them with candied fruit and barley-sugar cakes. No coin exchanged hands that I saw, only this ceremonial hospitality. I suspected from their manner that Madge was long known to them, and that her son was being groomed to continue this passage arrangement.

But most days were the same plodding routine. We rose, we ate, we walked. We stopped, we ate, we slept. One day I caught myself wondering if Molly would teach our child to make candles and tend bees. What could I teach her? Poisons and strangling techniques, I thought bitterly. No. Her letters and numbers she'd learn from me. She'd still be young enough when I returned for me to teach her that. And all Burrich had ever taught me about horses and dogs. That was the day when I realized I was looking ahead again, was planning for a life after I'd found Verity and somehow taken him safely back to Buck. My baby was just an infant now, I told myself, suckling at Molly's breast and looking about with wide eyes and seeing all new. She was too young to know something was missing, too young to know her father wasn't there. I'd be back with them soon, before she learned to say 'Pa', I'd be there to see her first steps.

That resolve changed something in me. I'd never looked forward to something so much. This was not an assassination that would end in someone's death. No, I looked forward to a life, and imagined teaching her things, imagined her growing up bright and pretty and loving her father, knowing nothing, ever, of any other life he'd ever led. She wouldn't remember me with a smooth face and a straight nose. She'd only know me as I was now. That was oddly important to me. So I would go to Verity because I had to, because he was my king and I loved him, and because he needed me. But finding him no longer marked the end of my journey, but the beginning. Once I had found Verity, I could turn about and come home to them. For a time, I forgot Regal.

So I thought to myself sometimes, and when I did I walked behind the sheep in their dust and stink and smiled a tightlipped smile behind the kerchief over my face. At other times, when I lay down alone at night, all I could think of was the warmth of a woman and a home and a child of my own. I think I felt every mile that stretched between us. Loneliness was a thing that ate at me then. I longed to know every detail of what was going on. Every night, every moment of quiet was a temptation to reach out with the Skill. But I understood Verity's admonition now. If

I Skilled to them, then Regal's coterie could find them as well as me. Regal would not hesitate to use them against me in any way he could imagine. So I hungered for knowledge of them, but dared not attempt to satisfy that hunger.

We came to one village that was almost worthy of the name. It had sprouted up like a fairy ring of mushrooms around a deep-water spring. It had an inn, a tavern and even several stores, all catering to travellers, with a scattering of houses surrounding it. We got there at midday, and Madge declared that we would have a rest, and not move on until the following morning. No one really objected. Once we'd watered our animals, we moved our beasts and wagons to the outskirts of town. The puppeteer decided to take advantage of the situation, and announced in the tavern and inn that his troupe would stage a performance for the whole town, with gratuities cheerfully accepted. Starling had already found a corner of the tavern to call her own and was introducing this Farrow town to some Buck ballads.

I was content to stay with the sheep on the outskirts of the town. I was soon the only one at our encampment. I did not especially mind. The horses' owner had offered me an extra copper if I'd keep an eye on them. They scarcely needed watching. They were hobbled, but even so, all the animals were grateful to stop for a bit and search out whatever grazing they could find. The bull was staked out and likewise occupied with scavenging grass. There was a sort of peace to being still and alone. I was learning to cultivate an emptiness of spirit. I could now go for long stretches without thinking of anything in particular. It made my endless waiting less painful. I sat on the tail of Damon's cart and stared out over the animals and the gentle undulating of the brush-spotted plain beyond them.

It did not last for long. In the late afternoon, the puppeteer's wagon came rattling into camp. Only Master Dell and the youngest apprentice were in it. The others had stayed in town to drink and talk and generally enjoy themselves. But the shouting of the master soon made it apparent that his youngest apprentice had disgraced herself with forgotten lines and incorrect movements. Her punishment was to stay in camp with the wagon. To this he added several sharp cuts with his strap. Both the snap of the leather and yelps of the girl were clearly audible across camp. I winced at the second one and was on my feet by the third one. I had no clear idea of my intention, and was actually relieved to see the master go striding off away from the wagon and back into town.

The girl wept noisily as she went about the task of unhitching the team and pegging it out. I'd noticed her before in a casual way. She was the youngest of the troupe, no more than sixteen, and seemed most often to be under her master's lash. Not that that was unusual. It was not uncommon for a master to have a lash to keep his apprentices devoted to their tasks. Neither Burrich nor Chade had ever taken a strap to me, but I'd had my share of cuffs and raps, and an occasional boot from Burrich if I wasn't moving fast enough to suit him. The puppeteer was no worse than many masters that I'd seen, and kinder than some. All of his underlings were well-fed and well-clothed. I suppose what irritated me about him was that one snap of his lash never seemed enough for him. It was always three or five or even more when he was in a temper.

The peace of the night was gone. Long after she'd finished staking out the horses, her deep sobbing rent the stillness. After a time I could not stand it. I went to the back of their travelling wagon and rapped on the small door. The weeping paused with a sniff. 'Who is it?' she asked hoarsely.

'Tom the shepherd. Are you all right?'

I'd hoped that she'd say she was and tell me to go away. Instead the door opened after a moment and she stood peering out at me. Blood was dripping from her jaw-line. I saw at a glance what had happened. The end of the strap had curled past her shoulder and the tip had bitten wickedly into her cheek. I didn't doubt that it hurt badly, but I suspected the amount of blood was scaring her even more. I saw a looking-glass set up on a table behind her and a bloody cloth beside it. For a moment we looked at one another wordlessly. Then, 'He's ruined my face,' she sobbed.

I couldn't think of words to say. Instead I stepped up into the wagon and took her by the shoulders. I sat her down. She'd been using a dry rag to poke at her face. Had she no sense at all? 'Sit still,' I told her tersely. 'And try to be calm. I'll be right back.'

I took her rag and damped it in cool water. I went back in and dabbed the blood away. As I suspected, the cut was not large, but it was bleeding profusely as cuts to the face or scalp often do. I folded the rag into a square and pressed it against her face. 'Hold that there. Press on it a bit, but don't move it. I'll be back.' I looked up to find her eyes fastened to the scar on my cheek as tears brimmed over from her eyes. I added, 'Skin as fair as yours doesn't scar all that easily. Even if it leaves a mark, it won't be large.'

The hugeness of her eyes at my words let me know I'd said exactly the wrong thing. I left the wagon, berating myself for getting involved at all.

I'd lost all my healing herbs and my pot of Burrich's ointment when I had abandoned my things in Tradeford. I'd noticed a flower that looked a bit like a stunted goldenrod in the area where the sheep were grazing, however, and some succulents sort of like bloodroot. So I pulled up one of the succulents, but it smelled wrong, and the juice from the leaves was sticky rather than like jelly. I washed my hands and then looked at the stunted goldenrod. It smelled right. I shrugged. I started out picking just a handful of leaves, but then decided as long as I was at it, I could restock a bit of what I'd lost. It appeared to be the same herb, but growing smaller and more straggly in this dry rocky soil. I spread out my harvest on the tail of the cart and sorted through it. The fatter leaves I left to dry. The smaller tips I crushed between two cleaned stones, and then took the resulting paste on one of the stones to the puppeteer's wagon. The girl looked at it with doubt, but nodded hesitantly when I told her, 'This will stop the bleeding. Soonest closed is smallest scar.'

When she took the rag away from her face, I saw that it had almost stopped bleeding. I smoothed on a fingertip's worth of the woundwort paste anyway. She sat quietly under my touch, and it was suddenly unnerving to recall that I had not touched a woman's face since I'd last seen Molly. This girl had blue eyes and they were wide open and looking up into my face. I looked aside from the earnest gaze. 'There. Now leave it alone. Don't wipe at it, don't touch it with your fingers, don't wash it. Let the scab form and then do your best to leave that alone.'

'Thank you,' she said in a tiny voice.

'Welcome,' I told her, and turned to leave.

'My name is Tassin,' she said to my back.

'I know. I've heard him roaring it at you,' I said. I started to go down the steps.

'He's an awful man. I hate him! I'd run away if I could.'

It didn't seem like a good time simply to walk away from her. I stepped off the wagon and paused. 'I know it's hard to feel a strap when you're trying hard. But . . . that's how it is. If you ran away and had no food, no place to sleep and your clothing all going to rags, that would be worse. Try to do better, so he won't take up the strap.' I believed so little of what I said, I could scarcely form the words. But those words seemed better than to tell her to leave now and run away. She wouldn't survive a day on the open prairie.

'I don't want to do better.' She'd found a spark of spirit, to be defiant. 'I don't want to be a puppeteer at all. Master Dell knew that when he bought my years.'

I edged away back toward my sheep, but she came down the steps and followed after me.

'There was a man I liked in our village. He'd made an offer for me, to be his wife, but had no money just then. He was a farmer, you see, and it was spring. No farmer has money in spring. He told my mother he'd pay a bride-price for me at harvest-time. But my mother said, "If he's poor now with one mouth to feed, he'll only be poorer after he has two. Or more." And then she sold me to the puppeteer, for half what he'd usually pay for an apprentice, because I wasn't willing.'

'They do it differently where I'm from,' I said awkwardly. I couldn't grasp what she was telling me. 'Parents pay a master to take on their child as apprentice, hoping the child can make a better life.'

She smoothed her hair back from her face. It was light brown, with a lot of curl to it. 'I've heard of that. Some do it that way, but most don't. They buy an apprentice, usually a willing one, and if he doesn't work out, then they can sell him for a drudge. Then you're not much better than a slave for six years.' She sniffed. 'Some say it makes an apprentice try harder, to know he may end up doing scut work in a kitchen or pumping a bellows in a smithy for six years if his master isn't pleased.'

'Well. It sounds to me like you'd better learn to like puppets,' I said lamely. I sat on the tail of my master's cart and looked out over my flock. She sat down next to me.

'Or hope someone buys me from my master,' she said despondently.

'You make yourself sound like a slave,' I said reluctantly. 'It's not that bad, is it?'

'Doing something you think is stupid, day after day?' she asked me. 'And being hit for not doing it perfectly? How is that better than being a slave?'

'Well, you're fed and clothed and sheltered. And he's giving you a chance to learn something, a trade that would let you travel all over the Six Duchies if you became good at it. You might end up performing for the King's Court at Buckkeep.'

She looked at me oddly. 'You mean Tradeford.' She sighed and shifted herself closer to me. 'It's lonely for me. All the others, they all want to be puppeteers. They get angry at me when I make mistakes, and always call me lazy and won't talk to me when they say I spoiled a performance. There's not one kind one among them; none of them would have cared about my face getting scarred as you did.'

There seemed nothing to reply to that. I didn't know the others well enough to agree or disagree. So I said nothing and we sat watching the sheep. The silence lengthened as the night got darker. I thought that soon I should kindle a fire.

'So,' she began after a few more minutes of my silence. 'How did you become a shepherd?'

'My parents died. My sister inherited. She didn't particularly care for me, and here I am.'

'What a bitch!' she said fiercely.

I took a breath to defend my fictitious sister, and then realized I'd only be extending the conversation. I tried to think of something I needed to go and do, but the sheep and other beasts were right there before us, grazing peacefully. Useless to hope that the others would soon return. Not with a tavern and new faces to talk to after our days on the road.

I finally made excuse that I was hungry and got up to gather stones and then dry dung and sticks for a fire. Tassin insisted on cooking. I was not truly hungry, but she ate with a hearty appetite, and fed me well from the puppeteer's travelling supplies. She made a pot of tea as well, and afterwards we sat by the fireside sipping it from heavy red porcelain mugs.

Somehow the silence had changed from awkward to companionable. It had been pleasant to sit and watch someone else prepare the meal. She had chattered at first, asking if I liked this sort of spice and did I make my tea strong, but not really listening for any answers. Seeming to find some sort of acceptance in my silence, she had gone on to speak more intimately of herself. With a sort of despair, she spoke of days spent learning and practising a thing she had no desire to learn nor practise. She spoke with a grudging marvel of the dedication of the other puppeteers, and their enthusiasm that she could not share. Her voice dwindled off and she looked up at me with eyes full of misery. She did not need to explain to me the loneliness she felt. She turned the talk to lighter things, the minor irritations she felt, the foods they ate that she disliked, the way one of the other puppeteers always smelled of old sweat, of one woman who reminded her to speak her lines by pinching her.

Even her complaints were pleasant in an odd way, filling my mind with her trivialities so that I could not focus on my larger problems. Being with her was in some ways like being with the wolf. Tassin was focused on the now, on this meal and this night, with little thought of anything else. From considering this my thoughts wandered to Nighteyes. I quested softly toward him. I could sense him, somewhere, alive, but could tell little more than that. Perhaps too great a distance separated us; perhaps he was too focused on his new life. Whatever the reason, his mind was not as open to me as it had once been. Perhaps he was simply becoming more attuned to the ways of his pack. I tried to feel glad that he had found such a life for himself, with many companions and possibly a mate.

'What are you thinking about?' Tassin asked.

She spoke so softly that I replied without thinking, still staring into the fire. 'That sometimes it only makes one more lonely to know that somewhere else, one's friends and family are well.'

She shrugged. 'I try not to think of them. I suppose my farmer found another girl, one whose parents would wait for a bride-price. As for my mother, I suspect her prospects were better without me. She was not so old that she could not catch another man.' She stretched, an oddly catlike gesture, then turned her head to gaze into my face and added, 'There's no sense in thinking of what's far away and what you haven't got. It will only make you unhappy. Be content with what you can have now.'

Our eyes were locked suddenly. There was no mistaking her meaning. For an instant I was shocked. Then she leaned across the small space between us. She put one hand on each side of my face. Her touch was gentle. She pushed the kerchief back from my hair, then used both hands to smooth the hair back from my face. She looked into my eyes as the tip of her tongue moistened my lips. She slid her hands down the sides of my face, down my neck to my shoulders. I was as entranced as a mouse looking at a snake. She leaned forward and kissed me, opening her mouth against mine as she did so. She smelled like sweet smoky incense.

I wanted her with a suddenness that dizzied me. Not as Tassin, but as woman and gentleness and closeness. It was lust that raced through me, and yet it was not that at all. It was like the Skill-hunger that eats at a man, demanding closeness and total communion with the world. I was unutterably weary of being alone. I caught her to me so quickly I heard her gasp of surprise. I kissed her as if I could devour her and somehow be less lonely by doing so. Suddenly we were prone and she was making small pleased sounds that suddenly changed to her pushing at my chest. 'Stop a moment,' she hissed. 'Just wait. There's a rock under me. And I mustn't spoil my clothes, give me your cloak to spread out . . .'

I watched her avariciously as she spread my cloak out on the earth by the fire. She lay down upon it and patted a place beside her. 'Well? Aren't you coming back?' she asked me flirtatiously. More lewdly, she added, 'Let me show you all I can do for you.' She smoothed her hands down the front of her shirt, inviting me to think of my hands doing the same.

If she had said nothing, if we had never paused, if she had simply looked up at me from the cloak ... but her question and her manner were all wrong, suddenly. All the illusion of gentleness and closeness were gone, replaced by the same sort of challenge another fighter might offer me in a practice-yard with staves. I am no better than any man. I didn't want to think, to consider anything. I longed to be able to simply throw myself down upon her and quench myself in her, but instead I heard myself asking, 'And if I get you with child?'

'Oh,' and she laughed lightly as if she had never considered such a thing. 'Then you can marry me, and buy my prentice years from Master Dell. Or not,' she added, as she saw my face change. 'A baby's not so large a thing to be rid of as a man might think. A few silvers for the right herbs ... but we needn't think of that now. Why worry about a thing that may never come to pass?'

Why indeed? I looked at her, wanting her with all the lust of my months alone and untouched. But I knew also that for that deeper hunger for companionship and understanding, she offered me no more solace than any man might find in his own hand. I shook my head slowly, more to myself than to her. She smiled up at me mischievously and reached a hand toward me.

'No.' I said the word quietly. She looked up at me, so incredulously amazed that I nearly laughed. 'This is not a good idea,' I said, and hearing the words aloud, I knew they were true. There was nothing lofty in it, no thoughts of undying faithfulness to Molly or shame that I had already left one woman with the burden of bearing a child alone. I knew those feelings, but they were not what came to me then. What I sensed was a hollowness in me that would only be made worse by laying myself down beside a stranger. 'It's not you,' I said as I saw her cheeks redden suddenly and the smile fade from her face. 'It's me. The fault's with me.' I tried to make my voice comforting. It was a waste.

She stood up suddenly. 'I know that, stupid,' she said scathingly. 'I only meant to be kind to you, nothing more.' She stalked angrily away from the fire, blending with the shadows quickly. I heard the slam of the wagon door.

I stooped slowly to pick my cloak up and shake the dust from it. Then, the night having become suddenly colder with a rising wind, I put it around my shoulders and sat down again to stare into my fire.

TWELVE

Suspicions

The use of the Skill is addictive. All students of this magic are warned of this from the very beginning. There is a fascination to this power that draws the user in, tempting him to use it more and more often. As the user's expertise and power increase, so does the lure of the Skill. The fascination of the Skill eclipses other interests and relationships. Yet it is a difficult attraction to describe to anyone who has not experienced the Skill itself. A rising covey of pheasant on a crisp autumn morning, or catching the wind's benefit perfectly in a boat's sails or the first mouthful of hot savoury stew after a cold and hungry day; these are all sensations that hover for only a moment. The Skill sustains that sensation, for as long as the strength of the user lasts.

It was very late when the others came back to our campsite. My master Damon was drunk and leaning companionably on Creece, who was drunk and irritable and reeked of Smoke. They dragged their blankets off the cart and rolled up in them. No one offered to relieve me in my watch. I sighed, doubting that I'd get any sleep until the next night.

Dawn came as early as it always does, and the caravan master was merciless in insisting that we rise and get ready for the road. I suppose she was wise. If she'd allowed them to sleep as long as they wanted, the earlier risers would have gone back to town, and she would have had to spend the day rounding them up. But it made for a miserable morning. Only the teamsters and the minstrel Starling seemed to have known when to stop drinking. We cooked and shared porridge while the others compared headaches and complaints.

I've noticed that drinking together, especially to excess, forms a bond between folk. So when the master decided his head ached too badly for him to drive the cart, he allotted that task to Creece. Damon slept in the cart as it jostled along while Creece drowsed over the reins as the pony followed the other wagons. They'd tied the bellwether to the tail of the cart, and the flock followed. Somewhat. To me fell the task of trotting behind in the dust, keeping the flock as well bunched as I could. The sky was blue but the day remained chill, with rising winds that stirred and carried the dust we raised. The night had been sleepless for me, and my head soon pounded with pain.

Madge called a brief halt at noon. Most of the caravan folk had recovered enough by then that they wished to eat. I drank from the water-casks on Madge's wagon, then wet my kerchief and sopped some of the dust from my face. I was trying to rinse grit from my eyes when Starling came up beside me. I stepped aside, thinking she wanted water. Instead, she spoke softly.

'I'd keep my kerchief on, were I you.'

I wrung it out and retied it about my head. 'I do. It does nothing to keep the dust from my eyes, though.'

Starling looked at me levelly. 'It's not your eyes you should worry about. It's that white shock of hair. You should black it with grease and ash tonight, if you get a private moment. It might make it a bit less noticeable.'

I looked questioningly at her, trying to keep my expression bland.

She smiled at me archly. 'King Regal's guard had been through that water-town just a few days before we arrived. They told the folk there that the King believed that the Pocked Man would be crossing Farrow. And you with him.' She paused, expecting me to say something. When I just looked at her, her grin widened. 'Or perhaps it's some other fellow with a broken nose, scar down his face, white streak in his hair, and . . .' she gestured toward my arm, 'a fresh sword-slash up his forearm.'

I found my tongue and a measure of my wits. I pushed back my sleeve, offered my arm for her inspection. 'A sword-slash? This is just a scratch I got off a nail-head in a tavern door. On my way out, a bit unwillingly. Take a look for yourself. It's almost healed now, anyway.'

She leaned over and looked at my arm obligingly. 'Oh. I see. Well. My mistake. Still,' and she met my eyes again, 'I'd keep your kerchief on anyway. To prevent anyone else from making the same mistake.' She paused, then canted her head at me. 'I'm a minstrel, you see. I'd rather witness history than make it. Or change it. But I doubt all the others in this caravan feel that way.'

I watched mutely as she strolled away, whistling. Then I drank again, being careful not to take too much, and went back to my sheep.

Creece was on his feet and helping, somewhat, for the rest of the afternoon. Even so, it seemed a longer, wearier day than I'd had in a while. There was nothing complicated about my task to make it so. The problem, I decided, was that I'd begun thinking again. I let my despair over Molly and our child drag me down. I'd let my guard down, I hadn't been fearful enough on my own behalf. Now it occurred to me that if Regal's guard managed to find me, they'd kill me. Then I'd never see Molly or our daughter. Somehow that seemed worse than the threat to my life.

At the evening meal that night, I sat back further from the fire than usual, even though it meant wrapping myself in my cloak against the cold. My silence was taken as normal. The rest of them talked, much more than usual, about the last evening in town. I gathered the beer had been good, the wine poor, while the resident minstrel had had small goodwill toward Starling for performing for his captive audience. The members of our caravan seemed to take it as a personal victory that Starling's songs had been well received by the villagers. 'You sang well, even if all you knew was those Buck ballads,' Creece even conceded magnanimously. Starling nodded to that dubious praise.

As she did every evening, Starling unwrapped her harp after the meal. Master Dell was giving his troupe a rare night off from their constant rehearsing, by which I gathered he had been pleased with his performers save Tassin. Tassin had not even a glance for me that evening, but instead perched by one of the teamsters, smiling up at his every word. I noticed that her injury was little more than a scratch on her face with some bruising around it. It would heal well.

Creece went off to stand night watch over our flock. I stretched out on my cloak just beyond reach of the firelight, thinking to drowse off immediately. I expected the others would soon be off to bed as well. The hum of their conversation was lulling, as was the lazy strumming of Starling's fingers on her harp-strings. Gradually the strumming changed to a rhythmic plucking, and her voice lifted in song.

I was floating at the edge of sleep when the words 'Antler Island Tower' jolted me awake. My eyes flew open as I realized she was singing about the battle there last summer, the *Rurisk's* first real engagement with the Red Ship Raiders. I recalled both too much and very little about that battle. As Verity had observed more than once, despite all Hod's weapons-instruction, I tended to revert to brawling in any sort of a fight. So I'd carried an axe into that battle and used it with a savagery I'd never expected of myself. Afterwards, it had been said that I'd killed the chief of the raiding party we'd cornered. I'd never known if that were true or not.

In Starling's song, it certainly was. My heart nearly stood still when I heard her sing of 'Chivalry's son, with eyes of flame, who carried his blood if not his name'. The song went on with a dozen improbable embellishments of blows I'd dealt and warriors I'd felled. It was strangely humiliating to hear those deeds sung of as noble and now almost legendary. I knew there were many fighters who dreamed of having songs sung of their exploits. I found the experience uncomfortable. I didn't recall the sun striking flames from my axe-head or that I fought as bravely as the stag on my crest. Instead I recalled the clinging smell of blood and treading on a man's entrails, a man who squirmed and moaned still. All the ale in Buckkeep that night had not been enough to bring me any sort of peace.

When the song was finally done, one of the teamsters snorted. 'So, that's the one ye daren't sing in the tavern last night, eh, Starling?'

Starling gave a deprecating laugh. 'Somehow I doubted it would be enjoyed. Songs about Chivalry's Bastard would not have been popular enough to earn me a penny there.'

'It's an odd song,' observed Dell. 'Here's the King offering gold for his head, and the guard telling all, beware, the Bastard has the Wit and used it to trick death. But your song makes him out to be some sort of hero.'

'Well, it's a Buck song, and he was well thought of in Buck, at least for a time,' Starling explained.

'But not any more, I'd wager. Save that any man would think well of a hundred gold coins if one could turn him over to the King's Guard,' one of the teamsters observed.

'Like as not,' Starling agreed easily. 'Though there's still some in Buck who would tell you that not all his tale has been told, and the Bastard was not so black as he's been tarred of late.'

'I still don't understand it. I thought he was executed for using the Wit to kill King Shrewd,' complained Madge.

'So some say,' Starling replied. 'Truth of it was, he died in his cell before he could be executed and was buried instead of burned. And the tale goes,' and here Starling's voice dropped to a near-whisper, 'that when spring came, not a leaf of greenery would grow on his grave. And an old wise woman, hearing this, knew that meant his Wit magic still slept in his bones and might be claimed by any bold enough to pull a tooth from his mouth. And so she went, by full moonlight, and took a manservant with a spade with her. She put him to digging up the grave. But he hadn't turned but a shovelful of earth before he found splintered wood from the Bastard's coffin.'

Starling paused theatrically. There wasn't a sound save the crackling of the fire.

'The box was empty, of course. And those that saw it said that the coffin had been splintered out from inside, not stove in. And one man told it to me that caught in the splintered edge of the coffin lid were the coarse grey hairs of a wolf's coat.'

A moment longer the silence held. Then, 'Not truly?' Madge asked Starling.

Her fingers ran lightly over her harp-strings. 'So I heard it told in Buck. But I also heard the Lady Patience, she that buried him, say it was all nonsense, that his body had been cold and stiff when she washed it and wrapped it in a gravecloth. And of the Pocked Man, that King Regal so fears, she declared he is no more than an old adviser of King Shrewd's, some old recluse with a scarred face, come out of his hermitage to keep alive a belief that Verity still lives and lend heart to those who must go on battling the Red Ships. So. I suppose you can choose to believe whichever you wish.'

Melody, one of the puppeteers, gave a mock shiver. 'Brrr. So. Sing us something merry now, to go to sleep on. I've no wish to hear more of your ghost tales before I seek my blankets tonight.'

So Starling willingly swept into a love ballad, an old one with a lilting refrain that Madge and Melody joined in singing. I lay in the darkness, pondering all I'd heard. I was uncomfortably aware that Starling had stirred it up intending for me to hear it. I wondered if she thought she were doing me a favour, or if she simply wished to see if any of the others had suspicions of me. One hundred gold coins for my head. That was enough to make a duke greedy, let alone a strolling minstrel. Despite my weariness, it was a long time before I dozed off that night.

The next day's drive was almost comforting in its monotony. I paced along behind my sheep, and tried not to think. It was not as easy to do as previously. It seemed that whenever I blanked my mind to my worries, I heard Verity's *Come to me* echoing inside my head. When we made camp that night, it was on the banks of a giant sinkhole with water at its centre. The talk about the fire was desultory. I think we were all more than a little weary of our trudging pace and longed to see the shores of Blue Lake. I wished simply to go to sleep, but I had first watch over the flock.

I climbed slightly up the hillside to where I could sit looking down on my woolly charges. The great bowl of the sinkhole cupped our whole caravan, with the small cook fire near the water showing like a star at the bottom of a well. Whatever wind blew passed us by, leaving us sheltered in a great stillness. It was almost peaceful.

Tassin probably thought she was being stealthy. I watched her come silently, her cloak pulled well up over her hair and about her face. She circled widely as if to pass by me. I did not follow her with my eyes, but listened to her as she went above me on the hillside and then came back down behind me. I caught her scent even in the still air and felt an involuntary anticipation. I wondered if I'd have the strength of will to refuse her a second time. Mistake it might be, but my body was all in favour of making it. When I judged her about a dozen steps away, I turned to look at her. She startled back from my gaze.

'Tassin,' I greeted her quietly, and then turned to look back at my sheep. After a moment, she came down the slope to stand a few steps away from me. I turned slightly and looked up at her without speaking. She pushed her hood back from her face and confronted me, challenge in her eyes and stance.

'You're him, aren't you?' she demanded breathlessly. There was a very slight edge of fear in her voice.

It was not what I'd expected her to say. I didn't have to pretend surprise. 'I'm him? I'm Tom the shepherd if that's the him you mean.'

'No, you're him, that Wit Bastard the King's Guard is seeking. Drew the teamster told me what they were saying in town, after Starling told that tale last night.'

'Drew told you I was a Wit Bastard?' I spoke carefully, as if baffled by her tumbling words. A terrible cold fear was welling up inside me.

'No.' A trace of anger mixed with her fear. 'Drew told me what the King's Guard said of him. A broken nose and a scar on the cheek and a white streak in his hair. And I saw your hair that night. You've a white streak in it.'

'Any man who's been hit on the head can have a white streak in his hair. It's an old scar.' I tilted my head and looked at her critically. 'I'd say your face is healing well.'

'You're him, aren't you?' She sounded even angrier that I'd tried to change the subject.

'Of course not. Look. He's got a sword-slash on his arm, hasn't he? Look at this.' I bared my right arm for her inspection. The knife-slash I'd given myself was down the back of my left forearm. I was gambling that she'd know a slash taken defending myself should have been on my sword-arm.

She scarcely glanced at my arm. 'Do you have any coin?' she asked me suddenly.

'If I'd had any coin, why would I have stayed in camp when the others went to town? Besides. Why would you care?'

'I wouldn't. But you would. You could use it to buy my silence. Otherwise, I might go to Madge with what I suspect. Or the teamsters.' She lifted her chin defiantly at me.

'Then they could look at my arm, as easily as you've done,' I said wearily. I turned away from her to look back over my sheep. 'You're being a silly little girl, Tassin, letting Starling's ghost tales get you all stirred up. Go back to bed.' I tried to sound disgusted with her.

'You've a scratch on your other arm. I saw it. Some might take it for a sword-slash.'

'Probably the same ones that would take you for intelligent,' I said derisively.

'Don't make mock of me,' she warned me in a voice gone flat with ugliness. 'I won't be made fun of.'

'Then don't say stupid things. What's the matter with you, anyway? Is this some sort of revenge? Are you angry because I wouldn't bed you? I told you, it's nothing to do with you. You're pretty to look at, and I don't doubt there'd be pleasure in touching you. But not for me.'

She spat suddenly on the ground beside me. 'As if I'd have let you. I was amusing myself, shepherd. No more than that.' She made a small sound in her throat. 'Men. How can you look at yourself and think anyone would want you for your own sake? You stink of sheep, you're skinny and your face looks like you've lost every fight you've ever been in.' She turned on her heel, then seemed to abruptly remember why she'd come. 'I won't tell any of them. Yet. But when we get to Blue Lake, your master must pay you something. See you bring it to me, or I'll have the whole town seeking you out.'

I sighed. 'Whatever amuses you, I'm sure you'll do. Create all the fuss you wish. When it comes to naught and folk laugh about it, it will probably give Dell one more reason to beat you.'

She turned away from me and went stalking off down the hillside. She lost her footing in the moonlight's uncertainty and nearly took a tumble. But she recovered herself and then glared back at me, as if daring me to laugh. I had no such inclination. Despite my defiance of her, my stomach was clenched up under my throat. A hundred gold coins. Spread a rumour of it, and that much money was enough to start a riot. After I was dead, they'd probably decide they had the wrong man.

I wondered how well I'd do at crossing the rest of the Farrow plains alone. I could leave right after Creece relieved me on watch. I'd go to the wagon and get my things quietly and sneak away into the night. How much farther could it be to Blue Lake anyway? I was pondering that as I watched yet another figure slip away from the campsite and come up the slope toward me.

Starling came quietly, but not stealthily. She lifted a hand to me in greeting before she sat down companionably at my side. 'I hope you didn't give her any money,' she greeted me affably.

'Umph,' I said, letting her take it however she wished.

'Because you're at least the third man who's supposedly got her pregnant on this trip. Your master had the honour of being the first accused. Madge's son was the second. At least I think he was. I don't know how many fathers she's selected for this possible child.'

'I haven't been with her, so she could scarcely accuse me of that,' I said defensively.

'Oh? Then you're probably the only man in the caravan who hasn't.'

That jolted me a bit. Then I thought about it and wondered if I would ever reach a place in which I ceased finding out how stupid I could be. 'So you think she's with child and is looking for a man to buy her out of her apprenticeship?'

Starling snorted. 'I doubt she's with child at all. She wasn't asking to be married, only for coin to buy herbs to shake the child loose. I think Madge's boy might have actually given her some. No. I don't think she wants a husband, just some money. So she looks for ways that allow her a bit of a tumble, and a man who might pay her for it afterwards.' She shifted, tossed aside an offending stone. 'So. If you haven't got her pregnant, what have you done to her?'

'I told you. Nothing.'

'Ah. That explains why she speaks so ill of you then. But only in the last day or so, so I supposed you "nothinged" her the night the rest of us went to town.'

'Starling,' I began warningly, and she raised a placating hand.

'I shan't say a word about whatever you didn't do to her. Not another word. That's not what I came up here to speak to you about anyway.'

She paused, and when I refused to ask the question, she did. 'What do you plan to do after we get to Blue Lake?'

I glanced at her. 'Collect my pay. Have a beer and a decent meal, a hot bath and a clean bed for one night at least. Why? What do you plan?'

'I thought I might go on to the Mountains.' She gave me a sideways glance.

'To seek your songworthy event there?' I tried to keep my question casual.

'Songs are more likely to be found clinging to a man than bound to a place,' she suggested. 'I thought you might be going to the Mountains as well. We could travel together.'

'You've still that idiotic notion that I'm the Bastard,' I accused her flatly.

She grinned. 'The Bastard. The Witted one. Yes.'

'You're wrong,' I said flatly. 'And even if you were right, why follow him to the Mountains? I'd take the chance for a bigger profit, and sell him to the King's Guard. With a hundred gold pieces, who'd need to make songs?'

Starling made a small sound of disgust. 'You've more experience of the King's Guard than I have, I'm sure. But even I've enough to know that a minstrel who tried to claim that reward would probably be found floating in the river a few days later. While some guardsmen became suddenly very wealthy. No. I've told you. I'm not after gold, Bastard. I'm after a song.'

'Don't call me that,' I warned her sharply. She shrugged and turned away. After a moment she twitched as if I'd poked her and then turned back to me with a grin widening across her face.

'Ah. I believe I've worked it out. That's how Tassin was squeezing you, isn't it? Asking for money to still her tongue.'

I made no reply.

'You're smart to refuse her. Give her any and she'll think she's right. If she truly believed you were the Bastard, she'd be holding her secret to sell to the King's Guard. Because she's had no experience of them, and would believe she might actually get to keep the gold.' Starling stood, stretching leisurely. 'Well. I'm back to bed while I may. But keep my offer in mind. I doubt you'll find a better one.' She swirled her cloak about herself theatrically, then bowed to me as if I were the King. I watched her stroll away from me down the hill, sure-footed as a goat even in the moonlight. She reminded me briefly of Molly.

I considered slipping away from the camp and going on to Blue Lake on my own. I decided that if I did, Tassin and Starling would only become certain that they had guessed correctly. Starling might try to follow and find me. Tassin would try to find a way to collect the reward. I wanted neither of those things. Better to stick it out and plod along as Tom the shepherd.

I lifted my eyes to the night sky. Clear and cold it arched above me. The dead of the night had a nasty chill to it of late. By the time I got to the Mountains, winter would be more than just a threat. If only I hadn't wasted those early months of summer being a wolf, I'd be in the Mountains by now. But that was another useless thought. The stars were close and bright tonight. It made the world seem a smaller place to have the sky so close. I felt suddenly that if I just opened up and reached for Verity, I would find him there, right at my fingertips. Loneliness swelled so suddenly inside me that I felt it would tear its way out of me. Molly and Burrich were no farther away than the closing of my eyes. I could go to them, could trade the hunger of not knowing for the pain of being unable to touch. The Skill walls, clutched so closely every waking moment since I had left Tradeford, now felt suffocating rather than shielding. I bowed my head to my drawn-up knees and hugged myself against the chill emptiness of the night.

After a time, the hunger passed. I lifted my head and looked out over the peaceful sheep, the cart and wagons, the motionless camp. A glance at the moon told me my watch was well over. Creece was never good about rousing himself to take his turn. So I stood and stretched and went down the hill to poke him from his warm blankets.

The next two days passed uneventfully, save that the weather grew colder and windier. On the evening of the third, just as we had settled for the night and I had taken up my first watch of the evening, I saw a dust cloud on the horizon. I thought little of it at first. We were on one of the more travelled caravan routes, and had stopped at a watering place. A wagon full of a tinker family had already been there. I assumed that whoever was raising the dust would also be seeking a water-place to rest for the night. So I sat and watched the dust get closer as the evening darkened. Slowly the dust resolved into figures on horseback, riding in an orderly formation. The closer they came, the more certain I became. King's Guards. The light was too weak for me to see the gold and brown of Regal's colours, but I knew.

It was all I could do to keep myself from leaping up and fleeing. Cold logic told me that if they were seeking me specifically, it would only take them a few minutes to ride me down. This vast plain offered me no near hiding places. And if they were not seeking me, to flee would only attract their attention, and make both Tassin and Starling certain in their suspicions. So I gritted my teeth and remained where I was, sitting with my stick across my knees watching the sheep. The riders bypassed me and the sheep and went directly to the water. I counted as they went past. Six of them. I recognized one of the horses, a buckskin colt Burrich had said would be a good courser someday. Seeing him reminded me too vividly of how Regal had plundered Buckkeep of every valuable thing before he left it to fend for itself. A tiny spark of anger ignited in me, one that somehow made it easier to sit and bide my time.

After a while, I decided that they were just on their way as we were, and had stopped only to water and rest for the night. Then Creece came lumbering out to find me. 'You're wanted in the camp,' he told me with ill-conceived irritability. Creece always liked to sleep as soon as he'd eaten. I asked him what had changed our schedule as he settled down in my place.

'King's Guards,' he huffed angrily. 'Pushing everybody about, demanding to see every member of our caravan. They searched all the wagons, too.'

'What are they looking for?' I asked idly.

'Damned if I know. Didn't care to get a fist in the face for asking, either. But you suit yourself about finding out.'

I took my staff with me as I walked back into the camp. My

short sword still hung at my side. I thought of concealing it, then decided against it. Anyone might carry a sword, and if I needed to draw it, I didn't want to be wrestling with my trousers.

The camp was like a stirred hornets' nest. Madge and her folk looked both apprehensive and angry. The guardsmen were currently harassing the tinker. One guardswoman kicked over a stack of tin pots with a fine clatter and then shouted something about searching anything she pleased, any way she pleased. The tinker stood by his wagon, his arms crossed on his chest. He looked as if he'd already been knocked down once. Two guardsmen had his wife and youngsters backed up against the tail of the wagon. The wife had a trickle of blood coming from her nose. She still looked ready to fight. I drifted into camp as silent as smoke and took a place beside Damon as if I'd always been there. Neither of us spoke.

The leader of the guards turned away from his confrontation with the tinker, and a shiver went up my back. I knew him. It was Bolt, favoured by Regal for his skill with his fists. I'd last seen him in the dungeon. He was the one who had broken my nose. I felt the beating of my heart pick up speed and heard my pulse in my ears. Darkness threatened the edges of my vision. I fought to breathe quietly. He paced to the centre of the camp and cast a disdainful eye over us. 'This is everyone?' he demanded more than queried.

We all bobbed nods. He cast his gaze over us and I looked down to avoid it. I forced my hands to be still, to stay away from both knife and sword. I tried not to let my tension show in my stance.

'As sorry a lot of vagabonds as I've ever seen.' His tone dismissed our importance. 'Caravan master! We've been riding all day. Have your boy see to our horses. We'll want food prepared, and more fuel gathered for the fire. And warm us some water for washing.' He ran his glance over us again. 'I want no trouble. The men we were looking for aren't here, and that's all we required to know. Just do as we ask, and there won't be any problems. You can go about your normal business.'

There were a few mutters of agreement, but mostly silence greeted this. He snorted his disdain for us, then turned to his riders and spoke quietly to them. Whatever orders he was giving did not seem to sit well with them, but the two that had cornered the tinker-woman came to heel at his words. They took over the fire Madge had built earlier, forcing the folk of our caravan to move off from it. Madge spoke quietly to her help, sending two off to care for the guards' horses, and another to fetch water and set it to warm. She herself strode heavily past our cart toward her own wagon and the food stores.

An uneasy semblance of order returned to the camp. Starling kindled a second, smaller fire. The puppeteer's troupe, the minstrel and the teamsters resettled next to it. The horse owner and her husband went quietly off to bed. 'Well, seems to have settled down,' Damon observed to me, but I noticed that he still twisted his hands nervously. 'I'm off to bed. You and Creece settle out the watches between you.'

I started to go back to my sheep. Then I paused and looked back around the camp. The guards were silhouettes around the fire now, lounging and talking, while a single one of them stood slightly back of the group keeping a general watch. He was looking toward the other fire. I followed his gaze. I could not decide if Tassin was looking back at him, or simply staring off at the other guards about their fire. Either way, I suspected I knew what was on her mind.

I turned aside and went to the back of Madge's wagon. She was scooping out beans and peas from sacks and measuring them into a soup kettle. I touched her lightly on the arm, and she jumped.

'Beg pardon. Could you use some help with that?'

She raised an eyebrow at me. 'Why would I?'

I glanced down at my feet and chose my lie carefully. 'I didn't care for how they looked at the tinker-woman, ma'am.'

'I know how to handle myself among rough men, shepherd. I couldn't be a caravan master if I didn't.' She measured salt into the kettle, then a handful of seasonings.

I nodded my head and said nothing. It was too obviously true for me to protest. But I did not leave, either, and after a few moments, she handed me a bucket and told me to fetch her some clean water. I obeyed her willingly, and when I brought it back,

I stood holding it until she took it from me. I watched her fill the soup kettle and stood at her elbow until she told me with some asperity to get out from under her feet. I apologized and backed away, upsetting her water bucket as I did so. So I took it and fetched her more fresh water in it.

After that, I went and got a blanket from Damon's cart, and rolled up in it for a few hours. I lay under the cart as if sleeping and watched, not the guardsmen, but Starling and Tassin. I noticed Starling did not take out her harp that night, as if she did not wish to call any attention to herself either. That somewhat reassured me about her. It would have been easy enough for her to visit their fire with her harp, to ingratiate herself with a few songs, and then offer to sell me. Instead she seemed as intent on watching Tassin as I was. Tassin rose once to leave on some excuse. I did not hear what Starling said quietly, but Tassin glared at her and Master Dell angrily ordered her back to her place. Certainly Dell wanted nothing to do with the guards in any way. But even after they had all gone off to bed, I could not relax. When it came time to relieve Creece on watch, I went reluctantly, not at all sure that Tassin would not choose the small hours of night in which to seek out the guards.

I found Creece sound asleep, and had to wake him to send him back to the cart. I sat down, my blanket around my shoulders, and thought of the six men down below, now sleeping around their fire. I had cause for true hatred of only one of them. I recalled Bolt to myself as he had been then, smirking as he drew on his leather gloves to beat me, sulking when Regal reprimanded him for breaking my nose lest it make me less presentable if the dukes wished to see me. I recalled the disdainful way he had performed his task for Regal, hammering easily past my token defence as I strove to keep Will and his Skill out of my mind.

Bolt hadn't even known me. He'd run his eyes over me and dismissed me, not even recognizing his own handiwork. I sat thinking for a bit about that. I supposed I had changed that much. Not just the scars he'd given me. Not just the beard and the workman's garb and the dirt of the road on me and my gauntness. FitzChivalry wouldn't have lowered his eyes before his gaze, would not have stood silent and let the tinker-folk fend for themselves.

FitzChivalry would not, perhaps, have poisoned all six guards for the sake of killing one. I wondered if I had grown wiser or wearier. Both, perhaps. It did not make me proud.

The Wit-sense gives me an awareness of other living things, all other living things, around me. I am seldom startled by anyone. So they did not take me by surprise. The dawn had just begun to blanch the blackness from the sky when Bolt and his guards came for me. I sat still, first feeling and then hearing their stealthy approach. Bolt had roused all five of his soldiers for the task.

With a sinking dismay, I wondered what had gone wrong with my poison. Had it lost its potency from being carried about so long? Been rendered useless by the cooking with the soup? I swear that for a moment my uppermost thought was that Chade would have not made this error. But I had no time to think about it. I glanced about at the gently undulating, near-featureless plain. Scrub-brush and a few rocks. Not even a gully or a mound for cover.

I could have run, and perhaps lost them for a time in the darkness. But in the end, that game was theirs. I'd have to come back for water eventually. If they did not track me down on the flat land by daylight on horseback, they could simply sit by the waterhole and wait me out. Besides, to flee was to admit I was FitzChivalry. Tom the shepherd would not run.

And so I looked up, startled and anxious when they came for me, but not, I hoped, betraying the heart-pounding fear I felt. I came to my feet, and when one seized me by an arm, I did not struggle but only looked up at him incredulously. Another guard came up from the other side, to take both my knife and my sword. 'Come down to the fire,' she told me gruffly. 'Captain wants a look at you.'

I went quietly, almost limply, and when they had reassembled at the campfire to present me to Bolt, I looked fearfully from one face to another, being careful not to single out Bolt. I was not sure I could look at him full face at close range and betray nothing. Bolt stood up, kicked at the fire to stir up the flames and then came to inspect me. I caught a glimpse of Tassin's pale face and hair peeking at me around the end of the puppeteer's wagon. For a time Bolt just stood looking at me. After a time, he pursed his mouth and gave his guards a disgusted look. With a small shake of his head, he let them know I wasn't what he'd wanted. I dared to take a deeper breath.

'What's your name?' Bolt suddenly demanded of me sharply.

I squinted at him across the fire. 'Tom, sir. Tom the shepherd. I've done nothing wrong.'

'Haven't you? Then you're the only man in the world who hasn't. You sound like a Buckman, Tom. Take off your kerchief.'

'I am, sir. From Buck, sir. But times are hard there.' I hastily dragged my kerchief off, then stood clutching and wringing it. I hadn't taken Starling's advice about staining my hair. That wouldn't have done any good during a close inspection. Instead, I had used my looking-glass and plucked out a good portion of the white hairs. Not all of them, but what I had now appeared more as a grey scattering of hair above my brow rather than a white streak. Bolt came around the fire to have a closer look at it. I flinched when he gripped me by the hair and tilted my head back to stare down into my face. He was as big and muscled as I remembered him. Every evil memory I had of him suddenly flooded my mind. I swear I even recalled the smell of him. The wretched sickness of fear filled me.

I offered him no resistance as he glared down at me. Nor did I meet his eyes, but rather shot frightened looks at him and then glanced away as if beseeching help. I noticed that Madge had come from somewhere and was standing, arms crossed on her chest, regarding us.

'Got a scar on your cheek, don't you, man?' Bolt demanded of me.

'Yes, sir, I do. Got it when I was a boy, fell out of a tree and a branch cut me . . .'

'You break your nose then, too?'

'No, sir, no, that was a tavern brawl, that was, about a year ago . . .'

'Take off your shirt!' he demanded.

I fumbled at the neck of it, then dragged it off over my head. I had thought he would look at my forearms and was prepared with my nail story for that. Instead he leaned over to look at a place between my shoulder and my neck, where a Forged one

had bitten a chunk out of me in a long ago fight. My bowels turned
to water. He looked at the gnarled scar there, then suddenly threw
his head back and laughed.

'Damn. I didn't think it was you, Bastard. I was sure it wasn't.
But that's the mark I remember seeing, the first time I drove you
into the floor.' He looked at the men standing around us, surprise
and delight still on his face. 'It's him! We've got him. The King's
got his Skill-wizards spread from the Mountains to the coast
looking for him, and he falls like fruit into our hands.' He licked
his lips as he ran his eyes over me gloatingly. I sensed a strange
hunger in him, one he almost feared. He seized me suddenly by
the throat and hauled me up on my toes. He brought his face
close to mine as he hissed, 'Understand me. Verde was a friend.
It's not a hundred gold pieces for you alive that keeps me from
killing you here. It's only my faith that my king can come up
with more interesting ways for you to die than I can improvise
here. You're mine again, Bastard, in the Circle. Or as much of
you as my king leaves for me anyway.'

He shoved me violently away from him into the fire. I stumbled
through it and was immediately seized by two men on the other
side. I looked from one to the other wildly. 'It's a mistake!' I cried
out. 'A terrible mistake!'

'Shackle him,' Bolt ordered them hoarsely.

Madge stepped suddenly forward. 'You're certain of this man?'
she asked him directly.

He met her eyes, captain to captain. 'I am. It's the Wit Bastard.'

A look of total disgust crossed Madge's face. 'Then take him
and welcome to him.' She turned on her heel and walked away.

My guards had been watching the conversation between Madge
and their captain rather than paying attention to the trembling
man between them. I chanced it all, breaking toward the fire as
I snapped my arms free of their careless grips. I shouldered a
startled Bolt aside and fled like a rabbit. I wove through the camp,
past the tinker's wagon, and saw only wide open country before
me. Dawn had greyed the plain to a featureless rumpled blanket.
No cover, no destination. I just ran.

I had expected men on foot after me, or men on horses. I
hadn't expected a man with a sling. The first rock hit me on the

flat of my left shoulder, numbing my arm. I kept running. I thought at first I'd taken an arrow. Then the bolt of lightning hit me.

When I woke up, my wrists were chained. My left shoulder ached horribly, but not as badly as the lump on my head. I managed to wiggle up to a sitting position. No one paid much attention to me. A shackle on each of my ankles was hooked to the length of chain that ran up and through a loop forged onto the chain that shackled my wrists together. A second, much shorter chain between my ankles was not even enough to let me take a full step. If I'd been able to stand.

I said nothing, did nothing. Shackled, I had no chance against six armed men. I didn't want to give them any excuse to brutalize me. Still, it took every bit of my will to sit quietly and consider my situation. The sheer weight of the chain was daunting, as was the chill of the iron biting into my flesh in the cold night air. I sat, head bowed, looking at my feet. Bolt noticed I was awake. He came to stand looking down at me. I kept my eyes on my own feet.

'Say something, damn you!' Bolt ordered me suddenly.

'You've got the wrong man, sir,' I said timidly. I knew there would be no convincing him of that, but perhaps I could shake his men's belief.

Bolt laughed. He went and sat back down by the fire. Then he lay back on his elbows. 'If I have, it's just too damn bad for you. But I know I don't. Look at me, Bastard. How was it you didn't stay dead?'

I shot him a fearful glance. 'I don't know what you mean, sir.'

It was the wrong response. He was tigerish in his speed, coming up from his reclining position to fly across the fire at me. I scrabbled to my feet but there was no escaping him. He seized me by my chains, drew me up, and slapped me stingingly. Then, 'Look at me,' he ordered.

I brought my eyes back to his face.

'How was it you didn't die, Bastard?'

'It wasn't me. You've got the wrong man.'

I got the back of his hand the second time.

Chade had once told me that, under torture, it is easier to resist questioning if you focus your mind on what you will say, rather than what you must not. I knew it was stupid and useless to tell Bolt I was not FitzChivalry. He knew I was. But having adopted that course, I stuck to it. The fifth time he hit me, one of his men spoke out behind me.

'With all respect, sir?'

Bolt flashed a furious look at the man. 'What is it?'

The man wet his lips. 'The captive was to be alive, sir. For the gold to be paid.'

Bolt turned his eyes back to me. It was unnerving to see the hunger in him, a craving such as Verity had for the Skill. This man liked to give pain. Liked to kill slowly. It only made him hate me all the more that he could not. 'I know that,' he said brusquely to the man. I saw his fist coming, but there was no way to avoid it.

When I came awake, it was full morning. There was pain. For a time, that was all I really knew. Pain, bad pain in one shoulder, and down my ribs on the same side. He'd probably kicked me, I decided. I didn't want to move any part of my face. Why, I wondered, is pain always worse when you're cold? I felt curiously detached from my situation. I listened for a time, with no desire at all to open my eyes. The caravan was getting ready to move on. I could hear Master Dell yelling at Tassin, who was crying that it was her money by right, that if he'd only help her get it, he could have his apprentice fee back and full welcome to it. He ordered her to get in the wagon. Instead I heard her footsteps crunching across the dry earth as she hurried over to me. But it was Bolt she spoke to in a whining voice. 'I was right. You didn't believe me, but I was right. I found him for you. If it weren't for me, you'd have ridden off after looking right at him. That gold is mine, by right. But I'll give you half and be more than happy. That's better than fair for you, you know it is.'

'I'd get in that wagon, were I you,' Bolt answered her coldly. 'Otherwise, once it leaves and we leave, you're left with nothing but a long walk.'

She had the sense not to argue with him, but she muttered dirty names to herself all the way back to the wagon. I heard

Dell tell her she was nothing but trouble and he'd be well rid of her at Blue Lake.

'Get him on his feet, Joff,' Bolt ordered someone.

They dashed water on me, and I got one eye open. I watched a guard pick up the slack of my chain and jerk on it. That woke a host of lesser pains. 'Get up!' she ordered me. I managed to nod. One of my teeth was loose. I could only see out of one eye. I started to lift my hands to my face to see how bad it was, but a tug on my chain prevented me. 'Does he ride or walk?' the one holding my chain asked Bolt as I staggered upright.

'I'd love to drag him, but it would slow us down too much. He rides. You double with Arno and put him on your horse. Tie him in the saddle and keep a tight grip on your horse's lead. He's playing dumb now, but he's mean and he's tricky. I don't know if he can do all the Wit things they say he can, but I don't want to find out. So keep a good grip on that lead rope. Where's Arno, anyway?'

'Off in the scrub, sir. His guts ain't too well today. He was up and down all night, dumping his sack.'

'Get him.' Bolt's tone made it plain that he wasn't interested in the man's problems. My guard hurried off, leaving me swaying on my feet. I lifted my hands to my face. I had only seen the one blow coming, but plainly there had been others. Endure, I told myself sternly. Live, and see what chances are offered you. I dropped my hands to find Bolt watching me.

'Water?' I asked in a slurry voice.

I didn't really expect any, but he turned to one of his other guards and made a small motion. A few moments later the fellow brought me a bucket of water and two dry biscuits. I drank and splashed my face. The biscuits were hard and my mouth was very sore, but I tried to get down what I could of them. I doubted I'd get much more in the day to come. I noticed then that my pouch was gone. I supposed Bolt had taken it while I was unconscious. My heart sank at the thought of Burrich's earring gone. As I gnawed gingerly at my biscuit, I wondered what he had thought of the powders in my pouch.

Bolt had us mounted and riding out before the caravan left. I caught one glimpse of Starling's face, but could not read her expression. Creece and my master carefully avoided even looking at me for fear of catching my taint. It was as if they had never known me at all.

They'd put me on a sturdy mare. My wrists were strapped tightly to the saddle pommel, making it impossible to ride comfortably or well even if I hadn't felt like a bag of broken bones. They hadn't taken the shackles off, only removed the short chain between my ankles. The longer chain to my wrists was looped up over the saddle. There was no way to avoid the chain's chafing. I had no idea what had become of my shirt, but I sorely missed it. The horse and motion would warm me somewhat, but not in any comfortable way. When a very pale-faced Arno was mounted behind his fellow guard, we set off, back toward Tradeford. My poison, I reflected ruefully, had done no more than give one man slack bowels. Such an assassin I was.

Come to me.

Would that I could, I told myself wearily as I was led off in the wrong direction. Would that I could. Every step the mare took rubbed my pains together. I wondered if my shoulder were broken or dislocated. I wondered at the strange sense of removal I felt from everything. And I wondered if I should hope to get to Tradeford alive, or try to get them to kill me before then. I could imagine no way of talking my way out of the chains, let alone fleeing in this flat land. I lowered my throbbing head and watched my hands as we rode. I shivered with the cold and the wind. I groped toward the mare's mind, but only succeeded in making her aware of my pain. She had no interest in jerking her head free and galloping away with me. She didn't much like the way I smelled of sheep, either.

The second time we halted for Arno to empty his guts, Bolt rode back and reined in beside me. 'Bastard!'

I turned my head slowly to look at him.

'How did you do it? I saw your body, and you were dead. I know a dead man when I see one. So how are you walking around again?'

My mouth wouldn't let me form words even if I'd had any. After a moment, he snorted at my silence. 'Well, don't count on it happening again. This time I'm cutting you up personally. I've got a dog at home. Eats anything. Figure he'll get rid of your liver and heart for me. What do you think of that, Bastard?'

I felt sorry for the dog, but I said nothing. When Arno staggered back to his horse, Joff helped him mount. Bolt spurred his horse back to the head of our column. We rode on.

The morning was not even half gone when Arno had his friend halt for the third time. He slipped down from the horse's back and staggered a few steps away to vomit. He doubled up, holding his aching guts as he did so, and then suddenly fell forward on his face in the dirt. One of the other guards laughed aloud, but when Arno only rolled over, groaning, Bolt ordered Joff to see what ailed him. We all watched as Joff dismounted and took water to Arno. Arno could not take the proffered water bottle and when Joff put it to his mouth the water just ran over his chin. He turned his head aside from it slowly and closed his eyes. After a moment, Joff looked up, her eyes wide with disbelief.

'He's dead, sir.' Joff's voice went a bit shrill on the words.

They scraped out a shallow grave for him and heaped rocks over the top. Two more guards had vomited before the burial was completed. Bad water was the consensus, though I caught Bolt looking at me with narrowed eyes. They hadn't bothered to take me off my horse. I hunched over my belly as if it pained me and kept my eyes down. It was no difficulty at all to look sick.

Bolt got his men remounted and we pushed on. By noon it was apparent that no one was well. One boy was swaying in his saddle as we rode. Bolt halted us for a brief rest but it turned into a longer one. No sooner would one man finish retching than another would begin. Bolt finally ordered them tersely back to their saddles despite their groaning complaints. We went on but at a gentler pace. I could smell the sour reek of sweat and puke on the woman who led my mare.

As we were going up a gentle rise, Joff fell from her saddle into the dust. I gave my mare a sharp nudge with my heels, but she only sidled sideways and put her ears back, too well-trained to gallop off with her reins dangling down from her bit. Bolt halted his troop, and every man immediately dismounted, some to puke, others to simply sink down in misery beside the horses. 'Make camp,' Bolt ordered, despite the early hour. Then he walked aside a little way, to crouch and retch dryly for a time. Joff didn't get up.

It was Bolt who walked back to me and cut my wrists loose from my saddle pommel. He gave a tug at my chain and I all but fell down on top of him. I staggered away a few steps, then sank down, my hands over my belly. He came to hunker down beside me. He grabbed the back of my neck, gripped it tightly. But I could feel his strength was not what it had been. 'What do you think, Bastard?' he asked me in a hoarse growl. He was very close to me and his breath and body stank of sickness. 'Was it bad water? Or something else?'

I made gagging sounds and leaned toward him as if to puke. He moved wearily away from me. Only two of his guards had managed to unsaddle their mounts. The others were collapsed miserably in the dirt. Bolt moved among them, cursing them uselessly but feelingly. One of the stronger guards finally began to gather the makings for a fire, while another crabbed down the line of horses, doing little more than uncinching saddles and dragging them from the horses' backs. Bolt came to fasten the hobble chain between my ankles.

Two more guards died that evening. Bolt himself dragged their bodies to one side, but could not find the strength to do more than that. The fire they had managed to kindle died soon for lack of fuel. The open night on the flat land seemed darker than anything I had ever known and the dry cold a part of the darkness. I heard the groans of the men, and one babbling about his guts, his guts. I heard the restless shifting of the unwatered horses. I thought longingly of water and warmth. Odd pains bothered me. My wrists were chafed raw from the shackles. They hurt less than my shoulder, but in an ever-present way I could not ignore. I guessed the blade-bone in my shoulder was at least fractured.

Bolt came staggering over to where I lay at dawn. His eyes were sunken, his cheeks drawn with his misery. He fell to his knees beside me and gripped my hair. I groaned. 'Are you dying, Bastard?' he asked me hoarsely. I moaned again and tried feebly to pull free of him. It seemed to satisfy him. 'Good. Good then.

Some were saying it was the Wit magic you'd put on us, Bastard.
But I think bad water can kill a man, be he Witted or honourable.
Still. Let's be sure of it, this time.'

It was my own knife that he drew out. As he dragged back on
my hair to expose my throat, I brought up my shackled hands to
crash the chain against his face. At the same time I *repelled* at
him with all the strength of Wit I could muster. He fell back
from me. He crawled a few paces away, then fell on his side in
the sand. I heard him breathing heavily. After a time, he stopped.
I closed my eyes, listening to that silence, feeling the absence of
his life like sunlight on my face.

After a time, when the day was stronger, I forced myself to
open my eye. It was harder to crawl over to Bolt's body. All
my aches had stiffened and combined to one pain that shrieked
whenever I moved. I went over his body carefully. I found Burrich's earring in his pouch. Odd to think that I stopped right
then and put it back in my ear lest I lose it. My poisons were
there as well. What wasn't in his pouch was the key to my
shackles. I started to sort my possessions out from his, but the
sun was pounding spikes into the back of my head. I simply put
his pouch at my belt. Whatever he'd had in there was mine now.
Once you've poisoned a man, I reflected, you might as well rob
him as well. Honour no longer seemed to have much to do with
my life.

Whoever had shackled me probably carried the key, I surmised.
I crawled to the next body, but found nothing in his pouch save
some Smoke herbs. I sat up, and became aware of faltering footsteps crunching over the dry earth toward me. I lifted my eyes,
squinted against the sunlight. The boy came slowly toward me,
his steps wavering. In one hand he had a waterskin. In the other
he held the key where I might see it.

A dozen steps away from me, he halted. 'Your life for mine,'
he croaked. He was swaying where he stood. I made no response.
He tried again. 'Water and the key to your bonds. Any horse you
want to take. I won't fight you. Only lift your Wit-curse off
me.'

He looked so young and pitiful standing there.

'Please,' he begged me abruptly.

I found myself shaking my head slowly. 'It was poison,' I told him. 'There's nothing I can do for you.'

He stared at me, bitterly, incredulous. 'Then I have to die? Today?' His words came out as a dry whisper. His dark eyes locked to mine. I found myself nodding.

'Damn you!' He shrieked the words, burning whatever life strength he had left. 'Then you die, too. You die right here!' He flung the key from us as far as he could, then staggered off in a feeble run, squawking and flailing at the horses.

The beasts had stood all night unpicketed, had even waited all morning hoping for grain and water. They were well-trained animals. But the smell of sickness and death and this boy's incomprehensible behaviour were too much for them. When he screamed suddenly and then fell face down almost among them, a big grey gelding threw up his head, snorting. I sent calming thoughts toward him, but he had thoughts of his own. He pranced nervously away, then suddenly decided this was a good decision and broke into a canter. The other horses followed his lead. Their hooves were not a thundering on the plain; rather they were the diminishing patter of a rainstorm as it vanishes, taking all hope of life with it.

The boy did not move again, but it was a time before he died. I had to listen to his soft weeping as I searched for the key. I wanted desperately to go look for waterskins instead, but I feared that if I turned away from the area where he had thrown it, I would never be able to decide which unremarkable stretch of sand held my salvation. So I crawled over it on my hands and knees, manacles cutting and chafing at my wrists and ankles, as I peered at the ground with my one good eye. Even after the sound of his weeping became too soft to hear, even after he died, I heard it still inside my mind. Sometimes I still can. Another young life ended senselessly, to no profit, as a result of Regal's vendetta with me. Or perhaps because of mine with him.

I did eventually find the key, just as I was certain that the setting sun would hide it forever. It was crudely made and turned very stiffly in the locks, but it worked. I opened the shackles, prying them out of my puffy flesh. The one on my left ankle had been so tight that my foot was cold and near numb. After a few minutes, pain flooded back into my foot with life. I didn't pay much attention. I was too busy seeking for water.

Most of the guards had drained their waterskins just as my poison had drained all fluids from their guts. The one the boy had shown me held only a few mouthfuls. I drank them very slowly, holding the water in my mouth for a long time before swallowing it. In Bolt's saddlebags I found a flask of brandy. I allowed myself one small mouthful of it, then capped it and set it aside. It was not much more than a day's walk back to the waterhole. I could make it. I'd have to.

I robbed the dead for what I needed. I went through the saddlebags and bundles on the heaped saddles. When I was finished, I wore a blue shirt that fit me in the shoulders, though it hung almost to my knees. I had dried meat and grain, lentils and peas, my old sword that I decided fit me best, Bolt's knife, a looking-glass, a small kettle, a mug and a spoon. I spread out a sturdy blanket and put these things on it. To them I added a change of clothing that was too large for me, but would be better than nothing. Bolt's cloak would be long on me, but it was the best made, so I took it. One of the men had carried some linen for bandaging and some salves. I took these, an empty waterskin and Bolt's flask of brandy.

I could have gone over the bodies for money and jewellery. I could have burdened myself with a dozen other perhaps-useful possessions. I found I wanted only to replace what I'd had, and to be away from the smell of the bloating bodies. I made the bundle as small and tight as I could, cinching it with leather straps from the horses' harness. When I lifted it to my good shoulder, it still felt much too heavy.

My brother?

The query seemed tentative, faint with more than distance. With disuse. As if a man spoke in a language he had not used in many years.

I live, Nighteyes. Stay with your pack, and live also.

Do you not need me? I felt his twinge of conscience as he asked this.

I always need you. I need to know you are alive and free.

I sensed his faint assent, but little more than that. After a time I wondered if I had not imagined his touch against my mind. But I felt oddly strengthened as I walked away from the bodies into the deepening night.

THIRTEEN

Blue Lake

Blue Lake is the terminus of the Cold River. It is also the name of the largest town on its shores. Early in King Shrewd's reign, the country surrounding the northeast side of the lake was renowned for its grainfields and orchards. A grape peculiar to its soil produced a wine with a bouquet no other could rival. Blue Lake wine was known not just throughout the Six Duchies, but was exported by the caravan load as far as Bingtown. Then came the long droughts and the lightning fires that followed them. The farmers and vintners of the area never recovered. Blue Lake subsequently began to rely more heavily on trade. The present-day town of Blue Lake is a trade town, where the caravans from Farrow and the Chalced States meet to barter for the goods of the Mountain folk. In summers, huge barges navigate the placid waters of the lake, but in winter the storms that sweep down from the mountains drive the barge folk from the lake and put an end to trade on the water.

The night sky was clear with an immense orange moon hanging low. The stars were true and I followed their guidance, sparing a few moments for weary wonderment that these were the same stars that had once shone down on me as I made my way home to Buckkeep. Now they guided me back to the Mountains.

I walked the night away. Not swiftly, and not steadily, but I knew that the sooner I got to water, the sooner I could ease my pains. The longer I went without water, the weaker I would become. As I walked, I moistened one of the linen bandages with Bolt's brandy, and dabbed at my face. I had looked at the damage briefly in the looking-glass. There was no mistaking that I had lost another fight. Most of it was bruising and minor cuts. I expected no new scars. The brandy stung on the numerous abrasions, but the moisture eased some of the scabbing so that I could open my mouth with minimal pain. I was hungry, but feared the salty dried meat would only accentuate my thirst.

I watched the sun come up over the great Farrow plain in a marvellous array of colours. The chill of the night eased and I loosened Bolt's cloak. I kept walking. With the increasing light, I scanned the ground hopefully. Perhaps some of the horses had headed back to the waterhole. But I saw no fresh tracks, only the crumble-edged hoofprints we had made yesterday, already being devoured by the wind.

The day was still young when I reached the water-place. I approached it cautiously, but my nose and my eyes told me it was blessedly deserted. I knew I could not depend on my luck that it would be that way long. It was a regular stopping place for caravans. My first act was to drink my fill. Then there was a certain luxury to building my own small fire, heating a kettle of water and adding lentils, beans, grain and dried meat to it. I set it on a stone close to the fire to simmer while I stripped and washed in the waterhole. It was shallow at one end, and the sun had almost warmed it. The flat blade of my left shoulder was still quite painful to touch or move, as were the chafed places on my wrists and ankles, the knot on the back of my head, my face in general . . . I left off cataloguing my pain for myself. I wasn't going to die from any of it. What more than that mattered?

The sun dried me while I shivered. I sloshed out my clothes and spread them on some brush. While the sun dried them, I wrapped myself in Bolt's cloak, drank brandy and stirred my soup. I had to add more water, and it seemed to take years for the dried beans and lentils to soften. I sat by my fire, occasionally adding some more branches or dried dung to it. After a time, I opened my eyes again and tried to decide if I were drunk, beaten or incredibly weary. I decided that was as profitable as cataloguing my pain. I ate the soup as it was, with the beans still a bit hard. I had more of the brandy with it. There wasn't much left. It was difficult to persuade myself to do it, but I cleaned the kettle and warmed more water. I cleaned the worst of my cuts, treated them with the salve, wrapped the ones that could be bandaged. One ankle looked nasty; I could not afford for it to become infected. I lifted my eyes to find the daylight fading. It seemed to have gone swiftly. With the last of my energy, I put out my fire, bundled up all my possessions, and moved away from the waterhole. I needed to sleep and I would not risk being discovered by other travellers. I found a small depression that was slightly sheltered from the wind by some tarry-smelling brush. I spread out the blanket, covered myself with Bolt's cloak and sank down into sleep.

I know that for a time I slept dreamlessly. Then I had one of those confusing dreams in which someone called my name, but I could not find who. A wind was blowing and it was rainy. I hated the sound of the blowing wind, so lonely. Then the door opened and Burrich stood in it. He was drunk. I felt both irritated and relieved. I had been waiting for him to come home since yesterday, and now he was here, he was drunk. How dared he be so?

A shivering ran over me, an almost awakening. And I knew that these were Molly's thoughts, it was Molly I was Skill-dreaming. I should not, I knew I should not, but in that edgeless dream state, I had not the will to resist. Molly stood up carefully. Our daughter was sleeping in her arms. I caught a glimpse of a small face, pink and plump, not the wrinkled red face of the newborn I'd seen before. To have already changed so much! Silently, Molly carried her to the bed and placed her gently on it. She turned up a corner of the blanket to keep the baby warm. Without turning around, she said in a low tight voice, 'I was worried. You said you'd be back yesterday.'

'I know. I'm sorry. I should have been, but . . .' Burrich's voice was hoarse. There was no spirit in it.

'But you stayed in town and got drunk,' Molly filled in coldly.

'I . . . yes. I got drunk.' He shut the door and came into the room. He moved to the fire to warm his red hands before it. His cloak was dripping and so was his hair, as if he had not bothered to pull the hood up as he walked home. He set a carry-sack down by the door. He took the soaked cloak off and sat down stiffly in the chair by the hearth. He leaned forward to rub his bad knee.

'Don't come in here when you're drunk,' Molly told him flatly.

'I don't. I'm not drunk. I know that's how you feel. I was drunk yesterday. I had a bit, earlier today, but I'm not drunk. Not now. Now I'm just . . . tired. Very tired.' He leaned forward and put his head in his hands.

'You can't even sit up straight.' I could hear the anger rising in Molly's voice. 'You don't even know when you're drunk.'

Burrich looked up at her wearily. 'Perhaps you're right,' he conceded, shocking me. He sighed. 'I'll go,' he told her. He rose, wincing as he put weight on his leg, and Molly felt a pang of guilt. He was still cold, and the shed where he slept at night was draughty and damp. But he'd brought it on himself. He knew how she felt about drunkards. Let a man have a drink or two, that was fine, she had a cup herself now and then, but to come staggering home like this and try to tell her . . .

'Can I see the baby for a moment?' Burrich asked softly. He had paused at the door. I saw something in his eyes, something Molly did not know him well enough to recognize, and it cut me to the bone. He grieved.

'She's right there, on the bed. I just got her to sleep,' Molly pointed out briskly.

'Can I hold her . . . just for a minute?'

'No. You're drunk and you're cold. If you touch her, she'll wake up. You know that. Why do you want to do that?'

Something in Burrich's face crumpled. His voice was hoarse as he said, 'Because Fitz is dead, and she's all I have left of him or his father. And sometimes . . .' He lifted a wind-roughened hand to rub his face. 'Sometimes it seems as if it's all my fault.' His voice went very soft on those words. 'I should never have let them take him from me. When he was a boy. When they first wanted to move him up to the keep, if I'd put him on a horse behind me and gone to Chivalry, maybe they'd both still be alive. I thought of that. I nearly did it. He didn't want to leave me, you know, and I made him. I nearly took him back to Chivalry instead. But I didn't. I let them have him, and they used him.'

I felt the trembling that ran suddenly through Molly. Tears stung suddenly at her own eyes. She defended herself with anger. 'Damn you, he's been dead for months. Don't try to get around me with drunkard's tears.'

'I know,' Burrich said. 'I know. He's dead.' He took a sudden deep breath, and straightened himself in that old familiar way. I saw him fold up his pains and weakness and hide them deep inside himself. I wanted to reach out and put a steadying hand on his shoulder. But that was truly me and not Molly. He started for the door, and then paused. 'Oh. I have something.' He fumbled inside his shirt. 'This was his. I . . . took it from his body, after he died. You should keep it for her, so she has something of her father's. He had this from King Shrewd.'

My heart turned over in my chest as Burrich stretched out his hand. There on his palm was my pin, with the ruby nestled in the silver. Molly just looked at it. Her lips were set in a flat line. Anger, or tight control of whatever she felt. So harsh a control even she did not know what she hid from. When she did not move toward him, Burrich set it carefully on the table.

It all came together for me suddenly. He'd gone up to the shepherd's cabin, to try again to find me, to tell me I had a daughter. Instead, what had he found? A decayed body, probably not much more than bones by now, wearing my shirt with the pin still thrust safely into the lapel. The Forged boy had been dark-haired, about my height and age.

Burrich believed I was dead. Really and truly dead. And he mourned me.

Burrich. Burrich, please, I'm not dead. Burrich, Burrich!

I rattled and raged around him, battering at him with every bit of my Skill-sense, but as always, I could not reach him. I came suddenly awake trembling and clutching at myself, feeling as if I were a ghost. He'd probably already gone to Chade. They'd both think me dead. A strange dread filled me at that thought. It seemed terribly unlucky to have all of one's friends believe one to be dead.

I rubbed gently at my temples, feeling the beginning of a Skill-headache. A moment later I realized my defences were down, that I'd been Skilling as fiercely as I was able toward Burrich. I slammed my walls up and then curled up shivering in the dusk. Will hadn't stumbled onto my Skilling that time, but I could not afford to be so careless. Even if my friends believed me dead, my enemies knew better. I must keep those walls up, must never take a chance of letting Will into my head. The new pain of the headache pounded at me, but I was too weary to get up and make tea. Besides, I had no elfbark, only the Tradeford woman's untried seeds. I drank the rest of Bolt's brandy instead, and went back to sleep. At the edge of awareness, I dreamed of wolves running. *I know you live. I shall come to you if you need me. You need but ask.* The reaching was tentative but true. I clung to the thought like a friendly hand as sleep claimed me.

In the days that followed, I walked to Blue Lake. I walked through wind carrying scouring sand in it. The scenery was rocks and scree, crackly brush with leathery leaves, low-growing fat-leaved succulents and far ahead, the great lake itself. At first the trail was no more than a scarring in the crusty surface of the plain, the cuts of hooves and the long ridges of the wagon paths fading in the ever-present cold wind. But as I drew closer to the lake, the land gradually became greener and gentler. The trail became more of a road. Rain began to fall with the wind, hard pattering rain that pelted its way through my clothes. I never felt completely dry.

I tried to avoid contact with the folk that travelled the road. There was no hiding from them in that flat country, but I did my best to look uninteresting and forbidding. Hard-riding messengers passed me on that trail, some headed toward Blue Lake, others back toward Tradeford. They did not pause for me, but that was small comfort. Sooner or later, someone was going to find five unburied King's Guards and wonder at that. And the tale of how the Bastard had been captured right in their midst would be too juicy a gossip for Creece or Starling to forbear telling. The closer I got to Blue Lake, the more folk were on the road, and I dared to hope I blended in with other travellers. For in the rich grassy pasture lands, there were holdings and even small settlements. One could see them from a great distance, the tiny hummock of a house and the wisp of smoke rising from a chimney. The land began to have more moisture in it, and brush gave way to bushes and trees. Soon I was passing orchards and then pastures with milk cows, and chickens scratching in the dirt by the side of the road. Finally I came to the town that shared the name of the lake itself.

Beyond Blue Lake was another stretch of flat land, and then the foothills. Beyond them, the Mountain Kingdom. And somewhere beyond the Mountain Kingdom was Verity.

It was a little unsettling when I considered how long it had taken me to come this far afoot compared to the first time when I had travelled with a royal caravan to claim Kettricken as bride for Verity. Out on the coast, summer was over and the winds of the winter storms had begun their lashing. Even here, it would not be long before the harsh cold of an inland winter seized the plains in the grip of the winter blizzards. I supposed the snow had already begun to fall in the Mountains. It would be deep before I reached the Mountains, and I did not know what conditions I would face as I travelled up into the heights to find Verity in the lands beyond. I did not truly know if he still lived; he had spent much strength helping me win free of Regal. Yet, *Come to me, come to me*, seemed to echo with the beating of my heart, and I caught myself keeping step to that rhythm. I would find Verity or his bones. But I knew I would not truly belong to myself again until I had done so.

Blue Lake town seems a larger city than it is because it sprawls so. I saw few dwellings of more than one storey. Most were low, long houses, with more wings added to the building as sons and daughters married and brought spouses home. Timber was plentiful on the other side of Blue Lake, so the poorer houses were of mud brick while those of veteran traders and fishers were of cedar plank roofed with wide shingles. Most of the houses were painted white or grey or a light blue, which made the structures seem even larger. Many had windows with thick, whorled panes of glass in them. But I walked past them and went to where I always felt more at home.

The waterfront was both like and unlike a seaport town. There were no high and low tides to contend with, only storm-driven waves, so many more houses and businesses were built out on pilings quite a way into the lake itself. Some fisherfolk were able to tie up literally at their own doorsteps, and others delivered their catch to a back door so that the fish merchant might sell it out the front. It seemed strange to smell water without salt or iodine riding the wind; to me the lake air smelled greenish and mossy. The gulls were different, with black-tipped wings, but in all other ways as greedy and thieving as any gulls I'd ever known. There were also entirely too many guardsmen for my liking. They prowled about like trapped cats in Farrow's gold and brown livery. I did not look in their faces, nor give them reason to notice me.

I had a total of fifteen silvers and twelve coppers, the sum of my funds and what Bolt had been carrying in his own purse. Some of the coins were a style I did not recognize, but the weights felt good in my hand. I assumed they'd be accepted. They were all I had to get me as far as the Mountains, and all I had that I might ever take home to Molly. So they were doubly valuable to me and I did not intend to part with any more than I must. But neither was I so foolish as to even consider heading into the Mountains without some provisions and some heavier clothes. So spend some I must, but I also hoped to find a way to work my passage across Blue Lake, and perhaps beyond.

In every town, there are always poorer parts, and shops or carts where folk deal in the cast-off goods of others. I wandered Blue Lake for a bit, staying always to the waterfront where trade seemed the liveliest, and eventually I came to streets where most of the shops were of mud brick even if they were roofed with shingles. Here I found weary tinkers selling mended pots and rag-pickers with their carts of well-worn wares and shops where one might buy odd crockery and the like.

From now on, I knew, my pack would be heavier, but it could not be helped. One of the first things I bought was a sturdy basket plaited from lake reeds with carry straps to go over my shoulders. I placed my present bundle inside it. Before the day was out, I had added padded trousers, a quilted jacket such as the Mountain folk wore and a pair of loose boots, like soft leather socks. They had leather lacing to secure them tightly to my calves. I also bought some woollen stockings, mismatched in colour but very thick, to wear beneath the boots. From another cart I purchased a snug woollen cap and a scarf. I bought a pair of mittens that were too large for me, obviously made by some Mountain wife to fit her husband's hands.

At a tiny herb stall, I was able to find elfbark, and so secured a small store of that for myself. In a nearby market, I bought strips of dried smoked fish, dried apples and flat cakes of very hard bread that the vendor assured me would keep well no matter how far I might travel.

I next endeavoured to book passage for myself on a barge across Blue Lake. Actually, I went to the waterfront hiring square, hoping to work my passage across. I swiftly found out no one was hiring. 'Look, mate,' a boy of thirteen loftily told me, 'everyone knows the big barges don't work the lake this time of year 'less there's gold in it. And there ain't this year. Mountain Witch shut down all the trade to the Mountains. Nothing to haul means no money worth taking the risk. And that's it, plain and simple. But even if the trade was open, you'd not find much going back and forth in winter. Summers is when the big barges can cross from this side to that. Winds can be iffy even then, but a good crew can work a barge, sail and oar, there and back again. But this time of year, it's a waste of time. The storms blow up every five days or so and the rest of the time the winds only blow one way, and if they aren't full of water, they're carrying ice and snow. It's a fine time to come from the Mountain side to Blue Lake town, if you don't mind getting wet and cold and chopping ice off your rigging all the way. But you won't find any of the big freight barges making the run from here to there until next spring. There's smaller boats that will take folk across, but passage on them is dear and for the daring. If you take ship on one of those, it's because you're willing to pay gold for the passage, and pay with your life if your skipper makes a mistake. You don't look as if you've got the coin for it, man, let alone to pay the King's tariff on the trip.'

Boy he might have been, but he knew what he spoke about. The more I listened, the more I heard the same thing. The Mountain Witch had closed the passes and innocent travellers were being attacked and robbed by Mountain brigands. For their own good, travellers and traders were being turned back at the border. War was looming. That chilled my heart, and made me all the more certain I must reach Verity. But when I insisted I had to get to the Mountains, and soon, I was advised to somehow avail myself of five gold pieces for the passage across the lake and good luck from there. In one instance, a man hinted he knew of a somewhat illegal endeavour in which I might gain that much in a month's time or less, if I were interested. I was not. I already had enough difficulties to contend with.

Come to me.

I knew that somehow, I would.

I found a very cheap inn, run down and draughty, but at least not smelling too much of Smoke. The clientele could not afford it. I paid for a bed and got a pallet in an open loft above the common room. At least heat also rose with the errant smoke from the hearth below. By draping my cloak and clothes over a chair by my pallet, I was finally able to dry them completely for the first time in days. Song and conversation, both rowdy and quiet, were a constant chorus to my first effort at sleep. There was no privacy and I finally got the hot bath I longed for at a bath-and-steamhouse five doors away. But there was a certain weary pleasure in knowing where I would sleep at night, if not how well.

I had not planned it, but it was an excellent way also to listen to the common gossip of Blue Lake. The first night I was there, I learned much more than I wished to of a certain young noble who had got not one, but two serving women with child and the intimate details of a major brawl in a tavern two streets away that had left Jake Ruddy-Nose without his namesake portion of anatomy, having had it bitten off by Crookram the Scribe.

The second night I was at the inn, I heard the rumour that twelve King's Guards had been found slaughtered by brigands half a day's ride past Jernigan's Spring. By the next night, someone had made the connection, and tales were told of how the bodies had been savaged and fed upon by a beast. I considered it quite likely that scavengers had found the bodies and fed from them. But as the tale was told, it was clearly the work of the Wit Bastard, who had changed himself into a wolf to escape his fetters of cold iron, and fallen upon the whole company by the light of a full moon to wreak his savage violence on them. As the teller described me, I had little fear of being discovered in their midst. My eyes did not glow red in firelight, nor did my fangs protrude from my mouth. I knew there would be other, more prosaic descriptions of me passed about. Regal's treatment of me had left me with a singular set of scars that were difficult to conceal. I began to grasp how difficult it had been for Chade to work with a pock-scarred face.

The beard I had once found an irritant now seemed natural to me. It grew in wiry curls that reminded me of Verity's and was just as unruly. The bruises and cuts Bolt had left on my face were mostly faded, though my shoulder still ached endlessly in the cold weather. The damp chill of the wintry air reddened my cheeks above my beard and fortunately made the edge of my scar less noticeable. The cut on my arm had long healed, but the broken nose I could do little about. It, too, no longer startled me when I saw it in a mirror. In a way, I reflected, I was as much Regal's creation now as Chade's. Chade had only taught me how to kill; Regal had made me a true assassin.

My third evening in the inn, I heard the gossip that made me cold.

'The King hisself, it was, aye, and the head Skill-wizard. Cloaks of fine wool with so much fur at the collar and hood you could scarcely see their faces. Riding black horses with gold saddles, fine as you please, and a score of brown and golds riding at their heels. Cleared the whole square so they might pass, did the guards. So I said to the fella next to me, hey, what's all this, you know? And he told me King Regal has come to town to hear for himself what the Mountain Witch has been doing to us, and to put an end to it. And more. Says he, the King himself has come to track down the Pocked Man and the Witted Bastard, for it's well known they work hand in glove with the Mountain Witch.'

I overheard this from a rheumy-eyed beggar who'd earned enough coin to buy a mug of hot cider and nurse it next to the inn fire. This bit of gossip earned him another round, while his patron told him yet again the tale of the Wit Bastard and how he had slaughtered a dozen of the King's Guard and drunk their blood for his magic. I found myself a turmoil of emotions. Disappointment that my poisons had evidently done nothing to Regal. Fear that I might be discovered by him. And a savage hope that I might have one more chance at him before I found my way to Verity.

I scarcely needed to ask any questions. The next morning found all of Blue Lake abuzz with the King's arrival. It had been many years since a crowned king had actually visited Blue Lake, and every merchant and minor noble intended to take advantage of the visit. Regal had commandeered the largest and finest inn in the town, blithely ordering that all the rooms be cleared for him and his retinue. I heard rumours that the innkeeper was both flattered and aghast at being chosen, for while it would certainly establish the reputation of his inn, there had been no mention of recompense, only a lengthy list of victuals and vintages that King Regal expected to be available.

I dressed in my new winter garments, pulled my wool cap down over my ears and set forth. The inn was found easily. No other inn at Blue Lake was three storeys high, nor could any boast so many balconies and windows. The streets outside the inn were thick with nobles attempting to present themselves to King Regal, many with comely daughters in tow. They were jostling elbow to elbow with minstrels and jugglers offering to entertain, merchants bearing samples of their finest wares as gifts, as well as those making deliveries of meat, ale, wine, bread, cheese and every other foodstuff imaginable. I did not attempt to get in, but listened mostly to those coming out. The tap-room was packed with guardsmen, and a rude lot were they, badmouthing the local ale and whores as if they got better in Tradeford. And King Regal was not receiving today, no, he felt poorly after his hasty trip, and had sent for the best stocks of merrybud to settle his complaints. Yes, there was to be a dinner this evening, a most lavish affair, my dear, only the very finest of folk to be invited. And did you see him, with that one eye gone like a dead fish's, fair give me the creeps, was I the King, I'd find a better made man to advise me, Skill or no. Such was the talk from a variety of folk leaving by front door and back, and I stored it all away as well as noting well which windows in the inn were curtained against the day's brief light. Resting, was he? I could aid him with that.

But there I found my dilemma. A few weeks ago, I would simply have slipped in and done my best to plant a knife in Regal's chest, and damn the consequences. But now I not only had Verity's Skill-command eating at me, but also the knowledge that if I survived, I had a woman and child awaiting me. I was no longer willing to trade my life for Regal's. This time, I needed a plan.

Nightfall found me on the roof of the inn. It was a cedar-shake roof, sharply peaked, and very slippery with frost. There were several wings to the inn, and I lay in the juncture of the pitched roofs between two of them, waiting. I was grateful to Regal for having chosen the largest and finest inn. I was up well above the level of the neighbouring buildings. No one was going to see me with a casual glance; they'd have to be looking for me. Even so, I waited till full dark before I half slid and half clambered down to the edge of the eaves. I lay there a time, calming my heart. There was nothing to hold on to. The roof had a generous eave, to shield the balcony below it. I would have to slide down, catch the eave with my hands in passing, and swing myself in if I was to land on the balcony. Otherwise, it was a three-storey drop to the street. I prayed I would not land upon the balcony's decoratively spiked railing.

I had planned well. I knew which rooms were Regal's bedchamber and sitting room, I knew the hour at which he would be at dinner with his guests. I had studied the door and window latches on several buildings in Blue Lake. I found nothing I was unfamiliar with. I had secured some small tools and a length of light line would provide my exit. I would enter and leave without a trace. My poisons waited in my belt pouch.

Two awls taken from a cobbler's shop earlier in the day provided my hand grips as I worked my way down the roof. I thrust them, not into the tough shakes, but between them so they caught on the overlapping shakes below. I was most nervous for the moments when part of my body dangled off the roof, with no clear view of what was happening below. At the crucial moment, I swung my legs a few times for impetus, and braced myself to let go.

Trap-trap.

I froze where I was, my legs curled under the eave of the roof while I clung to the two awls sunk between the shakes. I did not even breathe. It was not Nighteyes.

No. Small Ferret. Trap-trap. Go away. Trap-trap.

It's a trap?

Trap-trap for Wolf-Fitz. Old Blood knows, Big Ferret said, go with, go with, warn Wolf-Fitz. Rolf-Bear knew your smell. Trap-trap. Go away.

I almost cried out when a small warm body suddenly struck my leg and then ran up my clothes. In a moment, a ferret poked its whiskery face into mine. *Trap-trap*, he insisted. *Go away, go away.*

Dragging my body back up onto the roof was more difficult than lowering it down. I had a bad moment when my belt caught on the edge of the eaves. After a bit of wriggling, I got loose and slowly slithered back up onto the roof. I lay still a moment, catching my breath, while the ferret sat between my shoulders, explaining over and over. *Trap-trap.* A tiny, savagely predatory mind was his, and I sensed a great anger in him. I would not have chosen such a bond animal for myself, but someone had. Someone who was no more.

Big Ferret hurt to death. Tells little Ferret, go with, go with. Take the smell. Warn Fitz-Wolf. Trap-trap.

There was so much I wanted to ask. Somehow Black Rolf had interceded for me with the Old Blood. Since I had left Tradeford, I had feared that every Witted one I encountered would be against me. But someone had sent this small creature to warn me. And he had held to his purpose, even though his bond-partner was dead. I tried to learn more from him, but there was not much more in that small mind. Great hurt and outrage at the passing of his bond-partner. A determination to warn me. I would never learn who Big Ferret had been, nor how he had discovered this plan nor how his bond-beast had managed to conceal himself in Will's possessions. For that was who he showed me waiting silently in the room below. One-eye. The trap-trap.

Come with me? I offered him. Fierce as he was, he still seemed small and all alone. To touch minds with him was like seeing what remained of an animal cloven in two. The pain drove from his mind all save his purpose. There was room for only one other thing now.

No. Go with, go with. Hide in One-Eye's things. Warn Fitz-Wolf. Go with, go with. Find Old Blood-Hater. Hide-hide. Wait, wait. Old Blood-Hater sleep, Small Ferret kill.

He was a small animal, with a small mind. But an image of Regal, Old Blood-Hater, was fixed in that simple mind. I wondered how long it had taken Big Ferret to implant this notion firmly enough for him to carry it for weeks. Then I knew. A dying wish. The little creature had been driven all but mad by the death of his bond-human. This had been Big Ferret's last message to him. It seemed a futile errand for so small a beast.

Come with me, I suggested gently. *How can Small Ferret kill Old Blood-Hater?*

In an eye-blink he was at my throat. I actually felt the sharp teeth grip the vein in my throat. *Snip-snip when he sleeps. Drink his blood like a coney. No more Big Ferret, no more holes, no more coneys. Only Old Blood-Hater. Snip-snip.* He let go of my jugular and slipped suddenly inside my shirt. *Warm.* His small clawed feet were icy on my skin.

I had a strip of dried meat in my pocket. I lay on the roof and fed it to my fellow assassin. I would have persuaded him to come with me if I could, but I sensed he could no more change his mind than I could refuse to go to Verity. It was all he had left of Big Ferret. Pain, and a dream of revenge. *Hide-hide. Go with, go with the One-Eye. Smell the Old Blood-Hater. Wait until he sleeps. Then snip-snip. Drink his blood like a coney's.*

Yes-yes. My hunt. Trap-trap Fitz-Wolf. Go away, go away.

I took his advice. Someone had given much to send me this courier. I did not wish to face Will in any case. Much as I wanted to kill him, I knew now I was not his equal in the Skill. Nor did I wish to spoil Small Ferret's chance. There is honour among assassins, of a kind. It warmed my heart to know I was not Regal's only enemy. Soundless as the dark, I made my way over the inn roof and then down to the street by the stable.

I returned to my dilapidated inn, paid my copper and took a place at a plank table beside two other men. We ate the inn's potato and onion mainstay. When a hand fell on my shoulder, I did not startle so much as flinch. I had known there was someone behind me; I had not expected him to touch me. My hand went to my belt knife stealthily as I turned on my bench to face him. My table-mates went on eating, one noisily. No man in this inn professed an interest in any business save his own.

I looked up at Starling's smiling face and my guts turned over inside me. 'Tom!' she greeted me jovially, and claimed a seat at the table beside me. The man next to me gave over the space without a word, scraping his bowl along with himself over the stained table plank. After a moment I took my hand from my knife and put it back on the table's edge. Starling gave a small nod to that gesture. She wore a black cloak of good thick wool, trimmed with yellow embroidery. Small silver rings graced her ears now. She was entirely too pleased with herself to suit me. I said nothing, but only looked at her. She made a small gesture toward my bowl.

'Please, go on eating. I didn't mean to disturb your meal. You look as if you could use it. Short rations lately?'

'A bit,' I said softly. When she said no more, I finished the soup, wiping out the wooden bowl with the last two bites of coarse bread that had come with it. By then Starling had attracted the attention of a serving-girl, who brought us two mugs of ale. She took a long draw from hers, made a face, and then set it back on the table. I sipped at mine and found it no worse to the palate than the lake water that was the alternative.

'Well?' I said at last when she still had not spoken. 'What do you want?'

She smiled affably, toying with the handle of her mug. 'You know what I want. I want a song, one that will live after me.' She glanced about us, especially at the man who was still noisily sucking down his soup. 'Have you a room?' she asked me.

I shook my head. 'I've a pallet in the loft. And I've no songs for you, Starling.'

She shrugged her shoulders, a tiny movement. 'I've no songs for you right now, but I've got tidings that would interest you. And I've a room. At an inn some way from here. Walk there with me, and then we shall talk. There was a fine shoulder of pork roasting on the hearth fire when I left. It would likely be cooked by the time we got there.'

Every sense I had pricked up at the mention of meat. I could smell it, I could almost taste it. 'I couldn't afford it,' I told her bluntly.

'I could,' she offered blandly. 'Get your things. I'll share my room as well.'

'And if I decline?' I asked quietly.

Again she made the tiny shrugging motion. 'It's your choice.' She returned my gaze levelly. I could not decide if there was a threat in her small smile or not.

After a time I rose and went to the loft. When I returned, I had my things. Starling was waiting for me by the base of the ladder.

'Nice cloak,' she observed wryly. 'Haven't I seen it somewhere before?'

'Perhaps you have,' I said quietly. 'Would you like to see the knife that goes with it?'

Starling only smiled more broadly and made a small warding gesture with her hands. She turned and walked away, not looking back to see if I followed. Again, there was that curious mixture of trusting me and challenging me. I walked behind her.

Outside it was evening. The sharp wind that blew through the streets was full of lake damp. Even though it was not raining, I felt the moisture beading on my clothes and skin. My shoulder began to ache immediately. There were no street torches still burning; what little light there was escaped from shutters and doorsills. But Starling walked with sureness and confidence, and I followed, my eyes swiftly adjusting to the darkness.

She led me away from the waterfront, away from the poorer quarters of the town, up to the merchant streets and the inns that served the tradefolk of the town. It was not so far from the inn where King Regal was not truly staying at all. She opened an inn door that was inscribed with a tusked boar's head, and nodded to me to precede her. I did, but cautiously, glancing about well before I entered. Even after I saw no guardsmen, I was not sure if I were running my head into a snare or not.

This inn was bright and warm, with glass as well as shutters for its windows. The tables were clean, the reeds on the floor almost fresh, and the smell of roasting pork filled the air. A serving-boy walked by us with a tray full of brimming mugs, looked at me, then raised an eyebrow to Starling, obviously questioning her choice of men. Starling replied with a swooping bow, and in the process swept off her damp cloak. I followed suit more slowly, and then trailed after her as she led me to a table near the hearth.

She seated herself, then looked up at me. She was confident

she had me now. 'Let's eat before we talk, shall we?' she invited me engagingly, and indicated the chair opposite her. I took the offered seat, but turned it so my back was to the wall and I could command a view of the room. A small smile twitched at her mouth and her dark eyes danced. 'You've nothing to fear from me, I assure you. On the contrary, it is I who place myself at risk in seeking you out.'

She glanced about, then called to a boy named Oak that we wished two platters of the roast pork, some fresh bread and butter, and apple wine to go with it. He hastened off to fetch it, and served it out on our table with a charm and grace that bespoke his interest in Starling. He exchanged some small chatter with her, but noticed me very little, save to make a face of distaste as he stepped around my damp carry-basket. Another patron called him away, and Starling attacked her plate with appetite. After a moment, I sampled mine. I had not had fresh meat in some days, and the hot crackling fat on the pork almost made me dizzy with its savour. The bread was fragrant, the butter sweet. I had not tasted food this good since Buckkeep. For a second my appetite was all I considered. Then the taste of the apple wine put me suddenly in mind of Rurisk and how he had died of poisoned wine. I set my goblet carefully back on the table and recalled my caution. 'So. You sought me out, you say?'

Starling nodded as she chewed. She swallowed, wiped her mouth and added, 'And you were not easy to find, for I was not asking folk for news of you. Only looking with my own two eyes. I hope you appreciate that.'

I gave a half nod. 'And now that you have found me? What do you want of me? A bribe for your silence? If so, you'll have to content yourself with a few coppers.'

'No.' She took a sip of wine, then cocked her head to look at me. 'It is as I've told you. I want a song. It seems to me I've missed one already, not following you when you were . . . removed from our company. Though I hope you'll favour me with the details of exactly how you survived.' She leaned forward, the power of her trained voice dropping down to a confidential whisper. 'I can't tell you what a thrill that was for me, when I heard they'd found those six guardsmen dead. I had thought I was wrong about you, you see. I truly believed they had dragged off poor old Tom the shepherd as a scapegoat. Chivalry's son, I told myself, would never go as quietly as all that. And so I let you go and I didn't follow. But when I heard the news, it put a shiver up my spine as stood every hair on my body on end. "It was him," I chided myself. "The Bastard was there and I watched him taken away and never stirred a finger." You can't imagine how I cursed myself for doubting my instincts. But then I decided, well, if you survived, you'd still come here. You're on your way to the Mountains, aren't you?'

I just looked at her, a flat gaze that would have sent any Buckkeep stable-boy scuttling, and wiped the grin from the face of a Buck guard. But Starling was a minstrel. Singers of songs are never easily abashed. She went on with her meal, waiting for my answer. 'Why would I be going to the Mountains?' I asked her softly.

She swallowed, took a sip of wine, then smiled. 'I don't know why. To rally to Kettricken's aid perhaps? Whatever the reason, I suspect there's a song in it, don't you?'

A year ago, her charm and smile might have won me. A year ago I would have wanted to believe this engaging woman, I'd have wanted her to be my friend. Now she only made me tired. She was an encumbrance, a connection to avoid. I didn't answer her question. I only said, 'It's a foolish time to even think of going to the Mountains. The winds are against the trip; there will be no barge runs until spring; and King Regal has forbidden travel or trade between Six Duchies and the Mountains. No one's going to the Mountains.'

She nodded her agreement. 'I understand that the King's Guards pressed two barges and their crews a week ago, and forced them to attempt the trip. Bodies from at least one barge washed back to shore. Men and horses. No one knows if the other soldiers made it across or not. But,' she smiled with satisfaction and drew closer to me as she dropped her voice, 'I do know of one group who are still bound for the Mountains.'

'Who?' I demanded.

She made me wait a moment.

'Smugglers.' She spoke the word very softly.

'Smugglers?' I asked cautiously. It made sense. The tighter the restrictions on trade, the more profitable for those who managed it. There would always be men who would risk their lives for a profit.

'Yes. But that is not truly why I sought you out. Fitz, you must have heard that King Regal has come to Blue Lake. But it's all a lie, a trap to lure you in. You must not go there.'

'I knew that,' I told her calmly.

'How?' she demanded. She spoke quietly, but I could see how annoyed she was that I had known before she had told me.

'Perhaps a little bird told me,' I told her loftily. 'You know how it is, we Witted ones speak the tongues of all the animals.'

'Truly?' she asked me, gullible as a child.

I raised one eyebrow at her. 'It would be more interesting to me to know how you knew.'

'They tracked us down to question us. Everybody they could find from Madge's caravan.'

'And?'

'And such tales as we told. According to Creece, several sheep were lost along the way, dragged off at night without a sound. And when Tassin told of the night you tried to rape her, she said it was only then she noticed that your nails were black like a wolf's claws, and your eyes glowed in the darkness.'

'I never tried to rape her!' I exclaimed, and then hushed myself when the waiting-boy turned toward us inquiringly.

Starling leaned back in her chair. 'But such a fine tale as it made, it fair brought tears to my eyes. She showed the Skill-wizard the mark on her cheek where you'd clawed her, and said she would never have escaped you but for the wolfsbane that happened to grow nearby.'

'It sounds to me as if you should follow Tassin about if you are looking for a song,' I muttered disgustedly.

'Oh, but the tale I told was even better,' she began, then shook her head at the serving-boy as he approached. She pushed away her empty plate and glanced about the room. It was starting to fill with the evening's customers. 'I have a room upstairs,' she invited me. 'We can talk more privately there.'

This second meal had finally filled my belly. And I was warm.

I should have felt wary; but the food and the warmth were making me sleepy. I tried to focus my thoughts. Whoever these smugglers were, they offered the hope of getting to the Mountains. The only hope I'd had lately. I gave a small nod. She rose and I followed with my carry-basket.

The room upstairs was clean and warm. There was a feather bed on the bedframe, with clean wool blankets upon it. A pottery ewer of water and a washbasin rested on a small stand by the bed. Starling lit several candles in the room, driving the shadows back into the corners. Then she gestured me in. As she latched the door behind us, I sat down on the chair. Odd, how a simple, clean room could seem such a luxury to me now. Starling sat down on the bed.

'I thought you said you had no more coin than I did,' I commented.

'I didn't, back then. But since I came to Blue Lake, I've been in demand. Even more so since the guards' bodies were found.'

'How is that?' I asked her coldly.

'I'm a minstrel,' she retorted. 'And I was there when the Wit Bastard was taken. Do you think I can't tell the story of that well enough to be worth a coin or two?'

'So. I see.' I mulled over what she had told me, then asked, 'So, do I owe my glowing red eyes and fangs to your telling?'

She gave a snort of disdain. 'Of course not. Some street-corner ballad-maker came up with that.' Then she halted, and smiled almost to herself. 'But I'll admit to a bit of embroidery. As I tell it, Chivalry's Bastard was stoutly thewed and fought like a buck, a young man in the prime of his years, despite the fact that his right arm still bore the savage marks of King Regal's sword. And above his left eye, he'd a streak of white as wide as a man's hand in his hair. It took three guardsmen just to hold him, and he did not stop fighting, even when the leader of the guard struck him so hard it knocked the teeth from the front of his mouth.' She paused and waited. When I said nothing, she cleared her throat. 'You might thank me for making it a bit less likely that folk would recognize you on the street.'

'Thank you. I suppose. How did Creece and Tassin react to that?'

'They nodded all the while. My story only made theirs all the better, you see.'

'I see. But you still haven't told me how you know it was a trap.'

'They offered us money for you. If any of us had had word from you. Creece wanted to know how much. We had been taken up to the King's own sitting room for this questioning. To make us feel more important, I suppose. We were told the King himself felt ill after his long trip, and was resting right next door. While we were there, a servant came out, bringing the King's cloak and his boots to be cleaned of mud.' Starling gave me a small smile. 'The boots were immense.'

'And you know the size of the King's feet?' I knew she was correct. Regal had small hands and feet, and was more vain of them than many a court lady.

'I've never been to court. But a few of those better born at our keep had been up to Buckkeep for occasions. They spoke much of the handsome youngest prince, of his fine manners and dark, curling hair. And his tidy feet, and how well he danced on them.' She shook her head. 'I knew it was not King Regal in that room. The rest was easy to deduce. They had come to Blue Lake too promptly following the killings of the guards. They came for you.'

'Perhaps,' I conceded. I was beginning to have a high opinion of Starling's wits. 'Tell me more of the smugglers. How did you come to hear of them?'

She shook her head, smiling. 'If you strike a bargain with them, it will be through me. And I shall be a part of it.'

'How are they getting to the Mountains?' I asked.

She looked at me. 'If you were a smuggler, would you tell others what route you used?' Then she shrugged. 'I've heard gossip that smugglers have a way to cross the river. An old way. I know there was once a trade route that went upriver and then across. It fell out of favour when the river became so unpredictable. Since the bad fires a few years back, the river floods every year. When it does, it shifts in its bed. So the regular traders have come to rely more on boats than on a bridge that may or may not be intact.' She paused to gnaw briefly at a thumbnail. 'I think that at one time, there was a bridge a way upstream but after the river washed it out for the fourth consecutive year, no one had the heart to rebuild it. Someone else told me that in summer there is a pulley ferry, and that they used to cross on the ice in winter. In the years when the river freezes. Maybe they are hoping the river will freeze this year. My own thought is, when trade is stopped in one place, it starts in another. There will be a way across.'

I frowned. 'No. There must be another way to the Mountains.'

Starling seemed mildly insulted that I'd doubt her. 'Ask about it yourself, if you choose. You might enjoy waiting with the King's Guard that strut all about the waterfront. But most folk will tell you to wait for spring. A few will tell you that if you want to get there in the winter, you don't start from here. You could go south, around Blue Lake entirely. From there, I gather there are several trade routes to the Mountains, even in winter.'

'By the time I did that, it would be spring. I could get to the Mountains just as quickly by waiting it out here.'

'That's another thing I've been told,' Starling agreed smugly.

I leaned forward and put my head in my hands. *Come to me.* 'Are there no close, easy ways across that damnable lake?'

'No. If there were an easy way to cross, there would not still be guardsmen infesting the entire waterfront.'

There seemed no other choice for me. 'Where would I find these smugglers?'

Starling grinned broadly. 'Tomorrow, I will take you to them,' she promised. She rose and stretched. 'But tonight I must take myself to the Gilded Pin. I have not sung my songs there yet, but yesterday I was invited. I've heard their clients can be quite generous to travelling minstrels.' She stooped to gather up her well-wrapped harp. I rose as she picked up her still-damp cloak.

'I must be on my way as well,' I said politely.

'Why not sleep here?' she offered. 'Less chance of being recognized and a lot fewer vermin in this room.' A smile twisted the corner of her mouth as she looked at my hesitant face. 'If I wanted to sell you to the King's Guard, I could have done it. As alone as you are, FitzChivalry, you had better decide to trust someone.'

When she called me by my name, it was as if something twisted inside me. And yet, 'Why?' I asked her softly. 'Why do you aid me? And don't tell me it's the hope of a song that may never be.'

'That shows how little you understand minstrels,' she said. 'There is no more powerful lure for one than that. But I suppose there is more. No. I know there is.' She looked up at me suddenly, her eyes meeting mine squarely. 'I had a little brother. Jay. He was a guard stationed at the Antler Island Tower. He saw you fight the day the Raiders came.' She gave a brief snort of laughter. 'Actually, you stepped over him. You sank your axe into the man who had just struck him down. And waded deeper into the battle without even a glance back at him.' She looked at me from the corner of her eyes. 'That is why I sing "Antler Tower Raid" slightly different from any other minstrel. He told me of it, and I sing you as he saw you. A hero. You saved his life.'

She looked abruptly aside from me. 'For a time, anyway. He died later, fighting for Buck. But for a time, he lived because of your axe.' She stopped speaking, and swung her cloak around her shoulders. 'Stay here,' she told me. 'Rest. I won't be back until late. You can have the bed until then, if you want.'

She whisked out the door without waiting for a reply. I stood for a time staring at the closed door. FitzChivalry. Hero. Just words. But it was as if she had lanced something inside me, drained away some poison and now I could heal. It was the strangest feeling. Get some sleep, I advised myself. I actually felt as if I could.

FOURTEEN

Smugglers

There are few spirits so free as those of travelling minstrels, at least within the Six Duchies. If a minstrel is sufficiently talented, he can expect almost all rules of conduct to be suspended for him. They are permitted to ask the most prying of questions as a normal part of their trade. Almost without exception, a minstrel can presume hospitality anywhere from the King's own table to the lowliest hovel. They seldom marry in youth, though it is not unusual for them to bear children. Such children are free of the stigma of other bastards, and are frequently keep-raised to become minstrels themselves. It is expected of minstrels that they will consort with outlaws and rebels as well as nobles and merchants. They carry messages, bring news and hold in their long memories many an agreement and promise. At least, so it is in times of peace and plenty.

Starling came in so late, Burrich would have regarded it as early morning. I was awake the instant she touched the latch. I rolled quickly off her bed as she came in, then wrapped myself well in my cloak and lay down on the floor. 'FitzChivalry,' she greeted me fuzzily, and I could smell the wine on her breath. She stripped off her damp cloak, looked sideways at me, then spread it over me as an extra covering. I closed my eyes.

She dropped her outer clothing to the floor behind me with a fine disregard for my presence. I heard the give of the bed as she threw herself onto it. 'Um. Still warm,' she muttered, shouldering into the bedding and pillows. 'I feel guilty, taking your warm spot.'

Her guilt could not have been too sharp-edged, for in just a matter of moments her breathing went deep and even. I followed her example.

I awoke very early and left the inn. Starling didn't stir as I let myself out of her room. I walked until I found a bathhouse. The baths were almost deserted at this hour of the day; I had to wait while the first day's water was warmed. When it was ready, I stripped down and clambered gingerly in. I eased the ache in my shoulder in the deep, hot tub. I washed myself. Then I leaned back in the hot water and silence and thought.

I didn't like taking up with the smugglers. I didn't like linking up with Starling. I couldn't see any other choice. I could not think of how I'd bribe them to take me. I had little enough coin. Burrich's earring? I pondered. For a long time, I lay up to my chin in the water and refused to consider it. *Come to me.* I would find another way, I swore to myself. I would. I thought of what I had felt back in Tradeford when Verity had intervened to save me. That blast of Skill had left Verity without reserves. I did not know his situation, only that he had not hesitated to expend all he had for my sake. And if I had to choose between parting with Burrich's earring and going to Verity, I would choose Verity. Not because he had Skill-summoned me, nor even for the oath I had sworn to his father. For Verity.

I stood up and let the water stream off me. I dried off, spent a few minutes attempting to trim my beard, gave it up as a bad job, and went back to the Boar's Head. I had one bad moment on my way back to the inn. A wagon passed me as I strode along, none other than the wagon of Dell the puppeteer. I kept walking briskly and the young journeyman driving the wagon gave no sign of noticing me. Nonetheless, I was glad to reach the inn and get inside.

I found a corner table near the hearth and had the serving-boy bring me a pot of tea and a loaf of morning bread. This last proved to be a Farrow concoction full of seeds and nuts and bits of fruit. I ate slowly, waiting for Starling to descend. I was both impatient to be out to meet these smugglers, and reluctant to put myself in Starling's power. As the morning hours dragged by, I caught the serving-boy looking oddly at me twice. The third time I caught his stare, I returned it until he blushed suddenly and looked aside. I divined then the reason for his interest. I'd spent the night in Starling's room, and no doubt he wondered what would possess her to share quarters with such a vagabond. But it was still enough to make me uncomfortable. The day was more than halfway to noon anyway. I rose and went up the stairs to Starling's door.

I knocked quietly and waited. But it took a second round of louder knocking before I heard a sleepy reply. After a bit she came to the door, opened it a crack, then yawned at me and motioned me in. She wore only her leggings and a recently donned oversized tunic. Her curly dark hair was tousled all about her face. She sat down heavily on the edge of her bed, blinking her eyes as I closed and fastened the door behind me. 'Oh, you took a bath,' she greeted me, and yawned again.

'Is it that noticeable?' I asked her testily.

She nodded at me affably. 'I woke up once and thought you'd just left me here. I wasn't worried about it, though. I knew you couldn't find them without me.' She rubbed her eyes, and then looked at me more critically. 'What happened to your beard?'

'I tried to trim it. Without much success.'

She nodded in agreement. 'But it was a good idea,' she said comfortingly. 'It might make you look a bit less wild. And it might prevent Creece or Tassin or anyone else from our caravan from recognizing you. Here. I'll help you. Sit on that chair. Oh, and open the shutters, let some light in here.'

I did as she suggested, without much enthusiasm. She arose from the bed, stretched like a cat, and rubbed her eyes. She took a few moments to splash some water on her face, then worried her own hair back into order and fastened it with a couple of small combs. She belted the tunic to give it a shape, then slipped on her boots and laced them up. In a remarkably short time she was presentable. Then she came to me, and taking hold of my chin turned my face back and forth in the light with no shyness at all. I could not be as nonchalant as she was.

'Do you always blush so easily?' she asked me with a laugh. 'It's rare to see a Buck man able to flush so red. I suppose your mother must have been fair-skinned.'

I could think of nothing to say to that, so I sat silently as she rummaged in her pack and came up with a small pair of shears. She worked quickly and deftly. 'I used to cut my brothers' hair,' she told me as she worked. 'And my father's hair and beard, after my mother died. You've a nice shape to your jaw, under all this brush. What have you been doing with it, just letting it grow out anyway it pleased?'

'I suppose,' I muttered nervously. The scissors were flashing away right under my nose. She paused and brushed briskly at my face. A substantial amount of curly black hair fell to the floor. 'I don't want my scar to be visible,' I warned her.

'It won't,' she said calmly. 'But you will have lips and a mouth instead of a gap in your moustache. Tilt your chin up. There. Do you have a shaving blade?'

'Only my knife,' I admitted nervously.

'We'll make do then,' she said comfortingly. She walked to the door, flung it open, and used the power of a minstrel's lungs to bellow for the serving-boy to bring her hot water. And tea. And bread and some rashers of bacon. When she came back into the room, she cocked her head and looked at me critically. 'Let's cut your hair, too,' she proposed. 'Take it down.'

I moved too slowly to satisfy her. She stepped behind me, tugged off my kerchief and freed my hair from the leather thong. Unbound, it fell to my shoulders. She took up her comb and curried my hair roughly forward. 'Let's see,' she muttered as I gritted my teeth to her rough combing.

'What do you propose?' I asked her, but hanks of hair were already falling to the floor. Whatever she had decided was rapidly becoming a reality. She pulled hair forward over my face, then cut if off square above my eyebrows, tugged her comb through the rest of it a few times, then cut it off at jaw length. 'Now,' she told me, 'you look a bit more like Farrow merchant stock. Before you were obviously a Buckman. Your colouring is still Buck, but now your hair and clothes are Farrow. As long as you don't talk, folk won't be certain where you're from.' She considered a moment, then went to work again on the hair above my brow. After a moment she rummaged around and gave me a mirror. 'The white will be a lot less noticeable now.'

She was right. She had trimmed out most of the white hair,

and pulled forward black hair to fall over the stubble. My beard now hugged my face as well. I nodded a grudging approval. There was a knock at the door. 'Leave it outside!' Starling called through the door. She waited a few moments, then fetched in her breakfast and the hot water. She washed, then suggested I put a good edge on my knife while she ate. I did so, wondering as I honed the blade if I felt flattered or irritated at her refashioning of me. She was beginning to remind me of Patience. She was still chewing as she came to take the knife from my hand. She swallowed, then spoke.

'I'm going to give your beard a bit more shape. You'll have to keep it up, though, I'm not going to shave you every day,' she warned me. 'Now damp your face down well.'

I was substantially more nervous as she brandished the knife, especially as she worked near my throat. But when she was finished and I took up the looking-glass, I was amazed at the changes she had wrought. She had defined my beard, confining it to my jaw and cheek. The square-cut hair hanging over my brow made my eyes look deeper. The scar on my cheek was still visible, but it followed the line of my moustache and was less noticeable. I ran my hand lightly over my beard, pleased with how much less of it there was. 'It's quite a change,' I told her.

'It's a vast improvement,' she informed me. 'I doubt that Creece or Dell would recognize you now. Let's just be rid of this.' She gathered up the hair cuttings and opened the window to fling them out onto the wind. Then she shut it and brushed off her hands.

'Thank you,' I said awkwardly.

'You're welcome,' she told me. She glanced about the room, and breathed a small sigh. 'I'm going to miss that bed,' she told me. She set to packing with a swift efficiency. She caught me watching her and grinned. 'When you're a minstrel who wanders, you learn to do this quickly and well.' She tossed in the last items, then laced her pack shut. She swung it to one shoulder. 'Wait for me at the bottom of the back stairs,' she commanded. 'While I go and settle my bill.'

I did as she bade me, but waited substantially longer in the cold and wind than I had expected. Eventually she emerged, rosy-cheeked and ready for the day. She stretched herself like a little cat. 'This way,' she directed me.

I had expected to shorten my stride to accommodate her, but found that we matched pace easily. She glanced across at me as we strode away from the merchants' sector of town, and headed to the northern outskirts. 'You look different today,' she informed me. 'And it's not just the haircut. You've made up your mind about something.'

'I have,' I agreed with her.

'Good,' she said warmly as she took my arm companionably. 'I hope it's to trust me.' I glanced at her and said nothing. She laughed, but did not release my arm.

The wooden walkways of the merchants' section of Blue Lake soon disappeared and we walked in the street past houses that huddled against each other as if seeking shelter from the cold. The wind was a constant chill push against us as we strode along cobbled streets that gave way eventually to roads of packed earth that ran past small farmsteads. The road was rutted and muddy from the rains of the last few days. This day at least was fair, even if the blustery wind was cold. 'Is there much farther to go?' I finally asked of her.

'I'm not certain. I'm simply following directions. Watch for three stacked rocks at the side of the road.'

'What do you really know of these smugglers?' I demanded.

She shrugged a bit too casually. 'I know they are going to the Mountains, when no one else is. And I know they are taking the pilgrims with them.'

'Pilgrims?'

'Or whatever you wish to call them. They go to honour Eda's shrine in the Mountain Kingdom. They had bought passage on a barge earlier in the summer. But then the King's Guards claimed all the barges for their own use and shut down the borders to the Mountain Kingdom. The pilgrims have been stuck in Blue Lake since then, trying to find a way to continue their journey.'

We came to the three stacked rocks and a weedy track through a rocky, brambly pasture surrounded by a rock-and-pole fence. A few horses were grazing disconsolately. I noted with interest they were Mountain-bred, small and patchy-coated at this time of year.

A little house was set well back from the road. It was built of river-rock and mortar, with a sod roof. The small outbuilding behind it matched it. A thin trickle of smoke escaped its chimney, to be swiftly dispersed by the wind. A man sat on the fence, whittling at something. He lifted his eyes to regard us and evidently decided we were no threat. He made no challenge to us as we passed him and went to the door of the cottage. Just outside the cottage, fat pigeons cooed and strutted in a cote. Starling knocked at the door, but the answer came from a man who walked around the corner of the house. He had rough brown hair and blue eyes and was dressed like a farmer. He carried a brimming bucket of warm milk. 'Who do you seek?' he greeted us.

'Nik,' Starling replied.

'I know no Nik,' the man said. He opened the door and went into the house. Starling boldly followed him, and I trailed her with less confidence. My sword was at my hip. I put my hand closer to the hilt but not on it. I didn't want to provoke a challenge.

Inside the hut, a driftwood fire burned in the hearth. Most, but not all of the smoke was going up the chimney. A boy and a spotted kid shared a pile of straw in one corner. He regarded us with wide blue eyes, but said nothing. Smoked hams and sides hung low from the rafters. The man carried the milk to a table where a woman was chopping up fat yellow roots. He set the bucket down beside her work and turned to us mildly.

'I think you've come to the wrong house. Try down the road a way. Not the next house. That's where Pelf lives. But beyond, maybe.'

'Thank you kindly. We shall.' Starling smiled round at them all, and went to the door. 'Coming, Tom?' she asked me. I nodded pleasantly at the folk and followed her. We left the house and walked up the lane. When we were well away I asked her, 'Now what?'

'I'm not precisely sure. From what I overheard, I think we go to Pelf's house and ask for Nik.'

'From what you overheard?'

'You don't think I have personal knowledge of smugglers, do you? I was in the public baths. Two women were talking as they bathed. Pilgrims on their way to the Mountains. One was saying it might be their last chance at a bath for a while, and the other was saying she didn't care as long as they finally got to leave Blue Lake. Then one told the other where they were supposed to meet the smugglers.'

I said nothing. I suppose my expression said it all, for Starling asked me indignantly, 'Do you have any better ideas? This will either work out or it won't.'

'It may work out to us with our throats cut.'

'Then go back to town and see if you can do better.'

'I think if we did that, the man following us would decide we were certainly spies and do more than just follow us. Let us go on to Pelf, and see what comes of it. No, don't look back.'

We returned to the road and walked to the next farmstead. The wind had become stronger and I tasted snow on it. If we did not find this Nik soon, it was going to be a long, cold walk back to town.

Someone had once cared about this next farm. Once there had been a line of silver birches to either side of the drive. Now they were brittle scarecrows of trees, their branches long bare, bark peeling in the wind. A few survivors wept yellow coin leaves in the wind. Extensive pastures and fields had been fenced, but whatever stock they had held was long gone. The weedy fields went unplanted, the thistly pastures ungrazed. 'What happened to this land?' I demanded as we walked past the desolation.

'Years of drought. Then, a summer of fire. Out beyond these farmsteads, the riverbanks used to be covered with open oak forests and grazing land. Here, these were dairy farms. But out there, smallholders ran their goats in the free pasturage, and their haragars scavenged under the oaks for acorns. I've heard it was magnificent hunting as well. Then came the fire. It burned for over a month they say, so that a man could scarcely breathe and the river ran black with ash. Not just the forests and wild meadows, but hayfields and homes were torched by the flying sparks. After the years of drought, the river was no more than a trickle of itself. There was nowhere to flee from the fire. And after the fire came more hot dry days. But the winds that blew carried dust now as well as ash. Smaller streams choked with it. It blew until the rains finally came that fall. All the water that folk had prayed for for years came in one season. Floods of it. And when the water went down, well, you see what was left. Washed-out gravelly soil.'

'I recall hearing something of the sort.' It had been a conversation long ago. Someone . . . Chade? . . . had told me that the people held the King accountable for everything, even droughts and fires. It had meant little to me then, but to these farmers it must have seemed like the end of the world.

The house, too, spoke of a loving hand and better times. It was two storeys, built of timber, but its paint was long faded. Shutters were closed tight over the windows in the upper storey. There were two chimneys at either end of the house, but one was losing its stones. Smoke rose from the other one. A young woman stood before the door of the house. A fat grey pigeon perched on her hand and she was stroking it lightly. 'Good day,' she bid us in a pleasantly low voice as we approached. Her tunic was leather over a loose cream shirt of wool. She wore leather trousers as well, and boots. I put her age at about twelve, and knew she was some kin to the folk in the other house by her eyes and hair.

'Good day,' Starling returned to her. 'We are looking for Nik.'

The girl shook her head. 'You have come to the wrong house. There is no Nik here. This is Pelf's house. Perhaps you should seek further down the road.' She smiled at us, no more than puzzlement on her face.

Starling gave me an uncertain glance. I took her arm. 'We have been given poor directions. Come, let us take ourselves back to town and try again.' At that time I hoped no more than to get ourselves out of the situation.

'But . . .' she objected in confusion.

I had a sudden inspiration. 'Shush. We were warned these are not people to take lightly. The bird must have gone astray, or a hawk taken it. There is nothing more to be done here today.'

'A bird?' the girl piped suddenly.

'Only a pigeon. Good day to you.' I put my arm about Starling and turned her firmly. 'We did not mean to bother you.'

'Whose pigeon?'

I let my eyes meet hers for a moment. 'A friend of Nik's. Do not let it concern you. Come, Starling.'

'Wait!' the girl said suddenly. 'My brother is inside. Perhaps he knows this Nik.'

'I would not wish to bother him,' I assured her.

'No bother.' The bird on her hand stretched out his wings as she gestured to the door with it. 'Come inside out of the cold for a bit.'

'It is a cold day,' I conceded. I turned to confront the whittler just as he was emerging from the line of birches. 'Perhaps we should all go inside.'

'Perhaps.' The girl grinned at my shadow's discomfiture.

Within the door was a bare entry hall. The fine inlaid wood of the floor was scuffed and had gone unoiled for some time. Lighter spaces on the walls showed where paintings and tapestries had once hung. A bare staircase led to the upper floor. There was no light save what came in the thick windows. Inside, there was no wind, but it was not much warmer. 'Wait here,' the girl told us, and entered a chamber to our right, closing the door firmly behind her. Starling stood a bit closer to me than I wished. The whittler watched us expressionlessly.

Starling took a breath. 'Hush,' I told her before she could speak. Instead, she took my arm. I made the excuse of stooping to adjust my boot. As I straightened, I turned and put her on my left side. She immediately took hold of that arm. It seemed a very long time before the door opened. A tall man, brown-haired and blue-eyed, came out. He was dressed like the girl in leathers. A very long knife hung at his belt. The girl came on his heels, looking petulant. He had rebuked her, then. He scowled at us and demanded, 'What's this about?'

'My mistake, sir,' I said immediately. 'We were seeking one named Nik, and obviously we have come to the wrong house. Your pardon, sir.'

He spoke reluctantly. 'I've a friend with a cousin named Nik. I could give word of you to him, perhaps.'

I squeezed Starling's hand for silence. 'No, no, we wouldn't wish to trouble you. Unless you'd like to tell us where we could find Nik himself.'

'I could take a message,' he offered again. But it was not really an offer.

I scratched at my beard and considered. 'I've a friend whose cousin wished to send something across the river. He had heard that Nik might know someone who could take it for him. He promised my friend's cousin that he would send a bird, to let Nik know we were coming. For a fee, of course. That was all, a paltry matter.'

He gave a slow nod. 'I've heard of folks hereabouts who do such things. It's dangerous work, yes, treasonous work, too. They'd pay with their heads if the King's Guards caught them.'

'That they would,' I agreed readily. 'But I doubt that my friend's cousin would do business with the kind of folk who'd get caught. That was why he was wishing to speak to Nik.'

'And who was it sent you here to seek this Nik?'

'I forget,' I said coolly. 'I'm afraid I'm rather good at forgetting names.'

'Are you?' the man asked consideringly. He glanced at his sister and gave a small nod. 'May I offer you some brandy?'

'That would be most welcome,' I told him.

I managed to pry my arm free of Starling as we entered the chamber. As the door shut behind us, Starling sighed in the welcome warmth. This room was as opulent as the other was bare. Rugs coated the floor, tapestries lined the walls. There was a heavy oak table with a branch of white candles for illumination. A fire blazed in the huge hearth before a half circle of comfortable chairs. It was to this area our host led us. He snagged a glass decanter of brandy as he passed the table. 'Find some cups,' he peremptorily ordered the girl. She seemed to take no offence at it. I guessed his age at about twenty-five. Older brothers are not the kindest of heroes. She handed the whittler her pigeon, and gestured both of them out before she went to find cups.

'Now. You were saying,' he offered when we were settled before the fire.

'Actually, you were saying,' I suggested.

He was silent as his sister came back with cups. He passed them to us as he filled them and the four of us raised cups together.

'To King Regal,' he suggested.

'To my king,' I offered affably, and drank. It was good brandy, one Burrich would have appreciated.

'King Regal would see folk like our friend Nik swinging,' the man suggested.

'Or more likely in his Circle,' I suggested. I gave a small sigh. 'It's a dilemma. On the one hand, King Regal threatens his life. On the other hand, without King Regal's embargo on the mountain, what livelihood would Nik pursue? I heard all that his family's holdings grow these days is rocks.'

The man nodded in commiseration. 'Poor Nik. A man must do something to survive.'

'That he must,' I agreed. 'And sometimes to survive, a man must cross a river, even if his king forbids it.'

'Must he?' the man asked. 'Now that's a bit different from sending something across the river.'

'Not that different,' I told him. 'If Nik is good at his trade, the one should no more tax him than the other. And I'd heard Nik was good.'

'The best,' the girl said with quiet pride.

Her brother shot her a warning glance. 'What would this man be offering to cross?' he asked quietly.

'He'd offer it to Nik himself,' I said as softly.

For a few breaths the man looked into the fire. Then he stood and extended a hand. 'Nik Holdfast. My sister Pelf.'

'Tom,' I said.

'Starling,' the minstrel added.

Nik held his cup aloft again. 'To a bargain in the making,' he suggested, and again we drank. He sat and asked immediately, 'Shall we speak plainly?'

I nodded. 'The plainest possible. We had heard that you were taking a group of pilgrims over the river and across the border into the Mountain Kingdom. We seek the same service.'

'At the same price,' Starling chimed in smoothly.

'Nik, I don't like this,' Pelf broke in suddenly. 'Someone's tongue has been wagging too freely. I knew we should never have agreed to the first lot. How do we know . . .'

'Hush. I'm the one taking the risks, so I'll be the one to say what I will or will not do. You've naught to do but wait here and mind things while I'm gone. And see that your own tongue doesn't wag.' He turned back to me. 'It will be a gold each, up front. And another on the other side of the river. A third at the Mountain border.'

'Ah!' The price was shocking. 'We can't . . .' Starling dug her nails suddenly into my wrist. I shut my mouth.

'You will never convince me the pilgrims paid that much,' Starling said quietly.

'They have their own horses and wagons. Food supplies, too.' He cocked his head at us. 'But you look to be folk travelling with what's on your backs and no more.'

'And a lot easier to conceal than a wagon and team. We'll give you one gold now, and one at the Mountain border. For both of us,' Starling offered.

He leaned back in his chair and pondered a moment. Then he poured more brandy all round. 'Not enough,' he said regretfully. 'But I suspect it's all you have.'

It was more than I had. I hoped, perhaps, it was what Starling had. 'Take us over the river for that much,' I offered. 'From there, we're on our own.'

Starling kicked me under the table. She seemed to be speaking only to me as she said, 'He's taking the others to the Mountain border and across it. We may as well enjoy the company that far.' She turned back to Nik. 'It will have to take us all the way to the Mountains.'

Nik sipped at his brandy. He sighed heavily. 'I'll see your coin, begging your pardon, before we say it's a bargain.'

Starling and I exchanged glances. 'We'll require a private moment,' she said smoothly. 'Begging your pardon.' She rose and, taking my hand, led me to the corner of the room. Once there she whispered, 'Have you never bargained before in your life? You give too much, too fast. Now. How much coin do you truly have?'

For answer, I upended my purse in my hand. She picked through the contents as swiftly as a magpie stealing grain. She hefted the coins in her hand with a practised air. 'We're short. I thought you'd have more than this. What's that?' Her finger jabbed at Burrich's earring. I closed my hand around it before she could pick it up.

'Something very important to me.'

'More important than your life?'

'Not quite,' I admitted. 'But close. My father wore it, for a time. A close friend of his gave it to me.'

'Well, if it must go, I'll see that it goes dearly.' She turned away from me without another word and walked back to Nik. She took her seat, tossed the rest of her brandy down and waited for me. When I was seated, she told Nik, 'We'll give you what coin we have now. It's not as much as you ask. But at the Mountain border, I'll give you all my jewellery as well. Rings, earrings, all of it. What say you?'

He shook his head slowly. 'It's not enough for me to risk hanging over.'

'What's the risk?' Starling demanded. 'If they discover you with the pilgrims, you'll hang. You've already been paid for that risk in what they gave you. We don't increase your risk, only your supply burden. Surely it's worth that.'

He shook his head, almost reluctantly. Starling turned and held out her hand to me. 'Show it to him,' she said quietly. I felt almost sick as I opened my pouch and fingered out the earring.

'What I have might not seem like much at first glance,' I told him. 'Unless a person were knowledgeable about such things. I am. I know what I have and I know what it's worth. It's worth whatever trouble you'd have to go through for us.'

I spread it out on my palm, the fine silver net trapping the sapphire within. Then I picked it up by the pin and held it before the dancing fire. 'It's not just the silver or the sapphire. It's the workmanship. Look how supple is the silver net, see how fine the links.'

Starling reached one fingertip to touch it. 'King-in-Waiting Chivalry once owned it,' she added respectfully.

'Coins are more easily spent,' Nik pointed out.

I shrugged. 'If coins to spend are all a man wants, that is true. Sometimes there is pleasure in the owning of something, pleasure greater than coins in the pocket. But when it is yours, you could change it for coins, if you wished. Were I to attempt it now, in haste, I'd get but a fraction of its worth. But a man with your connections, and the time to bargain well, could get well over four golds for it. But if you'd rather, I could go back to town with it and . . .'

Greed had kindled in his eyes. 'I'll take it,' he conceded.

'On the other side of the river,' I told him. I lifted the jewellery and restored it to my ear. Let him look at it each time he looked at me. I made it formal. 'You undertake to get us both safely to the other side of the river. And when we get there, the earring is yours.'

'As your sole payment,' Starling added quietly. 'Though we will allow you to hold all our coins until then. As a surety.'

'Agreed, and here's my hand on it,' he acknowledged. We shook hands.

'When do we leave?' I asked him.

'When the weather's right,' he said.

'Tomorrow would be better,' I told him.

He rose slowly. 'Tomorrow, eh? Well, if the weather's right tomorrow, then is when we'll leave. Now I've a few things I need to attend to. I'll have to excuse myself, but Pelf can see to you here.'

I had expected to walk back to town for the night, but Starling bargained with Pelf, her songs for a meal for us, and then to prepare us a room for the night. I was a bit ill at ease to sleep among strangers, but reflected it might actually be safer than going back to town. If the food Pelf cooked for us was not as fine as we had enjoyed at Starling's inn the night before, it was still far better than onion and potato soup. There were thick slices of fried ham and apple sauce and a cake made with fruits and seeds and spices. Pelf brought us beer to go with it and joined us at table, speaking casually of general topics. After we'd eaten, Starling played a few songs for the girl, but I found I could scarcely keep my eyes open. I asked to be shown to a room, and Starling said she, too, was weary.

Pelf showed us to a chamber above Nik's elaborate room. It had been a very fine room once, but I doubted it had been regularly used for years. She had started a fire in the hearth there, but the long chill of disuse and the must of neglect still filled the room. There was an immense bed with a featherbed on it and greying hangings. Starling sniffed critically at it, and as soon as Pelf left, she busied herself in draping the blankets from the bed over a bench and setting it by the fire. 'They will both air and warm that way,' she told me knowledgeably.

I had been barring the door, and checking the latches on the windows and shutters. They all seemed sound. I was suddenly too weary to reply. I told myself it was the brandy followed by the beer. I dragged one chair to wedge it against the door while Starling watched me with amusement. Then I came back to the fire and sank down onto the blanket-draped bench and stretched my legs to the warmth. I toed my boots off. Well. Tomorrow I'd be on my way to the Mountains.

Starling came to sit beside me. For a time she didn't speak. Then she lifted a finger and batted at my earring with it. 'Was it truly Chivalry's?' she asked me.

'For a while.'

'And you'd give it up to get to the Mountains. What would he say?'

'Don't know. Never knew the man.' I suddenly sighed. 'By all accounts, he was fond of his little brother. I don't think he'd begrudge me spending it to get to Verity.'

'Then you do go to seek out your king.'

'Of course.' I tried in vain to stifle a yawn. Somehow it seemed foolish to deny it now. 'I'm not sure it was wise to mention Chivalry to Nik. He might make a connection.' I turned to look at her. Her face was too close. I couldn't bring her features into focus. 'But I'm too sleepy to care,' I added.

'You've no head for merrybud,' she laughed.

'There was no Smoke tonight.'

'In the cake. She told you it was spiced.'

'Is that what she meant?'

'Yes. That's what spiced means all over Farrow.'

'Oh. In Buck it means there's ginger. Or citron.'

'I know that.' She leaned against me and sighed. 'You don't trust these people, do you?'

'Of course not. They don't trust us. If we trusted them, they'd have no respect for us. They'd think us gullible fools, the sort who get smugglers into trouble by talking too much.'

'But you shook hands with Nik.'

'I did. And I believe he will keep his word. As far as it goes.'

We both fell silent, thinking about that. After a time, I started awake again. Starling sat up beside me. 'I'm going to bed,' she announced.

'Me, too,' I replied. I claimed a blanket and started to roll up in it by the fire.

'Don't be ridiculous,' she told me. 'That bed's big enough for four. Sleep in a bed while you can, for I bet we aren't going to see another one soon.'

I took very little persuading. The featherbed was deep, if a trifle smelly from damp. We each had a share of the blankets. I knew I should retain some caution but the brandy and the merrybud had unloosed the knot of my will. I fell into a very deep sleep.

Towards morning, I awoke once when Starling threw an arm over me. The fire had burned out and the room was cold. In her sleep she had migrated across the bed and was pressed up against my back. I started to ease away from her but it was too warm and companionable. Her breath was against the back of my neck. There was a woman smell to her that was not a perfume but a part of her. I closed my eyes and lay very still. Molly. The sudden desperate longing I felt for her was like a pain. I clenched my teeth to it. I willed myself into sleep again.

It was a mistake.

The baby was crying. Crying and crying. Molly was in her nightrobe with a blanket draped over her shoulders. She looked haggard and weary as she sat by the fire and rocked her endlessly. Molly sang a little song to her, over and over, but the tune had long since gone out of it. She turned her head slowly to the door as Burrich opened it. 'May I come in?' he asked quietly.

She nodded him in. 'What are you doing awake at this hour?' she asked him tiredly.

'I could hear her crying clear out there. Is she ill?' He went to the fire and poked it up a little. He added another piece of wood, then stooped to look in the baby's small face.

'I don't know. She just cries and cries and cries. She doesn't

even want to nurse. I don't know what's wrong with her.' There
was misery in Molly's voice far past the use of tears.

Burrich turned to her. 'Let me take her for a while. You go lie
down and try to rest a bit, or you'll both be ill. You can't do this
night after night.'

Molly looked up at him without comprehension. 'You want to
take care of her? You'd truly do that?'

'I may as well,' he told her wryly. 'I can't sleep through her
crying.'

Molly stood up as if her back ached. 'Warm yourself first. I'll
make some tea.'

For answer he took the babe from her arms. 'No, you go back
to bed for a while. No sense in all of us not sleeping.'

Molly seemed unable to grasp it. 'You truly don't mind if I go
back to bed?'

'No, go ahead, we'll be fine. Go on, now.' He settled the blanket
about her and then set the infant to his shoulder. She looked
very tiny with his dark hands against her. Molly walked slowly
across the room. She looked back at Burrich but he was looking
into the baby's face. 'Hush now,' he told her. 'Hush.'

Molly clambered into bed and pulled the blankets up over
herself. Burrich did not sit down. He stood before the fire, rocking
slightly on his feet as he patted the baby's back slowly.

'Burrich,' Molly called to him quietly.

'Yes?' He did not turn to look at her.

'There's no sense your sleeping in that shed in this weather.
You should move inside for the winter, and sleep by the hearth.'

'Oh. Well. It's not so very cold out there. It's all in what you're
used to, you know.'

A small silence fell.

'Burrich. I would feel safer, were you closer.' Molly's voice was
very small.

'Oh. Well. Then I suppose I shall be. But there's nothing you
need fear tonight. Go to sleep, now. Both of you.' He bent his
head and I saw his lips brush the top of the baby's head. Very
softly he began singing to her. I tried to make out the words, but
his voice was too deep. Nor did I know the language. The baby's
wailing became less determined. He began to pace slowly around

the room with her. Back and forth before the fire. I was with Molly as she watched him until she too, fell asleep to Burrich's soothing voice. The only dream I had after that was of a lone wolf, running, endlessly running. He was as alone as I was.

FIFTEEN

Kettle

Queen Kettricken was carrying Verity's child when she fled King-in-Waiting Regal to return to her Mountains. Some have criticized her, saying if she had remained at Buck and forced Regal's hand, the child would have been born safely there. Perhaps if she had, Buckkeep Castle would have rallied to her, perhaps all of Buck Duchy would have presented a more unified resistance to the Outislander Raiders. Perhaps the Coastal Duchies would have fought harder if they had had a queen at Buck. So some say.

The general belief of those who lived in Buckkeep Castle at the time and were well informed of the internal politics of the Farseer regency is very different. Without exception, they believed that both Kettricken and her unborn child would have met with foul play. It can be substantiated that even after Queen Kettricken had removed herself from Buckkeep, those who supported Regal as king did all that they could to discredit her, even to saying that the child she carried was not Verity's at all, but had been fathered by his bastard nephew FitzChivalry.

Whatever suppositions might be made about what would have happened if Kettricken had remained at Buckkeep are but useless speculations now. The historical fact is that she believed her child would have the best chance of surviving if born in her beloved Mountain Kingdom. She also returned to the Mountains in the hopes of being able to find Verity and restore her husband to power. Her search efforts, however, only yielded her grief. She found the battle site of his companions against unidentified attackers. The unburied remains were little more than scattered bones and draggled bits of clothing after the scavengers had finished with them. Among those remains, however, she found the blue cloak Verity had worn when she had last seen him, and his sheath knife. She returned to the royal residence at Jhaampe and mourned her husband as dead.

More distressing to her was that for months afterwards she received reports of sightings of folk in the garb of Verity's Guard in the mountains beyond Jhaampe. These individual guards were seen wandering alone by Mountain villagers. They seemed reluctant to have conversation with the villagers and despite their ragged condition often refused offers of aid or food. Without exception, they were described by those who saw them as 'pathetic' or 'piteous'. Some few of these men trickled in to Jhaampe from time to time. They seemed unable to answer her questions about Verity and what had become of him coherently. They could not even recall when they had parted company with him or under what circumstances. Without exception, they seemed almost obsessed with returning to Buckkeep.

In time she came to believe that Verity and his guard had been attacked, not only physically but by magic. The ambushers who struck at him with arrow and sword, and the false coterie that disheartened and confused his guard were, she surmised, in the employ of his younger brother, Prince Regal. This is what precipitated her unceasing ill will toward her brother-in-law.

I awoke to a hammering on the door. I shouted something back as I sat up disoriented and cold in the dark. 'We leave in an hour!' was the reply.

I fought my way clear of weltering blankets and Starling's sleepy embrace. I found my boots and pulled them on, and then my cloak. I snugged it around me against the chilly room. Starling's only move had been to immediately burrow into the warm place where I had lain. I leaned over the bed. 'Starling?' When there was no response, I reached down and shook her slightly. 'Starling! We leave in less than an hour. Get up!'

She heaved a tremendous sigh. 'Go ahead. I'll be ready.' She shouldered deeper into the blankets. I shrugged my shoulders and left her there.

Downstairs in the kitchen Pelf had stacks of griddle-cakes keeping warm by the cooking hearth. She offered me a plate with butter and honey and I was only too glad to accept. The house, so quiet a place the day before, was now thronged with folk. From the strong resemblances, this was a family business. The small boy with the spotted kid was sitting at a stool by the table, feeding the goat bits of griddle-cake. From time to time, I caught him staring at me. When I smiled back, the boy's eyes got wide. With a serious expression he arose and carried his plate off, with the goat skittering after him.

Nik strode through the kitchen, black wool cloak swirling about his calves. It was dotted with fresh snowflakes. He caught my eye in passing. 'Ready to go?'

I gave a nod.

'Good.' He gave me a glance on his way out. 'Dress warmly. Storm is just beginning.' He grinned. 'Perfect travelling weather for you and me.'

I told myself I had not expected to enjoy the trip. I had finished my breakfast before Starling came down the stairs. When she reached the kitchen, she surprised me. I had expected her to be sleepy. Instead she was brightly alert, her cheeks flushed and mouth laughing. As she came into the kitchen she was trading quips with one of the men, and getting the best of it. She did not hesitate when she got to table, but helped herself to a hearty serving of everything. When she looked up from her empty plate, she must have seen the surprise on my face.

'Minstrels learn to eat well when food is offered,' she said, and held her cup out to me. She was drinking beer with her break-fast. I filled her cup from the pitcher on the table. She had just set her mug down with a sigh when Nik came through the kitchen looking like a storm cloud. He caught sight of me and stopped in mid-stride. 'Ah. Tom. Can you drive a horse?'

'Certainly.'

'Well?'

'Well enough,' I said quietly.

'Good, then, we're ready to go. My cousin Hank was to drive, but he's breathing like a bellows this morning, took a cough in the night. His wife won't let him go. But if you can drive a cart . . .'

'He'll expect you to adjust your fee,' Starling broke in suddenly. 'By driving a horse for you, he's saved you the cost of a horse for himself. And what your cousin would have eaten.'

Nik was taken aback for a moment. He glanced from Starling to me. 'Fair is fair,' I observed. I tried not to smile.

'I'll make it right,' he conceded, and hastened out of the kitchen again. In a short time he was back. 'The old woman says she'll try you. It's her team and wagon, you see.'

It was still dark outside. Torches spluttered in the wind and snow. Folk hurried about, hoods up and cloaks well fastened. There were four wagons and teams. One was full of people, about fifteen of them. They huddled together, bags on their laps, heads bowed against the cold. A woman glanced toward me. Her face was full of apprehension. At her side, a child leaned against her. I wondered where they had all come from. Two men loaded a cask into the last wagon, then stretched a canvas over the whole load.

Behind the wagon loaded with passengers was a smaller two-wheeled cart. A little old woman swathed all in black sat erect on the seat. She was well bundled in cloak, hood and shawl, with a travelling blanket thrown across her knees as well. Her sharp black eyes watched me carefully as I walked around her rig. The horse was a speckled mare. She didn't like the weather and her harness was binding her. I adjusted it as best as I could, persuading her to trust me. When I was finished, I looked up to find the old woman watching me closely. Her hair was glistening black where it peeped from her hood, but not all of the white in it was snow. She pursed her lips at me but said nothing, even when I stowed my pack under the seat. I gave her 'Good day', as I climbed up on the seat beside her and took up the reins. 'I think I'm supposed to be driving for you,' I said genially.

'You think. Don't you know?' She peered at me sharply.

'Hank has been taken ill. Nik asked if I would drive your team. My name is Tom.'

'I don't like changes,' she told me. 'Especially not at the last minute. Changes say you weren't really ready in the first place, and now you're even less ready.'

I suspected I knew why Hank was suddenly feeling poorly. 'My name is Tom,' I introduced myself again.

'You already said that,' she informed me. She stared off into the falling snow. 'This whole trip was a bad idea,' she said aloud, but not to me. 'And no good is going to come of it. I can see that right now.' She kneaded her gloved hands in her lap. 'Damn old bones,' she said to the falling snow. 'If it weren't for my old bones, I'd not need a one of you. Not a one.'

I could think of nothing to reply to that, but was saved by Starling. She reined in beside me. 'Will you look at what they've given me to ride?' she challenged me. Her mount shook her black mane and rolled her eyes at me as if demanding that I look at what she was expected to carry.

'Looks fine to me. She's Mountain stock. They're all like that. But she'll go all day for you, and most of them have sweet tempers.'

Starling scowled. 'I told Nik that for what we're paying, I expected a proper horse.'

Nik rode past us at that moment. His mount was no larger than Starling's. He looked at her and then away, as if wary of her tongue. 'Let's go,' he said in a quietly carrying voice. 'It's better not to talk, and it's best to stay close to the wagon in front of you. It's easier to lose sight of each other in this storm than you might think.'

For all his soft voice, the command was instantly obeyed. There were no shouted commands nor calls of farewell. Instead the wagons in front of us rolled silently away from us. I stirred the reins and clucked to the team. The mare gave a snort of disapproval, but stepped out to the pace. We moved forward in near silence through a perpetual curtain of falling snow. Starling's pony tugged restlessly at her bit until Starling gave her her head. Then she trotted swiftly up to join the other horses at the front of the group. I was left sitting by the silent old woman.

I soon found the truth to Nik's warning. The sun came up, but the snow continued to fall so thickly the light seemed milky. There was a mother-of-pearl quality to the swirling snow that both dazzled and wearied the eye. It seemed an endless tunnel of white that we travelled through with only the tail of the other wagon to guide us.

Nik did not take us by the road. We went crunching off across the frozen fields. The thickly-falling snow soon filled in the tracks we left. In no time, there would be no trace of our passage. We travelled cross country until past noon, with the riders dismounting to take down fence railings and then restoring them in our wake. I glimpsed another farmhouse once through the swirling storm, but its windows were dark. Shortly after midday a final fence was opened for us. With a creak and a jolt, we came out of the field onto what had once been a road but was now little more than a trail. The only tracks on it were those we made ourselves, and the snow swiftly erased those.

And all that way, my companion had been as chilly and silent as the falling snow itself. From time to time, I watched her from the corner of my eye. She stared straight ahead, her body swaying to the motion of the wagon. She kneaded her hands restlessly in her lap as if they pained her. With little else to amuse myself, I spied upon her. Buck stock, obviously. The accent of my home was on her tongue still, though faded by many years of travel in other places. Her headscarf was the work of Chalced weavers, but the embroidery along the edges of her cloak, done black on black, was totally unfamiliar to me.

'You're a long way from Buck, boy,' she observed abruptly. She stared straight ahead as she said it. Something about her tone set my back up.

'As are you, old woman,' I replied.

She turned her whole face to look at me. I was not sure if I glimpsed amusement or annoyance in her bright crow eyes. 'That I am. Years and distance alike, a long way.' She paused, then asked abruptly, 'Why are you bound for the Mountains?'

'I want to see my uncle,' I replied truthfully.

She gave a snort of disdain. 'A Buck boy has an uncle in the Mountains? And you want to see him enough to put your head at risk?'

I looked over at her. 'He's my favourite uncle. You, I understand, go to Eda's shrine?'

'The others do,' she corrected me. 'I'm too old to pray for fertility. I seek a prophet.' Before I could speak, she added, 'He's my favourite prophet.' Almost, she smiled at me.

'Why don't you travel with the others in the wagon?' I asked her.

She gave me a chill look. 'They ask too many questions,' she replied.

'Ah!' I said, and grinned at her, accepting the rebuke.

After a few moments, she spoke again. 'I've been a long time on my own, Tom. I like to go my own way and keep my own counsels and decide for myself what I'll eat for my supper. Those ones, they're nice enough folk, but they scratch and peck like a flock of chickens. Left to themselves, not a one of them would make this journey alone. They all need the others to say, yes, yes, this is what we should be doing, it's worth the risk. And now that they've decided it, the decision is bigger than all of them. Not a one of them could turn back on their own.'

She shook her head at that, and I nodded thoughtfully. She said nothing more for a long time. Our trail had found the river. We followed it upstream, through a scanty cover of brush and very young trees. I could scarcely see it through the steadily-falling snow, but I could smell it and hear the rush of its passage. I wondered how far we'd go before we tried to cross it. Then I grinned to myself. I was certain Starling would know when I saw her this evening. I wondered if Nik was enjoying her company.

'What are you smirking about?' the old woman demanded suddenly.

'I was thinking on my friend the minstrel. Starling.'

'And she makes you smile like that?'

'Sometimes.'

'She's a minstrel, you say. And you? Are you a minstrel?'

'No. Just a shepherd. Most of the time.'

'I see.'

Our talk died off again. Then as evening began to fall, she told me, 'You may call me Kettle.'

'I'm Tom,' I replied.

'And that's the third time you've told me,' she reminded me.

I had expected we would camp at nightfall, but Nik kept us moving. We halted briefly while he took out two lanterns and hung them from a couple of the wagons. 'Just follow the light,' he told me tersely as he rode past us. Our mare did just that.

The light was gone and the cold getting intense when the wagon in front of us turned off the road and jolted into an opening in the trees by the river. Obediently I turned our mare to follow, and we bumped down off the road with a thud that made Kettle curse. I smiled: there were few Buckkeep guardsmen who could have done better.

In a short time we halted. I kept to my seat, wondering, for I could not see a thing. The river was a black sweeping force somewhere to our left. The wind off it added a new note of damp to the cold. The pilgrims in the wagon ahead of us were shifting restlessly and talking in soft whispers. I heard Nik's voice speaking and saw a man lead his horse past us. He took the lantern from the tail of the wagon as he went by. I followed its passage. In a moment man and horse had passed into a long, low building that had been invisible in the dark.

'Get down, go inside, we'll spend the night here,' Nik instructed us as he rode past us again. I dismounted and then waited to help Kettle down. As I offered her my hand, she looked almost startled.

'I thank you, kind sir,' she said quietly as I helped her down.

'You're welcome, my lady,' I replied. She took my arm as I guided her toward the building.

'Pretty damn well-mannered for a shepherd, Tom,' she observed in an entirely different voice. She gave a snort of laughter at the door and went inside, leaving me to go back and unhitch the mare. I shook my head at myself, but had to smile. I liked this old woman. I slung my pack over my shoulder and led the mare into the building where the others had gone. As I lifted her harness from her, I glanced around. It was one long open room. A fire had been kindled in a hearth at one end. The low-ceilinged building was of river-rock and clay with an earthen floor. The horses were at one end, crowding around a manger full of hay. As I turned our mare in with the others, one of Nik's men came bringing buckets of water to fill a trough. The depth of manure at that end of the room told me this building was frequently used by the smugglers.

'What was this place originally?' I asked Nik as I joined the others around the hearth.

'Sheep camp,' he told me. 'The shelter was for the early lambing. Then later, we'd shear here, after we'd washed the sheep in the river.' His blue eyes were afar for a time. Then he gave a harsh laugh. 'That was a long time ago. Now there's not enough feed for a goat, let alone sheep like we had.' He gestured at the fire. 'Best eat and sleep while you can, Tom. Morning comes early for us.' His glance seemed to linger on my earring as he passed me.

Food was simple. Bread and smoked fish. Porridge. Hot tea. Most of it was from the pilgrims' supplies, but Nik put in enough that they did not object to feeding his men and Starling and me. Kettle ate by herself, from her own stores, and brewed her own pot of tea. The other pilgrims were polite to her and she was courteous in return but there was plainly no bond between them save that they were all going to the same place. Only the three children of the party seemed unafraid of her, begging dried apples and stories from her until she warned them they would all be sick.

The shelter soon warmed, from the horses and folk in it as much as from the hearth. Door and window shutters were closed tight, to keep in light and sound as well as warmth. Despite the storm and lack of other travellers on our path, Nik was taking no chances. I approved of that in a smuggler. The meal had given me my first good look at the company. Fifteen pilgrims, of mixed age and gender, not counting Kettle. About a dozen smugglers, of which six had enough resemblance to Nik and Pelf that they were at least cousins. The others looked a mixed bunch, professionally tough and watchful. At least three were on watch at all times. They spoke little and knew their tasks well enough that Nik directed them very little. I found myself feeling confident that I would see at least the other side of the river, and probably the Mountain border. It was the most optimistic I'd felt in a long time.

Starling showed to her best advantage in such a company. As soon as we had eaten, she took out her harp, and despite Nik's frequent cautions to us to speak softly, he did not forbid the soft music and song she gave us. For the smugglers she sang an old ballad about Heft the highwayman, probably the most dashing robber that Buck had ever known. Even Nik was smiling at that song, and Starling's eyes flirted with him as she sang. To the pilgrims she sang about a winding river-road that carried folk home, and finished with a lullaby for the three children in our midst. By then more than just the children were stretched out on bedrolls. Kettle had peremptorily sent me out to fetch hers from the back of her cart. I wondered when I had been promoted from driver to servant, but said nothing as I fetched it for her. I supposed there was something about me that made all elderly folk assume my time was at their disposal.

I unrolled my own blankets next to Kettle's and lay down to seek sleep. Around me most of the others were already snoring. Kettle curled in her blankets like a squirrel in its nest. I could imagine how much her bones ached with the cold, but there was little I could do for her. Over by the hearth, Starling sat talking to Nik. From time to time, her fingers wandered lightly over her harp strings, their silvery notes a counterpoint to her low voice. Several times she made Nik laugh.

I was almost asleep.

My brother?

My whole body jerked with the shock of it. He was near.

Nighteyes?

Of course! Amusement. *Or do you have another brother now?*

Never! Only you, my friend. Where are you?

Where am I? Outside. Come to me.

I rose hastily and redonned my cloak. The man guarding the door frowned at me, but asked me no questions. I walked into the darkness, beyond the pulled-up wagons. The snow had ceased and the blowing wind had cleared a patch of starlit sky. Snow silvered the branches of every bush and tree. I was casting about for his presence when a solid weight hit me in the back. I was flung face-first in the snow and would have cried out, save that my mouth was full of snow. I managed to roll over and was trampled several times by a joyous wolf.

How did you know where to find me?

How do you know where to scratch when it itches?

I suddenly knew what he meant. I was not always aware of our bond. But to think of him now and to find him was suddenly no more difficult than to bring my two hands together in the dark. Of course I knew where he was. He was a part of me.

You smell like a female. You have taken a new mate?

No. Of course not.

But you share a den?

339

We travel together, as a pack. It is safer so.

I know.

For a time we sat in stillness of mind and body, simply adjusting to one another's physical presence again. I felt whole once more. I had peace. I had not known I had worried so much about him until the sight of him put my mind at rest. I sensed his unwilling agreement to that. He knew I had faced hardship and dangers alone. He had not thought I could survive them. But he had also missed me. He had missed my form of thinking, the sorts of ideas and discussions that wolves never shared amongst themselves. *Is that why you came back to me?* I asked him.

He stood up suddenly and shook himself all over. *It was time to come back,* he replied evasively. Then he added, *I ran with them. They finally allowed me to be part of their pack. We hunted together, we killed together, we shared meat. It was very good.*

But?

I wanted to be the leader. He turned and looked at me over his shoulder, his tongue lolling out. *I am used to being the leader, you know.*

Are you? And they would not accept you?

Black Wolf is very large. And quick. I am stronger than he is, I think, but he knows more tricks. It was much like when you fought Heart of the Pack.

I laughed quietly and he spun on me, lifting his lips in a mock snarl.

'Be easy,' I said quietly, warding him off with open hands. 'So. What happened?'

He flung himself down beside me. *He is still the leader. He still has the mate and the den.* He considered and I sensed him wrestling with the concept of the future. *It could be different, another time.*

'It could be,' I agreed. I scratched him gently behind the ear and he all but fell over in the snow. 'Will you go back to them, some day?'

He was having difficulty focusing on my words while I scratched his ears. I stopped and asked him again. He cocked his head to one side and regarded me with amusement. *Ask me on the some day, and I will be able to answer.*

One day at a time, I agreed with him. *I am glad you are here.*

But I still don't understand why you came back to me. You could have stayed with the pack.

His eyes met mine, and even in the darkness they gripped me. *You are called, are you not? Did not your king howl to you, 'Come to me'?*

I nodded unwillingly. *I am called.*

He stood suddenly, shook himself all over. He looked off into the night. *If you are called, I am called, too.* He did not admit it willingly.

You do not have to come with me. This call from my king binds me, not you.

In that, you are wrong. What binds you, binds me.

I do not understand how that could be, I said carefully.

Nor do I. But it is so. Come to me, he called to us. And for a time, I could ignore it. But no more.

I am sorry. I groped for a way to express it. *He has no right to you. I know that. I do not think he intended to call you. I do not think he intended to bind me. But it happened, and I must go to him.*

I stood up and dusted off the snow that was starting to melt on me. I felt ashamed. Verity, a man whom I trusted, had done this to me. That was bad enough. But through me it was imposed on the wolf. Verity had no right to put any demands on Nighteyes. For that matter, I had no right to put any demands on him. What had been between us had always been entered into voluntarily, a mutual giving on both sides with no laying-on of obligations. Now, through me, he was entrapped as surely as if I had caged him.

We share a cage, then.

I wish it were otherwise. I wish there were some way I could free you of this. But I do not even know how to free myself. Not knowing how you are bound, I do not know how to loose you. You and I, we share the Wit. Verity and I share the Skill. How could his Skill-sending have gone through me to seize you? You were not even with me when he summoned me.

Nighteyes sat very still in the snow. The wind had come up, and in the faint starlight I could see it ruffling his coat. *I am always with you, brother. You may not always be aware of me, but I am always with you. We are one.*

We share many things, I agreed. Uneasiness itched at me.

No. He turned to face me squarely, met my eyes as no wild wolf would have. *We do not share. We are one. I am no longer a wolf, you are no longer a man. What we are together, I have no name for. Perhaps the one who spoke to us of the Old Blood would have a word to explain it.* He paused. *See how much a man I am, that I speak of having a word for an idea? No word is needed. We exist, and we are whatever we are.*

I would set you free if I could.

Would you? I would not part from you.

That is not what I meant. I meant I would have for you a life of your own.

He yawned, then stretched. *I will have for us a life of our own. We shall win it together. So. Do we travel by night or by day?*

We travel by day.

He sensed what I meant. *You will stay with this huge pack to travel? Why not break free of it and run with me? We shall go faster.*

I shook my head. *It is not that simple. To travel where we must, I will need shelter, and I have none that is mine alone. I need the aid of this pack to survive in this weather.*

There followed a difficult half hour, as I tried to explain to him that I would need the support of the others in the caravan to reach the Mountains. Had I had a horse and provisions of my own, I would not have hesitated to trust to luck and strike out with the wolf. But on foot with only what I could carry myself, facing the deep snows and deeper cold of the Mountains, not to mention a river crossing? I would not be that great a fool.

We could hunt, Nighteyes insisted. We would curl together in the snow at night. He could take care of me as he always had. With persistence, I was able to convince him that I must continue to travel as I did. *Then I shall have to continue to sneak along like a stray dog, following all these folk?*

'Tom? Tom, are you out there?' There was irritated annoyance and worry in Nik's voice.

'Right here!' I stepped out of the bushes.

'What were you doing?' he demanded suspiciously.

'Pissing,' I told him. I made a sudden decision. 'And my dog has followed me from town and caught up with us here. I left him with friends, but he must have chewed his rope. Here, boy, come to heel.'

I'll chew your heel off for you, Nighteyes offered savagely, but he came, following me out into the cleared yard.

'Damn big dog,' Nik observed. He leaned forward. 'Looks more than half a wolf to me?'

'Some in Farrow have told me that. It's a Buck breed. We use them for herding sheep.'

You will pay for this. I promise you.

In answer I leaned down to pat his shoulder and then scratch his ears. *Wag your tail, Nighteyes.* 'He's a loyal old dog. I should have known he wouldn't be left behind.'

The things I endure for you. He wagged his tail. Once.

'I see. Well. You'd best get yourself inside and get some sleep. And next time, don't go off by yourself. For anything. At least, not without letting me know first. When my men are on watch, they get jumpy. They might cut your throat before they knew you.'

'I understand.'

I walked right past two of them.

'Nik, you don't mind, do you? The dog, I mean.' I tried to be affably abashed. 'He can stay outside. He's a real good watch-dog, actually.'

'Just don't expect me to feed him for you,' Nik growled. 'And don't let him be any trouble to us.'

'Oh, I'm sure he won't. Will you, boy?'

Starling chose that moment to come to the door. 'Nik? F . . . Tom?'

'We're right here. You were right, he was just pissing,' Nik said quietly. He took Starling's arm and began to guide her back into the shed.

'What's that?' she demanded, sounding almost alarmed.

I suddenly had to wager everything on her quick wits and our friendship. 'Just the dog,' I said quickly. 'Nighteyes must have chewed his rope. I warned Creece to watch him when I left him there, that he'd want to follow me. But Creece didn't listen, and here he is. I'll guess I'll have to take him to the Mountains with us after all.'

Starling was staring at the wolf. Her eyes were as wide and black as the night sky above us. Nik tugged at her arm and she finally turned back to the door. 'I suppose so,' she said faintly.

I silently thanked Eda and any other god that might be listening. To Nighteyes I said, 'Stay and guard, there's a good fellow.'

Enjoy it while you can, little brother. He flung himself down by the cart. I doubted that he'd stay there for more than a few heartbeats. I followed Starling and Nik inside. Nik shut the door firmly behind us and dropped the bolt in place. I pulled off my boots and shook out my snow-laden cloak before I wrapped myself in my blankets. Sleep was suddenly very close as I grasped the full relief I felt. Nighteyes was back. I felt whole. Safe, with the wolf at the door.

Nighteyes. I'm glad you're here.

You've an odd way of showing it, he replied, but I could sense he was more amused than upset.

Black Rolf sent me a message. Regal seeks to turn those of Old Blood against us. He offers them gold to hunt us down for him. We should not speak overly much.

Gold. What is gold to us, or those like us? Do not fear, little brother. I am here to take care of you again.

I closed my eyes and sank into sleep, hoping he was right. For an instant, as I teetered on the edge of wakefulness, I noticed that Starling had not spread her blankets by mine. She sat on her blankets on the other side of the room. By Nik. Heads together, they spoke softly about something. She laughed. I could not hear the words she next said, but the tone was a teasing challenge.

I almost felt a pang of jealousy. I rebuked myself for it. She was a companion, no more. What was it to me how she spent her nights? Last night she had slept against my back. This night she would not. I decided it was the wolf. She couldn't accept it. She was not the first. Knowing I was Witted was not the same thing as confronting my bond-animal. Well. That was how that was.

I slept.

Sometime in the night I felt a gentle groping. It was the barest brushing of the Skill across my senses. I came alert, but still, waiting. I felt nothing. Had I imagined it, dreamed it? A more chilling thought came to me. Perhaps it was Verity, too weakened to do more than reach for me. Perhaps it was Will. I lay still, longing to reach out, and fearing to. I wanted so badly to know that Verity was all right; since he had blasted Regal's coterie that night, I had felt nothing of him. *Come to me*, he had said. What if that had been his dying wish? What if all my seeking would yield me were bones? I pushed the fear away and tried to be open.

The mind I felt brush mine was Regal's.

I had never Skilled to Regal, had only suspected he was able to Skill. Even now, I doubted what I sensed. The strength of the Skill seemed Will's, but the feel of the thoughts was Regal's. *And you have not found the woman either?* The Skilling was not meant for me. He reached for someone else. I grew bolder, venturing closer. I tried to be open to his thoughts without reaching for them.

Not as of yet, my king. Burl. Hiding his trembling behind formality and courtesy. I knew Regal could sense it as clearly as I could. I even knew that he enjoyed it. Regal had never been able to grasp the difference between fear and respect. He had no belief in a man's respect for him unless it was tainted with fear. I had not thought he would extend that to his own coterie. I wondered what the threat was that he held over them.

And nothing of the Bastard? Regal demanded. There was no mistaking it now. Regal Skilled, using Will's strength. Did that mean he could not Skill by himself?

Burl steeled himself. *My king, I have found no sign of him. I believe he is dead. Truly dead, this time. He cut himself with a poisoned blade; the despair he felt at that moment of decision was absolute. No man could have pretended it.*

Then there should be a body, should there not?

Somewhere, my king, I am sure there is. Your guards have simply not found it yet. This from Carrod, who did not tremble with fear. He hid his fear even from himself, pretending it was anger. I understood how he might need to do that, but doubted the wisdom of it. It forced him to stand up to Regal. Regal did not appreciate a man who spoke his mind.

Perhaps I should put you in charge of riding the roads, looking for it, Regal suggested pleasantly. *At the same time, you might find the man who killed Bolt and his patrol.*

My lord king. . . Carrod began, but SILENCE! Regal overrode him. He drew freely on Will's strength to do it. The effort cost him nothing.

I believed him dead once before, and my trust in the word of others nearly got me killed. This time I will see him, see him hacked in pieces before I rest. Will's feeble attempt to trap the Bastard into betraying himself failed miserably.

Perhaps because he is already dead, Carrod ventured foolishly.

Then I witnessed a thing I wished I had not. A needle of pain, hot and piercing, he sent to Carrod with Will's Skill. In that sending, I finally glimpsed the whole of what they had become. Regal rode Will, not like a man rides a horse, to be thrown by the horse in anger, but as a tick or a leech bites into its victim and clings and sucks life from him. Waking or asleep, Regal was with him always, had access always to his strength. And now he spent it viciously, caring nothing for what it would cost Will. I had not known pain could be inflicted with Skill alone. A numbing blast of strength such as Verity had spent upon them, that I knew. But this was different. This was no show of force or temper. This was a display of purest vindictiveness. Somewhere, I knew, Carrod fell to the floor and thrashed in wordless agony. Linked as they were, Burl and Will must have shared a shadow of that pain. It surprised me that a member of a coterie was even capable of doing that to another. But then, it was not Will who sent the pain. It was Regal.

It passed, after a time. Perhaps in reality it only lasted an instant. For Carrod, it certainly lasted long enough. I sensed from him a faint mental whimpering. He was capable of no more than that just now.

I do not believe the Bastard died. I dare not believe it until I've seen his body. Someone killed Bolt and his men. So find his body and bring it to me, whether alive or dead. Burl. Remain where you are, and redouble your efforts. I am certain he is bound that way. Let no traveller pass you unchallenged. Carrod, I think perhaps you should join Burl. An indolent life does not seem to agree with your temperament. Be on your way tomorrow. And as you travel, do not be lazy.

Keep your minds upon your task. We know that Verity lives; he proved that to all of you most effectively. The Bastard will try to get to him. He must be stopped before he does so, and then my brother must be eliminated as a threat. These are the only tasks I have given you; why cannot you do them? Have you no thought for what will become of us should Verity succeed? Search for him, with Skill and men. Do not let folk forget what I have offered for his capture. Do not let them forget the punishment for aiding him. Am I understood?

Of course, my lord king. I shall spare no effort. Burl was quick to reply.

Carrod? I hear nothing from you Carrod. The threat of punishment hung over them all.

Please, my lord King. I shall do all, everything. Alive or dead, I shall find him for you. I shall.

Without even an acknowledgement, Will and Regal's presence vanished. I felt Carrod collapse. Burl lingered a moment longer. Did he listen, did he grope back toward my presence? I let my thoughts float free, my concentration dissipate. Then I opened my eyes and lay staring at the ceiling, thinking. The Skilling had left me queasy and trembling.

I am with you, my brother, Nighteyes assured me.

And I am glad that you are. I rolled over and tried to find sleep.

SIXTEEN

Bolthole

In many of the old legends and tales of the Wit, it is insisted that a Wit user eventually takes on many traits of his bond-animal. Some of the most frightening tales say that eventually a Witted one becomes capable of assuming the guise of that animal. Those who know intimately of such magic have assured me it is not so. It is true that a Witted one may, without realizing it, assume some of the physical mannerisms of his bond-animal, but one bonded to an eagle will not sprout wings, nor will one bonded to a horse begin to neigh. As time goes by, a Witted one grows in understanding of the bond-beast, and the longer a human and an animal are bonded, the greater will be the similarity of their mannerisms. The bond-animal is as likely to assume the mannerisms and traits of the human as the human is to adopt those of his beast. But this only happens over a long period of intense contact.

Nik agreed with Burrich's idea of when mornings began. I awoke to the sound of his men leading the horses out. A cold wind blew in the open door. Around me in the darkness the others were stirring. One of the children was crying at being awakened so early. Her mother shushed her. Molly, I thought with sudden longing. Somewhere hushing my child.

What's this?

My mate bore a cub. Far away.

Immediate concern. *But who will hunt meat to feed them? Should not we return to her?*

Heart of the Pack watches over her.

Of course. I should have known that. That one knows the meaning of pack, no matter how he denies it. All is well, then.

As I rose and bundled my blankets together, I wished I could accept it as blithely as he did. I knew Burrich would care for them. It was his nature. I recalled all the years he had watched over me as I had grown. Often I had hated him then; now I could not think of anyone else I would prefer to care for Molly and my baby. Save myself. I would much rather it was I watching over them, even rocking a crying babe in the middle of the night. Though I rather wished, just now, that the pilgrim woman would find a way to quiet her child. I was paying for my Skill-spying of the night before with a savage headache.

Food seemed to be the answer, for when the girl had a piece of bread and some honeycomb, she soon quieted. It was a hasty meal we shared, the only hot item being tea. I noticed Kettle was moving very stiffly and took pity on her. I fetched her a cup of hot tea to wrap her twisted fingers around while I rolled up her blankets for her. I had never seen hands so distorted by rheumatism; they reminded me of bird claws.

'An old friend of mine said that sometimes the sting of nettles actually relieved his hands when they ached,' I suggested to her as I tied her bundle.

'You find me nettles growing under the snow and I'll try them, boy,' she replied peevishly. But a few moments later she was offering me a dried apple from her small store. I accepted it with thanks. I loaded our things onto the cart and harnessed the mare while she finished her tea. I glanced about but saw nothing of Nighteyes.

Hunting, came the reply.

Wish I was with you. Good luck.

Aren't we supposed to speak but little, lest Regal hear us?

I didn't reply. It was a clear cold morning, almost shockingly bright after yesterday's snow. It was colder than it had been the day before; the wind off the river seemed to cut right through my garments, finding the gaps at cuffs and collars to poke its cold fingers through. I helped Kettle mount the cart, and then tucked one of her blankets around her in addition to her wraps. 'Your mother trained you well, Tom,' she said with genuine kindness.

I still winced at the remark. Starling and Nik stood talking together until everyone else was ready to go. Then she mounted her Mountain pony and took a place beside Nik at the head of our procession. I told myself that it was likely Nik Holdfast would make a better ballad than FitzChivalry anyway. If he could persuade her to go back with him at the Mountain border, my life would only be simpler.

I gave my mind to my task. There was really little to it, other than to keep the mare from lagging too far behind the pilgrims' wagon. I had time to see the country we traversed. We regained the little-used road we had been on the day before and continued to follow the river upstream. Along the river, it was sparsely treed, but a short distance away from the riverbank, it became a rolling, treeless terrain of brush and scrub. Gullies and washes cut our road on their way to the river. It seemed that at some time water had been plentiful here, perhaps in spring. But now the land was dry save for the crystal snow that blew loosely across it like sand and the river in its bed.

'Yesterday the minstrel made you smile to yourself. For whom is the frown today?' Kettle asked quietly.

'I was thinking it a shame, to see what this rich land has come to.'

'Were you?' she asked drily.

'Tell me of this seer of yours,' I said, mostly to change the subject.

'He is not mine,' she said with asperity. Then she relented. 'It is probably a fool's errand I go on. He whom I seek may not even be there. And yet what better use do I have for these years, than to chase a chimera?'

I kept silence. I was beginning to find it was the question she answered best. 'Do you know what's in this cart, Tom? Books. Scrolls and writings. Ones I've collected for years. I have gathered them in many lands, learned to read many tongues and letterings. In so many places, I found mention, over and over again, of the White Prophets. They appear at the junctures of history and shape it. Some say they come to set history on its proper course. There are those who believe, Tom, that all of time is a circle. All of history, a great wheel, turning inexorably. Just as seasons come and go, just as the moon moves endlessly through her cycle, so does time. The same wars are fought, the same plagues descend, the same folk, good or evil, rise to power. Humanity is trapped on that wheel, doomed endlessly to repeat the mistakes we have already made. Unless someone comes to change it. Far to the south, there is a land where they believe that for every generation, somewhere in the world there is a White Prophet. He or she comes, and if what is taught is heeded, the cycle of time moves into a better course. If it is ignored, all time is pushed into a darker path.'

She paused, as if waiting for me to say something. 'I know nothing of such teachings,' I admitted.

'I would not expect you to. It was in a far place I first studied such things. There they held that if such prophets fail, again and again, the repeating history of the world will grow more and more evil, until the entire cycle of time, hundreds of thousands of years, becomes a history of misery and wrong.'

'And if the prophet is heeded?'

'Each time one succeeds, it is easier for the next one. And when an entire cycle passes in which every prophet succeeds, time itself will finally stop.'

'So they work for the end of the world to come?'

'Not the end of the world, Tom. The end of time. To free humanity of time. For time is the great enslaver of us all. Time that ages us, time that limits us. Think how often you have wished to have more time for something, or wished you could go back a day and do something differently. When humanity is freed of time, old wrongs can be corrected before they are done.' She sighed. 'I believe this is the time for such a prophet to come. And my readings lead me to believe that this generation's White Prophet shall arise in the Mountains.'

'But you are alone on your quest. Do no others agree with you?'

'Many others. But few, very few, go to seek a White Prophet. It is the folk the Prophet is sent to who must heed him. Others should not interfere, lest they set all time awry forever.'

I was still puzzling over what she had said about time. It seemed to make a knot in my thinking. Her voice fell silent. I stared forward between the mare's ears and pondered. Time to go back and be honest with Molly. Time to follow Fedwren the scribe instead of being an assassin's apprentice. She had given me much to think about.

Our talk lapsed for some time.

Nighteyes reappeared shortly after noon. He came trotting pur-posefully out of the trees, to fall into place trotting beside our wagon. The mare gave him several nervous glances as she tried to puzzle out wolf smell and dog behaviour. I quested toward her and reassured her. He had been for some time on my side of the cart before Kettle caught sight of him. She leaned forward to look past me, then sat back again. 'There's a wolf beside our cart,' she observed.

'He's my dog. Though he has some wolf blood in him,' I admit-ted casually.

Kettle leaned forward to look at him again. She glanced up at my placid expression. Then she sat back. 'So they herd sheep with wolves in Buck these days.' She nodded, and said no more about him.

We pushed on steadily for the rest of the day. We saw no folk save ourselves, and only one small cabin sending up a trail of smoke in the distance. The cold and the blowing wind were a constant, but not one that became easier to ignore as the day went on. The faces of the pilgrims in the wagon in front of us became paler, noses redder, lips almost blue on one woman. They were packed together like fish in brine but all their closeness seemed to be no protection against the cold.

I moved my feet inside my boots to keep my toes awake, and shifted the reins from one hand to the other as I took turns warming my fingers under my arm. My shoulder ached, and the ache ran down my arm until even my fingers throbbed with it. My lips were dry but I dared not wet them lest they crack. Few things are as miserable to confront as constant cold. As for Kettle, I did not doubt it tortured her. She did not complain, but as the day went by she seemed to get smaller within her blanket as she curled closer on herself. Her silence seemed but further evidence of her misery.

We were still short of darkness when Nik turned our wagons away from the road and up a long trail nearly obscured by the blown snow. The only sign of it I could make out was that less grass stuck up above the snow, but Nik seemed to know it well. The mounted smugglers broke trail for the wagons. It was still heavy going for Kettle's little mare. I looked back behind us once to see the sweeping hand of the wind smoothing our trail out to no more than a ripple in the snowy landscape.

The land we crossed seemed featureless, but it undulated gently. We eventually crested the long rise we had ascended, and looked down onto a huddle of buildings that had been invisible from the road. Evening was drawing on. A single light shone in a window. As we wended our way down toward it, other candles were lit, and Nighteyes caught a trace of woodsmoke on the wind. We were expected.

The buildings were not old. They looked as if they had been recently completed. There was an ample barn. Wagons and all, we led the horses down into it, for the earth had been dug away so that the barn was half underground. This low profile was why we had not seen this place from the road, and I didn't doubt that was the reason for it. Unless a man knew this place was here, he'd never find it. The earth from the digging had been heaped up around the barn and other buildings. Inside the thick walls with the doors shut, we could not even hear the wind. A milk cow shifted in her stall as we unhitched the horses and put them in stalls. There was straw and hay and a trough of fresh water.

The pilgrims had got out of the wagon, and I was helping Kettle down when the barn door opened again. A lithe young woman with a mass of red hair piled on her head came storming in. Fists on her hips, she confronted Nik. 'Who are all these people and why have you brought them here? What good is a bolthole if half the countryside knows of it?'

Nik handed his horse to one of his men and turned to her. Without a word, he swept her into his arms and kissed her. But a moment later, she pushed him away. 'What are you . . .'

'They paid well. They've their own food, and can make do in here for the night. Then they'll be on their way to the Mountains tomorrow. Up there, no one cares what we do. There's no danger, Tel, you worry too much.'

'I have to worry for two, for you haven't the sense to. I've food ready, but not enough for all this lot. Why didn't you send a bird to warn me?'

'I did. Didn't it get here? Maybe the storm delayed it.'

'That's what you always say when you don't think to do it.'

'Let it go, woman. I've good tidings for you. Let's go back to your house and talk.' Nik's arm rested easily about her waist as they left. It was up to his men to settle us. There was straw to sleep in and plenty of space to spread it. There was a dug well with a bucket outside for water. There was a small hearth at one end of the barn. The chimney smoked badly, but it sufficed to cook on. The barn was not warm, save in comparison to the weather outside. But no one complained. Nighteyes had stayed outside.

They've a coop full of chickens, he told me. *And a pigeon coop, too.*

Leave them alone, I warned him.

Starling started to leave with Nik's men when they went up to the house, but they stopped her at the door. 'Nik says all of you are to stay inside tonight, in one place.' The man shot a meaningful glance at me. In a louder voice, he called, 'Get your water now, for we'll be bolting the door when we leave. It keeps the wind out better.'

No one was fooled by his comment, but no one challenged it. Obviously the smuggler felt the less we knew of his bolthole, the better. That was understandable. Instead of complaining we fetched water. Out of habit, I replenished the animals' trough. As I hauled the fifth bucket, I wondered if I would ever lose the reflex of seeing to the beasts first. The pilgrims had devoted themselves to seeing to their own comfort. Soon I could smell food cooking on the hearth. Well, I had dried meat and hard bread. It would suffice.

You could be hunting with me. There's game here. They had a garden this summer and the rabbits are still coming for the stalks.

He sprawled in the lee of the chicken house, the bloody remnants of a rabbit across his forepaws. Even as he ate, he kept one eye on the snow-covered garden patch, watching for other game. I chewed a stick of dry meat glumly while I heaped up straw for Kettle's bed in the stall next to her horse. I was spreading her blanket over it when she returned from the fire carrying her teapot.

'Who put you in charge of my bedding?' she demanded. As I

took a breath to reply, she added, 'Here's tea if you've a cup to your name. Mine's in my bag on the cart. There's some cheese and dried apples there as well. Fetch it for us, there's a good lad.'

As I did so, I heard Starling's voice and harp take up a tune. Singing for her supper, I didn't doubt. Well, it was what minstrels did, and I doubted she'd go hungry. I brought Kettle's bag back to her, and she portioned me out a generous share while eating lightly herself. We sat on our blankets and ate. During the meal, she kept glancing at me, and finally declared, 'You've a familiar cast to your features, Tom. What part of Buck did you say you were from?'

'Buckkeep Town,' I replied without thinking.

'Ah. And who was your mother?'

I hesitated, then declared, 'Sal Flatfish.' She had so many children running about Buckkeep Town, there was probably one named Tom.

'Fisherfolk? How did a fisherwoman's son end up a shepherd?'

'My father herded,' I extemporized. 'Between the two trades, we did well enough.'

'I see. And they taught you courtly courtesies to old women. And you've an uncle in the Mountains. Quite a family.'

'He took to wandering at an early age, and settled there.' The badgering was beginning to make me sweat a little. I could tell she knew it, too. 'What part of Buck did you say your family came from?' I asked suddenly.

'I didn't say,' she replied with a small smile.

Starling suddenly appeared at the door of the stall. She perched on the edge of it and leaned over. 'Nik said we'd cross the river in two days,' she offered. I nodded, but said nothing. She came around the end of the stall and casually tossed her pack down beside mine. She followed it to sit leaning against it, her harp on her lap. 'There are two couples down by the hearth, squabbling and bickering. Some water got into their travel bread, and all they can think to do is spit about whose fault it is. And one of the children is sick and puking. Poor little thing. The man who is so angry about the wet bread keeps going on about it's just a waste of food to feed the boy until he stops being sick.'

'That would be Rally. A more conniving, tight-fisted man I

never met,' Kettle observed genially. 'And the boy, Selk. He's been sick on and off since we left Chalced. And before, like as not. I think his mother thinks Eda's shrine can cure him. She's grasping at straws, but she has the gold to do so. Or did.'

It started off a round of gossiping between the two. I leaned in the corner and listened with half an ear and dozed. Two days to the river, I promised myself. And how much longer to the Mountains? I broke in to ask Starling if she knew.

'Nik says there's no way to tell that, it all depends on the weather. But he told me not to worry about it.' Her fingers wandered idly over the strings of her harp. Almost instantly, two children appeared in the door of the stall.

'Are you going to sing again?' asked the girl. She was a spindly little child of about six, her dress much worn. There were bits of straw in her hair.

'Would you like me to?'

For answer, they came bounding in to sit on either side of her. I had expected Kettle to complain at this invasion, but she said nothing, even when the girl settled comfortably against her. Kettle began to pick the straw from the child's hair with her twisted old fingers. The little girl had dark eyes and clutched a poppet with an embroidered face. When she smiled up at Kettle, I could see they were not strangers.

'Sing the one about the old woman and her pig,' the boy begged Starling.

I stood up and gathered my pack. 'I need to get some sleep,' I excused myself. I suddenly could not bear to be around the children.

I found an empty stall nearer the door of the barn and bedded down there. I could hear the mutter of the pilgrims' voices at their hearth. Some quarrelling still seemed to be going on. Starling sang the song about the woman, the stile and the pig, and then a song about an apple tree. I heard the footsteps of a few others as they came to sit and listen to the music. I told myself they'd be wiser to sleep, and closed my own eyes.

All was dark and still when she came to find me in the night. She stepped on my hand in the dark, and then near dropped her pack on my head. I said nothing, even when she stretched out beside me. She spread her blankets out to cover me as well, then wiggled in under the edge of mine. I didn't move. Suddenly I felt her hand touch my face questioningly. 'Fitz?' she asked softly in the darkness.

'What?'

'How much do you trust Nik?'

'I told you. Not at all. But I think he'll get us to the Mountains. For his own pride, if nothing else.' I smiled in the dark. 'A smuggler's reputation must be perfect, among those who know of it. He'll get us there.'

'Were you angry at me, earlier today?' When I said nothing, she added, 'You gave me such a serious look this morning.'

'Does the wolf bother you?' I asked her as bluntly.

She spoke quietly. 'It's true then?'

'Did you doubt it before?'

'The Witted part . . . yes. I thought it an evil lie they had told about you. That the son of a prince could be Witted . . . You did not seem a man who would share his life with an animal.' The tone of her voice left me no doubt as to how she regarded such a habit.

'Well. I do.' A tiny spark of anger made me forthright. 'He's everything to me. Everything. I have never had a truer friend, willing without question to lay his life down for mine. And more than his life. It is one thing to be willing to die for another. It is another to sacrifice the living of one's life for another. That is what he gives me. The same sort of loyalty I give to my king.'

I had set myself to thinking. I'd never put our relationship in those terms before.

'A king and a wolf,' Starling said quietly. More softly she added, 'Do you care for no one else?'

'Molly.'

'Molly?'

'She's at home. Back in Buck. She's my wife.' A queer little tremor of pride shivered through me as I said the words. My wife.

Starling sat up in the blankets, letting in a draught of cold air. I tugged at them vainly as she asked, 'A wife? You have a wife?'

'And a child. A little girl.' Despite the cold and the darkness, I grinned at those words. 'My daughter,' I said quietly, simply to hear how the words sounded. 'I have a wife and a daughter at home.'

She flung herself down in the darkness beside me. 'No you don't!' she denied it with an emphatic whisper. 'I'm a minstrel, Fitz. If the Bastard had married, the word would have gone round. In fact, there were rumours you were for Celerity, Duke Brawndy's daughter.'

'It was done quietly,' I told her.

'Ah. I see. You're not married at all. You've a woman, is what you're trying to say.'

The words stung me. 'Molly is my wife,' I said firmly. 'In every way that matters to me, she is my wife.'

'And in the ways that might matter to her? And a child?' Starling asked me quietly.

I took a deep breath. 'When I go back, that will be the first thing we remedy. It was promised to me, by Verity himself, that when he was king, I should marry whomever I wished.' Some part of me was aghast at how freely I was speaking to her. Another part asked, what harm could it do for her to know? And there was relief in being able to speak of it.

'So you do go to find Verity?'

'I go to serve my king. To lend whatever aid I may to Kettricken and Verity's heir-child. And then to go on, to beyond the Mountains, to find and restore my king. So he may drive the Red Ships from the Six Duchies coast and we may know peace again.'

For a moment all was silence save for the slicing wind outside the canvas. Then she snorted softly. 'Do even half of that, and I shall have my hero song.'

'I have no desire to be a hero. Only to do what I must to be free to live my own life.'

'Poor Fitz. None of us are ever free to do that.'

'You seem very free to me.'

'Do I? To me it seems as if every step I take carries me deeper into a mire, and the more I struggle, the more firmly I embed myself.'

'How is that?'

She gave a choked laugh. 'Look about you. Here I am, sleeping in straw and singing for my supper, gambling that there will eventually be a way to cross this river and go on to the Mountains. And if I get through all that, have I achieved my goal? No. I still must dangle after you until you do something songworthy.'

'You really needn't,' I said in some dismay at the prospect. 'You could go on your way, making your way as a minstrel. You seem to do well enough at it.'

'Well enough. Well enough for a travelling minstrel. You've heard me sing, Fitz. I've a good enough voice, and nimble enough fingers. But I am not extraordinary, and that is what it takes to win a position as keep minstrel. That's assuming there will be any more keeps in five years or so. I've no mind to sing to a Red Ship audience.'

For a moment we were both quiet, considering.

'You see,' she went on after a time, 'I've no one any more. Parents and brother gone. My old master gone, Lord Bronze gone, who was partial to me mostly for my master's sake. All gone when the keep burned. The Raiders left me for dead, you know, or I'd truly be dead.' For the first time, I heard hints of an old fear in her voice. She was quiet for a time, thinking of all that she would not mention. I rolled to face her. 'I've only myself to rely on. For now, for always. Only myself. And there's a limit to how long a minstrel can wander about singing for coins in inns. If you wish to be comfortable when you're old, you have to earn a place in a keep. Only a truly great song will do that for me, Fitz. And I've a limited amount of time in which to find one.' Her voice grew softer, her breath warm as she said, 'And so I shall follow you. For great events seem to happen in your wake.'

'Great events?' I scoffed.

She hitched herself closer to me. 'Great events. The abdication of the throne by Prince Chivalry. The triumph against the Red Ships at Antler Island. Were not you the one who saved Queen Kettricken from Forged Ones the night she was attacked, right before the Vixen Queen's Hunt? (Now there's a song I wish I had written.) To say nothing of precipitating the riots the night of Prince Regal's coronation. Let's see. Rising from the dead, making an attempt on Regal's life right inside Tradeford Hall and then escaping unscathed. Killing half a dozen of his guard single-handedly while manacled . . . I had a feeling I should have followed you that day. But I'd say I'd a good chance of witnessing something noteworthy if I but held onto your shirttail from now on.'

I'd never thought of those events as a list of things I'd caused. I wanted to protest that I had not caused any of them, that I had merely been caught up in the grinding wheels of history. Instead I just sighed. 'All I want to do is go home to Molly and our little daughter.'

'She probably longs for the same thing. It can't be easy for her, wondering when you'll come back, or if.'

'She doesn't wonder. She already believes me dead.'

After a time, Starling said hesitantly, 'Fitz. She thinks you dead. How can you believe she will be there waiting when you return, that she won't find someone else?'

I had played a dozen scenes in my head. That I might die before I returned home, or that when I returned, Molly would see me as a liar and a Witted one, that she would be repelled by my scars. I fully expected her to be angry at me for not letting her know I was alive. But I would explain that I had believed she had found another man and was happy with him. And then she'd understand and forgive me. After all, she was the one who had left me. Somehow I had never imagined returning home to find she had replaced me with someone else. Stupid. How could I not have foreseen that might happen, simply because it was the worst possible thing I could imagine? I spoke more to myself than Starling. 'I suppose I'd better get word to her. Send her a message, somehow. But I don't know exactly where she is. Nor who I'd entrust with such a message.'

'How long have you been gone?' she demanded to know.

'From Molly? Almost a year.'

'A year! Men,' Starling muttered softly to herself. 'They go off to fight or to travel and they expect their lives to be waiting for them when they get back. You expect the women who stay behind to keep the fields and raise the children and patch the roof and mind the cow, so that when you walk back in the door, you can find your chair still by the fire and hot bread on the table. Yes, and a warm, willing body in your bed, still waiting for you.' She was beginning to sound angry. 'How many days have you been gone from her? Well, that's how many days she has had to cope without you. Time doesn't stop for her just because you're gone. How do you think of her? Rocking your baby beside a warm hearth? How about this? The baby is inside, crying and untended on the bed, while she's out in the rain and wind trying to split wood for kindling because the fire went out while she was walking to and from the mill to get a bit of meal ground.'

I pushed the image away. No. Burrich wouldn't let that happen. 'In my mind, I see her in many ways. Not just in good times,' I defended myself. 'And she isn't completely alone. A friend of mine is looking after her.'

'Ah, a friend,' Starling agreed smoothly. 'And is he handsome, spirited and bold enough to steal any woman's heart?'

I snorted. 'No. He's older. He's stubborn, and cranky. But he's also steady and reliable and thoughtful. He always treats women well. Politely and kindly. He'll take good care of both her and the child.' I smiled to myself, and knew the truth of it as I added, 'He'll kill any man that even looks a threat at them.'

'Steady, kind and thoughtful? Treats women well?' Starling's voice rose with feigned interest. 'Do you know how rare a man like that is? Tell me who he is, I want him for myself. If your Molly will let him go.'

I confess I knew a moment's unease. I remembered a day when Molly had teased me, saying I was the best thing to come out of the stables since Burrich. When I had been sceptical as to whether that was a compliment, she had told me he was well regarded among the ladies, for all his silences and aloof ways. Had she ever looked at Burrich and considered him? No. It was me she had made love with that day, clinging to me although we could not be wed. 'No. She loves me. Only me.'

I had not intended to say the words aloud. Some note in my voice must have touched a kinder place in Starling's nature. She gave over tormenting me. 'Oh. Well, then. I still think you should send her word. So she has hope to keep her strong.'

'I will,' I promised myself. As soon as I reached Jhaampe. Kettricken would know some way by which I could get word back to Burrich. I could send back just a brief written message, not too plainly worded in case it was intercepted. I could ask him to tell her I was alive and I would return to her. But how would I get the message to him?

I lay silently musing in the dark. I did not know where Molly was living. Lacey would possibly know. But I could not send word via Lacey without Patience finding out. No. Neither of them must know. There had to be someone we both knew, someone I could trust. Not Chade. I could trust him, but no one would know how to find Chade, even if they knew him by that name.

Somewhere in the barn, a horse thudded a hoof against a stall wall. 'You're very quiet,' Starling whispered.

'I'm thinking.'

'I didn't mean to upset you.'

'You didn't. You just made me think.'

'Oh.' A pause. 'I am so cold.'

'Me, too. But it's colder outside.'

'That doesn't make me the least bit warmer. Hold me.'

It was not a request. She burrowed into my chest, tucking her head under my chin. She smelled nice. How did women always manage to smell nice? Awkwardly I put my arms around her, grateful for the added warmth but uneasy at the closeness. 'That's better,' she sighed. I felt her body relax against mine. She added, 'I hope we get a chance to bathe soon.'

'Me, too.'

'Not that you smell that bad.'

'Thank you,' I said a bit sourly. 'Mind if I go back to sleep now?'

'Go ahead.' She put a hand on my hip and added, 'If that's all you can think of to do.'

I managed to draw a breath. Molly, I told myself. Starling was so warm and near, smelling so sweet. Her minstrel's ways made nothing of what she suggested. To her. But what was Molly, truly, to me? 'I told you. I'm married.' It was hard to speak.

'Um. And she loves you, and you obviously love her. But we are the ones who are here, and cold. If she loves you that much would she begrudge you an added bit of warmth and comfort on such a cold night?'

It was difficult, but I forced myself to think about it a bit, then smiled to myself in the darkness. 'She wouldn't just begrudge me. She'd knock my head off my shoulders.'

'Ah.' Starling laughed softly into my chest. 'I see.' Gently she drew her body away from mine. I longed to reach out and pull her back to me. 'Perhaps we'd better just go to sleep, then. Sleep well, Fitz.'

So I did, but not right away and not without regrets.

The night brought us rising winds, and when the barn doors were unbolted in the morning, a fresh layer of snow greeted us. I worried that if it got much deeper, we'd have serious problems with the wagons. But Nik seemed confident and genial as he loaded us up. He bid a fond farewell to his lady and we set forth again. He led us away from the place by a different trail from the one we had followed to get there. This one was rougher, and in a few places the snow had drifted deep enough that the wagon bodies gouged a path through it. Starling rode beside us for part of the morning, until Nik sent a man back to ask her if she'd come ride with them. She thanked him cheerily for the invitation and promptly went to join him.

In the early afternoon, we came back to the road. It seemed to me that we had gained little by avoiding the road for so long, but doubtless Nik had had his reasons. Perhaps he simply did not want to create a beaten track to his hiding place. That evening our shelter was crude, some tumbledown huts by the riverbank. The thatched roofs were giving way, so there were fingers of snow on the floors in places and a great plume of snow that had blown in under the door. The horses had no shelter at all other than the lee of the cabin. We watered them at the river and they each got a portion of grain, but no hay awaited them here.

Nighteyes went with me to gather firewood, for while there was enough by the hearths to start a fire for a meal, there was not enough to last the night. As we walked down to the river to look for driftwood I mused on how things had changed between us. We spoke less than we once had, but I felt that I was more aware of him than I had ever been before. Perhaps there was less need to speak. But we had also both changed in our time apart. When I looked at him now, I sometimes saw the wolf first and then my companion.

I think you have finally begun to respect me as I deserve. There was teasing but also truth in that statement. He appeared suddenly in a patch of brush on the riverbank to my left, loped easily across the snowswept trail, and somehow managed to vanish in little more than snow dunes and leafless, scrubby bushes.

You're no longer a puppy, that's true.

Neither of us are cubs any more. We've both discovered that on this journey. You no longer think of yourself as a boy at all.

I trudged wordlessly through the snow and pondered that. I did not know quite when I had finally decided I was a man and not a boy any longer, but Nighteyes was right. Oddly, I felt a moment of loss for that vanished lad with the smooth face and easy courage.

I think I made a better boy than I do a man, I admitted ruefully to the wolf.

Why not wait until you've been at it a bit longer and then decide? he suggested.

The track we followed was barely a cart wide and visible only as a swatch where no brush poked up above the snow. The wind was busy sculpting the snow into dunes and banks. I walked into the wind, and my forehead and nose soon burned with its rough kiss. The terrain was little different from what we had passed for the last few days, but the experience of moving through it with only the wolf, silently, made it seem a different world. Then we came to the river.

I stood on top of the bank and looked across. Ice frosted the edges in places, and occasional knots of driftwood washing down the river sometimes carried a burden of dirty ice and clinging snow. The current was strong, as the swiftly bobbing driftwood showed. I tried to imagine it frozen over and could not. On the far side of that rushing flood were foothills dense with evergreens that gave onto a plain of oaks and willows that came right down to the water's edge. I suppose the water had stopped the fire's spread those years ago. I wondered if this side of the river had ever been as thickly treed as that.

Look, Nighteyes growled wistfully. I could feel the heat of his hunger as we eyed a tall buck that had come down to the river to water. He lifted his antlered head, sensing us, but regarded us calmly, knowing he was safe. I found my mouth watering with Nighteyes' thoughts of fresh meat. *Hunting will be much better on the other side.*

I hope so. He leaped from the bank to the snow-swathed gravel and rock of the river edge, and padded off upriver. I followed him less gracefully, finding dry sticks as I went. The walking was rougher down here, and the wind crueller, laden as it was with the river's cold. But it was also more interesting walking, somehow laden with more possibility. I watched Nighteyes range ahead of me. He moved differently now. He had lost a lot of his puppyish curiosity. The deer skull that once would have required a careful sniffing now got no more than a swift flipping over to be sure it was truly bare bones before he moved on. He was purposeful as he checked tangles of driftwood to see if game might be sheltering underneath it. He watched the undercut banks of the river as well, sniffing for game sign. He sprang upon and devoured a small rodent of some kind that had ventured out of a den under the bank. He dug briefly at the den's entrance, then thrust his muzzle in to snuff thoroughly. Satisfied there were no other inhabitants to dig out, he trotted on.

I found myself watching the river as I followed him. It became more daunting, not less, the more I saw of it. The depth of it and the strength of its current were attested to by the immense snaggle-rooted logs that swung and turned as the waters rushed them along. I wondered if the windstorm had been worse upriver to tear loose such giants, or if the river had slowly eaten away their foundations until the trees had tottered into the water.

Nighteyes continued to range ahead of me. Twice more I saw him leap and pin a rodent to the earth with his teeth and paws. I was not sure exactly what they were; they did not look like rats exactly, and the sleekness of their coats seemed to indicate they'd be at home in the water.

Meat doesn't really need a name, Nighteyes observed wryly, and I was forced to agree with him. He flipped his prey gleefully into the air and caught it again as it somersaulted down. He worried the dead thing fiercely and then launched it once more, dancing after it on his hind legs. For a moment his simple pleasure was contagious. He had the satisfaction of a successful hunt, meat to fill his belly and time to eat it unmolested. This time it went winging over my head, and I leaped up to catch the limp body and then fling it up higher still. He sprang high after it, all four legs leaving the ground. He seized it cleanly, then crouched, showing it to me, daring me to chase him. I dropped my armload of wood and sprang after him. He evaded me easily, then looped back to me, daring me, rushing past me just out of arm's reach as I flung myself at him.

'Hey!'

We both halted in our play. I got up slowly from the ground. It was one of Nik's men, standing far up the riverbank and staring at us. He carried his bow. 'Get some wood and come back now,' he ordered me. I glanced about, but could see no reason for the edgy tone to his voice. Nevertheless, I gathered my scattered armload of wood and headed back to the huts.

I found Kettle squinting at a scroll by the firelight, ignoring those who were trying to cook around her. 'What are you reading?' I asked her.

'The writings of Cabal the White. A prophet and seer of Kimoalan times.'

I shrugged. The names meant nothing to me.

'Through his guidance, a treaty was wrought that put an end to a hundred years of war. It enabled three folk to become one people. Knowledge was shared. Many kinds of foods that once grew only in the southern valleys of Kimoala came into common usage. Ginger, for instance. And kim-oats.'

'One man did that?'

'One man. Or two, perhaps, if you count the general he persuaded to conquer without destroying. Here, he speaks of him. "A catalyst was DarAles for his time, a changer of hearts and lives. He came not to be hero, but to enable the hero in others. He came, not to fulfil prophecies, but to open the doors to new futures. Such is ever the task of the catalyst." Above, he has written that it is in every one of us to be a catalyst in our own time. What do you think of that, Tom?'

'I'd rather be a shepherd,' I answered her truthfully. Catalyst was not a word I cherished.

That night I slept with Nighteyes at my side. Kettle snored

softly not far from me, while the pilgrims huddled together in one end of the hut. Starling had chosen to sleep in the other hut with Nik and some of his men. For a time, the sound of her harp and voice were occasionally borne to me on gusts of wind.

I closed my eyes and tried to dream of Molly. Instead I saw a burning village in Buck as the Red Ships pulled away from it. I joined a young lad as he put on sail in the dark, to ram his dory into the side of a Red Ship. He flung a burning lantern on board her and followed it with a bucket of cheap fish oil such as poor folk burned in their lamps. The sail blazed up as the boy sheered away from the burning ship. Behind him the curses and cries of the burning men rose with the flames. I rode with him that night, and felt his bitter triumph. He had nothing left, no family, no home, but he had spilled some of the blood that had spilled his. I understood the tears that wet his grinning face only too well.

SEVENTEEN

River Crossing

The Outislanders have always spoken mockingly of the Six Duchies folk, declaring us slaves of the earth, farmers fit only for grubbing in the dirt. Eda, the mother goddess who is thanked for plentiful crops and multiplying flocks, is disdained by the Outislanders as a goddess for a settled folk who have lost all spirit. The Outislanders themselves worship only El, the god of the sea. He is not a deity to offer thanks to, but a god to swear by. The only blessing he sends his worshippers are storms and hardships to make them strong.

In this they misjudged the people of the Six Duchies. They believed folk who planted crops and raised sheep would soon come to have no more spirit than sheep. They came amongst us slaughtering and destroying and mistook our concern for our folk for weakness. In that winter, the small folk of Buck and Bearns, Rippon and Shoaks, the fisherfolk and herders, goose-girls and pig-boys, took up the war that our wrangling nobles and scattered armies waged so poorly and made it their own. The small folk of a land can only be oppressed so long before they rise up in their own defence, be it against outlanders or an unjust lord of their own.

The others grumbled the next morning about the cold and the need for haste. They spoke longingly of hot porridge and hearth-cakes. There was hot water, but little more than that to warm our bellies. I filled Kettle's teapot for her and then went back to fill my cup with hot water. I squinted my eyes against the pain as I dug in my pack for my elfbark. My Skill-dream of the night before had left me feeling sick and shaky. The very thought of food made me ill. Kettle sipped her tea and watched as I used my knife to scrape shavings from a lump of bark into my mug. It was hard to make myself wait for the liquid to brew. The extreme bitterness of it flooded my mouth, but almost immediately I felt my headache ease. Kettle abruptly reached a claw-like hand to pluck the chunk of bark from my hand. She looked at it, sniffed it and, 'Elfbark!' she exclaimed. She gave me a look of horror. 'That's a vicious herb for a young man to be using.'

'It calms my headaches,' I told her. I took a breath to steel myself, then drank off the rest of the mug. The gritty remnants of bark stuck to my tongue. I forced myself to swallow them, then wiped out my mug and returned it to my pack. I held out my hand and she gave back the chunk of bark, but reluctantly. The look she was giving me was very strange.

'I've never seen anyone just drink it down like that. Do you know what that stuff is used for, in Chalced?'

'I've been told they feed it to galley slaves, to keep their strength up.'

'Strength up and hopes down. A man on elfbark is easily discouraged. Easier to control. It may dull the pain of a headache, but it dulls the mind as well. I'd be wary of it, were I you.'

I shrugged. 'I've used it for years,' I told her as I put the herb back in my pack.

'All the more reason to stop now,' she replied tartly. She handed me her pack to put back in the wagon for her.

It was mid-afternoon when Nik ordered our wagons to a halt. He and two of his men rode ahead, while the others assured us all was fine. Nik went ahead to ready the crossing place before we arrived there. I did not even need to glance at Nighteyes. He slipped away to follow Nik and his men. I leaned back on the seat and hugged myself, trying to stay warm.

'Hey, you. Call your dog back!' One of Nik's men commanded me suddenly.

I sat up and made a show of looking around for him. 'He's probably just scented a rabbit. He'll be back. Follows me everywhere, he does.'

'Call him back now!' the man told me threateningly.

So I stood up on the wagon seat and called Nighteyes. He did not come. I shrugged an apology at the men and sat down again. One continued to glare at me, but I ignored him.

The day had been clear and cold, the wind cutting. Kettle had been miserably silent all day. Sleeping on the ground had awakened the old pain in my shoulder to a constant jab. I did not even want to imagine what she was feeling. I tried to think only that we would soon be across the river, and that after that the Mountains were not far. Perhaps in the Mountains I would finally feel safe from Regal's coterie.

Some men pull ropes by the river. I closed my eyes and tried to see what Nighteyes did. It was difficult, for he directed his eyes at the men themselves, while I wished to study the task they did. But just as I discerned they were using a guideline to restring a heavier rope across the river, two other men on the far side began energetically digging through a pile of driftwood in the curve of a bank. The concealed barge was soon revealed, and the men went to work chopping away the ice that had formed on it.

'Wake up!' Kettle told me irritably, and gave me a poke in the ribs. I sat up to see the other wagon already in motion. I stirred the mare's reins and followed the others. We travelled a short way down the river-road before turning off it onto an open section of bank. There were some burned-out huts by the river that had apparently perished in the fires years ago. There was also a crude ramp of logs and mortar, much decayed now. On the far side of the river, I could see the remains of the old barge, half sunken. Ice covered parts of it, but dead grass also stuck up from it. It had been many seasons since it had floated. The huts on the other side were in as poor repair as the ones over here, for their thatched roofs had collapsed completely. Behind them rose gentle hills covered in evergreens. Beyond them, towering in the distance, were the peaks of the Mountain Kingdom.

A team of men had attached the revealed barge and were working it across the river to us. The bow was pointed into the current. The barge was tightly bridled to the pulley-line; even so the angry river strove to tear it loose and wash it downstream. It was not a large vessel. A wagon and team was going to be a snug fit. There were railings down the side of the barge, but other than that it was simply a flat, open deck. On our side, the ponies that Nik and his men had been riding had been harnessed to pull on the barge's tow-line while on the other side a team of patient mules backed slowly toward the water. As the barge came slowly toward us, her bow rose and fell as the river pushed against it. The current foamed and churned around its sides, while an occasional dip of the bow allowed a surge of water to fly up and over. It was not going to be a dry ride across.

The pilgrims muttered amongst themselves anxiously, but one man's voice suddenly rose to quell them. 'What other choice do we have?' he pointed out. Thereafter silence fell. They watched the barge come toward us with dread.

Nik's wagon and team were the first load across. Perhaps Nik did it that way to give the pilgrims courage. I watched as the barge was brought up snug to the old ramp and secured stern-in. I sensed the displeasure of his team, but also that they were familiar with this. Nik himself led them onto the barge and held their heads while two of his men scrambled about and tied the wagon down to the cleats. Then Nik stepped off, and waved his hand in signal. The two men stood, one by each horse's head, as the mule team on the other side took up the slack. The barge was cast off and moved out into the river. Laden, it sat more deeply in the water, but it did not bob as freely as it had. Twice the bow lifted high and then plunged back deeply enough to take a wash of water over it. All was silence on our side of the river as we watched the barge's passage. On the other side, it was pulled in and secured bow-first, the wagon unfastened, and the men drove it off and up the hill.

'There. You see. Nothing to worry about.' Nik spoke with an easy grin, but I doubted that he believed his own words.

A couple of men rode the barge back as it came across. They did not look happy about it. They clung to the railings and winced away from the flying spray off the river. Nevertheless they were both soaked by the time the barge reached our side and they stepped off. One man gestured Nik to one side and began to confer with him angrily, but he clapped him on the shoulders and laughed loudly as if it were all a fine joke. He held out his hand and they passed him a small pouch. He hefted it approvingly before hanging it from his belt. 'I keep my word,' he reminded them, and then strode back to our group.

The pilgrims went across next. Some of them wished to cross in the wagon, but Nik patiently pointed out that the heavier the load, the lower the barge rode in the river. He herded them onto the barge and made sure that each person had a good place to grip along the rail. 'You, too,' he called, motioning to Kettle and Starling.

'I'll go across with my cart,' Kettle declared, but Nik shook his head.

'Your mare isn't going to like this. If she goes crazy out there, you don't want to be on the barge. Trust me. I know what I'm doing.' He glanced at me. 'Tom? You mind riding across with the horse? You seem to handle her well.'

I nodded, and Nik said, 'There, now, Tom'll see to your mare. You go on, now.'

Kettle scowled, but had to own the sense of that. I helped her down, and Starling took her arm and walked her to the barge. Nik stepped onto the barge and spoke briefly to the pilgrims, telling them to simply hold on and not fear. Three of his men boarded the barge with them. One insisted on holding the smallest pilgrim child himself. 'I know what to expect,' he told the anxious mother. 'I'll see she gets across. You just have a care to yourself.' The little girl began to cry at that and her shrill wailing could be heard even over the rushing of the river water as the barge was pulled out onto the river. Nik stood beside me watching them go.

'They'll be fine,' he said, as much to himself as to me. He turned to me with a grin. 'Well, Tom, a few more trips and I'll be wearing that pretty earring of yours.'

I nodded to that silently. I'd given my word on the bargain but I was not happy about it.

Despite Nik's words, I heard him sigh with relief when the barge reached the other side. The drenched pilgrims scuttled off even as the men were securing it. I watched Starling help Kettle off, and then some of Nik's men hurried them up the bank and into the shelter of the trees. Then the barge was coming back to us again, bearing two more men. The pilgrims' empty wagon went next, along with a couple of ponies. The pilgrims' horses were not at all pleased. It took blindfolds and three men tugging to get them onto the barge. Once there and tied down, the horses still shifted as much as they could, snorting and shaking their heads. I watched them cross. On the other side, the team needed no urging to get the wagon swiftly off the barge. A man took the reins and the wagon rattled up the hill and out of sight.

The two men who rode back that time had the worst crossing yet. They were halfway across the river when an immense snag came in sight, bearing directly down on the barge. The clawing roots looked like a monstrous hand as the log bobbed in the fierce current. Nik shouted at our ponies and all of us sprang to help them haul on the rope, but even so the log struck the barge a glancing blow. The men on board yelled as the impact shook them from their grips on the railing. One was nearly flung off, but managed to catch a second post and hung on for dear life. Those two came off glaring and cursing, as if they suspected the mishap had been deliberate. Nik had the barge secured and himself checked all the lines fastening her to the pulley-rope. The impact had knocked one railing loose. He shook his head over that, and warned his men about it as they drove the last wagon aboard it.

Its crossing was no worse than any of the others. I watched with some trepidation, knowing that my turn was next. *Fancy a bath, Nighteyes?*

It will be worth it if there's good hunting on the other side, he replied, but I could sense he shared my nervousness.

I tried to calm myself and Kettle's mare as I watched them fasten the barge to the landing. I spoke soothingly to her as I led her down, doing all I could to assure her that she would be fine. She seemed to accept it, stepping calmly onto the scarred timbers of the deck. I led her out slowly, explaining it all as I went. She stood quietly as I tied her to a ring set in the deck. Two of Nik's men roped the cart down fast. Nighteyes leapt on, then sank down, belly low, his claws digging into the wood. He didn't like the way the river tugged at the barge greedily. Truth to tell, neither did I. He ventured over to crouch beside me, feet splayed.

'You go on across with Tom and the cart,' Nik told the soaked men who had already made one trip. 'Me and my boys will bring our ponies on the last trip. Stay clear of that mare, now, in case she decides to kick.'

They came aboard warily, eyeing Nighteyes almost as distrustfully as they watched the mare. They clustered at the back of the cart, and held on there. Nighteyes and I remained at the bow. I hoped we'd be out of reach of the mare's hooves there. At the last moment, Nik declared, 'I think I'll ride this one over with you.' He cast the barge off himself with a grin and a wave at his men. The mule team on the other side of the river started up, and with a lurch we moved out into the river.

Watching something is never the same as doing it. I gasped as the first slashing spray of river-water struck me. We were suddenly a toy in the clutches of an unpredictable child. The river rushed past us, tearing at the barge and roaring its frustration that it could not drag us free. The furious water near deafened me. The barge took a sudden plunge and I found myself gripping the railing as a surge of water flowed over the deck and clutched at my ankles in passing. The second time a plume of water smacked up from the bow and drenched us all, the mare screamed. I let go of my grip of the railing, intending to take hold of her headstall. Two of the men seemed to have the same idea. They were working their way forward, clinging to the cart. I waved them away and turned to the mare.

I will never know what the man intended. Perhaps to club me with the pommel of his knife. I caught the motion from the corner of my eye and turned to face him just as the barge gave another lurch. He missed me and staggered forward against the mare. The horse, already anxious, panicked into a frenzy of kicking. She threw her head wildly, slamming it against me so that I staggered away. I had almost caught my balance when the man made another flailing try at me. On the back of the cart, Nick was struggling with another man. He angrily shouted something about his word and his honour. I ducked my attacker's blow just as a crash of water came over the bow. The force of it washed me toward the centre of the barge. I caught hold of a cartwheel and clung there, gasping I clawed my sword half-free just as someone else grabbed me from behind. My first attacker came at me, grinning, his knife blade-first this time. Suddenly a wet furry body streaked past me. Nighteyes hit him squarely in the chest, slamming him back against the railing.

I heard the crack of the weakened post. Slowly, so slowly, wolf, man and railing went tipping toward the water. I lunged after them, dragging my assailant with me. As they went in, I managed to catch both the shattered remains of the post and Nighteyes' tail. I sacrificed my sword to do it. My grip was only on the end of his tail but I held on. His head came up, his front paws scrabbled frantically against the edge of the barge. He started to climb back on.

Then a booted foot came down with a smash on my shoulder. The dull ache in it exploded. The next boot caught me in the side of the head. I watched my fingers fly open, saw Nighteyes spun away from me, snatched by the river and borne off.

'My brother!' I cried aloud. The river swallowed my words, and the next slosh of water over the deck drenched me and filled my mouth and nose. When the water passed, I tried to get to my hands and knees. The man who had kicked me knelt beside me. I felt the press of his knife against my neck.

'Just stay where you are, and hold on,' he suggested grimly. He turned and yelled back at Nik. 'I'm doing this my way!'

I did not answer. I was questing out savagely, putting all my strength into reaching after the wolf. The barge surged under me, the river roared past, and I was drenched by spray and waves. Cold. Wet. Water in my mouth and nose, choking. I couldn't tell where I ended and Nighteyes began. If he still existed at all.

The barge scraped suddenly against the ramp.

They were clumsy in getting me to my feet on the other side. The one removed his knife before the second man had a good grip on my hair. I came up fighting, caring nothing for anything else they might do to me now. I radiated hate and fury and the panicky horse followed my lead. One man went down close enough to the mare that one of her hooves stove in his ribs. That left two, or so I thought. I shouldered one into the river. He managed to catch hold of the barge and clung there while I choked his companion. Nik shouted what sounded like a warning. I was squeezing his throat and bashing his head on the deck when the others fell on me. These ones wore their brown and gold openly. I tried to make them kill me, but they didn't. I heard other cries from far up the hillside and thought I recognized Starling's voice raised in anger.

After a time, I lay trussed on the snowy riverbank. A man stood guard over me with a drawn sword. I didn't know if he threatened me, or if he was charged with keeping the others from killing me. They stood in a circle, staring down at me avidly, like a pack of wolves who had just brought down a deer. I didn't care. Frantically, I quested out, caring nothing for anything they might do to me. I could sense that somewhere he fought for his life. My sense of him grew fainter and fainter as he put all his energies into simply surviving.

Nik was suddenly flung down beside me. One of his eyes was starting to puff shut and when he grinned at me, blood stained his teeth. 'Well, here we are, Tom, on the other side of the river. I said I'd bring you here, and here we are. I'll take that earring now, as we agreed.'

My guard kicked him in the ribs. 'Shut up,' he growled.

'This wasn't the agreement,' Nik insisted when he could take a breath.

He looked up at them all, tried to choose one to speak to. 'I had a deal with your captain. I told him I'd bring him this man, and in return, he offered me gold and safe passage. For me and the others.'

The sergeant gave a bitter laugh. 'Well, it wouldn't be the first deal Captain Mark made with a smuggler. Odd. Not a one of them ever profited us, hey, boys? And Captain Mark, he's down the river a way now, so it's hard to tell just what he promised you. Always liked his glory shows, did Mark. Well, now he's gone. But I know what my orders are, and that's to arrest all smugglers and bring them back to Moonseye. I'm a good soldier, I am.'

The sergeant stooped down and relieved Nik of the pouch of gold, and his own pouch as well. Nik struggled, and lost some blood in the process. I did not bother watching much of it. He'd sold me to Regal's guards. And how had he known who I was? Pillow talk with Starling, I told myself bitterly. I had trusted, and it had brought me what it always did. I did not even turn to look when they dragged him away.

I had but one true friend, and my foolishness had cost him. Again. I stared up at the sky and reached out of my body, threw my senses as wide as I could, questing, questing. I found him. Somewhere, his claws scrabbled and scratched at a steep and icy bank. His dense coat was laden with water, heavy with it so he could scarcely keep his head up. He lost his purchase, the river seized him again, and once more he spun around in it. It pulled him under and held him there, then threw him suddenly to the surface. The air he gasped in was laden with spray. He had no strength left.

Try! I commanded him. *Keep trying!*

And the fickle current flung him again against a riverbank, but this one was a tangle of dangling roots. His claws caught in them, and he hauled himself high, scrabbling at them as he choked out water and gasped in air. His lungs worked like bellows.

Get out! Shake off!

He gave me no answer at all, but I felt him haul himself out. Little by little, he gained the brushy bank. He crawled out like a puppy, on his belly. Water ran from him, forming a puddle around him where he cowered. He was so cold. Frost was already forming on his ears and muzzle. He stood up and tried to shake. He fell over. He staggered to his feet again and tottered a few more steps from the river. He shook again, water flying everywhere. The action both lightened him and stood his coat up. He stood, head down, and gagged out a gush of river-water. *Find shelter. Curl up and get warm*, I told him. He was not thinking very well. The spark that was Nighteyes had almost winked out. He sneezed violently several times, then looked around himself. *There*, I urged him. *Under that tree.* Snow had bent the evergreen's fronds almost to the ground. Beneath the tree was a little hollow, thickly floored with shed needles. If he crept in there, and curled up, he might get warm again. *Go on*, I urged him. *You can make it. Go on.*

'I think you kicked him too hard. He's just staring at the sky.'

'Did you see what that woman did to Skef? He's bleeding like a pig. He popped her a good one back.'

'Where'd the old one go? Did anyone find her?'

'She won't get far in this snow, so don't worry about it. Wake him up and get him on his feet.'

'He's not even blinking his eyes. He's hardly even breathing.'

'I don't care. Just take him to the Skill-wizard. After that, he's not our problem.'

I knew guards dragged me to my feet, I knew I was walked up the hill. I paid no attention to that body. Instead, I shook myself again, and then crept under the tree. There was just room to curl myself up. I put my tail over my nose. I flicked my ears a few times to shake the last of the water from them. *Go to sleep now. Everything's fine. Go to sleep.* I closed his eyes for him. He was still shivering, but I could feel a hesitant warmth creeping through him again. Gently I drew myself clear.

I lifted my head and looked out of my own eyes. I was walking up a trail, with a tall Farrow guard on either side of me. I didn't need to look back to know that others followed. Ahead of us, I saw Nik's wagons, pulled up in the shelter of the trees. I saw his men sitting on the ground with their hands bound behind them. The pilgrims, still dripping, huddled around a fire. Several guards stood around their group as well. I didn't see Starling or Kettle. One woman clutched her child to her and wept noisily over his shoulder. The boy did not appear to be moving. A man met my eyes, then turned aside to spit on the ground. 'It's the Witted Bastard's fault we've come to this,' I heard him say loudly. 'Eda scowls upon him! He tainted our pilgrimage!'

They marched me to a comfortable tent pitched in the lee of some great trees. I was shoved through the tent flaps and pushed down onto my knees on a thick sheepskin rug on an elevated wooden floor. One guard kept a firm grip on my hair as the sergeant announced, 'Here he is, sir. The wolf got Captain Mark, but we got him.'

A fat brazier of coals gave off a welcome heat. The interior of the tent was the warmest place I'd been in days. The sudden heat almost stupefied me. But Burl did not share my opinion. He sat in a wooden chair on the other side of the brazier, his feet out-stretched toward it. He was robed and hooded and covered over with furs as if there were nothing else between him and the night cold. He had always been a large-framed man; now he was heavy as well. His dark hair had been curled in imitation of Regal's. Displeasure shone in his dark eyes.

'How is it that you aren't dead?' he demanded of me.

There was no good answer to that question. I merely looked at him, expression bland, walls tight. His face flushed suddenly red and his cheeks appeared swollen with his anger. When he spoke, his voice was tight. He glared at the sergeant.

'Report properly.' Then, before the man could begin, he asked, 'You let the wolf get away?'

'Not let him, no sir. He attacked the captain. He and Captain Mark went into the river together, sir, and were carried off. Water that cold and swift, neither had a chance to survive. But I've sent a few men downriver to check the bank for the captain's body.'

'I'll want the wolf's body as well, if it's washed up. Be sure your men know that.'

'Yes sir.'

'Did you secure the smuggler, Nik? Or did he get away, as well?' Burl's sarcasm was heavy.

'No, sir. We have the smuggler and his men. We have those travelling with him as well, though they put up more of a fight than we expected. Some ran off in the woods, but we got them back. They claim to be pilgrims seeking Eda's shrine in the Mountains.'

'That concerns me not at all. What matters why a man broke the King's law, after he has broken it? Did you recover the gold the captain paid the smuggler?'

The sergeant looked surprised. 'No, sir. Gold paid to a smuggler? There was no sign of that. I wonder if it went downriver with Captain Mark. Perhaps he hadn't given it to the man . . .'

'I am not a fool. I know far more of what goes on than you think I do. Find it. All of it, and return it here. Did you capture all the smugglers?'

The sergeant took a breath and decided on the truth. 'There were a few with the pony team on the far side when we took down Nik. They rode off before . . .'

'Forget them. Where is the Bastard's accomplice?'

The sergeant looked blank. I believe he did not know the word.

'Did not you capture a minstrel? Starling?' Burl demanded again.

The sergeant looked uncomfortable. 'She got a bit out of control, sir. When the men were subduing the Bastard on the ramp. She lit into the man holding her and broke his nose. It took a bit to . . . get her under control.'

'Is she alive?' Burl's tone left no doubt of his contempt for their competence.

The sergeant flushed. 'Yes, sir. But . . .'

Burl silenced him with a look. 'Were your captain still alive, he would wish he were dead now. You have no concept of how to report, or of how to retain control of a situation. A man should have been sent to me immediately, to inform me of these events as they happened. The minstrel should not have been permitted to see what was happening, but secured immediately. And only an idiot would have tried to subdue a man on a barge in the middle of a strong current when all he had to do was wait for the barge to land. He'd have had a dozen swords at his command there. As for the smuggler's bribe, it will be returned to me, or you shall all go unpaid until it is made up. I am not a fool.' He glared around at everyone in the tent. 'This has been bungled. I will not excuse it.' He folded his lips tightly. When he spoke again, he spat out the words. 'All of you. Go.'

'Yes sir. Sir? The prisoner?'

'Leave him here. Leave two men outside, swords drawn. But I wish to speak to him alone.' The sergeant bowed and hastened out of the tent. His men followed him promptly.

I looked up at Burl and met his eyes. My hands were bound tightly behind me, but no one held me on my knees any more. I got to my feet and stood looking down on Burl. He met my gaze unflinchingly. When he spoke his voice was quiet. It made his words all the more threatening. 'I repeat to you what I told the sergeant. I am not a fool. I do not doubt that you already have a plan to escape. It probably includes killing me. I have a plan as well, and it includes my surviving. I am going to tell it to you. It's a simple plan, Bastard. I have always preferred simplicity. It is this. If you give me any trouble at all, I shall have you killed. As you have no doubt deduced, King Regal wishes you brought to him alive. If possible. Don't think that will prevent me from killing you if you become inconvenient. If you are thinking of your Skill, I will warn you my mind is well warded. If I even suspect you of trying it, we will try your Skill against my guard's sword. As for your Wit, well, it seems my problems are solved there, as well. But should your wolf materialize, he, too, is not proof against a sword.'

I said nothing.

'Do you understand me?'

I gave a single nod.

'That is as well. Now. If you give me no problems, you will be treated fairly. As will the others. If you are difficult at all, they, too, will share your privations. Do you understand that as well?' He met my gaze, demanding an answer.

I matched his quiet tone. 'Do you truly think I'd care if you spilled Nik's blood, now that he's sold me to you?'

He smiled. It turned me cold, for that smile had once belonged to the carpenter's genial apprentice. A different Burl now wore his skin. 'You're a wily one, Bastard, and have been since I've known you. But you've the same weakness of your father and the Pretender; you believe even one of these peasants' lives to be worth the equal of yours. Be any trouble to me, and they all pay, to the last drop of blood. Do you understand me? Even Nik.'

He was right. I had no stomach to visualize the pilgrims paying for my daring. I quietly asked, 'And if I am co-operative? What becomes of them, then?'

He shook his head over my foolishness in caring. 'Three years' servitude. Were I a less kindly man, I'd take a hand from each of them, for they have directly disobeyed the King's orders in attempting to cross the border and deserve to be punished as traitors. Ten years for the smugglers.'

I knew few of the smugglers would survive. 'And the minstrel?'

I do not know why he answered my question, but he did. 'The minstrel will have to die. You know that already. She knew who you were, for Will questioned her back in Blue Lake. She chose to help you, when she could have served her king instead. She is a traitor.'

His words ignited the spark of my temper. 'In helping me, she serves the true king. And when Verity returns, you will feel his wrath. There will be no one to shield you or the rest of your false coterie.'

For a moment, Burl only looked at me. I caught control of myself. I had sounded like a child, threatening another with his big brother's wrath. My words were useless, and worse than useless.

'Guards!' Burl did not shout. He scarcely lifted his voice at all, but the two were inside the tent instantly, swords drawn and pointed at my face. Burl behaved as if he did not notice the weapons. 'Bring the minstrel to us here. And see that she does not get "out of control" this time.' When they hesitated, he shook his head and sighed. 'Go on, now, both of you. Send your sergeant to me as well.' When they had departed, he met my eyes and made a face of discontent. 'You see what they give me to work with. Moonseye has ever been the refuse pile for Six Duchies soldiery. I have the cravens, the fools, the discontents, the connivers. And then I must face my king's displeasure when every task given them is botched.'

I think he actually expected me to commiserate with him. 'So, Regal has sent you here to join them,' I observed instead.

Burl gave me a strange smile. 'As King Shrewd sent your father and Verity here before me.'

That was true. I looked down at the thick sheepskin covering the floor. I was dripping on it. The warmth from the brazier was seeping into me, causing me to shiver as if my body were giving up cold it had hoarded. For an instant I quested away from myself. My wolf slept now, warmer than I was. Burl reached to a small table beside his chair and took up a pot. He poured a steaming cup of beef broth for himself and sipped at it. I could smell its savour. Then he sighed and leaned back in his chair.

'We've come a long way from where we began, haven't we?' He almost sounded regretful.

I bobbed my head. He was a cautious man, Burl, and I did not doubt that he would carry out his threats. I had seen the shape of his Skill, and seen, too, how Galen had bent and twisted it into a tool that Regal would use. He was loyal to an upstart prince. That Galen had forged into him; he could no longer separate it from his Skill. He had ambitions for power, and he loved the indolent life his Skill had earned him. His arms no longer bulged with the muscles of his work. Instead his belly stretched his tunics and the jowls of his cheeks hung heavy. He seemed a decade older than I was. But he would guard his position against anything that threatened it. Guard it savagely.

The sergeant reached the tent first, but his men came with Starling shortly afterwards. She walked between them and entered the tent with dignity despite her bruised face and swollen lip. There was an icy calm to her as she stood straight before Burl and gave him no greeting at all. Perhaps only I sensed the fury she contained. Of fear she showed no sign at all.

When she stood alongside me, Burl lifted his eyes to consider us both. He pointed one finger at her. 'Minstrel. You are aware that this man is FitzChivalry, the Witted Bastard.'

Starling made no response. It was not a question.

'In Blue Lake, Will, of Galen's Coterie, servant of King Regal, offered you gold, good honest coin, if you could help us track down this man. You denied all knowledge of where he was.' He paused, as if giving her a chance to speak. She said nothing. 'Yet, here we have found you, travelling in his company again.' He took a deep breath. 'And now he tells me that you, in serving him, serve Verity the Pretender. And he threatens me with Verity's wrath. Tell me. Before I respond to this, do you agree with this? Or has he misspoken on your behalf?'

We both knew he was offering her a chance. I hoped she'd have the sense to take it. I saw Starling swallow. She did not look at me. When she spoke, her voice was low and controlled. 'I need no one to speak for me, my lord. Nor am I any man's servant. I do not serve FitzChivalry.' She paused, and I felt dizzying relief. But then she took breath and went on, 'But if Verity Farseer lives, then he is true king of the Six Duchies. And I do not doubt that all who say otherwise will feel his wrath. If he returns.'

Burl sighed out through his nose. He shook his head regretfully. He gestured to one of the waiting men. 'You. Break one of her fingers. I don't care which one.'

'I am a minstrel!' Starling objected in horror. She stared at him in disbelief. We all did. It was not unheard of for a minstrel to be executed for treason. To kill a minstrel was one thing. To harm one was entirely another.

'Did you not hear me?' Burl asked the man when he hesitated.

'Sir, she's a minstrel.' The man looked stricken. 'It's bad luck to harm a minstrel.'

Burl turned away from him to his sergeant. 'You will see he receives five lashes before I retire this night. Five, mind you, and I wish to be able to count the separate welts on his back.'

'Yes, sir,' the sergeant said faintly.

Burl turned back to the man. 'Break one of her fingers. I don't care which one.' He spoke the command as if he had never uttered the words before.

The man moved toward her like a man in a dream. He was going to obey, and Burl was not going to stop the order.

'I will kill you,' I promised Burl sincerely.

Burl smiled at me serenely. 'Guardsman. Make that two of her fingers. I do not care which ones.' The sergeant moved swiftly, drawing his knife and stepping behind me. He set it to my throat and pushed me to my knees. I looked up at Starling. She glanced at me once, her eyes flat and empty, then looked away. Her hands, like mine, were bound behind her. She stared straight ahead at Burl's chest. Still and silent she stood, going whiter and whiter until the guardsman actually touched her. She cried out, a hoarse guttural sound as he gripped her wrists. Then she screamed, but her cry could not cover the two small snaps her fingers made as the man bent them backwards at the joints.

'Show me,' Burl commanded.

As if angry with Starling that he had had to do this, the man thrust her down on her face. She lay on the sheepskin before Burl's feet. After the scream, she had not made a sound. The two smallest fingers on her left hand stood out crazily from the others. Burl looked down at them, and nodded, satisfied.

'Take her away. See she is well guarded. Then come back and see your sergeant. When he is finished with you, come to me.' Burl's voice was even.

The guard seized Starling by her collar and dragged her to her feet. He looked both ill and angry as he prodded her out of the tent. Burl nodded to the sergeant. 'Let him up, now.'

I stood looking down at him, and he looked up at me. But there was no longer the slightest doubt as to who was in control of the situation. His voice was very quiet as he observed, 'Earlier you said you understood me. Now I know that you do. The journey to Moonseye can be swift and easy for you, FitzChivalry. And for the others. Or it can be otherwise. It is entirely up to you.'

I made no reply. None was needed. Burl nodded to the other guardsman. He took me from Burl's tent to another one. Four other guards inhabited it. He gave me both bread and meat and a cup of water. I was docile as he retied my hands in front of me so I could eat. Afterwards, he pointed me to a blanket in a corner, and I went like an obedient dog. They bound my hands behind me again and tied my feet. They kept the brazier burning all night, and always there were at least two watching me.

I did not care. I turned away from them and faced the wall of the tent. I closed my eyes, and went, not to sleep, but to my wolf. His coat was mostly dry, but still he slept in exhaustion. Both the cold and the battering of the river had taken their toll of him. I took what small comfort was left to me. Nighteyes lived, and now he slept. I wondered on which side of the river.

EIGHTEEN

Moonseye

Moonseye is a small but fortified town on the border between the Six Duchies and the Mountain Kingdom. It is a provisioning town and traditional stopping-place for trade caravans using the Chelika trail to the Wide Vale pass and the lands beyond the Mountain Kingdom. It was from Moonseye that Prince Chivalry negotiated his last great treaty with Prince Rurisk of the Mountain Kingdom. On the heels of finalizing this treaty came the discovery that Chivalry was father to an illegitimate son conceived with a woman from that area and already some six years old. King-in-Waiting Chivalry concluded his negotiations and immediately rode home to Buckkeep, where he offered his queen, father and subjects his deepest apologies for his youthful failure, and abdicated the throne to avoid creating any confusion as to the line of succession.

Burl kept his word. By day I walked, flanked by guards, my hands bound behind me. I was housed in a tent by night and my hands unbound that I might feed myself. No one was unnecessarily cruel to me. I do not know if Burl had ordered that I be strictly left alone, or if enough tales of the Witted, poisoning Bastard had been spread that no one ventured to bother me. In any case, my trek to Moonseye was no more unpleasant than foul weather and military provisions made it. I was sequestered from the pilgrims so I knew nothing of how Kettle, Starling and the pilgrims fared. My guards did not talk among themselves in my presence, so I had not even camp gossip for rumours. I dared not ask after any of them. Even to think of Starling and what they had done to her made me ill. I wondered if anyone would pity her enough to straighten and bind her fingers. I wondered if Burl would allow it. It surprised me how often I thought of Kettle and the children of the pilgrims.

I did have Nighteyes. My second night in Burl's custody, after a hasty feeding of bread and cheese, I was left alone in a corner of a tent that housed six men-at-arms as well. My wrists and ankles were well bound, but not cruelly tight, and a blanket flung over me. My guards soon became engrossed in a game of dice by the candle that lit the tent. It was a tent of good goat leather, and they had floored it with cedar boughs for their own comfort, so I did not suffer much from cold. I was aching and weary and the food in my belly made me drowsy. Yet I struggled to stay awake. I quested out toward Nighteyes, almost fearful of what I might find. I had had only the barest traces of his presence in my mind since I had bid him sleep. Now I reached for him and was jolted to feel him quite close by. He revealed himself as if stepping through a curtain, and seemed amused at my shock.

How long have you been able to do that?

A while. I had been giving thought to what the bear-man told us. And when we were apart, I came to know I had a life of my own. I found a place of my own in my mind.

I sensed a hesitancy to his thought, as if he expected me to rebuke him for it. Instead I embraced him, wrapping him in the warmth I felt for him. *I feared you would die.*

I fear the same for you, now. Almost humbly he added, *But I lived. And now at least one of us is free, to rescue the other.*

I am glad you are safe. But I fear there is little you can do for me. And if they catch sight of you, they will not rest until they have killed you.

Then they shall not catch sight of me, he promised lightly. He carried me off hunting with him that night.

The next day it took all of my concentration to stay on my feet and moving. A storm blew up. We attempted a military pace despite the snowy trails we followed and the shrieking winds that constantly buffeted us with threats of snow. As we moved away from the river and up into the foothills, the trees and underbrush were thicker. We heard the wind in the trees above us, but felt it less. The cold became dryer and more bitter at night the higher we went. The food I was given was enough to keep me on my feet and alive, but little more. Burl rode at the head of his procession, followed by his mounted guard. I walked behind in the midst of my guards. Behind us came the pilgrims flanked by regulars. Behind all that trailed the baggage train.

At the end of each day's march, I was confined to a swiftly-pitched tent, fed and then ignored until the next day's rising. My conversations were limited to accepting my meals, and to night-time thought-sharing with Nighteyes. The hunting on this side of the river was lush compared to where we had been. He found game almost effortlessly and was well on his way to rebuilding his old strength. He found it no trouble at all to keep pace with us and still have time to hunt. Nighteyes had just torn into a rabbit's entrails on my fourth night as a prisoner when he suddenly lifted his head and snuffed the wind.

What is it?

Hunters. Stalkers. He abandoned his meat and stood. He was on a hillside above Burl's camp. Moving toward it, slipping from tree to tree, were at least two dozen shadowy figures. A dozen carried bows. As Nighteyes watched, two crouched in the cover of a dense thicket. In a few moments, his keen nose caught the scent of smoke. A tiny fire glowed dully at their feet. They signalled the others, who spread out, noiseless as shadows. Archers sought vantage points while the others slipped into the camp below. Some went toward the picket-lines of the animals. With my own ears, I heard stealthy footsteps outside the tent where I lay trussed. They did not pause. Nighteyes smelled the stench of burning pitch. An instant later, two flaming bolts went winging through the night. They struck Burl's tent. In a moment, a great cry arose. As sleeping soldiers stumbled out of their tents and headed toward the blaze, the archers on the hillside rained arrows down on them.

Burl stumbled out of the burning tent, wrapping his blankets about himself as he came and bellowing orders. 'They're after the Bastard, you fools! Guard him at all costs!' Then an arrow went skipping past him over the frozen ground. He cried out and flung himself flat into the shelter of a supply wagon. A breath later two arrows thudded into it.

The men in my tent had leaped up at the first commotion. I

had largely ignored them, preferring Nighteyes' view of the events. But when the sergeant burst into the tent, his first order was, 'Drag him outside before they fire the tent. Keep him down. If they come for him, cut his throat!'

The sergeant's orders were followed quite literally. A man knelt on my back, his bared knife set to my throat. Six others surrounded us. All about us, in the darkness, other men scrambled and shouted. There was a second outcry as another tent went up in flames, joining Burl's that now blazed merrily and lit his end of the camp well. The first time I tried to lift my head and see what was happening, the young soldier on my back slammed my face back into the frozen ground energetically. I resigned myself to ice and gravel and looked through the wolf's eyes instead.

Had not Burl's guard been so intent on keeping me, and on protecting Burl, they might have perceived that neither of us were the targets of this raid. While arrows fell about Burl and his blazing tent, at the dark end of the camp the silent invaders were freeing smugglers and pilgrims and ponies. Nighteyes' spying had shown me that the archer who had fired Burl's tent wore the Holdfast features as clearly as Nik did. The smugglers had come after their own. The captives trickled out of the camp like meal from a holed sack while Burl's men guarded him and me.

Burl's assessment of his men had been correct. More than one man-at-arms waited out that raid in the shadow of a wagon or a tent. I did not doubt that they'd fight well if personally attacked, but no one ventured to lead a sortie against the archers on the hill. I suspected then that Captain Mark had not been the only man to have an arrangement with the smugglers. The fire they did return was ineffective, for the blazing tents in the camp had ruined their night vision, whereas the fire made silhouettes and targets of the archers who stood to return the smugglers' fire.

It was over in a remarkably short time. The archers on the hill continued to loose arrows down on us as they slipped away, and that fire held the attention of Burl's men. When the rain of missiles abruptly ceased, Burl immediately roared for his sergeant, demanding to know if I had been kept. The sergeant looked warningly about at his men, and then called back that they'd held them off me.

The rest of that night was miserable. I spent a good part of it face-down in the snow while a half-dressed Burl snorted and stamped all around me. The burning of his tent had consumed most of his personal supplies. When the escape of the pilgrims and smugglers was discovered, it seemed to be of secondary importance to the fact that no one else in camp had clothing of a size that would fit Burl.

Three other tents had been fired. Burl's riding-horse had been taken in addition to the smugglers' ponies. For all Burl's bellowed threats of dire vengeance, he made no effort to organize a pursuit. Instead he contented himself with kicking me several times. It was nearly dawn before he thought to ask if the minstrel, too, had been taken. She had. And that, he declared, proved that I had been the true target of the raid. He tripled the guard around me for the rest of that night, and for the next two days' journey to Moonseye. Not surprisingly, we saw no more of our attackers. They had got all they wished and vanished into the foothills. I had no doubt that Nik had boltholes on this side of the river as well. I could not feel any warmth toward the man who had sold me but I confessed to myself a grudging admiration that he had carried off the pilgrims with him when he escaped. Perhaps Starling could make a song of that.

Moonseye seemed a small town hidden in a fold of the mountains' skirts. There were few outlying farmsteads, and the cobbled streets began abruptly just outside the wooden palisade that surrounded the town. A sentry issued a formal challenge to us there from a tower above the walls. It was only after we had entered it that I appreciated what a thriving little city it was. I knew from my lessons with Fedwren that Moonseye had been an important military outpost for the Six Duchies before it had become a stopping-place for caravans bound for the other side of the Mountains. Now traders in amber and furs and carved ivory passed through Moonseye on a regular basis and enriched it in their passing. Or so it had been in the years since my father had succeeded in negotiating an open pass treaty with the Mountain Kingdom.

Regal's new hostilities had changed all that. Moonseye had reverted to the military holding it had been in my grandfather's day. The soldiers that moved through the streets wore Regal's gold and brown instead of Buck's blue, but soldiers are soldiers. The merchants had the weary, wary air of men rich only in their sovereign's scrip and wondering how redeemable it would prove in the long run. Our procession attracted the attention of the locals, but it was a surreptitious curiosity they showed us. I wondered when it had become bad luck to wonder too much about the King's business.

Despite my weariness, I looked about the town with interest. This was where my grandfather had brought me to abandon me to Verity's care, and where Verity had passed me on to Burrich. I had always wondered if my mother's folk had lived near Moonseye or if we had travelled far to seek out my father. But I looked in vain for any landmark or sign that would awaken some memory of my lost childhood in me. Moonseye looked to me both as strange and as familiar as any small town I had ever visited.

The town was thick with soldiers. Tents and lean-tos had been thrown up against every wall. It looked as if the population had recently increased a great deal. Eventually we came to a courtyard that the animals in the baggage train recognized as home. We were drawn up and then dismissed with military precision. My guard marched me off to a squat wooden building. It was windowless and forbidding. Inside was a single room where an old man sat on a low stool by a wide hearth where a welcoming fire burned. Less welcoming were three doors with small barred windows in them that opened off that room. I was shown into one, my bonds summarily cut, and then I was left alone.

As prisons go, it was the nicest one I'd ever been in. I caught myself in that thought and bared my teeth to it in something that was not quite a grin. There was a rope-laced bedstead with a bag of straw on it for a mattress. There was a chamber pot in the corner. Some light came in from the barred window, and some warmth. Not much of either, but it was still a great deal warmer than outside. It had not the severity of a serious prison. I decided it was a holding area for drunk or disruptive soldiers. It felt odd to take off my cloak and mittens and set them aside. I sat down on the edge of the bed and waited.

The only remarkable thing that happened that evening was that the meal offered meat and bread and even a mug of ale. The old man opened the door to pass me the tray. When he came to take the tray back, he left two blankets for me. I thanked him, and he looked startled. Then he shocked me by observing, 'You've your father's voice as well as his eyes.' Then he shut the door in my face, rather hastily. No one spoke further to me, and the only conversation I overheard were the curses and jibes of a dice game. From the voices I decided there were three younger men in the antechamber as well as the old key-holder.

As evening came on, they gave up their dice for quiet talk. I could make out little of what was said over the shrilling of the wind outside. I arose soundlessly from my bed and ghosted to the door. When I peered out of its barred window, I saw no less than three sentries on duty. The old man was asleep on his own bed in the corner, but these three in Regal's gold and brown took their duties seriously. One was a beardless boy, probably no more than fourteen. The other two moved like soldiers. One had a face more scarred than mine; I decided he was a brawler. The other wore a neatly-trimmed beard and was obviously in command of the other two. All were awake, if not exactly alert. The brawler was teasing the boy about something. The boy's face was sullen. Those two, at least, did not get along. From teasing the lad, the brawler went to endlessly complaining about Moonseye. The liquor was bad, there were too few women, and those there were were as cold as the winter itself. He wished the King would cut their leash and let them loose on the Mountain whore's thieving cut-throats. He knew they could cut a path to Jhaampe and take that tree-fort town in a matter of days. Where was the sense in waiting? On and on, he ranted. The others nodded to it as to a litany they knew well. I slipped away from the window and returned to my bed to think.

Nice cage.

At least they fed me well.

Not as well as I fed myself. A little warm blood in your meat is what you need. Will you escape soon?

As soon as I work out how.

I spent some time carefully exploring the limits of my cell.

Walls and floors of hewn plank, old and hard as iron to my fingers. A tightly-planked ceiling I could barely brush with my fingertips. And the wooden door with the barred window.

If I were getting out, it would have to be through the door. I returned to the barred window. 'Could I have some water?' I called out softly.

The youngster startled rather badly and the brawler laughed at him. The third guard looked at me, then went silently to take a dipper of water from a barrel in the corner. He brought it to the window and passed only the bowl of it through the bars. He let me drink from it, then withdrew it and walked away. 'How long are they going to hold me here?' I called after him.

'Till you're dead,' the brawler said confidently.

'We're not to speak to him,' the boy reminded him, and 'Shut up!' ordered their sergeant. The command included me. I stayed at the door, watching them, gripping the bars. It made the boy nervous but the brawler regarded me with the avaricious attention of a circling shark. It would take very little baiting to make that one want to hit me. I wondered if that could be useful. I was very tired of being hit, but it seemed the one thing I did well lately. I decided to press a little, to see what would happen. 'Why are you not to speak to me?' I asked curiously.

They exchanged glances. 'Get away from the window and shut up,' the sergeant ordered me.

'I just asked a question,' I objected mildly. 'What can be the harm in speaking to me?'

The sergeant stood up and I immediately backed away obediently.

'I'm locked up and there's three of you. I'm bored, that's all. Can't you at least tell me what you know about what's to become of me?'

'They'll do with you what should have been done the first time they killed you. Hanged over water and chopped into quarters and burned, Bastard,' the brawler offered me.

His sergeant rounded on him. 'Shut up. He's baiting you, you idiot. No one says another word to him. Not one. That's how a Witted one gets you into his power. By drawing you into talk. That's how he killed Bolt and his troop.' The sergeant shot me a savage look, then turned it on his men as well. They resumed their posts. The brawler gave me a sneering smile.

'I don't know what they've told you about me, but it's not true,' I offered. No one replied. 'Look, I'm no different from you. If I had some great magical power, do you think I'd be locked up like this? No. I'm just a scapegoat, that's all. You all know how it's done. If something goes wrong, someone has to take the blame for it. And I'm the one who's landed in the shit. Well, look at me and think of the stories you've heard. I knew Bolt when he was with Regal at Buckkeep. Do I look like a man who could take Bolt down?' I kept it up for the better part of their watch. I did not really think I could convince them I was an innocent man. But I could convince them that my talking or their replying was nothing to be feared. I told tales of my past life and misfortunes, certain they would be repeated all over the camp. Though what good that might do me, I did not know. But I stood at the door, gripping the bars at the window, and with very tiny motions, twisted at the bars I gripped. Back and forth I worked them against their settings. If they moved, I could not detect it.

The next day dragged for me. I felt that each hour that passed was one that brought danger closer to me. Burl had not come to see me. I felt sure he was holding me, waiting for someone to come and take me off his hands. I feared it would be Will. I did not think Regal would trust me to anyone else to transport. I did not want another encounter with Will. I did not feel I had the strength to withstand him. My work for the day consisted of jimmying at my bars and watching my captors. By the end of that day, I was ready to take a chance. After my evening meal of cheese and porridge, I lay down on my bed and composed myself to Skill.

I lowered my walls cautiously, fearing to find Burl waiting for me. I reached out of myself and felt nothing. I composed myself and tried again, with the same results. I opened my eyes and stared up into blackness. The unfairness of it sickened me. The Skill-dreams could come and take me at their will, but now when I sought that Skill-river, it eluded me completely. I made two more efforts before a throbbing headache forced me to give it up. The Skill was not going to help me get out of here.

That leaves the Wit, Nighteyes observed. He felt very near.

I don't really see how that is going to help me, either, I confided to him.

Nor do I. But I have dug out a spot under the wall, in case you are able to get out of your cage. It was not easy, for the ground is frozen and the logs of the wall were buried deep. But if you can get out of the cage, I can get you out of the city.

That is wise planning, I praised him. At least one of us was doing something.

Do you know where I den tonight? There was suppressed merriment in the thought.

Where do you den? I asked obediently.

Right under your feet. There was just space enough for me to crawl under here.

Nighteyes, this is foolish boldness. You may be seen or the marks of your digging discovered.

A dozen dogs have been here before me. No one will mark my coming and going. I have used the evening to see much of this men's warren. All of the buildings have spaces beneath them. It is very easy to slip from one to another.

Be careful, I warned him, but could not deny there was comfort in knowing him so close. I passed an uneasy night. The three guards were careful always to keep a door between us. I tried my charms on the old man the next morning when he passed me a mug of tea and two pieces of hard bread. 'So you knew my father,' I observed as he manoeuvred my food through the bars. 'You know, I have no memories of him. He never spent any time with me.'

'Count your blessings, then,' the old man replied shortly. 'Knowing the prince was not the same as liking him. Stiff as a stick he was. Rules and orders for us, while he was out making bastards. Yes, I knew your father. I knew him too well for my comfort.' And he turned away from the bars, dashing any hope I had of making him an ally. I retired to sit on my bed with my bread and tea and stare hopelessly at the walls. Another day had ticked endlessly by. I was sure it brought Will another day's journey closer to me. Another day closer to being dragged back to Tradeford. One day closer to death.

In the cold and the dark of the night, Nighteyes awoke me. *Smoke. A lot of it.*

I sat up in my bed. I went to the barred window and peered out. The old man was asleep in his cot. The boy and the brawler were playing at dice, while the other man carved at his nails with his belt knife. All was calm.

Where is the smoke coming from?

Shall I go and see?

If you would. Be careful.

When am I not?

A time passed, during which I stood to one side of my cell door and watched my guards. Then Nighteyes reached me again. *It's a big building, smelling of grain. It burns in two places.*

Does no one cry an alarm?

No one. The streets are empty and dark. This end of town is asleep.

I closed my eyes and shared his vision. The building was a granary. Someone had set two fires against it. One only smouldered, but the other was licking well up the dry wooden wall of the building.

Come back to me. Perhaps we can use this to our advantage.

Wait.

Nighteyes moved purposefully up the street, slipping from building to building as he went. Behind us, the granary fire began to crackle as it gained strength. He paused, sniffed the air and changed his direction. Soon he was looking at another fire. This one was eating eagerly into a covered pile of hay at the back of a barn. Smoke rose lazily, wisping up into the night. Suddenly, a tongue of flame leapt up and with an immense whoosh, the whole pile was ablaze. Sparks rode the heat into the night sky. Some still glowed as they settled onto roofs nearby.

Someone is setting those fires. Come back to me now!

Nighteyes came swiftly. On his way to me, he saw another fire nibbling at a pile of oily rags stuffed under the corner of a barracks. An errant breeze encouraged it to explore. The flames licked up a piling supporting the building, and curled eagerly along the bottom of the floor.

Winter had dried the wooden town with its harsh cold as thoroughly as any heat of summer. Lean-tos and tents spanned the spaces between the buildings. If the fires burned undetected much longer, all of Moonseye would be a cinder by morning. And I with it, if I were still locked in my cell.

How many guard you?

Four. And a locked door.

One of them will have the key.

Wait. Let us see if our odds get better. Or they may open the door to move me.

Somewhere in the cold town, a man raised his voice in a shout. The first fire had been spotted. I stood inside my cell, listening with Nighteyes' ears. Gradually the outcry increased, until even the guards outside my door stood, asking one another, 'What's that?'

One went to the door and opened it. Cold wind and the smell of smoke coiled into the room. The brawler drew his head back in and announced, 'Looks like a big fire at the other end of town.' In an instant, the other two men were leaning out the door. Their tense conversation woke the old man, who also came to have a look. Outside, someone ran past in the street, shouting, 'Fire! Fire down by the granary! Bring buckets!'

The boy looked to the officer. 'Should I go and see?'

For a moment the man hesitated but the temptation was too much. 'No. You stay here while I go. Stay alert.' He snatched up his cloak and headed out into the night. The boy looked disappointedly after him. He remained standing at the door, staring out into the night. Then, 'Look, there's more flames! Over there!' he exclaimed. The brawler swore, then snatched up his cloak.

'I'm going to go and have a look.'

'But we were told to stay and guard the Bastard!'

'You stay! I'll be right back, I just want to see what's going on!' He called the last words over his shoulder as he hurried away. The boy and the old man exchanged glances. The old man went back to his bed and lay down, but the boy continued to hang out the door. From my cell door I could see a slice of the street. A handful of men ran by, then someone drove a team and wagon past at a fast clip. Everyone seemed headed toward the fire.

'How bad does it look?' I asked.

'Can't see much from here. Just flames beyond the stables. A lot of sparks flying up.' The boy sounded disappointed to be so far from the excitement. He suddenly recalled whom he was speaking to. He abruptly drew in his head and shut the door. 'Don't talk to me!' he warned me and then went to sit down.

'How far from here is the granary?' I asked. He refused to even glance at me, but sat stony-eyed, staring at the wall. 'Because,' I went on conversationally, 'I just wondered what you were going to do if the fires spread this far. I wouldn't care to burn alive. They did leave you the keys, didn't they?' The boy glanced immediately toward the old man. His hand made an involuntary twitch toward his pouch as if to be sure he had them still, but neither made a reply. I stood by the barred window and watched him. After a time the boy went to the door and peered out again. I saw his jaw clench. The old man went to look over his shoulder.

'It's spreading, isn't it? A winter fire is a terrible thing. Everything dry as bones.'

The boy would not reply, but he turned to look at me. The old man's hand stole down to the key in his pouch.

'Come and bind my hands now and take me out of here. None of us want to be in this building if the flames come this far.'

A glance from the boy. 'I'm not stupid,' he told me. 'I won't be the one to die for letting you go free.'

'Burn where you stand, Bastard, for all I care,' the old man added. He craned his neck out the door again. Even from afar I could hear the sudden whoosh as some building vanished in an eruption of fire. The wind brought the smell of the smoke strongly now and I saw tension building in the boy's stance. I saw a man run past the open door, shouting something to the boy about fighting in the market square. More men ran past in the street, and I heard the jangle of swords and light armour as they ran. Ash rode on the winds now and the roaring of flames was louder than the gusting winds. Drifting smoke greyed the air outside.

Then suddenly boy and man came tumbling back into the room. Nighteyes followed them, showing every tooth he had. He filled the door and blocked their escape. The snarl he let loose was louder than the crackling of the flames outside.

'Unlock the door of my cell, and he won't hurt you,' I offered them.

Instead the boy drew his sword. He was good. He did not wait for the wolf to come in, but charged at him, weapon levelled, forcing Nighteyes back out of the door. Nighteyes avoided the blade easily, but he no longer had them cornered. The boy followed up his advantage, stepping out into the darkness to follow the wolf. The second the door was no longer blocked, the old man slammed it.

'Are you going to stay in here and burn alive with me?' I asked him conversationally.

In an instant, he had decided. 'Burn alone!' he spat at me. He flung the door open again and raced outside.

Nighteyes! He's the one with the key, the old one who runs away. I'll get it.

I was alone in my prison now. I half expected the boy to come back, but he did not. I grabbed the bars of the windows and shook the door against its latch. It barely budged. One bar felt slightly loose. I wrenched at it, bracing my feet against the door to lever at it with all my weight. An eternity later, one end twisted free. I bent it down and worked it back and forth until it came out in my hand. But even if all the bars came out, the opening would still be too small for me to get through. I tried, but the loose bar I gripped was too thick to get into the cracks around the door to pry at it. I could smell smoke everywhere now, thick in the air. The fire was close. I slammed my shoulder against the door but it didn't even shiver. I reached through the window and groped down. My straining fingers encountered a heavy metal bar. I walked my fingertips across it until I came to the lock that secured it in place. I could brush my fingers against it but no more. I couldn't decide if the room were truly getting warmer or if I were imagining it.

I was blindly bashing my iron bar against the lock and the braces that supported it when the outer door opened. A guard in gold and brown strode into the room, calling, 'I've come for the Bastard.' Then her glance took in the empty room.

In a moment, she pushed back her hood and became Starling. I stared at her in disbelief.

'Easier than I'd hoped,' she told me with a stark grin. It looked ghastly on her bruised face, more like a snarl.

'Maybe not,' I said faintly. 'The cell's locked.'

Her grin became a look of dismay. 'The back of this building is smouldering.'

She snatched my bar with her unbandaged hand. Just as she lifted it to smash at the lock, Nighteyes appeared in the door. He padded into the room and dropped the old man's pouch on the floor. Blood had darkened the leather.

I looked at him, suddenly aghast. 'You killed him?'

I took from him what you needed. Hurry. The back of this cage burns.

For a moment I could not move. I looked at Nighteyes and wondered what I was making of him. He had lost some of his clean wildness. Starling's eyes went from him, to me, to the pouch on the floor. She did not move.

And some of what makes you a man is gone from you. We have no time for this, my brother. Would not you kill a wolf if it would save my life?

I didn't need to answer that. 'The key is in that pouch,' I told Starling.

For a moment she just stared down at it. Then she stooped and fumbled the heavy iron key out of the leather pouch. I watched her fit it into the keyhole, now praying that I had not dented the mechanism too badly. She turned the key, jerked loose the hasp and then lifted the bar from the door. As I came out she ordered me, 'Bring the blankets. You'll need them. The cold outside is fierce.'

As I snatched them up, I could feel the heat radiating from the back wall of my cell. I grabbed up my cloak and mittens. Smoke was beginning to slink in between the planks. We fled with the wolf at our heels.

No one took any notice of us outside. The fire was beyond battling. It held the town and raced wherever it willed. The people I saw were engaged in the selfish business of salvage and survival. A man trundled a barrow of possessions past us with no more than a warning look. I wondered if they were his. Down the street I could see a stable afire. Frantic grooms were dragging horses out but the screams of the panicked animals still within were shriller than the wind. With a tremendous crash a building across the street collapsed, wheezing hot air and ash toward us in a terrible sigh. The wind had spread the fire throughout all Moonseye. The fire sped from building to building, and the wind carried burning sparks and hot ash beyond the walls to the forest above. I wondered if even the deep snows would be enough to stop it. 'Come on!' Starling yelled angrily and I realized I had been standing and gawking. Clutching the blankets I followed her wordlessly. We ran through the winding streets of the burning town. She seemed to know the way.

We came to a crossroads. Some sort of struggle had taken place there. Four bodies sprawled in the street, all in Farrow colours. I paused, to stoop over a soldier and take the fallen woman's knife and the pouch at her belt.

We neared the gates of the town. Suddenly a wagon rattled up beside us. The two horses drawing it were mismatched and lathered. 'Get in!' someone shouted at us. Starling leaped into the wagon without hesitation.

'Kettle?' I asked, and 'Hurry up!' was her reply. I climbed in and the wolf leaped easily up beside me. She did not wait to see us settled but slapped the reins on the horses. The wagon plunged forward with a lurch.

Ahead of us were the gates. They were open and unmanned, swinging on their hinges in the wind from the fire. To one side I caught a glimpse of a sprawled body. Kettle did not even slow the team. We were through the gates without a backwards glance, and rattling down the dark road, to join others fleeing the destruction with carts and barrows. Most seemed bound toward the few outlying homesteads to seek shelter for the night, but Kettle kept our horses moving. As the night about us grew darker and folk fewer, Kettle stirred the horses to a faster clip. I peered ahead into the darkness.

I realized Starling was looking back behind us. 'It was only supposed to be a diversion,' she said in an awestruck voice. I turned to look back.

An immense orange glow silhouetted the palisade of Moonseye in black. Sparks rose thick as swarming bees into the night sky above it. The roar of the flames was like storm winds. As we watched, a building caved in and another wave of sparks rose into the air.

'A diversion?' I peered at her through the darkness. 'You did all that? To free me?'

Starling shot me an amused glance. 'Sorry to disappoint you. No. Kettle and I came along for you, but that was not what this was about. Most of that is the work of Nik's family. Revenge against those who broke faith with them. They went in to find them and kill them. Then they left.' She shook her head. 'It's too complicated to explain it all right now, even if I understood it. Evidently the King's Guard at Moonseye has been corrupt for years. They've been well paid to see nothing of the Holdfast smugglers. And the smugglers have seen to it that the men posted here enjoyed some of the better things in life. I gather that Captain Mark enjoyed the best of the profits. He was not alone, but neither was he generous about sharing.

'Then Burl was sent here. He knew nothing of the arrangement. He brought a huge influx of soldiers with him, and tried to impose military discipline here. Nik sold you to Mark. But when Nik was selling you to Mark, someone saw a chance to sell Mark and his arrangement to Burl. Burl saw a chance to take you, and clean up a ring of smugglers. But Nik Holdfast and his clan had paid well for safe passage for the pilgrims. Then the soldiers broke faith with them, and the Holdfast promise to the pilgrims was broken.' She shook her head. Her voice went tight. 'Some of the women were raped. One child died of the cold. One man will never walk again because he tried to protect his wife.' For a time, the only sounds were the noises of the wagon and the distant roaring of the fires. Her eyes were very black as she looked back at the burning town. 'You've heard of honour among thieves? Well, Nik and his men have avenged theirs.'

I was still staring back at the destruction of Moonseye. I cared not a whit for Burl and his Farrowmen. But there had been merchants there, and traders, families and homes. The flames were devouring them all. And Six Duchies soldiers had raped their captives as if they were lawless raiders instead of King's

Guards. Six Duchies soldiers, serving a Six Duchies king. I shook my head. 'Shrewd would have hanged them all.'

Starling cleared her throat. 'Don't blame yourself,' she told me. 'I learned long ago not to blame myself for evil done to me. It wasn't my fault. It wasn't even your fault. You were just the catalyst that started the chain of events.'

'Don't call me that,' I begged her. The wagon rumbled on, carrying us deeper into the night.

NINETEEN

Pursuit

The peace between the Six Duchies and the Mountain Kingdom was relatively new at the time of King Regal's reign. For decades, the Mountain Kingdom had controlled all trade through the passes with as tight a grip as the Six Duchies had on all trade on the Cold and Buck Rivers. Trade and passage between the two regions had been capriciously managed by both powers, to the detriment of both. But during the reign of King Shrewd, mutually beneficial trade agreements were worked out between King-in-Waiting Chivalry of the Six Duchies and Prince Rurisk of the Mountains. The peace and prosperity of this arrangement was secured further when, over a decade later, the Mountain princess Kettricken became the bride of King-in-Waiting Verity. Upon the untimely death of her older brother, Rurisk, on the very eve of her wedding, Kettricken became the sole heir to the Mountain crown. Thus it appeared for a time that the Six Duchies and the Mountain Kingdom might share a monarch and eventually become one land.

Circumstances put all such hope to ruin, however. The Six Duchies were threatened from without by the Raiders, and torn within by the bickering of princes. King Shrewd was murdered, King-in-Waiting Verity disappeared while on a quest, and when Prince Regal claimed the throne for his own, his hatred for Kettricken was such that she felt obliged to flee to her native Mountains for the sake of her unborn child. Self-proclaimed 'King' Regal saw this somehow as a reneging on a promised surrender of territory. His initial endeavours to move troops into the Mountain Kingdom, ostensibly as 'guards' for trading caravans, were repulsed by the Mountain folk. His protestations and threats prompted the closing of the Mountain borders to Six Duchy trade. Thwarted, he embarked on a vigorous campaign of discrediting Queen Kettricken and building patriotic hostility toward the Mountain King-

dom. His eventual goal seemed obvious: to take, by force if necessary, the lands of the Mountain Kingdom as a Six Duchies province. It seemed a poor time for such a war and such a strategy. The lands he justly possessed were already under siege by an outside enemy, one he seemed unable or disinclined to defeat. No military force had ever conquered the Mountain Kingdom, and yet this was what he seemed intent upon doing. Why he so desperately desired to possess this territory was a question that initially baffled everyone.

The night was clear and cold. The bright moonlight was enough to show us where the road ran, but not more than that. For a time I simply sat in the wagon, listening to the crunching of the horses' hooves on the road and trying to absorb all that had happened. Starling took the blankets we had brought from my cell and shook them out. She gave me one and draped one across her own shoulders. She sat huddled and apart from me, looking out the back of the wagon. I sensed she wanted to be left alone. I watched the orange glow that had been Moonseye dwindle in the distance. After a time, my mind started working again.

'Kettle?' I called over my shoulder. 'Where are we going?'

'Away from Moonseye,' she said. I could hear the weariness in her voice.

Starling stirred and glanced at me. 'We thought you would know.'

'Where did the smugglers go?' I asked.

I felt more than saw Starling shrug. 'They wouldn't tell us. They said if we went after you, we had to part company with them. They seemed to believe Burl would send soldiers after you, no matter how badly Moonseye had been hit.'

I nodded, more to myself than to her. 'He will. He's going to blame the whole raid on me. And it will be said that the raiders were actually from the Mountain Kingdom, soldiers sent to free me.' I sat up, easing away from Starling. 'And when they catch us, they'll kill you both.'

'We didn't intend that they should catch us,' Kettle observed.

'And they won't,' I promised. 'Not if we act sensibly. Pull up the horses.'

Kettle scarcely needed to stop them. They had slowed to a weary walk long ago. I tossed my blanket at Starling and went around the team. Nighteyes launched himself from the wagon and followed me curiously. 'What are you doing?' Kettle demanded as I unbuckled the harness and let it fall to the snowy ground.

'Changing this over so they can be ridden. Can you ride bareback?' I was using the guard's knife to hack through the reins as I spoke. She'd have to ride bareback, whether she could or not. We had no saddles.

'I suppose I'll have to,' she observed grumpily as she clambered down from the wagon. 'But we aren't going to get very far very fast, doubled on these horses.'

'You and Starling will do fine,' I promised her. 'Just keep going.'

Starling was standing in the bed of the wagon looking down on me. I didn't need the moonlight to know there was disbelief on her face. 'You're leaving us here? After we came back for you?'

That wasn't how I'd seen it. 'You are leaving me here,' I told her firmly. 'Jhaampe is the only large settlement, once you've turned your back on Moonseye and headed toward the Mountain Kingdom. Ride steadily. Don't go directly to Jhaampe. That's what they'll expect us to do. Find one of the smaller villages and hide there for a time. Most of the Mountain folk are hospitable. If you hear no rumours of pursuit, go on to Jhaampe. But get as far as you can as fast as you can before you stop to ask for shelter or food.'

'What are you going to do?' Starling asked in a low voice.

'Nighteyes and I are going our own way. As we should have a long time ago. We travel fastest alone.'

'I came back for you,' Starling said. Her voice was close to breaking at my betrayal. 'Despite all that had happened to me. Despite . . . my hand . . . and everything else . . .'

'He's drawing them off our trail,' Kettle suddenly said.

'Do you need help to mount?' I asked Kettle quietly.

'We don't need any help from you!' Starling declared angrily. She shook her head. 'When I think of all I've been through, following you. And all we did to free you . . . You'd have burned alive in that cell back there but for me!'

'I know.' There was no time to explain all of it to her. 'Goodbye,' I said quietly. And I left them there, walking away from them into the forest. Nighteyes walked at my side. The trees closed in around us and they were soon lost to sight.

Kettle had seen quickly to the heart of my plan. As soon as Burl had the fires under control, or perhaps before, he would think of me. They'd find the old man killed by a wolf, and never believe I had perished in my cell. There would be pursuit. They'd send out riders on all the roads into the mountains, and they'd soon catch up with Kettle and Starling. Unless the hunters had another, more difficult trail to follow. One that cut cross-country, headed directly to Jhaampe. Due west.

It would not be easy. I had no specific knowledge of what lay between me and the capital city of the Mountain Kingdom. No towns, most likely, for the Mountain Kingdom was sparsely populated. The folk were mostly trappers, hunters and nomadic herders of sheep and goats who tended to live in isolated cabins or tiny villages surrounded by ample hunting and trapping range. There would be little chance for me to beg or steal food or supplies. What worried me more was that I might find myself on the edge of an unscalable ridge or having to ford one of the many swift cold rivers that swept fiercely down the ravines and narrow valleys.

Useless to worry until we find ourselves blocked, Nighteyes pointed out. *If it happens, then we must simply find a way around it. It may slow us down. But we will never get there at all if we stand still and worry.*

So we hiked the night away, Nighteyes and I. When we came to clearings, I studied the stars, and tried to travel as close to due west as I could. The terrain proved every bit as challenging as I had expected it to be. Deliberately I chose routes kinder to a man and wolf afoot than to men on horseback. We left our trail up brushy hillsides and through tangled thickets in narrow gorges. I comforted myself as I forged through such places by imagining Starling and Kettle making good time on the roads. I tried not to think that Burl would send out enough trackers to follow more than one trail. No. I had to get a good lead on them and then lure Burl to send them after me in full force.

The only way I could think of to do that was to represent myself as a threat to Regal. One that must be dealt with immediately.

I lifted my eyes to the top of a ridge. Three immense cedars stood together in a clump. I would stop there, build a tiny fire, and try to Skill. I had no elfbark, I reminded myself, so I would have to make provisions to rest well afterwards.

I will watch over you, Nighteyes assured me.

The cedars were huge, their reaching branches interweaving overhead so thickly that the ground beneath was bare of snow. The soil was thickly carpeted with fragrant bits of cedar frond that had fallen over time. I scraped myself up a couch of them to keep my body off the cold earth and then gathered a good supply of firewood. For the first time, I looked inside the pouch I had stolen. There was a fire flint. Also five or six coins, some dice, a broken bracelet, and folded up in a scrap of fabric, a lock of fine hair. It summarized too neatly a soldier's life. I scraped away a bit of earth and buried the hair, the dice, and the bracelet together. I tried not to wonder if it were a child or a lover that she had left behind. Her death was none of my doing, I reminded myself. Still, a chill voice whispered the word 'catalyst' in the back of my mind. But for me, she would be alive still. For a moment, I felt old and weary and sick. Then I forced myself to set both the soldier and my own life aside. I kindled the fire and fed it up well. I stacked the rest of my firewood close to hand. I wrapped myself in my cloak and lay back on my cedar frond bed. I took a breath, closed my eyes and Skilled.

It was as if I had tumbled into a swift river. I had not been prepared to succeed so easily, and was nearly swept away. Somehow the Skill-river seemed deeper and wilder and stronger here. I did not know if it were a waxing of my own abilities or something else. I found and centred myself and resolutely firmed my will against the temptations of the Skill. I refused to consider that from here I might fling my thoughts to Molly and our child, might see as with my own eyes how she was growing and how they both fared. Nor would I reach for Verity, much as I longed to. The strength of this Skilling was such I had no doubt I could find him. But that was not what I was here for. I was here to taunt an enemy and must be on my guard. I set every ward I could that would not seal me off from the Skill, and turned my will toward Burl.

I extended myself, feeling for him cautiously. I was ready to fling up my walls in an instant if attacked. I found him easily and was almost startled at how unaware of my touch he was.

Then his pain jolted through me.

I drew back, faster than a startled sea anemone in a tide pool. I shocked myself by opening my eyes and staring up into cedar boughs burdened with snow. Sweat slicked my face and back.

What was that? Nighteyes demanded.

You know as much as I do, I told him.

It had been purest pain. Pain independent of an injury to the body, pain that was not sorrow or fear. Total pain, as if every part of the body, inside and out, were immersed in fire.

Regal and Will were causing it.

I lay shaking in the aftermath, not of the Skilling, but Burl's pain. It was a monstrosity larger than my mind could grasp. I tried to sort out all I had sensed in that brief moment. Will, and perhaps some shadow of Carrod's Skill, immobilizing Burl for this punishment. From Carrod there had been poorly-masked horror and distaste for this task. Perhaps he feared it would some day be turned upon him again. Will's strongest emotion had been wrath that Burl had had me in his power and somehow let me slip away. But beneath the wrath was a sort of fascination with what Regal was doing to Burl. Will did not take any pleasure in it. Not yet.

But Regal did.

There had been a time when I had known Regal. Never well, it was true. Once he had been simply the younger of my uncles, the one who did not like me at all. He had vented it boyishly, in shoves and clandestine pinches, in teasing and tattling. I had not liked it, I had not liked him, but it had been almost understandable. It had been a boy's jealousy that the favoured eldest son had created yet another rival for King Shrewd's time and attention. At one time he had been simply a pampered young prince, envious that his elder brothers were in line for the throne ahead of him. He had been spoiled and rude and selfish.

But he had been human.

What I had felt from him just now was so far beyond what I could understand in terms of cruelty that it was almost incompre-

hensible. Forged Ones had lost their humanity, but in their emptiness was the shadow of what they had been. Had Regal opened
his breast and showed me a nest of vipers, I could not have been
more shocked. Regal had thrown humanity aside, to embrace
something darker. And this was the man the Six Duchies now
called King.

This was the man who would send troops after Starling and
Kettle.

'I'm going back,' I warned Nighteyes, and did not give him time
to object. I closed my eyes and flung myself into the Skill-river. I
opened myself wide to it, drawing its cold strength into me without thought that too much of it would devour me. At the instant
Will became aware of me, I spoke to them. 'You will die at my
hand, Regal. As certainly as Verity will reign again as King.' Then
I smashed that gathered power against them.

It was almost as instinctive as a clenched fist. I did not plan
it, but suddenly I understood this was what Verity had done to
them back in Tradeford. There was no message, nothing but a
furious unleashing of strength upon them. I opened wide to them
and showed myself, then when they turned to me, I willed myself
to blast them with every bit of Skill I had gathered. Like Verity,
I held back nothing of my strength. I believe if there had been
only one, I would have succeeded in burning the Skill right out
of him. Instead, they shared the jolt. I will never know what
effect it had on Burl. Perhaps he was grateful for my savagery, for
it shattered Will's concentration and released him from Regal's
sophisticated torture. I felt Carrod's shriek of terror as he broke
off his Skilling. I think Will might have stood and challenged
me, had not Regal feebly commanded him *Break it off, you fool,
do not risk me for your vengeance!* In the blinking of an eye, they
were gone.

The day was strong when I was next aware. Nighteyes was
lying almost on top of me and there was blood on his coat. I
pushed feebly at him and he moved immediately. He stood up
and sniffed my face. I smelled my own blood with him; it was
revolting. I sat up suddenly and the world spun around me. I
became slowly aware of the clamour of his thoughts.

Are you all right? You were trembling and then you began to bleed

*from your nose. You have not been here, I have not been able to hear
you at all!*

'I'm all right,' I soothed him hoarsely. 'Thank you for keeping
me warm.'

My fire was down to a few embers. I reached carefully for my
wood and added a few sticks to the fire. It seemed as if my hands
were a long way away from me. When I had the fire burning, I
sat and warmed myself. Then I stood and staggered a few steps
to where the snow began. I rubbed a handful across my face to
cleanse it of the taste and smell of blood. I put a bit of clean
snow in my mouth for my tongue felt thick and clotted.

Do you need to rest? Do you need food? Nighteyes asked me
anxiously.

Yes and yes. But most of all, we needed to flee. I had no doubt
that what I had done would bring them after me. I had done
what I had wanted, and beyond all my expectations, it had been
real. I had given them a reason to fear me. Now they would never
rest until they'd destroyed me. I had also shown them plainly
where I was; they'd have a feel for where to send their men. I
must not be here when they arrived. I went back to my fire and
kicked earth onto it. I stamped it to be sure it was out. Then we
fled.

We travelled as swiftly as I could manage. There was no question that I held Nighteyes back. He would look at me pityingly
as I toiled up a hill, hip-deep in snow that he but spread toes
and ran lightly over. It was not unusual that when I begged for
a rest and stopped to lean against a tree, he would range ahead,
searching out the best trail. When both light and my strength
were near exhausted and I would stop to build a fire for the night,
he would disappear to return with meat for both of us. Most often
it was white snow hares, but once it was a fat beaver that had
ventured too far from its iced-over pond. I made pretence to
myself that I cooked my meat, but it was a very brief searing over
a fire. I was too tired and too hungry to do more. The meat diet
put no fat on my flesh, but it did keep me alive and moving. I
had little of true sleep, for I had to constantly replenish my fire
to keep from freezing and rise several times a night to stamp
feeling back into my feet. Endurance. That was what it was all

about. Not swiftness or great strength, but a miserly eking out of my ability to force myself to keep moving every day.

I kept my Skill-walls up tight, but even so I was aware of Will's battling against them. I did not think he could track me as long as I guarded myself, but I was not certain of that. The constant mental wariness was yet another draw on my strength. Some nights I longed simply to drop all my guards and let him in, to finish me off once and for all. But at such times, all I had to do was recall what Regal was now capable of doing. Without fail it put a bolt of terror through me and inspired me to push myself all the harder to increase the distance between us.

When I arose on the fourth dawn of our travelling, I knew we were deep within the Mountain Kingdom. I had seen no sign of pursuit since we had left Moonseye. Surely this deep within Kettricken's own land, we were safe.

How much farther is this Jhaampe, and what shall we do when we get there?

I don't know how much farther. And I don't know what we shall do.

For the first time, I considered it. I forced myself to think of all that I had not permitted myself to consider before. I knew nothing truly of what had become of Kettricken since the time I had sent her from the King's side to flee into the night. She had had no word from me or about me. Kettricken would have borne the child by now. By my reckoning, her babe would be close in age to my own daughter. I suddenly found myself very curious. I could hold that babe and say to myself, 'This must be how it feels to hold my daughter.'

Except that Kettricken believed me dead. Executed by Regal and long buried would be what she had heard. She was my queen and Verity's wife. Surely I could reveal to her how I had survived. But to tell the truth to her would be like dropping a pebble in a pond. Unlike Starling or Kettle or anyone else who had deduced who I was, Kettricken had known me before. It would not be rumour or legend, not a wild tale of someone who had glimpsed me for a moment, but a fact. She could say to others who had known me, 'Yes, I saw him, and he truly lives. How? Why, by his Wit, of course.'

I trudged along behind Nighteyes through the snow and cold and thought what that would mean to Patience when word reached her. Shame, or joy? Hurt that I had not revealed myself to her? Through Kettricken, word could be sent, to spread to those I had known. Eventually, it would reach Molly and Burrich. What would it do to Molly, to hear it from afar like that, not only that I was alive and had not returned to her, but that I was tainted with the Wit? It had cut me to the heart to know she had kept from me the knowledge that she carried our child. That had been my first true glimpse of how betrayed and hurt she must have felt by all the secrets I had kept from her over the years. To have one more and one of such magnitude pushed in her face might end whatever feelings she might still have for me. My chances of rebuilding a life with her were small enough; I could not bear for them to dwindle further.

And all the others, the stable-folk I had known, the men I had rowed and fought alongside, the common soldiers of Buckkeep would find out as well. However I might feel about the Wit, I had already seen the disgust in one friend's eyes. I had seen how it had changed even Starling's attitude toward me. What would folks think of Burrich, that he had had a Witted one in his stable and tolerated me? Would he be discovered as well? I gritted my teeth. I would have to remain dead. Better, perhaps, to by-pass Jhaampe altogether and press on to find Verity. Save that, without supplies I had as much chance of that as Nighteyes had of passing himself off as a lapdog.

And there was one other small matter. The map.

When Verity had departed Buckkeep, it had been on the strength of a map. It was an old one that Kettricken had unearthed in the Buckkeep libraries. It had been faded and ancient, made in the days of King Wisdom, who had first visited the Elderlings and enlisted them to the aid of the Six Duchies. The detail of the map had faded, but both Kettricken and Verity had been convinced that one of the marked trails led to where King Wisdom had first encountered those elusive beings. Verity had left Buckkeep determined to follow the map into the regions beyond the Mountain Kingdom. He had taken with him the fresh copy of the map he had made. I had no idea of what had become of the older map; probably carried off to Tradeford when Regal had looted Buckkeep's libraries. But the style of the map and the unusual characteristics of the bordering had made me long suspect that the map was a copy of yet an older map. The bordering was in the Mountain style; if the original were to be found anywhere, it would be in the libraries of Jhaampe. I had had some access to them in the months of my convalescence in the Mountains. I knew their library was both extensive and well kept. Even if I did not find the original of that particular map, I might perhaps find others that covered the same area.

During my time in the Mountains, I had also been impressed with what a trusting folk they were. I had seen few locks and no guards such as we had at Buckkeep. It would be no trick to get into the royal residence. Even if they had established a practice of setting guards, the walls were only made of layers of barkcloth that had been plastered over with clay and painted. I felt confident I could get in one way or another. Once within, it would not take me long to rifle through their library and steal what I needed. I could resupply at the same time.

I had the grace to be ashamed of that thought. I also knew that shame would not keep me from doing it. Once again, I had no choice. I slogged up yet another ridge through the snow and it seemed to me my heart beat out that phrase over and over. No choice, no choice, no choice. Never any choice about anything. Fate had made me a killer, a liar and a thief. And the harder I tried to avoid those roles, the more firmly I was pushed into them. Nighteyes padded at my heels, and fretted about my black mood.

So distracted were we that we crested the ridge and both of us stood, foolishly outlined, in full view of the troop of horsemen on the road below us. The yellow and brown of their jackets stood out against the snow. I froze like a startled deer. Even so, we might have escaped their notice were it not for the pack of hounds with them. I took it in at a glance. Six hounds, not wolf-hounds, thank Eda, but short-legged rabbit-hounds, unsuited to this weather or terrain. There was one long-legged dog, a gangly, curly-backed mongrel. He and his handler moved separately from the pack. The pursuit was using whatever it had to find us. There were a dozen men on horseback, however. Almost instantly the mongrel threw his head up and bayed. In an instant the hounds took it up, milling, heads raised to snuff, and giving cry as they found our scents. The huntsman controlling the hounds lifted a hand and pointed up at us as we took to our heels. The mongrel and his handler were already racing toward us.

'I didn't even know there was a road there,' I panted apologetically to Nighteyes as we fled down the hillside. We had a very brief advantage. We went downhill following our own trail, while the hounds and horsemen in pursuit of us must come up a hill of unbroken snow. I hoped that by the time they reached the ridge we had just left, we could be out of view in the brushy ravine below us. Nighteyes was holding back, loath to leave me behind. The hounds were baying and I heard the voices of men raised in excitement as they took up the chase.

RUN! I commanded Nighteyes.

I will not leave you.

I'd have small chance if you did, I admitted. My mind worked frantically. *Get to the bottom of the ravine. Lay as much false trail as you can, loop around, go downstream following the ravine. When I get there, we'll flee uphill. It may delay them a while.*

Fox tricks! he snorted, and then raced past me in a blur of grey and vanished into the thick brush of the ravine. I tried to drive myself faster through the snow. Just before I reached the brushy ravine's edge, I looked back. Dogs and horsemen were just cresting the ridge. I gained the shelter of the snow-cloaked brush and scrabbled down the steep side. Nighteyes had left enough tracks there for a whole pack of wolves. Even as I paused for a quick breath, he raced past me in yet another direction.

Let's get out of here!

I did not wait for his reply, but took off up the ravine as fast as my legs would carry me. The snow was shallower at the very bottom for the overhanging trees and brush had caught and held most of it. I went half doubled over, knowing that if I snagged on the branches they would dump their cold loads upon me. The belling of the hounds rang in the freezing air. I listened to it as I pushed my way on. When I heard their excitement give way to a frustrated canine yelling, I knew they had reached the muddled trail at the bottom of the ravine. Too soon; they were there too soon and would be coming too fast.

Nighteyes!

Silence, fool! The hounds will hear you! And that other.

My heart near stopped in my chest. I could not believe how stupid I had been. I toiled on through the snowy brush, my ears straining after what was happening behind us. The huntsmen had liked the false trail Nighteyes had left and were all but forcing the hounds along it. There were too many men on horseback for the narrowness of the ravine. They were getting in one another's way, and perhaps fouling our true trail. Time gained, but only a bit of it. Then suddenly I heard alarmed cries and a wild yelping of hounds. I picked up a confused babble of doggy thoughts. A wolf had sprung down on them and raced right through the centre of their pack, slashing as he went, dashing off right through the very legs of the horses the men rode behind them. One man was down and having trouble catching his wild-eyed mount. A dog had lost most of one floppy ear and was agonized with it. I tried to shut my mind to his pain. Poor beast, and all for none of your own gain. My legs were like lead and my mouth dry, but I tried to force speed from myself, to use well the time Nighteyes had gained at such risk to himself. I wanted to cry out to him to leave off his taunting, to flee with me, but dared not betray to the pack the true direction of our retreat. Instead I pushed myself on.

The ravine was getting narrower and deeper. Vines and brambles and brush grew from the steepening sides and dangled down. I suspected I walked on top of a winter-frozen stream. I began to look for a way out of it. Behind me the hounds were yelping again, baying out to one another that they had the true trail now, follow the wolf, the wolf, the wolf. I knew then with certainty that Nighteyes had shown himself to them once more and was deliberately drawing them away from me. *Run, boy, run!* He flung the thought to me, uncaring that the hounds would hear him. There was a wild merriment to him, a hysterical silliness to his thought. It reminded me of the night I had chased Justin through the halls of Buckkeep, to slaughter him in the Great Hall before all the guests at Regal's King-in-Waiting ceremony. Nighteyes was in a frenzy that had carried him past worrying over his own survival. I plunged on, my heart in my throat for him, fighting the tears that pricked the corners of my eyes.

The ravine ended. Before me was a glistening cascade of ice, a memorial to the mountain stream that cut this canyon during the summer months. The ice hung in long, rippled icicles down the face of a rocky crack in the mountain, gleaming with a faint sheen of moving water still. The snow at its base was crystalline. I halted, suspecting a deep pool, one I might unwittingly find under a layer of too-thin ice. I lifted my eyes. The walls here were mostly undercut and overgrown. In other places, bare slabs of rock showed through the drapery of snow. Runty saplings and twiggy brush grew in a scattering, leaning out to catch the sunlight from above. None of it looked promising for a climb. I turned to double back on my trail and heard a single howl rise and fall. Neither hound nor wolf, it could only be the mongrel dog. Something in the certainty of his cry convinced me he was on my trail. I heard a man shout encouragement and the dog yelped again, closer. I turned to the wall of the ravine and started to climb. I heard the man halloo to the others, calling and whistling for them to follow him, he had a man's tracks here, never mind the wolf, it was just a Wit-trick. In the distance the hounds suddenly took up a different yelping. In that moment, I knew that Regal had finally found what he had sought. A Witted one to hunt me. Old Blood had been bought.

I jumped and caught at a sapling leaning out from the wall of the ravine. I hauled myself up, got my feet on it, balanced and reached for another above me. When I put my weight on it, its roots tore loose from the rocky soil. I fell, but managed to catch myself on the first tree again. Up again, I told myself fiercely. I stood on it, and heard it crack under my weight. I reached up to grab handfuls of twiggy brush leaning down from the undercut bank. I tried to go up quickly, to not let my weight hang from any sapling or bush for more than a few moments. Handfuls of twigs broke off in my grip, tufts of old grasses pulled free, and I found myself scrabbling along the lip of the ravine but not getting any higher. I heard a shout below me and against my will I glanced back and down. A man and dog were in the clearing below. As the mongrel bayed up at me, the man was nocking an arrow to his bow. I hung helpless above them, as easy a shot as a man could wish.

'Please,' I heard myself gasp, and then heard the tiny unmistakable sound of a bowstring being released. I felt it hit me, a fist in the back, one of Regal's old tricks from my childhood, and then a deeper, hotter pain inside me. One of my hands had let go. I had not commanded it to, it had simply come unhooked from its grip. I swung from my right hand. I could hear, so clearly, the yelping of the dog as it smelled my blood. I could hear the rustle of the man's garment as he drew another arrow from his quiver.

Pain bit again, deep into my right wrist. I cried out as my fingers let go. In a reflex of terror, my legs scrabbled fiercely against the yielding brush that dangled over the undercut bank. And somehow I was rising, my face brushing crusty snow. I found my left arm and made vague swimming motions with it. *Get your legs up!* Nighteyes snapped at me. He made not a sound, for his teeth were set firmly in the sleeve and flesh of my right arm as he dragged me up. The chance at living rejuvenated me. I kicked wildly and then felt solid ground under my belly. I clawed my way forward, trying to ignore the pain that centred in my back, but spread out from there in red waves. If I had not seen the man loose an arrow, I would have believed I had a pole as thick as a wagon axle sticking out of my back.

Get up, get up! We have to run.

I don't recall how I got to my feet. I heard dogs scrabbling up the cliff behind me. Nighteyes stood back from the edge and met them as they came up. His jaws tore them open and he flung their bodies back down on the rest of the pack. When the curly-backed mongrel fell, there was a sudden lessening in the yelping below. We both knew his agony, and heard the screams of the man below as his bond-animal bled to death in the snow. The other huntsman was calling his dogs off, angrily telling the others it would do no good to send them up to be slaughtered. I could hear the men yelling and cursing as they turned their weary horses and started back down the ravine, to try and find a place where they could get up and after us, to try and pick up our trail again.

Run! Nighteyes told me. We would not speak of what we had just done. There was a sensation of terrible warmth running down my back that was also a spreading coldness. I put my hand to my chest, almost expecting to feel the arrowhead and shaft sticking out there. But no, it was buried deep. I staggered after Nighteyes, my consciousness awash in too much sensation, too many kinds of pain. My shirt and cloak tugged against the arrow-shaft as I moved, a tiny wiggling of the wood that was echoed by the arrowhead deep inside me. I wondered how much further damage it was doing. I thought of the times I had butchered arrow-slain deer, of the black puddingy flesh full of blood that one found around such a wound. I wondered if he'd got my lung. A lung-shot deer didn't go far. Did I taste blood in the back of my throat . . . ?

Don't think about it! Nighteyes commanded me savagely. *You weaken us both. Just walk. Walk and keep walking.*

So he knew as well as I did that I could not run. I walked and he walked at my side. For a time. Then I was walking blindly forward in the dark, not even caring in which direction I went, and he was not there. I groped for him, but could not find him. Somewhere afar I heard the yelping of dogs again. I walked on. I blundered into trees. Branches scratched my face but it was all right because my face was numb. The shirt on my back was a slushy sheet of frozen blood that moved chafingly against my skin. I tried to pull my cloak more closely around me, but the sudden pain nearly drove me to my knees. Silly me. I had forgotten it would drag against the arrow-shaft. Silly me. Keep walking, boy. I walked on.

I bumped into another tree. It released a shower of snow on me. I staggered clear and kept on walking. For a long time. Then I was sitting in the snow, getting colder and colder. I had to get up. I had to keep moving.

I walked again. Not for very long, I don't think. Under the shelter of some great evergreens where the snow was shallow, I sank to my knees. 'Please,' I said. I had not the strength to weep for mercy. 'Please.' I could not think whom I was asking.

I saw a hollow between two thick roots. Pine needles were thick on the ground there. I huddled into the small space. I could not lie down for the arrow sticking out of my back. But I could lean my forehead against the friendly tree and cross my arms on my chest. I made myself small, folding my legs under me and sinking into the space between the roots. I would have been cold save I was too tired. I sank into sleep. When I woke up, I'd build a fire and get warm. I could imagine how warm I'd be, could almost feel it.

My brother!

I'm here, I told him calmly. *Right here.* I quested out to touch him reassuringly. He was coming. The ruff around his throat was spiky with frozen saliva, but not a tooth had got through. He had one slash down the side of his muzzle but it was not bad. He'd led them in circles and then harried their horses from behind before leaving them plunging through a snow-covered swale of deep grass in the dark. Only two of their dogs were left alive and one of the horses was limping so badly the rider had doubled up with another.

Now he came to find me, surging up the snowy slopes easily. He was tired, yes, but the energy of triumph surged through him. The night was crisp and clean around him. He caught the scent and then the tiny eye-flicker of the hare that crouched beneath a bush, hoping he'd pass by. We did not. A single, sudden sideways pounce and the hare was in his jaws. We clutched it by its bony head and snapped its spine with one shake. We trotted on, the meat a welcome dangling weight from his jaws. We would eat well. The night forest was silver and black around us.

Stop. My brother, do not do this.

Do what?

I love you. But I do not wish to be you.

I hovered where I was. His lungs working so strongly, drawing in the cold night air past the hare's head in his mouth. The slight sting of the slash down his muzzle, his powerful legs carrying his lean body so well.

You do not wish to be me, either, Changer. Not really.

I was not sure he was correct. With his eyes I saw and smelled myself. I had wedged myself into the space between the roots of the great tree, and was curled up as small as an abandoned pup. My blood smell was strong on the air. Then I blinked, and I was looking down into the darkness of my crooked elbow over my face. I lifted my head slowly, painfully. Everything hurt and all the pain traced back to that arrow centred in my back.

I smelled rabbit guts and blood. Nighteyes stood beside me, feet braced on the carcass as he tore it open. *Eat, while it's hot.*

I don't know if I can.

Do you want me to chew it for you?

He was not jesting. But the only thing more revolting than eating was the thought of eating disgorged meat. I managed a tiny shake of my head. My fingers were almost numb, but I watched my hand pinch up the small liver and carry it up to my mouth. It was warm and rich with blood. Suddenly I knew Nighteyes was right. I had to eat. Because I had to live. He had torn the hare apart. I picked up a portion and bit into the warm meat. It was tough but I was determined. Without thinking, I had nearly abandoned my body for his, nearly climbed in beside him into that perfect healthy wolf's body. I had done it once before, with his consent. But now we both knew better. We would share, but we could not become one another. Not without both of us losing.

Slowly I sat up. I felt the muscles of my back move against the arrow, protesting at the way it snagged them. I could feel the weight of the shaft. When I imagined it sticking out of me, I nearly lost the food I'd eaten. I forced myself to a calm I did not feel. Suddenly, oddly, an image of Burrich came to me. That deadly stillness in his face when he had flexed his knee and watched the old wound pulling open. Slowly I reached my hand back. I walked my fingers up my spine. It made the muscles pull against the arrow. Finally my fingers touched the sticky wood of the arrow-shaft. Even that light touch was a new sort of pain. Awkwardly I closed my fingers around the shaft, closed my eyes and tried to pull on it. Even if there had been no pain involved, it would have been difficult. But the agony rocked the world around me, and when it steadied, I found myself on my hands and knees with my head hanging down.

Shall I try?

I shook my head, remaining as I was. I was still afraid I'd faint. I tried to think. If he pulled it out, I knew I'd pass out. If the bleeding was bad, I'd have no way to stop it. No. Best to leave it in there. I gathered all my courage. *Can you break it off?*

He came close to me. I felt his head against my back. He turned his head, manoeuvred his jaws so that his back teeth would close

on the shaft. Then he closed his jaws. There was a snick, like a
gardener pruning a sapling, and a shiver of new pain. A wave of
giddiness washed over me. But somehow I reached back and
tugged my blood-sodden cloak free of the stub of arrow. I pulled
it closer around me, shuddering. I closed my eyes.

No. Build a fire first.

I peeled my eyes open again. It was all too hard. I scraped
together all the twigs and sticks within easy reach. Nighteyes
tried to help, fetching branches to me, but it still took an eternity
before I had a tiny flame dancing. Slowly I added sticks. About
the time I had the fire burning, I realized the day was dawning.
Time to move on again. We stayed only to finish eating the rabbit
and to let me get my hands and feet thoroughly warm. Then we
started off again, Nighteyes leading me unpityingly onwards.

TWENTY

Jhaampe

Jhaampe, the capital city of the Mountain Kingdom, is older than Buckkeep, just as the ruling line of the Mountain Kingdom is older than the house of Farseer. As a city, Jhaampe is as far removed in style from the fortress city of Buckkeep as the Farseer monarchs are different from the philosopher guides of the Sacrifice lineage that rule the Mountains.

There is no permanent city such as we know. There are few permanent buildings. Instead, along the carefully-planned and garden-bordered roads are spaces where the nomadic folk of the Mountains may come and go. There is a designated space for the market, but the merchants migrate in a procession that parallels that of the seasons. A score of tents may spring up overnight and their inhabitants swell the population of Jhaampe for a week or a month, only to disappear without a trace when their visiting and trading is over. Jhaampe is an ever-changing city of tents populated by the vigorous outdoor-dwelling folk of the mountains.

The homes of the ruling family and the companions that choose to stay year round with them are not at all like our castles and halls. Instead, their dwellings centre around great trees, living still, their trunks and branches patiently trained over scores of years to provide a framework for the building. This living structure is then draped with a fabric woven of tree-bark fibres and reinforced with a latticework. Thus the walls can take on the gently curving shapes of a tulip bud or the dome of an egg. A clay coating is spread over the fabric layer and this in turn is painted with a shiny resinous paint in the bright hues the mountain folk enjoy. Some are decorated with fanciful creatures or patterns but most are left simple. Purples and yellows predominate, so that to come upon the city growing in the shade of the great mountain trees is like coming upon a patch of crocus in springtime.

About these homes and at the intersections of the roads in this
nomadic 'city' are the gardens. Each is unique. One may centre around
an unusually-shaped stump or an arrangement of stones or a graceful
bit of wood. They may contain fragrant herbs or bright flowers or any
combination of plants. One notable one has at its heart a bubbling
spring of steaming water. Here grow plants with fleshy leaves and
exotically-scented flowers, denizens of some warmer clime brought here
to delight the mountain-dwellers with their mystery. Often visitors leave
gifts in the gardens when they depart, a wooden carving or a graceful
pot or perhaps merely an arrangement of bright pebbles. The gardens
belong to no one, and all tend them.

At Jhaampe can also be found hot springs, some of water that can
scald a man, others merely a gently bubbling warmth. These have been
confined, both as public baths and as a source of heat in some of the
smaller dwellings. In every building, in every garden, at every turn
the visitor finds the austere beauty and simplicity of colour and form
that are the Mountain ideal. The overall impression that one carries
away is of tranquility and joy in the natural world. The chosen simplicity of life there may lead the visitor to question his own choice in
life.

It was night. I recall little more than that it followed long days
of pain. I moved my staff and took another step. I moved my
staff again. We were not going quickly. A scurrying of snowflakes
in the air was more blinding than the darkness. I could not get
away from the circling wind that carried them. Nighteyes wove
a pacing path around me, guiding my hesitant steps as if it could
hurry me. From time to time he keened anxiously. His body
was tight with fear and weariness. He smelled wood smoke and
goats. . . . *not to betray you, my brother. But to help you. Remember
that. You need someone with hands. But if they try to mistreat you,
you have but to call and I shall come. I shall not be far . . .*

I could not make my mind focus on his thoughts. I felt his
bitterness that he could not help me and his fear that he was
leading me into a trap. I thought we had been arguing but I could
not remember what I had been insisting on. Whatever it was,
Nighteyes had won, simply by virtue of knowing what he wanted.

My feet slipped on the packed snow of the road and I went to my knees. Nighteyes sat down beside me and waited. I tried to lie down and he seized my wrist in his jaws. He tugged gently, but the thing in my back burst into sudden flames. I made a noise.

Please, my brother. There are huts ahead, and lights within them. Fires and warmth. And someone with hands, who can cleanse the foul wound in your back. Please. Get up. Just once more.

I lifted my hanging head and tried to see. There was something in the road ahead of us, something the road forked and went around on either side. The silver moonlight gleamed on it but I could not make out what it was. I blinked hard, and it became a carved stone, taller than a man. It had not been shaped to be an object, but was simply smoothed into a graceful shape. At its base, bare twiggy limbs recalled summer shrubbery. An irregular wall of smaller stones bordered it. Snow garnished all. It reminded me of Kettricken somehow. I tried to rise but could not. Beside me, Nighteyes whined in agony. I could not frame a thought to reassure him. It took all my strength to remain on my knees.

I did not hear footsteps but I felt a sudden increase in the tension thrumming through Nighteyes. I lifted my head again. Far ahead of me, past the garden, someone came walking through the night. Tall and slender, draped in heavy fabric, hood pulled forward so far it was almost a cowl. I watched the person come. Death, I thought. Only death could come so silently, gliding so smoothly through this icy night. 'Run away,' I whispered to Nighteyes. 'No sense in letting him take both of us. Run away now.'

For a wonder, he obeyed me, slipping away silently from my side. When I turned my head, I could not see him, but I sensed he was not far. I felt his strength leave me as if I had taken off a warm coat. Part of me tried to go with him, to cling to the wolf and be the wolf. I longed to leave this battered body behind.

If you must, my brother. If you must, I will not turn you away.

I wished he had not said it. It did not make it easier to resist the temptation. I had promised myself I would not do that to him, that if die I must, I would die and leave him free and clean of me to carve his own life. Yet as the moment for dying grew nearer there seemed so many good reasons to forsake that promise.

The healthy wild body, that simple life in the now called to me.

Slowly the figure drew nearer. A great shivering of cold and pain racked me. I could go to the wolf. I summoned the last of my strength to defy myself. 'Here!' I croaked to Death. 'Here I am. Come and take me and let it be done at last.'

He heard me. I saw him halt and stand stiffly as if afraid. Then he came with sudden haste, his white cloak swirling in the night wind. He stood by me, tall and slender and silent. 'I've come to you,' I whispered. Abruptly he knelt by me, and I glimpsed the chiselled ivory of his bony face. He put his arms around me and lifted me to bear me away. The pressure of his arm on my back was agonizing. I fainted.

Warmth was seeping back into me, bringing pain with it. I sprawled on my side, within walls, for the wind surged like the ocean outside. I smelled tea and incense, paint and wood-shavings and the wool rug I lay on. My face burned. I could not stop the shuddering that ran through me, though every wave of it awakened the searing pain in my back. My hands and feet throbbed.

'The knots of your cloak-strings are frozen. I'm going to cut them. Lie still now.' The voice was curiously gentle, as if unused to such a tone.

I managed to get an eye open. I was lying on the floor. My face was turned toward a stone hearth where a fire burned. Someone leaned over me. I saw the glitter of a blade nearing my throat, but I could not move. I felt it sawing and honestly could not tell if it tasted my flesh. Then my cloak was being lifted back. 'It's frozen to your shirt,' someone muttered. I almost thought I knew the voice. A gasp. 'It's blood. All this is frozen blood.' My cloak made an odd tearing sound as it was peeled loose. Then someone sat down on the floor beside me.

I turned my eyes up slowly but could not lift my head to see a face. Instead I saw a slender body clothed in a soft robe of white wool. Hands the colour of old ivory pushed the cuffs of his sleeves up. The fingers were long and thin, the wrists bony. Then he rose abruptly to get something. For a time I was alone. I closed my eyes. When I opened them a wide vessel of blue pottery was by my head. Steam rose from it and I smelled willow and rowan. 'Steady,' said the voice, and for a moment one of those hands rested on my shoulder reassuringly. Then I felt spreading warmth on my back.

'I'm bleeding again,' I whispered to myself.

'No. I'm soaking the shirt loose.' Once again, the voice was almost familiar. I closed my eyes. A door opened and shut and a gust of cold air wafted across me. The man beside me paused. I felt him glance up. 'You might have knocked,' he said with mock severity. I felt again the spreading warmth of water on my back. 'Even one such as I occasionally has other guests.'

Feet crossed hastily to me. Someone lowered herself fluidly to the floor beside me. I saw the folding of her skirts as she sank down. A hand pushed the hair back from my face. 'Who is he, holy one?'

'Holy one?' There was bitter humour in his voice. 'If you would speak of holes, you should speak of him, not me. Here, look at his back.' He spoke softer then. 'As to who he is, I have no idea.'

I heard her give a gasp. 'All of that is blood? How does he yet live? Let us get some warmth to him, and clean away the blood.' Then she tugged at my mittens and dragged them free of my hands. 'Oh, his poor hands, his fingers all gone black at the ends!' she exclaimed in horror.

That I did not want to see or know. I let go of everything.

For a time, it seemed as if I were a wolf again. I stalked an unfamiliar village, alert for dogs or anyone stirring about, but all was white silence and snow falling in the night. I found the hut I sought and prowled about it, but dared not enter it. After a time, it seemed I had done all I could about something. So I went hunting. I killed, I ate, I slept.

When I opened my eyes again, the room was washed with the pale light of day. The walls curved. I thought at first my eyes would not focus, and then I recognized the shape of a Mountain dwelling. Slowly I took in detail. Thick rugs of wool on the floor, simple wooden furniture, a window of greased hide. On a shelf, two dolls leaned their heads together beside a wooden horse and tiny cart. A huntsman puppet dangled in a corner. On a table were bits of brightly-painted wood. I smelled the clean shavings and the fresh paint. Puppets, I thought. Someone was making puppets. I was belly down on a bed with a blanket over me. I was warm. The skin of my face and my hands and feet burned unpleasantly but that could be ignored, for the great pain that bored into my back took precedence. My mouth was not so dry. Had I drunk something? I seemed to recall the spill of warm tea in my mouth but it was not a definite memory. Feet in felted wool slippers approached my bed. Someone bent down and lifted the blanket off me. Cool air flowed across my skin. Deft hands moved over me, prodding the area around my wound. 'So thin. Were he better fleshed, I'd say he had more chance,' said an old woman's voice sadly.

'Will he keep his toes and fingers?' A woman's voice, close by. A young woman. I could not see her but she was near. The other woman bent over me. She handled my hands, bending the fingers and pinching at the ends of them. I winced and tried feebly to pull away. 'If he lives, he'll keep his fingers,' she said, not unkindly but factually. 'They will be tender, for he must shed all the skin and flesh that was frozen. By themselves, they are not too bad. The infection in his back is what may kill him. There's something inside that wound. An arrowhead and part of the shaft by the look of it.'

'Cannot you take it out?' Ivory-hands spoke from somewhere in the room.

'Easily,' the woman replied. I realized she was speaking the tongue of Buck, with a Mountain accent. 'But he will certainly bleed and he has not much blood left he can part with. And the foulness of his wound may spread in fresh-flowing blood to poison all his body.' She sighed. 'Would that Jonqui were alive still. She was very wise in this type of thing. It was she who pulled from Prince Rurisk the arrow that had pierced his chest. The wound bubbled with his very life's breath and still she did not let him die. I am not such a healer as she, but I will try. I will send my apprentice with a salve for his hands and feet and face. Rub his skin well with it each day, and do not be dismayed at the shedding of skin. As for his back, that we must keep a drawing poultice on, to suck the poisons from it as best we may. Food and drink you must get into him, as much as he will take. Let him rest.

And a week hence, we will pull that arrow and hope he has built the strength to live through it. Jofron. Know you a good drawing poultice?'

'One or two. Bran and goosegrass is a good one,' she offered.

'It will do well. Would that I could stay and tend him, but I have many another to see to. Cedar Knoll was attacked last night. A bird has come with tidings that many were injured before the soldiers were driven off. I cannot tend one and leave many. I must leave him in your hands.'

'And in my bed,' Ivory-hands said dolefully. I heard the door close behind the healer.

I drew in a deeper breath but found no strength to speak.

Behind me, I heard the man moving about the hut, the small sounds of water poured and crockery moved. Footsteps came closer. 'I think he's awake,' Jofron said softly.

I gave a small nod against my pillow.

'Try to get this down him, then,' suggested Ivory-hands. 'Then let him rest. I shall return with bran and goosegrass for your poultice. And some bedding for myself, for I suppose he must stay here.' A tray was passed over my body and came into my view. There were a bowl and a cup on it. A woman sat beside me. I could not turn my head to see her face, but the fabrics of her skirt were Mountain-woven. Her hand spooned up a bit from the bowl and offered it to me. I sipped at it cautiously. Some sort of broth. From the cup wafted the scents of chamomile and valerian. I heard a door slide open, and then shut. I felt a waft of cold air move through the room. Another spoonful of broth. A third.

'Where?' I managed to say.

'What?' she asked, leaning closer. She turned her head and leaned down to see my face. Blue eyes. Too close to my own. 'Did you say something?'

I refused the spoon. It was suddenly too much effort to eat, even though what I had taken had heartened me. The room seemed darker. When next I awoke night was deep around me. All was silent save for the muted crackling of a fire in the hearth. The light it cast was fitful, but enough to show me the room. I felt feverish and very weak and horribly thirsty. There was a cup of water on a low table near my bed. I tried to reach for it, but the pain in my back stopped my arm's movement. My back felt taut with the swollen wound. Any movement awakened it. 'Water,' I mouthed, but the dryness of my mouth made it a whisper. No one came.

Near the hearth, my host had made up a pallet for himself. He slept like a cat, lax, but with that aura of constant wariness. His head was pillowed on his outstretched arm and the fire glazed him with light. I looked at him and my heart turned over in my chest.

His hair was smoothed back sleek on his skull, confined to a single plait, baring the clean lines of his face. Expressionless and still, it seemed a chiselled mask. The last trace of boyishness had been burned away, leaving only the clean planes of his lean cheeks and high forehead and long straight nose. His lips were narrower, his chin firmer than I recalled. The dance of the firelight lent colour to his face, staining his white skin with its amber. The Fool had grown up in the time we had been apart. It seemed too much change for twelve months, and yet this year had been longer than any in my life. For a time I simply lay and looked at him.

His eyes opened slowly, as if I had spoken to him. For a time he stared back at me without a word. Then a frown creased his brow. He sat up slowly, and I saw that truly he was ivory, his hair the colour of fresh-ground flour. It was his eyes that stopped my heart and tongue. They caught the firelight, yellow as a cat's. I finally found my breath. 'Fool,' I sighed sadly. 'What have they done to you?' My parched mouth could barely shape the words. I reached out my hand to him, but the movement pulled the muscles of my back and I felt my injury open again. The world tilted and slid away.

Safety. That was my first clear sensation. It came from the soft warmth of the clean bedding, the herb fragrance of the pillow beneath my head. Something warm and slightly damp pressed gently on my wound and muffled its stab. Safety clasped me as gently as the cool hands that held my frostbitten hand between them. I opened my eyes and the firelit room slowly swam into focus.

He was sitting by my bed. There was a stillness about him that was not repose as he stared past me and into the darkened room.

He wore a plain robe of white wool with a round collar. The simple clothes were a shock after the years of seeing him in motley. It was like seeing a garish puppet stripped of its paint. Then a single silver tear tracked down one cheek beside the narrow nose. I was astonished.

'Fool?' My voice came out as a croak this time.

His eyes came instantly to mine and he dropped to his knees beside me. His breath came and went raggedly in his throat. He snatched up the cup of water and held it to my mouth while I drank. Then he set it aside, to take up my dangling hand and clasp it gently. He spoke softly as he did this, more to himself than to me. 'What have they done to me, Fitz? Gods, what have they done to you, to mark you so? What has become of me, that I did not even know you though I carried you in my arms?' His cool fingers moved tentatively down my face, tracing the scar and the broken nose. He leaned down suddenly to rest his brow against mine. 'When I recall how beautiful you were,' he whispered brokenly, and then fell silent. The warm drip of his tear against my face felt scalding.

He sat up abruptly, clearing his throat. He wiped his sleeve across his eyes, a child's gesture that unmanned me even more. I drew a deeper breath and gathered myself. 'You've changed,' I managed to say.

'Have I? I imagine I have. How could I not have changed? I thought you dead, and all my life for naught. Then now, this moment, to be given back both you and my life's purpose . . . I opened my eyes to you and thought my heart would stop, that madness had finally claimed me. Then you spoke my name. Changed, you say? More than you can imagine, as much as you have plainly changed yourself. This night, I hardly know myself.' It was as close as I had ever heard the Fool come to babbling. He took a breath, and his voice cracked on his next words. 'For a year, I have believed you dead, Fitz. For a whole year.'

He had not released my hand. I felt the trembling that went through him. He stood suddenly, saying, 'We both need something to drink.' He walked away from me across the darkened room. He had grown, but it was in shape rather than size. I doubted he was much taller, but his body was no longer a child's.

He was lean and slight as ever, muscled as tumblers are. He brought a bottle from a cabinet, two simple cups. He uncorked the bottle and I smelled the warmth of the brandy before he poured. He came back to sit by my bed and offer me a cup. I managed to wrap my hand around it despite my blackened fingertips. He seemed to have recovered some of his aplomb. He looked at me over the rim as he drank. I lifted my head and tipped a spill of mine into my mouth. Half went down my beard and I choked as if I had never had brandy before. Then I felt the hot race of it in my belly. The Fool shook his head as he gently wiped my face.

'I should have listened to my dreams. Over and over, I dreamed you were coming. It was all you ever said, in the dream. I am coming. Instead I believed so firmly that I had failed somehow, that the Catalyst was dead. I could not even see who you were when I picked you up from the ground.'

'Fool,' I said quietly. I wished he would stop speaking. I simply wanted to be safe for a time, and think of nothing. He did not understand.

He looked at me and grinned his old sly Fool's smile. 'You still don't understand, do you? When word reached us that you were dead, that Regal had killed you . . . my life ended. It was worse, somehow, when the pilgrims began to trickle in, to hail me as the White Prophet. I knew I was the White Prophet. I've known it since I was a child, as did those who raised me. I grew up, knowing that some day I would come north to find you and that between the two of us we would put time in its proper course. All of my life, I knew I would do that.

'I was not much more than a child when I set out. Alone, I made my way to Buckkeep, to seek the Catalyst that only I would recognize. And I found you, and I knew you, though you did not know yourself. I watched the ponderous turning of events and marked how each time you were the pebble that shifted that great wheel from its ancient path. I tried to speak to you of it, but you would have none of it. The Catalyst? Not you, oh, no!' He laughed, almost fondly. He drained off the rest of his brandy at a gulp, then held my cup to my lips. I sipped.

He rose, then, to pace a turn about the room and then halted to refill his cup. He came back to me again. 'I saw it all come to the tottering brink of ruin. But always you were there, the card never dealt before, the side of the die that had never before fallen uppermost. When my king died, as I knew he must, there was an heir to the Farseer line, and FitzChivalry yet lived, the Catalyst that would change all things so that an heir would ascend to the throne.' He gulped his brandy again and when he spoke the scent of it rode his breath. 'I fled. I fled with Kettricken and the unborn child, grieving, yet confident that all would come to pass as it must. For you were the Catalyst. But when word came to us that you were dead . . .' He halted abruptly. When he tried to speak again, his voice had gone thick and lost its music. 'It made of me a lie. How could I be the White Prophet if the Catalyst were dead? What could I predict? The changes that could have been, had you lived? What would I be but a witness as the world spun deeper and deeper into ruin? I had no purpose any more. Your life was more than half of mine, you see. It was in the interweaving of our doings that I existed. Worse, I came to wonder if any part of the world were truly what I believed it. Was I a White Prophet at all, or was it but some peculiar madness, a self-deception to console a freak? For a year, Fitz. A year. I grieved for the friend I had lost, and I grieved for the world that somehow I had doomed. My failure, all of it. And when Kettricken's child, my last hope, came into the world still and blue, what could it be but my doing somehow?'

'No!' The word burst from me with a strength I had not known I had. The Fool flinched as if I had struck him. Then, 'Yes,' he said simply, carefully taking my hand again. 'I am sorry. I should have known you did not know. The Queen was devastated at the loss. And I. The Farseer heir. My last hope crumbled away. I had held myself together, telling myself, well, if the child lives and ascends the throne, perhaps that will have been enough. But when she was brought to bed with naught but a dead babe for all her travails . . . I felt my whole life had been a farce, a sham, an evil jest played on me by time. But now . . .' He closed his eyes a moment. 'Now I find you truly alive. So I live. And again, suddenly, I believe. Once more I know who I am. And who my Catalyst is.' He laughed aloud, never dreaming how his words chilled my blood. 'I had no faith. I, the White Prophet, did not believe my own foreseeing! Yet here we are, Fitz, and all will still come to pass as it was ever meant to do.'

Again he tipped the bottle to fill his cup. The liquor, when he poured it, was the colour of his eyes. He saw me staring and grinned delightedly. 'Ah, you say, but the White Prophet is no longer white? I suspect it is the way of my kind. I may gain more colour now, as the years pass.' He made a deprecating motion. 'But that is of little import. I have already talked too much. Tell me, Fitz. Tell me all. How did you survive? Why are you here?'

'Verity calls me. I must go to him.'

The Fool drew in breath at my words, not a gasp, but a slow inhalation as if he took life back into himself. He almost glowed with pleasure at my words. 'So he lives! Ah!' Before I could speak more, he lifted his hands. 'Slowly. Tell me all, in order. These are words I have hungered to hear. I must know everything.'

And so I tried. My strength was small and sometimes I felt myself borne up on my fever so that my words wandered and I could not recall where I had left off my tale of the past year. I got as far as Regal's dungeon, then could only say, 'He had me beaten and starved.' The Fool's quick glance at my scarred face and the casting aside of his eyes told me he understood. He, too, had known Regal too well. When he waited to hear more, I shook my head slowly.

He nodded, then put a smile on his face. 'It's all right, Fitz. You are weary. You have already told me what I most longed to hear. The rest will keep. For now, I shall tell you of my year.' I tried to listen, clinging to the important words, storing them in my heart. There was so much I had wondered for so long. Regal had suspected the escape. Kettricken had returned to her rooms to find that her carefully-chosen and packed supplies were gone, spirited away by Regal's spies. She had left with little more than the clothes on her back and a hastily-grabbed cloak. I heard of the evil weather the Fool and Kettricken had faced the night they slipped away from Buckkeep.

She had ridden my Sooty and the Fool had battled headstrong Ruddy all the way across the Six Duchies in winter. They had reached Blue Lake at the end of the winter storms. The Fool had supported them and earned their passage on a ship by painting his face and dying his hair and juggling in the streets. What colour had he painted his skin? White, of course, all the better to hide the stark white skin that Regal's spies would be watching for.

They had crossed the lake with little incident, passed Moonseye and travelled into the Mountains. Immediately Kettricken had sought her father's aid in finding what had become of Verity. He had, indeed, passed through Jhaampe but nothing had been heard of him since. Kettricken had put riders on his trail and even joined in the search herself. But all her hopes had come to grief. Far up in the mountains, she had found the site of a battle. The winter and the scavengers had done their work. No one man could be identified, but Verity's buck standard was there. The scattered arrows and hewn ribs of one body showed it was men and not the beasts or elements that had attacked them. There were not enough skulls to go with the bodies and the scattering of the bones made the number of dead uncertain. Kettricken had clung to hope until a cloak had been found that she remembered packing for Verity. Her hands had embroidered the buck on the breast patch. A tumble of mouldering bones and ragged garments were beneath it. Kettricken had mourned her husband as dead.

She had returned to Jhaampe to pendulum between devastated grief and seething rage at Regal's plots. Her fury had solidified into a determination that she would see Verity's child upon the Six Duchies throne, and a fair reign returned to the folk. Those plans had sustained her until the stillbirth of her child. The Fool had scarcely seen her since, save to catch glimpses of her pacing through her frozen gardens, her face as still as the snows that overlay the beds.

There was more, shuffled in with his account, of both major and minor news for me. Sooty and Ruddy were both alive and well. Sooty was in foal to the young stallion despite her years. I shook my head over that. Regal had been doing his best to provoke a war. The roving gangs of bandits that now plagued the Mountain folk were thought to be in his pay. Shipments of grain that had been paid for in spring had never been delivered, nor had the Mountain traders been permitted to cross the border with their wares. Several small villages close to the Six Duchies border had been found looted and burned with no survivors. King Eyod's wrath, slow to stir, was now at white heat. Although the Mountain folk had no standing army as such, there was not one inhabitant who would not take up arms at the word of their Sacrifice. War was imminent.

And he had tales of Patience, the Lady of Buckkeep, brought erratically by word of mouth passed among merchants and on to smugglers. She did all she could to defend Buck's coast. Money was dwindling, but the folk of the land gave to her what they called the Lady's Levy and she disposed of it as best she could amongst her soldiers and sailors. Buckkeep had not fallen yet, though the Raiders now had encampments up and down the whole coastline of the Six Duchies. Winter had quieted the war, but spring would bathe the coast in blood once more. Some of the smaller keeps spoke of treaties with the Red Ships. Some openly paid tribute in the hopes of avoiding Forging.

The Coastal Duchies would not survive another summer. So said Chade. My tongue was silent as the Fool spoke of him. He had come to Jhaampe by secret ways in high summer, disguised as an old pedlar, but made himself known to the Queen when he arrived. The Fool had seen him then. 'War agrees with him,' the Fool observed. 'He strides about like a man of twenty. He carries a sword at his hip and there is fire in his eyes. He was pleased to see how her belly swelled with the Farseer heir, and they spoke bravely of Verity's child on the throne. But that was high summer.' He sighed. 'Now I hear he has returned. I believe because the Queen has sent word of her stillbirth. I have not been to see him yet. What hope he can offer us now, I do not know.' He shook his head. 'There must be an heir to the Farseer throne,' he insisted. 'Verity must get one. Otherwise . . .' He made a helpless gesture.

'Why not Regal? Would not a child from his loins suffice?'

'No.' His eyes went afar. 'No. I can tell you that quite clearly, yet I cannot tell you why. Only that in all futures I have seen, he makes no child. Not even a bastard. In all times, he reigns as the last Farseer, and ushers in the dark.'

A shiver walked over me. He was too strange when he spoke

of such things. And his odd words had brought another worry into my mind. 'There were two women. A minstrel Starling, and an old woman pilgrim, Kettle. They were on their way here. Kettle said she sought the White Prophet. I little thought he might be you. Have you heard aught of them? Have they reached Jhaampe town?'

He shook his head slowly. 'No one has come seeking the White Prophet since winter closed on us.' He halted, reading the worry in my face. 'Of course, I do not know of all who come here. They may be in Jhaampe. But I have heard nothing of two such as that.' He reluctantly added, 'Bandits prey on roadside travellers now. Perhaps they were . . . delayed.'

Perhaps they were dead. They had come back for me, and I had sent them on alone.

'Fitz?'

'I'm all right. Fool, a favour?'

'I like not that tone already. What is it?'

'Tell no one I am here. Tell no one I am alive, just yet.'

He sighed. 'Not even Kettricken? To tell her that Verity lives still?'

'Fool, what I have come to do, I intend to do alone. I would not raise false hopes in her. She has endured the news of his death once. If I can bring him back to her, then will be time enough for true rejoicing. I know I ask much. But let me be a stranger you are aiding. Later, I may need your aid in obtaining an old map from the Jhaampe libraries. But when I leave here, I would go alone. I think this quest is one best accomplished quietly.' I glanced aside from him and added, 'Let FitzChivalry remain dead. Mostly, it is better so.'

'Surely you will at least see Chade?' He was incredulous.

'Not even Chade should know I live.' I paused, wondering which would anger the old man more: that I had attempted to kill Regal when he had always forbidden it, or that I had so badly botched the task. 'This quest must be mine alone.' I watched him and saw a grudging acceptance in his face.

He sighed again. 'I will not say I agree with you completely. But I shall tell no one who you are.' He gave a small laugh. Talk fell off between us. The bottle of brandy was empty. We were reduced to silence, staring at one another drunkenly. The fever and the brandy burned in me. I had too many things to think of and too little I could do about any of them. If I lay very still, the pain in my back subsided to a red throb. It kept pace with the beating of my heart.

'Too bad you didn't manage to kill Regal,' the Fool observed suddenly.

'I know. I tried. As a conspirator and an assassin, I'm a failure.'

He shrugged for me. 'You were never really good at it, you know. There was a naiveté to you that none of the ugliness could stain, as if you never truly believed in evil. It was what I liked best about you.' The Fool swayed slightly where he sat, but righted himself. 'It was what I missed most, when you were dead.'

I smiled foolishly. 'A while back, I thought it was my great beauty.'

For a time the Fool just looked at me. Then he glanced aside and spoke quietly. 'Unfair. Were I myself, I would never have spoken such words aloud. Still. Ah, Fitz.' He looked at me and shook his head fondly. He spoke without mockery, making almost a stranger of himself. 'Perhaps half of it was that you were so unaware of it. Not like Regal. Now there's a pretty man, but he knows it too well. You never see him with his hair tousled or the red of the wind on his cheeks.'

For a moment I felt oddly uncomfortable. Then I said, 'Nor with an arrow in his back, more's the pity,' and we both went off into the foolish laughter that only drunks understand. It woke the pain in my back to a stabbing intensity however, and in a moment I was gasping for breath. The Fool rose, steadier on his feet that I would have expected, to take a drippy bag of something off my back and replace it with one almost uncomfortably warm from a pot on the hearth. That done, he came again to crouch beside me. He looked directly in my eyes, his yellow ones as hard to read as his colourless ones had been. He laid one long cool hand along my cheek and then gentled the hair back from my eyes.

'Tomorrow,' he told me gravely. 'We shall be ourselves again. The Fool and the Bastard. Or the White Prophet and the Catalyst, if you will. We will have to take up those lives, as little as we care for them, and fulfil all fate has decreed for us. But for here, for now, just between us two, and for no other reason save I am me and you are you, I tell you this. I am glad, glad that you are alive. To see you take breath puts the breath back in my lungs. If there must be another my fate is twined around, I am glad it is you.'

He leaned forward then and for an instant pressed his brow to mine. Then he breathed a heavy sigh and drew back from me. 'Go to sleep, boy,' he said in a fair imitation of Chade's voice. 'Tomorrow comes early. And we've work to do.' He laughed unevenly. 'We've the world to save, you and I.'

TWENTY-ONE

Confrontations

Diplomacy may very well be the art of manipulating secrets. What would any negotiation come to, were not there secrets to either share or withhold? And this is as true of a marriage pact as it is of a trade agreement between kingdoms. Each side knows truly how much it is willing to surrender to the other to get what it wishes; it is in the manipulation of that secret knowledge that the hardest bargain is driven. There is no action that takes place between humans in which secrets do not play a part, whether it be a game of cards or the selling of a cow. The advantage is always to the one who is shrewder in what secret to reveal and when. King Shrewd was fond of saying that there was no greater advantage than to know your enemy's secret when he believed you ignorant of it. Perhaps that is the most powerful secret of all to possess.

The days that followed were not days for me, but disjointed periods of wakefulness interspersed with wavery fever dreams. Either my brief talk with the Fool had burned my last reserves, or I finally felt safe enough to surrender to my injury. Perhaps it was both. I lay on a bed near the Fool's hearth and felt wretchedly dull when I felt anything at all. Overheard conversations rattled against me. I slipped in and out of awareness of my own misery, but never far away, like a drum beating the tempo of my pain was Verity's *come to me, come to me*. Other voices came and went through the haze of my fever but his was a constant.

'She believes you are the one she seeks. I believe it, too. I think you should see her. She has come a long and weary way, seeking the White Prophet.' Jofron's voice was low and reasonable.

I heard the Fool set down his rasp with a clack. 'Tell her she is mistaken, then. Tell her I am the White Toymaker. Tell her the White Prophet lives further down the street, five doors down on the left.'

'I will not make mock of her,' Jofron said seriously. 'She has travelled a vast distance to seek you and on the journey lost all but her life. Come, holy one. She waits outside. Will not you talk to her, just for a bit?'

'Holy one,' the Fool snorted with disdain. 'You have been reading too many old scrolls. As has she. No, Jofron.' Then he sighed, and relented. 'Tell her I will talk with her two days hence. But not today.'

'Very well.' Jofron plainly did not approve. 'But there is another one with her. A minstrel. I don't think she will be put off as easily. I think she is seeking him.'

'Ah, but no one knows he is here. Save you, me and the healer. He wishes to be left alone for a time, while he heals.'

I moved my mouth. I tried to say I would see Starling, that I had not meant to turn Starling away.

'I know that. And the healer is still at Cedar Knoll. But she is a smart one, this minstrel. She has asked the children for news of a stranger. And the children, as usual, know everything.'

'And tell everything,' the Fool replied glumly. I heard him fling down another tool in annoyance. 'I see I have but one choice then.'

'You will see them?'

A snort of laughter from the Fool. 'Of course not. I mean that I will lie to them.'

Afternoon sun slanting across my closed eyes. I woke to voices, arguing.

'I only wish to see him.' A woman's voice, annoyed. 'I know he is here.'

'Ah, I suppose I shall admit you are right. But he sleeps.' The Fool, with his maddening calm.

'I still would see him.' Starling, pointedly.

The Fool heaved a great sigh. 'I could let you in to see him. But then you would wish to touch him. And once you had touched him, you would wish to wait until he awakened. And once he awakened, you would wish to have words with him. There would be no end to it. And I have much to do today. A toymaker's time is not his own.'

'You are not a toymaker. I know who you are. And I know who he truly is.' The cold was flowing in the open door. It crept under my blankets, tightened my flesh and tugged at my pain. I wished they would shut it.

'Ah, yes, you and Kettle know our great secret. I am the White Prophet, and he is Tom the shepherd. But today I am busy, prophesying puppets finished tomorrow, and he is asleep. Counting sheep, in his dreams.'

'That's not what I mean.' Starling lowered her voice, but it carried anyway. 'He is FitzChivalry, son of Chivalry the Abdicated. And you are the Fool.'

'Once, perhaps, I was the Fool. It is common knowledge here in Jhaampe. But now I am the Toymaker. As I no longer use the other title, you may take it for yourself if you wish. As for Tom, I believe he takes the title Bed Bolster these days.'

'I will be seeing the Queen about this.'

'A wise decision. If you wish to become her Fool, she is certainly the one you must see. But for now, let me show you something else. No, step back, please, so you can see it all. Here it comes.' I heard the slam and the latch. 'The outside of my door,' the Fool announced gladly. 'I painted it myself. Do you like it?'

I heard a thud as of a muffled kick, followed by several more. The Fool came humming back to his work table. He took up the wooden head of a doll and a paintbrush. He glanced over at me. 'Go back to sleep. She won't get in to see Kettricken any time soon. The Queen sees few people these days. And when she does, it's not likely she'll be believed. And that is the best we can do for now. So sleep while you may. And gather strength, for I fear you will need it.'

*   *   *

Daylight on white snow. Belly down in the snow amongst the trees, looking down on a clearing. Young humans at play, chasing one another, leaping and dragging one another down to roll over and over in the snow. They are not so different from cubs. Envious. We never had other cubs to play with while we were growing. It is like an itch, the desire to race down and join in. They would be frightened, we caution ourselves. Only watch. Their shrill yelps fill the air. Will our she-cub grow to be like these, we wonder? Braided hair flies behind as they race through the snow chasing one another.

'Fitz. Wake up. I need to talk to you.'

Something in the Fool's tone cut through both fog and pain. I opened my eyes, then squinted painfully. The room was dark, but he had brought a branch of candles to the floor by my bedside. He sat beside them, looking into my face earnestly. I could not read his face; it seemed that hope danced in his eyes and at the corners of his mouth, but also he seemed braced as if he brought me bad tidings. 'Are you listening? Can you hear me?' he pressed.

I managed a nod. Then, 'Yes.' My voice was so hoarse I hardly knew it. Instead of getting stronger for the healer to pull the arrow, I felt as if the wound were getting stronger. Each day the area of pain spread. It pushed always at the edge of my mind, making it hard to think.

'I have been to dine with Chade and Kettricken. He had tidings for us.' He tilted his head and watched my face carefully as he said, 'Chade says there is a Farseer child in Buck. Just a babe yet, and a bastard. But of the same Farseer lineage as Verity and Chivalry. He swears it is so.'

I closed my eyes.

'Fitz. Fitz! Wake up and listen to me. He seeks to persuade Kettricken to claim the child. To either say that it is her rightful child by Verity, hidden by a false stillbirth to protect her from assassins. Or to say the child is Verity's bastard, but that Queen Kettricken chooses to legitimize her and claim her as heir.'

I could not move. I could not breathe. My daughter, I knew. Kept safe and hidden, guarded by Burrich. To be sacrificed to the throne. Taken from Molly, and given to the Queen. My little girl, whose name I didn't even know. Taken to be a princess and in time a queen. Put beyond my reach forever.

'Fitz!' The Fool put his hand on my shoulder and squeezed it gently. I knew he longed to shake me. I opened my eyes.

He peered into my face. 'Have you nothing to say to me?' he asked carefully.

'May I have some water?'

While he got it for me, I composed myself. He helped me drink. By the time he took the cup, I had decided what question would be most convincing. 'What did Kettricken say to the news that Verity had fathered a bastard? It could scarcely bring her joy.'

The uncertainty I had hoped for spread across the Fool's face. 'The child was born at the end of harvest. Too late for Verity to have sired it before he left on his quest. Kettricken grasped it faster than I did.' He spoke almost gently. 'You must be the father. When Kettricken asked Chade directly, he said as much.' He cocked his head to study me. 'You did not know?'

I shook my head slowly. What was honour to one such as I? Bastard and assassin, what claim did I have to nobility of soul? I spoke the lie I would always despise. 'I could not have fathered a child born at harvest. Molly had turned me out of her bed months before she left Buck.' I tried to keep my voice steady as I spoke. 'If the mother is Molly, and she claims the child is mine, she lies.' I strove to be sincere as I added, 'I am sorry, Fool. I have fathered no Farseer heir for you, nor do I intend to.' It was no effort to let my voice choke and tears mist my eyes. 'Strange.' I shook my head against the pillow. 'That such a thing could bring me such pain. That she could seek to pass the babe off as mine.' I closed my eyes.

The Fool spoke gently. 'As I understand it, she has made no claims for the child. As of yet, I believe she knows nothing of Chade's plan.'

'I suppose I should see both Chade and Kettricken. To tell them I am alive and reveal the truth to them. But when I am stronger. Just now, Fool, I would be alone,' I begged him. I wanted to see neither sympathy nor puzzlement on his face. I prayed he would believe my lie even as I despised myself for the foul thing I had said of Molly. So I kept my eyes closed, and he took his candles and went away.

I lay for a time in the dark, hating myself. It was better this way, I told myself. If ever I returned to her, I could make all right. And if I did not, at least they would not take our child from her. I told myself over and over again I had done the wise thing. But I did not feel wise. I felt traitorous.

I dreamed a dream at once vivid and stultifying. I chipped black stone. That was the entire dream, but it was endless in its monotony. I was using my dagger as a chisel and a rock as a hammer. My fingers were scabbed and swollen from the many times my grip had slipped and I'd struck them instead of the dagger hilt. But it didn't stop me. I chipped black stone. And waited for someone to come and help me.

I awoke one evening to find Kettle sitting by my bed. She looked even older than I recalled. Hazy winter daylight seeped through a parchment window to touch her face. I studied her for a time before she realized I was awake. When she did, she shook her head at me. 'I should have guessed, from all your strangeness. You were bound for the White Prophet yourself.' She leaned closer and spoke in a whisper. 'He will not allow Starling in to see you. He says you are too weak for so lively a visitor. And that you wish no one to know you are here, just yet. But I'll take word of you to her, shall I?'

I closed my eyes.

A time of bright morning and a knock at the door. I could not sleep, nor could I stay awake for the fever that racked me. I had drunk willowbark tea until my belly was sloshing. Still my head pounded, and I was always shivering or sweating. The knock came again, louder, and Kettle set down the cup she had been plaguing me with. The Fool was at his work table. He put aside his carving tool, but Kettle called, 'I'll get it!' and opened the door, even as he was saying, 'No, let me.'

Starling pushed in, so abruptly that Kettle exclaimed in surprise. Starling came past her, into the room, shaking snow from her cap and cloak. She shot the Fool a look of triumph. The Fool merely nodded cordially at her as if he had been expecting her. He turned back to his carving without a word. The bright sparks of anger in her eyes grew hotter, and I sensed her satisfaction in something. She shut the door loudly behind her and came into the room like the northwind herself. She dropped to sit cross-legged on the floor beside my bed. 'So, Fitz. I'm so glad to finally see you again. Kettle told me you were hurt. I'd have come to see you before, but I was turned away at the door. How are you today?'

I tried to focus my mind. I wished she would move more slowly and speak more softly. 'It's too cold in here,' I complained petulantly. 'And I've lost my earring.' I had only discovered the loss that morning. It fretted me. I could not recall why it was so important, but my mind would not let go of it either. The very thought made my headache worse.

She stripped off her mittens. One hand was bandaged still. She touched my forehead with the other. Her hand was blessedly cold. Odd that cold could feel so good. 'He's burning up!' she accused the Fool. 'Haven't you the sense to give him willowbark tea?'

The Fool shaved off another curl of wood. 'There's a pot of it there by your knee, if you haven't overset it. If you can get him to drink any more of it, you're a better man than I.' Another curl of wood.

'That would not be hard,' Starling said in an ugly little voice. Then, in a kinder tone, to me, 'Your earring isn't lost. See, I have it right here.' She took it from the pouch at her belt. One small part of me worked well enough to notice that she was warmly dressed in the Mountain style now. Her hands were cold and a bit rough as she put the earring back in my ear for me. I found a question.

'Why did you have it?'

'I asked Kettle to bring it to me,' she told me bluntly. 'When *he* would not let me in to see you. I had to have a token, something to prove to Kettricken that all I told her was true. I have been to her and spoken to her and her counsellor, this very day.'

The Queen's name broke through my wandering thoughts and gave me a moment of focus. 'Kettricken! What have you done?' I cried in dismay. 'What have you told her?'

Starling looked startled. 'Why, all she must know so that she will help you on your quest. That you are truly alive. That Verity is not dead, and that you will seek him. That word must be sent to Molly that you are alive and well, so that she shall not lose heart but will keep your child safe until you return. That . . .'

'I trusted you!' I cried out. 'I trusted you with my secrets and you have betrayed me. What a fool I've been!' I cried out in despair. All, all was lost.

'No, I am the Fool.' He broke into our conversation. He walked slowly across the room and stood looking down on me. 'The more so that I had believed you trusted me, it seems,' he went on, and I had never seen him so pale. 'Your child,' he said to himself. 'A true child of Farseer lineage.' His yellow eyes flickered like a dying fire as they darted from Starling to me. 'You know what such tidings mean to me. Why? Why lie to me?'

I did not know what was worse, the hurt in the Fool's eyes, or the triumph in the glance Starling gave him.

'I had to lie, to keep her mine! The child is mine, not a Farseer heir!' I cried out desperately. 'Mine and Molly's. A child to grow and love, not a tool for a kingmaker. And Molly must not hear I am alive from any save me! Starling, how could you have done this to me? Why was I such an idiot, why did I talk of such things at all to anyone?'

Now Starling looked as injured as the Fool. She stood up stiffly and her voice was brittle. 'I but sought to help you. To help you do what you must do.' Behind Starling, the wind gusted the door open. 'That woman has a right to know her husband is alive.'

'To which woman do you refer?' asked another icy voice. To my consternation, Kettricken swept into the room with Chade at her heels. She regarded me with a terrible face. Grief had ravaged her, had carved deep lines beside her mouth and eaten the flesh from her cheeks. Now anger raged in her eyes as well. The blast of cold wind that came with them cooled me for an instant. Then the door was closed and my eyes moved from face to familiar face. The small room seemed crowded with staring faces, with cold eyes looking at me. I blinked. There were so many of them and so close, and all stared at me. No one smiled. No welcome, no joy. Only the savage emotions that I had wakened with all the changes I had wrought. Thus was the Catalyst greeted. No one wore any expression I'd hoped to see.

None save Chade. He crossed the room to me in long strides, stripping off his riding gloves as he came. When he threw back the hood of his winter cloak, I saw that his white hair was bound back in a warrior's tail. He wore a band of leather across his brow, and centred on his forehead was a medallion of silver. A buck with antlers lowered to charge. The sigil Verity had given to me. Starling moved hastily from his path. He gave her not a glance as he folded easily to sit on the floor by my bed. He took my hand in his, narrowed his eyes at the sight of the frostbite. He held it softly. 'Oh, my boy, my boy, I believed you were dead. When Burrich sent me word he had found your body, I thought my heart would break. The words we had when last we parted . . . but here you are, alive if not well.'

He bent and kissed me. The hand he set to my cheek was callused now, the pocks scarcely visible on the weathered flesh. I looked up in his eyes and saw welcome and joy. Tears clouded my own as I had to demand, 'Would you truly take my daughter for the throne? Another bastard for the Farseer line . . . Would you have let her be used as we have been used?'

Something grew still in his face. The set of his mouth hardened into resolve. 'I will do whatever I have to do to see a true-hearted Farseer on the Six Duchies throne again. As I am sworn to do. As you are sworn also.' His eyes met mine.

I looked at him in dismay. He loved me. Worse, he believed in me. He believed that I had in me that strength and devotion to duty that had been the backbone of his life. Thus he could inflict on me things harder and colder than Regal's hatred of me could imagine. His belief in me was such that he would not hesitate to plunge me into any battle, that he would expect any sacrifice of me. A dry sob suddenly racked me and tore at the arrow in my back. 'There is no end!' I cried out. 'That duty will

hound me into death. Better I were dead! Let me be dead then!'
I snatched my hand away from Chade, heedless of how much
that motion hurt. 'Leave me!'

Chade didn't even flinch. 'He is burning with fever,' he said
accusingly to the Fool. 'He doesn't know what he's saying. You
should have given him willowbark tea.'

A terrible smile crooked the Fool's lips. Before he could reply,
there was a sharp shredding sound. A grey head was forced through
the greased hide window, flashing a muzzle full of white teeth.
The rest of the wolf soon followed, oversetting a shelf of potted
herbs onto some scrolls set out below them. Nighteyes sprang,
nails skittering on the wood floor, and slid to a halt between me
and the hastily-standing Chade. He snarled all round. *I will kill
them all for you, if you say so.* I dropped my head down to my
pillows. My clean, wild wolf. This was what I had made of him.
Was it any better than what Chade had made of me?

I looked around them again. Chade was standing, his face
very still. Every single face held some shock, some sadness, some
disappointment that I was responsible for. Despair and fever shook
me. 'I'm sorry,' I said weakly. 'I have never been what you thought
I was,' I confessed. 'Never.'

Silence filled up the room. The fire crackled briefly.

I dropped my face to my pillow and closed my eyes. I spoke
the words I was compelled to say. 'But I shall go and find Verity.
Somehow, I will bring him back to you. Not because I am what
you believe me to be,' I added, slowly lifting my head. I saw hope
kindle in Chade's face. 'But because I have no choice. I have
never had any choices.'

'You do believe Verity is alive!' The hope in Kettricken's voice
was savagely hungry. She swept toward me like an ocean storm.

I nodded my head. Then, 'Yes,' I managed. 'Yes, I believe he
lives. I have felt him strongly with me.' Her face was so close,
huge in my sight. I blinked my eyes, and then could not focus
them.

'Why has not he returned then? Is he lost? Injured? Does he
have no care for those he left behind?' Her questions rattled
against me like flung stones, one after another.

'I think,' I began, and then could not. Could not think, could not speak. I closed my eyes. I listened to a long silence. Nighteyes whined, then growled deep in his throat.

'Perhaps we should all leave for a time,' Starling ventured unevenly. 'Fitz is not up to this just now.'

'You may leave,' the Fool told her grandly. 'Unfortunately I still live here.'

Going hunting. It is time to go hunting. I look to where we came in, but the Scentless One has blocked that way, covering it over with another piece of deerskin. Door, part of us knows that is the door and we go to it, to whine softly and prod at it with our nose. It rattles against its catch like a trap about to spring shut. The Scentless One comes, stepping lightly, warily. He stretches his body past me, to put a pale paw on the door and open it for me. I slip out, back into a cool night world. It feels good to stretch my muscles again, and I flee the pain and the stuffy hut and the body that does not work to this wild sanctuary of flesh and fur. The night swallows us and we hunt.

It was another night, another time, before, after, I did not know, my days had come unlinked from one another. Someone lifted a warm compress from my brow and replaced it with a cooler one. 'I'm sorry, Fool,' I said.

'Thirty-two,' said a voice wearily. Then, 'Drink,' it added more gently. Cool hands raised my face. A cup lapped liquid against my mouth. I tried to drink. Willowbark tea. I turned my face away in disgust. The Fool wiped my mouth and sat down on the floor beside my bed. He leaned companionably close against it. He held his scroll up to the lamplight and went on reading. It was deep night. I closed my eyes and tried to find sleep again. All I could find were things I'd done wrong, trusts I'd betrayed.

'I'm so sorry,' I said.

'Thirty-three,' said the Fool without looking up.

'Thirty-three what?' I asked.

He glanced over at me in surprise. 'Oh. You're truly awake and talking?'

'Of course. Thirty-three what?'

'Thirty-three "I'm sorrys". To various people, but the greatest number of them to me. Seventeen calls for Burrich. I lost count of your calls for Molly, I'm afraid. And a grand total of sixty-two "I'm coming, Verity".'

'I must be driving you crazy. I'm sorry.'

'Thirty-four. No. You've just been raving, rather monotonously. It's the fever, I suppose.'

'I suppose.'

The Fool went back to reading. 'I'm so tired of lying on my belly,' I ventured.

'There's always your back,' the Fool suggested, to see me wince. Then, 'Do you want me to help you shift to your side?'

'No. That just hurts more.'

'Tell me if you change your mind.' His eyes went back to the scroll.

'Chade hasn't been back to see me,' I observed.

The Fool sighed and set aside his scroll. 'No one has. The healer came in and berated us all for bothering you. They're to leave you alone until she pulls the arrow out. That's tomorrow. Besides. Chade and the Queen have had much to discuss. Discovering that both you and Verity are still alive has changed everything for them.'

'Another time, he would have included me.' I paused, knowing I was wallowing in self-pity, but unable to stop myself. 'I suppose they feel they cannot trust me any more. Not that I blame them. Everyone hates me now. For the secrets I kept. For all the ways I failed them.'

'Oh, not everyone hates you,' the Fool chided gently. 'Only me, really.'

My eyes darted to his face. His cynical smile reassured me. 'Secrets,' he said, and sighed. 'Someday I shall write a long philosophical treatise on the power of secrets, when kept or told.'

'Do you have any more brandy?'

'Thirsty again? Do have some more willowbark tea.' There was acid courtesy in his voice now, overladen with honey. 'There's plenty you know. Buckets of it. All for you.'

'I think my fever is down a bit,' I offered humbly.

He lifted a hand to my brow. 'So it is. For now. But I do not think the healer would approve of you getting drunk again.'

'The healer is not here,' I pointed out.

He arched a pale eyebrow at me. 'Burrich would be *so* proud of you.' But he rose gracefully and went to the oak cabinet. He stepped carefully around Nighteyes sprawled on the hearth in heat-soaked sleep. My eyes travelled to the patched window and then back to the Fool. I supposed some sort of agreement had been worked out between them. Nighteyes was so deeply asleep he was not even dreaming. His belly was full as well. His paws twitched when I quested toward him, so I withdrew. The Fool was putting the bottle and two cups on a tray. He seemed too subdued.

'I am sorry, you know.'

'So you have told me. Thirty-five times.'

'But I am. I should have trusted you and told you about my daughter.' Nothing, not a fever, not an arrow in my back would keep me from smiling when I said that phrase. My daughter. I tried to speak the simple truth. It embarrassed me that it seemed a new experience. 'I've never seen her, you know. Only with the Skill, anyway. It's not the same. And I want her to be mine. Mine and Molly's. Not a child that belongs to a kingdom, with some vast responsibility to grow into. Just a little girl, picking flowers, making candles with her mother, doing . . .' I floundered and finished, 'whatever it is that ordinary children are allowed to do. Chade would end that. The moment that anyone points to her and says, "There, she could be the Farseer heir," she's at risk. She'd have to be guarded and taught to fear, to weigh every word and consider every action. Why should she? She isn't truly a royal heir. Only a bastard's bastard.' I said those harsh words with difficulty, and vowed never to let anyone say them to her face. 'Why should she be put in such danger? It would be one thing if she were born in a palace and had a hundred soldiers to guard her. But she has only Molly and Burrich.'

'Burrich is with them? If Chade chose Burrich, it is because he thinks him the equal of a hundred guards. But far more discreet,' the Fool observed. Did he know how that would wrench me? He brought the cups and the brandy and poured for me. I managed to pick up my own cup. 'To a daughter. Yours and Molly's,' he offered and we drank. The brandy burned clean in my throat.

'So,' I managed. 'Chade knew all along and sent Burrich to guard her. Even before I knew, they knew.' Why did I feel they had stolen something from me?

'I suspect so, but I am not certain.' The Fool paused, as if wondering at the wisdom of telling me. Then I saw him discard the reserve. 'I've been putting pieces together, counting back the time. I think Patience suspected. I think that's why she started sending Molly to take care of Burrich when his leg was injured. He didn't need that much care, and he knew it as well as Patience did. But Burrich is a good ear, mostly because he talks so little himself. Molly would need someone to talk to, perhaps someone that had once kept a bastard himself. That day we were all up in his room . . . you had sent me there, to see what he could do for my shoulder? The day you locked Regal out of Shrewd's rooms to protect him . . .' for a moment he seemed caught in that memory. Then he recovered. 'When I came up the stairs to Burrich's loft I heard them arguing. Well, Molly arguing, and Burrich being silent, which is his strongest way to argue. So, I eavesdropped,' he admitted frankly. 'But I didn't hear much. She was insisting he could get some particular herb for her. He wouldn't. Finally, he promised her he would tell no one, and bade her to think well and do what she wished to do, not what she thought was wisest. Then they said no more, so I went in. She excused herself and departed. Later, you came and said she had left you.' He paused. 'Actually, looking back, I was as dull-witted as you, not to have worked it out just from that.'

'Thank you,' I told him drily.

'You're welcome. Though I will admit we all had much on our minds that day.'

'I'd give anything to be able to go back in time and tell her that our child would be the most important thing in the world for me. More important than king or country.'

'Ah. So you would have left Buckkeep that day, to follow her and protect her.' The Fool quirked an eyebrow at me.

After a time, I said, 'I couldn't.' The words choked me and I washed them down with brandy.

'I know you couldn't have. I understand. You see, no one can avoid fate. Not as long as we are trapped in time's harness, anyway. And,' he said more softly, 'no child can avoid the future that fate decrees. Not a fool, not a bastard. Not a bastard's daughter.'

A shiver walked up my spine. Despite all my disbelief, I feared. 'Are you saying that you know something of her future?'

He sighed and nodded. Then he smiled and shook his head. 'That is how it is, for me. I know something of a Farseer's heir. If that heir is she, then doubtless, years from now, I shall read some ancient prophecy and say, ah, yes, there it is, it was foretold how it would come to be. No one truly understands a prophecy until it comes true. It's rather like a horseshoe. The smithy shows you a bit of iron stock and you say, it will never fit. But after it's been through the fire and hammered and filed, there it is, fitting perfectly to your horse's hoof as it would never fit any other.'

'It sounds as if you are saying prophets shape their prophecies to be true after the fact.'

He cocked his head. 'And a good prophet, like a good smith, shows you that it fits perfectly.' He took the empty glass from my hand. 'You should be sleeping, you know. Tomorrow the healer is going to draw the arrowhead out. You will need your strength.'

I nodded, and suddenly found my eyes were heavy.

Chade gripped my wrists and pulled down firmly. My chest and cheek pressed against the hard wooden bench. The Fool straddled my legs and pinned my hips down with his leaning weight. Even Kettle had her hands on my bare shoulders, pressing me down on the unyielding bench. I felt like a hog trussed for slaughter. Starling stood by with lint bandaging and a basin of hot water. As Chade drew my hands down tight, I felt as if my whole body might split open at the rotten wound in my back. The healer squatted beside me. I caught a glimpse of the pincers she held. Black iron. Probably borrowed from the blacksmith's shed.

'Ready?' she asked.

'No,' I grunted. They ignored me. It wasn't me she was talking to. All morning she had worked on me as if I were a broken toy, prodding and pressing the foul fluids of infection from my back while I squirmed and muttered curses. All had ignored my imprecations, save the Fool, who had offered improvements on them. He was very much himself again. He had persuaded Nighteyes to go outside. I could sense the wolf prowling about the door. I had tried to convey to him what was to be done. I'd pulled enough quills from him in our time together that he had some idea of necessary pain. He still shared my dread.

'Go ahead,' Chade told the healer. His head was close to mine, his beard scratching my shaven cheek. 'Steady my boy,' he breathed into my ear. The cold jaws of the pincers pressed against my inflamed flesh.

'Don't pant. Hold still,' the healer told me severely. I tried. It felt as if she were plunging them into my back seeking for a grip. After an eternity of probing, the healer said, 'Hold him.' I felt the jaws of the pincers clench. She pulled, ripping my spine up and out of my body.

Or so it felt. I recall that first grating of metal head against bone, and all my resolutions not to scream were forgotten. I roared out my pain and my consciousness together. I tumbled again into that vague place that neither sleep nor wakefulness could reach. My feverish days had made it entirely too familiar to me.

Skill-river. I was in it and it was in me. Only a step away, it had always been only a step away. Surcease from pain and loneliness. Swift and sweet. I was tattering away in it, coming undone like a piece of knitting comes unravelled when the right thread is tugged. All my pain was coming undone as well. *No.* Verity forbade it firmly. *Back you go, Fitz.* As if he shooed a small child away from the fire. I went.

Like a diver surfacing, I came back to the hard bench and voices over me. The light seemed dim. Someone exclaimed about blood and called for a cloth full of snow. I felt it pressed to my back while a sopping red rag was tossed to the Fool's rug. The stain spread out on the wool and I flowed with it. I was floating and the room was full of black specks. The healer was busy by the fire. She drew another smith's tool from the flames. It glowed and she turned to look at me. 'Wait!' I cried in horror and half reared up off the bench, only to have Chade catch me by the shoulders.

'It has to be done,' he told me harshly and held me in a grip of iron as the healer came near. At first I felt only pressure as she held a hot brand to my back. I smelled the burning of my own flesh and thought I did not care, until a spasm of pain jerked me more sharply than a hangman's noose. The black rose up to drag me down. 'Hung over water and burned!' I cried out in despair. A wolf whined.

Rising. Coming up, nearer and nearer the light. The dive had been deep, the waters warm and full of dreams. I tasted the edge of consciousness, took a breath of wakefulness.

Chade. '. . . but surely you could have told me, at least, that he was alive and had come to you. Eda and El in a knot, Fool, how often have I trusted you with my closest counsels?'

'Almost as often as you have not,' the Fool replied tartly. 'Fitz asked me to keep his presence here a secret. And it was, until that minstrel interfered. What would it have hurt if he had been left alone to rest completely before that arrow came out? You've listened to his ravings. Do they sound to you like a man at peace with himself ?'

Chade sighed. 'Still. You could have told me. You know what it would have meant to me, to know he was alive.'

'You know what it would have meant to me, to know there was a Farseer heir,' the Fool retorted.

'I told you as soon as I told the Queen!'

'Yes, but how long had you known she existed? Since you sent Burrich to keep watch over Molly? You knew Molly carried his child when last you came to visit, yet you said nothing.'

Chade took a sharp breath, then cautioned. 'Those are names I'd as soon you did not speak, not even here. Not even to the Queen have I given those names. You must understand, Fool. The more folk who know, the greater the risk to the child. I'd never have revealed her existence, save that the Queen's child died and we believed Verity dead.'

'Save your hope of keeping secrets. A minstrel knows Molly's name; minstrels keep no secrets.' His dislike of Starling glittered in his voice. In a colder tone, he added, 'So what did you really plan to do, Chade? Pass off Fitz's daughter as Verity's? Steal her from Molly and give her to the Queen, to raise as her own?' The Fool's voice had gone deadly soft.

'I . . . the times are hard and the need so great . . . but . . . not steal her, no. Burrich would understand, and I think he could make the girl understand. Besides. What can she offer the child? A penniless candlemaker, bereft of her trade . . . how can she care for her? The child deserves better. As does the mother, truly, and I would do my best to see she was provided for, also. But the baby cannot be left with her. Think, Fool. Once others knew the babe was of Farseer lineage she could only be safe on the throne, or in line for it. The woman listens to Burrich. He could make her see that.'

'I'm not so sure you could make Burrich see that. He gave one child up to royal duty. He may not feel it's a wise choice a second time.'

'Sometimes all the choices are poor ones, Fool, and still a man must choose.'

I think I made some small sound, for they both came to me quickly. 'Boy?' Chade demanded anxiously. 'Boy, are you awake?'

I decided I was. I opened one eye a crack. Night. Light from the hearth and a few candles. Chade and the Fool and a bottle of brandy. And me. My back felt no better. My fever felt no less. Before I could even try to ask, the Fool held a cup to my lips. Damnable willowbark tea. I was so thirsty, I drank it all. The next cup he offered was meat broth, wonderfully salty. 'I'm so thirsty,' I managed to say when I'd finished it. My mouth felt sticky with thirst, thick with it.

'You've lost a lot of blood,' Chade explained needlessly.

'Do you want more broth?' the Fool asked.

I managed the tiniest nod. The Fool took the cup and went to the hearth. Chade leaned close and whispered, strangely urgent, 'Fitz. Tell me one thing. Do you hate me, boy?'

For a moment, I didn't know. But the thought of hating Chade

457

meant too great a loss to me. Too few folk in the world cared for me. I could not hate even one of them. I shook my head a tiny bit. 'But,' I said slowly, carefully forming the thick words, 'don't take my child.'

'Do not fear,' he told me gently. His old hand smoothed my hair back from my face. 'If Verity's alive, there will be no need of it. For the time being, she is safest where she is. And if King Verity returns and assumes his throne, he and Kettricken will get children of their own.'

'Promise?' I begged.

He met my eyes. The Fool brought the broth to me, and Chade stepped aside to make room for him. This cup was warmer. It was like life itself flowing back into me. When it was gone, I could speak more strongly. 'Chade,' I said. He had walked over to the hearth and was staring into it. He turned back to me when I spoke.

'You did not promise,' I reminded him.

'No,' he agreed gravely. 'I did not promise. Times are too uncertain for that promise.'

For a long time I just looked at him. After a time, he gave his head a tiny shake and looked aside. He could not meet my eyes. But he offered me no lies. So it was up to me.

'You can have me,' I told him quietly. 'And I will do my best to bring Verity back, and do all I can to restore to him his throne. You can have my death, if that is what it takes. More than that, you can have my life, Chade. But not my child's. Not my daughter's.'

He met my eyes and nodded slowly.

Recovery was a slow and painful business. It seemed to me that I should have relished each day in a soft bed, each mouthful of food, each moment of safe sleep. But it was not so. The frostbitten skin on my fingers and toes peeled and snagged on everything, and the new skin beneath was horribly tender. Every day the healer came to poke at me. She insisted that the wound on my back must be kept open and draining. I grew weary of the foul-smelling bandages she took away, and wearier still of her picking at my wound to see that it did not close too soon. She reminded me of a crow on a dying animal, and when I tactlessly told her so one day, she laughed at me.

After a few days, I was moving about again, but never carelessly. Every step, every reach of a hand was a cautious thing. I learned to keep my elbows snug to my sides to decrease the pull of muscles in my back, learned to walk as if I balanced a basket of eggs on my head. Even so, I wearied quickly, and too strenuous a stroll might bring the fever back at night. I went daily to the baths and though soaking in the hot water eased my body, I could not be there even a moment without recalling that here was where Regal sought to drown me, and there was where I had seen Burrich clubbed to the ground. *Come to me, come to me*, would begin the siren call in my head then, and my mind would soon be full of thoughts and wonderings about Verity. It was not conducive to a peaceful spirit. Instead I would find myself planning every detail of my next journey. I made a mental list of the equipment I must beg from Kettricken and debated long and hard over taking a riding animal. In the end I decided against it. There was no grazing for one; my capacity for unthinking cruelty was gone. I would not take a horse or pony simply to have it die. I knew, too, that soon I must ask leave to search the libraries to see if there might be found a precursor to Verity's map. I dreaded seeking out Kettricken for she had not summoned me at all.

Every day I reminded myself of these things, and every day I put it off one more day. As of yet, I still could not walk the length of Jhaampe without stopping to rest. Conscientiously, I began to force myself to eat more and to push the limits of my strength. Often the Fool joined me on my strengthening walks. I knew he hated the cold, but I welcomed his silent companionship too much to suggest he stay warm within. He took me once to see Sooty, and that placid beast welcomed me with such pleasure that I returned every day thereafter. Her belly was swelling with Ruddy's foal; she'd drop early in spring. She seemed healthy enough, but I fretted over her age. I took an amazing amount of comfort from the old mare's gentle presence. It pulled at my injury to lift my arms to groom her, but I did anyway, and Ruddy as well. The spirited young horse needed more handling than he was getting. I did my best with him, and missed Burrich every moment of it.

The wolf came and went as he pleased. He joined the Fool and me on our walks, and strolled into the hut afterwards at our heels. It was almost distressing to see how swiftly he adapted. The Fool muttered about the claw marks on his door and the shed fur on his rugs, but they liked each other well enough. A wolf puppet began to emerge in sections from chunks of wood on the Fool's work table. Nighteyes developed a taste for a certain seedcake that was also the Fool's favourite. The wolf would stare fixedly at him whenever the Fool was eating it, drooling great pools of saliva onto the floor until the Fool would relent and give him a share. I scolded them both about what sweets could do to his teeth and coat and was ignored by both of them. I suppose I felt a bit of jealousy at how quickly he came to trust the Fool, until Nighteyes asked pointedly one day, *Why should not I trust whom you trust?* I had no answer to that.

'So. When did you become a toymaker?' I asked the Fool idly one day. I was leaning on his table, watching his fingers thread the limbs and torso of a jumping jack onto his stick framework. The wolf was sprawled out under the table, deeply asleep.

He shrugged one shoulder. 'It became obvious once I was here that King Eyod's court was no place for a Fool.' He gave a short sigh. 'Nor did I truly have the desire to be the Fool for anyone save King Shrewd. That being so, I cast about for some other means to earn my bread. One evening, quite drunk, I asked myself what I knew best. "Why, being a puppet," I replied to myself. Jerked about by the strings of fate, and then tossed aside to crumple in a heap. That being so, I decided that I would no longer dance to the string's pull, but would pull the strings. The next day I put my resolution to the test. I soon discovered a liking for it. The simple toys I grew up with and the ones that I saw in Buck seem wondrously strange to Mountain children. I found I needed to have few dealings with the adults, which suited me well. Children here learn to hunt and fish and weave and harvest at a very early age, and whatever they garner is their own. So I trade for what I need. Children, I have found, are much more swift to accept the unusual. They admit their curiosity, you see, rather than disdaining the object that arouses it.' His pale fingers tied a careful knot. Then he picked his creation up and set it to dancing for me.

I watched its gay prancing with a retroactive desire to have possessed such a thing of brightly-painted wood and finely-sanded edges. 'I want my daughter to have things such as that,' I heard myself say aloud. 'Well-made toys and soft bright shirts, pretty hair ribbons and dolls to clutch.'

'She will,' he promised me gravely. 'She will.'

The slow days passed. My hands began to look normal again and even to have some calluses on them again. The healer said I might go with no bandaging on my back. I began to feel restless but knew I did not yet have the strength to leave. My disquiet in turn agitated the Fool. I did not realize how much I paced until the evening he rose from his chair and shoved his table over into my path to divert me from my course. We both laughed, but it did not dispel the underlying tension. I began to believe I destroyed peace wherever I went.

Kettle visited often and drove me to distraction with her knowledge of the scrolls concerning the White Prophet. Too often they mentioned a Catalyst. Sometimes the Fool was drawn into her discussions. More often he simply made noncommittal noises as she tried to explain it all to me. I almost missed her dour taciturnity. I confess, too, that the more she talked, the more I wondered how a woman of Buck had ever chanced to wander so far from her homeland, to become a devotee of a distant teaching that would someday lead her back to her homeland. But the old Kettle showed through when she deflected my slyly-posed questions.

Starling came, though not as often as Kettle, and usually when the Fool was out and about on errands. It seemed that they could not be in the same room without striking sparks from one another. As soon as I was able to move about at all, she began to persuade me to take outside walks with her, probably to avoid the Fool. I suppose they did me good, but I took no enjoyment in them. I had had my fill of winter cold and usually her conversation made me feel both restless and spurred. Her talk was often of the war back in Buck, snippets of news overheard from Chade and Kettricken, for she was often with them. She played for them in the evenings, as best she could with her damaged hand and a borrowed harp. She lived in the main hall of the royal residence. This taste of a court life seemed to agree with her. She was frequently enthused and animated. The bright clothes of the Mountain folk set off her dark hair and eyes, while the cold brought colour to her face. She seemed to have recovered from all misfortune, to be once more filled with life. Even her hand was healing well, and Chade had helped her barter for wood to make a new harp. It shamed me that her optimism only made me feel older and weaker and more wearied. An hour or two with her wore me out as if I had been exercising a headstrong filly. I felt a constant pressure from her to agree with her. Often I could not.

'He makes me nervous,' she told me once, in one of her frequent diatribes against the Fool. 'It's not his colour; it's his manner. He never says a kind or simple word to anyone, not even to the children who come to trade for his toys. Have you marked how he teases and mocks them?'

'He likes them, and they like him,' I said wearily. 'He does not tease them to be cruel. He teases them as he teases everyone. The children enjoy it. No child wishes to be spoken down to.' The brief walk had tired me more than I wished to admit to her. And it was tedious constantly to defend him to her.

She made no reply. I became aware of Nighteyes shadowing us. He drifted from the shelter of a cluster of trees to the snow-laden bushes of a garden. I doubted his presence was a great secret, and yet he was uneasy about strolling openly through the streets. It was strangely comforting to know he was close by.

I tried to find another topic. 'I have not seen Chade in some days now,' I ventured. I hated to fish for news of him. But he had not come to me and I would not go to him. I did not hate him, but I could not forgive his plans for my child.

'I sang for him last night.' She smiled at the recollection. 'He was at his most witty. He can even bring a smile to Kettricken's face. It is hard to believe he lived in such isolation for years. He draws people to himself like a flower draws bees. He has a most gentlemanly way of letting a woman know she is admired. And . . .'

'Chade?' The word burst from me incredulously. 'Gentlemanly?'

'Of course,' she said in amusement. 'He can be quite charming, when he has the time. I sang for him and Kettricken the other night, and he was quite gracious in his thanks. A courtier's tongue he has.' She smiled to herself, and I could see that whatever Chade had said had stayed pleasantly with her. To try to envision Chade as a charmer of women required my mind to bend in an unaccustomed direction. I could think of nothing to say, and so left her in her pleasant reverie. After a time, she added unexpectedly, 'He will not be going with us, you know.'

'Who? Where?' I could not decide if my recent fever had left me slow-witted or if the minstrel's mind jumped about like a flea.

She patted my arm comfortingly. 'You are getting tired. We had best turn back. I can always tell when you are wearied, you ask the most inane questions.' She took a breath and returned to her topic. 'Chade will not be going with us to seek Verity. He has to go back to Buck, to pass the word of your quest and hearten the folk there. Of course, he will respect your wishes and make no mention of you. Only that the Queen has set forth to find the King and restore him to the throne.'

She paused, and tried to say casually, 'He has asked me to devise some simple ditties for him, based on the old songs so they may be easily learned and sung.' She smiled at me and I could tell how pleased she was he had asked this of her. 'He will spread them among the taverns and inns of the road and like seeds they will sprout and trail from there. Simple songs saying that Verity will return to set things right and that a Farseer heir will rise to the throne to unite the Six Duchies in both victory and peace. He says it is most important to keep the heart in the people, and to keep before them the image of Verity returning.'

I sorted my way back through her chatter of songs and prophecies. 'Us, you said. Us, who? And going where?'

She stripped off her glove and set her hand to my forehead

quickly. 'Are you feverish, again? A bit, perhaps. Let us turn back now.' As we began retracing our steps through the quiet streets, she added patiently, 'Us, you and I and Kettricken, going to find Verity. Had you forgotten that was why you came to the Mountains? Kettricken says the way will be hard. It is not terribly difficult to travel to the scene of the battle. But if Verity went on from there, then it is on one of the ancient paths marked on her old map, and they may not be paths at all any more. Her father is plainly not enthused with her undertaking. His mind is fixed only on the waging of war against Regal. "While you seek your husband king, your false brother seeks to make our folks his slaves!" he has told her. So she must gather what supplies are given to her willingly, and take only such folk as would go with her rather than stay to fight Regal. There are not many of those, to be sure, and . . .'

'I wish to go back to the Fool's house,' I said faintly. My head was spinning and my stomach churning. I had forgotten that this had been the way of it at King Shrewd's court. Why had I expected it to be different here? The plans would be made, the arrangements undertaken, and then they would tell me what they wished me to do and I would do it. Had not that always been my function? To go to such and such a place, and kill that certain man, a man I'd never met before, all on someone else's say? I did not know why it suddenly shocked me so to find that all their momentous planning had moved on without any words from me, as if I were no more than a horse in a stall, waiting to be saddled, mounted and reined to the hunt.

Well, was not that the bargain I had offered Chade, I reminded myself. That they could have my life, if they would but leave my child alone. Why be surprised? Why even be concerned at all? I should simply go back to the Fool's, to sleep and eat and build my strength until called for.

'Are you all right?' Starling asked me suddenly, anxiously. 'I don't think I have ever seen you so pale.'

'I'm fine,' I assured her dully. 'I was just thinking it would be pleasant to help the Fool make the puppets for a time.'

She frowned again. 'I still do not understand what you see in him. Why do not you come to stay in a room near Kettricken and me? You need little tending any more; it is time you resumed your rightful place at the Queen's side.'

'When the Queen summons me, I will go to her,' I said dutifully. 'That will be time enough.'

TWENTY-TWO

Departure

Chade Fallstar occupies a unique niche in the history of the Six Duchies. Although he was never acknowledged, his strong physical resemblance to the Farseers makes it almost certain that he was blood-related to the royal line. Be that as it may, who he was pales in significance compared to what he was. Some have said he was a spy for King Shrewd for decades before the Red Ship Wars. Others have linked his name to that of Lady Thyme, who almost certainly was a poisoner and thief for the royal family. These beliefs can never be substantiated.

What can be known, without a doubt, was that he emerged into public life following the desertion of Buckkeep by the Pretender, Regal Farseer. He put his services at the beck and call of Lady Patience. She was able to draw on his established network of people throughout the Six Duchies, both to gather information and to distribute resources for the defence of the coastline. There is much evidence to suggest that initially he endeavoured to remain a private and secretive figure. His unique appearance made this difficult and he eventually abandoned all attempts. Despite his years, he became something of a hero, a dashing old man, if you will, coming and going from inns and taverns at all hours, eluding and taunting Regal's guardsmen, bringing news and passing funds for the defence of the Coastal Duchies. His exploits made him admired. Always he bade the folk of the Six Duchies to take heart and foretold to them that King Verity and Queen Kettricken would return, to lift from their backs the yokes of taxation and warfare under which they suffered. While a number of songs have been made of his deeds, the most accurate is the song cycle 'Chade Fallstar's Reckoning', attributed to Queen Kettricken's minstrel, Starling Birdsong.

*   *   *

My memory rebels at recalling those last days in Jhaampe. A bleakness of spirit settled on me, one that remained unchanged by friendship or brandy. I could find no energy, no will to bestir myself. 'If fate is some great wave that is going to bear me up and dash me against a wall, regardless of what I choose, why then I choose to do nothing. Let it do with me as it will,' I declared grandiosely, if a trifle drunkenly to the Fool one evening. To this he said nothing. He simply continued sanding the shags into the wolf-puppet's coat. Nighteyes, wakeful but silent, lay at the Fool's feet. When I was drinking he shielded his mind from me and expressed his disgust by ignoring me. Kettle sat in the hearth corner, knitting and alternating between looking disappointed or disapproving. Chade sat in a straight-backed chair across the table from me. A cup of tea was before him and his eyes were cold as jade. Needless to say, I was drinking alone, for the third straight night. I was testing to the limits Burrich's theory that while drinking could solve nothing, it could make the unbearable tolerable. It did not seem to be working for me. The more I drank, the less tolerable my situation seemed. And the more intolerable I became to my friends.

The day had brought me more than I could bear. Chade had come to see me finally, to say that Kettricken wished to see me on the morrow. I allowed as I would be there. With a bit of prodding from Chade, I agreed that I would be presentable – washed, shaven, cleanly attired and sober. None of which I was at that moment. It was a poor time for me to endeavour to match wits or words with Chade, but my judgment was such that I attempted it. I asked bellicose and accusing questions. He answered them calmly. Yes, he had suspected Molly carried my child, and yes, he had urged Burrich to become her protector. Burrich had already been seeing that she had money and shelter, he had been reluctant to share her dwelling, but when Chade had pointed out the dangers to her and the child if anyone else figured out the circumstances, Burrich had agreed. No, he had not told me. Why? Because Molly had coerced Burrich into promising her he would not tell me of her pregnancy. His condition for guarding her as Chade requested was that Chade would also respect that promise. Initially Burrich had hoped I would puzzle out for myself why Molly had disappeared. He had also confided to Chade that as soon as the child was born he would consider himself freed of his promise and would tell me, not that she was pregnant, but that I had a child. Even in my state, I could see that that was about as devious as Burrich had ever managed to be. A part of me appreciated the depth of his friendship that he'd bend his promise that far for me. But when he had gone to tell me of my daughter's birth, he had instead discovered evidence of my death.

He had gone straight to Buck, to leave words with a stonemason there, who passed word to another and so on until Chade came to meet Burrich at the fish-docks. They had both been incredulous. 'Burrich could not believe that you had died. I could not understand why you had still been there. I had left word with my watchers, all up and down the river road, for I had been sure you would not flee to Bingtown, but would immediately set out for the Mountains. I had been so sure that despite all you had endured, your heart was true. It was what I told to Burrich that night; that we must leave you alone, to discover for yourself where your loyalty was. I had wagered Burrich that left to your own devices you would be like an arrow released from a bow, flying straight to Verity. That, I think, was what shocked us both the most. That you had died there, and not on the road to your king.'

'Well,' I declared with a drunkard's elaborate satisfaction, 'you were both wrong. You both thought you knew me so well, you both thought you had crafted such a tool as could not defy your purposes. But I did NOT die there! Nor did I go to seek my king. I went to kill Regal. For myself.' I leaned back in my chair and crossed my arms on my chest. Then sat up abruptly at the uncomfortable pressure on my healing injury. 'For myself!' I repeated. 'Not for my king or Buck or any of the Six Duchies. For me, I went to kill him. For me.'

Chade merely looked at me. But from the hearth corner where Kettle rocked, her old voice rose in complacent satisfaction. 'The White Scriptures say, "He shall thirst for the blood of his own kin, and his thirst shall go unslaked. The Catalyst shall hunger for a hearth and children in vain, for his children shall be another's, and another's child his own . . ."'

'No one can force me to fulfil any such prophecies!' I vowed in a roar. 'Who made them, anyway?'

Kettle went on rocking. It was the Fool who answered me. He spoke mildly, without looking up from his work. 'I did. In my childhood, in the days of my dreaming. Before I knew you anywhere, save in my dreams.'

'You are doomed to fulfil them,' Kettle told me gently.

I slammed my cup back onto the table. 'Damned if I will!' I shouted. No one jumped or replied. In a terrible instant of crystalline recall, I heard Molly's father's voice from his chimney corner. 'Damn you, girl!' Molly had flinched but ignored him. She had known there was no reasoning with a drunk. 'Molly,' I moaned soddenly and put my head down on my arms to weep.

After a time, I felt Chade's hands on my shoulders. 'Come, boy, this avails you nothing. To bed with you. Tomorrow you must face your queen.' There was far more patience in his voice than I deserved, and I suddenly knew the depths of my churlishness.

I rubbed my face on my sleeve and managed to lift my head. I did not resist as he helped me to my feet and steered me toward the cot in the corner. As I sat down on the edge of it, I said quietly, 'You knew. You knew all along.'

'Knew what?' he asked me tiredly.

'Knew all this about the Catalyst and the White Prophet.'

He blew air out through his nose. 'I "know" nothing of that. I knew something of the writings about them. Recall that things were comparatively settled before your father abdicated. I had many long years after I had taken to my tower, when my king did not require my services for months at a time. I had much time for reading, and many sources for scrolls. So I had encountered some of the foreign tales and writings that deal with a Catalyst and a White Prophet.' His voice became milder, as if he'd forgotten the anger in my question.

'It was only after the Fool had come to Buckkeep, and I had quietly discovered that he had a strong interest in such writings, that my own interest was piqued. You yourself once told me that he had referred to you as the Catalyst. So I began to wonder . . . but in truth, I give all prophecies small credence.'

I lay back gingerly. I could almost sleep on my back again. I rolled to my side, kicked off my boots and dragged a blanket up over me.

'Fitz?'

'What?' I asked Chade grudgingly.

'Kettricken is angry with you. Do not expect her patience tomorrow. But keep in mind that she is not only our queen. She is a woman who has lost a child and been kept in suspense over her husband's fate for over a year, hounded away from her adopted country, only to have trouble dog her steps to her native land. Her father is understandably bitter. He turns a warrior's eyes toward the Six Duchies and Regal, and has no time for quests to search for the brother of his enemy, even if he believed he lived. Kettricken is alone, more grievously alone than you or I can imagine. Find tolerance for the woman. And respect for your queen.' He paused uncomfortably. 'You will need both tomorrow. I can be of little help to you with her.'

I think he went on after that, but I had ceased to listen. Sleep soon dragged me under its waves.

It had been some time since Skill-dreams had troubled me. I do not know if my physical weakness had finally banished my dreams of battle, or if my constant guard against Regal's coterie had blocked them from my mind. That night my brief respite ended. The strength of the Skill-dream that snatched me from my body was as if a great hand had reached inside me, seized me by the heart and dragged me out of myself. I was suddenly in another place.

It was a city, in the sense that folk dwelt there in great numbers. But the folk were unlike any I had ever seen, nor had I ever seen such dwellings. The buildings soared and spiralled to airy heights. The stone of the walls seemed to have flowed into their forms. There were bridges of delicate tracery and gardens that both cascaded down and tendrilled up the sides of the structures. There were fountains that danced and others that pooled silently. Everywhere brightly-clad people moved through the city, as numerous as ants.

Yet all was silent and still. I sensed the flow of folk, the play of the fountains, the perfume of the unfolding blossoms in the gardens. All was there, but when I turned to behold it, it was gone. The mind could sense the delicate tracery of the bridge but the eye saw only the fallen rubble gone to rust and rot. Frescoed walls had been wind-polished away to roughly plastered bricks. A turn of the head changed a leaping fountain to weedy dust in a cracked basin. The hastening crowd in the market spoke only with the voice of a racing wind heavy with stinging sand. I moved through this ghost of a city, bodiless and seeking, unable to decipher why I was there or what was drawing me. It was neither light nor dark there, neither summer nor winter. I am outside time, I thought to myself, and wondered if this was the ultimate hell of the Fool's philosophy or the final freedom.

I saw at last, far ahead of me, a small figure plodding along one of the vast streets. His head was bowed to the wind and he held his cloak's hem over his mouth and nose as he walked to shield him from the sand-laden wind. He was not a part of the ghostly crowd but moved through the rubble, skirting the places where some unrest in the earth had sunken or ridged the paved street. I knew in that instant of sighting him that this was Verity. I knew by the jerk of life I felt in my chest, and knew then that what had pulled me here was the tiny pebble of Verity's Skill that hid still within my own consciousness. I sensed also that the danger to him was extreme. Yet I saw nothing to threaten him. He was at a great distance from me, seen through the hazy shadows of buildings that had been, veiled in the ghosts of a market-day crowd. He trudged heavily along, alone and immune to the ghost city, and yet entwined in it. I saw nothing, but danger loomed over him like a giant's shadow.

I hastened after him and in the blinking of an eye was beside him. 'Ah,' he greeted me. 'So you have come at last, Fitz. Welcome.' He did not pause as he walked, nor turn his head. Yet I felt a warmth as if he had clasped my hand in greeting, and I felt no need to reply. Instead I saw with his eyes the lure and the danger.

A river flowed ahead. It was not water. It was not glistening stone. It partook of both those things, but was neither. It sliced through the city like a gleaming blade, sliding out of the riven mountain behind us and continuing until it disappeared into a more ancient river of water. Like a seam of coal bared by a cutting tide, or gold veining quartz, it lay exposed on the earth's body. It was magic. Purest ancient magic, inexorable and heedless of men, flowed there. The river of Skill I had so tediously learned to navigate was to this magic as the bouquet of wine is to wine. That which I glimpsed with Verity's eyes had a physical existence as concrete as my own. I was immediately drawn to it as a moth is drawn to a candle flame.

It was not just the beauty of that shining flow. The magic filled every one of Verity's senses. The sound of its rushing was musical, a running of notes that kept one waiting and listening, in the certainty that the sound was building to something. The wind carried its scent, elusive and changeable, one moment the edge of lemon blossoms and the next a smoky coiling of spices. I tasted it on every breath, and longed to plunge myself into it. I was suddenly sure that it could quench every appetite I had ever suffered, not just those of my body but the vague yearnings of my soul as well. I longed for my body to be here as well, that I might experience it as completely as Verity did.

Verity paused, lifting his face. He drew in a deep breath, air laden with Skill as fog is laden with moisture. Suddenly I could taste in the back of Verity's throat a hot metallic tang. The longing he had felt for it suddenly became an all-consuming desire. He thirsted for it. When he got to it, he would throw himself on his knees and drink his fill. He would be filled with all the consciousness of the world, he would partake of the whole and become the whole. At last he would know completion.

But Verity himself would cease to exist.

I drew back in fascinated horror. I don't think there is anything more frightening than to encounter the true will for self-destruction. Despite my own attraction to the river, it touched off an anger in me. This was not worthy of Verity. Neither the man nor the prince I had known could be capable of such a cowardly act. I looked at him as if I had never seen him.

And realized how long it had been since I had seen him.

The bright blackness of his eyes had become a dull darkness. The cloak that the wind snapped about him was a rent rag of a thing. The leather of his boots had long ago cracked, the stitches of the seams giving way and gaping open. The steps he took were uncertain, uneven things. Even if the wind had not buffeted him, I doubted his stride would have been steady. His lips were pale and cracked and his flesh had a greyish overtone to it as if the very blood of his body had forsaken it. There had been summers when he Skilled against the Red Ships to such an extent that the flesh and muscle fell from his body, leaving him a gaunt skeleton of a man with no physical stamina. Now he was a man of stamina alone, ropy muscles stretched on a framework of bones that was scarcely cloaked in flesh at all. He was the embodiment of weary purpose. Only his will kept him upright and moving. Toward the magic flow.

I do not know where I found my own will to resist it. Possibly it was because I had paused and focused myself on Verity for an instant, and seen all that the world would lose if he ceased to exist as himself. Whatever the source of my strength, I pitted it against his. I threw myself into his path but he walked through me. There was nothing to me, here. 'Verity, please, stop, wait!' I cried and flung myself at him, a furious feather on the wind. I had no effect on him. He didn't even pause.

'Someone has to do it,' he said quietly. Three steps later he added, 'For a time, I hoped it would not be me. But over and over, I have asked myself, "Who else, then?"' He turned to look at me with those burnt-to-ashes eyes. 'No other answer has ever come. It has to be me.'

'Verity, stop,' I pleaded, but he continued to walk. Not hurrying, not lagging, but simply trudging along the way a man does when he has measured the distance he must go and matched his strength to it. He had the endurance to get there if he walked.

I withdrew a bit, feeling my strength ebbing. For a moment, I feared I would lose him by being drawn back to my sleeping body. Then I realized an equally potent fear. Linked so long, and even now being pulled along after him, I might find myself drowned alongside him in that vein of magic. If I had had a body in that realm, I probably would have seized onto something and held on. As I pleaded with Verity to stop and listen to me, I instead anchored myself in the only other way I could imagine. I reached with my Skill, grasping after those others whose lives touched mine: Molly, my daughter, Chade and the Fool, Burrich and Kettricken. I had no true Skill-links with any of them so my grip was a tenuous one at best, lessened by my frantic fear that at any moment Will or Carrod or even Burl might somehow become aware of me. It seemed to me that it slowed Verity. 'Please wait,' I said again.

'No,' he said quietly. 'Don't seek to dissuade me, Fitz. It's what I have to do.'

I had never thought to measure my Skill-strength against Verity's. I had never imagined we could be opposed to each other. But as I proceeded to batter myself against him, I felt very much like a child kicking and screaming as his father calmly carried him off to bed. Verity not only ignored my attack, I sensed that his will and concentration were elsewhere. He moved implacably on toward the black flow and my consciousness was borne along with him. Self-preservation lent a frantic new strength to my struggles. I strove to push him away, to drag him back, but it availed me nothing.

But there was a terrible duality to my struggle. I longed for him to win. If he overpowered me and dragged me down with him, then I need take no responsibility for it. I could open myself to that flow of power and be quenched in it. It would be an end to all torments, surcease at last. I was so tired of doubts and guilts, so weary of duties and debts. If Verity carried me into that flow of Skill with him I could finally surrender with no shame.

There came a moment when we stood on the brink of that iridescent flow of power. I stared down at it with his eyes. There was no gradual shore. Instead there was a knife's edge brink where solid earth gave way to a streaming otherness. I stared at it, seeing it as a foreign thing in our world, a warping of our very world's nature. Ponderously Verity lowered himself to one knee. He stared into that black luminescence. I did not know if he hesitated to say farewell to our world, or if he paused to gather his will to destroy himself. My will to resist was suspended. This was a door to an otherness I could not even imagine. Hunger and curiosity drew us closer to the brink.

In the next moment he plunged his hands and forearms into the magic.

I shared that sudden knowledge with him. So I screamed with him as the hot current ate the flesh and muscle from his arms. I swear I felt the acid lick of it across the bared bones of his fingers and wrist and forearm. I knew his pain. Yet it was crowded from his features by the rapturous smile that overwhelmed his face. My link with him was suddenly a clumsy thing that barred me from sensing in full what he felt. I longed to be beside him, to bare my own flesh to that magic river. I shared his conviction that he could end all pain if only he would give in and plunge the rest of himself into the stream. So easy. All he had to do was lean forward a bit and let go. He crouched over the stream on his knees, sweat dripping from his face only to disappear as tiny puffs of steam when it fell into the flow. His head was bowed, and his shoulders moved up and down with the strength of his panting. Then he begged me suddenly, in a tiny voice, 'Pull me back.'

I had not had the strength to oppose his determination. But when I joined my will to his and together we fought the terrible allure of the power, it was just enough. He was able to draw his forearms and hands free from the stuff, though it felt as if he drew them out of solid stone. It gave him up reluctantly and as he staggered back I sensed in full for a moment what he had shared. There was the oneness of the world flowing there, like a single sweet note drawn out purely forever. It was not the song of humanity but an older, greater song of vast balances and pure being. Had Verity surrendered to it, it would have ended all his torments.

Instead, he tottered to his feet and turned away from it. He carried his forearms stretched out before him, palms up, the fingers curled into cups as if he begged something. In shape they had not changed. But now arms and fingers gleamed silver with the power that had penetrated and fused with his flesh. As he began to walk away from the stream with the same studied purposefulness with which he had approached it, I felt how his arms and hands burned as if with frostbite.

'I don't understand,' I said to him.

'I don't want you to. Not yet.' I felt a duality in him. The Skill burned in him like a forge-fire of incredible heat, but the strength of his body was only sufficient to keep him walking. It was effortless for him to shield my mind from the pull of that river now. But for him to move his own body up the path taxed both his flesh and his will. 'Fitz. Come to me. Please.' It was no Skill-order this time, not even the command of a prince, only the plea of a man to another. 'I have no coterie, Fitz. Only you. If the coterie that Galen created for me had been true, then I would have more faith that what I must do is possible. Yet not only are they false to me, but they seek to defeat me. They peck at me like birds on a dying buck. I do not think their attacks can destroy me, but I fear they may weaken me enough that I do not succeed. Or worse yet, that they may distract me and succeed in my place. We cannot allow that, boy. You and I are all that stand between them and their triumph. You and I. The Farseers.'

I was not there in any physical sense. Yet he smiled at me and lifted one terrible gleaming hand to cup my face. Did he intend what he did? I do not know. The jolt was as powerful as if a warrior had slammed his shield into my face. But not pain. Awareness. Like sunlight bursting through clouds to illuminate a clearing in the forest. Everything suddenly stood out clearly, and I saw all the hidden reasons and purposes for what we did, and I understood with a painful purity of enlightenment why it was necessary I follow the path before me.

Then all was gone, and I dwindled off into blackness. Verity was gone and my understanding with him. But for one brief instant, I had glimpsed the completeness of it. Only I remained now, but my self was so tiny I could only exist if I held on with all my might. So I did.

From a world away I heard Starling cry out in fear, 'What's wrong with him?' And Chade replied gruffly, 'It's only a seizure, such as he has from time to time. His head, Fool, hold his head or he'll dash his own brains out.' Distantly I felt hands gripping and restraining me. I surrendered myself to their care and sank into the darkness. I came to, for a bit, some time later. I recall little of it. The Fool raised my shoulders and steadied my head that I could drink from a cup a concerned Chade held to my lips. The familiar bitterness of elfbark puckered my mouth. I had a glimpse of Kettle standing over me, lips folded in a tight line of disapproval. Starling stood away, her eyes huge as a cornered animal's, not deigning to touch me. 'That should bring him round,' I heard Chade say as I sank into a deep sleep.

The next morning I arose early despite my pounding head and sought the baths. I slipped out so silently that the Fool did not waken, but Nighteyes arose and ghosted out with me.

Where did you go, last night? he demanded, but I had no answer for him. He sensed my reluctance to think about it. *I go to hunt now,* he informed me tartly. *I advise you to drink but water after this.* I assented humbly and he left me at the door of the bathhouse.

Within was the mineral stink of the hot water that bubbled up from the earth. The Mountain folk trapped it in great tanks, and channelled it through pipes to other tubs so that one might choose the heat and depth one wished. I scrubbed myself off in a washing tub, then submerged myself in the hottest water I could stand and tried not to recall the scalding of the Skill on Verity's forearms. I emerged red as a boiled crab. At the cool end of the bath-hut there were several mirrors on the wall. I tried not to see my own face as I shaved. It reminded me too vividly of Verity's. Some of the gauntness had left it in the last week or so, but the streak of white at my brow was back and showed even more plainly when I bound my hair back in a warrior's tail. I would not have been surprised to see Verity's handprint on my face, or to find my scar eradicated and my nose straightened, such had been the power of that touch. But Regal's scar on my face stood out pallidly against my steam-reddened face. Nothing had improved the broken nose. There was no outward sign of my encounter last night at all. Again and again, my mind circled back to that moment, to that touch of purest power. I fumbled to recall it and almost could. But the absolute experience of it, like pain or pleasure, could not be recalled in full, but only in pale memory. I knew I had experienced something extraordinary. The pleasures of Skilling, which all Skill-users were cautioned against, were like a tiny ember compared to the bonfire of knowing, feeling and being that I had briefly shared last night.

It had changed me. The anger I had been nursing toward Kettricken and Chade was gutted. I could find the emotion still, but I could not bring it back in force. I had briefly seen, not only my child, but the entire situation from all possible views. There was no malice in their intent, nor even selfishness. They believed in the morality of what they did. I did not. But I could no longer deny entirely the sense of what they sought. It left me feeling soulless. They would take my child away from Molly and me. I could hate what they did, but I could not focus that anger at them.

I shook my head, drawing myself back to the moment. I looked at myself in the mirror, wondering how Kettricken would see me. Did she still see the young man who had dogged Verity's steps and so often served her at court? Or would she look at my scarred face and think she did not know me, that the Fitz she had known was gone? Well, she knew by now how I had gained my scars. My queen should not be surprised. I would let her judge who stood behind those marks.

I braced my nerves, then turned my back to the mirror. I looked over my shoulder. The centre of injury in my back reminded me of a sunken red starfish in my flesh. Around it the skin was tight and shiny. I flexed my shoulders and watched the skin tug against the scar. I extended my sword arm and felt the tiny pull of resistance there. Well, no sense worrying about it. I pulled on my shirt.

I returned to the Fool's hut to clothe myself afresh and found to my surprise that he was dressed and ready to accompany me. Clothes were laid out on my cot: a white loose-sleeved shirt of soft warm wool, and dark leggings of a heavier woollen weave. There was a short dark surcoat to match the leggings. He told me that Chade had left them. It was all very simple and plain.

'It suits you,' the Fool observed. He himself was dressed much as he did every day, in a woollen robe, but this one was dark blue with embroidery at the sleeves and hem. It was closer to what I had seen the Mountain folk wear. It accentuated his pallor far more than the white one had, and made plainer to my eyes the slight tawniness his skin, eyes and hair were beginning to possess. His hair was as fine as ever. Left to itself, it still seemed to float freely around his face, but today he was binding it back.

'I did not know Kettricken had summoned you,' I observed, to which he grimly replied, 'All the more reason to present myself. Chade came to check on you this morning, and was concerned to find you gone. I think he half fears that you have run off with the wolf again. But in case you had not, he left a message for you. Other than those who have been in this hut, no one in Jhaampe has been told your true name. Much as it must surprise you to find that the minstrel had that much discretion. Not even the healer knows who she healed. Remember, you are Tom the shepherd until such time as Queen Kettricken feels she can speak more plainly to you. Understand?'

I sighed. I understood all too well. 'I never knew Jhaampe to host intrigue before,' I observed.

He chuckled. 'You have visited here only briefly before this. Believe me, Jhaampe breeds intrigues every bit as convoluted as Buckkeep did. As strangers here, we are wise to avoid being drawn into them, as much as we can.'

'Save for the ones we bring with us,' I told him, and he smiled bitterly as he nodded.

The day was bright and crisp. The sky glimpsed overhead through the dark evergreen boughs was an endless blue. A small breeze ran alongside us, rattling dry snow crystals across the frozen tops of the snow banks. The dry snow squeaked under our boots and the cold roughly kissed my freshly-shaven cheeks. From further off in the village, I could hear the shouts of children at play. Nighteyes pricked his ears to that, but continued to shadow us. The small voices in the distance reminded me of sea-birds crying and I suddenly missed the shores of Buck acutely.

'You had a seizure last night,' the Fool said quietly. It was not quite a question.

'I know,' I said briefly.

'Kettle seemed very distressed by it. She questioned Chade most closely about the herbs he prepared for you. And when they did not rouse you as he had said they would, she went off in her corner. She sat there most of the night, knitting loudly and peering at him disapprovingly. It was a relief to me when they all finally left.'

I wondered if Starling had stayed, but did not ask it. I did not even want to know why it mattered to me.

'Who is Kettle?' the Fool asked abruptly.

'Who is Kettle?' I asked, startled.

'I believe I just said that.'

'Kettle is . . .' It suddenly seemed odd that I knew so little about someone I had travelled with so long. 'I think she grew up in Buck. And then she travelled, and studied scrolls and prophecies, and returned to seek the White Prophet.' I shrugged at the scantiness of my knowledge.

'Tell me. Do you find her . . . portentous?'

'What?'

'Do you not feel there is something about her, something that . . .' He shook his head angrily. It was the first time I had ever seen the Fool searching for words. 'Sometimes, I feel she is significant. That she is wound up with us. Other times, she seems but a nosy old woman with an unfortunate lack of taste in her choice of companions.'

'You mean me,' I laughed.

'No. I mean that interfering minstrel.'

'Why do you and Starling dislike one another so?' I asked tiredly.

'It is not dislike, dear Fitzy. On my part, it is disinterest. Unfortunately, she cannot conceive of a man who could look at her with no interest in bedding her. She takes my simple dismissal of her as an insult, and strives to make of it some lack or fault in me. Whilst I take offence at her proprietary attitude toward you. She has no true affection for Fitz, you know, only for being able to say she knew FitzChivalry.'

I was silent, fearing that what he said was true. And so we came to the palace at Jhaampe. It was as unlike Buckkeep as I could imagine. I have heard it said that the dwellings at Jhaampe owe their origins to the dome-shaped tents some of the nomadic tribes still use. The smaller dwellings were still tent-like enough that they did not startle me as the palace still did. The living heart tree that was its centrepole towered immensely above us. Other secondary trees had been patiently contorted over years to form supports for the walls. When this living framework had been established, mats of bark cloth had been draped gracefully over them to form the basis for the smoothly curving walls. Plastered with a sort of clay and then painted in bright colours, the houses would always remind me of tulip buds or mushroom caps. Despite its great size, the palace seemed organic, as if it had sprouted up from the rich soil of the ancient forest that sheltered it.

Size made it a palace. There were no other outward signs, no flags, no royal guards flanking the doors. No one sought to bar our entrance. The Fool opened the carved wood-framed doors of a side entrance, and we went in. I followed him as he threaded his way through a maze of freestanding chambers. Other rooms were on platforms above us, reached by ladders or, for the grander ones, staircases of wood. The walls of the chambers were flimsy things, with some temporary rooms of no more than barkcloth tapestries stretched on frameworks. The inside of the palace was only slightly warmer than the forest outside. The individual chambers were heated by free-standing braziers in the winter.

I followed the Fool to a chamber whose outer walls were decorated with delicate illustrations of water birds. This was a more permanent room, with sliding wooden doors likewise carved with birds. I could hear the notes of Starling's harp from within and the murmur of low voices. He tapped at the door, waited briefly and then slid it open to admit us. Kettricken was within, and the Fool's friend Jofron and several other people I did not recognize. Starling sat on a low bench to one side, playing softly while Kettricken and the others embroidered a quilt on a frame that almost filled the room. A bright garden of flowers was being created on the quilt top. Chade sat not far from Starling. He was dressed in a white shirt and dark leggings with a long wool vest, gaily embroidered, over the shirt. His hair was pulled back in a grey warrior's tail, with the leather band on his brow bearing the buck sigil. He looked decades younger than he had at Buckkeep. They spoke together more softly than the music.

Kettricken looked up, needle in hand, and greeted us calmly. She introduced me to the others as Tom, and politely asked if I were recovering well from my injury. I told her I was, and she bade me be seated and rest myself a bit. The Fool circled the quilt, complimented Jofron on her stitchery, and when she invited him, he took a place beside her. He took up a needle and floss, threaded it and began adding butterflies of his own invention to one corner of the quilt while he and Jofron talked softly of gardens they had known. He seemed very at ease. I felt at a loss, sitting idly in a room full of quietly occupied people. I waited for Kettricken to speak to me, but she went on with her work. Starling's eyes met mine and she smiled, but stiffly. Chade avoided my glance, looking past me as if we were strangers.

There was conversation in the room, but it was soft and intermittent, mostly requests for a skein of thread to be passed, or comments on each other's work. Starling played the old familiar Buck ballads, but wordlessly. No one spoke to me or paid me any mind. I waited.

After a time, I began to wonder if it were a subtle form of punishment. I tried to remain relaxed, but tension repeatedly built up in me. Every few minutes I would remember to unclench my jaws and loosen my shoulders. It took some time for me to see a similar anxiety in Kettricken. I had spent many times attending my lady in Buckkeep when she had first come to court. I had seen her lethargic at her needlework, or lively in her garden, but now she sewed furiously, as if the fate of the Six Duchies depended on her completing this quilt. She was thinner than I recalled, the bones and planes of her face showing more plainly. Her hair, a year after she had cut it to mourn Verity, was still too short for her to confine it well. The pale strands of it constantly crept forward. There were lines in her face, around her eyes and mouth and she frequently chewed on her lips, a thing I had never seen her do before.

The morning seemed to drag on, but finally one of the young men sat up straight, then stretched and declared his eyes were getting too weary to do any more today. He asked the woman at his side if she had a mind to hunt with him today, and she readily agreed. As if this were some sort of signal, the others began to rise and stretch and make their farewells to Kettricken. I was struck at their familiarity with her, until I recalled that here she was not regarded as Queen, but as eventual Sacrifice to the Mountains. Her role among her own folk would never be seen as that of ruler, but as guide and co-ordinator. Her father King Eyod was known among his own folk as the Sacrifice, and was expected to be ever and always unselfishly available to his folk to help in any way they might require. It was a position that was both less regal than that of Buck royalty, and more beloved. I wondered idly if it might not have suited Verity more to have come here and been Kettricken's consort.

'FitzChivalry.'

I looked up to Kettricken's command. Only she, I, Starling, Chade, and the Fool remained in the room. I almost looked to Chade for direction. But his eyes had excluded me earlier. I sensed I was on my own here. The tone of Kettricken's voice made this a formal interview. I stood straight, and then managed a rather stiff bow. 'My queen, you summoned me.'

'Explain yourself.'

The wind outside was warmer than her voice. I glanced up at her eyes. Blue ice. I lowered my gaze and took a breath. 'Shall I report, my queen?'

'If it will explain your failures, do so.' That startled me. My eyes flew to hers, but though our glances met, there was no meeting. All the girl in Kettricken had burned away, as the impurities are burned and beaten from iron ore in a foundry. With it seemed to have gone any feeling for her husband's bastard nephew. She sat before me as ruler and judge, not friend. I had not expected to feel that loss so keenly.

Despite my better judgment, I let ice creep into my own voice. 'I shall submit to my queen's judgment on that,' I offered.

She was merciless. She had me start not with my own death, but days before that, when we had first begun plotting to whisk King Shrewd secretly from Buckkeep and Regal's reach. I stood before her, and had to admit that the Coastal Dukes had approached me with the offer of recognizing me as King-in-Waiting rather than Regal. Worse, I had to tell her that although I had refused that, I had promised to stand with them, assuming the command of Buckkeep Castle and the protection of Buck's coast. Chade had once warned me that it was as close to treason as made no difference. But I was tired to death of all my secrets, and I relentlessly bared them. More than once I wished Starling were not in the room, for I dreaded hearing my own words made into a song denouncing me. But if my queen deemed her worthy of confidence, it was not my place to question it.

So on I went, down the weary track of days. For the first time, she heard from me how King Shrewd had died in my arms, and how I had hunted down and killed both Serene and Justin in the Great Hall before everyone. When it came to my days in Regal's dungeon, she had no pity on me. 'He had me beaten and starved, and I would have perished there if I had not feigned death,' I said. It was not good enough for her.

No one, not even Burrich, had known a full telling of those days. I steeled myself and launched into it. After a time, my voice began to shake. I faltered in my telling. Then I looked past her at the wall, took a breath, and went on. I glanced at her once, to find her gone white as ice. I stopped thinking of the events behind my words. I heard my own voice dispassionately relating all that had happened. I heard Kettricken draw in her breath when I spoke of Skilling to Verity from my cell. Other than that, there was not a sound in the room. Once my eyes wandered to Chade. I found him sitting, deathly still, his jaw set as if he endured some torment of his own.

I forged my way on through the story, telling without judgment of my own resurrection by Burrich and Chade, of the Wit-magic that made it possible and of the days that followed. I told of our angry parting, of my journeys in detail, of the times when I could sense Verity and the brief joinings we shared, of my attempt on Regal's life, and even of how Verity had unwittingly implanted into my soul his command to come to him. On and on, my voice getting huskier as my throat and mouth dried with the telling. I did not pause nor rest until I had finished telling her of my final staggering trek into Jhaampe. And when at last my full tale of days was told out to her, I continued to stand, emptied and weary. Some people say there is a relief in the sharing of cares and pains. To me there was no catharsis, only an unearthing of rotting corpses of memories, a baring of still suppurating wounds. After a time of silence, I found the cruelty to ask, 'Does my account excuse my failures, my queen?'

But if I had thought to rend her, I failed there also. 'You make no mention of your daughter, FitzChivalry.'

It was true. I had not made mention of Molly and the child. Fear sliced through me like a cold blade. 'I had not thought of her as pertaining to my report.'

'She obviously must,' Queen Kettricken said implacably. I

forced myself to look at her. She clasped her hands before her. Did they tremble, did she feel any remorse for what she said next? I could not tell. 'Given her lineage, she much more than "pertains" to this discussion. Ideally, she should be here, where we could guarantee a measure of safety to the Farseer heir.'

I imposed calm on my voice. 'My queen, you are mistaken in naming her so. Neither I nor she have any legitimate claim to the throne. We are both illegitimate.'

Kettricken was shaking her head. 'We do not consider what is or is not between you and her mother. We consider only her bloodline. Regardless of what you may claim for her, her lineage will claim her. I am childless.' Until I heard her speak that word aloud, I did not grasp what her depth of pain was. A few moments ago, I had thought her heartless. Now I wondered if she were completely sane any more. Such was the grief and despair that one word conveyed. She forced herself on. 'There must be an heir to the Farseer throne. Chade has advised me that alone I cannot rally the people to protect themselves. I am too foreign to their eyes still. But no matter how they see me, I remain their queen. I have a duty to do. I must find a way to unite the Six Duchies and repulse the invaders from our shores. To do that, they must have a leader. I had thought to offer you, but he has said that they will not accept you either. That matter of your supposed death and use of Beast magic is too big an obstacle. That being so, there remains only your child of the Farseer line. Regal has proven false to his own blood. She, then, must be Sacrifice for our people. They will rally to her.'

I dared to speak. 'She is only an infant, my queen. How can she . . .'

'She is a symbol. It is all the people will require of her right now, that she exist. Later, she will be their queen in truth.'

I felt as if she had knocked the wind from me. She spoke on. 'I shall be sending Chade to fetch her here, where she may be kept safe and properly educated as she grows.' She sighed. 'I would like her mother to be with her. Unfortunately, we must present the child as mine, somehow. How I hate such deceptions. But Chade has convinced me of the necessity. I hope he will also be able to convince your daughter's mother.' More to herself, she added, 'We shall have to say that we said my child was stillborn to make Regal believe there was no heir to threaten. My poor little son. His people will never even know he was born. And that, I suppose, is how he is Sacrifice for them.'

I found myself looking at Kettricken closely, and finding there remained very little of the Queen I had known at Buckkeep. I hated what she was saying; it outraged me. Yet my voice was gentle as I asked, 'Why is any of this necessary, my queen? King Verity lives. I shall find him and do all I can to return him to you. Together, you shall rule at Buckkeep, and your children after you.'

'Shall he? Will we? Will they?' Almost she shook her head in denial. 'It may be, FitzChivalry. But for too long I put my faith in believing that things would turn out as they should. I will not fall prey to those expectations again. Some things must be made certain before further risks can be taken. An heir to the Farseer line must be assured.' She met my eyes calmly. 'I have made up the declaration and given a copy to Chade, with another to be kept safely here. Your child is heir to the throne, FitzChivalry.'

I had been keeping my soul intact with a tiny hope for so long. For so many months, I had lured myself along with the idea that when all was over and done, I could somehow go back to Molly and win again her love, that I could claim my daughter as my own. Other men might dream of high honours or riches or deeds of valour sung by minstrels. I wanted to come to a small cot as the light faded, to sit in a chair by a fire, my back aching from work, my hands rough with toil, and hold a little girl in my lap while a woman who loved me told me of her day. Of all the things I had ever had to give up simply by virtue of the blood I carried, that was the dearest. Must I now surrender that? Must I become to Molly forever the man who had lied to her, who had left her with child and never returned, and then caused that child to be stolen from her as well?

I had not meant to speak aloud. I did not realize I had until the Queen replied. 'That is what it is to be Sacrifice, FitzChivalry. Nothing can be held back for oneself. Nothing.'

'I will not acknowledge her, then.' The words burned my tongue to speak them. 'I will not claim her as mine.'

'You need not, for I shall claim her as mine. No doubt she will carry the Farseer looks. Your blood is strong. For our purposes, it is sufficient that I know the child is yours. You have already acknowledged that to Starling the minstrel. To her you said you had fathered a child with Molly, a candlemaker from Buckkeep Town. In all of the Six Duchies, the witness of a minstrel is recognized by law. She has already set her hand to the document, with her oath that she knows the child to be a true Farseer. FitzChivalry,' she went on and her voice was almost kind, though my ears rang to hear her words and I near reeled where I stood, 'no one can escape fate. Not you, nor your daughter. Step back and see this is why she came to be. When all circumstances conspired to deny the Farseer line an heir, somehow one was yet made. By you. Accept, and endure.'

They were the wrong words. She might have been raised to them, but I had been told, 'The fight is not over until you have won it.' I lifted my eyes and looked around at them all. I don't know what they saw on my face but their faces became still. 'I can find Verity,' I said quietly. 'And I will.'

They were silent.

'You want your king,' I said to Kettricken. I waited until I saw assent in her face.

'I want my child,' I said quietly.

'What are you saying?' Kettricken demanded coldly.

'I am saying that I want the same things you do. I wish to be with the one I love, to raise our child with her.' I met her eyes. 'Tell me I can have that. It is all I have ever wanted.'

She met my eyes squarely. 'I cannot make you that promise, FitzChivalry. She is too important for simple love to claim her.'

The words struck me as both utterly absurd and completely true. I bowed my head in what was not assent. I stared a hole into the floor, trying to find other choices, other ways.

'I know what you will say next,' Kettricken said bitterly. 'That if I claim your child for the throne, you will not help me find Verity. I have considered long and well, knowing that this will sever me from your help. I am prepared to seek him out on my own. I have the map. Somehow, I shall . . .'

'Kettricken.' I cut into her speech with her name said quietly, bereft of her title. I had not meant to. I saw it startled her. I found myself slowly shaking my head. 'You do not understand. Were Molly standing here before me with our daughter, still I would have to seek my king. No matter what is done to me, no matter how I am wronged. Still, I must seek Verity.'

My words changed the faces in the room. Chade lifted his head and looked at me with fierce pride shining in his eyes. Kettricken turned aside, blinking at tears. I think she may have felt slightly ashamed. To the Fool, I was once more his Catalyst. In Starling there bloomed the hope that I might still be worthy of a legend.

But in me there was the overriding hunger for the absolute. Verity had shown it to me, in its pure physical form. I would answer my king's Skill-command and serve him as I had vowed. But another call beckoned me now as well. The Skill.

TWENTY-THREE

The Mountains

One might suppose that the Mountain Kingdom, with its sparse hamlets and scattered folk, was a new realm but recently gathered together. In truth, its history far predates any of the written records of the Six Duchies. To call this region a kingdom is truly a misnomer. In ancient times, the diverse hunters, herders and farmers, both nomadic and settled, gradually gave their allegiance to a Judge, a woman of great wisdom, who resided at Jhaampe. Although this person has come to be called the King or Queen of the Mountains by outsiders, to the residents of the Mountain Kingdom, he or she is still the Sacrifice, the one who is willing to give all, even life, for the sake of those who are ruled. The first Judge who lived at Jhaampe is now a shadowy figure of legend, her deeds known only by the songs of her that Mountain folk still sing.

Yet old as those songs are, there is an even older rumour of a more ancient ruler and capital city. The Mountain Kingdom, as we know it today, consists almost entirely of the wandering folk and settlements on the eastern flanks of the Mountains. Beyond the Mountains lie the icy shores that border the White Sea. Some few trade routes still meander through the sharp teeth of the Mountains to reach the hunting folk who live in that snowy place. To the south of the Mountains are the unsettled forests of the Rain Wilds, and somewhere the source of the Rain River that is the boundary of the Chalced States. These are the only lands and folks that have been truly charted beyond the Mountains. Yet there have always been legends of another land, one locked and lost in the peaks beyond the Mountain Kingdom. As one travels deeper in the Mountains, past the boundaries of the folk who owe allegiance to Jhaampe, the land becomes even more rugged and unyielding. Snow never leaves the taller peaks, and some valleys host only glacial ice. In some areas, it is said that great steams and smokes *pour up from cracks in the mountains and that the earth may tremble quietly or wrench itself in violent shakings. There are few reasons for anyone to venture into that region of scree and cliffs. Hunting is easier and more profitable on the greener slopes of the mountains. There is insufficient grazing to lure any shepherd's flocks.*

Regarding that land, we have the usual tales that distant lands spawn. Dragons and giants, ancient tumbledown cities, savage unicorns, treasure hoards and secret maps, dusty streets paved with gold, valleys of eternal spring where the water rises steaming from the ground, dangerous sorcerers spell-locked in caves of gems and ancient sleeping evils embedded in the earth. All are said to reside in the ancient, nameless land beyond the boundaries of the Mountain Kingdom.

Kettricken truly had expected me to refuse to help her search for Verity. In the days of my convalescence she had determined she would seek for him on her own, and to that end she had mustered supplies and animals. In the Six Duchies, a queen would have had the royal treasury to draw on, as well as the enforced largesse of her nobles. Such was not the case in the Mountain Kingdom. Here, while King Eyod remained alive, she was no more than a younger relative of the Sacrifice. While it was expected that she would succeed him some day, it gave her no right to command the wealth of her people. In truth, even were she Sacrifice, she would not have had access to riches and resources. The Sacrifice and his immediate family lived simply within their beautiful dwelling. All of Jhaampe, the palace, the gardens, the fountains, all belonged to the folk of the Mountain Kingdom. The Sacrifice did not want for anything, but neither did he possess excess.

So Kettricken turned, not to royal coffers and nobles eager to curry favour, but to old friends and cousins for what she needed. She had approached her father, but he had told her, firmly but sadly, that finding the King of the Six Duchies was her concern, not that of the Mountain Kingdom. Much as he grieved with his daughter over the disappearance of a man she loved, he could not divert supplies from defending the Mountain Kingdom from Regal of the Six Duchies. Such was the bond between them that she could accept his refusal with understanding. It shamed me to

think of the rightful Queen of the Six Duchies turning to the
charity of her relatives and friends. But only when I was not
nursing my resentment toward her.

She had designed the expedition to her convenience, not mine.
I approved of little of it. In the few days before we departed, she
deigned to consult me on some aspects of it, but my opinions
were overridden as often as they were listened to. We spoke to
one another civilly, without the warmth of either anger or friendship. There were many areas where we disagreed, and when we
did, she did as she judged wisest. Unspoken but implied was that
my judgment in the past had been faulty and short-sighted.

I wanted no beasts of burden that might starve and freeze. Block
as I might, the Wit left me vulnerable to their pain. Kettricken,
however, had procured half a dozen creatures that she claimed
did not mind snow and cold, and browsed rather than grazed.
They were jeppas, creatures native to some of the remoter parts
of the Mountain Kingdom. They reminded me of long-necked
goats with paws instead of hooves. I had small faith that they
would be able to carry enough to make them worth the nuisance
of dealing with them. Kettricken told me calmly that I would
soon get used to them.

It all depends on how they taste, Nighteyes suggested philosophi-
cally. I was prone to agree with him.

Her choice of companions for the expedition irked me even
more. I saw no sense to her risking herself, but on that point I
knew better than to argue. I resented Starling's going, once I
discovered what she had bargained to be allowed to go. Her reason
was still to find a song that would make her reputation. She had
bought her place in our group by her unspoken trade that only
if she were allowed to go would she make written record that
Molly's child was mine also. She knew I felt she had betrayed
me, and wisely avoided my company after that. With us would
go three cousins of Kettricken's, all big, stoutly-muscled folk well
practised in travelling through the Mountains. It would not be a
large party. Kettricken assured me that if six were not enough to
find Verity, then six hundred would not suffice. I agreed with her
that it was easier to supply a smaller party, and that often they
travelled faster than large groups.

Chade was not to be of our party. He was going back to Buck-keep, to bear the tidings to Patience that Kettricken would seek out Verity, and to plant the seeds of rumour that there was, indeed, an heir to the Six Duchies throne. He would also be seeing Burrich and Molly and the child. He had offered to let Molly and Patience and Burrich know that I was still alive. The offer had come awkwardly, for he knew full well that I hated the part he had played in claiming my daughter for the throne. But I swallowed my anger and spoke to him politely and was rewarded with his solemn promise that he would say nothing of me to any of them. At the time it seemed like the wisest course. I felt that only I could fully explain to Molly why I had acted as I had. And she had already mourned me as dead once. If I did not survive this quest, she would not grieve any more than she had.

Chade came to bid me farewell the night he left for Buck. At first we both tried to pretend that all was well between us. We talked of small things that had once mattered to both of us. I felt genuine loss when he told me of Slink's death. I tried to talk him into taking Ruddy and Sooty with him, to return them to Burrich's care. Ruddy needed a firmer hand than he was getting, and the stallion could be far more than transportation to Burrich. His stud service could be sold or traded, and Sooty's foal represented more wealth to come. But Chade shook his head and said he must travel swiftly and attract no attention. One man with three horses was a target for bandits if nothing else. I had seen the vicious little gelding Chade had for a mount. Bad-tempered as he was, he was tough and agile, and Chade assured me, very swift in a chase over bad terrain. He grinned as he said it, and I knew that that particular ability of the horse had been well tested. The Fool was right, I thought to myself then bitterly. War and intrigue did agree with him. I looked at him, in his tall boots and swirling cloak, at the rampant buck he wore so openly on his brow above his green eyes, and tried to equate him with the gentle-handed old man who had schooled me in how to kill people. His years were there still, but he carried them differently. Privately I won-dered what drugs he used to prolong his energy.

Yet as different as he was, he was still Chade. I wanted to reach out to him and know that there was still a bond of some kind between us, but I could not. I could not understand myself. How could his opinion still matter so much to me, when I knew he was willing to take my child and my happiness for the sake of the Farseer throne? I felt it as a weakness in myself that I could not find the strength of will to hate him. I reached for that hatred, and came up with only a boyish sulkiness that kept me from clasping his hand at his departure or wishing him well. He ignored my surliness, which made me feel even more childish.

After he was gone, the Fool gave me the leather saddlebag he had left for me. Inside was a very serviceable sheath knife, a small pouch of coins and a selection of poisons and healing herbs, including a generous supply of elfbark. Wrapped and carefully labelled that it should be used only with the greatest caution and in greatest need was a small paper of carris seed. In a battered leather sheath was a plain but serviceable short sword. I felt a sudden anger at him that I could not explain. 'It is so typical of him,' I exclaimed and dumped the bag out on the table for the Fool to witness. 'Poison and knives. That is what he thinks of me. This is still how he sees me. Death is all he can imagine for me.'

'I doubt he expected you to use them on yourself,' the Fool observed mildly. He pushed the knife away from the marionette he was stringing. 'Perhaps he thought you might use them to protect yourself.'

'Don't you understand?' I demanded of him. 'These are gifts for the boy Chade taught to be an assassin. He can't see that isn't who I am any longer. He can't forgive me for wanting a life of my own.'

'Any more than you can forgive him for no longer being your benevolent and indulgent tutor,' the Fool observed drily. He was knotting the strings from the control paddles to the marionette's limbs. 'It's a bit of a threat, isn't it, to see him stride about like a warrior, putting himself joyfully in danger for something he believes in, flirting with women, and generally acting as if he'd claimed a life of his own for himself?'

It was like a dash of cold water in the face. Almost, I had to admit my jealousy that Chade had boldly seized what still eluded me. 'That isn't it at all!' I snarled at the Fool.

The marionette he was working on wagged a rebuking finger at me while the Fool smirked at me over his head. It had an uncanny resemblance to Ratsy. 'What I see,' he observed to no one in particular, 'is that it is not Verity's buck head he wears on his brow. No, the sigil he chose is more like one, oh, let me see, one that Prince Verity chose for his bastard nephew. Do not you see a resemblance?'

I was silent for a time. Then, 'What of it?' I asked grudgingly.

The Fool swung his marionette to the floor, where the bony creature shrugged eerily. 'Neither King Shrewd's death, nor Verity's supposed death flushed that weasel out of hiding. Only when he believed you murdered did anger flare up in him hot enough for him to fling aside all hiding and pretence and declare he would yet see a true Farseer on the throne.' The marionette wagged a finger at me.

'Are you trying to say he does this for me, for my sake? When the last thing I would wish is to see the throne claim my child?'

The marionette crossed its arms and wagged its head thoughtfully. 'It seems to me that Chade has always done what he thought was best for you. Whether you agreed or not. Perhaps he extends that to your daughter. She would be, after all, his great grand-niece, and the last living remnant of his bloodline. Excluding Regal and yourself, of course.' The marionette danced a few steps. 'How else would you expect a man that old to provide for a child so young? He does not expect to live forever. Perhaps he thought she would be safer astride a throne than ridden over by another who wished to claim it.'

I turned away from the Fool and made some pretence of gathering clothing to wash. It would take me a long time to think through what he had said.

I was willing to accept Kettricken's choice of tents and clothing for her expedition, and honest enough to be grateful that she saw fit to provide for my clothing and shelter as well. Had she excluded me totally from her entourage, I could not have completely faulted her. Instead, Jofron came one day bearing a stack of clothing and bedding for me, and to measure my feet for the sacklike boots the Mountain folk favoured. She proved merry company, for she and the Fool exchanged playful barbs all the while. His fluency in Chyurda exceeded my own, and at times I was hard pressed to follow the conversation, while half of the Fool's word-plays escaped me. I wondered in passing exactly what went on between those two. When I had first arrived, I had thought her some sort of disciple to him. Now I wondered if she had not affected that interest simply as an excuse to be near him. Before she left, she measured the Fool's feet as well, and asked him questions as to what colours and trims he wished worked into the boots.

'New boots?' I asked him after she had gone. 'As little as you venture outside, I would scarcely think you need them.'

He gave me a level look. The recent merriment faded from his face. 'You know I must go with you,' he pointed out calmly. He smiled an odd smile. 'Why else do you think we have been brought together in this far place? It is by the interaction of the Catalyst and the White Prophet that the events of this time shall be returned to their proper course. I believe that if we succeed, the Red Ships will be driven from the Six Duchies coast, and a Farseer will inherit a throne.'

'That would seem to fit most of the prophecies,' Kettle agreed from her hearth corner. She was tying off the last row of knitting on a thick mitten. 'If the plague of the mindless hunger is Forging, and your actions put a stop to that, that would fit another prophecy as well.'

Kettle's knack of providing a prophecy for every occasion was beginning to grate on me. I took a breath, and then asked the Fool, 'And what does Queen Kettricken say about your joining her party?'

'I haven't discussed it with her,' he replied blithely. 'I am not joining her, Fitz. I am following you.' A sort of bemusement came over his face. 'I have known since I was a child that together we should do this task. It had not occurred to me to question that I would go with you. I have been making preparations since the day you arrived here.'

'As have I,' Kettle observed quietly.

We both turned to stare at her. She feigned not to notice as she tried on the mitten and admired its fit.

'No.' I spoke bluntly. Bad enough to look forward to dying pack animals. I was not going to witness the death of another friend. It was too obvious to voice that she was hopelessly too old for such a trek.

'I thought you might stay here, in my home,' the Fool offered more gently. 'There is plenty of firewood for the rest of the winter and some supplies of meal and –'

'I expect to die on the journey, if it's any comfort to you.' She took off the mitten and set it with its mate. Casually she inspected what was left of her skein of wool. She began to cast on stitches, the yarn flowing effortlessly through her fingers. 'And you needn't worry about me before then. I've made provision for myself. Done a bit of trading, and I have the food and such that I'll need.' She glanced up at me from her needles, and added quietly, 'I have the wherewithal to see this journey through to the end.'

I had to admire her calm assumption that her life was still her own, to do with as she wished. I wondered when I had begun to think of her as a helpless old woman that someone would have to look after now. She looked back down to her knitting. Needlessly, for her fingers continued to work whether she watched them or not. 'I see you understand me,' she said quietly. And that was that.

I have never known any expedition to get off exactly as planned. Generally, the larger one is, the more difficulties it has. Ours was no exception. The morning before we were scheduled to depart, I was rudely shaken out of my sleep.

'Get up, Fitz, we have to leave now,' Kettricken said tersely.

I sat up slowly. I was wide awake instantly, but my healing back still did not encourage me to move swiftly. The Fool was sitting on the edge of his bed, looking more anxious than I had ever seen him. 'What is it?' I demanded.

'Regal.' I had never heard so much venom in one word. Her face was very white and she knotted and unknotted her fists at her side. 'He has sent a courier under a truce flag to my father, saying that we harbour a known traitor to the Six Duchies. He says that if we release you to him, he will see it as a sign of good faith with the Six Duchies and will not consider us an enemy. But if we do not, he will loose the troops he has poised on our borders, for he will know that we plot with his enemies against him.' She paused. 'My father is considering what to do.'

'Kettricken, I am but the excuse,' I protested. My heart was hammering in my chest. Nighteyes whined anxiously. 'You must know it has taken him months to mass those troops. They are not there because I am here. They are in place because he plans to move against the Mountain Kingdom no matter what. You know Regal. It is all a bluff to see if he can get you to turn me over to him. Once you do, he will find some other pretext to attack.'

'I am not a simpleton,' she said coldly. 'Our watchers have known of the troops for weeks. We have been doing what we can to prepare ourselves. Always our mountains have been our strongest defence. But never before have we confronted an organized foe in such numbers. My father is Sacrifice, Fitz. He must do whatever will best serve the Mountain Kingdom. So now he must ponder if by turning you over, he will have a chance to treat with Regal. Do not think my father is stupid enough to trust him. But the longer he can delay an attack against his people, the better prepared they will be.'

'It sounds as if there is little left to decide,' I said bitterly.

'There was no reason for my father to make me privy to the courier's message,' Kettricken observed. 'The decision is his.' Her eyes met mine squarely, and held a shadow of our old friendship. 'I think perhaps he offers me a chance to spirit you away. Before I would be defying his orders to turn you over to Regal. Perhaps he thinks to tell Regal you have escaped but he intends to track you down.'

Behind Kettricken, the Fool was pulling on leggings under his nightshirt.

'It will be harder than I had planned,' Kettricken confided in me. 'I cannot involve any other Mountain folk in this. It will have to be you, I and Starling. Alone. And we must leave now, within the hour.'

'I'll be ready,' I promised her.

'Meet me behind Joss's woodshed,' she said, and left.

I looked at the Fool. 'So. Do we tell Kettle?'

'Why are you asking me?' he demanded.

I gave a small shrug. Then I got up and began dressing hastily. I thought of all the small ways in which I was not prepared and then gave it up as useless. In a very short time, the Fool and I shouldered our packs. Nighteyes rose, stretched thoroughly, and went to the door to precede us. *I shall miss the fireplace. But the hunting will be better.* He accepted all so calmly.

The Fool took a careful look around the hut, and then closed the door behind us. 'That's the first place I've ever lived that was solely mine,' he observed as we walked away from it.

'You leave so much behind to do this,' I said awkwardly, thinking of his tools, his half-finished puppets, even the plants growing inside by the window. Despite myself, I felt responsible for it. Perhaps it was because I was so glad that I was not going on alone.

He glanced over at me and shrugged. 'I take myself with me. That's all I truly need, or own.' He glanced back at the door he had painted himself. 'Jofron will take good care of it. And of Kettle, too.'

I wondered if he left behind more than I knew.

We were nearly to the woodshed when I saw some children racing down the path toward us. 'There he is!' one cried, pointing. I shot a startled glance at the Fool, then braced myself, wondering what was to come. How could one defend oneself against children? At a loss, I awaited the attack. But the wolf did not wait. He sank low to his belly in the snow, even his tail flat. As the children closed the distance, he suddenly shot forward straight at the leader. 'NO!' I cried aloud in horror, but none of them paid me any heed. The wolf's front paws struck the boy's chest, to drive him down hard in the snow. In a flash Nighteyes was up and after the others, who fled, shrieking with laughter as one after another he caught up with them and mowed them down. By the time he'd felled the last one, the first boy was up and after him, vainly trying to keep up with the wolf and making wild grabs at his tail as Nighteyes flashed by him, tongue lolling.

He felled them all again, twice more, before he halted in one of his racing loops. He watched the children getting to their feet, then glanced over his shoulder at me. He folded his ears down abashedly, then looked back to the children, his tail wagging low.

One girl was already digging a chunk of fatbread out of her pocket while another teased him with a strip of leather, snaking it over the snow and trying to get him involved in a tug-of-war. I feigned not to notice.

I'll catch up with you later, he offered.

No doubt, I told him drily. The Fool and I kept walking. I glanced back once to see the wolf, teeth set in the leather and all four feet braced while two boys dragged at the other end of it. I surmised that I now knew how he had been spending his afternoons. I think I felt a pang of envy.

Kettricken was already waiting. Six laden jeppas were roped together in a train. I wished now I had taken the time to learn more about them, but I had assumed the others would have the care of them. 'We're still taking all of them?' I asked in dismay.

'It would take too long to unpack the loads and repack with only what we need. Perhaps later we'll abandon the extra supplies and animals. But for now, I simply wish to be gone as soon as possible.'

'Then let's leave,' I suggested.

Kettricken looked pointedly at the Fool. 'What are you doing here? Wishing Fitz farewell?'

'I go where he does,' the Fool said quietly.

The Queen looked at him and something in her face almost softened. 'It will be cold, Fool. I have not forgotten how you suffered from the cold on the way here. Where we go, now, the cold will linger long after spring has reached Jhaampe.'

'I go where he does,' the Fool repeated quietly.

Kettricken shook her head to herself. Then she shrugged. She strode to the head of the line of jeppas and snapped her fingers. The lead animal flapped his hairy ears and followed her. The others followed him. Their obedience impressed me. I quested briefly toward them and found such a strong herd instinct at work that they scarcely thought of themselves as separate animals. As long as the lead animal followed Kettricken, there would be no problems with the others.

Kettricken led us along a trail that was little more than a path. It wound mostly behind the scattered cottages that housed the winter residents of Jhaampe. In a very short time we left the last of the huts behind and travelled through ancient forest. The Fool and I walked behind the string of animals. I watched the one in front of us, marking how his wide, flat feet spread on the snow much as the wolf's did. They set a pace slightly faster than a comfortable walk.

We had not gone too far before I heard a shout behind us. I flinched and glanced hastily over my shoulder. It was Starling, coming at a run, her pack jouncing on her shoulders. When she came up to us, she said accusingly, 'You left without me!'

The Fool grinned. I shrugged. 'I left when my queen commanded it,' I observed.

She glared at us, and then hurried past us, floundering through the loose snow beside the trail to pass the jeppas and catch up with Kettricken. Their voices carried clearly in the cold air. 'I told you I was leaving right away,' the Queen said tersely. 'Then I did.'

To my amazement, Starling had the sense to be quiet. For a brief time she struggled along in the loose snow beside Kettricken. Then she gradually gave it up, letting first the jeppas, and then the Fool and I pass her. She fell in behind me. I knew our pace would be difficult for her to match. I felt sorry for her. Then I thought of my daughter, and did not even look back to see if she were keeping up.

It was the beginning of a long, uneventful day. The path led always uphill, never steeply, but the constant grade was taxing. Kettricken did not let up on the pace, but kept us moving steadily. None of us talked much. I was too busy breathing, and trying to ignore the gradually increasing ache in my back. Sound flesh covered the arrow-wound now, but the muscles under it still complained of their new healing.

Great trees towered above us. Most of the trees were evergreens, some of kinds I had never seen before. They made a perpetual twilight of the brief winter day's greyness. There was little underbrush to struggle with; most of the scenery was of the staggered ranks of immense trunks and a few low swooping branches. For the most part, the live branches of the trees began far over our heads. From time to time, we passed patches of smaller deciduous trees that had sprung up in areas of open forest made by a great tree's demise. The path was well packed, evidently used often by animals and by folk on skis. It was narrow, and if one did not pay attention, it was easy to step off the path and sink surprisingly deep in the unpacked snow. I tried to pay attention.

The day was mild, by mountain standards, and I soon discovered that the clothing Kettricken had procured for me was very efficient at keeping me warm. I loosened my coat at the throat and then the collar of my shirt to let body heat escape. The Fool threw back the fur-rimmed hood of his coat, to reveal that he wore a gay woollen hat within it. I watched the tassel on the end of it bobbing as he walked. If the pace bothered him, he said nothing about it. Perhaps, like me, he had no breath left to complain.

Shortly after midday, Nighteyes joined us.

'Good doggie!' I observed aloud to him.

That pales in comparison to what Kettle is calling you, he observed smugly. *I pity you all when the old bitch catches up with the pack. She has a stick.*

Is she following us?

She tracks quite well, for a noseless human. Nighteyes trotted past us, moving with surprising ease even in the unpacked snow to the side of the trail. I could tell he was enjoying the ripple of unease that his scent pushed through the trailing jeppas. I watched him as he passed them all and then Kettricken. Once he was in the lead, he ranged confidently ahead, just as if he knew where we were going. I soon lost sight of him, but I did not worry. I knew he would circle back often to check on us.

'Kettle is following us,' I told the Fool.

He shot me a questioning look.

'Nighteyes says she is quite angry with us.'

His shoulders rose and fell in a quick sigh. 'Well. She has a right to her own decision,' he observed to himself. Then, to me, he added, 'It still unnerves me a bit when you and the wolf do that.'

'Does it bother you? That I am Witted?'

'Does it bother you to meet my eyes?' he rejoined.

It was enough. We kept walking.

Kettricken held us to a steady pace for as long as the daylight

Robin Hobb

lasted. A trampled area under the shelter of some of the great trees was our stopping-place. While it did not look frequently used, we were on some sort of traders' trail to Jhaampe. Kettricken was matter-of-fact in her total command of us. She gestured Starling to a small rick of dry firewood protected from the snow by canvas. 'Use some to get a fire started, and then take care to replace at least as much as we use. Many folk stop here, and in foul weather, a life may depend on that wood being there.' Starling meekly obeyed.

She directed the Fool and I as we assisted her in setting up a shelter. When we were finished, we had a tent shaped rather like the cap of a mushroom. That done, she portioned out the tasks of unloading bedding and moving it into the tent, unloading the animals and picketing the lead animal, and melting snow for water. She herself shared fully in the tasks. I watched the efficiency with which she established our camp and saw to our needs. With a pang, I realized she reminded me of Verity. She would have made a good soldier.

Once our basic camp was established, the Fool and I exchanged glances. I went to where Kettricken was checking our jeppas. Those hardy beasts were already at work nibbling bud tips and bark from the smaller trees that fronted one side of the camp. 'I think Kettle may be following us,' I told her. 'Do you think I should go back and look for her?'

'To what end?' Kettricken asked me. The question sounded callous, but she went on, 'If she can catch up with us, then we will share what we have. You know that. But I suspect that she will weary before she gets here, and turn back to Jhaampe. Perhaps she has already turned back.'

And perhaps she has become exhausted and sunk down by the side of the trail, I thought to myself. But I did not go back. I recognized in Kettricken's words the harsh practicality of the Mountain folk. She would respect Kettle's decision to follow us. Even if her attempt to do so killed her, Kettricken would not interfere with her own will for herself. I knew that among the Mountain folk, it was not unusual for an old person to choose what they called Sequestering, a self-imposed exile where cold might put an end to all infirmities. I, too, respected Kettle's right

502

to choose her life-path, or die in the attempt. But it did not stop me from sending Nighteyes back down our trail to see if she was still coming. I chose to believe it was only curiosity on my part. He had just returned to camp with a bloody white hare in his jaws. At my request, he stood, stretched and woefully commanded me, *Guard my meat, then*. He disappeared into the gathering dusk.

The evening meal of porridge and hearth-cakes was just finished cooking when Kettle came into camp with Nighteyes at her heels. She stalked up to the fire and stood warming her hands at it as she glowered at the Fool and me. The Fool and I exchanged a glance. It was a guilty one. I hastily offered Kettle the cup of tea I had just poured for myself. She took it and drank it before she said accusingly, 'You left without me.'

'Yes,' I admitted. 'We did. Kettricken came to us and said we must leave right away, so the Fool and I –'

'I came anyway,' she announced triumphantly, cutting through my words. 'And I intend to go on with you.'

'We are fleeing,' Kettricken said quietly. 'We can't slow our pace for you.'

Sparks near leaped from Kettle's eyes. 'Did I ask you to?' she asked the Queen tartly.

Kettricken shrugged. 'Just so you understand,' she said quietly.

'I do,' Kettle replied as quietly. And it was settled.

I had watched this interchange with a sort of awe. I felt an increase in respect for both of the women afterwards. I think I fully grasped then how Kettricken perceived herself. She was the Queen of the Six Duchies and she did not doubt it. But unlike many, she had not hidden behind a title or taken offence at Kettle's quick reply to her. Instead, she had answered her, woman to woman, with respect but also authority. Once more I had glimpsed her mettle and found I could not fault it.

We all shared the yurt that night. Kettricken filled a small brazier with coals from our fire and brought it within. It made the shelter surprisingly comfortable. She posted a watch and included both Kettle and herself in that duty. The others slept well. I lay awake for a time. I was once more on my way to find Verity. That brought a tiny measure of release from the incessant Skill-command. But I was also on my way to the river where he had laved his hands in raw Skill. That seductive image lurked always at the edge of my mind now. Resolutely I pushed the temptation from my mind, but that night my dreams were full of it. We broke camp early, and were on our way before the day was fairly born. Kettricken bid us discard a second, smaller yurt that had been brought along to accommodate our original larger party. She left it carefully stowed at the stopping-place where another might find and make use of it. The freed beast was loaded instead with the bulk of the packs the humans had carried. I was grateful, for the throbbing of my back was unceasing now.

For four days Kettricken held us to that pace. She did not say if she truly expected pursuit. I did not ask. There were no real opportunities for private talk with anyone. Kettricken always led, followed by the animals, the Fool and me, Starling, and, often trailing us by quite a distance, Kettle. Both women kept their promises. Kettricken did not slow the pace for the old woman, and Kettle never complained of it. Each night she came into camp late, usually accompanied by Nighteyes. She was usually just in time to share our food and shelter for the night. But she arose the moment Kettricken did the next day and never complained.

The fourth night, when we were all within the tent and settling down to sleep, Kettricken suddenly addressed me. 'FitzChivalry, I would have your thoughts on something,' she declared.

I sat up, intrigued by the formality of her request. 'I am at your service, my queen.'

Beside me, the Fool muffled a snicker. I suppose we both looked a bit odd, sitting in a welter of blankets and furs and addressing one another so formally. But I kept my demeanour.

Kettricken added a few bits of dry wood to the brazier to bring up a flame and light. She took out an enamelled cylinder, removed the cap and coaxed out a piece of vellum. As she gently unrolled it, I recognized the map that had inspired Verity to his quest. It seemed odd to look at the faded map in this setting. It belonged to a much more secure time in my life, when hot meals of good food were taken for granted, when my clothes were tailored to fit me and I knew where I would sleep each night. It seemed unfair that my whole world had changed so much since I had last seen the map, but that it remained unchanged, an ageing flap of vellum with a worn tracery of lines on it. Kettricken held it flat on her lap and tapped a blank spot on it. 'This is about where we are,' she told me. She took a breath as if bracing herself. She tapped another spot, likewise unmarked. 'This is about where we found the signs of a battle. Where I found Verity's cloak and . . . the bones.' Her voice quavered a bit on the words. She looked up suddenly and her eyes met mine as they had not since Buck-keep. 'You know, Fitz, it is hard for me. I gathered up those bones and thought they were his. For so many months, I believed him dead. And now, solely on your word of some magic that I do not possess or understand, I try to believe he is alive. That there is hope still. But . . . I have held those bones. And my hands cannot forget the weight and chill of them, nor my nose that smell.'

'He lives, my lady,' I assured her quietly.

She sighed again. 'Here is what I would ask you. Shall we go directly to where the trails are marked on this map, the ones that Verity said he would follow? Or do you wish to be taken to the battle-site first?'

I thought for a time. 'I am sure you gathered from that place all there was to gather, my queen. Time has passed, part of a summer and more than half of a winter since you were last there. No. I can think of nothing I might find there that your trackers did not when the ground was bared of snow. Verity lives, my queen, and he is not there. So let us not seek him there, but where he said he would go.'

She nodded slowly, but if she took heart from my words, she did not show it. Instead, she tapped the map again. 'This road here shown is known to us. It was a trade road once, and although no one even recalls what its destination was, it is still used. The more remote villages and the solitary trappers have their paths to it, and they then follow it down to Jhaampe. We could have been travelling on it all this time, but I did not wish to. It is too well used. We have come by the swiftest route, if not the widest. Tomorrow, however, we shall cross it. And when we do, we shall set our backs toward Jhaampe and follow it up into the Moun-tains.' Her finger traced it on the map. 'I have never been to that part of the Mountains,' she said simply. 'Few have, other than trappers or occasional adventurers who go to see if the old tales are true. Usually they bring back tales of their own that are even stranger than the ones that prompted them to go adventuring.'

I watched her pale fingers walk slowly across the map. The faint lines of the ancient road diverged into three separate trails with different destinations. It began and ended, that road, with no apparent source or destination. Whatever had once been marked at the end of those lines had faded away into inky ghosts. Neither of us had any way of knowing which destination Verity had chosen. Though they did not look far separated on the map, the terrain of the Mountains could mean they were days or even weeks apart. I also had small trust in such an old map being reliably to scale.

'Where are we going first?' I asked her.

She hesitated briefly, then her finger tapped one of the trail ends. 'Here. I think this one would be closest.'

'Then that is a wise choice.'

She met my eyes again. 'Fitz. Could not you simply Skill to him, and ask him where he is? Or bid him come to us? Or at least ask him why he has not returned to me?'

At each small shake of my head, her eyes grew wilder. 'Why not?' she demanded in a shaking voice. 'This great and secret magic of the Farseers cannot even call him to us in such need?'

I kept my eyes on her face, but wished there had been fewer listening ears. Despite all Kettricken knew of me, I still felt very uneasy speaking of the Skill with anyone save Verity. I chose my words carefully. 'By Skilling to him, I might place him in great danger, my lady. Or draw trouble down on us.'

'How?' she demanded.

I briefly considered the Fool, Kettle and Starling. It was hard to explain to myself the uneasiness I felt at speaking bluntly of a magic that had been guarded as a secret for so many generations. But this was my queen and she had asked me a question. I lowered my eyes and spoke. 'The coterie Galen made was never loyal to the King. Not to King Shrewd, not to King Verity. Always they were the tool of a traitor, used to cast doubt on the King's abilities and undermine his ability to defend his kingdom.'

From Kettle came a small gasp of indrawn breath, while Kettricken's blue eyes went steely grey with cold. I continued. 'Even now, were I to openly Skill to Verity, they might find a way to listen. By such a Skilling, they might find him. Or us. They have grown strong in the Skill, and ferreted out ways of using it that I have never learned. They spy on other Skill-users. They can, using only the Skill, inflict pain, or create illusion. I fear to Skill to my king, Queen Kettricken. That he has not chosen to Skill to me makes me believe my caution is the same as his.'

Kettricken had gone snow pale as she mulled my words. Softly she asked, 'Always disloyal to him, Fitz? Speak plainly. Did not they aid in defending the Six Duchies at all?'

I weighed my words as if I were reporting to Verity himself. 'I have no proof, my lady. But I would guess that Skill-messages of Red Ships were sometimes never relayed, or were deliberately delayed. I think the commands that Verity Skilled forth to the coterie members in the watchtowers were not passed on to the keeps they were to guard. They obeyed him enough that Verity could not tell his messages and commands had been delivered hours after he had sent them. To his dukes, his efforts would appear inept, his strategies untimely or foolish.' My voice trailed away at the anger that blossomed in Kettricken's face. Colour came up in her cheeks, angry roses.

'How many lives?' she asked harshly. 'How many towns? How many dead, or worse, Forged? All for a prince's spite, all for a spoiled boy's ambition for the throne? How could he have done it, Fitz? How could he have stood to let people die simply to make his brother look foolish and incompetent?'

I did not have any real answer to that. 'Perhaps he did not think they were people and towns,' I heard myself say softly. 'Perhaps to him they were only game pieces. Possessions of Verity's to be destroyed if he could not win them for himself.'

Kettricken closed her eyes. 'This cannot be forgiven,' she said quietly to herself. She sounded ill with it. With an oddly gentle finality, she added, 'You will have to kill him, FitzChivalry.'

So odd, to be given that royal command at last. 'I know that, my lady. I knew it when last I tried.'

'No,' she corrected me. 'When last you attempted it, it was for yourself. Did not you know that had angered me? This time, I tell you that you must kill him for the sake of the Six Duchies.' She shook her head, almost surprised. 'It is the only way in which he can be Sacrifice for his people. To be killed for them before he can hurt them any more.'

She looked around abruptly at the circle of silent people huddled in bedding, staring at her. 'Go to sleep,' she told all of us, as if we were wilful children. 'We must get up early again tomorrow and once more travel swiftly. Sleep while you can.'

Starling went outside to take up her first night's watch. The others lay back and as the flames from the brazier fell and the light dimmed, I am sure they slept. But despite my weariness, I lay and stared into the darkness. About me were only the sounds of people breathing, of the night wind barely moving through the trees. If I quested out, I could sense Nighteyes prowling about, ever alert for the unwary mouse. The peace and stillness of the winterbound forest was all around us. They all slept deeply, save for Starling on watch.

No one else heard the rushing drive of the Skill-urge that grew stronger within me every day of our journeying. I had not spoken to the Queen of my other fear: that if I reached out to Verity with the Skill, I would never return, but would instead immerse myself in that Skill river I had glimpsed and be forever borne away on it. Even to think on that temptation brought me quivering to the edge of acquiescence. Fiercely I set my walls and boundaries, putting every guard between me and the Skill that I had ever been taught. But tonight I set them, not just to keep Regal and his coterie out of my mind, but to keep myself in it.

TWENTY-FOUR

The Skill Road

What is the true source of magic? Is one born with it in the blood, as some dogs are born to follow a scent while others are best at herding sheep? Or is it a thing that may be won by any with the determination to learn? Or rather are magics inherent to the stones and waters and earths of the world, so that a child imbibes abilities with the water he drinks or the air he breathes? I ask these questions with no concept of how to discover the answers. Did we know the source, could a wizard of great power be deliberately created by one desiring to do so? Could one breed for magic in a child as one breeds a horse for strength or speed? Or select a babe, and begin instruction before the child could even speak? Or build one's house where one might tap the magic where the earth is richest with it? These questions so frighten me that I have almost no desire to pursue the answers, save that if I do not, another may.

It was early afternoon when we came to the wide trail marked on the map. Our narrow path merged into it as a stream joins a river. For some days we were to follow it. Sometimes it led us past small villages tucked into sheltered folds of the Mountains, but Kettricken hastened us past them without stopping. We passed other travellers on the road, and these she greeted courteously, but firmly turned aside all efforts at conversation. If any recognized her as Eyod's daughter, they gave no sign of it. There came a day, however, when we passed the entire day without so much as a glimpse of another traveller, let alone a village or hut. The trail grew narrower, and the only tracks upon it were old ones, blurred by fresh snow. When we rose the next day and set forth upon it, it soon dwindled to no more than a vague track through the trees.

Several times Kettricken paused and cast about, and once she made us backtrack and then go on in a new direction. Whatever signs she was following were too subtle for me.

That night, when we camped, she again took out her map and studied it. I sensed her uncertainty, and came to sit beside her. I asked no questions and offered no advice, only gazing with her at the map's worn markings. Finally she glanced up at me.

'I think we are here,' she said. Her finger showed me the end of the trade trail we had followed. 'Somewhere north of us, we should find this other road. I had hoped there would be some ancient connecting trail between the two. It was an idea that made sense to me, that this old road would perhaps connect to one even more forgotten. But now . . .' she sighed. 'Tomorrow, I suppose we blunder on and hope for luck to aid us.'

Her words did not put heart into any of us.

Nevertheless, the next day we moved on. We moved steadily north, through forest that seemed to have been forever untouched by an axe. Branches laced and intertwined high above us, while generations of leaves and needles lay deep beneath the uneven blanketing of snow that had filtered down to the forest floor. To my Wit-sense, these trees had a ghostly life that was almost animal, as if they had acquired some awareness simply by virtue of their age. But it was an awareness of the greater world of light and moisture, soil and air. They regarded our passage not at all, and by afternoon I felt no more significant than an ant. I had never thought to be disdained by a tree.

As we travelled on, hour after hour, I am sure I was not the only one to wonder if we had lost our way completely. A forest this old could have swallowed a road a generation ago. Roots would have lifted its cobbles, leaves and needles blanketed it. What we sought might no longer exist except as a line on an old map.

It was the wolf, ranging well ahead of us as always, who found it first.

I like this not at all, he announced.

'The road is that way,' I called to Kettricken ahead of me. My puny human voice seemed like a fly's buzzing in a great hall. I was almost surprised when she heard me and looked back. She took in my pointing hand, then, with a shrug, led her pack sheep in a more westerly direction. We still walked for some time before I saw an arrow-straight break in the clustering trees ahead of us. A stripe of light penetrated the forest there.

What is wrong with it?

The wolf shook himself all over as if to rid his coat of water. *It is too much of man. Like a fire to cook meat over.*

I do not understand.

He lay back his ears. *Like a great force made small and bent to a man's will. Always fire seeks a way to escape containment. So does this road.*

His answer made no sense to me. Then we came to the road. Kettricken led her pack sheep down onto it. I hesitated. The wide road was a straight cut through the trees, its surface lower than that of the forest floor, as when a child drags a stick through sand and leaves a trough behind. The forest trees grew alongside it and leaned over it, but none of them had sent roots thrusting out into the road, nor had any saplings sprouted up from it. Neither had the snow that covered the road's surface been marred, not even by a bird's track. There were not even the muted signs of old tracks covered with snow. No one had trodden this road since the winter snows had begun. As far as I could see, no game trails even crossed it.

I stepped down onto the road's surface.

It was like walking into trailing cobwebs face first. A piece of ice down the back. Stepping into a hot kitchen after being out in an icy wind. It was a physical sensation that seized me, as sharply as any of those others, and yet as indescribable as wet or dry is. I halted, transfixed. Yet none of the others showed any awareness of it as they hopped down from the lip of the forest onto the road surface. Starling's only comment, to herself, was that at least here the snow was shallower and the walking better. She did not even ask herself why the snow should be shallower on the road, but only hurried after the trailing line of jeppas. I was still standing on the road, looking about me, some minutes later when Kettle stepped out of the trees and onto the road's surface. She, too, halted. For an instant, she seemed startled and muttered something.

'Did you say Skill-wrought?' I demanded of her.

Her eyes jumped to me as if she had been unaware of me standing right there before her. She glared. For a moment she didn't speak. Then, 'I said "Hell-rot!"' she declared. 'Near twisted my ankle jumping down. These mountain boots are no stiffer than socks.' She turned away from me and trudged off after the others. I followed her. For some reason, I felt as if I were wading in water, save without the resistance of water. It is a difficult sensation to describe. As if something flowed uphill around me and hurried me along with its current.

It seeks a way to escape containment, the wolf observed again sourly. I glanced up to find him trotting along beside me, but on the lip of the forest rather than on the smooth road surface. *You'd be wiser to travel up here, with me.*

I thought about it. *I seem to be all right. Walking is easier here. Smoother.*

Yes, and fire makes you warmer, right up until the time it burns you.

I had no reply to that. Instead I walked alongside Kettle for a way. After days of travelling single file on the narrow trail, this seemed easier and more companionable. We walked all the rest of the afternoon on the ancient road. It climbed ever upward, but always angling across the faces of the hills, so that the going was never too steep. The only things that ever marred the smooth coat of snow on its surface were occasional dead branches dropped from trees above, and most of these were decaying into sawdust. Not once did I see any animal tracks, either on the road or crossing it.

Not even a sniff of any game, Nighteyes confirmed woefully. *I shall have to range this night to find fresh meat for myself.*

You could go now, I suggested.

I trust you not alone upon this road, he informed me sternly.

What could harm me? Kettle is right here beside me, so I would not be alone.

She is as bad as you are, Nighteyes insisted stubbornly. But despite my questions, he could not explain to me what he meant.

Yet as afternoon deepened into evening, I began to have notions of my own. Time and again, I caught my mind drifting in vivid daydreams, musings so engrossing that coming out of them was like waking with a start. And like many a dream, they popped like bubbles, leaving me with almost no recall of what I had been thinking. Patience giving military commands as if she were Queen of the Six Duchies. Burrich bathing a baby and humming as he did so. Two people I did not know, setting charred stones upon one another as they rebuilt a house. Foolish, bright-coloured images they seemed, but edged so vividly that almost I believed my own musings. The easy walking on the road that had seemed so pleasant at first began to seem an involuntary hurrying, as if a current urged me on independent of my own will. Yet I could not have been hurrying much, for Kettle kept pace with me all the afternoon. Kettle broke in often on my thoughts, to ask me trivial questions, to draw my attention to a bird overhead, or to ask if my back was bothering me. I endeavoured to answer, but moments later I could not recall what we had been talking about. I could not blame her for frowning at me, so muddle-witted was I, but neither could I seem to find a remedy for my absent mind. We passed a fallen log across the road. I thought something odd about it, and intended to mention it to Kettle but the thought fled before I could master it. So caught up was I in nothing at all, that when the Fool hailed me, I startled. I peered ahead, but could not even see the jeppas any more. Then, 'FitzChivalry!' he shouted again, and I turned around, to find I had walked past not only him, but our whole expedition. Kettle at my side muttered to herself as she turned back.

The others had halted and were already unloading the jeppas. 'Surely you don't mean to pitch the tent in the centre of the road?' Kettle asked in alarm.

Starling and the Fool looked up from where they were stretch-ing out the goat leather shape of the yurt. 'Fear ye the hurrying throngs and carts?' the Fool asked sarcastically.

'It's flat and level. Last night, I had a root or a rock under my bedding,' Starling added.

Kettle ignored them and spoke to Kettricken. 'And we'd be in full view for anyone who stepped onto this road for quite a way in both directions. I think we should move off and camp under the trees.'

Kettricken glanced about. 'It's nearly dark, Kettle. And I do not think we have a great deal to fear from pursuit. I think . . .'

I flinched when the Fool took my arm and walked me to the edge of the road. 'Climb up,' he told me gruffly when we got to the edge of the forest. I did, scrambling up to stand once more on forest moss. Once I was there, I yawned, feeling my ears pop. Almost right away, I felt more alert. I glanced back to the road where Starling and Kettricken were gathering up the yurt hides to move them. Kettle was already dragging the poles off the road. 'So, we've decided to camp off the road,' I observed stupidly.

'Are you all right?' the Fool asked me anxiously.

'Of course. My back is no worse than usual,' I added, thinking he referred to that.

'You were standing there, staring off up the road, paying no heed to anyone. Kettle says you've been like that most of the afternoon.'

'I've been a bit muddled,' I admitted. I dragged off my mitten to touch my own face. 'I don't think I'm getting a fever. But it was like that . . . bright-edged fever thoughts.'

'Kettle says she thinks it's the road. She said that you said it was Skill-wrought.'

'She said I said? No. I thought that was what she said when we came onto it. That it was Skill-wrought.'

'What is "Skill-wrought"?' the Fool asked me.

'Shaped by the Skill,' I replied, then added, 'I suppose. I've never heard of the Skill used to make or shape something.' I looked wondering back at the road. It flowed so smoothly through the forest, a pure white ribbon, vanishing off under the trees. It drew the eye, and almost I could see what lay beyond the next fold of the forested hillside.

'Fitz!'

I jerked my attention back to the Fool in annoyance. 'What?' I demanded.

He was shivering. 'You've just been standing there, staring off down the road since I left you. I thought you'd gone to get firewood, until I looked up and saw you standing here still. What is the matter?'

I blinked my eyes slowly. I had been walking in a city, looking at the bright yellow and red fruit heaped high in the market stalls. But even as I groped after that dream, it was gone, leaving only a confusion of colour and scent in my mind. 'I don't know. Perhaps I am feverish. Or just very weary. I'll go get the wood.'

'I'm going with you,' the Fool announced.

By my knee, Nighteyes whined anxiously. I looked down at him. 'What's the matter?' I asked him aloud.

He looked up at me, the fur between his eyes ridged with worry. *You do not seem to hear me. And your thoughts are not . . . thoughts.*

I'll be all right. The Fool is with me. Go and hunt. I can feel your hunger.

And I feel yours, he answered ominously.

He left then, but reluctantly. I followed the Fool into the woods, but did little more than carry the wood he picked up and handed to me. I felt as if I could not quite wake up. 'Have you ever been studying something tremendously interesting, only to suddenly look up and realize hours have passed? That is how I feel just now.'

The Fool handed me another stick of wood. 'You are frightening me,' he informed me quietly. 'You speak much as King Shrewd did in the days he was weakening.'

'But he was drugged then, against pain,' I pointed out. 'And I am not.'

'That is what is frightening,' he told me.

We walked together back to camp. We had been so slow that Kettle and Starling had gathered some fuel and got a small fire going already. The light of it illuminated the dome-shaped tent and the folk moving around it. The jeppas were shadows drifting nearby as they browsed. As we piled our wood by the fire for later use, Kettle looked up from her cooking.

'How are you feeling?' she demanded.

'Better, somewhat,' I told her.

I glanced about for any chores that needed doing, but camp had been set without me. Kettricken was inside the tent, poring over the map by candlelight. Kettle stirred porridge by the fire while, strange to say, the Fool and Starling conversed quietly. I stood still, trying to recall something I'd meant to do, something

I'd been in the middle of doing. The road. I wanted another look at the road. I turned and walked toward it.

'FitzChivalry!'

I turned, startled at the sharpness in Kettle's call. 'What is it?'

'Where are you going?' she asked. She paused, as if surprised by her own question. 'I mean, is Nighteyes about? I haven't seen him for a bit.'

'He went to hunt. He'll be back.' I started toward the road again.

'Usually he's made his kill and come back by now,' she continued.

I paused. 'There's not much game near the road, he said. So he's had to go further.' I turned away again.

'Now there's a thing that seems odd,' she went on. 'There's no sign of human traffic on the road. And yet the animals avoid it still. Doesn't game usually follow whatever path is easiest?'

I called back to her, 'Some animals do. Others prefer to keep to cover.'

'Go and get him, girl!' I heard Kettle tell someone sharply.

'Fitz!' I heard Starling call, but it was the Fool who caught up with me and took me by the arm.

'Come back to the tent,' he urged me, tugging at my arm.

'I just want to have another look at the road.'

'It's dark. You'll see nothing now. Wait until morning, when we're travelling on it again. For now, come back to the tent.'

I went with him, but told him irritably, 'You're the one who is acting strange, Fool.'

'You'd not say that, had you seen the look on your face but a moment ago.'

The rations that night were much the same as they had been since we left Jhaampe: thick grain porridge with some chopped dried apple in it, some dried meat, and tea. It was filling, but not exciting. It did nothing to distract me from the intent way the others watched me. I finally set down my tea mug and demanded, 'What?'

No one said anything at first. Then Kettricken said, bluntly, 'Fitz, you don't have a watch tonight. I want you to stay in the tent and sleep.'

'I'm fine, I can stand a watch,' I began to object, but it was my queen who ordered, 'I tell you to stay within the tent tonight.'

For a moment I fought my tongue. Then I bowed my head. 'As you command. I am, perhaps, overly tired.'

'No. It is more than that, FitzChivalry. You scarcely ate tonight, and unless one of us forces you to speak you do nothing save gaze off into the distance. What distracts you?'

I tried to find an answer to Kettricken's blunt question. 'I do not know. Exactly. At least, it is a difficult thing to explain.' The only sound was the tiny crackling of the fire. All eyes were on me. 'When one is trained to Skill,' I went on more slowly, 'one becomes aware that the magic itself has a danger to it. It attracts the attention of the user. When one is using the Skill to do a thing, one must focus one's attention tightly on the intent and refuse to be distracted by the pulling of the Skill. If the Skill-user loses that focus, if he gives in to the Skill itself, he can become lost in it. Absorbed by it.' I lifted my eyes from the fire and looked around at their faces. Everyone was still save for Kettle, who was nodding ever so slightly.

'Today, since we found the road, I have felt something that is almost like the pull of the Skill. I have not attempted to Skill; actually, for some days, I have blocked the Skill from myself as much as I can, for I have feared that Regal's coterie may try to break into my mind and do me harm. But despite that, I have felt as if the Skill were luring me. Like a music I can almost hear, or a very faint scent of game. I catch myself straining after it, trying to decide what calls me . . .'

I snapped my gaze back to Kettle, saw the distant hunger in her eyes. 'Is it because the road is Skill-wrought?'

A flash of anger crossed her face. She looked down to her old hands curled in her lap. She gave a sigh of exasperation. 'It might. The old legends that I have heard say that when a thing is Skill-wrought, it can be dangerous to some folk. Not to ordinary people, but to those who have an aptitude for the Skill but have not been trained in it. Or to those whose training is not advanced far enough for them to know how to be wary.'

'I have never heard of any legends about Skill-wrought things.' I turned to the Fool and Starling. 'Have either of you?'

Both shook their heads slowly.

'It seems to me,' I said carefully to Kettle, 'that someone as well-read as the Fool should have come across such legends. And certainly a trained minstrel should have heard something about them.' I continued to look at her levelly.

She crossed her arms on her chest. 'I am not to blame for what they have not read or heard,' she said stiffly. 'I only tell you what I was told, a long time ago.'

'How long ago?' I pressed. Across from me, Kettricken frowned, but did not interfere.

'A very long time ago,' Kettle replied coldly. 'Back when young men respected their elders.'

The Fool's face lit with a delighted grin. Kettle seemed to feel she had won something, for she set her tea mug in her porridge bowl with a clatter and handed them to me. 'It is your turn to clean the dishes,' she told me severely. She got up and stamped away from the fire and into the tent.

As I slowly gathered the dishes to wipe them out with clean snow, Kettricken came to stand beside me. 'What do you suspect?' she asked me in her forthright way. 'Do you think she is a spy, an enemy among us?'

'No. I do not think she is an enemy. But I think she is . . . something. Not just an old woman with a religious interest in the Fool. Something more than that.'

'But you don't know what?'

'No. I don't. Only I have noticed that she seems to know a deal more about the Skill than I expect her to. Still, an old person gathers much odd knowledge in a lifetime. It may be no more than that.' I glanced up to where the wind was stirring the treetops. 'Do you think we shall have snow tonight?' I asked Kettricken.

'Almost certainly. And we shall be fortunate if it stops by morning. We should gather more firewood, and stack it near the tent's door. No, not you. You should go within the tent. If you wandered off now, in this darkness and with snow to come, we'd never find you.'

I began to protest, but she stopped me with a question. 'My Verity. He is more highly trained than you are in the Skill?'

'Yes, my lady.'

'Do you think this road would call to him, as it does to you?'

'Almost certainly. But he has always been far stronger than I in matters of Skill or stubbornness.'

A sad smile tweaked her lips. 'Yes, he is stubborn, that one.' She sighed suddenly, heavily. 'Would that we were only a man and a woman, living far from both sea and mountains. Would that things were simple for us.'

'I wish for that as well,' I said quietly. 'I wish for blisters on my hands from simple work and Molly's candles lighting our home.'

'I hope you get that, Fitz,' Kettricken said quietly. 'I truly do. But we've a long road to tread between here and there.'

'That we do,' I agreed. And a sort of peace bloomed between us. I did not doubt that if circumstances demanded it, she would take my daughter for the throne. But she could no more have changed her attitude about duty and sacrifice than she could have changed the blood and bones of her body. It was who she was. It was not that she wished to take my child from me.

All I needed do to keep my daughter was to bring her husband safely back to her.

We went to bed later that night than had become our custom. All were wearier than usual. The Fool took first watch despite the lines of strain in his face. The new ivory cast his skin had taken on made him look terrible when he was cold, like a statue of misery carved from old bone. The rest of us did not notice the cold much when we were moving during the day, but I don't think the Fool was ever completely warm. Yet he bundled himself warmly and went to stand outside in the rising wind without a murmur of complaint. The rest of us lay down to sleep.

The storm was, at first, a thing that was happening above us, in the treetops. Loose needles fell rattling against the yurt's skin and as the storm grew more intense, small branches and occasional dumps of icy snow. The cold grew stronger and became a thing that crept in at every gap of blanket or garment. Midway through Starling's watch, Kettricken called her in, saying the storm would stand watch for us now. When Starling entered, the wolf slunk in at her heels. To my relief, no one objected very loudly. When Starling commented that he carried snow in with him, the Fool replied that he had less on him than she did. Nighteyes came immediately to our part of the tent, and lay down between the Fool and the outer wall. He set his great head on the Fool's chest and heaved a sigh before closing his eyes. I almost felt jealous.

He's colder than you are. Much colder. And, in the city, where hunting was so poor, he often shared food with me.

So. He is pack, then? I asked with a trace of amusement.

You tell me, Nighteyes challenged me. *He saved your life, fed you from his kills and shared his den with you. Is he pack with us or not?*

I suppose he is, I said after a moment's consideration. I had never seen things in quite that light before. Unobtrusively, I shifted in my bedding to be slightly closer to the Fool. 'Are you cold?' I asked him aloud.

'Not so long as I keep shivering,' he told me miserably. Then he added, 'Actually, I'm warmer with the wolf between me and the wall. He gives off a lot of heat.'

'He's grateful for all the times you fed him in Jhaampe.'

The Fool squinted at me through the tent's dimness. 'Really? I did not think animals carried memories for that long.'

That startled me into thinking about it. 'Usually, they don't. But tonight, he recalls that you fed him and is grateful.'

The Fool lifted a hand to scratch carefully around Nighteyes' ears. Nighteyes made a puppy growl of pleasure and happily snuggled closer. I wondered again at all the changes I was seeing in him. More and more often, his reactions and thoughts were a mixture of human and wolf.

I was too tired to give it much thought. I closed my eyes and started to sink into sleep. After a time, I realized that my eyes were tightly shut, my jaw clenched, and I was no closer to sleep. I wanted to simply let go of consciousness, so weary was I, but the Skill so threatened and lured me that I could not relax enough to sleep. I kept shifting, trying to find a physical position that was more relaxing, until Kettle on the other side of me pointedly asked me if I had fleas. I tried to be still.

I stared up into the darkness of the tent's ceiling, listening to the blowing wind outside and the quiet breathing of my companions inside. I closed my eyes and relaxed my muscles, trying to at least rest my body. I wanted so desperately to fall asleep. But Skill-dreams tugged at me like tiny barbed hooks in my mind until I thought I should scream. Most were horrible. Some sort of Forging ceremony in a coastal village, a huge fire burning in a pit, and captives dragged forward by jeering Outislanders and offered the choice of being Forged or flinging themselves into the pit. Children were watching. I jerked my mind back from the flames.

I caught my breath and calmed my eyes. Sleep. In a night chamber in Buckkeep Castle, Lacey was carefully removing lace from an old wedding gown. Her mouth was pinched shut with disapproval as she picked out the tiny threads that secured the ornate work. 'It will bring a good price,' Patience said to her. 'Perhaps enough to supply our watchtowers for another month. He would understand what we must do for Buck.' She held her head very upright, and there was more grey in the black of her hair than I recalled as her fingers unfastened the strings of tiny pearls that glistened in scalloping at the neckline of the gown. Time had aged the white of the gown to ivory, and the luxuriant breadth of the skirts cascaded over their laps. Patience cocked her head suddenly as if listening, a puzzled frown on her face. I fled.

I used all my will to pry my eyes open. The fire in the small brazier burned small, shedding a reddish light. I studied the poles that supported the taut hides. I willed my breath to calmness. I dared not think of anything that might lure me out of my own life, not Molly, not Burrich, not Verity. I tried to find some neutral image to rest my mind upon, something with no special connotations to my life. I called up a bland landscape. A smooth blank plain of land cloaked in white snow, a peaceful night sky over it. Blessed stillness . . . I sank into it as into a soft featherbed.

A rider comes, swiftly, leaning low, clinging to his horse's neck, urging him on. There is a simple safe beauty to the duo, the running horse, the man's streaming cloak echoed by the horse's flowing tail. For a time, there is no more than this, the dark horse and rider cleaving the snowy plain under an open moonlit night. The horse runs well, an effortless stretching and gathering of muscles and the man sits him lightly, almost appearing to ride above him rather than on his back. The moon glints silver off the man's brow, glistening upon the rampant buck badge that he wears. Chade.

Three riders and horses appear. Two come from behind, but those horses are running wearily, heavily. The lone rider will outdistance them if the chase goes much longer. The third pursuer cuts the plain at an angle to the others. The piebald horse runs with a will, unmindful of the deeper snow he churns through in pursuit. His small rider sits him high and well, a woman or a young man. The moonlight dances lightly along a drawn blade. For a time it looks as if the young rider will intersect with Chade's path of flight, but the old assassin has seen him. He speaks to his horse, and the gelding puts on a burst of speed, incredible to see. He leaves the two lumbering pursuers far behind, but the piebald reaches the packed trail now and his legs stretch long as he endeavours to catch up. For a time, it looks as if Chade will escape cleanly, but the piebald horse is fresher. The gelding cannot maintain his burst of speed, and the even pace of the piebald slowly eats into his lead. The gap closes gradually but relentlessly. Then the piebald is running right behind the black gelding. The gelding slows and Chade turns in the saddle and lifts an arm in greeting. The other rider shouts to him, her voice thin in the cold air. 'For Verity the true King!' She tosses a bag to him, and he throws a packet to her. Abruptly they separate, the two horses both veering from the trodden path to go wide of one another. The hoofbeats dwindle in the night.

The labouring mounts of the pursuers are lathered and wet, steaming in the cold air. Their riders pull them up, cursing, when they reach the place where Chade and his cohort separated. Snatches of conversation mixed with curses float on the air. 'Damned Farseer partisans!' and 'No way to tell which one has it now!' and finally, 'Not going back to face a lash over this mess.' They seem to have reached an agreement, for they let their horses breathe, and then proceed more slowly, following the trodden path away from wherever they have come.

I found myself briefly. Strange to discover I was smiling even though sweat misted my face. The Skilling was strong and true. I was breathing deep with the strain of it. I tried to draw back from it, but the sweet rush of knowing was too keen. I was elated at Chade's escape, elated to know that there were partisans who worked on Verity's behalf. The world stretched out wide before me, tempting as a tray of sweet cakes. My heart chose instantly.

A baby is wailing, in that endless, hopeless way that infants have. My daughter. She is lying on a bed, still wrapped in a blanket that is beaded with rain. Her face is red with the earnestness of her screaming. The pent frustration in Molly's voice is frightening as she says, 'Be quiet. Can't you just be quiet!'

Burrich's voice, stern and weary. 'Don't be cross at her. She's only a babe. She's probably just hungry.'

Molly stands, lips pinched tight, arms folded tightly across her chest. Her cheeks are red, her hair has gone to wet strands. Burrich is hanging up his dripping cloak. They have all been somewhere, together, and just returned. The ashes are dead in the fireplace, the cottage cold. Burrich goes to the hearth and awkwardly kneels by it, favouring his knee, and begins to select kindling to build a fire. I can feel the tension in him, and I know how he strives to contain his temper. 'Take care of the baby,' he suggests quietly. 'I'll get the fire going and put some water to boil.'

Molly takes off her cloak and moves deliberately to hang it by his. I know how she hates to be told what to do. The baby continues wailing, as remorseless a demand as the winter wind outside. 'I am cold, and tired, and hungry, and wet. She's going to have to learn that sometimes she just has to wait.'

Burrich leans down to blow on a spark, curses softly when it does not catch. 'She is cold and hungry and tired and wet, too,' he points out. His voice is getting crisper. He continues doggedly with his fire-making. 'And she is too small to do anything about it. So she cries. Not to torment you, but to tell you she needs help. It's like a puppy yelping, woman, or a chick cheeping. She doesn't do it to annoy.' His voice is rising on every sentence.

'Well, it annoys me!' Molly declares, and turns to the fight. 'She will just have to cry it out. I'm too tired to deal with her. And she's getting spoiled. All she does is cry to be held. I never have a moment to myself any longer. I can't even sleep a night through. Feed the baby, wash the baby, change the baby, hold the baby. That's all my life is any more.' She lists off her grievances aggressively. That glint is in her eye, the same one I'd seen when she defied her father, and I know she expects Burrich to stand and advance on her. Instead, he blows on a tiny glow and grunts in satisfaction when a narrow tongue of flame licks up and kindles a curl of birch bark. He doesn't even turn to look at Molly or the wailing child. Twig after twig he sets on the tiny fire, and I marvel that he cannot be aware of Molly seething behind him. I would not be so composed were she behind me and wearing that expression.

Only when the fire is well established does he rise, and then he turns, not to Molly but to the child. He walks past Molly as if she is not there. I do not know if he sees how she steels herself not to flinch from the sudden blow she half-expects from him. It wrings my heart to see this scar her father has left on her. Burrich leans over the baby, speaking in his calming voice as he unwraps her. I watch in a sort of awe as he competently changes her napkin. He glances about, then takes up a wool shirt of his that is hanging on a chair back and wraps her in it. She continues to wail, but on a different note. He props her against his shoulder and uses his free hand to fill the kettle and set it on the fire. It is as if Molly is not there at all. Her face has gone white and her eyes are huge as he begins to measure out grain. When he finds the water is not yet boiling, he sits down with the baby and pats her back rhythmically. The wailing becomes less determined, as if the baby is wearying of crying.

Molly stalks over to them. 'Give me the baby. I'll nurse her now.'

Burrich slowly turns his eyes up to her. His face is impassive. 'When you're calm, and want to hold her, I'll give her to you.'

'You'll give her to me now! She's my child!' Molly snaps and reaches for her. Burrich stops her with a look. She steps back. 'Are you trying to make me ashamed?' she demands. Her voice is going shrill. 'She's my child. I have a right to raise her as I see fit. She doesn't need to be held all the time.'

'That's true,' he agrees blandly, but makes no move to give her the child.

'You think I'm a bad mother. But what do you know about children, to say I'm wrong?'

Burrich gets up, staggers a half step on his bad leg, and regains his balance. He takes up the measure of grain. He sprinkles it over the boiling water, then stirs it to wet it evenly. Then he puts a tight lid on the pot and pulls it slightly back from the fire's reach. All this while balancing the babe in the crook of one arm. I can tell he has been thinking when he answers, 'Not babies, perhaps. But I know about young things. Colts, puppies, calves, piglets. Even hunting cats. I know if you want them to trust you, you touch them often when they are small. Gently, but firmly, so they believe in your strength, too.'

He was warming to his subject. I'd heard this lecture a hundred times before, usually delivered to impatient stable-boys. 'You don't shout at them, or make sudden moves that look threatening. You give them good feed and clean water, and keep them clean and give them shelter from the weather.' His voice drops accusingly as he adds, 'You don't take out your temper on them, or confuse punishment with discipline.'

Molly looks shocked at his words. 'Discipline comes from punishment. A child learns discipline when she is punished for doing something wrong.'

Burrich is shaking his head. 'I'd like to "punish" the man that beat that into you,' he says, and an edge of his old temper creeps into his voice. 'What did you really learn from your father taking his temper out on you?' he demands. 'That to show tenderness to your baby is a weakness? That to give in and hold your child when she cries because she wants you is somehow not an adult thing to do?'

'I don't want to talk about my father,' Molly declares suddenly, but there is uncertainty in her voice. She reaches for the baby like a child clutching at a favourite toy and Burrich lets her take the infant. Molly sits on the hearthstones and opens her blouse. The baby seeks her breast greedily and is instantly silent. For a time the only sounds are the wind muttering outside, the bubbling of the porridge pot and the small stick noises of Burrich feeding the fire. 'You did not always keep your patience with Fitz when he was little,' Molly mutters chidingly.

Burrich gives a brief snort of laughter. 'I don't think anyone would have been eternally patient with that one. When I got

525

him, he was five or six, and I knew nothing of him. And I was a young man, with many other interests. You can put a colt in a corral, or tie a dog up for a time. Not so with a child. You can never forget you have a child for even an instant.' He shrugs his shoulders helplessly. 'Before I knew it, he'd become the centre of my life.' An odd little pause. 'Then they took him from me, and I let them . . . And now he's dead.'

A silence. I wanted desperately to reach to them both, then, to tell them that I lived. But I could not. I could hear them, I could see them, but I could not reach them. Like the wind outside the house, I roared and pounded at the walls, to no avail.

'What am I going to do? What will become of us?' Molly asks abruptly of no one. The despair in her voice is rending. 'Here I am. No husband, and a child, and no way to make my own way in the world. Everything I saved is gone.' She looks at Burrich. 'I was so stupid. I always believed he would come to find me, that he would marry me. But he never did. And now he never will.' She begins to rock as she clutches the baby to her. Tears spill unheeded down her cheeks. 'Don't think I didn't hear that old man today, the one that said he'd seen me in Buckkeep Town and I was the Wit-Bastard's whore. How long before that tale races through Capelin Beach? I daren't go to town any more, I can't hold up my head.'

Something goes out of Burrich at her words. He slumps, elbow on knee, head in his hand. He mutters, 'I thought you had not heard him. Had he not been half as old as god, I'd have made him answer for his words.'

'You can't challenge a man for speaking the truth,' Molly says dispiritedly.

That brings Burrich's head up. 'You're not a whore!' he declares hotly. 'You were Fitz's wife. It's not your fault if not all were privy to it.'

'His wife,' Molly says mockingly to herself. 'I was not, Burrich. He never married me.'

'Such was how he spoke of you to me. I promise you, I know this. Had he not died, he would have come to you. He would. He always intended to make you his wife.'

'Oh, yes, he had many intentions. And he spoke many lies.

Intentions are not deeds, Burrich. If every woman who had heard a man promise marriage were a wife, well, there'd be a spate less of bastards in the world.' She straightens up and wipes the tears from her face with a weary finality. Burrich makes no answer to her words. She looks down into the little face that is finally at peace. The babe has gone to sleep. She slips her little finger into the child's mouth to free her nipple from the babe's sleepy grip on it. As Molly does up her blouse, she smiles weakly. 'I think I feel a tooth coming through. Maybe she's just colicky from teething.'

'A tooth? Let me see!' Burrich exclaims and comes to bend over the baby as Molly carefully pushes down her pink lower lip to reveal a tiny half-moon of white showing in her gum. My daughter pulls away from the touch, frowning in her sleep. Burrich takes her gently from Molly and carries her over to the bed. He settles her into it, still wrapped in his shirt. By the fire, Molly takes the lid off the kettle and gives the porridge a stir.

'I'll take care of you both,' Burrich offers awkwardly. He is looking down at the child as he speaks. 'I'm not so old I can't get work, you know. As long as I can swing an axe, we can trade or sell firewood in town. We'll get by.'

'You're not old at all,' Molly says absently as she sprinkles a bit of salt into the porridge. She goes to her chair and drops into it. From a basket by her chair, she takes up a piece of mending and turns it about in her hands, deciding where to begin. 'You seem to wake up new each day. Look at this shirt. Torn out at the shoulder seam as if a growing boy did it. I think you get younger each day. But I feel as if I get older with every passing hour. And I can't live on your kindness forever, Burrich. I've got to get on with my life. Somehow I just can't think how to begin, just now.'

'Then don't worry about it, just now,' he says comfortingly. He comes to stand behind her chair. His hands lift as if he will put them on her shoulders. Instead he crosses his arms on his chest. 'Soon it will be spring. We'll put in a garden and the fish runs will begin again. There may be some hiring work down in Capelin Beach. You'll see, we'll get by.'

His optimism reaches something in her. 'I should start now

and make some straw hives. With great good luck, I might chance on a swarming of bees.'

'I know a flowering field up in the hills where the bees work thick in summer. If we set out hives there, would the bees move in to them?'

Molly smiles to herself. 'They are not like birds, silly. They only swarm when the old hive has too many bees. We might get a swarm that way, but not until high summer or autumn. No. Come spring, when the bees first stir, we'll try to find a bee tree. I used to help my father hunt bees when I was smaller, before I grew wise enough to winter a hive over. You put out a dish of warmed honey to draw them. First one, and then another will come. If you are good at it, and I am, you can find the bee line and follow it back to the bee tree. That is only the start, of course. Then you have to force the swarm out of the tree and into the hive you've made ready. Sometimes, if the bee tree is small, you can simply cut it down and take the bee gum home with you.'

'Bee gum?'

'The part of the tree they nest in.'

'Don't they sting you?' Burrich asks incredulously.

'Not if you do it right,' she tells him calmly.

'You'll have to teach me how,' he says humbly.

Molly twists in her seat to look up at him. She smiles, but it is not like her old smile. It is a smile that acknowledges that they are pretending it will all go as they plan. She knows too well now that no hope can be completely trusted. 'If you'll teach me to write my letters. Lacey and Patience started, and I can read a bit, but the writing comes harder to me.'

'I'll teach you and then you can teach Nettle,' he promises her.

Nettle. She has named my daughter Nettle, after the herb she loves, though it leaves great rashes on her hands and arms if she is careless when she gathers it. Is that how she feels about our daughter, that she brings pain even as she brings enjoyment? It pains me to think it is so. Something tugs at my attention, but I cling fiercely where I am. If this is as close as I can come to Molly right now, then I will take what I can and cling to it.

No. Verity speaks firmly. *Come away now. You put them in danger. Do you think they would scruple to destroy them, if they thought by doing so they could hurt and weaken you?*

Abruptly I am with Verity. He is somewhere cold and windy and dark. I try to see more of what is around us, but he blocks my eyes. So effortlessly he has brought me here against my will, so effortlessly he closes off my vision. The strength of Skill on him is frightening. Yet I can sense he is tired, weary almost to death despite this vast power. The Skill is like a strong stallion and Verity is the fraying rope that tethers it. It pulls at him every minute and every minute he resists it.

We are coming to you, I tell him needlessly.

I know. Hurry. And do this no more, think of them no more, and give no thought at all to the names of those who would do us harm. Every whisper here is a shout. They have powers you do not imagine, in strengths you cannot defy. Where you go, your enemies may follow. So leave no trail.

But where are you? I demand as he thrusts me away from him.

Find me! he commands me, and slams me back into my own body and life.

I sat up in my blankets, convulsively gasping for air. It reminded me of wrestling and being slammed down on the flat of my back. For a moment I made tiny sounds as I sought to fill my lungs. Finally I drew a full breath. I looked about me in the darkness. Outside the tent, the windstorm howled. The brazier was a small red glow in the centre that illuminated little more than Kettle's huddled form sleeping close to it.

'Are you all right?' the Fool asked me quietly.

'No,' I said softly. I lay back down beside him. I was suddenly too tired to think, too tired to say another word. The sweat on my body chilled and I began to shiver. The Fool surprised me by putting an arm around me. I moved closer to him gratefully, sharing warmth. The sympathy of my wolf wrapped me. I waited for the Fool to say something comforting. He was too wise to try. I fell asleep longing for words that did not exist.

TWENTY-FIVE

Strategy

Six Wisemen came to Jhaampe-town
Climbed a hill, and never came down
Found their flesh and lost their skins
   Flew away on stony wings.

Five Wisemen came to Jhaampe-town
   Walked a road not up nor down
Were torn to many and turned to one
   In the end, left a task half-done.

Four Wisemen came to Jhaampe-town
   They spoke in words without a sound
   They begged their Queen to let them go
And what became of them, no one can know.

Three Wisemen came to Jhaampe-town
They'd helped a king to keep his crown.
   But when they tried to climb the hill
   Down they came in a terrible spill.

Two Wisemen came to Jhaampe-town
   Gentle women there they found.
Forgot their quest and lived in love
Perhaps were wiser than ones above.

One Wiseman came to Jhaampe-town.
   He set aside both queen and crown
   Did his task and fell asleep
Gave his bones to the stones to keep.

No wise men go to Jhaampe-town
To climb the hill and never come down.
'Tis wiser far and much more brave
To stay at home and face the grave.

'Fitz? Are you awake?' The Fool was bending over me, his face very close to mine. He seemed anxious.

'I think so.' I shut my eyes. Images and thoughts flickered through my mind. I could not decide which of them were mine. I tried to remember if it was important to know that.

'Fitz!' This was Kettricken, shaking me.

'Make him sit up,' Starling suggested. Kettricken promptly gripped me by my shirt front and hauled me into a sitting position. The sudden change dizzied me. I could not understand why they wanted me to be awake in the middle of the night. I said so.

'It's midday,' Kettricken said tersely. 'The storm hasn't let up since last night.' She peered at me closely. 'Are you hungry? Would you like a cup of tea?'

While I was trying to decide, I forgot what she had asked me. There were so many people talking softly, I could not sort my thoughts from theirs. 'I beg your pardon,' I told the woman politely. 'What did you ask me?'

'Fitz!' The pale man hissed in exasperation. He reached behind me and dragged a pack over to him. 'He has elfbark in here, for tea. Chade left it with him. It should bring him back to himself.'

'He doesn't need that,' an old woman said sharply. She crawled closer to me, reached up and gripped my ear. She pinched it tightly.

'Ouch! Kettle!' I rebuked her, and tried to pull away. She kept her painful hold.

'Wake up!' she told me sternly. 'Right now!'

'I'm awake!' I promised her and after a scowl at me, she let go of my ear. While I looked about me in some confusion, she muttered angrily, 'We're too close to that damnable road.'

'It's still stormy outside?' I asked bewilderedly.

'You've only been told that six times,' Starling retorted, but I could hear the worry that underlay her words.

'I had ... nightmares last night. I didn't sleep well.' I looked around at the circle of folk clustered around the small brazier. Someone had braved the wind for a fresh supply of wood. A kettle hung on a tripod over the brazier, heaped full of melting snow. 'Where's Nighteyes?' I asked as soon as I missed him.

'Hunting,' Kettricken said and, *With very little luck*, came the echo from the hillside above us. I could feel the wind past his eyes. He had folded his ears back from it. *Nothing is moving in this storm. I don't know why I bother.*

Come back and stay warm, I suggested. At that moment, Kettle leaned over and pinched my arm savagely. I jerked back from it with a cry.

'Pay attention to us!' she snapped at me.

'What are we doing?' I demanded as I sat rubbing my arm. No one's behaviour made any sense to me today.

'Waiting for the storm to pass,' Starling told me. She leaned closer to me, peering into my face. 'Fitz, what is the matter with you? I feel as if you're not really here.'

'I don't know,' I admitted. 'I feel caught in a dream. And if I don't concentrate on staying awake, I start to fall right back to sleep.'

'Then concentrate,' Kettle advised me roughly. I could not understand why she seemed so angry with me.

'Maybe he should just sleep,' the Fool suggested. 'He seems tired, and from all the leaping and yelping he did in his sleep last night, his dreams were scarcely restful.'

'So he will get more rest staying awake now than from going back to dreams like that,' Kettle insisted mercilessly. She poked me suddenly in the ribs. 'Talk to us, Fitz.'

'About what?' I hedged.

Kettricken moved quickly to the attack. 'Did you dream of Verity last night?' she demanded. 'Is Skilling last night what has left you so dazed today?'

I sighed. One does not answer a direct question from one's queen with a lie. 'Yes,' I told her, but as her eyes lit I had to add, 'But it was a dream that will bring you small comfort. He is alive, in a cold, windy place. He would let me see no more than that, and when I asked where he was, he simply told me to find him.'

'Why would he behave so?' Kettricken asked. The hurt on her face was as if Verity himself had shoved her away.

'He warned me severely against all Skilling. I had been ... watching Molly and Burrich.' It was so hard to admit this, for I wanted to speak nothing of what I had seen there. 'Verity came and took me away from there, and warned me that our enemies might find them through me and hurt them. I believe that is why he concealed his surroundings from me. Because he feared that if I knew them, somehow Regal or his coterie might come to know them.'

'Does he fear that they seek for him also?' Kettricken asked wonderingly.

'So it seems to me. Though I have felt no tremor of their presence, he seems to believe they will seek him out, either by the Skill or in the flesh.'

'Why should Regal bother to do so, when all believe Verity dead?' Kettricken asked me.

I shrugged. 'Perhaps to make certain that he never returns to prove them all wrong. I do not truly know, my queen. I sense that my king conceals much from me. He warned me that the powers of the coterie are many and strong.'

'But surely Verity is as strong?' Kettricken asked with a child's faith.

'He masters a storm of power such as I have never witnessed, my lady. But it takes all his will to control it.'

'All such control is an illusion,' Kettle mumbled to herself. 'A trap to deceive the unwary.'

'King Verity is scarcely unwary, Dame Kettle!' Kettricken retorted angrily.

'No, he is not,' I agreed in a conciliatory tone. 'And the words were mine, not Ver ... King Verity's, my lady. I only seek to make you understand that what he now does is beyond my comprehension. All I can do is trust that he knows what he is about. And do as he has ordered me.'

'To find him,' Kettricken agreed. She sighed. 'Would that we could leave now, this very minute. But only a fool defies a storm such as this one.'

'While we bide here, FitzChivalry is in constant danger,' Kettle informed us. All eyes turned to her.

'What makes you say so, Kettle?' Kettricken asked.

She hesitated. 'Anyone can see it is so. Unless he is kept talking, his thoughts drift, his eyes become empty. He cannot sleep at night without the Skill coming upon him. It is obvious that the road is at fault.'

'While these things are so, it is not at all obvious to me that the road is the problem. A lingering fever from his injury could be at fault, or . . .'

'No.' I risked interrupting my queen. 'It is the road. I have no fever. And I did not feel this way before I travelled on it.'

'Explain this to me,' Kettricken commanded.

'I don't understand it myself. I can only suppose that Skill was somehow used to construct that road. It runs straighter and more level than any road I have ever known. No tree intrudes upon it, despite how little it is used. There are no animal tracks upon it. And did you mark the one tree we passed yesterday, the log that had fallen across the road? The stump and the uppermost branches were still almost sound . . . but all of the trunk that had fallen upon the road itself was rotted away to almost nothing. Some force moves still in that road, to keep it so clear and true. And I think whatever it is, it is related to the Skill.'

Kettricken sat a moment considering this. 'What do you suggest we do?' she asked me.

I shrugged. 'Nothing. For now. The tent is well pitched here. We'd be foolish to try to move it in this wind. I must simply be aware of the danger to myself, and endeavour to avoid it. And tomorrow, or whenever the wind falls, I should walk beside the road instead of upon it.'

'That will be little better for you,' Kettle grumbled.

'Perhaps. But as the road is our guide to Verity, it would be foolish to leave it. Verity survived this path, and he walked it alone.' I paused, thinking that I now understood better some of the fragmented Skill-dreams I had had of him. 'I will manage, somehow.'

The circle of faces doubtfully regarding me were not reassuring.

'You must, I suppose,' Kettricken concluded dolefully. 'If there is any way we can assist you, FitzChivalry . . .'

'There is none that I can think of,' I admitted.

'Save to keep his mind occupied as best we can,' Kettle offered. 'Do not let him sit idly, nor sleep overmuch. Starling, you have your harp, have you not? Could not you play and sing for us?'

'I have *a* harp,' Starling corrected her sourly. 'It's a poor thing compared to my old one that was taken from me at Moonseye.' For a moment her face emptied and her eyes turned inward. I wondered if that were how I looked when the Skill pulled at me. Kettle reached to pat her softly on one knee, but Starling flinched to the touch. 'Still, it's what I have, and I'll play it, if you think it will help.' She reached behind her for her pack and drew from it a bundled harp. As she drew the harp from its wrappings, I could see that it was little more than a framework of raw wood with strings stretched across it. It had the essential shape of her old harp, but with none of its grace and polish. It was to Starling's old harp what one of Hod's practice blades was to a fine sword: a thing of utility and function, no more than that. But she settled it on her lap and began tuning it. She began the opening notes of an old Buck ballad when she was interrupted by a snowy nose poking its way into the tent door.

'Nighteyes!' The Fool welcomed him.

I've meat to share. This came as a proud announcement. *More than enough to gorge well on.*

It was not an exaggeration. When I crawled out of the tent to see his kill, it was a sort of boar. The tusks and coarse hair were much the same as those I had hunted before, but this creature had larger ears and the coarse hair was mottled black and white. When Kettricken joined me, she exclaimed over it, saying she had seen few of them before, but they were known to roam the forests and had a reputation as vicious game best left alone. She scratched the wolf behind the ear with a mittened hand and praised him overmuch for his bravery and skill, until he fell over in the snow overcome with pride in himself. I looked at him, lolling near on his back in the snow and wind and could not help but grin. In an instant he had flipped to his feet, to give me a nasty pinch on the leg and demand that I open its belly for him.

The meat was fat and rich. Kettricken and I did most of the butchering, for the cold savaged the Fool and Kettle mercilessly and Starling begged off for the sake of a harpist's hands. Cold and damp were not the best things for her still-healing fingers. I did not much mind. Both the task and the harsh conditions kept my mind from wandering as I worked, and there was an odd pleasure to being alone with Kettricken, even under such circumstances, for in sharing this humble work, we both forgot station and past and became but two people in the cold rejoicing in a richness of meat. We cut off long skewering strips that would cook swiftly over the little brazier in sufficient quantity for all of us to gorge. Nighteyes took the entrails for himself, revelling in the heart and liver and guts and then a front leg with the satisfaction of bones to crack. He brought this gristly prize into the tent with him, but no one made comment on the snowy, bloody wolf that lay along one side of the tent wall and noisily chewed his meat save to praise him. I thought him insufferably satisfied with himself and told him so; he but informed me that I had never made so difficult a kill alone, let alone dragged it back intact to share. All the while the Fool scratched his ears.

Soon the rich smell of cooking filled the tent. It had been some days since we had had fresh meat of any kind, and the cold we had endured made the fat taste doubly rich to us. It brought our spirits up and we could almost forget the howling of the wind outside and the cold that pressed so fiercely against our small shelter. After we were all sated with meat, Kettle made tea for us. I know of nothing more warming than hot meat and tea and good fellowship.

This is pack, Nighteyes observed in contentment from his corner. And I could do no more than agree.

Starling cleansed her fingers of grease and took her harp back from the Fool who had asked to see it. To my surprise, he leaned over it with her, and traced down the frame with a pale fingernail saying, 'Had I my tools here, I could shave the wood here, and here, and smooth a curve like so along this side. I think it might fit your hands better.'

Starling looked at him hard, caught between suspicion and hesitancy. She studied his face for mockery, but found none. Carefully she observed, as if she spoke to us all, 'My master who taught me harping was good at the making of harps as well. Too good, perhaps. He tried to teach me, and I learned the basics, but he could not stand to watch me "fumble and scrape at fine wood" as he put it. So I never learned for myself the finer points of shaping the frame. And with this hand still stiff . . .'

'Were we back at Jhaampe, I could let you fumble and scrape as much as you wanted. To do so is truly the only way to learn. But for here, for now, even with such knives as we have, I think I might bring a more graceful shape out of this wood.' The Fool spoke openly.

'If you would,' she accepted quietly. I wondered when they had set aside their hostilities and realized I had not, for some days, paid much attention to anyone save myself. I had accepted that Starling wanted little more to do with me than to be present if I did something of vast import. I had not made any of friendship's demands upon her. Both Kettricken's rank and her grief had imposed a barrier between us that I had not ventured to breach. Kettle's reticence about herself made any true conversation difficult. But I could think of no excuse for how I had excluded the Fool and the wolf from my thoughts lately.

When you throw up walls against those who would use Skill against you, you lock more than your Skill-sense inside, Nighteyes observed.

I sat pondering that. It seemed to me that my Wit and my feeling for people had dimmed somewhat of late. Perhaps my companion was right. Kettle poked me suddenly, sharply. 'Don't wander!' she chided me.

'I was just thinking,' I said defensively.

'Well, think aloud then.'

'I've no thoughts worth sharing just now.'

Kettle glowered at me for being unco-operative.

'Recite then,' commanded the Fool. 'Or sing something. Anything to keep yourself focused here.'

'That's a good idea,' Kettle agreed, and it was my turn to glower at the Fool. But all eyes were on me. I took a breath and tried to think of something to recite. Almost everyone had a favourite story or bit of poetry memorized. But most of what I had possessed had to do with the poisoning herbs or others of the assassin's arts. 'I know one song,' I finally admitted. '"Crossfire's Sacrifice".'

Now Kettle scowled, but Starling struck up the opening notes with an amused smile on her face. After one false start, I launched into it, and carried it off fairly well, though I saw Starling flinch a time or two at a soured note. For whatever reason, my choice of song displeased Kettle, who sat grim and staring at me defiantly. When I had finished, the turn was passed to Kettricken, who sang a hunting ballad from the Mountains. Then it was the Fool's turn, and he humoured us with a ribald folk song about courting a milk-maid. I believe I saw grudging admiration from Starling for that performance. That left Kettle, and I had expected her to beg off. Instead, she sang the old children's nursery rhyme about 'Six Wise Men went to Jhaampe-town, climbed a hill and never came down', all the time eyeing me as if each word from her cracked old voice were a barb meant just for me. But if there was a veiled insult there, I missed it, as well as the reason for her ill-will.

Wolves sing together, Nighteyes observed, just as Kettricken suggested, 'Play us something we all know, Starling. Something to give us heart.' So Starling played that ancient song about gathering flowers for one's beloved, and we all sang along, some with more heart than others.

As the last note died away, Kettle observed, 'The wind's dropping.'

We all listened, and then Kettricken crawled from the tent. I followed her, and we stood quiet for a time in a wind that had gone quieter. Dusk had stolen the colours from the world. In the wake of the wind, snow had begun thickly falling. 'The storm has almost blown itself out,' she observed. 'We can be on our way tomorrow.'

'None too soon for me,' I said. *Come to me, come to me* still echoed in the beating of my heart. Somewhere up in those Mountains, or beyond them, was Verity.

And the river of Skill.

'As for me,' Kettricken said quietly, 'would that I had followed my instincts a year ago, and gone to the ends of the map. But I reasoned that I could do no better than Verity had done. And I feared to risk his child. A child I lost anyway, and thus failed him both ways.'

'Failed him?' I exclaimed in horror. 'By losing his child?'

'His child, his crown, his kingdom. His father. What did he entrust me with that I did not lose, FitzChivalry? Even as I rush to be with him again, I wonder how I can meet his eyes.'

'Oh, my queen, you are mistaken in this, I assure you. He would not perceive that you have failed him, but fears only that he abandoned you in the greatest of danger.'

'He only went to do what he knew he must,' Kettricken said quietly. And then added plaintively, 'Oh, Fitz, how can you speak for what he feels, when you cannot even tell me where he is?'

'Where he is, my queen, is but a bit of information, a spot on that map. But what he feels, and what he feels for you . . . that is what he breathes, and when we are together in the Skill, joined mind to mind, then I know such things, almost whether I would or no.' I recalled the other times I had been privy unwillingly to Verity's feelings for his queen, and was glad the night hid my face from her.

'Would this Skill were a thing I could learn . . . do you know, how often and how angry I have felt with you, solely because you could reach forth to the one I longed for, and know his mind and heart so easily? Jealousy is an ugly thing, and always I have tried to set it aside from me. But sometimes it seems so monstrously unfair that you are joined to him in such a way, and I am not.'

It had never occurred to me that she might feel such a thing. Awkwardly, I pointed out, 'The Skill is as much curse as it is gift. Or so it has been to me. Even if it were a thing I could gift you with, my lady, I do not know that is a thing one would do to a friend.'

'To feel his presence and his love for even a moment, Fitz . . . for that I would accept any curse that rode with it. To know his touch again, in any form . . . can you imagine how I miss him?'

'I think I can, my lady,' I said quietly. Molly. Like a hand gripping my heart. *Chopping hard winter turnips on the table-top. The knife was dull, she would ask Burrich to put an edge on it if he ever came in from the rain. He was cutting wood to take down to the village and sell tomorrow. The man worked too hard, his leg would be hurting him tonight.*

'Fitz? FitzChivalry!'

I snapped back to Kettricken shaking me by the shoulders.

'I'm sorry,' I said quietly. I rubbed at my eyes and laughed. 'Irony. All my life, it has been so difficult to use the Skill. It came and went like the wind in a ship's sails. Now, I am here, and suddenly Skilling is as effortless as breathing. And I hunger to use it, to find out what is happening to those I love best. But Verity warns me I must not, and I must believe he knows best.'

'As must I,' she agreed wearily.

We stood a moment longer in the dimness, and I fought a sudden impulse to put my arm around her shoulders and tell her it would be all right, that we would find her husband and king. Briefly, she seemed that tall slender girl who had come from the Mountains to be Verity's bride. But now she was the Queen of the Six Duchies, and I had seen her strength. Surely she needed no comfort from one such as I.

We cut more slices of meat from the freezing boar and then rejoined our companions in the tent. Nighteyes was sleeping contentedly. The Fool had Starling's harp clutched between his knees and was using a skinning knife as a makeshift draw-knife to gentle some of the frame's lines. Starling sat beside him, watching and trying not to look anxious. Kettle had taken off a little pouch she wore about her neck, opened it and was sorting out a handful of polished stones. As Kettricken and I built up the small fire in the brazier and prepared to cook the meat, Kettle insisted on explaining the rules of a game to me. Or attempting to. She finally gave up, exclaiming, 'You'll understand it when you've lost a few times.'

I lost more than a few times. She kept me at it for long hours after we had eaten. The Fool continued to shave wood from Starling's harp, with many pauses to put a fresh edge on the knife. Kettricken was silent, almost moody, until the Fool noticed her melancholy mood and began to tell tales of Buckkeep life before she had come there. I listened with one ear, and even I was drawn back to those days when the Red Ships were no more than a tale and my life had been almost secure if not happy. Somehow the talk rounded into the various minstrels that had played at Buck-keep, both famous and lesser, and Starling plied the Fool with questions about them.

I soon found myself caught up in the play of the stones. It was strangely soothing: the stones themselves were red, black and white, smoothly polished and pleasant to hold. The game involved each player randomly drawing stones from the pouch and then placing them on the intersections of lines on a patterned cloth. It was a game at once simple and complex. Each time I won a game, Kettle immediately introduced me to more complicated strategies. It engrossed me and freed my mind from memories or ponderings. When finally all the others were already drowsing in their sleeping skins, she set up a game on the board and bade me study it.

'It can be won decisively in one move of a black stone,' she told me. 'But the solution is not easy to see.'

I stared at the game layout and shook my head. 'How long did it take you to learn to play?'

She smiled to herself. 'As a child, I was a fast learner. But I will admit you are faster.'

'I thought this game came from some far land.'

'No, it is an old Buck game.'

'I've never seen it played before.'

'It was not uncommon when I was a girl, but it was not taught to everyone. But that is of no matter now. Study the layout of the pieces. In the morning, tell me the solution.'

She left the pieces set up on the cloth by the brazier. Chade's long training of my memory served me well. When I lay down, I visualized the board and gave myself one black stone with which to win. There was quite a variety of possible moves, as a black stone could also claim the place of a red stone and force it to another intersection, and a red stone had similar powers over a white. I closed my eyes, but held onto the game, playing the stone in various ways until I finally fell asleep. Either I dreamed of the game, or of nothing at all. It kept the Skill-dreams safely at bay but when I awoke in the morning, I still had no solution to the puzzle she had set me.

I was the first one awake. I crawled out of the tent and returned with a pot packed full of new wet snow to melt for morning tea. It was substantially warmer outside than it had been in days. It cheered me, even as it made me wonder if spring were already a reality in the lowlands. Before my mind could start wandering, I returned to puzzling about the game. Nighteyes came to rest his head on my shoulder where I sat.

I'm tired of dreaming of rocks. Lift up your eyes and see the whole thing, little brother. It is a hunting pack, not isolated hunters. See. That one. Put the black there, and do not use the red to displace a white, but set it there to close the trap. That is all.

I was still wondering at the marvellous simplicity of Nighteyes' solution when Kettle awoke. With a grin she asked me if I had solved it yet. In answer, I took a black stone from the pouch and made the moves the wolf had suggested. Kettle's face went slack with astonishment. Then she looked up at me in awe. 'No one has ever figured it out that rapidly,' she told me.

'I had help,' I admitted sheepishly. 'It's the wolf's game, not mine.'

Kettle's eyes grew round. 'You are jesting with an old woman,' she rebuked me carefully.

'No. I am not,' I told her, as I seemed to have hurt her feelings. 'I thought about it for most of the night. I believe I even dreamed about game strategies. But when I woke, it was Nighteyes who had the solution.'

She was silent for a time. 'I had thought that Nighteyes was . . . a clever pet. One who could hear your commands even if you did not speak them aloud. But now you say he can comprehend a game. Will you tell me he understands the words I speak?'

Across the tent, Starling was propped up on one elbow, listening to the conversation. I tried to think of a way to dissemble, then rejected it fiercely. I squared my shoulders as if I were reporting to Verity himself and spoke clearly. 'We are Wit-bound. What I hear and understand, he comprehends as I do. What interests him, he learns. I do not say he could read a scroll, or remember a song. But if a thing intrigues him, he thinks on it, in his own way. As a wolf, usually, but sometimes almost as anyone might . . .' I struggled to try and put in words something I myself did not understand perfectly. 'He saw the game as a pack of wolves driving game. Not as black and red and white markers. And he saw where he would go, were he hunting with that pack, to make their kill more likely. I suppose that sometimes I see things as he sees them . . . as a wolf. It is not wrong, I believe. Only a different way of perceiving the world.'

There was still a trace of superstitious fear in Kettle's eyes as she glanced from me to the sleeping wolf. Nighteyes chose that moment to let his tail rise and fall in a sleepy wag to indicate he was fully cognizant that we spoke of him. Kettle gave a shiver. 'What you do with him . . . is it like Skilling from human to human, only to a wolf?'

I started to shake my head, but then had to shrug. 'The Wit begins more as a sharing of feelings. Especially when I was a child. Following smells, chasing a chicken because it would run, enjoying food together. But when you have been together as long as Nighteyes and I have, it starts to be something else. It goes beyond feelings, and it's never really words. I am more aware of the animal that my mind lives inside. He is more aware of . . .'

Thinking. Of what comes before and after choosing to do an action. One becomes aware that one is always making choices, and considers what the best ones are.

Exactly. I repeated his words aloud for Kettle. By now Nighteyes was sitting up. He made an elaborate show of stretching and then sat looking at her, his head cocked to one side.

'I see,' she said faintly. 'I see.' Then she got up and left the tent.

Starling sat up and stretched. 'It gives one an entirely different outlook on scratching his ears,' she observed. The Fool answered her with a snort of laughter, sat up in his bedding, and immediately reached to scratch Nighteyes behind the ears. The wolf fell over on him in appreciation. I growled at both of them and went back to making tea.

We were not as swift to be packed and on our way. A thick layer of damp snow overlay everything, making breaking camp that much more difficult. We cut up what was left of the boar and took it with us. The jeppas were rounded up; despite the storm, they had not wandered far. The secret seemed to be in the bag of sweetened grain that Kettricken kept to lure the leader.

When we were loaded and finally ready to leave, Kettle announced that I must not be allowed to walk on the road, and that someone must always be with me. I bristled a bit at that, but they ignored me. The Fool volunteered quickly to be my first partner. Starling gave him an odd smile and a shake of her head over that. I accepted their ridicule by sulking manfully. They ignored that, too.

In a short time the women and the jeppas were moving easily up the road, while the Fool and I scrabbled alongside on the berm that marked the edge of it. Kettle turned to shake her walking stick. 'Get him further away than that!' she scolded the Fool. 'Get to where you can just see us to follow us. Go on, now. Go on.'

So we obediently edged back into the woods. As soon as we were out of sight of the others, the Fool turned to me and excitedly demanded, 'Who is Kettle?'

'You know as much as I do,' I pointed out shortly. And added a question of my own, 'What is between you and Starling now?'

He lifted his eyebrows at me and winked slyly.

'I doubt that very much,' I retorted.

'Ah, not all are as immune to my wiles as you are, Fitz. What can I tell you? She pines for me, she yearns for me in the depths of her soul, but knows not how to express it, poor thing.'

I gave it up as a bad question. 'What do you mean by asking me, "Who is Kettle?"'

He gave me a pitying glance. 'It is not so complex a question, princeling. Who is this woman who knows so much of what troubles you, who suddenly fishes out of a pocket a game I have only seen mentioned once in a very old scroll, who sings for us "Six Wise Men Went to Jhaampe-Town" with two additional verses I've never heard anywhere. Who, oh light of my life, is Kettle, and why does so ancient a woman choose to spend her last days hiking up a mountain with us?'

'You're in fine spirits this morning,' I observed sourly.

'Aren't I?' he agreed. 'And you are almost as adept at avoiding my question. Surely, you must have some musings on this mystery to share with a poor Fool?'

'She doesn't give me enough information about herself to base any wondering on,' I returned.

'So. What can we surmise about one who guards her tongue as closely as all that? About someone who seems to know something of the Skill as well? And the ancient games of Buck, and old poetry? How old do you suppose she is?'

I shrugged. 'She didn't like my song about Crossfire's coterie,' I offered suddenly.

'Ah, but that could easily have been just your singing. Let's not grasp at straws, here.'

In spite of myself, I smiled. 'It has been so long since your tongue has had an edge to it, it's almost a relief to hear you mock me.'

'Had I known you missed it, I would have been rude to you much sooner.' He grinned. Then he grew more serious. 'FitzChivalry, mystery hovers about that woman like flies on . . . spilt beer. She absolutely reeks of omens and portents and prophecies coming into focus. I think it is time one of us asked her a few direct questions.' He smiled at me. 'Your best chance will be when she is shepherding you along this afternoon. Be subtle, of course. Ask her who was king when she was a girl. And why she was exiled.'

'Exiled?' I laughed aloud. 'There's a leap of the imagination.'

'Do you think so? I don't. Ask her. And be sure to tell me whatever she doesn't say.'

'And in return for all this, you will tell me what is truly going on between you and Starling?'

He gave me a sideways glance. 'Are you sure you want to know? The last time we made such a trade, when I gave you the secret you'd bargained for, you found you did not want it.'

'Is this such a secret?'

He arched one eyebrow at me. 'You know, I am hardly certain of the answer to that myself. Sometimes you surprise me, Fitz. More often, you don't, of course. Most often I surprise myself. Such as when I volunteer to slog through loose snow and dodge trees with some bastard when I could be parading up a perfectly straight avenue with a string of charming jeppas.'

I got as little information from him the rest of the morning. When afternoon came, it was not Kettle, but Starling who was my walking companion. I expected that to be uncomfortable. I still had not forgotten that she had bargained her knowledge of my child in order to be part of this expedition. But somehow in the days since we had begun our journey, my anger had become a weary wariness toward her. I knew now there was no bit of information she would scruple to use against me, and so I guarded my tongue, resolving to say nothing at all of Molly or my daughter. Not that it would do much good now.

But to my surprise, Starling was affable and chatty. She plied me with questions, not about Molly, but about the Fool, to the point at which I began to wonder if she *had* conceived a sudden affection for him. There had been a few times at court when women had taken an interest in him and pursued him. To those who were attracted by the novelty of his appearance, he had been mercilessly cruel in exposing the shallowness of their interest. There had been one gardener maid who was impressed with his wit so much that she was tongue-tied in his presence. I heard kitchen gossip that she left bouquets of flowers for him at the base of his tower stairs, and some surmised that she had occasionally been invited to ascend those steps. She had had to leave Buckkeep Castle to care for her elderly mother in a distant town, and that had been where it ended, as far as I knew.

Yet as slight as this knowledge of the Fool was, I kept it from Starling, turning aside her questions with banalities that the two of us were childhood friends whose duties had left us very little time for socializing. This was actually very close to the truth, but I could see it both frustrated and amused her. Her other questions were as odd. She asked if I had ever wondered what his true name was. I told her that not being able to recall the name my own mother had given me had left me chary of asking others such questions. That quieted her for a time, but then she demanded to know how he had dressed as a child. My descriptions of his seasonal motleys did not suit her, but I truthfully told her that until Jhaampe I had never seen him dressed in other than his jester's clothes. By afternoon's end, her questions and my answers had more of sparring in them than conversation. I was glad to join the others in a camp, pitched at quite a distance from the Skill road.

Even so, Kettle kept me busy, letting me do her chores as well as my own for the sake of occupying my mind. The Fool concocted a respectable stew from our supplies and the pork. The wolf contented himself with another leg off the animal. When the meal things were finally cleared away, Kettle immediately set out the game cloth and pouch of stones. 'Now we shall see what you have learned,' she promised me.

But half a dozen games later, she squinted up at me with a frown. 'You were not lying!' she accused me.

'About what?'

'About the wolf devising the solution. Had you mastered that strategy yourself, you would play a different game now. Because someone gave you the answer rather than your discovering it yourself, you don't fully understand it.'

At the moment the wolf rose and stretched. *I weary of stones and cloth*, he informed me. *My hunting is more fun, and offers real meat at the end of it.*

So you are hungry?

No. Bored. He nosed the flap of the tent open and slipped out into the night.

Kettle watched him go with pursed lips. 'I was about to ask if you could not team together to play this game. It would interest me to see how you played.'

'I think he suspected that,' I muttered, a bit disgruntled that he had not invited me to join him.

Five games later, I grasped the brilliant simplicity of Nighteyes' noose tactic. It had lain before me all that time, but suddenly it was as if I saw the stones in motion rather than resting on the vertices of the cloth's pattern. In my next move, I employed it to win easily. I won the next three games handily, for I saw how it could be employed in a reverse situation as well.

At the third win, Kettle cleared the cloth of stones. Around us the others had already sunk into sleep. Kettle added a handful of twigs to the brazier to give us one last burst of light. Rapidly her knotted old fingers set out the stones on the cloth. 'Again, this is your game, and it is your move,' she informed me. 'But this time, you have only a white stone to place. A little weak white stone, but it can win for you. Think well on this one. And no cheating. Leave the wolf out of it.'

I stared at the situation to fix the game in my mind and then lay down to sleep. The game she had set out for me looked hopeless. I did not see how it could be won with a black stone, let alone a white one. I do not know if it were the stone game or our distance from the road, but I sank quickly into a sleep that was dreamless until near dawn. Then I joined the wolf in his wild running. Nighteyes had left the road far behind him and was joyously exploring the surrounding hillsides. We came on two snow cats feeding off a kill, and for a time he taunted them, circling just out of reach to make them hiss and spit at us. Neither would be lured from the meat and after a time we gave off the game to head back for the yurt. As we approached the tent, we circled stealthily about the jeppas, scaring them into a defensive bunch and then nudging them along to mill about just outside the tent. When the wolf crept back into the tent, I was still with him as he poked the Fool rudely with an icy nose.

It is good to see you have not lost all spirit and fun, he told me as I unlocked my mind from his and roused up in my own body.

Very good, I agreed with him. And rose to face the day.

TWENTY-SIX

Signposts

*One thing I have learned well in my travels. The riches of one region
are taken for granted in another. Fish we would not feed to a cat in
Buckkeep is prized as a delicacy in the inland cities. In some places
water is wealth, in others the constant flooding of the river is both an
annoyance and a peril. Fine leather, graceful pottery, glass as trans-
parent as air, exotic flowers . . . all of these I have seen in such
plentiful supply that the folk who possess them no longer see them as
wealth.*

*So perhaps, in sufficient quantity, magic becomes ordinary. Instead
of a thing of wonder and awe, it becomes the stuff of roadbeds and
signposts, used with a profligacy that astounds those who have it not.*

That day I travelled, as before, across the face of a wooded hillside.
At first the flank of the hill was broad and gentle. I could walk
in sight of the road and only slightly below it on the hillside.
The huge evergreens held most of the burden of winter snow
above me. The footing was uneven and there were occasional
patches of deep snow but walking was not too difficult. By the
end of that day, however, the trees were beginning to dwindle
in size and the slope of the hill was markedly steeper. The road
hugged the hillside, and I walked below it. When it came time
to camp that night, my companions and I were hard pressed to
find a level place to pitch the tent. We scrabbled quite a way
down the hill before we found a place where it levelled. When
we did have the yurt up, Kettricken stood looking back up at the
road and frowning to herself. She took out her map and was
consulting it by the waning daylight when I asked her what the
matter was.

She tapped the map with a mittened finger and then gestured to the slope above us. 'By tomorrow, if the road keeps climbing and the slopes get steeper, you won't be able to keep pace with us. We'll be leaving the trees behind us by evening tomorrow. The country is going to be bare, steep and rocky. We should take firewood with us now, as much as the jeppas can easily carry.' She frowned. 'We may have to slow our pace to allow you to match us.'

'I'll keep up,' I promised her.

Her blue eyes met mine. 'By the day after tomorrow, you may have to join us on the road.' She looked at me steadily.

'If I do, then I'll have to cope with it.' I shrugged and tried to smile despite my uneasiness. 'What else can I do?'

'What else can any of us do?' she muttered to herself in reply.

That night when I had finished cleaning the cooking pots, Kettle once again set out her cloth and stones. I looked at the spread of pieces and shook my head. 'I haven't worked it out,' I told her.

'Well, that is a relief,' she told me. 'If you, or even if you and your wolf had, I would have been too astonished for words. It's a difficult problem. But we shall play a few games tonight, and if you keep your eyes open and your wits sharp, you may see the solution to your problem.'

But I did not, and lay down to sleep with gamecloth and pieces scattered in my brain.

The next day's walk went as Kettricken had foretold. By noon I was scrabbling through brushy places and over tumbles of bared rock with Starling at my heels. Despite the breathless effort the terrain demanded, she was full of questions, and all about the Fool. What did I know of his parentage? Who had made his clothing for him? Had he ever been seriously ill? It had become routine for me to answer her by giving her little or no information. I had expected her to weary of this game, but she was as tenacious as a bull-dog. Finally, I rounded on her in exasperation and demanded to know exactly what it was about him that fascinated her so.

A strange look came to her face, as one who steels oneself to a dare. She started to speak, paused, and then could not resist.

Her eyes were avid on my face as she announced, 'The Fool is a woman, and she is in love with you.'

For a moment it was as if she had spoken in a foreign language. I stood looking down on her and trying to puzzle out what she had meant. Had she not begun to laugh, I might have thought of a reply. But something in her laughter offended me so deeply that I turned my back on her and continued making my way across the steep slope.

'You're blushing!' she called from behind me. Merriment choked her voice. 'I can tell from the back of your neck! All these years, and you never even knew? Never even suspected?'

'I think it's a ridiculous idea,' I said without even looking back.

'Really? What part of it?'

'All of it,' I said coldly.

'Tell me you absolutely know that I'm wrong.'

I didn't dignify her taunt with an answer. I did forge through a patch of thick brush without pausing to hold the branches back for her. I know she knew I was getting angry because she was laughing. I pushed my way clear of the last of the trees and stood looking out over a nearly-sheer rockface. There was almost no brush, and cracked grey stone pushed up in icy ridges through the snow. 'Stay back!' I warned Starling as she pushed up beside me. She looked around me and sucked in her breath.

I looked up the steep hillside to where the road was scored across the mountain's face like a gouge in a piece of wood. It was the only safe way across that sheer mountain face. Above us was the steep boulder-strewn mountainside. It was not quite sheer enough to call it a cliff. There was a scattering of wind-warped trees and bushes, some with roots straggling over the rocky soil as much as in it. Snow frosted it unevenly. Climbing up to the road would be a challenge. The slope we traversed had been getting steeper all morning. I should not have been surprised, but I had been so intent on picking the best path that it had been some time since I had looked up to the road.

'We'll have to return to the road,' I told Starling and she nodded mutely.

It was easier said than done. In several places I felt rock and scree slew under my feet, and more than once I went on all fours.

I could hear Starling panting behind me. 'Only a little further!' I called back to her as Nighteyes came toiling up the slope beside us. He passed us effortlessly, moving by leaps up the slope until he reached the edge of the road. He disappeared over the edge of it, and then returned to stand on the lip looking down at us. In a moment the Fool appeared beside him, to gaze down at us anxiously. 'Need any help?' he called down.

'No. We'll make it!' I called back up to him. I paused, crouching and clinging to the trunk of a stunted tree, to catch my breath and wipe the sweat from my eyes. Starling halted behind me. And suddenly I felt the road above me. It had a current like a river, and as the current of a river stirs the air to wind over it, so did the road. It was a wind not of winter cold, but of lives, both distant and near. The Fool's strange essence floated on it, and Kettle's close-mouthed fear and Kettricken's sad determination. They were as separate and recognizable as the bouquets of different wines.

'FitzChivalry!' Starling emphasized my name by hitting me between the shoulder blades.

'What?' I asked her absently.

'Keep moving! I can't cling here much longer, my calves are cramping!'

'Oh.' I found my body and climbed the remaining distance to the lip of the road. The flowing Skill made me effortlessly aware of Starling behind me. I could feel her placing her feet and gripping the scraggly mountain willow at the edge of the cliff. I stood for an instant on the lip of the road's edge. Then I stepped down, onto the smooth surface of the road, slipping into its pull like a child slipping into a river.

The Fool had waited for us. Kettricken was at the head of the line of jeppas, looking back anxiously to watch us join them. I took a deep breath and felt as if I were gathering myself together. Beside me, Nighteyes suddenly flipped my hand with his nose.

Stay with me, he suggested. I felt him groping for a firmer grip on our bond. That I could not help him alarmed me. I looked down into his deep eyes and suddenly found a question.

You're on the road. I didn't think animals could come on the road.

He gave a sneeze of disgust. *There's a difference between thinking* an action is wise and doing it. And you might have noticed that the jeppas have been travelling on the road for some days.

It was too obvious. Why do the wild animals avoid it then?

Because we still depend on ourselves for survival. The jeppas depend on humans, and will follow them into any danger, no matter how foolish it seems to them. Thus they have not the sense to run from a wolf, either. Instead they flee back to you humans when I scare them. It's a lot like horses or cattle and rivers. Left to themselves, they swim them only if death is right behind them, from predators or starvation. But humans convince them to swim rivers any time the human wishes to be on the other side. I think they are rather stupid.

So why are you on this road? I asked him with a smile.

Do not question friendship, he told me seriously.

'Fitz!'

I startled, and turned to Kettle. 'I'm fine,' I told her, even as I knew I was not. My Wit-sense usually made me very aware of others around me. But Kettle had walked up right behind me and I'd not noticed until she spoke to me. Something about the Skill road was dulling my Wit. When I did not think specifically of Nighteyes, he faded into a vague shadow in my mind.

I'd be less than that, were I not striving to stay with you, he pointed out worriedly.

'It will be all right. I just have to pay attention,' I told him.

Kettle assumed I was speaking to her. 'Yes, you do.' Pointedly she took my arm and started me walking. The others had gone ahead. Starling was walking with the Fool, and singing some love ditty as she walked, but he was looking over his shoulder worriedly at me. I gave him a nod and he nodded back uneasily. Beside me, Kettle pinched my arm. 'Pay attention to me. Talk to me. Tell me. Have you solved the game problem I gave you?'

'Not yet,' I admitted. The days were warmer, but the wind that blew past us now still brought the threat of ice on the higher mountain peaks. If I thought about it, I could feel the cold on my cheeks, but the Skill road bade me ignore it. The road was steadily climbing now. Even so, I seemed to walk effortlessly on its surface. My eyes told me that we were going uphill, but I strode along as easily as if it were down.

Another pinch from Kettle. 'Think about the problem,' she

bade me curtly. 'And do not be deceived. Your body labours and is cold. Simply because you are not constantly aware of it does not mean you can ignore it. Pace yourself.'

Her words seemed both foolish and wise. I realized that by hanging onto my arm, she was not only supporting herself but was forcing me to walk more slowly. I shortened and slowed my stride to match hers. 'The others seem to take no harm from it,' I observed to her.

'True. But they are neither old nor Skill-sensitive. They will ache tonight, and tomorrow they will slow their pace. This road was built with the assumption that those who used it would be either unaware of its more subtle influences, or trained in how to manage them.'

'How do you know so much about it?' I demanded.

'Do you want to know about me, or about this road?' she snapped angrily.

'Both, actually,' I told her.

She didn't answer that. After a time she asked me, 'Do you know your nursery rhymes?'

I don't know why it made me so angry. 'I don't know!' I retorted. 'I don't recall my earliest childhood, when most children learn them. I suppose you could say I learned stable rhymes instead. Shall I recite for you the fifteen points of a good horse?'

'Recite for me instead "Six Wisemen went to Jhaampe-town"!' she snarled. 'In my days, children were not only taught their learning rhymes, they knew what they meant. This is the hill in the poem, you ignorant pup! The one no wise man goes up and expects to come down again!'

A shiver walked down my spine. There have been a few times in my life when I have recognized some symbolic truth in a way that stripped it down to its most frightening bones. This was one. Kettle had brought to the forefront of my mind a thing I had known for days. 'The Wisemen were Skilled ones, weren't they?' I asked softly. 'Six, and five, and four . . . coteries, and the remains of coteries . . .' My mind skipped up the stair of logic, substituting intuition for most of the steps. 'So that's what became of the Skilled ones, the old ones we could not find. When Galen's coterie did not work well, and Verity needed more help to defend

Buck, Verity and I sought for older Skilled ones, folk who had been trained by Solicity before Galen became Skillmaster,' I explained to Kettle. 'We could find few records of names. And they had all either died, or disappeared. We suspected treachery.'

Kettle snorted. 'Treachery would be nothing new to coteries. But what more commonly happened is that as people grew in the Skill, they became more and more attuned to it. Eventually the Skill called them. If one were strong enough in the Skill, one could survive the trip up this road. But if she were not, she perished.'

'And if one succeeded?' I asked.

Kettle gave me a sidelong glance, but said nothing.

'What is at the end of this road? Who built it, and where does it lead?'

'Verity,' she said quietly at last. 'It leads to Verity. You and I need know no more than that.'

'But you know more than that!' I accused her. 'As do I. It leads to the source of all Skill as well.'

Her glance became worried, then opaque. 'I know nothing,' she told me sourly. Then, as conscience smote her, 'There is much I suspect, and many half-truths have I heard. Legends, prophecies, rumours. Those are what I know.'

'And how do you know them?' I pressed.

She turned to regard me levelly. 'Because I am fated to do so. Even as you are.'

And not another word on the subject would she say. Instead, she set up hypothetical game boards and demanded to know what moves I would make, given a black, red or white stone. I tried to focus on the tasks, knowing that she gave them to me to keep my mind my own. But ignoring the Skill-force of that road was rather like ignoring a strong wind or a current of icy water. I could choose not to pay attention to it, but that did not make it stop. In the midst of puzzling out game strategy, I would wonder at the pattern of my own thoughts and believe them not my own at all, but those of another whom I had somehow tapped. While I could keep the game puzzle in front of me, it did not stop the gallery of voices whispering in the back of my mind.

The road wound up and up. The mountain itself rose nearly

sheer on our left, and dropped off as abruptly on our right. This road went where no sane builders would have placed it. Most trade routes meandered between hills and over passes. This one traversed the face of a mountain, carrying us ever higher. By the time the day was fading, we had fallen far behind the others. Nighteyes raced ahead of us and then came trotting back to report that they had come to a resting-place, wide and level, where they were setting up the tent. With the coming of night, the mountain winds bit more fiercely. I was glad to think of warmth and rest, and persuaded Kettle to try to hurry.

'Hurry?' she asked. 'You are the one who keeps slowing. Keep up, now.'

The last march before rest always seems longest. So the soldiers of Buckkeep always told me. But that night I felt we waded through cold syrup, so heavy did my feet seem. I think I kept pausing. I know that several times Kettle tugged at my arm and told me to come along. Even when we rounded a fold in the mountainside and saw the lit tent ahead of us, I could not seem to make myself move faster. Like a fever dream, my eyes brought the tent closer to me, and then set it afar. I plodded on. Multitudes whispered around me. The night dimmed my eyes. I had to squint to see in the cold wind. A crowd streamed past us on the road, laden donkeys, laughing girls carrying baskets of bright yarn. I turned to watch a bell merchant pass us. He carried a rack high on his shoulder, and dozens of brass bells of every shape and tone jingled and rang as he walked along. I tugged at Kettle's arm to bid her turn and see it, but she only seized my hand in a grip of iron and hurried me on. A boy strode past us, going down to the village with a basketful of bright mountain flowers. Their fragrance was intoxicating. I pulled free of Kettle's grip. I hurried after him, to buy a few for Molly to scent her candles.

'Help me!' Kettle called. I looked to see what was the matter, but she was not by me. I couldn't find her in the crowd.

'Kettle!' I called. I glanced back but then realized I was losing the flower-monger. 'Wait!' I called to him.

'He's getting away!' she cried, and there was fear and desperation in her voice.

Nighteyes suddenly hit me from behind, his front paws striking my shoulders. His weight and speed threw me face first on the thin layer of snow covering the road's smooth surface. Despite my mittens, I skinned the palms of my hands and the pain in my knees was like fire. 'Idiot!' I snarled at him and tried to rise, but he caught me by one ankle and flipped me down onto the road again. This time I could look down over the edge into the abyss below. My pain and astonishment had stilled the night, the folk had all vanished, leaving me alone with the wolf.

'Nighteyes!' I protested. 'Let me up!'

Instead he seized my wrist in his jaws, clamped his teeth down and began to drag me on my knees away from the road's edge. I had not known he had such strength, or rather, I had never supposed it would be turned on me. I swatted at him ineffectually with my free hand, all the while yelling and trying to get to my feet. I could feel blood running on my arm where one tooth had sunk in.

Kettricken and the Fool suddenly flanked me, seizing me by my upper arms and hoisting me to my feet. 'He's gone mad!' I exclaimed as Starling raced up behind them. Her face was white, her eyes huge.

'Oh, wolf,' she exclaimed, and dropped to one knee to give him a hug. Nighteyes sat panting, obviously enjoying her embrace.

'What is the matter with you?' I demanded of him. He looked up at me, but did not reply.

My first reaction was a stupid one. I lifted my hands to my ears. But that had never been how I had heard Nighteyes. He whined as I did so, and I heard that clearly. It was just a dog's whine. 'Nighteyes!' I cried. He reared up to stand on his hind legs, his front paws on my chest. He was so big he could almost look me in the eye. I caught an echo of his worry and desperation, but no more than that. I quested out toward him with my Wit-sense. I could not find him. I could not sense any of them. It was as if they had all been Forged.

I looked around at their frightened faces and realized they were talking, no, almost shouting, something about the edge of the road and the black column and what was the matter, what was the matter? For the first time it struck me how ungainly speech was. All of those separate words, strung together, every voice mouthing them differently, and this was how we communicated with each other. 'Fitz, fitz, fitz,' they shouted, my name, meaning me, I suppose, but each voice sounding the word differently, and each with a different image of whom they spoke to and why they needed to speak to me. The words were such awkward things, I could not concentrate on what they were trying to convey by them. It was like dealing with foreign traders, pointing and holding up fingers, smiling or frowning, and guessing, always guessing at what the other truly meant.

'Please,' I said. 'Hush. Please!' I only wanted them to be silent, to stop their noises and mouthings. But the sound of my own words caught my attention. 'Please,' I said again, marvelling at all the ways my mouth must move to make that inexact sound. 'Hush!' I said again, and realized the word meant too many things to have any real meaning at all.

Once, when I was very new to Burrich, he had told me to unharness a team. It was when we were still getting a measure of one another, and no task any sane man would give a child. But I managed, climbing all over the docile beasts, and unfastening every shining buckle and clasp until the harness lay in pieces on the ground. When he came to see what was taking me so long, Burrich had been mutely astounded but unable to fault that I had done what he had told me to do. As for me, I had been amazed at how many pieces there were to something that had seemed to be all one thing when I had started in on it.

So it was for me then. All these sounds to make a word, all these words to frame a thought. Language came apart in my hands. I had never stopped to consider it before. I stood before them, so drenched in the Skill-essence on that road that speech seemed as childishly awkward as eating porridge with one's fingers. Words were slow and inexact, hiding as much meaning as they revealed. 'Fitz, please, you have to . . .' began Kettricken, and so engrossed did I become in considering every possible meaning those five words might have that I never heard the rest of what she said.

The Fool took hold of my hand and led me into the tent. He pushed at me until I sat down, and took off my hat and mittens and outer coat. Without a word, he put a hot mug into my hands. That I could understand, but the rapid, worried conversation of the others was like the frightened squawking of a coop full of chickens. The wolf came and lay down beside me, to rest his big head on one of my thighs. I reached down to stroke the broad skull and finger the soft ears. He pressed closer against me as if pleading. I scratched him behind the ears, thinking that might be what he wanted. It was terrible not to know.

I was not much use to anyone that evening. I tried to do my share of the chores, but the others kept taking them out of my hands. Several times I was pinched, or poked and bid, 'Wake up!' by Kettle. One time I became so fascinated by the motion of her mouth as she scolded me that I didn't realize when she walked away from me. I don't remember what I was doing when the back of my neck was seized in her claw-like grip. She dragged my head forward and kept her hold while she tapped each stone in turn on her gamecloth. She put a black stone in my hand. For a time I just stared at the markers. Then suddenly I felt that shift in perception. There was no space between me and the game. For a time I tried my pebble in various positions. I finally found the perfect move, and when I set my stone in place, it was as if my ears had suddenly cleared, or like blinking sleep from my eyes. I lifted my eyes to consider those around me.

'Sorry,' I muttered inadequately. 'Sorry.'

'Better now?' Kettle asked me softly. She spoke as if I were a toddler.

'I'm more myself now,' I told her. I looked up at her, suddenly desperate. 'What happened to me?'

'The Skill,' she said simply. 'You just aren't strong enough in it. You nearly followed the road where it no longer goes. There is some sort of marker there, and once the road diverged there, one track going down into the valley and the other continuing across the mountainside. The downhill path is sheared off, carried away in a cataclysm years ago. There is nothing but tumbled stone at the bottom, but one can just see where the road emerges from the ruin and continues. It vanishes in another jumble of stone in the distance. Verity could not have gone there. But you nearly followed its memory to your death.' She paused and looked at me severely. 'In my days . . . you haven't been trained enough to do what you've been doing, let alone face this challenge. If this is the best you were taught ... Are you certain Verity is alive?' she suddenly demanded of me. 'That he survived this trial alone?'

I decided one of us had to stop keeping secrets. 'I saw him, in a Skill-dream. In a city, with folk such as we passed today. He laved his hands and arms in a magic river, and walked away laden with power.'

'God of fishes!' Kettle swore. Something of horror and something of awe lit in her face.

'We passed no folk today,' Starling objected. I had not been aware she had seated herself by me until she spoke. I jumped, startled that someone could get that close to me and I had not sensed it.

'All those who have ever trodden this road have left something of themselves upon it. Your senses are muffled to those ghosts, but Fitz walks here naked as a new-born child. And as naive.' Kettle leaned back suddenly against her bedroll, and all the lines in her face deepened. 'How can such a child be the Catalyst?' she asked of no one in particular. 'You don't know how to save yourself from yourself. How are you going to save the world?'

The Fool leaned over from his bedroll suddenly to take my hand. Something like strength flowed into me with that reassuring touch. His tone was light, but his words sank into me. 'Competence was never guaranteed in the prophecies. Only persistence. What does your White Colum say? "They come like raindrops against the stone towers of time. But in time it is always the rain that prevails, not the tower."' He gave my hand a squeeze.

'Your fingers are like ice,' I told him as he let go.

'I am cold past belief,' he agreed with me. He drew his knees up to his chest and wrapped his arms around them. 'Cold and tired. But persistent.'

I lifted my eyes from him to find Starling with a knowing smile on her face. Gods, how it irked me. 'I have elfbark in my pack,' I suggested to the Fool. 'It gives warmth as well as strength.'

'Elfbark.' Kettle scowled, as if it were disgusting. But after a moment's reflection, she said excitedly, 'Actually, that might be a good idea. Yes. Elfbark tea.'

When I took the drug out of my pack, Kettle snatched it out of my hands as if I might cut myself on it. She muttered to herself as she measured tiny portions of it into mugs for us. 'I've seen what kind of doses you expose yourself to,' she chided me, and brewed the tea herself. She put none of it in the tea she prepared for Kettricken, Starling and herself.

I sipped at my hot tea, tasting first the acrid bite of the elfbark and then the warmth of it in my belly. Its enervating heat spread through me. I watched the Fool, and saw him relax in its embrace, even as his eyes began to sparkle with it.

Kettricken had her map out and was frowning over it. 'FitzChivalry, study this with me,' the Queen suddenly commanded. I moved around the brazier to sit next to her. I was scarcely settled before she began. 'I believe we are here,' she told me. Her finger tapped the first juncture of the trail that was marked on the map. 'Verity said he would visit all three places that were marked on the map. I believe that when this map was made, the road that you nearly followed tonight was intact. Now it is no longer there. And has not been there for some time.' Her blue eyes met mine. 'What do you suppose Verity did when he reached this point?'

I considered a moment. 'He's a pragmatic man. This other, second destination looks no more than three or four days from here. I think he might go there first, seeking the Elderlings there. And this third one is but, oh, seven days past there. I think he would decide it would be fastest to visit those two places first. Then, if he had no success there, he might return here, to try and find a way down to . . . whatever's there.'

She wrinkled her brow. I suddenly recalled how smooth it had been when she was first his bride. Now I seldom saw her without lines of care and worry in her face. 'He has been gone long, my husband. Yet it did not take us all that long to reach here. Perhaps he has not yet returned because he is down there. Because it took him so long to find a way down there to continue his journey.'

'Perhaps,' I agreed uneasily. 'Bear in mind that we are well supplied and travel together. By the time Verity reached this far, he would have been alone, and with few resources.' I refrained from telling Kettricken that I suspected he had been injured in that last battle. There was no sense in giving her more anxiety. Against my will, I felt a part of me groping out toward Verity. I shut my eyes and resolutely sealed myself in again. Had I imagined a taint upon the Skill-current, a too-familiar feeling of insidious power? I set my walls again.

'. . . split the party?'

'I beg pardon, my queen,' I said humbly.

I did not know if the look in her eyes were exasperation or fear. She took my hand and held it firmly. 'Attend me,' she commanded. 'I said, tomorrow we shall seek a way down. If we see anything that looks promising, we will attempt it. But I think we should give such a search no more than three days. If we find nothing, we should move on. But an alternative is to split the party. To send . . .'

'I do not think we should split the party,' I said hastily.

'You are most likely correct,' she conceded. 'But it takes so long, so very long, and I have been alone with my questions too long.'

I could think of nothing to say to that, so I pretended to be busy rubbing Nighteyes' ears.

My brother. It was a whisper, no more, but I looked down at Nighteyes beside me. I rested a hand on his ruff, strengthening the bond with a touch. *You were as empty as an ordinary human. I could not make you even feel me.*

I know. I don't know what happened to me.

I do. You are moving ever farther from my side to the other side. I fear you will go too far and be unable to return. I feared it had already happened today.

What do you mean, my side, and the other side?

'Can you hear the wolf again?' Kettricken asked me worriedly. I was surprised, when I looked up, to see how anxiously she regarded me.

'Yes. We are together again,' I told her. A thought occurred to me. 'How did you know we were unable to communicate?'

She shrugged. 'I suppose I assumed it. He seemed so anxious and you seemed so distant from everyone.'

She has the Wit. Don't you, my queen?

I can not say for certain that something passed between them. Once, long before in Buckkeep, I thought I had sensed Kettricken using the Wit. I suppose she well could have been using it then, for my own sense of it was so diminished I could scarce sense my own bond-animal. In any case Nighteyes lifted his head to look at her and she returned his gaze steadily. With a small frown, Kettricken added, 'Sometimes I wish I could speak to him as you do. Had I his speed and stealth at my disposal, I could be more certain of the safety of the road, both before us and behind. He might be able to find a path down, one not apparent to our eyes.'

If you can keep your Wits about you enough to tell her what I see, I would not mind doing such a task.

'Nighteyes would be most pleased to help you in such a way, my queen,' I offered.

She gave a weary smile. 'Then, I suppose, if you can keep aware of both of us, you may serve as go-between.'

Her eerie echoing of the wolf's thought unsettled me, but I only nodded my assent. Every aspect of conversation now demanded my complete attention, or it slipped away from me. It was like being horribly tired and having to constantly fight off sleep. I wondered if it were this hard for Verity.

There is a way to ride it, but lightly, lightly, like mastering an ill-tempered stallion who rebels against every touch of the rein or heel. But you are not ready to do so yet. So fight it, boy, and keep your head above water. Would that there were another way for you to come to me. But there is only the road, and you must follow it – No, make no reply to me. Know that there are others that listen avariciously if not as keenly as I. Be wary.

Once, in describing my father Chivalry, Verity had said that when he Skilled it was like being trampled by a horse, that Chivalry would rush into his mind, dump out his messages and flee. I now had a better understanding of what my uncle had meant. I felt rather like a fish suddenly deserted by a wave. There was that gaping sense of something missing in the instant after Verity's departure. It took me a moment to remember I was a person. Had I not been fortified already with the elfbark, I think I might have fainted. As it was, the drug was increasing its hold on me. I had a sense of being muffled in a warm soft blanket. My weariness was gone, but I felt muted. I finished the little that was left in my cup and waited for the flush of energy that elfbark usually gave me. It didn't come.

'I don't think you used enough,' I told Kettle.

'You have had plenty,' she said with asperity. She sounded like Molly did when she thought I was drinking too much. I braced myself, expecting images of Molly to fill my mind. But I stayed within my own life. I do not know if I felt relieved or disappointed. I longed to see her and Nettle. But Verity had warned me . . . belatedly I announced to Kettricken, 'Verity Skilled to me. Just now.' Then I cursed myself as a churl and a lackwit as I saw the hope flush her face. 'It was not really a message,' I amended hastily. 'Just a warning reminder to me that I am to avoid Skilling. He still believes there may be others seeking me that way.'

Her face fell. She shook her head to herself. Then she looked up to demand, 'He had no word at all for me?'

'I do not know if he realizes you are with me,' I hastily side-stepped the question.

'No words,' she said dully as if she had not heard me. Her eyes were opaque as she asked, 'Does he know how I have failed him? Does he know about . . . our child?'

'I do not believe he does, my lady. I sense no such grief in him, and well I know how it would grieve him.'

Kettricken swallowed. I cursed my clumsy words, and yet, was it my place to utter words of comfort and love to his wife? She straightened up abruptly, then rose. 'I think I shall bring in a bit more firewood for tonight,' she announced. 'And grain the jeppas. There is scarcely a twig for them to browse on here.'

I watched her leave the tent for the dark and still cold outside. No one spoke a word. After a breath or two, I rose and followed her. 'Don't be long,' Kettle warned me enigmatically. The wolf shadowed after me.

Outside the night was clear and cold. The wind was no worse than usual. Familiar discomforts can almost be ignored. Kettricken was neither fetching wood nor graining the jeppas. I was sure both tasks had already been done earlier. Instead she was standing at the edge of the cloven road, staring out over the blackness of cliff at her feet. She stood tall and stiff as a soldier reporting to his sergeant and made not a sound. I knew she was crying.

There is a time for courtly manners, a time for formal protocol and a time for humanity. I went to her, took her by the shoulders and turned her to face me. She radiated misery and the wolf beside me whined high. 'Kettricken,' I said simply. 'He loves you. He will not blame you. He will grieve, yes, but what kind of a man would not? As for Regal's deeds, they are Regal's deeds. Do not take the blame for those to yourself. You could not have stopped him.'

She wiped a hand across her face and did not speak. She looked past me, her face a pale mask in the starlight. She sighed heavily, but I could sense her strangling on her sorrow. I set my arms about my Queen and pulled her to me, pressing her face to my shoulder. I stroked her back, feeling the terrible tension there. 'It's all right,' I lied to her. 'It's going to be all right. In time, you'll see. You'll be together again, you'll make another child, both of you will sit in the Great Hall at Buckkeep and listen to the minstrels sing. There will be peace again, somehow. You've never seen Buckkeep at peace. There will be time for Verity to hunt and fish, and you'll ride at his side. Verity will laugh and shout and roar through the halls like the north wind again. Cook used to chase him out of the kitchen for slicing the meat from the roast before it was cooked through, he would come home from the chase that hungry. He'd come right in and cut the leg off a cooking fowl, that he would, and carry it about with him, telling stories in the guardroom, waving it about like a sword . . .'

I patted her back as if she were a child and told her tales of the bluff, hearty man I remembered from my boyhood. For a time her forehead rested on my shoulder and she was completely still. Then she coughed once, as if starting to choke, but instead terrible sobs welled up from her. She cried suddenly and unabashedly as a child that has taken a bad fall and is hurt as well as frightened. I sensed these were tears that had long gone unshed, and I did not try to help her stop. Instead I went on talking and patting her, scarcely hearing what I was saying myself, until her sobs began to quiet and her shaking to still. At last she drew away from me a little, to grope in her pocket for a kerchief. She wiped her face and eyes and blew her nose before she tried to speak.

'I'm going to be all right,' she said. To hear the strength of her belief in those words made my heart ache. 'It's just . . . It's hard just now. Waiting to tell him all these terrible things. Knowing how they will hurt him. They taught me so many things about being Sacrifice, Fitz. From the beginning, I knew I might have terrible sorrows to bear. I am strong enough ... to bear these things. But no one warned me that I might come to love the man they'd choose for me. To bear my sorrow is one thing. To bring sorrow to him is another.' Her throat closed on the words and she bowed her head. I feared she might begin to weep again. Instead when she lifted her head she smiled at me. Moonlight touched the silver wetness on her cheeks and lashes. 'Sometimes I think only you and I see the man beneath the crown. I want him to laugh, and roar about, and leave his bottles of ink open and his maps scattered about. I want him to put his arms about me and hold me. Sometimes I want those things so much, I forget about the Red Ships and Regal and . . . everything else. Sometimes I think that if we could only be together again, all the rest would come right as well. It is not a very worthy thought to have. A Sacrifice is supposed to be more . . .'

A glint of silver behind her caught my eyes. I saw the black column over her shoulder. It leaned at a cant over the broken edge of the road, half its stone support gone. I did not hear the rest of what she said. I wondered how I had not seen it before. It gleamed brighter than the moon on the sparkling snow. It was hewn of black stone webbed with glittering crystal. Like moonlight on a rippling river of Skill. I could decipher no writing on its surface. The wind was screaming behind me as I reached out and ran a hand down that smooth stone. It welcomed me.

TWENTY-SEVEN

The City

There runs through the Mountain Kingdom an old trade trail that serves none of the present-day towns of the Mountain Kingdom. Portions of this old highway appear as far south and east as the shore of Blue Lake. The trail is not named, no one recalls who constructed it, and few use it even for the stretches that remain intact. In places the road has been gradually destroyed by the freezing swells that are common to the Mountains. In other places flooding and landslides have reduced it to rubble. Occasionally an adventurous Mountain youth will undertake to trace the road to its source. Those who return have tall tales of ruined cities and steaming valleys where sulphurous ponds smoke, and they speak too, of the forbidding nature of the territory the road spans. No game and poor hunting, they say, and it is not recorded anywhere that anyone has ever been impressed enough to make a return trip to the road's end.

I stumbled to my knees in the snowy street. I got to my feet slowly, groping for a memory. Had I got drunk? The queasiness, the dizziness were right for that. But not this darkly gleaming and silent city. I looked all around me. I was in a town square of some sort, standing in the shadow of a looming stone memorial of some kind. I blinked my eyes, squeezed them shut, then opened them again. The nebulous light still fogged me. I could scarcely see more than an arm's length in any direction. I waited in vain for my eyes to adjust to the vague starlight. But soon I began to shiver, so I began to walk silently through the empty streets. My natural wariness came back first, followed by a dim recollection of my companions, the tent, the sundered road. But between that hazy memory and my standing up in this street, there was nothing.

I looked back the way I had come. Darkness had swallowed
the road behind me. Even my footprints were being filled in by
the slowly falling damp snowflakes. I blinked snowflakes from my
eyelashes and peered about me. I saw the damply glistening sides
of stone buildings to either side of the street. My eyes could make
no sense of the light. It was sourceless and evenly insufficient.
There were no looming shadows or especially dark alleys. But
neither could I make out where I was going. The heights and
styles of the buildings, the destinations of the streets remained a
mystery.

I felt panic rise in me and fought it down. The sensations I
had reminded me too vividly of how I had been Skill-deceived
in Regal's manor. I was terrified to grope out with the Skill lest
I encounter Will's taint in this city. But if I moved blindly on,
trusting that I was not being deceived, I might blunder into a trap.
In the shelter of a wall, I paused and forced myself to composure. I
tried once more to recall how I had come here, how long ago I
had left my companions and why. Nothing came to me. I quested
out with my Wit-sense, trying to find Nighteyes, but I sensed
nothing else alive. I wondered if there were truly no living creatures nearby, or if my Wit-sense had once more failed. I had no
answers to that either. When I listened, I heard only wind. I
smelled only damp stone, fresh snow and somewhere, perhaps,
river water. Panic rose in me once more and I leaned back against
the wall.

The city suddenly sprang to life around me. I perceived I was
leaning up against the wall of an inn. From within I heard the
sounds of a shrill piping instrument and voices lifted in an
unfamiliar song. A wagon rumbled past in the street, and then
a young couple darted past the mouth of the alley, hand in
hand, laughing as they ran. It was night in this strange city,
but it was not sleeping. I lifted my eyes to the impossible
heights of their strangely-spired buildings, and saw lights
burning in the upper storey. In the distance, a man called loudly
to someone.

My heart was hammering. What was wrong with me? I steeled
myself and found the resolve to go forth and find out what I could
about this strange city. I waited until another keg-laden ale-wagon

had rumbled past the mouth of my alley. Then I stepped away from the wall.

And in that instant, all was once more quiet, gleaming darkness. Gone was the song and laughter from the tavern; no one passed in the streets. I ventured to the mouth of the alley and peered cautiously in both directions. Nothing. Only softly falling wet snow. At least, I told myself, the weather was milder here than it had been on the road above. Even if I had to spend the entire night out of doors, I would not suffer too much.

I wandered a time through the city. At every intersection, I chose the widest road to follow, and soon realized a pattern of always going gently downhill. The river smell grew stronger. I paused once to rest on the edge of a great circular basin that might have enclosed a fountain or been a washing court. Immediately the city once more sprang to life around me. A traveller came and watered his horse at the dry basin so close that I could have reached out to touch him. He noticed me not at all, but I marked well the strangeness of his garb and the odd shape of the saddle the horse wore. A group of women walked past me, talking and laughing quietly together. They wore long, straight garments that hung softly from their shoulders and fluttered about their calves as they walked. All wore their long fair hair loose to their hips, and their boots rang on the cobbled street. When I rose to speak to them, they vanished and the light with them.

Twice more I woke the city before I realized all it took was the touch of my hand on a crystal-veined wall. It took an unreasonable amount of courage but I began to walk with just my fingers trailing along the buildings' sides. When I did so, the city bloomed into life about me as I walked. It was night and the quiet snow still fell. The passing wagons left no tracks in it. I heard the slamming of doors that had long since rotted away and saw folk walk lightly over a deep gully some wild rainstorm had created down one street. It was hard to dismiss them as ghosts when they called greetings aloud to one another. I was the one who was ignored and invisible as I drifted along.

At length I came to a wide black river flowing smoothly under the starlight. Several ghost quays ran out into it and two immense ships were anchored out in the river. Lights shone from their decks. Hogsheads and bales waited dockside to be loaded. A huddle of folk were engaged in some game of chance and someone's honesty was being loudly disputed. They dressed differently from the river-rats who came into Buck and the language was different, but in all else that I could tell, they were the same breed. As I watched, a fight broke out and spread to become a general brawl. It dispersed quickly when the whistle of the night-watch sounded, combatants fleeing in all directions before the city guard arrived.

I lifted my hand from the wall. I stood a moment in the snow-spangled darkness, letting my eyes adjust. Ships, quays, river folk were all gone. But the quiet black water still flowed, steaming in the colder air. I walked toward it, feeling the road go rough and broken under my feet as I advanced. The waters of this river had risen and fallen over this street, working their damage with no one to oppose them. When I turned my back to the river and studied the skyline of the city, I could see the faint silhouettes of fallen spires and crumpled walls. Once again I quested out about me; once again I found no life.

I turned back to the river. Something in the general configuration of the land tugged at my memory. It was not precisely here, I knew that, but I felt sure that this was the river where I had seen Verity lave his hands and arms and bring them out gleaming with magic. Cautiously I walked over broken paving stones right down to the edge of the river. It looked like water, it smelled like water. I crouched down beside it and thought. I had heard tales of pools of tarry mud covered over with water; I knew well how oil floated upon water. Perhaps beneath the black water there flowed another river, one of silver power. Perhaps, further upstream or down, was the tributary of pure Skill I had seen in my vision.

I drew off my mitten and bared my arm. I set my hand upon the flow of the water, feeling its icy kiss against my bare palm. Senses straining, I tried to detect whether there was Skill beneath that surface; I felt nothing. But perhaps if I plunged in my arm and hand, they would come up gleaming with strength. I dared myself to reach in to discover for myself.

That was as far as my courage went. I was no Verity. I knew

the strength of his Skilling, and I had seen how his immersion in the magic had tried his will. I was no match for it. He had marched alone up the Skill road while I . . . My mind darted back to that puzzle. When had I left the Skill road and my companions? Perhaps I never had. Perhaps all this was a dream. I reached up and patted cold water on my face. I felt no different. I set my nails to my face and scratched the skin until it hurt. It proved nothing to me but only made me wonder if I could dream pain. I had found no answers in this strange dead city, only more questions.

With great resolve I turned my steps back the way I had come. Visibility was poor and the clinging snow was rapidly filling my footprints. With reluctance I set my fingers to the stone of a wall. It was easier to trace my way back that way, for the living city had had more landmarks than the cold cinders of it did. Yet as I hurried through the snowy streets, I wondered when all these folk had been here. Did I view the events of a night a hundred years ago? Had I come here another night would I view the same events played out or see a different night from the city's history? Or did these shades of folk perceive themselves as living now, was I an odd cold shadow that crept through their lives? I forced myself to stop wondering about things I had no answer to. I had to trace my way back the way I had come.

Either I came to the end of places I could remember or I took a wrong turning. The result was the same. I found myself wandering up a road I was sure was unfamiliar. I trailed my fingers down the fronts of a row of shops, all locked up tight for the night. I passed two lovers locked in an embrace in a doorway. A ghost dog padded past me without giving me so much as a curious sniff.

Despite the milder weather, I was getting cold. And tired. I glanced up at the sky. It would soon be morning. By daylight, I could perhaps climb up one of the buildings and get the lay of the land. Perhaps when I awoke, I would recall how I came here. Foolishly, I cast about for some overhanging eave or shed where I might shelter before it occurred to me that there was no reason not to go inside one of the buildings. Even so, I felt queer as I chose a door and walked through it. While I touched a wall, I saw a dim interior. Tables and shelves were laden with fine pottery and glassware. A cat slept by a banked hearth. When I lifted my hand from the wall, all was cold and pitch-black. So I trailed my fingers along the wall, nearly stumbling over the crumbling remains of one of the tables. I stooped, and gathered together the bits by touch and took them to the hearth. By great perseverance, I made a true fire of them where the ghost fire burned.

When it was going well and I stood over it to warm myself, its flickering light showed me a different view of the room. Bare walls and debris-strewn floor. There was no trace of the fine crockery and glassware, though there were a few more bits of wood from long-fallen shelves. I thanked my luck that they had been made of good oak, for surely they would have rotted to splinters long ago if they had not. I decided to lay my cloak on the floor to save me from the stone's chill and trust my fire to keep me warm enough. I lay down and closed my eyes and tried not to think of ghost cats or what phantom folk slept in their beds on the floor above me.

I tried to set my Skill-walls before I slept, but it was rather like drying one's feet while standing in a river. The closer I came to sleep, the harder it was to recall where those boundaries lay. How much of my world was me and how much was the folk I cared about? I dreamed first of Kettricken, Starling, Kettle and the Fool wandering about with torches while Nighteyes ran back and forth, back and forth whining. It was not a comfortable dream and I turned away from it and drifted deeper into myself. Or so I supposed.

I found the familiar hut. I knew the simple room, the rough table, the tidy hearth, the narrow bed so neatly made. Molly sat in her nightrobe by the hearth, rocking Nettle and singing softly a song about stars and starfish. I could recall no lullabies and was as charmed by it as Nettle. The baby's wide eyes were on Molly's face as her mother sang. She gripped one of Molly's forefingers in her small fist. Molly sang the song over and over and over, but I found no boredom there. It was a scene I could watch for a month, for a year, and never know tedium.

But the babe's eyelids slid shut, once, to open quickly. They closed more slowly a second time, and stay closed. Her tiny pursed mouth moved as if she suckled in her sleep. Her black hair had begun to curl. Molly lowered her face to brush her lips across Nettle's forehead.

Molly rose wearily and carried the baby to her bed. She pulled open the blanket, nestled the child in, and then went back to the table to blow out the single candle there. By the light from the hearth, I watched her ease into bed beside the child and draw the blankets up over them both. She closed her eyes and sighed and did not stir again. I watched over her leaden sleep, recognizing it as the sleep of exhaustion. I knew sudden shame. This hard, bare life was not anything I ever envisioned for her, let alone our child. Were it not for Burrich, life would be even harder for them. I fled from seeing them this way, promising myself that things would get better, that somehow I would make things better for them. When I returned.

'I expected that by the time I returned, things would be better. But this is too good to trust, in a way.'

It was Chade's voice. He leaned over a table in a darkened room, studying a scroll. A branch of candles lit his face and the unrolled map before him. He looked tired but in good spirits. His grey hair was dishevelled. His white shirt was half open and loose of his breeches so it hung about his hips like a skirt. The old man was lean and muscular where before he was skinny. He took a long draw from a steaming mug and shook his head over something. 'Regal seems to gain no ground in his war against the Mountains. In every attack against the border towns, the Usurper's troops feint and then withdraw. There is no concerted effort to seize territory they have ravaged, no massing of troops to force their way to Jhaampe. What is his game?'

'Come here and I'll show you.'

Chade looked up from his scroll, half amused and half annoyed. 'I've a serious question to ponder. I'll not find the answer to this in your bed.'

The woman threw back the bedding and rose, to pad softly over to the table. She moved like a stalking cat. Her nakedness was not vulnerability, but armour. Her long brown hair had pulled loose of its warrior tail to reach past her shoulders. She was not young, and long ago a sword had left its tracks down her ribs. She was still breathtaking in a formidable, female way. She bent over the map beside him and pointed to something. 'Look here. And here. And here. Were you Regal, why would you attack all these places at once, with forces too small to hold any of them?'

When Chade did not answer, she moved her finger to tap another spot on the map. 'None of those attacks came as any great surprise. Mountain troops that had been gathered here were diverted to these two villages. Another second force from this location went to the third village. Now, see where the Mountain troops were not?'

'There's nothing along there worth having.'

'Nothing,' she agreed. 'But once there was a trade route that went through the lesser pass, here, and thence into the heart of the Mountains. It bypasses Jhaampe, and is little used any more for that reason. Most traders want a route that will allow them to sell and trade in Jhaampe as well as the lesser towns.'

'Of what value is that to Regal? Does he seek to take and hold it?'

'No. No troops have been seen there at all.'

'Where does the trail lead?'

'Now? Nowhere save a few scattered villages. But it is good travelling for a small force moving fast.'

'Where does it go?'

'It dwindles away at Shishoe.' She tapped another spot on the map. 'But it would carry that hypothetical band of warriors deep into Mountain territory. Well behind all the troops watching and guarding the border. West of Jhaampe and unsuspected.'

'But what would be their goal?'

The woman shrugged casually, and smiled to see Chade's eyes leave the map. 'Perhaps an assassination attempt on King Eyod? Perhaps an attempt to recapture this bastard that is supposed to be sheltering in the Mountains. You tell me. This is more your trade than mine. Poison the wells at Jhaampe?'

Chade suddenly paled. 'It's been a week. They'll already be in place, their plot already in motion.' He shook his head. 'What am I to do?'

'Were it I, I'd send a swift courier to King Eyod. A lass on a horse. Alert him that there may be spies at his back.'

'I suppose that's best,' Chade agreed. There was a sudden weariness in his voice. 'Where are my boots?'

'Relax. The messenger was sent yesterday. By now King Eyod's trackers will be working the trail. He has very good trackers. I can vouch for that.'

Chade looked at her consideringly in a way that had nothing to do with her nakedness. 'You know the quality of his trackers. Yet you sent one of your own lasses to his very doorstep, with a missive penned by your own hand, to warn him.'

'I saw no good in letting such tidings wait.'

Chade smoothed his short beard over his jaw. 'When first I asked your aid, you told me you'd work for coin, not patriotism. You told me that to a horse thief, one side of the border was as good as another.'

She stretched, rolling her shoulders. She stepped to face him, placing her hands on his hips in calm assumption. They were nearly of a height. 'Perhaps you have won me to your side.'

His green eyes gleamed like a hunting cat's. 'Have I?' he mused as he drew her closer.

I came to myself with a small start and shifted uncomfortably. I felt ashamed to have spied on Chade, and envious of him as well. I poked a bit at my fire and lay down again, reminding myself that Molly also slept alone, save for the small warmth of our daughter. It was little comfort and my sleep was restless for the remainder of the night.

When I opened my eyes again, a square of watery sunlight overlay me from the unshuttered window. My fire had burned to a few coals, but I was not that cold. In the light of day, the chamber I was in was dismal. I went and peered into a second room, seeking a stairway to the upper storeys that might offer me a better view of the city. Instead I saw the sagging remnants of wooden steps I dared not trust even for a brief ascent. The damp was heavier as well. The dank cold stone walls and floor reminded me of the dungeons of Buckkeep. I left the shop, stepping out into a day that seemed almost warm. Last night's snow was retreating into puddles. I took off my hat and let the gentler wind move against my hair. Spring, some part of me whispered. The edge of spring was in the air.

I had expected that daylight would vanquish the phantom denizens of the city. Instead, the light seemed to make them stronger. Black stone with quartz-like veins had been used widely in constructing the city and I had but to touch any piece of it to see the city's life awaken around me. But even when I touched nothing I still seemed to catch glimpses of folk, to hear the murmur of their chatter and sense the tumult of their passage. I walked for some time, seeking a tall, mostly intact building that would offer me the view I sought. By daylight, the city was far more ruined than I had suspected. Whole domes of roofs had fallen in, and some buildings had great cracks green with moss running up their walls. In others, outer walls had fallen away entirely, exposing the inner chambers and filling the street below with rubble I must clamber over. Few of the taller buildings were totally intact and some leaned drunkenly against one another. I finally saw a likely building with a tall spire peeping up above its neighbours, and made my way toward it.

When I reached it, I wasted some little time in standing and staring up at it. I wondered if it had been a palace. Great lions of stone guarded the entrance steps. The exterior walls were of the same shining black stone I had come to regard as the common building material for the city, but affixed to them were silhouettes of folk and beasts all cut from some gleaming white stone. The stark contrast of white on black and the grand scale of these images made them almost overwhelming. A giant of a woman gripped an immense plough behind a team of monstrous oxen. A winged creature, perhaps a dragon, took an entire wall to himself. I slowly climbed the wide stone steps to the entryway. It seemed to me that as I did so, the murmuring of the city grew louder and more insistently real. A grinning young man came hastening down the steps, a scroll gripped in one hand. I sidestepped to avoid colliding with him, but as he hastened past I felt not the slightest sense of his being. I turned to stare after him. His eyes had been yellow as amber.

The great wooden doors were closed and had been latched, but so rotted were they that one cautious push tore the lock free.

One door swung open while the other sagged gratefully down to collapse on the floor. I peered in before I entered. Streaked and dusty windows of thick glass admitted the winter sunlight. Dust motes from the settling door danced in the air. I half expected bats or pigeons or a scurrying rat or two. There was nothing, not even a scent of animal habitation. Like the road, the city was avoided by wild beasts. I stepped inside, my boots scuffing lightly on the dusty floors.

There were the tatters of ancient hangings, a collapsed wooden bench. I lifted my eyes to a ceiling far above my head. This chamber alone could have held the entire exercise grounds at Buckkeep. I felt tiny. But across the chamber from me were stone steps marching up into the gloom. As I crossed to them, I heard the businesslike mutter of talk, and suddenly the stairs were peopled with tall robed folk coming and going. Most gripped scrolls or clutched papers, and the tone of their conversation was that of people discussing weighty matters. They were subtly different from any folk I had ever been among. The colours of their eyes were too bright; the bones of their bodies were elongated. But for all that, much else about them was ordinary. This must have been some chamber of laws or ruling, I decided. Only such matters put lines upon so many brows and scowls on so many faces. There were a number of folk in yellow robes and black leggings, bearing a sort of insignia plates upon their shoulders, and these I judged to be officials. As I climbed first one staircase, and then another from the second floor, these yellow-robes increased in number.

The stairs were somewhat lit by the wide windows at each landing. The first showed me only the upper storey of the next building. On the second landing, I gained a view of some roofs. The third floor I had to cross to reach another stairway. Judging by the generous tatters on the walls, this floor had been even more opulent. I began to perceive ghostly furniture as well as people, as if the magic were stronger here. I kept to the edges of the walkways, loath to feel the un-touch of folk walking through me. There were many cushioned benches for waiting, another sure sign of officialdom, and many lesser scribes sitting at tables recording information from the scrolls presented to them.

I went up yet another flight of stairs, but was frustrated in my quest for a clear view of the city by an immense window of stained glass. The image presented was one of a woman and a dragon. They did not appear to be at odds, but instead stood as if speaking to one another. The woman in this window had black hair and black eyes and wore a band of bright red on her brow. She carried something in her left hand, but whether it was weapon or wand of office I could not tell. The immense dragon wore a jewelled collar, but nothing else in its stance or demeanour suggested domestication. I stared at the window, light gleaming through its dusty colours, for several long minutes before I could go on. I felt it had some significance I could not quite grasp. At last I turned away from it to survey this upper chamber.

This floor was better lit than the other ones had been. It was all one huge open chamber, but substantially smaller than the main floor had been. Tall narrow windows of clear glass alternated with stretches of wall ornately decorated with friezes of battles and agrarian scenes. I was drawn to the artwork, but resolutely directed my steps to another staircase. This was not broad, but was a spiralling stair that I hoped led up to the tower I had glimpsed from outside the building. The city spirits seemed less numerous here.

The climb was steeper and longer than I had expected it to be. I opened both my coat and my shirt before I reached the top. The winding steps were lit at intervals by windows scarce wider than arrow-slits. At one a young woman stood staring out over the city, an air of hopelessness in her lavender eyes. She seemed so real I found myself begging her pardon as I stepped around her. She paid no heed, of course. Again I had the eerie feeling that I was the ghost here. There were a few landings on this stair and doors leading to chambers, but these were locked and time seemed to have been more merciful here. The dry air of the upper levels had preserved the wood and metal. I wondered what lay behind their undisturbed fastness. Gleaming treasure? The knowledge of the ages? Mouldering bones? None gave to my shovings, and as I continued up, I hoped I would not find a locked door as my reward at the top of the tower.

The whole city was a mystery to me. The ghost life that teemed through it was such a contrast to its utter desertion now. I had seen no sign of battle; the only upheavals I had seen in the city seemed to be the result of the earth's deep unease. Here I passed more locked doors; I wonder if Eda herself knew what was behind them. No one locks a door unless he expects to return. I wondered where they had gone, the folk of this town who still moved here as ghosts. Why was this river city abandoned, and when? Had this been the home of the Elderlings? Were they the dragons I had seen on the buildings and in the stained-glass window? Some folk enjoy a puzzle; it gave me a pounding headache to complement the nagging hunger that had been growing in me since daybreak.

I reached at last the upper tower chamber. It opened all around me, a round chamber with a domed ceiling. Sixteen panels made up the walls of the room and eight were of thick glass, streaked and filthy. They subdued the winter sunlight flooding into the room through them, making it at once lit and gloomy. One of the windows was shattered and lay in shards both within and without the chamber, for a narrow parapet ran around the outside of the tower. A great round table was partially collapsed in the centre of the room. Two men and three women, all armed with pointers, were gesturing at where the table had once dominated the chamber, discussing something. One of the men seemed quite angry. I stepped around the phantom table and bureaucrats. A narrow door opened easily out onto the balcony.

There was a wooden railing running about the edge of the parapet but I did not trust it. Instead I walked a slow circuit of that tower, caught between wonder and fear of falling. On the south side, a wide river valley spread out before me. In the far distance was an edging of dark blue hills that held up the pale winter sky. The river wound, a fat lazy snake, through the near part of the valley. In the distance I could see other towns on the river. Beyond the river was a wide green valley, thickly treed or populated with tidy farmsteads which blinked in and out of existence when I shook my head to clear my eyes of ghosts. I saw a wide black bridge across the river and the road continuing on beyond it. I wondered where it led. Briefly I saw bright towers glinting in the distance. I pushed the ghosts away from my mind and saw a distant lake with steam rising off it in the watery sunlight. Was Verity out there somewhere?

My eyes wandered to the southeast and widened at what I saw there. Perhaps there was the answer to some of my questions. A whole section of the city was gone. Simply gone. No crumble of ruins was there, no fire-blackened rubble. Only a great and sudden rift gaped in the earth, as if some vast giant had driven in a giant wedge and split it wide. The river had filled it in, a shining tongue of water intruding into the city. The remains of buildings teetered on its edge still, streets ended abruptly at the water. My eyes traced this huge wound in the earth. Even at this distance, I could tell that the great crack extended beyond the far shore of the river. The destruction had plunged like a spear deep into the heart of the city. The placid water shone silver under the winter sky. I wondered if some sudden earthquake had been the death blow to this city. I shook my head. Too much of it remained standing still. No doubt it had been a great disaster, but it did not explain the city's death to me.

I walked slowly around to the north side of the tower. The city spread out at my feet, and beyond it I saw vineyards and grainfields. And beyond them, a forested stretch with the road running through it. Several days' ride away were the mountains. I shook my head to myself. By all my bearings, I must have come from there. Yet I did not recall the intervening journey at all. I leaned back against the wall and wondered what to do. If Verity were somewhere in this city, I felt no tingle of his presence. I wished I could recall why I had left my companions and when. *Come to me, come to me*, whispered through my bones. An overwhelming dreariness rose up in me and I longed simply to lie down where I was and die. I tried to tell myself it was the elfbark. It felt more like the after-effects of near-constant failure. I went back into the central chamber to get out of the chill winter wind.

As I stepped back in through the shattered window, a stick rolled under my foot and I nearly fell. When I recovered, I glanced down and wondered that I had not noticed before. At the base of the broken window were the remains of a small fire. Soot had smudged some of the hanging glass remaining in the side part of the window frame. I stooped to touch it cautiously; my finger came away black. It was not very fresh, but neither was it older than a few months; otherwise the winter storms would have weathered more of it away. I stepped away and tried to make my weary mind work. The fire was made from wood, but it had included sticks as from trees or bushes. Someone had deliberately carried small twigs up here to kindle this fire. Why? Why not use the remains of the table? And why climb this high to make a fire? For the view?

I sat down beside the remains of the fire and tried to think. When I leaned my back against the stone wall, it gave more substance to the arguing phantoms around the table. One shouted something at another, and then drew an imaginary line with his pointer over the collapsed table. One of the women crossed her arms across her chest and looked stubborn, while another smiled coldly and tapped with her own stick on the table. Cursing myself for an idiot, I leaped to my feet to look down at the ancient ruins of the table.

The second that I perceived it was a map, I was sure Verity had made the fire. A foolish grin spread wide across my face. Of course. A tall-windowed tower looking out over the city and surrounding countryside, and in the centre of the room, a great table holding the most peculiar map I had ever seen. It was not drawn on paper, but made of clay to mimic the rolling countryside. It had cracked in the collapsing of the table, but I could see how the river had been wrought of shining chips of black glass. There were tiny models of the buildings of the city beside the arrow-straight roads, tiny fountains filled with blue chips of glass, even twigs leafed with green wool to represent the greater trees in the city. At intervals throughout the city, small crystals of stone were fixed in the map. I suspected they represented compass points. All was there, even tiny squares to represent stalls in the market. Despite its ruin, it delighted the eye with its detail. I smiled, very certain that within months of Verity returning to Buckkeep, there would be a similar table and map in his Skill-tower.

I bent over it, ignoring the phantoms, to retrace my steps. I located the map tower easily. As luck would have it that section of the map was much cracked, but I still was fairly certain of my path as my fingers walked where my feet had the night before. Once more I marvelled at the straightness of the roads and the precise intersections where they met. I was not certain exactly where I had first 'awakened' the night before, but I was able to select a section of the city that was not too large and say with certainty it was within that square. My eye returned to the tower and I carefully noted the number of intersections and the turns I must make to return to my starting-point. Perhaps once there, if I cast about, I might find something that would awaken my memories of the missing days. I wished suddenly for a bit of paper and a quill to sketch out the surrounding area. When I did so, the meaning of the fire was instantly clear.

Verity had used a burnt stick to make his map. But upon what? I glanced around the room, but there were no hangings on these walls. Instead the walls between the windows were slabs of white stone, incised with . . . I stood up to get a closer look. Wonder overtook me. I put my hand on the cold white stone, and then peered out of the dirty window beside it. My fingers traced the river I could see in the distance, then found the smooth track of the road that crossed it. The view out of each window was represented by the panel beside it. Tiny glyphs and symbols might have been the names of towns or holdings. I scrubbed at the window, but most of the dirt was on the outside.

The significance of the broken window was suddenly clear. Verity had broken out that pane, for a clearer view of what lay beyond it. And then he had kindled that fire and used a burnt stick to copy something, probably to the map he had been carrying since Buckkeep. But what? I went to the broken window and studied the panels to either side of it. A hand had smeared the left one, wiping dust away from it. I set my own hand upon the print of Verity's palm in the dust. He had cleared this panel and stared out the window, and then copied something down. I could not doubt that it was his destination. I wondered if what was marked on the panel somehow co-ordinated with the markings on the map he had carried. I wished in vain that I had Kettricken's copy with me to compare the two.

Out of the window, I could see the mountains to the north of me. I had come from there. I studied the view and then tried to relate it to the etched panel beside me. The flickering ghosts of the past were no help. One moment I looked out over a forested countryside; the next I was looking at vineyards and grainfields. The only feature that was in common to both views was the black ribbon of road that went straight as an arrow to the mountains. My fingers tracked the road up the panel. There in the distance it reached the mountains. Some glyphs were marked there, where the road diverged. And a tiny sparkle of crystal had been embedded in the panel there.

I put my face close to the panel and tried to study the tiny glyphs there. Did they match the markings on Verity's map? Were they symbols Kettricken would recognize? I left the tower room and hastened down the stairs, passing through phantoms that seemed to grow stronger and stronger. I heard their words clearly now and caught glimpses of the tapestries that had once graced the walls. There were many dragons depicted on them. 'Elderlings?' I asked of the echoing stone walls, and heard my words shivering up and down the stairs.

I sought something to write upon. The tattered tapestries were damp rags that crumbled at a touch. What wood there was was old and rotten. I broke down the door to one inner chamber, hoping to find its contents well preserved. Inside, I found the interior walls lined with wooden racks of pigeonholes, each holding a scroll. They looked substantial, as did the writing implements on the table in the centre of the room. But my groping fingers found little more than the ghosts of paper, crisp and fragile as ashes. My eyes showed me a stack of fresh vellums on a corner shelf. My groping fingers pushed away rotted debris, finally to find a usable fragment no bigger than my two hands. It was stiff and yellowed, but it might serve. A heavy stoppered glass pot held the dried remnants of an ink. The wooden handles of their writing implements were gone, but the metal tips had survived and they were long enough for me to grasp firmly. Armed with these supplies, I returned to the map-room.

Spittle restored the ink to life and I honed the metal nib on the floor until it shone clean again. I rekindled the remnants of Verity's fire, for the afternoon was becoming overcast and the light through the dusty windows was dimming. I knelt in front of the panel Verity's hand had dusted and copied as much as I could of the road, mountains and other features onto the scrap of stiffened leather. Painstakingly I squinted at the tiny glyphs and transferred as many of them as I could to the vellum. Perhaps Kettricken could make sense of them. Perhaps when we compared this clumsy map of mine to the map she carried, some common feature would make sense. It was all I had to go on. The sun was setting outside and my fire no more than embers when I finally finished. I looked down on my scratchings ruefully. Neither Verity nor Fedwren would have been impressed with my work. But it would have to do. When I was certain the ink was set and would not smear, I put the vellum inside my shirt to carry it. I would not chance rain or snow on it to blur my markings.

I left the tower as night was falling. My ghostly companions had long since gone home to hearth and supper. I walked the streets among scores of folk seeking their homes or venturing out for an evening's pleasure. I passed inns and taverns that seemed to blaze with light and heard merry voices from within. It was becoming harder and harder for me to see the truth of the empty streets and abandoned buildings. It was a special misery to walk with my belly growling and my throat dry past inns where phantoms filled themselves with ghostly cheer and shouted aloud to one another in greeting.

My plans were simple. I would go to the river and drink. Then I would do my best to return to the first place I remembered in the city. I would find some sort of shelter in that vicinity for the night, and by morning light I would head back toward the mountains. I hoped if I went by the path I had probably used to come here, something would stimulate my memory.

I was kneeling by the river's edge, one palm flat on the paving stone, drinking cold water when the dragon appeared. One moment the sky above me was empty. Then there was a great golden light on everything and the noise of great wings beating, like the whirring of a pheasant's wings in flight. About me folk cried out, some in startlement and some in delight. The creature dived down on us and circled low. The wake of wind it put out set the ships to rocking and the river to rippling. Once more it circled and then without warning it plunged completely out of sight in the river. The golden light it had shed was extinguished and the night seemed all the darker by comparison.

I jerked back reflexively from the dream wave that leaped against the shore as the river absorbed the dragon's impact. All around me, people were staring expectantly at the water. I followed their gazes. At first I saw nothing. Then the water parted and a great head emerged from the river. Water dripped from it and ran gleaming down the golden serpentine neck that next appeared. All the tales I had ever been told had alluded to dragons as worms or lizards or snakes. But as this one emerged from the river, holding out its dripping wings, I found myself thinking of birds. Graceful cormorants rising out of the sea from a dive after fish, or brightly-plumaged pheasants came to my mind as the huge creature emerged. It was fully as large as one of the ships and the spread of its wings put the canvas sails to shame. It paused on the riverbank and preened the water from its scaled wings. The word scale does no justice to the ornate plates that sheathed its wings, yet feather is too airy a word to describe them. Could a feather be made of finely beaten gold, perhaps it might come close to the dragon's plumage.

I was transfixed with delight and wonder. The creature ignored me, emerging from the river so close to me that had it been real, I would have been soaked by the water that dripped from its outstretched wings. Every drop that fell back into the river carried the unmistakable shimmer of raw magic with it. The dragon paused on the riverbank, its four great clawed feet sinking deep in the damp earth as it carefully folded its wings and then preened its long, forked tail. Golden light bathed me and illuminated the gathering crowd. I turned away from the dragon to regard them. Welcome shone in their faces and great deference. The dragon had the bright eyes of a gyrfalcon and the carriage of a stallion as it strode up to them. The folk parted to make way for it, murmuring respectful greetings.

'Elderling,' I said aloud to myself. I followed it, my fingers trailing the building fronts, one with the entranced crowd, as it paraded slowly up the street. Folk poured from taverns to add their greetings and swelled the crowd that followed it. Obviously this was no common event. I do not know what I hoped to discover by following it. I do not think I really thought of anything at that time, save to follow this immense, charismatic creature. I understood now the reason why the main streets of this city had been built so wide. It was not to allow the passage of wagons, but so that nothing might impede one of these great visitors.

It paused once before a great stone basin. Folk rushed forward to vie for the honour of working a windlass of sorts. Bucket after bucket rose on a loop of chain, each spilling its cargo of liquid magic into the basin. When the basin brimmed with the shimmering stuff, the Elderling gracefully bowed its neck and drank. Ghost-Skill it might be, but even the sight of it awakened that insidious hunger in me. Twice more the basin was filled and twice more the Elderling drank it down before it proceeded on its way. I followed, marvelling at what I had seen.

Ahead of us suddenly loomed that great gash of destruction that marred the city's symmetrical form. I followed the ghostly procession to the lip of it, only to see everyone, man, woman and Elderling, vanish completely as they strode unconcernedly out into the space. In a short time I stood alone on the edge of that gaping crevasse, hearing only the wind whispering over the still deep water. A few patches of stars showed through the overcast sky and were reflected in the black water. Whatever other secrets of the Elderlings I might have learned had been swallowed long ago in that great cataclysm.

I turned and walked slowly away, wondering where the Elderling had been bound and for what purpose. I shuddered again as I recalled how it had drunk down the silver gleaming power.

It took me some time to retrace my steps first to the river. Once there, I focused my mind on recalling what I had seen in the map-room earlier that day. My hunger was a hollow thing that rattled against my ribs now, but I resolutely ignored it as I threaded my way through the streets. My strength of will carried me through a knot of brawling shadows but my resolution failed me when the city guard came charging down the streets on their massive horses. I leaped to one side to let them pass, and winced as I heard the sounds of their falling truncheons. Unreal as it was, I was glad to leave the noisy discord behind me. I made a right turn up a slightly narrower street and walked on past three more intersections.

I halted. Here. This was the plaza where I had been kneeling in the snow the night before. There, that pillar standing at its centre, I recalled some sort of monument or sculpture looming over me. I walked toward it. It was made of the same ubiquitous black stone veined with gleaming crystal. To my weary eyes it seemed to gleam brighter with the same mysterious unlight the other structures gave off. The faint shining outlined on its side glyphs cut deep into its surface. I walked slowly around it. Some, I was sure, were familiar and perhaps twin to those I had copied earlier in the day. Was this then some sort of guidepost, labelled with destinations according to compass headings? I reached out a hand to trace one of the familiar glyphs.

The night bent around me. A wave of vertigo swept over me. I clutched at the column for support, but somehow missed it and went stumbling forward. My outstretched hands found nothing and I fell face forward into crusted snow and ice. For a time I just lay there, my cheek against the icy road, blinking my useless eyes at the blackness of the night. Then a warm, solid weight hit me. *My brother!* Nighteyes greeted me joyously. He thrust his cold nose into my face and pawed at my head to rouse me. *I knew you would come back. I knew it!*

TWENTY-EIGHT

The Coterie

Part of the great mystery that surrounds the Elderlings is that the few images we have of them bear small resemblance to each other. This is true not only of tapestries and scrolls that are copies of older works and hence might contain errors, but also of the few images of Elderlings that have survived from King Wisdom's time. Some of the images bear superficial resemblances to the legends of dragons, featuring wings, claws, scaly skin and great size. But others do not. In at least one tapestry, the Elderling is depicted as similar to a human, but gold of skin and great of size. The images do not even agree in the number of limbs that benevolent race possessed. They may have as many as four legs and two wings also, or have no wings at all and walk upon two legs as a man.

It has been theorized that so little was written about them because knowledge of the Elderlings at that time was regarded as common knowledge. Just as no one sees fit to create a scroll that deals with the most basic attributes of what a horse is, for it would serve no useful purpose, so no one thought that one day Elderlings would be the stuff of legends. To a certain degree, this makes sense. But one has only to look about at all the scrolls and tapestries in which horses are featured as the stuff of common life to find a flaw. Were Elderlings so accepted a part of life, surely they would have been more often depicted.

After a very confusing hour or two, I found myself back in the yurt with the others. The night seemed all the colder for having spent an almost warm day in the city. We huddled in the tent in our blankets. They had told me I had vanished from the lip of the cliff only the night before; I had told them of all I had encountered in the city. There had been a certain amount of disbelief on everyone's part. I had felt both moved and guilty to see how much anguish my disappearance had caused them. Starling had obviously been weeping, while both Kettle and Kettricken had the owly look of folks who had not slept. The Fool had been the worst, pale and silent with a slight trembling to his hands. It had taken a bit of time for all of us to recover. Kettle had cooked a meal twice the size of what we usually had and all save the Fool had eaten heartily. He had not seemed to have the energy. While the others sat in a circle around the brazier listening to my tale, he was already curled in his blankets, the wolf snug beside him. He seemed completely exhausted.

After I had been over the events of my adventure for the third time, Kettle commented cryptically, 'Well, thank Eda you were dosed with elfbark before you were taken; otherwise you would never have kept your wits at all.'

'You say "taken"?' I pressed immediately.

She scowled at me. 'You know what I mean.' She looked about at all of us staring at her. 'Through the guidepost or whatever it is. They must have something to do with it.' A silence met her words. 'It seems obvious to me, that's all. He left us at one, and arrived there at one. And returned to us the same way.'

'But why didn't they take anyone else?' I protested.

'Because you are the only Skill-sensitive one among us,' she pointed out.

'Are they Skill-wrought as well?' I asked her bluntly.

She met my glance. 'I looked at the guidepost by daylight. It is hewn of black stone with wide threads of shining crystal in it. Like the walls of the city you describe. Did you touch both posts?'

I was silent a moment, thinking. 'I believe so.'

She shrugged. 'Well, there you are. A Skill-imbued object can retain the intent of its maker. Those posts were erected to make travel easier for those who could master them.'

'I've never heard of such things. How do you know them?'

'I am only speculating on what seems obvious to me,' she told me stubbornly. 'And that is all I am going to say. I'm going to sleep. I'm exhausted. We all spent the entire night and most of the day looking for you and worrying about you. What hours we could rest, that wolf never stopped howling.'

Howling?

I called you. You did not answer.

I did not hear you, or I would have tried.

I begin to fear, Little Brother. Forces pull at you, taking you to places I cannot follow, closing your mind to mine. This, right now, is as close as I have ever come to being accepted into a pack. But if I lost you, even it would be lost to me.

You will not lose me, I promised him, but I wondered if it was a promise I could keep.

'Fitz?' Kettricken asked in a nudging voice.

'I am here,' I assured her.

'Let us look at the map you copied.'

I took it out and she drew out her own map. We compared the two. It was hard to find any similarities, but the scales of the maps were different. At last we decided that the piece I had copied down in the city bore a superficial resemblance to the portion of trail that was drawn on Kettricken's map. 'This place,' I gestured to one destination marked on her map, 'would seem to be the city. If that is so, then this corresponds to this, and this to this.'

The map Verity had set out with had been a copy of this older, faded map. On that one the trail I now thought of as the Skill road had been marked, but oddly, as a path that began suddenly in the Mountains and ended abruptly at three separate destinations. The significance of those endpoints had once been marked on the map, but those markings had faded into inky smears. Now we had the map I had copied in the city, with those three endpoints on it also. One had been the city itself. The other two were now our concern.

Kettricken studied the glyphs I had copied from the city's map. 'I've seen such markings, from time to time,' she admitted uneasily. 'No one truly reads them anymore. A handful of them are still known. One encounters them mostly in odd places. In a few places in the Mountains, there are raised stones that have such marks. There are some at the west end of the Great Chasm Bridge. No one knows when they were carved, or why. Some are thought to mark graves, but others say they marked land boundaries.'

'Can you read any of them?' I asked her.

'A few. They are used in a challenge game. Some are stronger than others . . .' her voice trailed off as she studied my scratchings. 'None match exactly the ones I know,' she said at last, disappointment heavy in her voice. 'This one is almost like the one for "stone". But the others I have never seen at all.'

'Well, it's one of the ones that was marked here.' I tried to make my voice cheery. 'Stone' conveyed nothing at all to me. 'It seems closest to where we are. Shall we go there next?'

'I would have liked to see the city,' the Fool said softly. 'I should have liked to see the dragon, too.'

I nodded slowly. 'It is a place and a thing worth seeing. Much knowledge is there, if only we had the time to ferret it out. Did not I have Verity always in my head with his "come to me, come to me" I think I would have been more curious to explore.' I had said nothing to them of my dreams of Molly and Chade. Those were private things, as was my ache to be home with her again.

'Doubtless you would have,' Kettle agreed. 'And doubtless got yourself into more trouble that way. I wonder, did he so bind you to keep you on the road and protect you from distractions?'

I would have challenged her again on her knowledge, had not the Fool repeated softly, 'I would have liked to see the city.'

'We should all sleep now. We are up at first light, to travel hard tomorrow. It heartens me to think that Verity had been there before FitzChivalry, even as it fills me with foreboding. We must get to him quickly. I can no longer stand wondering each night why he never returned.'

'Comes the Catalyst, to make stone of flesh and flesh of stone. At his touch shall be wakened the dragons of the earth. The sleeping city shall tremble and waken to him. Comes the Catalyst.' The Fool's voice was dreamy.

'The writings of White Damir,' Kettle added reverently. She looked at me and for a moment was annoyed. 'Hundreds of writings and prophecies and they all terminate in you?'

'Not my fault,' I said inanely. I was already rucking my way into my blankets. I thought longingly of the almost warm day I had had. The wind was blowing and I felt chilled to the bone.

I was drowsing off when the Fool reached over to pat my face with a warm hand. 'Good you're alive,' he muttered.

'Thank you,' I said. I was summoning up Kettle's game board and pieces in an effort to keep my mind to myself for the night. I had just begun to contemplate the problem. Suddenly I sat up, exclaiming, 'Your hand is warm! Fool! Your hand is warm!'

'Go to sleep,' Starling chided me in an offended tone.

I ignored her. I dragged the blanket down from the Fool's face and touched his cheek. His eyes opened slowly. 'You're warm,' I told him. 'Are you all right?'

'I don't feel warm,' he informed me miserably. 'I feel cold. And very, very tired.'

I began building up the fire in the brazier hastily. Around me the others were stirring. Starling across the tent had sat up and was peering at me through the gloom.

'The Fool is never warm,' I told them, trying to make them understand my urgency. 'Always, when you touch his skin, it is cool. Now he's warm.'

'Indeed?' Starling asked in an oddly sarcastic voice.

'Is he ill?' Kettle asked tiredly.

'I don't know. I've never known him to be ill in my whole life.'

'I am seldom ill,' the Fool corrected me quietly. 'But this is a fever I have known before. Lie down and sleep, Fitz. I'll be all right. I expect the fever will have burned out by morning.'

'Whether it has or not, we must travel tomorrow morning,' Kettricken said implacably. 'We have already lost a day lingering here.'

'Lost a day?' I exclaimed, almost angrily. 'Gained a map, or more detail for one, and knowledge that Verity had been to the city. For myself, I doubt not that he went there as I did, and perhaps returned to this very spot. We have not lost a day, Kettricken, but gained all the days it would have taken us to find a way down to what remains of the road down there and then tramp to the city. And back again. As I recall, you had proposed spending a day just to seek for a way down that slide. Well, we did, and we found the way.' I paused. I took a breath and imposed calm on my voice. 'I will not seek to force any of you to my will. But if the Fool is not well enough to travel tomorrow, I shall not travel either.'

A glint came into Kettricken's eyes, and I braced myself for battle. But the Fool forestalled it. 'I shall travel tomorrow, well or not,' he assured us both.

'That's settled, then,' Kettricken said swiftly. Then, in a more human voice she asked, 'Fool, is there anything I can do for you? I would not use you so harshly, were not the need so great. I have not forgotten, and never shall, that without you I would never have reached Jhaampe alive.'

I sensed a story I was not privy to, but kept my questions to myself.

'I will be fine. I am just . . . Fitz? Could I beg some elfbark of you? That warmed me last night as nothing else has.'

'Certainly.' I was rummaging in my pack for it when Kettle spoke out warningly.

'Fool, I counsel you against it. It is a dangerous herb, and almost always more damaging than good. Who knows but you are ill tonight because you had some the night before last?'

'It is not that potent a herb,' I said disdainfully. 'I've used it for a number of years, and taken no lasting ill from it.'

Kettle gave a snort. 'None that you are wise enough to see, anyway,' she said sarcastically. 'But it is a warming herb that gives energy to the flesh, even if it is deadening to the spirit.'

'I always found it restored me rather than deadened me,' I countered as I found the small packet and opened it. Without my asking her, Kettle got up to put water on to boil. 'I never noticed it dulling my mind,' I added.

'The one taking it seldom does,' she retorted. 'And while it may boost your physical energy for a time, you must always pay for it later. Your body is not to be tricked, young man. You will know that better when you are as old as I.'

I fell silent. As I thought back over the times I had used elfbark to restore myself, I had the uncomfortable suspicion that she was at least partly right. But my suspicion was not enough to keep me from brewing two cups rather than just one. Kettle shook her head at me, but lay back down and said no more. I sat beside the

Fool as we drank our tea. When he handed me back the empty mug, his hand seemed warmer, not cooler.

'Your fever is rising,' I warned him.

'No. It is just the heat of the mug on my skin,' he suggested.

I ignored him. 'You are shaking all over.'

'A bit,' he admitted. Then his misery broke through and he said, 'I am cold as I have never been before. My back and my jaws ache from shaking with it.'

Flank him, suggested Nighteyes. The big wolf shifted to press more closely against him. I added my blankets to those covering the Fool and then crawled in beside him. He said not a word but his shivering lessened somewhat.

'I can't recall that you were ever ill at Buckkeep,' I said quietly.

'I was. But very seldom, and I kept to myself. As you recall, the healer had little tolerance for me, and I for him. I would not have trusted my health to his purges and tonics. Besides, what works for your kind sometimes does nothing for mine.'

'Is your kind so vastly different from mine?' I asked after a time. He had brought us close to a topic we had seldom even mentioned.

'In some ways,' he sighed. He lifted a hand to his brow. 'But sometimes I surprise even myself.' He took a breath, then sighed it out as if he had endured some pain for an instant. 'I may not even be truly ill. I have been going through some changes in the past year. As you have noticed.' He added the last in a whisper.

'You have grown, and gathered colour,' I agreed softly.

'That is a part of it.' A smile twitched over his face, then faded. 'I think I am almost an adult now.'

I snorted softly. 'I have counted you as a man for many years, Fool. I think you found your manhood before I did mine.'

'Did I? How droll!' he exclaimed softly, and for a moment sounded almost like himself. His eyes sagged shut. 'I am going to sleep now,' he told me.

I made no reply. I shouldered deeper into the blankets beside him and set my walls once more. I sank into a dreamless rest that was not cautionless sleep.

I awoke before first light with a foreboding of danger. Beside me, the Fool slept heavily. I touched his face, and found it warm still and misted with sweat. I rolled away from him, tucking the blankets in tight around him. I added a twig or two of precious fuel to the brazier and began drawing my clothes on quietly. Nighteyes was immediately alert.

Going out?

Just to sniff about.

Shall I come?

Keep the Fool warm. I won't be long.

Are you sure you'll be all right?

I'll be very careful. I promise.

The cold was like a slap. The darkness, absolute. After a moment or two, my eyes adjusted but even so I could see little more than the tent itself. An overcast had blotted the stars even. I stood still in the icy wind, straining my senses to find what had disturbed me. It was not the Skill but my Wit that quested out into the darkness for me. I sensed our party, and the hunger of the huddled jeppas. Grain alone would not keep them long. Another worry. Resolutely I set it aside and pushed my senses further. I stiffened. Horses? Yes. And riders? I thought so. Nighteyes was suddenly beside me.

Can you scent them?

The wind is wrong. Shall I go see?

Yes. But be unseen.

Of course. See to the Fool. He whimpered when I left him.

In the tent, I quietly woke Kettricken. 'I think there may be danger,' I told her softly. 'Horses and riders, possibly on the road behind us. I'm not certain yet.'

'By the time we are certain, they will be here,' she said dourly. 'Wake everyone. I want us up and ready to move by light.'

'The Fool is still feverish,' I said, even as I stooped and shook Starling's shoulder.

'If he stays here, he won't be feverish, he'll be dead. And you with him. Has the wolf gone to spy for us?'

'Yes.' I knew she was right, but it was still hard to force myself to shake the Fool to consciousness. He moved like a man in a daze. While the others bundled our gear, I hurried him into his coat and nagged him into an extra pair of leggings. I wrapped him in all our blankets and stood him outside while the rest of us struck the tent and loaded it. Of Kettricken I asked quietly, 'How much weight can a jeppa bear?'

'More than the Fool weighs. But they are too narrow to straddle comfortably, and they are skittish with a live load. We might put him on one for a way, but it would be uncomfortable for him and the jeppa would be difficult to control.'

It was the answer I had expected, but it did not make me happy.

'What news from the wolf?' she asked me.

I reached for Nighteyes, and was dismayed to find what an effort it was to touch minds with him. 'Six riders,' I told her.

'Friend or foe?' she asked.

'He has no way to know,' I pointed out to her. To the wolf I asked, *How do the horses look?*

Delicious.

Large, like Sooty? Or small, like Mountain horses?

Between. One pack mule.

'They are on horses, not Mountain ponies,' I told Kettricken. She shook her head to herself. 'Most of my folk do not use horses this high in the Mountains. They would use ponies, or jeppas. Let us decide they are enemies and act accordingly.'

'Run or fight?'

'Both, of course.'

She had already taken her bow from one of the jeppas' loads. Now she strung it to have it ready. 'First we look for a better place to stage an ambush. Then we wait. Let's go.'

It was easier said than done. Only the smoothness of the road made it possible at all. Light was only a rumour as we started that day. Starling led the jeppas ahead. I brought the Fool behind them, while Kettle with her staff and Kettricken with her bow followed us. At first I let the Fool try to walk on his own. He lurched slowly along, and as the jeppas drew inexorably away from us, I knew it would not do. I put his left arm across my shoulders and my arm about his waist and hurried him along. In a short time he was panting and struggling to keep his feet from dragging. The unnatural warmth of his body was frightening. Cruelly, I forced him on, praying for cover of some sort.

When we came to it, it was not the kindness of trees, but the cruelty of sharp stone. A great portion of the mountain above the road had given way and cascaded down. It had carried off more than half the road with it, and left what remained heaped high with stone and earth. Starling and the jeppas were looking at it dubiously when the Fool and I limped up. I set him down on a stone, where he sat, eyes closed and head bowed. I pulled the blankets more closely around him, and then went to stand by Starling.

'It's an old slide,' she observed. 'Maybe it won't be that hard to scramble across it.'

'Maybe,' I agreed, my eyes already looking for a place to attempt it. Snow overlay the stone, cloaking it. 'If I go first, with the jeppas, can you follow with the Fool?'

'I suppose.' She glanced over at him. 'How bad is she?'

There was only worry in Starling's voice, so I swallowed my annoyance. 'He can stagger along, if he has an arm to lean on. Don't start to follow until the last animal is up and moving across it. Then follow our tracks.'

Starling bobbed her head in agreement but did not look happy. 'Shouldn't we wait for Kettricken and Kettle?'

I thought. 'No. If those riders do catch up with us, I don't want to be here with stone at my back. We cross the slide.'

I wished the wolf were with us, for he was twice as sure-footed as I and much quicker of reflex.

Can't come to you without their seeing me. It's sheer rock above and below the road here, and they are between you and me.

Don't fret about it. Just watch them and keep me alerted. Do they travel swiftly?

They walk their horses and argue much among themselves. One is fat and weary of riding. He says little but he does not hasten. Be careful, my brother.

I took a deep breath, and, as no place looked better than any other, simply followed my nose. At first it was just a scattering of loose stone across the road, but beyond that was a wall of great boulders, rocky soil and loose sharp-edged stone. I picked my way up this treacherous footing. The lead jeppa followed me and the others came behind her unquestioningly. I soon found that blowing snow had frozen across the rocks in thin sheets, often covering hollows and cracks beneath them. I stepped carelessly on one and thrust my leg down to my knee in a crack. I extricated myself carefully and proceeded.

When I took a moment and looked around me my courage almost failed. Above was a great slope of slide debris going up to a sheer wall of rock. I walked on a hillside of loose rock and stone. Looking ahead, I could not see where it ended. If it gave way, I would tumble and slide with it to the edge of the road and shoot off it into the deep valley beyond. There would be nothing, not a twig of greenery, not a boulder of any size that I could cling to. Small things became suddenly frightening. The jeppa's nervous tugging at the lead rope I clutched, a sudden shift in the push of the breeze, even my hair blowing in my eyes were abruptly life-threatening. Twice I dropped to all fours and crawled. The rest of the way, I went at a crouch, looking before I placed a foot and trusting my weight to it slowly.

Behind me came the line of jeppas, all following the lead beast. They were not as cautious as I. I heard stone shift beneath them, and small scatterings of rock that they loosened went pebbling and bounding down the slope, to shoot off in space. Each time it happened, I feared it would waken other rocks and set them sliding. They were not roped together, save for the lead I had on the first beast. At any moment I dreaded to see one go slipping down the hillside. They were strung out behind me like corks on a net, and far behind them came Starling and the Fool. I stopped once to watch them and cursed myself as I realized the difficulty of the task I had given her. They came at half my crawling pace, with Starling gripping the Fool and watching footing for both of them. My heart was in my mouth when she stumbled once and the Fool sprawled flat beside her. She looked up then and saw me staring back at her. Angrily she lifted an arm and motioned to me to go on. I did. There was nothing else I could do.

The dump of rock and stone ended as abruptly as it had begun. I scrabbled down to the road's flat surface with gratitude. Behind me came the lead jeppa, and then the other beasts, jumping from scarp to rock to road like goats as they descended. As soon as they were all down, I scattered some grain on the road to keep them well bunched and clambered back up the slide's shoulder.

I could see neither Starling nor the Fool.

I wanted to run back across the face of the slide. Instead I forced myself to go slowly, picking my way back along the tracks the jeppas and I had left. I told myself that I should be able to see their brightly coloured garments in this dull landscape of greys and blacks and whites. And finally I did. Starling was sitting quite still in a patch of scree with the Fool stretched out beside her on the stones.

'Starling!' I called to her softly.

She looked up. Her eyes were huge. 'It all started to move around us. Little rocks and then bigger ones. So I stopped still to let it settle. Now I can't get the Fool up and I can't carry her.' She fought the panic in her voice.

'Sit still. I'm coming.'

I could plainly see where a section of the surface rock had broken loose and started tumbling. Rolling pebbles had left their tracks over the snowy surface. I sized up what I could see and wished I knew more of avalanches. The movement of stone seemed to have begun well above them and to have flowed past them. We were still a good way above the edge, but once the scree began moving, it would swiftly carry us over the edge. I made my heart cold and relied on my head.

'Starling!' I called to her softly again. It was needless; her attention was entirely focused on me. 'Come to me. Very slowly and carefully.'

'What about the Fool?'

'Leave him. Once you are safe, I will go back for him. If I come to you, all three of us will be at risk.'

It is one thing to see the logic of something. It is another to force oneself to keep a resolve that smacks of cowardice. I do not know what Starling was thinking as she got slowly to her feet. She never straightened up entirely, but ventured toward me one slow step at a time, crouched over. I bit my lip and kept silent though I longed to urge her to hurry. Twice small herds of pebbles were loosened by her steps. They went cascading downhill, rousing others to join them as they flowed down the incline and then bounded over the edge. Each time she froze in a crouch, her eyes fixed desperately on me. I stood and stupidly wondered what I would do if she started to slide with the rocks. Would I fling myself uselessly after her, or watch her go and keep forever the memory of those dark eyes pleading?

But at last she reached the relative stability of the larger rocks where I stood. She clutched at me and I held her, feeling the trembling that rattled through her. After a long moment, I gripped her upper arms firmly and held her a little apart from me. 'You have to go on, now. It's not far. When you get there, stay there and keep the jeppas bunched together. Do you understand?'

She gave a quick nod and then took a deep breath. She stepped free of me and began cautiously to follow the trail the jeppas and I had left. I let her get a safe distance away before I took my first cautious steps toward the Fool.

The rocks shifted and grated more noticeably under my greater weight. I wondered if I would be wiser to walk higher or lower on the slope than she had. I thought of going back to the jeppas for a rope, but could think of nothing to secure it to. And all the while I kept moving forward, one cautious step at a time. The Fool himself did not move.

Rocks began to move around my feet, tapping against my ankles as they tumbled past me, slipping out from under my feet. I halted where I was, frozen by the gravel hurrying past me. I felt one of my feet start to slip, and before I could control myself, I plunged forward a step. The exodus of small rocks became swifter and more determined. I did not know what to do. I thought of flinging myself flat and spreading my weight, but decided swiftly it would only make it more easy for the tumbling rocks to carry me with them. Not one of the moving stones was bigger than my fist, but there were so many of them. I froze where I was and counted ten breaths before the rattlings settled again.

It took every scrap of courage I could muster to take the next step. I studied the ground for a time and selected a place that looked least unstable. I eased my weight to that foot and chose a place for my next step. By the time I reached the Fool's prone body, my shirt was sweated to my back and my jaw ached from clenching it. I eased myself down beside him.

Starling had lifted the blanket's corner to shelter his face, and he still lay covered like a dead man. I lifted it away, to look down at his closed eyes. He was a hue I had never seen before. The deathly white of his skin at Buckkeep had taken on a yellowish cast in the Mountains, but now he was a terrible dead colour. His lips were dry and chapped, his eyelashes crusted yellow. And he was still warm to the touch.

'Fool?' I asked him gently, but he made no response. I spoke on, hoping some part of him would hear me. 'I'm going to have to lift you and carry you. The footing is bad, and if I slip, we're going to fall all the way. So once I have you up in my arms, you must be very, very still. Do you understand?'

He took a slightly deeper breath. I took it for assent. I knelt downhill of him and worked my hands and arms under his body. As I straightened up, the arrow scar in my back screamed. I felt sweat pop out on my face. I knelt upright for a moment, the Fool in my arms, mastering my pain and gaining my balance. I shifted one leg to get my foot under me. I tried to stand up slowly, but as I did so rocks began cascading past me. I fought a terrible urge to clutch the Fool to me and run. The rattling and scattering of loose shale went on and on and on. When it finally ceased, I was trembling with the effort of standing perfectly still. I was ankle-deep in loose scree.

'FitzChivalry?'

I turned my head slowly. Kettricken and Kettle had caught up. They were standing uphill of me, well off the patch of loosened stone. They both looked sickened at my predicament. Kettricken was the first to recover.

'Kettle and I are going to cross above you. Stay where you are, and be as still as you can. Did Starling and the jeppas make it across?' I managed a small nod. I had not the spit to speak.

'I'll get a rope and come back. I'll be as quick as it is safe to be.'

Another nod from me. I had to twist my body to watch them, so I did not. Nor did I look down. The wind blew past me, the stone ticked under my feet, and I looked down into the Fool's face. He did not weigh much, for a man grown. He had always been slight and bird-boned, relying on his tongue for defence rather than fist and muscle. But as I stood and held him, he grew weightier and weightier in my arms. The circle of pain in my back slowly expanded, and somehow managed to make my arms ache with it.

I felt him give a slight twitch in my arms. 'Be still,' I whispered.

He prised his eyes open and looked up at me. His tongue sought to moisten his lips. 'What are we doing?' he croaked.

'We're standing very still in the middle of an avalanche,' I whispered back. My throat was so dry it was hard to talk.

'I think I could stand,' he offered weakly.

'Don't move!' I ordered him.

He took a slightly deeper breath. 'Why are you always near when I get into these sort of situations?' he wondered hoarsely.

'I could ask you the same,' I retorted, unfairly.

'Fitz?'

I twisted my screaming back to look up at Kettricken. She was silhouetted against the sky. She had a jeppa with her, the lead one. She had a coil of rope looped on one shoulder. The other end was fixed to the jeppa's empty pack harness.

'I'm going to throw the rope to you. Don't try to catch it, let it go past you and then pick it up and wrap it around yourself. Understand?'

'Yes.'

She could not have heard my answer, but she nodded back to me encouragingly. In a moment the rope came flopping and uncoiling past me. It unsettled a small amount of pebbles, but their scurrying motion was enough to make me sick. The length of the rope sprawled across the rock, less than an arm's length from my foot. I looked down at it and tasted despair. I steeled my will.

'Fool, can you hold onto me? I have to try to pick up the rope.'

'I think I can stand,' he offered again.

'You may have to,' I admitted unwillingly. 'Be ready for anything. But whatever else, hold onto me.'

'Only if you promise to hold onto the rope.'

'I'll do my best,' I promised grimly.

My brother, they have stopped where we camped last night. Of the six men –

Not now, Nighteyes!

Three have gone down as you did, and three remain with the horses.

Not now!

The Fool shifted his arms to get an awkward hold on my shoulders. The damnable blankets that had swathed him were everywhere I didn't want them to be. I clutched at the Fool with my left arm and got my right hand and arm somewhat clear even though my arm was still under him. I fought a ridiculous impulse to laugh. It was all so stupidly awkward and dangerous. Of all the ways I had thought I might die, this one had never occurred to me. I met the Fool's eyes and saw the same panicky laughter in them. 'Ready,' I told him, and crouched toward the rope. Every taut muscle in my body screeched and cramped.

My fingers failed to touch the rope by a handsbreadth. I glanced up to where Kettricken and the jeppa were anxiously poised. It came to me that I had no idea what was supposed to happen once I had the rope. But my muscles were already extended too far to stop and ask questions. I forced my hand to the rope, even as I felt my right foot sliding out from under me.

Everything happened simultaneously. The Fool's grip on me tightened convulsively as the whole hillside beneath us seemed to break into motion. I grasped the rope but was still sliding downhill. Just before it tightened I managed to flip one wrap around my wrist. Above us and to the east of us, Kettricken led the sure-footed jeppa on. I saw the animal stagger as it took part of our weight. It dug in its feet and kept moving across the slide zone. The rope tightened, biting into my wrist and hand. I held on.

I don't know how I scrabbled my feet under me, but I did, and made a semblance of walking as the hill kept rattling away beneath me. I found myself swinging like a slow pendulum with the taut rope providing me just enough resistance to keep me atop the rattling stone sliding downhill past me. Suddenly I felt firmer footing. My boots were full of tiny pebbles, but I ignored them as I kept my grip on the rope and moved steadily across the slide area. By now we were far downhill of the original path I had chosen. I refused to look down and see how close we were to the edge. I concentrated on keeping my awkward grip on the Fool and the rope and keeping my feet moving.

Abruptly, we were out of danger. I found myself in an area of bigger rocks, free of the loose scree that had nearly ended our lives. Above us, Kettricken kept moving steadily and so did we, and then we were climbing down onto the blessedly level road bed. In a few more minutes we were all on flat snowy ground. I dropped the rope and slowly sagged down with the Fool. I closed my eyes.

'Here. Drink some water.' It was Kettle's voice, and she was offering me a waterskin as Kettricken and Starling pried the Fool out of my arms. I drank some water and shook for a short while. Every part of me hurt as if bruised. As I sat recovering, something pushed into the front of my mind. I suddenly staggered to my feet.

'Six of them, and three have gone down as I did, he said.'

All eyes turned to me at my blurted words. Kettle was getting water down the Fool, but he did not look much better. Her mouth was pursed with worry and displeasure. I knew what she feared. But the fear the wolf had given me was more compelling.

'What did you say?' Kettricken asked me gently, and I realized they thought my mind was wandering again.

'Nighteyes has been following them. Six men on horses, one pack animal. They stopped at our old campsite. And he said that three of them went down as I did.'

'Meaning to the city?' Kettricken asked slowly.

To the city, Nighteyes echoed. It chilled me to see Kettricken nod as if to herself.

'How can that be?' Starling asked softly. 'Kettle told us the signpost only worked for you because you had had Skill-training. It didn't affect any of the rest of us.'

'They must be Skilled ones,' Kettle said softly and looked at me questioningly.

There was only one answer. 'Regal's coterie,' I said and shuddered. The sickness of dread rose in me. They were so horribly close, and they knew how to hurt me so badly. An overwhelming fear of pain flooded my mind. I fought panic.

Kettricken patted my arm awkwardly. 'Fitz. They'll not get past that slide easily. With my bow, I can pick them off as they cross.' Kettricken offered these words. There was irony in my queen offering to protect the royal assassin. Somehow it steadied me, even as I knew her bow was no protection from the coterie.

'They don't need to come here to attack me. Or Verity.' I took a deep breath, and suddenly heard an additional fact in my words. 'They don't need to physically follow us here to attack us. So why have they come all this way?'

The Fool leaned up on an elbow. He rubbed at his pasty face. 'Maybe they don't come here to pursue you at all,' he suggested slowly. 'Maybe they want something else.'

'What?' I demanded.

'What did Verity come here for?' he demanded. His voice was weak but he seemed to be thinking very carefully.

'The aid of the Elderlings? Regal never believed in them. He saw it only as a way to get Verity out of his path.'

'Perhaps. But he knew the tale he spread of Verity's death was a fabrication of his own. You yourself say that his coterie waited and spied upon you. In what hopes, if not to discover Verity's whereabouts? By now, he must wonder as much as the Queen does, why Verity has not returned. And Regal must wonder, what errand was so important that the Bastard turned aside from killing him to set forth on it. Look behind you, Fitz. You have left a trail of blood and mayhem. Regal must wonder where it all leads.'

'Why would they go down into the city?' I asked, and then a worse question, 'How did they know how to go down into the city? I blundered into it, but how did they know?'

'Perhaps they are far stronger than you in the Skill. Perhaps the guidepost spoke to them, or perhaps they came here already knowing much more than you did.' Kettle spoke carefully, but there was no 'perhaps' in her voice.

It was all suddenly clear to me. 'I don't know why they are here. But I know I am going to kill them before they can get to Verity, or trouble me any further.' I heaved myself to my feet.

Starling sat staring at me. I think she realized at that moment exactly what I was. Not some romanticized princeling in exile who would eventually do some heroic task, but a killer. And not even a very competent one.

'Rest a bit first,' Kettricken advised me. Her voice was steady and accepting.

I shook my head. 'I wish I could. But the opportunity they've given me is now. I don't know how long they'll be in the city. I hope they'll spend some time there. I'm not going down to meet them, you see. I'm no match for them in the Skill. I can't fight their minds. But I can kill their bodies. If they've left their horses, guards and supplies behind them, I can take those things from them. Then when they come back, they'll be trapped. No food, no shelter. No game to hunt around here, even if they remembered how to hunt. I won't get a chance as good as this again.'

Kettricken was nodding reluctantly. Starling looked ill. The Fool had sagged back into his bedding. 'I should be going with you,' he said quietly.

I looked at him and tried to keep amusement out of my voice. 'You?'

'I've just a feeling . . . that I should go with you. That you should not go alone.'

'I won't be alone. Nighteyes is waiting for me.' I quested out briefly and found my comrade. He was crouched on his belly in the snow, downtrail of the guards and horses. They had built a small fire and were cooking food over it. It was making the wolf hungry.

Shall we have horse tonight?

We shall see, I told him. I turned to Kettricken. 'May I take your bow?'

She handed it over reluctantly. 'Can you shoot it?' she asked.

It was a very fine weapon. 'Not well, but well enough. They've no cover worth mentioning, and they aren't expecting an attack. If I'm lucky, I can kill one before they know I'm even around.'

'You'll shoot one without even issuing a challenge?' Starling asked faintly.

I looked into the sudden disillusionment in her eyes. I closed my eyes and focused on my task instead. *Nighteyes?*

Shall I drive the horses over the cliff, or just down the trail? They've already scented me and are getting anxious. But the men pay no attention.

I'd like the supplies they are carrying, if it can be managed. Why did killing a horse bother me more than killing a man?

We'll see, Nighteyes replied judiciously. *Meat is meat*, he added.

I slung Kettricken's quiver over my back. The wind was kicking up again, promising more snow. The thought of crossing the slide area again turned my bowels to water. 'There is no choice,' I reminded myself. I looked up to see Starling turning away from me. She had evidently taken my remark as her reply. Well, it would serve there as well. 'If I fail, they will come after you,' I said carefully. 'You should get as far from here as you can; travel until you can't see any more. If all goes well, we'll catch up with you soon enough.' I crouched down beside the Fool. 'Can you walk at all?' I asked him.

'For a way,' he said dully.

'If I must, I can carry him.' Kettricken spoke with quiet certainty. I looked at the tall woman and believed her. I gave a short nod of my head.

'Wish me luck,' I told them, and turned back to the slide zone.

'I'm coming with you,' Kettle announced abruptly. She stood up from retying her boots. 'Give me the bow. And follow where I walk.'

I was speechless for a moment. 'Why?' I demanded at last.

'Because I know what I'm doing crossing that rock. And I'm more than "good enough" with a bow. I'll wager I can drop two of them before they know we're there.'

'But –'

'She is very good on the slide,' Kettricken observed calmly. 'Starling, take the jeppas. I'll bring the Fool.' She gave us an unreadable look. 'Catch up as soon as you can.'

I recalled that I'd tried to leave Kettle behind once before. If she was going with me, I wanted her to be with me, not coming up behind me when I didn't expect it. I glared at her, but nodded.

'The bow,' she reminded me.

'Can you really shoot well?' I asked her as I grudgingly surrendered it.

A funny smile twisted her face. She looked down at her crooked fingers. 'I would not tell you I could do a thing if I could not. Some of my old skills are still mine,' she said quietly.

We set out to clamber back up onto the tumbled rock. Kettle went first, her probing staff in hand, and I came behind her, one staff length back as she had bid me. She didn't say a word to me as she glanced back and forth between the ground at her feet and where she wished to take us. I could not discern what it was that decided her path, but the loose stone and crystalline snow remained quiet under her short steps. She made it look easy enough that I began to feel foolish.

They are eating now. And no one keeps a watch.

I relayed the information to Kettle, who nodded grimly. To myself I fretted and wondered if she would be able to do what needed doing. To be good with a bow is one thing. To shoot a man down while he is eating his dinner peacefully is another. I thought of Starling's objection, and wondered what kind of man would show himself and issue a challenge before trying to kill all three men. I touched the hilt of my short sword. Well, it was what Chade had promised me so long ago. Killing for my king, with none of the honour or glory of the soldier on the battlefield. Not that any of my battle memories had much of honour or glory in them.

We were suddenly clambering down from the loose rock of the slide area, going very quietly and carefully. Kettle spoke very softly. 'We've a way to go yet. But when we get there, let me choose my spot, and get my first shot off. As soon as the man is down, show yourself and draw their attention. They may not look for me, and I may get another clean shot.'

'Have you done this sort of thing before?' I asked softly.

'It's not that different from our game, Fitz. From here, let us go silently.'

I knew then she had not killed this way before, if she had ever killed a human before at all. I began to doubt the wisdom of giving her the bow. At the same time, I was selfishly grateful for her companionship. I wondered if I were losing my courage.

Perhaps you are learning that a pack is best for such things.

Perhaps.

There was little cover on the road. Above and below us, the mountainside rose sheer. The road itself was flat and bare. We rounded a shoulder of the mountain and their camp was in plain sight. All three guards still sat carelessly about the fire, eating and talking. The horses caught our scent and shifted with small snortings. But as the wolf had kept them uneasy for some time, the men paid them no mind. Kettle set an arrow to her bow as we walked and carried it ready. In the end, it was simple. Ugly mindless slaughter, but simple. She let go her arrow when one of the men noticed us. It took him through the chest. The other two leaped to their feet, turned to see us, and dived for their weapons. But in that short space of time, Kettle had nocked another arrow and let fly as the helpless wretch drew a sword clear. Nighteyes came suddenly from behind to bear the last man down and hold him until I could rush in to finish him with a sword.

It had happened swiftly, almost quietly. Three dead men sprawled in the snow. Six sweating, restless horses, one impassive mule. 'Kettle. See what food they have on the horses,' I told her, to stop her awful staring. She swung her gaze to me, then slowly nodded.

I went over the bodies, to see what they might tell me. They did not wear Regal's colours, but the origin of two were plain in the features of their faces and the cut of their clothes. Farrowmen. The third one, when I turned him over, near stopped my heart. I'd known him in Buckkeep. Not well, but enough to know his name was Tallow. I crouched looking down into his dead face, ashamed that I could recall no more of him than that. I supposed he had gone on to Tradeford when Regal moved the court there; many of the servants had. I tried to tell myself it did not matter where he had begun; he had ended here. I closed my heart and did my tasks.

I tumbled the bodies off the cliff's edge. While Kettle went through their stores and sorted out what she thought we two could carry back, I stripped the horses of every bit of harness and tack. This followed the bodies down the cliff. I went through their bags, finding little besides warm clothes. The pack animal carried only their tent and such things. No papers. What need would coterie members have of written instructions?

Drive the horses well down the road. I doubt they'll come back here on their own.

That much meat, and you want me to just chase it away?

If we kill one here, it's more than we can eat and carry. Whatever we left would feed those three when they return. They were carrying dry meat and cheese. I'll see your belly is full tonight.

Nighteyes was not pleased, but he heeded me. I think he chased the horses further and faster than he truly needed to, but at least he left them alive. I had no idea what their chances were in the mountains. Probably end up in a snowcat's belly, or as a feast for the ravens. I was suddenly horribly tired of it all.

'Shall we go on?' I asked Kettle needlessly, and she nodded. It was a good trove of food she had packed for us to carry, but I privately wondered if I'd be able to stomach any of it. What little we could not carry nor the wolf stuff down, we kicked over the edge. I looked around us. 'Dare I touch it, I'd try to push that pillar over the edge, too,' I told Kettle.

She gave me a look as if she thought I had asked it of her. 'I fear to touch it also,' she said at last, and we both turned away from it.

Evening crept across the mountains as we went up the road, and night came swift on her heels. I followed Kettle and the wolf across the landslide in near darkness. Neither of them seemed afraid, and I was suddenly too weary to care if I survived the trek. 'Don't let your mind wander,' Kettle chided me as we finally came down off the tumble of stone and onto the road again. She took my arm and gripped it tightly. We walked for a time in almost blackness, simply following the straight flat road before us as it cut across the face of the mountain. The wolf went ahead of us, coming back frequently to check on us. *Camp's not much farther*, he encouraged me after one such trip.

'How long have you been doing this?' Kettle asked me after a time.

I didn't pretend to misunderstand the question. 'Since I was about twelve,' I told her.

'How many men have you killed?'

It was not the cold question it sounded. I answered her seriously. 'I don't know. My . . . teacher advised me against keeping a count. He said it wasn't a good idea.' Those weren't his exact words. I remembered them well. 'How many doesn't matter after one,' Chade had said. 'We know what we are. Quantity makes you neither better nor worse.'

I pondered now what he had meant by that as Kettle said to the dark, 'I killed once before.'

I made no reply. I'd let her tell me about it if she wished, but I really didn't want to know.

Her arm in mine began to tremble slightly. 'I killed her, in a temper. I didn't think I could, she had always been stronger. But I lived and she died. So they burned me out, and turned me out. Sent me into exile forever.' Her hand found mine and gripped it tightly. We kept on walking. Ahead of us, I spied a tiny glow. It was most likely the brazier burning inside the tent.

'It was so unthinkable, to do what I had done,' Kettle said wearily. 'It had never happened before. Oh, between coteries, certainly, once in a great while, for rivalry for the King's favour. But I Skill-duelled a member of my own coterie, and killed her. And that was unforgivable.'

TWENTY-NINE

The Rooster Crown

There is a game played among the Mountainfolk. It is a complex game to learn, and a difficult one to master. It features a combination of cards and rune chips. There are seventeen cards, usually about the size of a man's hand and made from any light-coloured wood. Each of these cards features an emblem from Mountain lore, such as the Old Weaver-Man or She Who Tracks. The renderings of these highly stylized images are usually done in paint over a burnt outline. The thirty-one rune chips are made from a grey stone peculiar to the Mountains, and are incised with glyphs for Stone, Water, Pasture, and the like. The cards and stones are dealt out to the players, usually three, until no more remain. Both cards and runes have traditional weights that are varied when they are played in combination. It is reputed to be a very old game.

We walked the rest of the way to the tent in silence. What she had told me was so immense I could not think of anything to say. It would have been stupid to voice the hundreds of questions that sprang up in me. She had the answers, and she would choose when to give them to me. I knew that now. Nighteyes came back to me silently and swiftly. He slunk close to my heels.

She killed within her pack?

So it seems.

It happens. It is not good, but it happens. Tell her that.

Not just now.

No one said much as we came into the tent. No one wanted to ask. So I quietly said, 'We killed the guards and drove off the horses and threw their supplies off the cliff.'

Starling only stared at us, without comprehension. Her eyes

were wide and dark, bird-like. Kettricken poured mugs of tea for us and quietly added the stores of food we had brought to our own dwindling supplies. 'The Fool is a bit better,' she offered by way of conversation.

I looked at him sleeping in his blankets and doubted it. His eyes had a sunken look. Sweat had plastered his fine hair to his skull and his restless sleep had stood it up in tufts. But when I set my hand to his face, it was almost cool to the touch. I snugged the blanket closer around him. 'Did he eat anything?' I asked Kettricken.

'He drank some soup. I think he'll be all right, Fitz. He was sick once before, for a day or so in Blue Lake. It was the same, fever and weakness. He said then that it might not be a sickness, but only a change his kind go through.'

'He said somewhat the same to me yesterday,' I agreed. She put a bowl of warm soup in my hands. For an instant it smelled good. Then it smelled like the remains of the soup the panicked guards had spilled on the snowy road. I clenched my jaws.

'Did you see the coterie members at all?' Kettricken asked me.

I shook my head, then forced myself to speak. 'No. But there was a big horse there, and the clothing in his bags would have fit Burl. In another there were blue garments such as Carrod favours. And austere things for Will.'

I said their names awkwardly, in a way fearing to name them, lest I summon them. In another way, I was naming those I had killed. Skilled or not, the Mountains would make an end of them. Yet I took no pride in what I had done, nor would I completely believe it until I saw their bones. All I knew for now was that it was not likely they would attack me this night. For an instant I imagined them returning to the pillar, expecting to find food and fire and shelter awaiting them. They would find cold and dark. They would not see the blood on the snow.

I realized the soup was getting cold. I forced myself to eat it, mouthfuls that I simply swallowed, not wishing to taste. Tallow had played the penny whistle. I had a sudden memory of him sitting on the back steps outside the scullery, playing for a couple of kitchen maids. I shut my eyes, wishing vainly that I could recall something evil about him. I suspected his only crime had been serving the wrong master.

'Fitz.' Kettle instantly poked me.

'I wasn't wandering,' I complained.

'You would have, soon. Fear has been your ally this day. It has kept you focused. But you must sleep sometime tonight, and when you do, you must have your mind well warded. When they get back to the pillar, they will recognize your handiwork and come hunting you. Do you not think so?'

I knew it was so, but it was still unsettling to hear it spoken aloud. I wished Kettricken and Starling were not listening and watching us.

'So. We shall have a bit of our game again, shall we?' Kettle cajoled.

We played four chance games. I won twice. Then she set up a game with almost entirely white pieces, and gave me one black stone with which to win. I tried to focus my mind on the game, knowing it had worked before, but I was simply too tired. I found myself thinking that it had been over a year since I had left Buckkeep as a corpse. Over a year since I had slept in a real bed I called my own. Over a year since meals had been reliable. Over a year since I had held Molly in my arms, over a year since she had bid me leave her alone forever.

'Fitz. Don't.'

I lifted my eyes from the gamecloth to find Kettle watching me closely.

'You can't indulge that. You have to be strong.'

'I am too tired to be strong.'

'Your enemies were careless today. They did not expect you to discover them. They won't be careless again.'

'I hope they'll be dead,' I said with a cheer I did not feel.

'Not that easily,' Kettle replied, unknowing of how her words chilled me. 'You said it was warmer down in the city. Once they see they've no supplies, they'll go back to the city. They have water there, and I'm sure they took at least some supplies for the day. I don't think we can disregard them yet. Do you?'

'I suppose not.'

Nighteyes sat up beside me with an anxious whine. I quelled

my own despair and then quieted him with a touch. 'I just wish,' I said quietly, 'that I could simply sleep for a time. Alone in my mind, dreaming my own dreams, without fearing where I'll go or who might attack me. Without fearing that my hunger for the Skill will overcome me. Just simple sleep.' I spoke to her directly, knowing now she understood well what I meant.

'I can't give you that,' Kettle told me calmly. 'All I can give you is the game. Trust it. It's been used by generations of Skill-users to keep such dangers at bay.'

And so I bent to the board once more, and fixed the game in my mind, and when I lay down by the Fool that night, I kept it before my eyes.

I hovered that night, like a nectar bird, somewhere between sleep and wakefulness. I could reach a place just short of sleep and keep myself there by contemplating Kettle's game. More than once, I drifted back to wakefulness. I would become cognizant of the dim light from the brazier and the sleeping forms beside me. Several times I reached out to check the Fool; each time his skin seemed cooler and his own sleep deeper. Kettricken, Starling and Kettle rotated through watches that night. I noticed that the wolf shared Kettricken's. They still did not trust me to remain wary through one, and I was selfishly grateful for that.

Just short of dawn, I stirred once more to find all still quiet. I checked the Fool, and then lay back and closed my eyes, hoping to find a few more moments of rest. Instead, in horrific detail, I beheld a great eye, as if the closing of my own eyes had opened this one. I struggled to open my own eyes again, I floundered desperately toward wakefulness, but I was held. There was a terrible pull on my mind, like the sucking pull of an undertow on a swimmer. I resisted with all my will. I could feel wakefulness just above me, like a bubble I could break into, if only I could touch it. But I could not. I struggled, grimacing my face, trying to pull my wayward eyes open.

The eye watched me. One single immense dark eye. Not Will's. Regal's. He stared at me, and I knew he took delight in my struggles. It seemed effortless for him to hold me there, like a fly under a glass bowl. Yet even in my panic, I knew that if he could have done more than hold me, he would. He had got past my walls, but had not the power to do more than threaten me. That was still enough to make my heart pound with terror.

'Bastard,' he said fondly. The word broke over my mind like a cold ocean wave. I was drenched in its threat. '*Bastard, I know about the child. And your woman. Molly. Tit for tat, Bastard.*' He paused and his amusement grew as my terror swelled. '*Now there's a thought. Has she pretty tits, Bastard? Would I find her amusing?*'

'NO!'

I wrenched clear of him, sensing for an instant Carrod, Burl, and Will as well. I flung myself free.

I came awake abruptly. I scrabbled from my bedding and fled outside, bootless and uncloaked. Nighteyes followed at my heels, snarling in every direction. The sky was black and scattered with stars. The air was cold. I drew breath after shuddering breath of it, trying to still the sick fear in me. 'What is it?' Starling demanded fearfully. She was on watch outside the tent.

I just shook my head at her, unable to voice the horror of it. After a time, I turned and went back inside. Sweat was coursing down my body as if I had been poisoned. I sat down in my muddle of blankets. I could not stop panting. The more I tried to still my panic, the greater it became. *I know about the child. And your woman.* Those words echoed and echoed through me. Kettle stirred in her bedding, then rose and came across the tent to sit behind me. She set her hands on my shoulders. 'They broke through to you, did they?'

I nodded, tried to swallow with a dry throat.

She reached for a waterskin and handed it to me. I took a drink, almost choked, and then managed another swallow. 'Think about the game,' she urged me. 'Clear your mind of everything but the game.'

'The game!' I cried out savagely, jerking both the Fool and Kettricken awake. 'The game? Regal knows about Molly and Nettle. He threatens them. And I am powerless! Helpless.' I felt the panic building in me again, the unfocused fury. The wolf whined, then growled deep in his throat.

'Can't you Skill to them, warn them somehow?' Kettricken asked.

'No!' Kettle cut in. 'He should not even think of them.'

Kettricken gave me a look that mingled apology and righteousness. 'I fear Chade and I were correct. The princess will be safer in the Mountain Kingdom. Do not forget that his task was to fetch her. Take heart. Perhaps even now Nettle is with him, on her way to safety, out of Regal's reach.'

Kettle called my gaze away from the Queen. 'Fitz. Focus on the game. Only on the game. His threats could be a ploy, to trick you into betraying them. Don't talk about them. Don't think about them. Here. Look here.' Her trembling old hands moved my blanket away and spread out the gamecloth. She spilled stones into her hand, and plucked out white ones to re-create the problem. 'Solve this. Focus on this, and this only.'

It was next to impossible. I looked at the white stones and thought it all a stupid task. What players could be so clumsy and short-sighted as to let the game degrade into such a clutter of white stones? It was not a problem worth solving. But neither could I lie down and sleep. I scarcely dared blink lest I see that eye again. Had it been Regal's whole countenance or both his eyes it would not perhaps have seemed so awful. But the disembodied eye seemed all-seeing and constant, inescapable. I stared at the game pieces until the white stones seemed to float above the junctures of the lines. One black stone, to bring a winning pattern out of this chaos. One black stone. I held it in my hand, rubbing it with my thumb.

All the next day, as we followed the road down the mountain's flank, I held the stone in my bare hand. My other arm was about the Fool's waist, his arm around my neck. These two things kept my mind focused.

The Fool seemed somewhat better. His body was no longer feverish, but he seemed unable to stomach food or even tea. Kettle forced water on him until he simply sat and refused it, shaking his head wordlessly. He seemed as indisposed to talk as I was. Starling and Kettle with her staff led our weary little procession. The Fool and I followed the jeppas, while Kettricken with her bow strung kept our rear guarded. The wolf prowled restlessly up and down the line, now ranging ahead, now loping up our back trail.

Nighteyes and I had gone back to a sort of wordless bond. He understood that I did not wish to think at all, and did his best not to distract me. It was still unnerving to sense him trying to use the Wit to communicate with Kettricken. *No sign of anyone behind us,* he would tell her as he trotted past on one of his endless trips. Then he would go ranging far ahead of the jeppas and Starling, only to come back to Kettricken and assure her in passing that all was clear ahead of us. I tried to tell myself that she merely had faith that Nighteyes would let me know if he found anything amiss on his scouting trips. But I suspected she was becoming more and more attuned to him.

The road led us very swiftly downwards. As we descended the land changed. By late afternoon, the slope above the road was gentling and we began to pass twisted trees and mossy boulders. Snow faded and became patchy on the hillside while the road was dry and black. Dry tufts of grass showed green at their bases just off the shoulder of the road. It was hard to make the hungry jeppas keep moving. I made a vague Wit-effort to let them know that there would be better browsing ahead, but I doubt that I had enough familiarity with them to make any lasting impression on them. I tried to limit my thoughts to the fact that firewood would be more plentiful tonight, and to gratitude that the lower the road carried us the warmer grew the day.

At one time, the Fool made a gesture to a low growing plant that had tiny white buds on it. 'It would be spring in Buckkeep by now,' he said in a low voice, and then added quickly, 'I'm sorry. Pay no attention to me, I'm sorry.'

'Are you feeling any better?' I asked him, resolutely thrusting spring flowers and bees and Molly's candles out of my mind.

'A little.' His voice shook and he took a quick breath. 'I wish we could walk more slowly.'

'We'll camp soon,' I told him, knowing that we could not slow our pace now. I felt a growing urgency and had developed the notion it came from Verity. I pushed that name, too, from my mind. Even walking down the wide road in daylight, I feared that Regal's eye was only a blink away and that if I glimpsed it they would once more hold me under their power. For an instant I hoped Carrod and Will and Burl were cold and hungry, but then realized I could not safely think of them, either.

'You were sick like this before,' I observed to the Fool, mostly to think of something else.

'Yes. In Blue Lake. My lady queen spent the food money on a room that I might be in out of the rain.' He turned his head to stare at me. 'Do you think that might have caused it?'

'Caused what?'

'Her child to be stillborn . . .'

His voice dwindled off. I tried to think of words. 'I don't think it was any one thing, Fool. She simply suffered too many misfortunes while she was carrying the babe.'

'Burrich should have gone with her and left me. He would have taken better care of her. I wasn't thinking clearly at the time . . .'

'Then I'd be dead,' I pointed out. 'Among other things. Fool, there is no sense in trying to play that game with the past. Here is where we are today, and we can only make our moves from here.'

And in that instant, I suddenly perceived the solution to Kettle's game problem. It was so instantly clear that I wondered how I could not have seen it. Then I knew. Each time I had studied the board, I wondered how it could have got into such a sorry condition. All I had seen were the senseless moves that had preceded mine. But those moves had no longer mattered, once I held the black stone in my hand. A half-smile crooked my lips. My thumb rubbed the black stone.

'Where we are today,' the Fool echoed, and I felt his mood shadow mine.

'Kettricken said that you might not truly be ill. That it might be . . . peculiar to your kind.' I was uncomfortable coming even that close to a question regarding this.

'It could be. I suppose. Look.' He drew off his mitten, then reached up and dragged his nails down his cheek. Dry white trails followed them. He rubbed at it and the skin powdered away beneath his hands. On the back of his hand, the skin was peeling as if it had been blistered.

'It's like a sunburn peeling away. Do you think it's the weather you've been in?'

'That, too, is possible. Save that if it is like last time, I shall itch and peel over every bit of my body. And gain a bit more colour in the process. Are my eyes changing?'

I obliged him by meeting his gaze. Familiar as I was with him, it was still not an easy task. Had those colourless orbs darkened a trifle more? 'Perhaps they are a bit darker. No more than ale held up to the light. What will happen to you? Will you continue to have fevers and gain colour?'

'Perhaps. I don't know,' he admitted after a few moments had passed.

'How could you not know?' I demanded. 'What were your elders like?'

'Like you, foolish boy. Human. Somewhere back in my blood-line, there was a White. In me, as rarely happens, that ancient blood is given form again. But I am no more White than I am human. Did you think that one such as I was common to my people? I have told you. I am an anomaly, even among those who share my mixed lineage. Did you think White Prophets were born every generation? We would not be taken so seriously if we were. No. Within my lifetime, I am the only White Prophet.'

'But could not your teachers, with all those records you said they kept, tell you anything of what to expect?'

He smiled, but bitterness was in his voice. 'My teachers were too certain that they knew what to expect. They planned to pace my learning, to reveal what they thought I should know when they thought I should know it. When my prophecies were different from what they had planned, they were not pleased with me. They tried to interpret my own words for me! There have been other White Prophets, you see. But when I tried to make them see that I was the White Prophet, they could not accept it. Writing after writing they showed to me, to try to convince me of my effrontery in insisting on such a thing. But the more I read, the more my certainty grew. I tried to tell them my time was nearly upon me. All they could counsel was that I should wait and study more to be certain. We were not on the best terms when I left. I imagine they were quite startled to find I was gone so young from them, even though I had prophesied it for years.' He gave me a strangely apologetic smile. 'Perhaps if I had stayed to complete my schooling, we would know better how to save the world.'

I felt a sudden sinking in the pit of my stomach. So much had I come to rely on a belief that the Fool, at least, knew what we were about. 'How much do you truly know of what is to come?'

He took a deep breath, then sighed it out. 'Only that we do it together, Fitzy-fitz. Only that we do it together.'

'I thought you had studied all those writings and prophecies . . .'

'I did. And when I was younger, I dreamed many dreams, and even had visions. But it is as I have told you before; nothing is a precise fit. Look you, Fitz. If I showed you wool and a loom and a set of shears, would you look at it and say, oh, that is the coat I will someday wear? But once you have the coat on, it is easy to look back and say, oh, those things foretold this coat.'

'What is the good of it, then?' I demanded in disgust.

'The good of it?' he echoed. 'Ah. I have never quite thought of it in those terms before. The good of it.'

We walked for a time in silence. I could see what an effort it was for him to keep to the pace, and wished vainly there had been a way to keep one of the horses and get it past the slide area.

'Can you read weather signs, Fitz? Or animal tracks?'

'Some, for weather. I am better at animal tracks.'

'But in either one, are you always sure you are right?'

'Never. You don't really know until the next day dawns, or you bring the beast to bay.'

'So it is with my reading of the future. I never know . . . please, let us stop, even if for only a bit. I need to get my breath, and take a sip of water.'

I obliged him reluctantly. There was a mossy boulder just off the road, and he seated himself there. Not too far from the road were evergreens of a type I did not know. It rested my eyes to look on trees again. I left the road to sit beside him, and was instantly aware of a difference. As subtle as bees' humming was the working of the road, but when it suddenly ceased, I felt it. I yawned to pop my ears, and suddenly felt more clear-headed.

'Years ago I had a vision,' the Fool observed. He drank a bit more water, then passed the skin to me. 'I saw a black buck rising from a bed of shining black stone. When first I saw the black walls of Buckkeep rising over the waters, I said to myself, "Ah, that is what that meant!" Now I see a young bastard whose sigil is a buck walking on a road wrought from black stone. Maybe that is what the dream signified. I don't know. But my dream was duly recorded, and someday, in years to come, wise men will agree as to what it signified. Probably after both you and I are long dead.'

I asked a question that had long prickled me. 'Kettle says there is a prophecy about my child . . . the child of the Catalyst . . .'

'That there is,' the Fool confirmed calmly.

'Then you think Molly and I are doomed to lose Nettle to the throne of the Six Duchies?'

'Nettle. You know, I like her name. Very much, I do.'

'You did not answer my question, Fool.'

'Ask me again in twenty years. These things are so much easier when one looks back.' The sideways glance he gave me told me he would say no more on that topic. I tried a new tack.

'So you came, all that way, so that the Six Duchies would not fall to the Red Ships.'

He gave me an odd look, then grinned as if astonished. 'Is that how you see it? That we do all this to save your Six Duchies?' When I nodded, he shook his head. 'Fitz, Fitz. I came to save the world. The Six Duchies falling to the Red Ships is but the first pebble in the avalanche.' He took another deep breath. 'I know the Red Ships seem disaster enough to you, but the misery they make to your folk is no more than a pimple on the world's buttocks. Were that all, were it simply one set of barbarians seizing land from another, it would be no more than the ordinary working of the world. No. They are the first stain of poison spreading in a stream. Fitz, do I dare tell you this? If we fail, the spread is fast. Forging takes root as a custom, nay, as an amusement for the high ones. Look at Regal and his "King's Justice". He has succumbed to it already. He pleasures his body with drugs and deadens his soul with his savage amusements. Aye, and spreads the disease to those around him, until they take no satisfaction in a contest of skill that draws no blood, until games are only amusing if lives are wagered on the outcome! The very coinage of life becomes debased. Slavery spreads, for if it is accepted to take a man's life for amusement, then how much wiser to take it for profit?'

His voice had grown in strength and passion as he spoke. Now he caught his breath suddenly and leaned forward over his knees. I set a hand on his shoulder, but he only shook his head. After a moment, he straightened. 'I declare, talking to you is more wearying than hiking. Take me at my word, Fitz. As bad as the Red Ships are, they are amateurs and experimenters. I have seen visions of what the world becomes in the cycle when they prosper. I vow it shall not be this cycle.'

He heaved himself to his feet with a sigh and crooked out his arm. I took it and we resumed our walking. He had given me much to think about, and I spoke little. I took advantage of the gentling countryside to walk alongside the road rather than upon it. The Fool did not complain of the uneven ground.

As the road plunged ever deeper into the valley, the day warmed and the foliage increased. By evening, the terrain had mellowed so much that we were able to pitch the tent, not only off the road, but quite a distance from the road. Before bedtime, I showed Kettle my solution to her game, and she nodded as if well pleased. She immediately began to set out a new puzzle. I stopped her.

'I do not think I will need that tonight. I am looking forward to truly sleeping.'

'Are you? Then you shouldn't look forward to waking up again.'

I looked shocked.

She resumed setting out her pieces. 'You are one against three, and those three a coterie,' she observed more gently. 'And possibly those three are four. If Regal's brothers could Skill, he most likely has some ability. With the aid of the others, he could learn to lend his strength to them.' She leaned closer to me and lowered her voice, although the others were all busy with camp chores. 'You know it is possible to kill with the Skill. Would he wish to do less than that to you?'

'But if I sleep off the road –' I began.

'The force of the road is like the wind that blows alike on all. The ill wishes of a coterie are like an arrow that targets only you. Besides. There is no way you can sleep and not worry about the woman and the child. And every time you think of them, it is possible the coterie sees them through your eyes. You must crowd them out of your mind.'

I bent my head over the gamecloth.

I awoke the next morning to the pattering of rain on the tent skins. I lay for a time listening to it, grateful that it was not snow but dreading a day of walking in rain. I sensed the others waking up around me with a keenness I had not felt in days. I felt almost as if I had rested. Across the tent, Starling observed sleepily, 'We walked from winter to spring yesterday.'

Next to me the Fool shifted, scratched and muttered, 'Typical minstrel. Exaggerate everything.'

'I see you are feeling better,' Starling retorted.

Nighteyes thrust his head into the tent, a bloody rabbit dangling in his jaws. *The hunting is better, too.*

The Fool sat up in his blankets. 'Is he offering to share that?'

My kill is your kill, little brother.

Somehow it stung to hear him call the Fool 'brother'. *Especially when you've already eaten two this morning?* I asked him sarcastically.

No one forced you to lie in bed all dawn.

I was silent a moment. *I have not been much companion to you lately,* I apologized.

I understand. It is no longer just we two. Now we are pack.

You are right, I told him humbly. *But this evening, I intend to hunt with you.*

The Scentless One may come too, if he wishes. He could be a good hunter, did he try, for his scent could never give him away.

'He not only offers to share meat, he invites you to hunt with us this evening.'

I had expected the Fool to decline. Even at Buck he had never shown any inclination toward hunting. Instead he inclined his head gravely toward Nighteyes and told him, 'I would be honoured.'

We struck camp speedily and were soon on our way. As before I walked beside the road rather than upon it, and felt clearer-headed for it. The Fool had eaten voraciously at breakfast and now seemed almost his old self. He walked upon the road, but within hailing distance and kept up a merry chattering to me all day. Nighteyes ranged ahead and behind as always, frequently at a gallop. All of us seemed infected with the relief of warmer weather. The light rain soon gave way to a streaky sunlight, and the earth steamed fragrantly. Only my constant ache over Molly's safety and a nagging fear that at any time Will and his cohorts might attack my mind kept it from being a lovely day. Kettle had warned me about letting my mind dwell on either problem, lest I attract the coterie's attention. So I carried my fear inside me like a cold black stone, resolutely telling myself there was absolutely nothing I could do.

Odd thoughts popped into my head all day. I could not see a flower bud without wondering if Molly would have used it for scent or colour in her work. I found myself wondering if Burrich was as good with a wood axe as he was with a battle axe, and if it would be enough to save them. If Regal knew of them, he would send soldiers after them. Could he know of them without knowing exactly where they were?

'Stop that!' Kettle reprimanded me sharply, with a light rap of her walking stick. I jolted back to full awareness. The Fool glanced over at us curiously.

'Stop what?' I demanded.

'Thinking those thoughts. You know what I mean. Were you thinking of anything else, I would not have been able to walk up behind you. Find your discipline.'

I did, and reluctantly dredged up the game problem from the night before to concentrate on.

'That's better,' Kettle told me in quiet approval.

'What are you doing back here?' I asked suddenly. 'I thought you and Starling were leading the jeppas.'

'We've come to a fork in the road. And another pillar. Before we proceed, we want the Queen to see it.'

The Fool and I hastened ahead, leaving Kettle to go back and tell Kettricken of the juncture. We found Starling sitting on some ornamental stonework at the side of the road while the jeppas browsed greedily. The juncture of the road was marked by a great paved circle, surrounded by open grassy meadow, with another monolith at its centre. I would have expected it to be crowned with moss and scarred by lichen. Instead the black stone was smooth and clean save for dust deposited by wind and rain. I stood staring up at the stone, studying the glyphs while the Fool wandered about. I was wondering if any of the markings on this one matched the markings I had copied to the map when the Fool exclaimed, 'There was a village here, once!' He gestured wide with his hands.

I glanced up, and saw what he meant. There were indentations in the meadows where stunted grass cloaked old, paved walkways. A wide, straight way that might have been a street once ran through the meadow and off beneath the trees. Moss- and vine-shrouded upthrusts were all that remained of cottage and shop walls that had lined it. Trees grew where once hearths had burned and folk had dined. The Fool found a large block of stone and climbed upon it to spy in all directions. 'It might have been a sizeable town, at one time.'

It made sense. If this road had been the highway for commerce that I had seen in my Skill-seeing, then it was only natural that a town or market would spring up at every crossroads. I could imagine it on a bright spring day, when farmers brought fresh eggs and new spring greens to town and weavers hung out their new goods to tempt the buyers and . . .

For half an instant, the circle about the pillar thronged with folk. The vision began and ended at the pavement stones. Only within the virtue of the black stone did the people laugh and gesture and barter with one another. A girl crowned with a twist of green vine came through the crowd, glancing back over her shoulder at someone. I swear she caught my eye and winked at me. I thought I heard my name called and turned my head. Upon a dais stood a figure dressed in a flowing garment that shimmered with the glint of gold thread. She wore a gilded wooden crown decorated with cunningly carved and painted rooster heads and tail feathers. Her sceptre was no more than a feather duster but she gestured with it royally as she issued some decree. In the circle about me, folk roared with laughter. I could only stare at her ice-white skin and colourless eyes. She looked right at me.

Starling slapped me, hard. My head snapped on my neck with the force of her blow. I looked at her in astonishment, blood pooling in my mouth where my teeth had cut my cheek. She lifted her clenched fist again, and I realized she had not slapped me. I stepped back hastily, catching her wrist as her fist went by. 'Stop it!' I cried angrily.

'You . . . stop it!' she panted. 'And make her stop it, too!' She gestured angrily to where the Fool perched still upon his stone, frozen in artful mime of a statue. He did not breathe nor blink. But as I watched he slowly toppled over, falling like a stone.

I expected him to change it to a handspring in mid-fall, to come flashing to his feet as he so often had when he amused King Shrewd's court. Instead he measured his length in the meadow grass and lay still.

For a moment I stood stunned. Then I raced to his side. I seized the Fool under the arms and dragged him away from both the black circle and the black stone he had climbed upon. Some instinct made me take him into shade and lean him back against the trunk of a live oak. 'Get water!' I snapped at Starling, and her scolding and fluttering ceased. She ran back to the loaded jeppas and got a waterskin.

I put my fingers alongside his throat and found his life pulsing steadily there. His eyes were only half-closed and he lay like a man stunned. I called his name and patted at his cheek until Starling returned with the water. I unstoppered the skin and let a cold stream of it spatter down over his face. For a time there was no response. Then he gasped, snorted out water and sat up abruptly. His eyes were blank. Then his gaze met mine and he grinned wildly. 'Such a folk and such a day! It was the announcing of Realder's dragon, and he had promised he would fly me . . .' He frowned suddenly and looked about in confusion. 'It fades, like a dream it fades, leaving less than its shadow behind . . .'

Kettle and Kettricken were suddenly with us as well. Starling tattled out all that had happened while I helped the Fool to drink some water. When she was finished, Kettricken looked grave, but it was Kettle who lashed out at us. 'The White Prophet and the Catalyst!' she cried in disgust. 'Rather name them as they are, the Fool and the Idiot. Of all the careless, foolish things to do! He has no training at all, how is he to protect himself from the coterie?'

'Do you know what happened?' I demanded, cutting into her tirade.

'I . . . well, of course not. But I can surmise. The stone he clambered on must be a Skill-stone, the same stuff as the road and the pillars. And somehow this time the road seized you both with its power instead of just you.'

'Did you know it could happen?' I didn't wait for her reply. 'Why didn't you warn us?'

'I didn't know!' she retorted, and then added guiltily, 'I only suspected, and I never thought either of you would be so foolish as to . . .'

'Never mind!' the Fool cut in. Abruptly he laughed and stood up, pushing away my arm. 'Oh, this! This is such as I have not felt in years, not since I was a child. The certainty, the power of it. Kettle! Would you hear a White Prophet speak? Then hearken to this, and be glad as I am glad. We are not only where we must be, we are when we must be. All junctures coincide, we draw closer and closer to the centre of the web. You and I.' He clasped my head suddenly between his two hands and placed his brow against mine. 'We are even who we must be!' He freed me suddenly and spun away. He launched the handspring I had expected earlier, came to his feet, curtseyed deeply and laughed aloud again, exultantly. We all gawked at him.

'You are in great danger!' Kettle told him severely.

'I know,' he replied, almost sincerely, and then added, 'as I said. Exactly where we need to be.' He paused, then asked me suddenly, 'Did you see my crown? Wasn't it magnificent? I wonder if I shall be able to carve it from memory?'

'I saw the rooster crown,' I said slowly. 'But what to make of any of this, I do not know.'

'You don't?' He cocked his head at me, then smiled pityingly. 'Oh, Fitzy-fitz, I would explain it if I could. It is not that I wish to keep secrets, but these secrets defy telling in mere words. They are more than half a feeling, a grasping of rightness. Can you trust me in this?'

'You are alive again,' I said wonderingly. I had not seen such light in his eyes since the days when he had made King Shrewd bellow with laughter.

'Yes,' he said gently. 'And when we have finished, I promise that you will be, also.'

The three women stood glaring and excluded. When I looked at the outrage on Starling's face, the rebuke in Kettle's and the exasperation in Kettricken's, I suddenly had to grin. Behind me the Fool chuckled. And try as we might, we could not explain to their satisfaction exactly what had happened. Nevertheless, we wasted quite some time in attempting it.

Kettricken took out both maps and consulted them. Kettle insisted on accompanying me when I took my map back to the central pillar to compare the glyphs on it to the ones on the map. They shared a number of marks in common, but the only one that Kettricken recognized was the one she had named before. Stone. When I reluctantly offered to see if this pillar might not transport me as the other one had, Kettricken adamantly refused. I am ashamed to admit I was greatly relieved. 'We began together, and I intend that we shall finish together,' she said darkly. I knew she suspected that the Fool and I were keeping something from her.

'What do you propose then?' I asked her humbly.

'What I first suggested. We will follow that old road that goes off through the trees. It appears to match what is marked here. It cannot take us more than two marches to reach the end of it. Especially if we start now.'

And with no more announcement than that, she got up and clicked to the jeppas. The leader came immediately and the rest obediently fell into line behind her. I watched her long even strides as she led them off down the shady road.

'Well, get along, both of you!' Kettle snapped at the Fool and me. She shook her walking stick and I almost suspected she wished she could prod us along like errant sheep. But the Fool and I both fell obediently into line behind the jeppas, leaving Starling and Kettle to follow us.

That night the Fool and I left the tent's shelter and went with Nighteyes. Both Kettle and Kettricken had been dubious as to the wisdom of this, but I had assured them I would act with all caution. The Fool had promised not to let me out of his sight. Kettle rolled her eyes at this, but said nothing. Plainly we were both still suspected of being idiots, but they let us leave anyway. Starling was sulkily silent, but as we had not had words, I assumed her pique had some other source. As we left the fireside, Kettricken said quietly, 'Watch over them, wolf,' and Nighteyes replied with a wave of his tail.

Nighteyes led us swiftly away from the grassy road and up into the wooded hills. The road had been leading us steadily downwards into more sheltered country. The woods that we moved through were open groves of oaks with wide meadows between. I saw sign of wild boar but was relieved when we did not encounter any. Instead, the wolf ran down and killed two rabbits that he graciously allowed me to carry for him. As we were returning to the camp by a roundabout path we came on a stream. The water was icy and sweet and cress grew thick along one bank. The Fool and I tickled for fish until our hands and arms were numb with the cold water. As I hauled out a final fish, its lashing tail splashed the enthusiastic wolf. He leaped back from it then snapped at me in rebuke. The Fool playfully scooped up another handful and flung it at him. Nighteyes leaped, jaws wide to meet it. Moments later, all three of us were involved in a water battle, but I was the only one who landed bodily in the stream when the wolf sprang on me. Both Fool and wolf were laughing heartily as I staggered out, soaked and chilled. I found myself laughing also. I could not recall the last time I had simply laughed aloud about so simple a thing. We returned to camp late, but with fresh meat, fish, and watercress to share.

There was a small, welcoming fire burning outside the tent. Kettle and Starling had already made porridge for our meal, but Kettle volunteered to cook again for the sake of the fresh food. While she was preparing it, Starling stared at me until I demanded, 'What?'

'How did you all get so wet?' she asked.

'Oh. By the stream where we got the fish. Nighteyes pushed me in.' I gave him a passing nudge with my knee as I headed toward the tent. He made a mock snap at my leg.

'And the Fool fell in as well?'

'We were throwing water at one another,' I admitted wryly. I grinned at her, but she did not smile. Instead she gave a small snort as if disdainful. I shrugged and went into the tent. Kettricken glanced up at me from her map, but said nothing. I rucked through my pack and found clothes that were dry if not clean. Her back was turned so I changed hastily. We had grown accustomed to granting one another the privacy of ignoring such things.

'FitzChivalry,' she said suddenly in a voice that commanded my attention.

I dragged my shirt down over my head and buttoned it. 'Yes, my queen?' I came to kneel beside her, thinking she wanted to consult on the map. Instead, she set it aside and turned to me. Her blue eyes met mine squarely.

'We are a small company, all dependent on one another,' she abruptly told me. 'Any kind of strife within our group serves the purpose of our enemy.'

I waited, but she said no more. 'I do not understand why you tell me this,' I said humbly at last.

She sighed and shook her head. 'I feared as much. And perhaps I do more harm than good to speak of it at all. Starling is tormented by your attentions to the Fool.'

I was speechless. Kettricken speared me with a blue glance, then looked aside from me again. 'She believes the Fool is a woman and that you kept a tryst with her tonight. It chagrins her that you disdain her so completely.'

I found my tongue. 'My lady queen, I do not disdain Mistress Starling.' My outrage had rendered me formal. 'In truth, she is the one who has avoided my company and put a distance between us since finding that I am Witted and sustain a bond with the wolf. Respecting her wishes, I have not pressed my friendship upon her. As to what she says of the Fool, surely you must find it as ludicrous as I do.'

'Should I?' Kettricken asked me softly. 'All I can truthfully say I know of it is that he is not a man like other men.'

'I cannot disagree with that,' I said quietly. 'He is unique among all the people I have ever known.'

'Cannot you show some kindness to her, FitzChivalry?' Kettricken burst out suddenly. 'I do not ask that you court her, only that you do not let her be rent with jealousy.'

I folded my lips, forced my feelings to find courteous answer.

'My queen, I will offer her, as I ever have, my friendship. She has given me small sign of late of even wanting that, let alone more. But as to that topic, I do not disdain her nor any other woman. My heart is given already. It is no more right to say that I disdain Starling than it is to say that you disdain me because your heart is filled with my Lord Verity.'

Kettricken shot me an oddly startled look. For a moment she seemed flustered. Then she looked down at the map she still gripped. 'It is as I feared. I have only made it worse by speaking to you. I am so tired, Fitz. Despair drags at my heart always. To have Starling moody is like sand against raw flesh to me. I but sought to put things right between you. I beg your pardon if I have intruded. But you are a comely youth still, and it will not be the last time you have such cares.'

'Comely?' I laughed aloud, both incredulous and bitter. 'With this scarred face and battered body? It haunts my nightmares that when next Molly sees me, she shall turn aside from me in horror. Comely.' I turned aside from her, my throat suddenly too tight to speak. It was not that I mourned my appearance so much as I dreaded that Molly must look some day on my scars.

'Fitz,' Kettricken said quietly. Her voice was suddenly that of a friend, not the Queen. 'I speak to you as a woman, to tell you that although you bear scars, you are far from the grotesque you seem to believe yourself. You are, still, a comely youth, in ways that have nothing to do with your face. And were my heart not full with my Lord Verity, I would not disdain you.' She reached out a hand and ran cool fingers down the old split down my cheek, as if her touch could erase it. My heart turned over in me, an echo of Verity's embedded passion for her amplified by my gratitude that she would say such a thing to me.

'You well deserve my lord's love,' I told her artlessly from a full heart.

'Oh, do not look at me with his eyes,' she said dolefully. She rose suddenly, clasping the map to her breast like a shield, and left the tent.

THIRTY

Stone Garden

Dimity Keep, a very small holding on the coast of Buck, fell shortly before Regal crowned himself King of the Six Duchies. A great many villages were destroyed in that dread time, and there has never been a true count made of all the lives that were lost. Small keeps like Dimity were frequent targets for the Red Ships. Their strategy was to attack simple villages and the smaller holdings to weaken the overall defence line. Lord Bronze, to whom the Keep of Dimity was entrusted, was an old man, but nonetheless he led his men in defending his small castle. Unfortunately, heavy taxation for general coastline protection had drained his resources for some time, and Dimity Keep's defences were in poor repair. Lord Bronze was among the first to fall. The Red Ships took the keep almost easily, and reduced it with fire and sword to the rubble-strewn mound that it is today.

Unlike the Skill road, the road we travelled the next day had experienced the full ravages of time. Doubtless once a wide thoroughfare, the encroachments of the forest had narrowed it to little more than a track. While to me it seemed almost carefree to march down a road that did not at every moment threaten to steal my mind from me, the others muttered about the hummocks, upthrust roots, fallen branches and other obstacles we scrambled through all day. I kept my thoughts to myself and enjoyed the thick moss that overlay the once-cobbled surface, the branchy shade of the bud-leafed trees that overarched the road and the occasional patter of fleeing animals in the underbrush.

Nighteyes was in his element, racing ahead and then galloping back to us, to trot purposefully along beside Kettricken for a time. Then he would go ranging off again. At one time he came dashing back to the Fool and me, tongue lolling, to announce that tonight we would hunt wild pig, for their sign was plentiful. I relayed this to the Fool.

'I did not lose any wild pigs. Therefore, I shall not hunt for any,' he replied loftily. I rather agreed with his sentiments. Burrich's scarred leg had made me more than wary of the great tusked animals.

Rabbits, I suggested to Nighteyes. *Let us hunt rabbits.*

Rabbits for rabbits, he snorted disdainfully, and dashed off again.

I ignored the insult. The day was just pleasantly cool for hiking and the verdant forest smells were like a homecoming to me. Kettricken led us on, lost in her own thoughts, while Kettle and Starling followed us, caught up in talk. Kettle still tended to walk more slowly, though the old woman seemed to have gained stamina and strength since our journey had begun. But they were a comfortable distance behind us when I quietly asked the Fool, 'Why do you allow Starling to believe you are a woman?'

He turned to me, waggled his eyebrows and blew me a kiss. 'And am I not, fair princeling?'

'I'm serious,' I rebuked him. 'She thinks you are a woman and in love with me. She thought that we had a tryst last night.'

'And did we not, my shy one?' He leered at me outrageously.

'Fool,' I said warningly.

'Ah.' He sighed suddenly. 'Perhaps the truth is, I fear to show her my proof, lest ever afterwards she find all other men a disappointment.' He gestured meaningfully at himself.

I looked at him levelly until he grew sober. 'What does it matter what she thinks? Let her think whatever is easiest for her to believe.'

'Meaning?'

'She needed someone to confide in and, for a time, chose me. Perhaps it was easier for her to do that if she believed I was a woman, also.' He sighed again. 'That is one thing that in all my years among your folk I have never become accustomed to. The great importance that you attach to what gender one is.'

'Well it is important . . .' I began.

'Rubbish!' he exclaimed. 'Mere plumbing, when all is said and done. Why is it important?'

I stared at him, at a loss for words. It all seemed so obvious to me as to not need saying. After a time, I said, 'Could you not simply tell her you are a man and let the issue be laid to rest?'

'That would scarcely lay it to rest, Fitz,' he replied judiciously. He clambered over a fallen tree and waited for me to follow. 'For then she would need to know why, if I am a man, I do not desire her. It would have to be either a fault in me, or something I perceived as a fault in her. No. I do not think anything needs to be said on that topic. Starling, however, has the minstrel's failing. She thinks that everything in the world, no matter how private, should be a topic for discussion. Or better yet, made into a song. Ah, yes!'

He struck a sudden pose in the middle of the forest trail. His stance was so artfully reminiscent of Starling when she readied herself to sing that I was horrified. I glanced back at her as the Fool launched into sudden, hearty song:

> 'Oh, when the Fool pisses
> Pray tell, what's the angle?
> Did we take down his pants
> Would he dimple or dangle?'

My eyes darted from Starling to the Fool. He bowed, an embroidery of the elaborate bow that often marked the end of her performances. I wanted at once to laugh aloud and to sink into the earth. I saw Starling redden and start forward, but Kettle caught at her sleeve and said something severely. Then they both glared at me. It was not the first time that one of the Fool's escapades had embarrassed me, but it was one of the most keenly-edged ones. I made a helpless gesture back at them, then rounded on the Fool. He was capering down the path ahead of me. I hastened to catch up with him.

'Did you ever stop to think you might hurt her feelings?' I asked him angrily.

'I gave it as much thought as she gave to whether such an allegation might hurt mine.' He rounded on me suddenly, wagging a long finger. 'Admit it. You asked that question with never a thought as to whether it would hurt my vanity. How would you feel if I demanded proof that you were a man? Ah!' His shoulders slumped suddenly and he seemed to lose all energy. 'Such a thing to waste words on, with all else we must confront. Let it go, Fitz, and I will as well. Let her refer to me as "she" as much as she wishes. I will do my best to ignore it.'

I should have left it alone. I did not. 'It is only that she thinks that you love me,' I tried to explain.

He gave me an odd look. 'I do.'

'I mean, as a man and a woman love.'

He took a breath. 'And how is that?'

'I mean . . .' It half-angered me that he pretended not to understand me. 'For bedding. For . . .'

'And is that how a man loves a woman,' he interrupted me suddenly, 'for bedding?'

'It's a part of it!' I felt suddenly defensive but could not say why.

He arched an eyebrow at me and said calmly, 'You are confusing plumbing and love again.'

'It's more than plumbing!' I shouted at him. A bird abruptly flew off, cawing. I glanced back at Kettle and Starling, who exchanged puzzled glances.

'I see,' he said. He thought a bit as I strode ahead of him on the path. Then, from behind me he called out, 'Tell me, Fitz, did you love Molly or that which was under her skirts?'

Now it was my turn to be affronted. But I was not going to let him baffle me into silence. 'I love Molly and all that is a part of her,' I declared. I hated the heat that rose in my cheeks.

'There, now you have said it,' the Fool replied as if I had proven his point for him. 'And I love you, and all that is a part of you.' He cocked his head and the next words held a challenge. 'And do you not return that to me?'

He waited. I desperately wished I had never started this discussion. 'You know I love you,' I said at last, grudgingly. 'After all that has been between us, how can you even ask? But I love you as a man loves another man . . .' Here the Fool leered at me mockingly. Then a sudden glint lit his eyes, and I knew that he was about to do something awful to me.

He leaped to the top of a fallen log. From that height, he gave Starling a triumphant look and cried dramatically, 'He loves me, he says! And I love him!' Then with a whoop of wild laughter he leapt down and raced ahead of me on the trail.

I ran my hand back through my hair and then slowly clambered over the log. I heard Kettle laughing and Starling's angry comments. I walked silently through the forest, wishing I'd had the sense to keep my mouth shut. I was certain that Starling was simmering with fury. Lately she had had almost no words for me. I had accepted that she found my Wit something of an abomination. She was not the first to be dismayed by it; at least she showed some tolerance for me. But now the anger she carried would have a more personal bite to it. One more small loss of what little I had left. A part of me greatly missed the closeness we had shared for a time. I missed the human comfort of having her sleep against my back, or suddenly take my arm when we were walking. I thought I had closed my heart against those needs, but I suddenly missed that simple warmth.

As if that thought had opened a breach in my walls, I suddenly thought of Molly. And Nettle, both in danger because of me. Without warning, my heart was in my throat. I must not think of them, I warned myself, and reminded myself that there was nothing I could do. There was no way I could warn them without betraying them. There was no possible way I could reach them before Regal's henchmen did. All I could do was trust to Burrich's strong right arm, and cling to the hope that Regal did not truly know where they were.

I jumped over a trickling creek and found the Fool waiting for me on the other side. He said nothing as he fell into pace beside me. His merriment seemed to have deserted him.

I reminded myself that I scarcely knew where Molly and Burrich were. Oh, I knew the name of a nearby village, but as long as I kept that to myself, they were safe.

'What you know, I can know.'

'What did you say?' I asked the Fool uneasily. His words had replied so exactly to my thoughts that it sent a chill up my spine.

'I said, what you know, I can know,' he repeated absently.

'Why?'

'Exactly my thought. Why would I wish to know what you know?'

'No. I mean, why did you say that?'

'In truth, Fitz, I've no idea. The words popped into my head and I said them. I often say things I have not well considered.' The last he said almost as an apology.

'As do I,' I agreed. I said no more to him, but it bothered me. He seemed, since the incident at the pillar, to be much more of the Fool I remembered from Buckkeep. I welcomed his sudden growth in confidence and spirits but I also worried that he might have too much faith in events flowing as they should. I also recalled that his sharp tongue was more prone to bare conflicts than resolve them. I myself had felt its edge more than once, but in the context of King Shrewd's court, I had expected it. Here, in such a small company, it seemed to cut more sharply. I wondered if there were any way I could soften his razor humour. I shook my head to myself, then resolutely dredged up Kettle's latest game problem and kept it before my mind even as I clambered over forest debris and sidestepped hanging branches.

As late afternoon wore on, our path led us deeper and deeper into a valley. At one point the ancient trail afforded a view of what lay below us. I glimpsed the green-beaded, trailing branches of willows coming into leaf and the rose-tinged trunks of paper birches presiding over a deeply grassed meadow. Beyond I saw the brown standing husks of last year's cattails deeper in the vale. The lush rankness of the grasses and ferns foretold swampland as surely as the green smell of standing water did. When the ranging wolf came back wet to his knees, I knew I was right.

Before long we came to where an energetic stream had long ago washed out a bridge and devoured the road to either side of it. Now it trickled shining and silver in a gravelly bed, but the fallen trees on either bank attested to its floodtime fury. A chorus of frogs stilled suddenly at our approach. I went rock to rock to get past it with dry feet. We had not gone far before a second stream crossed our path. Given a choice of wet feet or wet boots, I chose the former. The water was icy. The only kindness was that it numbed my feet from the stones in its bed. On the far side I put my boots back on. Our small company had closed its ranks as the trail grew more difficult. Now we continued to march silently together. Blackbirds called and early insects hummed.

'So much life here,' Kettricken said softly. Her words seemed to hang in the still sweet air. I found myself nodding in agreement. So much life around us, both green and animal. It filled my Wit-sense and seemed to hang in the air like a mist. After the barren stones of the mountains and the deserted Skill road, this abundance of life was heady.

Then I saw the dragon.

I halted in my tracks and lifted my arms out in a sudden gesture for both stillness and silence that all seemed to recognize. All of my companions' gazes followed mine. Starling gasped and the hackles on the wolf stood up. We stared at it, as unmoving as it was.

Golden and green, he sprawled under the trees in their dappled shade. He was far enough off the trail that I could only see patches of him through the trees, but those were impressive enough. His immense head, as long as a horse's body, rested deep in the moss. His single eye that I could see was closed. A great crest of feather-scales, rainbow-hued, lay lax about his throat. Similar tufts above each eye looked almost comical, save that there could be nothing comical about a creature so immense and so strange. I saw a scaled shoulder, and winding between two trees, a length of tail. Old leaves were heaped about it like a sort of nest.

After a long breathless moment, we exchanged glances. Kettricken raised her eyebrows at me, but I deferred to her with a tiny shrug. I had no concept of what dangers it might present, or how to face them. Very slowly and silently I drew my sword. It suddenly looked like a very silly weapon. As well face a bear with a table-knife. I don't know how long our tableau held. It seemed an endless time. My muscles were beginning to ache with the strain of remaining motionless. The jeppas shifted impatiently, but held their places in line as long as Kettricken kept their leader still. At last Kettricken made a small silent motion, and slowly started our party forward again.

When I could no longer see the slumbering beast, I began to breathe a bit easier. Just as quickly, reaction set in. My hand ached from gripping my sword hilt and all my muscles suddenly went rubbery. I wiped my sweaty hair back from my face. I turned to exchange a relieved look with the Fool, only to find him staring beyond me with unbelieving eyes. I turned hastily, and like flocking birds, the others mimed my gesture. Yet again we halted, silently transfixed, to stare at a sleeping dragon.

This one sprawled in the deep shade of evergreen trees. Like the first, she nestled deep in moss and forest debris. But there the resemblance ended. Her long sinuous tail was coiled and wrapped around her like a garland, and her smoothly scaled hide shone a rich, coppery brown. I could see wings folded tight to her narrow body. Her long neck was craned over her back like a sleeping goose's and the shape of her head was bird-like also, even to a hawk-like beak. From the creature's brow spiralled up a shining horn, wickedly sharp at the tip. The four limbs folded beneath her put me more in mind of a hind than a lizard. To call both these creatures dragons seemed a contradiction, yet I had no other word for beings such as these.

Again we stood silent and staring while the jeppas shifted restlessly. Abruptly Kettricken spoke. 'I do not think they are living beings. I think they are clever carvings of stone.'

My Wit-sense told me otherwise. 'They are alive!' I cautioned her in a whisper. I started to quest toward one, but Nighteyes near panicked. I drew my mind-touch back. 'They sleep very deeply, as if still hibernating from the cold weather. But I know they are alive.'

While Kettricken and I were speaking, Kettle went to decide it for herself. I saw Kettricken's eyes widen, and turned to look back at the dragon, fearing it was awakening. Instead I saw Kettle place her withered hand on the creature's still brow. Her hand seemed to tremble as she touched it, but then she smiled, almost sadly, and stroked her hand up the spiralling horn. 'So beautiful,' she mused. 'So cunningly wrought.'

She turned back to us all. 'Mark how last year's vine twined about her tail tip. See how deeply she lies in the fallen leaves of a score of years. Or perhaps a score of scores. Yet each tiny scale still gleams, so perfectly fashioned is she!'

Starling and Kettricken started forward with exclamations of wonder and delight, and were soon crouched by the sculpture, calling each other's attention to crafted detail after detail. The individual scales of each wing, the fluidly graceful looping of the tail coils and every other marvel of the artist's design were admired. Yet while they pointed and touched so avidly, the wolf and I held back. Hackles stood up all along Nighteyes' back. He did not growl; instead he gave a whine so high it was almost like a whistle. After a moment, I realized the Fool had not joined the others. I turned to find him regarding it from afar, as a miser might look on a pile of gold larger even than his dreams. There was the same sort of wideness to his eyes. Even his pale cheeks seemed to hold a rosy flush.

'Fitz, come and see! It is only cold stone, carved so well as to appear alive. And look! There is another, with the antlers of a stag and the face of a man!' Kettricken lifted a hand to point and I glimpsed yet another figure sprawled sleeping on the forest floor. They all departed the first effigy to regard this new one, exclaiming anew over the beauty and details of it.

I moved myself forward on leaden feet, the wolf pressed tightly to my side. When I stood next to the horned one, I could see for myself the fuzzy sac of spider webs affixed in the hollow of one hoofed foot. The creature's ribs did not move with the pumping of any lungs, nor did I feel any body warmth at all. I finally forced myself to set a hand to the cold, carved stone. 'It's a statue,' I said aloud, as if to force myself to believe what my Wit-sense denied. I looked around me, past the stag-man that Starling still admired, to where Kettle and Kettricken stood smiling by yet another sculpture. Its boar-like body sprawled on its side, and the tusks that protruded from its snout were as long as I was tall. In all ways it resembled the forest pig that Nighteyes had killed, save for its immense size and the wings tucked close to its side.

'I spy at least a dozen of these things,' the Fool announced. 'And, behind those trees, I found another carved column such as we have seen before.' He set a curious hand to the skin of the sculpture, then almost winced away at the cold contact.

'I cannot believe they are lifeless stone,' I told him.

'I, too, have never seen such realistic detail in a carving,' he agreed.

I did not try to tell him he had misunderstood me. Instead, I stood pondering a thing. Here, I sensed life, but there was only cold stone under my hand. It had been the opposite with Forged ones; savage life obviously motivated their bodies, yet my Wit-sense regarded them as but cold stone. I groped for some sort of connection but found only the odd comparison.

I glanced about me but found my companions scattered throughout the forest, moving from sculpture to sculpture, and calling to one another in delight as they discovered new ones under clambering ivy or engulfed in fallen leaves. I drifted after them slowly. It seemed to me that this might be the destination marked on the map. It almost certainly was, if the old mapmaker had had his scale correct. And yet, why? What was important about these statues? The significance of the city I had seen at once; it might have been the original habitation of the Elderlings. But this?

I hastened after Kettricken. I found her by a winged bull. He slept, legs folded under him, powerful shoulders bunched, heavy muzzle dropped to his knees. It was a perfect replica of a bull in every way, from its wide sweep of horns to its tufted tail. His cloven hooves were buried beneath the forest loam, but I did not doubt they were there. She had stretched her arms wide to span the sweep of his horns. Like all the others, he had wings, folded in repose on his wide black back.

'May I see the map?' I asked her, and she started out of her reverie.

'I've already checked it,' she told me quietly. 'I am convinced this is the marked area. We passed the remains of two stone bridges. That corresponds to what is shown on the map. And the marking on the column the Fool found corresponds to one you copied in the city for this destination. I think we are on what were once the shores of a lake. That is how I've been reading the map, anyway.'

'The shores of a lake.' I nodded to myself as I considered what Verity's map had shown me. 'Perhaps. Perhaps it silted in and became swamp. But then, what do all these statues signify?'

She made a vague gesture around at the forest. 'A garden or park of some kind, perhaps?'

I looked around us and shook my head. 'Not like any garden

I've ever seen. The statues seem random. Should not a garden possess unity and theme? At least, so Patience taught me. Here I see only sprawled statues, with no sign of paths or beds or . . . Kettricken? Are all the statues of sleeping creatures?'

She frowned to herself for a moment. 'I believe so. And I think that all are winged.'

'Perhaps it is a graveyard,' I ventured. 'Perhaps there are tombs beneath these creatures. Perhaps this is some strange heraldry, marking the burial places for different families.'

Kettricken looked about us, considering. 'Perhaps it is so. But why would that be marked on the map?'

'Why would a garden?' I countered.

We spent the rest of the afternoon exploring the area. We found a great many more animals. There were all kinds and a variety of styles, but all were winged and sleeping. And they had been here a very long time. A closer examination showed me that these great trees had grown around the statues, the statues had not been placed around them. Some were almost captured by the encroaching moss and leaf mould. Of one, little remained to be seen save a great toothed snout projecting from a boggy bit of ground. The bared teeth shone silver and the tips were sharp.

'Yet I found not a single one with a chip or a crack. Every one looks as perfect as the day it was created. Nor can I decide how the colours were put to the stone. It does not feel like paint or stain, nor does it appear weathered by the years.'

I was expounding my thoughts slowly to the others as we sat about our campfire that evening. I was trying to work Kettricken's comb through my wet hair. In the late afternoon, I had slipped away from the others, to wash thoroughly for the first time since we had left Jhaampe. I had also attempted to wash out some of my clothes. When I returned to camp, I had found that all of the others had had much the same ideas. Kettle was moodily draping wet laundry on a dragon to dry. Kettricken's cheeks were pinker than usual and she had rebraided her wet hair into a tight queue. Starling seemed to have forgotten her earlier anger at me. Indeed, she seemed to have forgotten entirely about the rest of us. She stared at the flames of the campfire, a musing look on her face, and I could almost see the tumbling words and notes as she fit them together. I wondered what it was like, if it was like solving the game puzzles that Kettricken set for me. It seemed odd to watch her face, knowing a song was unfolding in her mind.

Nighteyes came to lean his head against my knee. *I do not like denning in the midst of these living stones*, he confided to me.

'It does seem as if at any moment they might awaken,' I observed.

Kettle had settled with a sigh to the earth beside me. She shook her old head slowly. 'I do not think so,' she said quietly. She almost sounded as if she grieved.

'Well, as we cannot fathom their mystery, and what remains of the road has ended here, we shall leave them tomorrow and resume our journey,' Kettricken announced.

'What will you do,' the Fool asked quietly, 'if Verity is not at the last map destination?'

'I do not know,' Kettricken confided to us quietly. 'Nor shall I worry about it until it happens. I still have an action left to take; until I have exhausted it, I shall not despair.'

It struck me then that she spoke as if considering a game, with one final move left that might yet lead to victory. Then I decided that I had spent too much time focusing on Kettle's game problems. I yanked a last snarl from my hair and pulled it back into a tail.

Come hunt with me before the last light is gone, the wolf suggested.

'I think I shall hunt with Nighteyes tonight,' I announced as I stood and stretched. I raised one eyebrow at the Fool, but he seemed lost in thought and made no response. As I stepped away from the fire, Kettricken asked me, 'Are you safe, alone?'

'We are far from the Skill road. This has been the most peaceful day I've known in some time. In some ways.'

'We may be far from the Skill road, but we are still in the heart of a land once occupied by Skill-users. They have left their touch everywhere. You cannot say, while you walk these hills, that you are safe. You should not go alone.'

Nighteyes whined low in his throat, anxious to be gone. I longed to go hunt with him, to stalk and chase, to move through the night with no human thoughts. But I would not discount Kettle's warning.

'I'll go with him,' Starling offered suddenly. She rose, dusting her hands on her hips. If anyone besides myself thought it was strange, no one made sign of it. I expected at least a mocking farewell from the Fool, but he continued to gaze off into the darkness. I hoped he was not getting sick again.

Do you mind if she goes with us? I asked Nighteyes.

In reply he gave a small sigh of resignation, and trotted away from the fire. I followed him more slowly and Starling followed me.

'Shouldn't we catch up with him?' she asked me several moments later. The forest and the deepening dusk were closing in around us. Nighteyes was nowhere to be seen, but then, I did not need to see him.

I spoke, not in a whisper, but very low. 'When we hunt, we move independently of one another. When one of us starts up some game, the other comes swiftly, either to intercept, or to join in the chase.'

My eyes had adjusted to the dark. Our quest led us away from the statues, into a forest night innocent of man's workings. Spring smells were strong, and the songs of frogs and insects were all around us. I soon struck a game trail and began to move along it. Starling came behind me, not silently, but not awkwardly either. When one moves through the forest by day or by night, one can either move with it or against it. Some people know how to do it instinctively; others never learn. Starling moved with the forest, ducking under hanging branches and sidestepping others as we wove our way through the night. She did not try to force her way through the thickets we encountered, but turned her body to avoid being caught on the twiggy branches.

You are so aware of her, you will not see a rabbit if you step on it! Nighteyes chided me.

At that moment, a hare started from a bush right beside my path. I sprang after it, going doubled over to follow it on the game trail. It was far faster than me, but I knew it would most likely circle. I also knew that Nighteyes was moving swiftly to intercept it. I heard Starling hurrying after me but had no time to think of her as I kept the hare in sight as it dodged around trees and under snags. Twice I nearly had it, and twice it doubled away from me. But the second time it doubled, it raced straight into the jaws of the wolf. He sprang, pinned it to the earth with his front paws, then seized its small skull in his jaws. As he stood, he gave it a sharp shake, snapping its neck.

I was opening its belly and spilling its entrails out for the wolf when Starling caught up with us. Nighteyes snapped the guts up with relish. *Let's find another*, he suggested, and moved swiftly off into the night.

'He always gives up the meat to you like that?' Starling asked me.

'He doesn't give it up. He lets me carry it. He knows that now is the best hunting, and so he hopes to kill again swiftly. If not, he knows I will keep meat safe for him, and that we will share later.' I secured the dead hare to my belt. I started off through the night, the warm body flopping lightly against my thigh as I walked.

'Oh.' Starling followed. A short time later, as if in answer to something I'd said, she observed, 'I do not find your Wit-bond with the wolf offensive.'

'Neither do I,' I replied quietly. Something in her choice of words nettled me. I continued to prowl along the trail, eyes and ears alert. I could hear the soft pad, pad, pad of Nighteyes' feet off to my left and ahead of me. I hoped he would scare game toward me.

A short time later, Starling added, 'And I will stop calling the Fool "she". Whatever I may suspect.'

'That's good,' I told her noncommittally. I did not slow my pace.

I truly doubt you will be much good as hunter this night.

This is not of my choosing.

I know.

'Do you want me to apologize as well?' Starling asked in a low strained voice.

'I . . . uh,' I stammered, and fell silent, unsure of what this was all about.

'Very well then,' she said in an icily determined voice. 'I apologize, Lord FitzChivalry.'

I rounded on her. 'Why are you doing this?' I demanded. I

spoke in a normal voice. I could sense Nighteyes. He was already topping the hill, hunting alone now.

'My lady queen bid me stop spreading discord within the company. She said that Lord FitzChivalry carried many burdens I could not know of, and did not deserve to bear also my disapproval,' she informed me carefully.

I wondered when all this had come to pass, but dared not ask it. 'None of this is necessary,' I said quietly. I felt oddly shamed, like a spoiled child who had sulked until the other children gave in. I took a deep breath, determined simply to speak honestly and see what came of it. 'I do not know what made you withdraw your friendship, save that I disclosed my Wit to you. Nor do I understand your suspicions of the Fool, or why they seem to anger you. I hate this awkwardness between us. I wish we could be friends, as we were before.'

'You do not despise me, then? For giving my witness that you claimed Molly's child as your get?'

I groped inside me after the lost feelings. It had been long since I had even thought about it. 'Chade already knew of them,' I said quietly. 'He would have found a way, even if you had not existed. He is very . . . resourceful. And I have come to understand that you do not live by the same rules that I do.'

'I used to,' she said softly. 'A long time ago. Before the keep was sacked and I was left for dead. After that, it was hard to believe in the rules. Everything was taken from me. All that was good and beautiful and truthful was laid waste by evil and lust and greed. No. By something even baser than lust and greed, some drive I could not even understand. Even while the Raiders were raping me, they seemed to take no pleasure in it. At least, not the kind of pleasure . . . They mocked my pain and struggling. Those who watched were laughing as they waited.' She was looking past me into the darkness of the past. I believe she spoke as much to herself as me, groping to understand something that defied meaning. 'It was as if they were driven, but not by any lust or greed that could be sated. It was a thing they could do to me, so they did it. I had always believed, perhaps childishly, that if you followed the rules, you would be protected, that things like that would not happen to you. Afterwards, I felt . . . tricked.

Foolish. Gullible, that I had thought ideals could protect me. Honour and courtesy and justice . . . they are not real, Fitz. We all pretend to them, and hold them to us like shields. But they guard only against folk who carry the same shields. Against those who have discarded them, they are no shields at all, but only additional weapons to use against their victims.'

I felt dizzied for an instant. I had never heard a woman speak of something like that so dispassionately. Mostly it was not spoken of at all. The rapes that occurred during a raid, the pregnancies that might follow, even the children that Six Duchies women bore to the Red Ship Raiders were seldom spoken of as such. I suddenly realized we had been standing still a long time. The chill of the spring night was reaching me. 'Let's go back to the camp,' I suggested abruptly.

'No,' she said flatly. 'Not yet. I fear I may cry, and if I do, I'd rather do it in the dark.'

It was getting close to full dark. But I led her back to a wider game trail, and we found a log to sit down on. Around us, the frogs and insects filled the night with mating songs.

'Are you all right?' I asked her after we had sat some time in the silence.

'No. I am not,' she said shortly. 'I need to make you understand. I did not sell your child cheaply, Fitz. I did not betray you casually. At first, I did not even think of it that way. Who would not want her daughter to become a princess, and eventually a queen? Who would not want lovely clothes and a fine home for his child? I did not think that you or your woman would see it as a misfortune befalling her.'

'Molly is my wife,' I said quietly, but I truly believe she did not hear me.

'Then, even after I knew it would not please you, I did it anyway. Knowing it would buy me a place here, at your side, witnessing . . . whatever it is you are going to do. Seeing strange sights no minstrel has ever sung of before, like those statues today. Because it was my only chance at a future. I must have a song, I must witness something that will assure me forever of a place of honour among minstrels. Something that will guarantee me my soup and wine when I am too old to travel from keep to keep.'

'Couldn't you have settled for a man to share your life and children?' I asked quietly. 'It seems to me you have no problem catching a man's eye. Surely there must be one that . . .'

'No man wants a barren woman to wed,' she said. Her voice went flat, losing its music. 'At the fall of Dimity Keep, Fitz, they left me for dead. And I lay there among the dead, sure that I would die soon, for I could not imagine continuing to live. Around me buildings were burning and injured folk were screaming and I could smell flesh scorching . . .' She stopped speaking. When she resumed, her voice was a bit more even. 'But I didn't die. My body was stronger than my will. On the second day, I dragged myself to water. Some other survivors found me. I lived, and was better off than many. Until two months later. By then I was sure that what had been done to me was worse than killing me. I knew I carried a child fathered by one of those creatures.

'So I went to a healer, who gave me herbs that did not work. I went to her again, and she warned me, saying if they had not worked, then I had better leave it to happen. But I went to another healer, who gave me a different potion. It . . . made me bleed. I shook the child loose from me, but the bleeding did not stop. I went back to the healers, both of them, but neither could help me. They said it would stop on its own, in time. But the one told me that it was likely I would never have other children.' Her voice tightened, then thickened. 'I know you think it slatternly, the way I am with men. But once you have been forced, it is . . . different. Ever after. I say to myself, well, I know that it can happen to me at any time. So this way, at least I decide with whom and when. There will never be children for me, and hence there will never be a permanent man. So why should not I take my pick of what I can have? You made me question that for a time, you know. Until Moonseye. Moonseye proved me right again. And from Moonseye I came to Jhaampe, knowing that I was free to do whatever I must do to assure my own survival. For there will be no man and no children to look after me when I am old.' Her voice went brittle and uneven as she said, 'Sometimes I think it were better had they Forged me . . .'

'No. Never say that. Never.' I feared to touch her, but she turned suddenly and burrowed her face against me. I put an arm around her and found her trembling. I felt compelled to confess my stupidity. 'I did not understand. When you said Burl's soldiers had raped some of the women . . . I did not know you had suffered that.'

'Oh.' Her voice was very small. 'I had thought you deemed it unimportant. I have heard it said in Farrow that rape bothers only virgins and wives. I thought perhaps you felt that to one such as I, it was no more than my due.'

'Starling!' I felt an irrational flash of anger that she could have believed me so heartless. Then I thought back. I had seen the bruises on her face. Why had not I guessed? I had never even spoken to her of how Burl had broken her fingers. I had assumed she had known how that had sickened me, that she knew it was Burl's threat of greater damage to her that had kept me leashed. I had thought that she withdrew friendship from me because of my wolf. What had she believed of my distance?

'I have brought much pain into your life,' I confessed. 'Do not think I do not know the value of a minstrel's hands. Or that I discount the violation of your body. If you wish to speak of it, I am ready to listen. Sometimes, talking helps.'

'Sometimes it does not,' she countered. Her grip on me suddenly tightened. 'The day you stood before us all, and spoke in detail of what Regal had done to you. I bled for you that day. It did not undo anything that was done to you. No. I do not want to talk about it, or think about it.'

I lifted her hand and softly kissed the fingers that had been broken on my account. 'I do not confuse what was done to you with who you are,' I offered. 'When I look at you, I see Starling Birdsong the minstrel.'

She nodded her face against me, and I knew it was as I surmised. She and I shared that fear. We would not live as victims.

I said no more than that, but only sat there. It came to me again that even if we found Verity, even if by some miracle his return would shift the tides of war and make us victors, for some the victory would come far too late. Mine had been a long and weary road, but I still dared to believe that at the end of it there might be a life of my own choosing. Starling had not even that. No matter how far inland she might flee, she would never escape the war. I held her closer and felt her pain bleed over into me. After a time, her trembling stilled.

'It's full dark,' I said at last. 'We had best go back to the camp.'

She sighed, but she straightened up. She took my hand. I started to lead her back to camp, but she tugged back on my hand. 'Be with me,' she said simply. 'Just for here and just for now. With gentleness and friendship. To take the . . . other away. Give me that much of yourself.'

I wanted her. I wanted her with a desperation that had nothing to do with love, and even, I believe, little to do with lust. She was warm and alive and it would have been sweet and simple human comfort. If I could have been with her, and somehow arisen from it unchanged in how I thought of myself and what I felt for Molly, I would have done so. But what I felt for Molly was not something that was only for when we were together. I had given Molly that claim to me; I could not rescind it simply because we were apart for a time. I did not think there were words that could make Starling understand that in choosing Molly I was not rejecting her. So instead I said, 'Nighteyes comes. He has a rabbit.'

Starling stepped close to me. She ran a hand up my chest to the side of my neck. Her fingers traced the line of my jaw and caressed my mouth. 'Send him away,' she said quietly.

'I could not send him far enough that he would not know everything of what we shared,' I told her truthfully.

Her hand on my face was suddenly still. 'Everything?' she asked. Her voice was full of dismay.

Everything. He came and sat down beside us. Another rabbit dangled in his jaws.

'We are Wit-bonded. We share everything.'

She took her hand from my face and stood clear of me. She stared down at the dark shape of the wolf. 'Then all I just told you . . .'

'He understands it in his own way. Not as another human would, but . . .'

'How did Molly feel about that?' she abruptly demanded.

I took a sharp breath. I had not expected our conversation to take this turn. 'She never knew,' I told her. Nighteyes started back to the camp. I followed him more slowly. Behind me came Starling.

'And when she does know?' Starling pressed. 'She will just accept this . . . sharing?'

'Probably not,' I muttered unwillingly. Why did Starling always make me think of things I had avoided considering?

'What if she forces you to choose between her and the wolf?'

I halted in my tracks for an instant. Than I started walking again, a bit faster. The question hung around me, but I refused to think about it. It could not be, it could never come to that. Yet a voice whispered inside me, 'If you tell Molly the truth, it will come to that. It must.'

'You are going to tell her, aren't you?' Starling relentlessly asked me the one question I was hiding from.

'I don't know,' I said grimly.

'Oh,' she said. Then after a time, she added, 'When a man says that, it usually means, "No, I won't, but from time to time, I'll toy with the idea, so I can pretend I eventually intend to do it."'

'Would you please shut up?' There was no strength in my words.

Starling followed me silently. After a time, she observed, 'I don't know who to pity. You, or her.'

'Both of us, perhaps,' I suggested stonily. I wanted no more words about it.

The Fool was on watch when we got back to camp. Kettle and Kettricken were asleep. 'Good hunting?' he asked in a comradely way as we approached.

I shrugged. Nighteyes was already gnawing his way through the rabbit he had carried. He sprawled contentedly by the Fool's feet. 'Good enough.' I held up the hare. The Fool took it from me and casually hung it from the tent pole.

'Breakfast,' he told me calmly. His eyes darted to Starling's face, but if he could tell she had been weeping, he made no jest of it. I don't know what he read in my face, for he made no comment on it. She followed me into the tent. I pulled off my boots and sank gratefully into my bedding. When I felt her settle herself against my back a few moments later, I was not very surprised. I decided it meant she had forgiven me. It did not make it easy to fall asleep.

But eventually I did. I had set up my walls, but somehow I managed a dream of my very own. I dreamed that I sat by Molly's bed and watched over her as she and Nettle slept. The wolf was at my feet, while in the chimney corner the Fool sat on a stool and nodded to himself, well pleased. Kettle's gamecloth was spread on the table, but instead of stones, it had tiny statues of different dragons in white and black. The red stones were ships, and it was my move. I had the piece in my hand that could win the game, but I only wished to watch Molly sleep. It was almost a peaceful dream.

THIRTY-ONE

Elfbark

There are a number of old 'White Prophecies' that relate to the betrayal of the Catalyst. White Colum says of this event, 'By his love is he betrayed, and his love betrayed also.' A lesser-known scribe and prophet, Gant the White, goes into more detail. 'The heart of the Catalyst is bared to a trusted one. All confidence is given, and all confidence betrayed. The child of the Catalyst is given into his enemies' hands by one whose love and loyalty are above question.' The other prophecies are more oblique, but in each case the inference is that the Catalyst is betrayed by one who has his implicit trust.

Early the next morning, as we ate toasted bits of rabbit meat, Kettricken and I consulted her map again. We scarcely needed it any more, we both knew it so well. But it was a thing to set between us and point at as we discussed things. Kettricken traced a fading line on the battered scroll. 'We shall have to return to the column in the stone circle, and then follow the Skill road for some little way beyond it. Right up to our final destination, I believe.'

'I have no great wish to walk upon that road again,' I told her honestly. 'Even walking beside it strains me. But I suppose there is no help for it.'

'None that I can see.'

She was too preoccupied to offer much sympathy. I looked at the woman. The once gleaming blonde hair was a short scruffy braid. Cold and wind had weathered her face, chapping her lips and etching fine lines at the corners of her eyes and mouth, to say nothing of the deeper worry lines in her brow and between her eyes. Her clothing was travel-stained and worn. The Queen of the Six Duchies could not even have passed muster as a chambermaid in Tradeford. I suddenly wanted to reach out to her. I could think of no way to do so. So I simply said, 'We will get there, and we will find Verity.'

She lifted her eyes to meet mine. She tried to put faith into her gaze and voice as she said, 'Yes, we will.' I heard only courage.

We had torn down and moved our camp so often, it no longer took any thought. We moved as a unit, almost as a single creature. Like a coterie, I thought to myself.

Like a pack, Nighteyes corrected me. He came to push his head against my hand. I paused and scratched his ears and throat thoroughly. He closed his eyes and laid back his ears in pleasure. *If your mate makes you send me away, I shall miss this greatly.*

I won't let that happen.

You believe she will make you choose.

I refuse to think about it just now.

Ah! He fell over on his side then rolled to his back so I could scratch his belly. He bared his teeth in a wolfish smile. *You live in the now and refuse to think of what may come. But I, I find I can think of little else save what may come to be. These times have been good for me, my brother. Living with others, hunting together, sharing meat. But the howling bitch had it aright last night. Cubs are needed to make a pack. And your cub . . .*

I cannot think of that just now. I must think only of what I must do today to survive, and all I must do before I can hope to go home.

'Fitz? Are you all right?'

It was Starling, coming to take me by the elbow and give me a small shake. I looked at her, wakened from my bemusement. The howling bitch. I tried not to grin. 'I'm fine. I was with Nighteyes.'

'Oh.' She glanced down at the wolf, and I saw her struggle again to grasp just what we shared. Then she shrugged it off. 'Ready to leave?'

'If everyone else is.'

'They seem to be.'

She went to help Kettricken load the final jeppa. I glanced about for the Fool, and saw him sitting silently on top of his pack. His hand rested lightly upon one of the stone dragons and he had a faraway look on his face. I walked up softly behind him. 'Are you all right?' I asked quietly.

He did not jump. He never startled. He just turned his pale gaze up to meet mine. The look on his face was a lost yearning with none of his usual sharp wit to it. 'Fitz. Have you ever felt you recalled something, but when you groped after it, there was nothing there?'

'Sometimes,' I said. 'I think it happens to everyone.'

'No. This is different,' he insisted quietly. 'Since I stood on that stone the day before yesterday, and suddenly glimpsed the old world that was here . . . I keep having odd half-memories. Like him.' He stroked the dragon's head gently, a lover's caress to the wedge-shaped reptilian head. 'I can almost remember knowing him.' He suddenly fixed me with a pleading look. 'What did you see, back then?'

I gave a small shrug. 'It was like a market plaza, with shops around it, and folk plying their trades. A busy day.'

'Did you see me?' he asked very quietly.

'I'm not sure.' I suddenly felt very uneasy, speaking about it. 'Where you were, there was someone else. She was like you, in a way. No colour to her, and behaving, I think, as a jester. You spoke of her crown, carved like rooster heads and tails.'

'Did I? Fitz, I can recall little of what I said immediately afterward. I only recall the feeling, and how swiftly it faded. Briefly, I was connected to everything. Part of it all. It was wonderful, like feeling a surge of love or glimpsing something perfectly beautiful or . . .' He struggled for words.

'The Skill is like that,' I told him softly. 'What you felt is the pull of it. It is what a Skill-user must constantly resist, lest he be swept away on it.'

'So that was Skilling,' he observed to himself.

'When you first came out of it, you were ecstatic. You said something about somebody's dragon that you were to introduce. It made small sense. Let me think. Realder's dragon. And he had promised to fly you.'

'Ah. My dream last night. Realder. That was your name.' He caressed the statue's head as he spoke. When he did so, the oddest thing happened. My Wit-sense of the statue surged and Nighteyes came springing to my side, every hackle on his back standing erect. I know the hair on the back of my neck stood up as well, and I recoiled, expecting the statue suddenly to stir to life. The Fool shot us a puzzled glance. 'What is it?'

'The statues seem alive to us. To both Nighteyes and me. And when you spoke that name, it almost seemed to stir.'

'Realder,' the Fool repeated experimentally. I caught my breath as he said it, but felt no response. He glanced at me and I shook my head. 'Just stone, Fitz. Cold and beautiful stone. I think perhaps your nerves are fraying.' He took my arm companionably and we walked away from the statues and back to the faded trail. The others were already out of sight, save for Kettle. She stood leaning on her stick and glaring back at us. Instinctively I quickened my pace. When we got to the place where she waited, she took my other arm, and then imperiously waved at the Fool to precede us. We followed him, but at a slower pace. When he was a substantial distance ahead of us, she squeezed my arm in a grip of steel and demanded, 'Well?'

For an instant I looked at her blankly. Then, 'I haven't worked it out yet,' I apologized to her.

'That much is plain,' she told me severely. She sucked on her teeth for a moment, frowned at me, nearly spoke, and then shook her head briskly at herself. She did not let go of my arm.

For much of the rest of the day, as I walked silently by her side, I pondered the game puzzle.

I do not think there is anything quite so tedious as retracing one's steps when one is desperate to get somewhere. Now that we were no longer following an ancient road near invisible in overgrowth, we followed our own trampled way back through the marshy forest and up into the hills, and made better speed leaving than we had in getting there. With the shifting of the seasons, the daylight was lingering longer, and Kettricken pushed our march to the edge of dusk. Thus it was that we found ourselves only one hill away from the plaza of black stone when we made our camp that night. I think it was for my sake that Kettricken chose to camp on the ancient road for another night. I had no desire to sleep any closer to that crossroads than I must.

Shall we hunt? Nighteyes demanded as soon as our shelter was set.

'I'm going hunting,' I announced to the others. Kettle glanced up disapprovingly.

'Stay well away from the Skill road,' she warned me.

The Fool surprised me by coming to his feet. 'I shall go with them. If the wolf doesn't mind.'

The Scentless One is welcome.

'You are welcome to go with us. But are you sure you feel that strong?'

'If I get tired, I can come back,' the Fool pointed out.

As we strode off into the deepening dusk, Kettricken was poring over her map and Kettle was on watch. 'Don't be long, or I shall come and find you,' she warned me as I left. 'And stay away from the Skill road,' she repeated.

Somewhere above the trees, a full moon sailed. Light from her crept and snaked down in silvery spills through the newly leafed branches to illuminate our way. For a time we simply travelled together through the pleasantly open woods. The wolf's senses supplemented mine. The night was alive with the smells of growing things and the calls of tiny frogs and night insects. The night air had a crisper bite to it than the day did. We found a game trail and followed it. The Fool kept pace with us, saying not a word. I breathed in deeply and then sighed it out. Despite everything else, I heard myself say, *This is good.*

Yes. It is. I shall miss it.

I knew he was thinking of what Starling had said the night before. *Let us not think of tomorrows that may never come. Let us just hunt,* I suggested, and we did. The Fool and I kept to the trail and the wolf veered off through the woods, to spook game back toward us. We moved with the forest, sliding near noiselessly through the night, every sense alert. I came across a porcupine trundling along through the night, but I did not feel like clubbing it to death, let alone gingerly skinning it before we could eat. I wanted simple meat tonight. With great difficulty, I persuaded Nighteyes to seek other prey with me. *If we do not find anything else, we can always come back for it. They are not exactly swift of foot,* I pointed out to him.

He agreed grudgingly, and we quartered out again. On an open hillside still warm from the sun, Nighteyes spotted the flick of an ear and the glint of a bright eye. In two bounds he was on top of the rabbit. His spring started another rabbit that fled toward the top of the hill. I gave chase, but the Fool called out he was going back now. Halfway up the hill, I knew I would not catch him. I was tired from the long day of walking and the rabbit was in fear of its life. By the time I reached the top of the hill, it was nowhere in sight. I halted, panting. The night wind moved lightly through the trees. On it I caught a scent, at once strange and oddly familiar. I could not identify it, but all the connotations to it were unpleasant. While I stood, nostrils flared, trying to place it, Nighteyes raced soundlessly up to me. *Be small!* he ordered me.

I didn't pause to think, but obeyed, crouching where I was and peering about for danger.

No! Be small in your mind.

This time I instantly grasped what he meant, and threw my Skill walls up in a panic. His keener nose had instantly associated the faint scent on the air with the scent of Burl's clothing in his saddlebags. I crouched as small as I could make myself and set and reset my boundaries about my mind, even as I pleaded with reality that it was next to impossible that he be here.

Fear can be a powerful spur to the mind. I suddenly grasped what should always have been obvious. We were not that far from the crossroads plaza and the black guidepost there. The symbols carved on the guidepost columns did not merely indicate where the adjacent roads led; they also indicated where the signposts could transport one. Anywhere there was a column, one could be transported to the next column. From the ancient city to any marked location was no more than a step away. All three of them could be but steps away from me right now.

No. There is only the one, and he is not even close to us. Use your nose, if not your brain, Nighteyes scathingly reassured me. *Shall I kill him for you?* he offered casually.

Please. But be careful of yourself.

Nighteyes snorted softly in disdain. *He is fatter far than that wild pig I killed. He puffs and sweats just to walk down the trail. Lie still, little brother, while I get rid of him.* Silent as death, the wolf moved off through the forest.

I crouched an eternity, waiting to hear something, a snarl, a scream, the noises of someone running through the brush. There was nothing. I flared my nostrils but could catch no trace of the elusive scent. Suddenly I could no longer stand to crouch and wait. I surged to my feet and followed the wolf, as silently lethal as he. Before, when we had been hunting, I had not paid much attention to where we had gone. Now I perceived that we had approached closer to the Skill road than I had suspected; that our campsite was not that far from it at all.

Like a strain of distant music, I was suddenly aware of their Skilling. I halted where I stood. I willed my mind to stillness, and let their Skill brush my senses while I made no response.

I'm close. Burl, breathless with both excitement and fear. I sensed him poised and waiting. *I feel him, he draws near.* A pause. *Oh, I like not this place. I like it not at all.*

Be calm. A touch is all it will take. Touch him as I showed you, and his walls will come down. Will spoke, master to apprentice.

And if he has a knife?

He won't have time to use it. Believe me. No man's walls can stand before that touch, I promise you. All you need do is touch him. I will come through you and do the rest.

Why me? Why not you or Carrod?

Would you really rather have Carrod's task? Besides. You are the one who had the Bastard in your power and was stupid enough to try to hold him in a cage. Go and complete the task you should have finished long ago. Or would you care to feel our king's wrath again?

I felt Burl shiver. And I trembled, too, for I felt him. Regal. The thoughts were Will's, but somehow, somewhere, Regal heard them, too. I wondered if Burl knew as plainly as I did that no matter whether he killed the Bastard or not, Regal would enjoy giving him pain again. That the memory of torturing him was so pleasurable a one that Regal could no longer think of him at all without being reminded of how completely it had satiated him. Briefly.

I was glad I was not Burl.

There! That was the Bastard! Find him!

I should have died then, by all rights. Will had found me, had found my careless thought floating in the air. My brief sympathy for Burl was all it had taken. He bayed on my trail like a hound. *I have him!*

There was a moment of poised tension. My heart hammered against my ribs as I sent the Wit questing out all around me. Nothing bigger than a mouse was close by. I found Nighteyes down the hill from me, moving with swift stealth. Yet Burl had said he drew near to me. Had he found a way to shield himself from my Wit-sense? The thought made my knees weak.

Somewhere far down the hill, I heard the crash of a body through brush and a man's shout. The wolf was on him, I thought. *No, brother, not I.*

I could scarcely understand the wolf's thought. I reeled with a Skill-impact, yet could feel no source for it. My senses contradicted each other, as if I plunged into water and felt it as sand. With no clear idea of what I did, I began a shambling run down the hill.

This is not him! Will, in great anger and agitation. *What is this? Who is this?*

A pause of consternation. *It's that freak thing, the Fool!* Then vast anger. *Where is the Bastard? Burl, you clumsy moron! You have betrayed us all to him.*

But it was not I, but Nighteyes who charged down on Burl. Even at my distance, I could hear his snarls. In the dark woods below, a wolf launched himself at Burl, and the Skill-shriek he sent up at the sight of those ravening jaws coming toward his face was such that Will was distracted. In that instant, I slammed up my walls, and raced to join my wolf in the physical attack on Burl.

I was doomed to disappointment. They were much farther away than I had thought them. I never even got a glimpse of Burl, save through the wolf's eyes. Fat and clumsy as the wolf might think Burl, he proved an excellent runner when the wolf was at his heels. Even so, Nighteyes would have pulled him down if he had had any farther to go than he did. At his first spring, Nighteyes got only his cloak as Burl spun. His second attack tore legging and flesh, but Burl fled as if uninjured. Nighteyes saw him reach the edge of the black flagged plaza and race up to the column, one hand outstretched pleadingly. His palm slapped the shining stone, and Burl suddenly vanished into the column. The wolf braced his legs to halt, his feet skittering on the slick stone. He cowered back from the standing stone as if Burl had leaped into a blazing bonfire. He halted a handspan from it, snarling furiously, not only in anger but in savage fear. All this I knew, although I was a hillside away, running and stumbling in the dark.

Suddenly there was a wave of Skill. It made no physical manifestation, yet the impact flung me to the ground and drove the breath out of me. It left me dazed, ears ringing, helplessly open to anyone who might wish to possess me. I lay there, sick and stunned. Perhaps that was what saved me, that at that moment I felt absolutely no trace of Skill within myself.

But I heard the others. There was no sense to their Skilling, only awestruck fear. Then they faded in the distance, as if the Skill river itself washed them away. I almost went reaching after them, in my amazement at what I sensed. They seemed to have been shattered to fragments. Their dwindling bewilderment washed against me. I closed my eyes.

Then I heard Kettle frantically calling my name. Panic stained her voice.

Nighteyes!

I'm already on my way. Catch up! the wolf told me grimly. I did as I was told.

I was scratched, dirty, and one trouser leg was torn at the knee when I reached the yurt. Kettle was standing outside it, waiting for me. The fire had been built up as a beacon. At the sight of her the pounding of my heart lessened somewhat. I had half-believed that they were being attacked. 'What's wrong?' I demanded as I charged up to her.

'The Fool,' she said, and added, 'We heard an outcry and raced outside. Then I heard the wolf snarling. We went toward the sound and found the Fool.' She shook her head. 'I am not sure what has happened to him.'

I started to push past her into the tent, but she caught me by the arm. She was surprisingly strong for an old woman. She halted me to face her. 'You were attacked?' she demanded.

'In a way.' Briefly I told her what had happened. Her eyes widened as I spoke of that Skill-wave.

When I was finished, she nodded to herself, grimly confirming her suspicions. 'They reached for you and seized him instead. He has not the faintest idea of how to protect himself. For all I know, they have him still.'

'What? How?' I asked numbly.

'Back there at the plaza. You two were Skill-linked, however briefly, by the strength of the stone and the strength of who you are. It leaves a . . . sort of a path. The more often two are linked, the stronger it becomes. With frequency it becomes a bond, like a coterie bond. Others who are Skilled can see such bonds, if they look for them. Often they are like back doors, unguarded ways into a Skilled one's mind. This time, however, I would say they found the Fool in your stead.'

The look on my face made her let go of my arm. I pushed my way into the tent. There was a tiny fire burning in the brazier. Kettricken knelt by the Fool, speaking to him low and earnestly. Starling sat unmoving in her bedding, pale and staring at him, while the wolf restlessly prowled the crowded interior of the tent. His hackles still stood high.

I went quickly to kneel by the Fool. At first glimpse of him, I recoiled. I had expected him to lie limply unconscious. Instead he was rigid, his eyes open and his eyeballs twitching about as if he watched some terrible struggle we could not witness. I touched his arm. The rigidity of his muscles and the coolness of his body reminded me of a corpse. 'Fool?' I asked him. He gave no sign at all of hearing me. 'Fool!' I cried louder, and leaned over him. I shook him, lightly at first and then more violently. It had no effect.

'Touch him and Skill to him,' Kettle instructed me gruffly. 'But be careful. If they still have him, you put yourself at risk as well.'

It shames me to say that I froze for an instant. As much as I loved the Fool, I feared Will still. I reached at last, a second and an eternity later, to put my hand on his brow.

'Don't be afraid,' Kettle told me uselessly. And then added that which almost paralysed me: 'If they have him and hold him still, it is only a matter of time before they use the link between you to take you as well. Your only choice is to battle them from his mind. Go on, now.'

She set her hand to my shoulder, and for one eerie moment, it was Shrewd's hand on my shoulder, drawing Skill-strength from me. Then she gave me a reassuring little pat. I closed my eyes, felt the Fool's brow under my hand. I dropped my Skill walls.

The Skill river flowed, full to floodtime, and I fell into it. A moment to gain orientation. I knew an instant of terror as I sensed Will and Burl at the very edges of my perception. They were in great agitation about something. I recoiled from them as if I had brushed a hot stove, and narrowed my focus. The Fool, the Fool, only the Fool. I sought for him, I almost found him. Oh, he was passing strange, and surpassing strange. He darted and eluded me, like a bright gold carp in a weedy pool, like the motes that dance before one's eyes after being dazzled by the sun. As well to clutch at the moon's reflection in a still midnight pond as to seek a grip on that bright mind. I knew his beauty and his power in the briefest flashes of insight. In a moment I understood and marvelled at all that he was, and in the next I had forgotten that understanding.

Then, with an insight worthy of the stone game, I knew what to do. Rather than attempt to seize him, I surrounded him. I made no effort to invade or capture, but simply to encompass all that I saw of him and hold it separate from harm. It reminded me of when I had first been learning to Skill. Often Verity had done this for me, helping me contain myself when the current of the Skill threatened to spill me wide to the world. I steadied the Fool as he gathered himself back into himself.

I suddenly felt a cool clasping of my wrist. 'Stop it,' he begged gently. 'Please,' he added, and it smote me that he thought he needed that word. I withdrew from my seeking and opened my eyes. I blinked a few times, and then was surprised to find myself shivering with the cold sweat that cloaked me. It was impossible for the Fool to look any paler than he always was, but there was a tentative look to his eyes and mouth, as if he were not sure he was awake. My eyes met his, and I felt almost a jolt of awareness of him. A Skill-bond, thin as a thread, but there. Had not my nerves been so raw from reaching after him, I probably would not have felt it at all.

'I did not like that,' he said quietly.

'I am sorry,' I told him gently. 'I thought they had hold of you, so I went seeking you.'

He waved a hand feebly. 'Oh, not you. I meant the others.' He swallowed as if sickened. 'They were within me. In my mind, in my memories. Smashing and befouling like evil, lawless children. They . . .' His eyes went glassy.

'Was it Burl?' I suggested gently.

'Ah. Yes. That is his name, though he scarce remembers it himself these days. Will and Regal have taken him over for their own uses. They came through him into me, thinking they had found you . . .' His voice dwindled off. 'Or so it seems. How could I know such a thing?'

'The Skill brings strange insights. They cannot overcome your mind without showing much of their own,' Kettle informed him grudgingly. She took a small pot of steaming water off the brazier. To me she added, 'Give me your elfbark.'

I immediately reached for my pack to dig it out, but I could not resist asking her chidingly, 'I thought you said this herb was not beneficial.'

'It isn't,' she said tersely. 'For Skill-users. But for him, it may give him the protection he cannot provide for himself. They will try this again, I do not doubt. If they can invade him, even for a moment, they will use him to find you. It is an old trick.'

'One I have never heard of,' I pointed out as I handed her my bag of elfbark. She shook some into a cup, and added boiling water. Then she calmly put my bag of herbs into her pack. It was obviously not an oversight, and I dismissed as useless asking for them back.

'How do you know so much about Skill matters?' the Fool asked her pointedly. He was recovering some of his spirit.

'Perhaps I learned by listening instead of asking personal questions all the time,' she snapped at him. 'Now, you are going to drink this,' she added, as if she regarded the topic as settled. If I had not been so anxious, it would have been humorous to see the Fool so deftly quelled.

The Fool took the cup but looked over at me. 'What was that, that happened at the last? They held me, and then suddenly, it was all earthquake and flood and fire at once.' He knitted his brow. 'And then I was gone, scattered. I could not find myself. Then you came . . .'

'Would anyone care to explain to me what has happened this night?' Kettricken asked a bit testily.

I half expected Kettle to answer but she kept silent.

The Fool lowered his mug of tea. 'It is a hard thing to explain, my queen. Like two ruffians bursting into your bedchamber, dragging you from your bed and shaking you, all the while calling you by another's name. And when they discovered I was not the Fitz, they were very angry with me. Then came the earthquake and I was dropped. Down several flights of stairs. Metaphorically speaking, of course.'

'They let you go?' I asked delightedly. I instantly turned to Kettle. 'They are not as clever as you feared, then!'

Kettle scowled at me. 'Nor you as clever as I had hoped,' she muttered darkly. 'Did they let him go? Or did a Skill blast shake them loose? And if so, whose power was that?'

'Verity,' I said with sudden certainty. Comprehension washed over me. 'They attacked Verity tonight as well! And he defeated them!'

'Of what do you speak?' Kettricken demanded in her Queen's voice. 'Who attacked my king? What knowledge of these others who attack the Fool does Kettle have?'

'No personal knowledge, my lady, I assure you!' I declared hastily.

'Oh, do shut up!' Kettle snapped at me. 'My queen, I have a scholar's knowledge, if you will, of one who has studied but cannot do a thing. Since Fool and Catalyst were joined for that moment back in the plaza, I feared they might share a bond the Skill-users could turn against them. But either the coterie does not know this, or something distracted them tonight. Perhaps the Skill wave that Fitz spoke of.'

'This Skill wave . . . you believe it was Verity's doing?' Kettricken's breath was suddenly swift, her colour heightened.

'Only from him have I ever felt such strength,' I told her.

'Then he lives,' she said softly. 'He lives.'

'Perhaps,' said Kettle sourly. 'To blast with Skill like that can kill a man. And it may not have been Verity at all. It may have been a failed effort by Will and Regal to get at Fitz.'

'No. I told you. It scattered them like chaff in a wind.'

'And I told you. They may have destroyed themselves in trying to kill you.'

I had thought that Kettricken would chide her, but both she and Starling stared wide-eyed in astonishment at Kettle's sudden professing of Skill knowledge. 'How kind of you both to have warned me so well,' the Fool said with acid courtesy.

'I didn't know . . .' I began my protest, but again Kettle overrode me.

'It would have done no good to warn you, save to put your mind to dwelling on it. We can make this comparison. It has taken all our combined effort to keep Fitz both focused and sane on the Skill road. He would never have survived his journey into the city, had not his senses been numbed with elfbark first. Yet these others travel the road and use the Skill beacons freely. Obviously their strength overmatches his by much. Ah, what to do, what to do?'

No one replied to her questioning of herself. She looked up suddenly at the Fool and me accusingly. 'This cannot be right. It simply cannot be right. The Prophet and the Catalyst, and you are scarcely more than boys. Green to manhood, untrained in Skill, full of pranks and lovesick woes. These are the ones sent to save the world?'

The Fool and I exchanged glances, and I saw him take a breath to reply to her. But at that moment, Starling snapped her fingers. 'And that is what makes the song!' she exclaimed suddenly, her face transfigured with delight. 'Not a song of heroic strength and mighty-thewed warriors. No. A song of two, graced only with friendship's strength. Each possessed of a loyalty to a king that would not be denied. And that in the refrain . . . "Green of manhood", something, ah . . .'

The Fool caught my eye, glanced meaningfully down at himself. 'Green manhood? I really should have showed her,' he said quietly.

And despite everything, despite even the glowering of my queen, I burst out laughing.

'Oh, stop it,' Kettle rebuked us, with such discouragement in her voice that I was instantly sober. 'It is neither the time for songs nor knavery. Are you both too foolish to see the danger you are in? The danger you put all of us in with your vulnerability?' I watched her as she reluctantly took my elfbark out of her pack again and put her kettle back to boil. 'It is the only thing I can think of to do,' she apologized to Kettricken.

'What is that?' she asked.

'To drug the Fool at least with elfbark. It will deafen him to them, and hide his thoughts from them.'

'Elfbark doesn't work like that!' I objected indignantly.

'Doesn't it?' Kettle turned on me fiercely. 'Then why was it used traditionally for years for just that purpose? Given to a royal bastard young enough, it could destroy any potential for Skill use. Often enough was that done.'

I shook my head defiantly. 'I've used it for years, to restore my strength after Skilling. So has Verity. And it has never . . .'

'Sweet Eda's mercy!' Kettle exclaimed. 'Tell me you are lying, please!'

'Why should I lie about this? Elfbark revives a man's strength, though it may bring on melancholy spirits following use. Often I would carry elfbark tea up to Verity in his Skill-tower, to sustain him.' My telling faltered. The dismay on Kettle's face was too sincere. 'What?' I asked softly.

'Elfbark is well known among Skilled ones as a thing to avoid,' she said quietly. I heard every word, for no one in the tent even seemed to be breathing. 'It deadens a man to Skill, so that he can neither use the Skill himself, nor may others reach through its fog to Skill to him. It is said to stunt or destroy Skill talent in the young, and to impede its development in older Skill-users.' She looked at me with pity in her eyes. 'You must have been strongly talented, once, to retain even a semblance of Skilling.'

'It cannot be . . .' I said faintly.

'Think,' she bade me. 'Did ever you feel your Skill-strength wax strong after using it?'

'What of my lord Verity?' Kettricken suddenly demanded.

Kettle shrugged reluctantly. She turned to me. 'When did he start using it?'

It was hard for me to focus my mind on her words. So many things were suddenly in a different light. Elfbark had always cleared my head of the pounding that heavy Skilling brought on. But I had never tried to Skill immediately after I had used elfbark. Verity had, I knew that. But how successfully, I did not know. My erratic talent for Skilling . . . could that have been my elfbark use? Like a lightning bolt was the immense knowledge that Chade had made a mistake in giving it to Verity and me. Chade had made a mistake. It had never occurred to me, somehow, that Chade could be wrong or mistaken. Chade was my master, Chade read and studied and knew all the old lore. But he had never been taught to Skill. A bastard like myself, he had never been taught to Skill.

'FitzChivalry!' Kettricken's command jerked me back to myself.

'Uh, so far as I know, Verity began to use it in the early years of the war. When he was the only Skill-user to stand between us and the Red Ships. I believe he had never used the Skill so intensely as then, nor been as exhausted by it. So Chade began to give him elfbark. To keep up his strength.'

Kettle blinked a few times. 'Unused, the Skill does not develop,' she said, almost to herself. 'Used, it grows, and begins to assert itself, and one learns, almost instinctively, the many uses to which it may be put.' I found myself nodding faintly to her soft words. Her old eyes came up suddenly to meet mine. She spoke without reservation. 'You are most likely stunted, both of you. By the elfbark. Verity, as a man grown, may have recovered. He may have seen his Skill grow in the time he has spent away from the herb. As you seem to have. Certainly he seems to have mastered the road alone.' She sighed. 'But I suspect those others had not used it, and their talents and usage of Skill had grown and outstripped what yours is. So now you have a choice, FitzChivalry, and only you can make it. The Fool has nothing to lose by using the drug. He cannot Skill, and by using it, he may keep the coterie from finding him again. But you . . . I can give you this, and it will deaden you to the Skill. It will be harder for them to reach you, and much harder for you to reach out. You might be safer that way. But you will be once more thwarting your talent. Enough elfbark may kill it off completely. And only you can choose.'

I looked down at my hands. Then I looked up at the Fool. Once more, our eyes met. Hesitantly, I groped toward him with my Skill. I felt nothing. Perhaps it was only my own erratic talent cheating me again. But it seemed likely to me that Kettle had been right; the elfbark the Fool had just drunk had deadened him to me.

As Kettle spoke, she had been taking the kettle from the fire. The Fool held his cup out to her wordlessly. She gave him a pinch more of the bitter bark and filled it again with water. Then she looked at me, quietly waiting. I looked at the faces watching me, but found no help there. I picked up a mug from the stacked crockery. I saw Kettle's old face darken and her lips tightened, but she said nothing to me. She simply reached into the pouch of elfbark, working her fingers to get to the bottom where the bark had crushed itself into powder. I looked into the empty mug, waiting. I glanced back up at Kettle. 'You said the Skill blast might have destroyed them?'

Kettle shook her head slowly. 'It is not a thing to count on.'

There was nothing I could count on. Nothing that was certain.

Then I set the mug down and crawled over to my blankets. I was suddenly tremendously weary. And frightened. I knew Will was out there somewhere, seeking me. I could hide myself in elfbark, but it might not be enough to stave him off. It might only weaken my already-stunted defences against him. Abruptly I knew I would sleep not at all that night. 'I'll take the watch,' I offered and stood again.

'He should not stand alone,' Kettle said grumpily.

'His wolf watches with him,' Kettricken told her confidently. 'He can aid Fitz against this false coterie as no one else can.'

I wondered how she knew that, but dared not ask her. Instead I took up my cloak and went to stand outside by the dwindling fire, watching and waiting like a condemned man.

THIRTY-TWO

Capelin Beach

The Wit is held in much disdain. In many areas it is regarded as a perversion, with tales told of Witted ones coupling with beasts to gain this magic, or offering blood sacrifice of human children to gain the gift of the tongues of beasts and birds. Some tale-tellers speak of bargains struck with ancient demons of the earth. In truth, I believe the Wit is as natural a magic as a man can claim. It is the Wit that lets a flock of birds in flight suddenly wheel as one, or a school of fingerlings hold place together in a swiftly flowing stream. It is also the Wit that sends a mother to her child's bedside just as the babe is awakening. I believe it is at the heart of all wordless communication, and that all humans possess some small aptitude for it, recognized or not.

The next day we once more reached the Skill road. As we trailed past the forbidding pillar of stone, I felt myself drawn to it. 'Verity may be but one stride away for me,' I said quietly.

Kettle snorted. 'Or your death. Have you taken complete leave of your senses? Do you think any one Skill-user could stand against a trained coterie?'

'Verity did,' I replied, thinking of Tradeford and how he had saved me. The rest of that morning, she walked with a thoughtful look on her face.

I did not endeavour to get her to speak, for I carried a burden of my own. I felt within me a nagging sense of loss. It was almost the irritating sensation of knowing one had forgotten something, but was unable to recall what. I had left something behind. Or I had forgotten to do something important, something I had been intending to do. By late afternoon, with a sinking feeling, I grasped what was missing.

Verity.

When he had been with me, I had seldom been sure of his presence. Like a hidden seed waiting to unfurl was how I had thought of him. The many times I had sought him within myself and failed to find him suddenly meant nothing. This was not a doubt or a wondering. This was a growing certainty. Verity had been with me for over a year. And now he was gone.

Did it mean he was dead? I could not be certain. That immense wave of Skill I had felt could have been him. Or something else, something that had forced him to withdraw into himself. That was probably all it was. It was a miracle that his Skill touch upon me had lasted as long as it had. Several times I started to speak of it to Kettle or Kettricken. Each time, I could not justify it. What would I say: Before this, I could not tell if Verity was with me, and now I cannot feel him at all? At night by our fires, I studied the lines in Kettricken's face and asked myself what point there was in increasing her worry. So I pushed my worries down and kept silent.

Continuous hardship makes for monotony and days that run together in the telling. The weather was rainy, in a fitful, windy way. Our supplies were precariously low, so that the greens we could gather as we walked and whatever meat Nighteyes and I could bring down at night became important to us. I walked beside the road instead of on it, but remained constantly aware of its Skill-murmur, like the muttering of a river of water beside me. The Fool was kept well dosed with elfbark tea. Very soon he began to exhibit both the boundless energy and bleak spirits that were elfbark's properties. In the Fool's case, it meant endless cavorting and tumbling tricks as we made our way along the Skill road, and a cruelly bitter edge to his wits and tongue. He jested all too often of the futility of our quest, and to any encouraging remark he riposted with savage sarcasm. By the end of the second day, he reminded me of nothing so much as an ill-mannered child. He heeded no one's rebukes, not even Kettricken's, nor did he recall that silence could be a virtue. It was not so much that I feared his endless prattle and edged songs would bring the coterie down on us as that I worried his constant noise might mask their approach. Pleading with him to be quiet did me as little good as roaring at him to shut up. He wore on my nerves until I dreamed of throttling him, nor do I think I was alone in that impulse.

The kinder weather was the only way in which our lot improved on those long days as we followed the Skill road. The rain became lighter and more intermittent. The leaves opened on the deciduous trees that flanked the road and the hills about us greened almost overnight. The health of the jeppas improved with the browse, and Nighteyes found plentiful small game. The shorter hours of sleep told on me, but letting the wolf hunt alone would not have solved it. I feared to·sleep any more. Worse, Kettle feared to let me sleep.

Of her own accord, the old woman took charge of my mind. I resented it, but was not so stupid as to resist. Both Kettricken and Starling had accepted her knowledge of the Skill. I was no longer permitted to go off alone, or in the sole company of the Fool. When the wolf and I hunted at night, Kettricken went with us. Starling and I shared a watch, during which, at Kettle's urging, she kept my mind busy with learning to recite both songs and stories from Starling's repertoire. During my brief hours of sleep Kettle watched over me, a dark stewing of elfbark at her elbow where, if need be, she could pour it down my throat and douse my Skill. All of this was annoying, but worst was during the day when we walked together. I was not allowed to speak of Verity, or the coterie, or anything that might touch upon them. Instead, we worked at game problems, or gathered wayside herbs for the evening meal, or I recited Starling's stories for her. At any time when she suspected my mind was not fully with her, she might give me a sharp rap with her walking stick. The few times I tried to direct our talk with questions about her past, she loftily informed me that it might lead to the very topics we must avoid.

There is no more slippery task than to refrain from thinking of something. In the midst of my busywork, the fragrance of a wayside flower would bring Molly to my mind, and from thence to Verity who had called me away from her was but a skip of thought. Or some chance nattering of the Fool would call to my thoughts King Shrewd's tolerance for his mockery, and recall to me how my king had died and at whose hands. Worst of all was

Kettricken's silence. She could no longer speak to me of her anxiety over Verity. I could not see her without feeling how she longed to find him, and then rebuking myself for thinking of him. And so the long days of our travelling passed for me.

Gradually the countryside around us changed. We found ourselves descending deeper and deeper into valley after winding valley. For a time our road paralleled that of a milky grey river. In places its rising and fallings had gnawed the road at its side to no more than a footpath. We came at length to an immense bridge. When we first glimpsed it from a distance, the spider web delicacy of its span reminded me of bones, and I feared that we would find it reduced to splintered fragments of reaching timbers. Instead we crossed on a creation that arched over the river needlessly high, as if in joy that it could. The road we crossed on shone black and shining, while the archwork that graced above and below the span was a powdery grey. I could not identify what it was wrought from, whether true metal or strange stone, for it had more the look of a spun thread than hammered metal or chiselled rock. The elegance and grace of it stilled even the Fool for a time.

After the bridge, we climbed a series of small hills, only to begin another descent. This time the valley was narrow and deep, a steep-sided cleft in the earth as if some giant had long ago cleaved it with a war-axe. The road clung to one side of it and followed it inexorably down. We could see little of where we were going, for the valley itself seemed full of clouds and greenery. This puzzled me until the first rivulet of warm water cut our pathway. It bubbled up steamily from a spring right beside the road, but had long ago disdained the ornately carved stone walls and drainage channel some vanished engineer had placed to contain it. The Fool made great show of considering its stench and whether it should be attributed to rotten eggs or some flatulence of the earth itself. For once not even his rudeness could make me smile. It was for me as if his knavery had gone on too long, the merriment fled and only the crudity and cruelty left.

We came in early afternoon to a region of steaming pools. The lure of hot water was too much to resist, and Kettricken let us make camp early. We had the long-missed comfort of hot water for soaking our weary bodies in, though the Fool disdained it because of its smell. To me it smelled no worse than the steaming waters that rose to feed the baths in Jhaampe, but for once I was just as glad to forgo his company. He went off in search of more potable water, while the women took over the largest pool and I sought out the relative privacy of a smaller one at some distance. I soaked for a time, and then decided to pound some of the dirt from my clothing. The mineral stink of the water was far less than the odour my own body had left on them. That done, I spread my garments on the grass to dry and went to lie once more in the water. Nighteyes came to sit on the bank and watch me in puzzlement, his tail tucked neatly around his feet.

It feels good, I told him needlessly, for I knew he could sense my pleasure.

It must have something to do with your lack of fur, he decided at last.

Come in and I'll scrub you off. It would help you shed off your winter undercoat, I offered him.

He gave a disdainful sniff. *I think I'd prefer to scratch it off a bit at a time.*

Well, you needn't sit and watch me and be bored. Go hunting if you wish.

I would, but the high bitch has asked me to watch you. So I shall.

Kettricken?

So you name her.

How asked you?

He gave me a puzzled glance. *As you would. She looked at me and I knew her mind. She worried that you were alone.*

Does she know you hear her? Does she hear you?

Almost, at times. He lay down abruptly on the sward and stretched, curling his pink tongue. *Perhaps when your mate bids you set me aside, I shall bond to her.*

Not funny.

He made no reply to me, but rolled over and proceeded to roll about scratching his back. The topic of Molly was now an edge of uneasiness between us, a rift I dared not approach and one he obsessively peered into. I wished abruptly that we were as we once had been, joined and whole, living only in the now. I leaned

675

back, resting my head on the bank, half in and half out of the water. I closed my eyes and thought of nothing.

When I opened them again, the Fool was standing looking down on me. I startled visibly. So did Nighteyes, springing to his feet with a growl. 'Some guardian,' I observed to the Fool.

He has no scent, and walks lighter than falling snow! the wolf complained.

'He is always with you, isn't he?' the Fool observed.

'One way or another,' I agreed and lay back in the water. I would have to get out soon. The late afternoon was becoming evening. The additional chill in the air only made the hot water more soothing. After a moment, I glanced over at the Fool. He was still just standing and staring at me. 'Is something wrong?' I asked him.

He made an inconclusive gesture, and then sat down awkwardly on the bank. 'I've been thinking about your candlemaker girl,' he said suddenly.

'Have you?' I asked quietly. 'I've been doing my best not to.'

He thought about this for a bit. 'If you die, what will become of her?'

I rolled over on my belly and propped myself on my elbows to stare at the Fool. I half expected this was the lead line to some new mockery of his, but his face was grave. 'Burrich will take care of her,' I said quietly. 'For as long as she needs help. She's a capable woman, Fool.' After a moment's consideration, I added, 'She took care of herself for years before . . . Fool, I've never really taken care of her. I was near her, but she always stood on her own.' I felt both shamed and proud as I said that. Shamed that I had given her so little besides trouble, and proud that such a woman had cared for me.

'But you would at least want me to take word to her, would you not?'

I shook my head slowly. 'She believes me dead. They both do. If in fact I die, I'd just as soon let her believe I died in Regal's dungeons. For her to learn otherwise would only tar me blacker in her eyes. How could you explain to her that I did not come to her immediately? No. If something happens to me, I wish no tales told her.' Bleakness gripped me once more. And if I survived and went back to her? That was almost worse to consider. I tried to imagine standing before her and explaining to her that once more, I had put my king ahead of her. I clenched my eyes tight shut at the thought of it.

'Still, when all this is done and gone, I should like to see her again,' the Fool observed.

I opened my eyes. 'You? I did not know that you had even spoken to one another.'

The Fool seemed a bit taken aback at this. 'But, that is, I meant for your sake. To see for myself that she is well provided for.'

I felt oddly touched. 'I don't know what to say,' I told him.

'Say nothing, then. Tell me only where I may find her,' he suggested with a smile.

'I don't precisely know that myself,' I admitted to him. 'Chade knows. If . . . if I do not live through what we must do, ask it of him.' It felt unlucky to speak of my own death, so I added, 'Of course, we both know we shall survive. It is foretold, is it not?'

He gave me an odd look. 'By whom?'

My heart sank. 'By some White Prophet or other, I had hoped,' I muttered. It occurred to me that I had never asked the Fool if my survival was foretold. Not every man survives winning a battle. I found my courage. 'Is it foretold that the Catalyst lives?'

He appeared to be thinking hard. He suddenly observed, 'Chade leads a dangerous life. There is no assurance that he will survive either. And if he does not, well, surely you must have some idea of where the girl is. Will not you tell me?'

That he had not answered my question seemed suddenly answer enough. The Catalyst did not survive. It was like being hit by a wave of cold salt water. I felt tumbled in that cold knowledge, drowning in it. I'd never hold my daughter, never feel Molly's warmth again. It was almost a physical pain, and it dizzied me.

'FitzChivalry?' the Fool pressed me. He lifted a hand to suddenly cover his mouth tightly, as if he could speak no more. His other hand rose to grip his wrist suddenly. He looked sickened.

'It's all right,' I said faintly. 'Perhaps it's better that I know what is to come.' I sighed and racked my brain. 'I've heard them speak of a village. Burrich goes there to buy things. It cannot be far. You could start there.'

The Fool gave a tiny nod of encouragement to me. Tears stood in his eyes.

'Capelin Beach,' I said quietly.

A moment longer he sat staring at me. Then he suddenly toppled over sideways.

'Fool?'

There was no response. I stood, the warm water running off me and looked over at him. He sprawled on his side as if asleep. 'Fool!' I called irritably. When there was still no response, I waded out of the pond and over to him. He lay on the grassy bank, miming the deep, even breathing of sleep. 'Fool?' I asked again, half expecting him to come leaping up in my face. Instead he made a vague motion as if I disturbed his dreaming. It irritated me beyond words that he could go so abruptly from serious words to some kind of knavery. Yet it was typical of his behaviour over the past few days. There was suddenly no relaxation or peace left in the hot water. Still dripping, I began to gather my clothes. I refused to look at him as I brushed and shook most of the water from my body. The clothing I pulled on was slightly damp anyway. The Fool slept on as I turned away from him and walked back to camp. Nighteyes trailed at my heels.

Is it a game? he asked me as we walked.

Of a kind, I suppose, I told him shortly. *Not one I enjoy.*

The women were already back at the camp. Kettricken was poring over her map while Kettle gave the jeppas tiny shares of the remaining grain. Starling was sitting by the fire, worrying a comb through her hair, but looked up as I approached. 'Did the Fool find clean water?' she asked me.

I shrugged. 'Not when I last saw him. At least, if he had, he wasn't carrying it with him.'

'We've enough in the waterskins to get by with, anyway. I just prefer fresh for the tea.'

'Me, too.' I sat down by the cook fire and watched her. She seemed to give no thought to her fingers at all as they danced over her hair, binding the wet shining hair into smooth braids. She coiled them to her head and pinned them down securely.

'I hate wet hair flapping around my face,' she observed, and I realized I had been staring. I glanced away, embarrassed.

'Ah, he can still blush,' she laughed. Then added, pointedly, 'Would you like to borrow my comb?'

I lifted my hand to my own draggled hair. 'I suppose I should,' I muttered.

'Truly,' she agreed, but did not pass it to me. Instead she came to kneel behind me. 'How did you do all this?' she wondered aloud as she began to tug the comb through it.

'It just gets that way,' I mumbled. Her gentle touch, the soft tugging at my scalp felt incredibly good.

'It's so fine, that's the problem. I never met a Buck man with hair so fine.'

My heart moved sideways in my chest. A Buck beach on a windy day, and Molly on a red blanket beside me, her blouse not quite laced. She had told me I was considered the best thing to have come out of the stables since Burrich. 'I think it is your hair. It is not as coarse as most Buck men.' One brief interlude, of flirtatious compliments and idle talk and her sweet touch under the open sky. I almost smiled. But I could not recall that day without also recalling that, like so many of our times together, it had ended in quarrelling and tears. My throat closed up and I shook my head, trying to clear the memories away.

'Sit still,' Starling chided me with a sharper tug on my hair. 'I've almost got it smooth. Brace yourself, this is the last snarl.' She caught hold of my hair above it, and ripped out the snarl with a swift jerk that I almost didn't feel. 'Give me the thong,' she told me, and took it from me to bind my hair back for me.

Kettle came back from tending the jeppas. 'Any meat?' she asked me pointedly.

I sighed. 'Not yet. Soon,' I promised. I hauled myself to my feet wearily.

'Watch him, wolf,' Kettle asked Nighteyes. He gave a slight wag of his tail and then led me away from the camp.

It was past dark when we returned to camp. We were well pleased with ourselves, for we brought, not rabbit, but a cloven-hoofed creature rather like a small kid, but with a silkier hide. I had opened its belly at the kill site, both to let Nighteyes have the entrails and to lighten it for carrying. I slung the meat over my shoulder, but regretted that after a short time. Whatever biting vermin it had been carrying were only too happy to transfer to my neck. I would have to wash myself again this night.

I grinned at Kettle as she came to meet me and unslung the kid to hold it up for her inspection. But instead of congratulations, she only demanded, 'Have you any more elfbark?'

'I gave you all I had,' I told her. 'Why? Have we run out? The way it makes the Fool behave, I'd almost welcome that news.'

She gave me an odd look. 'Did you quarrel?' she demanded. 'Did you strike him?'

'What? Of course not!'

'We found him by the pool where you bathed,' she said quietly. 'Twitching in his sleep like a dreaming dog. I woke him, but even awake, he seemed vague. We brought him back here, but he only sought his blankets. Since then, he has been sleeping like a dead thing.'

We had reached the cook fire and I dropped the kid beside it and hurried into the tent, Nighteyes pushing his way in front of me.

'He revived, but only for a bit,' Kettle continued. 'Then he dropped off to sleep again. He behaves like a man recovering from exhaustion, or a very long illness. I fear for him.'

I scarcely heard her. Once in the tent, I dropped to my knees beside him. He lay on his side, curled in a ball. Kettricken knelt by him, her face clouded with worry. He looked to me simply like a man sleeping. Relief warred with irritation in me.

'I've given him almost all the elfbark,' Kettle was going on. 'If I give him what's left now, we have no reserves if the coterie tries to attack him.'

'Is there no other herb . . .' Kettricken began, but I interrupted her.

'Why don't we simply let him sleep? Perhaps this is just the end of his other illness. Or maybe an effect of the elfbark itself. Even with potent drugs, one can only trick the body so long, and then it makes its demands known.'

'That is true,' Kettle agreed reluctantly. 'But this is so unlike him . . .'

'He has been unlike himself since the third day he was using the elfbark,' I pointed out. 'His tongue too sharp, his jibes too cutting. If you asked me, I would say I prefer him asleep to awake these days.'

'Well. Perhaps there is something to what you say. We will let him sleep then,' Kettle conceded. She took a breath, as if to say more, but did not. I went back outside to prepare the kid for cooking. Starling followed me.

For a time, she just sat silently watching me skin it out. It was not that large an animal. 'Help me build up the fire and we'll roast the whole thing. Cooked meat will keep better in this weather.'

The whole thing?

Except a generous portion for you. I worked my knife around a knee joint, snapped the shank free and cut the remaining gristle.

I'll want more than bones, Nighteyes reminded me.

Trust me, I told him. By the time I was finished, he had the head, hide, all four shanks, and one hind quarter to himself. It made it awkward to fasten the meat to a spit, but I managed. It was a young animal, and though it did not have much fat, I expected the meat would be tender. The hardest part would be waiting for it to be cooked. The flames licked their tips against it, searing it, and the savoury smell of roasting meat taunted me.

'Are you so angry with the Fool?' Starling asked me quietly.

'What?' I glanced over my shoulder at her.

'In the time we have travelled together, I have come to see how you are with one another. Closer than brothers. I would have expected you to sit beside him and fret, as you did when he was ill. Yet you behave as if nothing is wrong with him at all.'

Minstrels, perhaps, see too clearly. I pushed my hair back from my face and thought. 'Earlier today, he came to me and we talked. About what he would do, for Molly, if I did not live to return to her.' I looked at Starling and shook my head. When my throat went tight, it surprised me. 'He does not expect me to survive. And when a prophet says such a thing, it is hard to believe otherwise.'

The look of dismay on her face was not comforting. It gave the lie to her words when she insisted, 'Prophets are not always right. Did he say, for certain, that he had seen your death?'

'When I asked him, he would not answer,' I replied.

'He should not have even brought up such a topic,' Starling suddenly exclaimed angrily. 'How can he expect you to have heart for whatever you must do, when you believe it will be your death?'

I shrugged my shoulders at her silently. I had refused to think of it the whole time we had been hunting. Instead of going away, the feelings had only built up. The misery I suddenly felt was overwhelming. Yes, and the anger, too. I was furious at the Fool for telling me. I forced myself to consider it. 'The tidings are scarcely his doing. And I cannot fault his intent. Yet it is hard to face one's death, not as a thing that will happen someday, somewhere, but as something that will likely occur before this summer loses its green.' I lifted my head and looked around the verdant wild meadow that surrounded us.

It is amazing how different a thing appears when you know it is the last one you will have. Every leaf on every limb stood out, in a multitude of greens. Birds sang challenges to one another, or winged by in flashes of colour. The smells of the cooking meat, of the earth itself, even the sound of Nighteyes cracking a bone between his jaws were all suddenly unique and precious things. How many days like this had I walked through blindly, intent only on having a mug of ale when I got to town or what horse must be taken for shoeing today? Long ago, in Buckkeep, the Fool had warned me that I should live each day as if it were significant, as if every day the fate of the world depended on my actions. Now I suddenly grasped what he had been trying to tell me. Now, when the days left to me had dwindled to where I might count them.

Starling put her hands on my shoulders. She leaned down and put her cheek against mine. 'Fitz, I am so sorry,' she said quietly. I scarcely heard her words, only her belief in my death. I stared at the meat cooking over the flames. It had been a live kid.

Death is always at the edge of now. Nighteyes' thought was gentle. *Death stalks us, and he is ever sure of his kill. It is not a thing to dwell on, but it is something we all know, in our guts and bones. All save humans.*

With shock, I beheld what the Fool had been trying to teach me about time. I suddenly wished to go back, to have again each separate day to spend. Time. I was trapped in it, fenced into a tiny piece of now that was the only time I could influence. All the soons and tomorrows I might plan were ghost things that might be snatched from me at any moment. Intentions were nothing. Now was all I had. I suddenly stood up.

'I understand,' I said aloud. 'He had to tell me, to push me. I have to stop acting as if there is a tomorrow when I can put things right. It all has to be done now, right away, with no concern for tomorrow. No belief in tomorrow. No fears for tomorrow.'

'Fitz?' Starling drew back from me a little way. 'You sound as if you are going to do something foolish.' Her dark eyes were full of worry.

'Foolish,' I said to myself. 'Foolish as the Fool is. Yes. Could you watch the meat, please?' I asked Starling humbly.

I did not wait for her reply. I stood as she stepped free of me and went into the yurt. Kettle sat by the Fool, simply watching him sleep. Kettricken was mending a seam in her boot. They both glanced up as I came in. 'I need to talk to him,' I said simply. 'Alone, if you would not mind.'

I ignored their puzzled glances. I already wished I had not told Starling what the Fool had told me. Doubtless she would tell the others, but just now I did not want to share it with them. I had something important to tell the Fool, and I would do it now. I did not wait to watch them leave the yurt. Instead I sat down beside the Fool. I touched his face gently, feeling the coolness of his cheek. 'Fool,' I said quietly. 'I need to talk to you. I understand. I think I finally understand what you've been trying to teach me all along.'

It took me several more efforts before he stirred to wakefulness. I finally shared some of Kettle's concern. This was not the simple sleep of a man at a day's end. But finally he opened his eyes and peered up at me through the gloom. 'Fitz? Is it morning?' he asked.

'Evening. And there is fresh meat roasting, and soon it will be done. I think a good meal will help put you right.' I started to hesitate, then recalled my new resolution. Now. 'I was angry at you earlier, for what you told me. But now I think I understand why. You are right, I have been hiding in the future and wasting my days.' I took a breath. 'I want to give Burrich's earring over to you, into your keeping. Af . . . afterwards, I'd like you to take it to him. And tell him I did not die outside some shepherd's hut, but keeping my oath to my king. That will mean something to him, it may pay him back a bit for all he has done for me. He taught me to be a man. I don't want that left unsaid.'

I unfastened the catch of the earring and drew it from my ear. I pressed it into the Fool's lax hand. He lay on his side, listening silently. His face was very grave. I shook my head at him.

'I have nothing to send Molly, nothing for our child. She'll have the pin Shrewd gave me so long ago, but little more than that.' I was trying to keep my voice steady, but the importance of my words was choking me. 'It may be wisest not to tell Molly that I lived past Regal's dungeons. If that can be managed. Burrich would understand the reason for such a secret. She has mourned me as dead once, there is no sense in telling her otherwise. I am glad you will seek her out. Make toys for Nettle.' Against my will, tears stung my eyes.

The Fool sat up, his face full of concern. He gripped my shoulder gently. 'If you want me to find Molly, you know I will, if it comes to that. But why must we think of such things now? What do you fear?'

'I fear my death.' I admitted it. 'But fearing it will not stop it. So I make what provisions I can. As I should have, long ago.' I met his smoky eyes squarely. 'Promise me.'

He looked down at the earring in his hand. 'I promise. Though why you think my chances are better than yours, I do not know. Nor do I know how I will find them, but I will.'

I felt great relief. 'I told you earlier. I know only that their cottage is near a village called Capelin Beach. There is more than one Capelin Beach in Buck, that is true. But if you tell me you will find her, I believe you will.'

'Capelin Beach?' His eyes went distant. 'I think I recall . . . I thought I had dreamed that.' He shook his head and almost smiled. 'So I am now a party to one of the closest-held secrets in Buck. Chade told me that not even he knew precisely where Burrich had hidden Molly away. He had only a place to leave a message for Burrich, so Burrich might come to him. "The fewer who know a secret, the fewer can tell it," he told me. Yet it seems to me I have heard that name before. Capelin Beach. Or dreamed it, perhaps.'

My heart went cold. 'What do you mean? Have you had a vision of Capelin Beach?'

He shook his head. 'Not a vision, no. Yet a nightmare toothier than most, so that when Kettle found and woke me, I felt I had not slept at all, but had been fleeing for my life for hours.' He shook his head again slowly and rubbed at his eyes, yawning. 'I do not even recall lying down to sleep outside. But that is where they found me.'

'I should have known something was wrong with you,' I apologized. 'You were by the hot spring, speaking to me of Molly and . . . things. And then you suddenly lay down and went to sleep. I thought you were mocking me,' I admitted sheepishly.

He gave a tremendous yawn. 'I do not even recall seeking you out,' he admitted. He sniffed suddenly. 'Did you say there was meat roasting?'

I nodded. 'The wolf and I got a kid. It's young and should be tender.'

'I'm hungry enough to eat old shoes,' he declared. He threw back his bedding and left the tent. I followed him.

That meal was a better time than we had had in days. The Fool seemed weary and pensive, but had abandoned his barbed humour. The meat, though not tender as fat lamb, was better than anything we had had in weeks. By the end of the meal, I shared Nighteyes' sleepy satiation. He curled up outside by Kettricken to share her watch while I sought my blankets in the tent.

I had half expected the Fool to be wakeful after he had slept so much of the afternoon away. Instead he was first to his blankets and deeply asleep before I had even dragged my boots off. Kettle set out her gamecloth and gave me a problem to consider. I lay down to get what rest I could while Kettle watched over my sleep.

But I got small rest that night. No sooner had I dozed off than the Fool began to twitch and yip in his sleep. Even Nighteyes poked his head in the tent door to see what it was about. It took Kettle several tries to rouse him, and when he dozed off again, he slipped right back into his noisy dreams. That time I reached over to shake him. But when I touched his shoulder, awareness of him surged through me. For an instant, I shared his night terror. 'Fool, wake up!' I cried out to him, and as if in answer to that command, he sat up.

'Let go, let go!' he cried desperately. Then, looking round and finding that no one held him, he dropped back to his bedding. He turned his eyes to meet mine.

'What were you dreaming?' I asked him.

He thought, then shook his head. 'It's gone, now.' He took a shuddering breath. 'But I fear it waits for me, should I close my eyes. I think I shall see if Kettricken wants some company. I would rather be awake than face . . . whatever it was I was facing in my dreams.'

I watched him leave the tent. Then I lay back in my blankets. I closed my eyes. I found it, faint as a silver shining thread. There was a Skill-bond between us.

Ah. Is that what that is? the wolf marvelled.

Can you feel it, too?

Only sometimes. It is like what you had with Verity.

Only weaker.

Weaker? I think not. Nighteyes considered. *Not weaker, my brother. But different. Fashioned more like a Wit-bond than a Skill-joining.*

He looked up at the Fool as the Fool came out of the tent. After a time, the Fool frowned to himself and looked down at Nighteyes.

You see, said the wolf. *He senses me. Not clearly, but he does. Hello, Fool. My ears itch.*

Outside the tent, the Fool reached down suddenly to scratch the wolf's ears.

THIRTY-THREE

The Quarry

There are legends, among the Mountain folk, of an ancient race, much gifted with magic and knowing many things now lost to men forever. These tales are in many ways similar to the tales of elves and Old Ones that are told in the Six Duchies. In some cases, the tales are so similar as to be obviously the same story adapted by different folk. The most obvious example of this would be the tale of The Flying Chair of the Widow's Son. Among the Mountain folk, that Buck tale becomes The Flying Sled of the Orphan Boy. Who can tell which telling was first?

The folk of the Mountain Kingdom will tell you that that ancient race is responsible for some of the more peculiar monuments that one may chance upon in their forests. They are also credited with lesser achievements, such as some of the games of strategy that Mountain children still play, and for a very peculiar wind instrument, powered not by a man's lungs, but by breath trapped in an inflated bladder. Tales are also told of ancient cities far back in the mountains that were once the dwelling of these beings. But nowhere in all their literature, spoken or written, have I found any account of how these people ceased to be.

Three days later we reached the quarry. We had had three days of hiking through suddenly hot weather. The air had been full of the scents of opening leaves and flowers and the whistles of birds and the drones of insects. To either side of the Skill road, life burgeoned. I walked through it, senses keen, more aware of being alive than I had ever been. The Fool had spoken no more about whatever he had foreseen for me. For that I was grateful.

I had found Nighteyes was right. Knowing was hard enough. I would not dwell on it.

Then we came to the quarry. At first it seemed to us that we had simply come to a dead end. The road ramped down into a worked gorge of bare stone, an area twice the size of Buckkeep Castle. The walls of the valley were vertically straight and bare, scarred where immense blocks of black stone had been quarried from it. In a few places, cascading greenery from the earth at the edge of the quarry covered the sheared rock sides. At the lower end of the pit, rain water had collected and stagnated greenly. There was little other vegetation, for there was precious little soil. Beneath our feet, past the end of the Skill road, we stood on the raw black stone the road had been wrought from. When we looked up at the looming cliff across from us, black stone veined with silver met our eyes. On the floor of the quarry a number of immense blocks had been abandoned amidst piles of rubble and dust. The huge blocks were bigger than buildings. I could not imagine how they had been cut, let alone how they would have been hauled away. Beside them were the remains of great machines, reminding me somewhat of siege engines. Their wood had rotted, their metal rusted. Their remains hunched together like mouldering bones. Silence brimmed the quarry.

Two things about the place immediately caught my attention. The first was the black pillar that reared up in our pathway, incised with the same ancient runes we had encountered before. The second was the absolute absence of animal life.

I came to a halt by the pillar. I quested out, and the wolf shared my searching. Cold stone.

Perhaps we shall learn to eat rocks, now? the wolf suggested.

'We shall have to do our hunting elsewhere tonight,' I agreed.

'And find clean water,' added the Fool.

Kettricken had stopped by the pillar. The jeppas were already straying away, searching disconsolately for anything green. Possessing the Skill and the Wit sharpened my perceptions of other folk. But for the moment, I sensed nothing from her. Her face was still and empty. A slackness came over it, as if she aged before my eyes. Her eyes wandered over the lifeless stone, and by chance turned to me. A sickly smile spread over her mouth.

'He's not here,' she said. 'We've come all this way, and he isn't here.'

I could think of nothing to say to her. Of all the things I might have expected at the end of our quest, an abandoned stone quarry seemed unlikeliest. I tried to think of something optimistic to say. There was nothing. This was the last location marked on our map, and evidently the final destination of the Skill road as well. She sank down slowly to sit flat on the stone at the pillar's base. She just sat there, too weary and discouraged to weep. When I looked to Kettle and Starling, I found them staring at me as if I were supposed to have an answer. I did not. The heat of the warm day pressed down on me. For this, we had come so far.

I smell carrion.

I don't. It was the last thing I wanted to think about just now.

I didn't expect you would, with your nose. But there is something very dead not far from here.

'So go roll in it and have done with it,' I told him with some asperity.

'Fitz,' Kettle rebuked me as Nighteyes trotted purposefully away.

'I was talking to the wolf,' I told her lamely. The Fool nodded, almost vacantly. He had not been at all himself. Kettle had insisted that he continue taking the elfbark, though our small supply limited him to a very weak dose of the same bark brewed over again. From time to time, I thought I caught a brief hint of the Skill-bond between us. If I looked at him, he would sometimes turn and return my look, even across camp. It was little more than that. When I spoke of it to him, he said he sometimes felt something, but was not sure what it was. Of what the wolf had told me, I made no mention. Elfbark tea or no, he remained solemn and lethargic. His sleep at night did not seem to rest him; he moaned or muttered through his dreams. He reminded me of a man recovering from a long illness. He hoarded his strength in many small ways. He spoke little; even his bitter merriment had vanished. It was but one more worry for me to bear.

It's a man!

The stench of the corpse was thick in Nighteyes' nostrils. I nearly retched with it. Then, 'Verity,' I whispered to myself in horror. I set out at a run in the direction the wolf had taken.

The Fool followed more slowly in my wake, drifting like down on the wind. The women watched us go without comprehension.

The body was wedged between two immense blocks of stone. It was huddled as if even in death it sought to hide. The wolf circled it restlessly, hackles up. I halted at some distance, then tugged the cuff of my shirt down over my hand. I lifted it to cover my nose and mouth. It helped a bit, but nothing could have completely drowned that stink. I walked closer, steeling myself to what I knew I must do. When I got close to the body, I reached down, seized hold of its rich cloak, and dragged it out into the open.

'No flies,' the Fool observed almost dreamily.

He was right. There were no flies and no maggots. Only the silent rot of death had been at work on the man's features. They were dark, like a ploughman's tan, only darker. Fear had contorted them, but I knew it was not Verity. Yet I had stared at him for some moments before I recognized him. 'Carrod,' I said quietly.

'A member of Regal's coterie?' the Fool asked, as if there could be another Carrod about.

I nodded. I kept my shirt cuff over my nose and mouth as I knelt beside him.

'How did he die?' the Fool asked. The smell did not seem to bother him, but I did not think I could speak without gagging. I shrugged. To answer I would have had to take a breath. I reached gingerly to tug at his clothes. The body was both stiff and softening. It was hard to examine it, but I could find no sign of any violence on him. I took a shallow breath and held it, then used both hands to unbuckle his belt. I pulled it free of the body with his purse and knife still on it, and hastily retreated with it.

Kettricken, Kettle and Starling came up on us as I was coaxing the mouth of his purse open. I did not know what I had hoped to find, but I was disappointed. A handful of coins, a flint, and a small whetstone were all he carried. I tossed it to the ground, and rubbed my hand down my trouser leg. The stench of death clung to it.

'It was Carrod,' the Fool told the others. 'He must have come by the pillar.'

'What killed him?' Kettle asked.

I met her gaze. 'I don't know. I believe it was the Skill. Whatever it was, he tried to hide from it. Between those rocks. Let's get away from this smell,' I suggested. We retreated back to the pillar. Nighteyes and I came last and more slowly. I was puzzled. I realized I was putting everything I could into keeping my Skill walls strong. Seeing Carrod dead had shocked me. One less coterie member, I told myself. But he was here, right here in the quarry when he died. If Verity had killed him with the Skill, perhaps that meant Verity had been here as well. I wondered if we would stumble across Burl and Will somewhere in the quarry, if they too had come here to attack Verity. Colder was my suspicion that it was more likely we would find Verity's body. But I said nothing to Kettricken of these thoughts.

I think the wolf and I sensed it at the same time. 'There's something alive back there,' I said quietly. 'Deeper in the quarry.'

'What is it?' the Fool asked me.

'I don't know.' A shivering ran all over me. My Wit-sense of whatever was back there ebbed and flowed. The more I tried for a feel of what it was, the more it eluded me.

'Verity?' Kettricken asked. It broke my heart to see hope quicken once more in her eyes.

'No,' I told her gently. 'I don't think so. It doesn't feel like a human. It's like nothing I've ever sensed before.' I paused and added, 'I think you should all wait here while the wolf and I go see what it is.'

'No.' Kettle spoke, not Kettricken, but when I glanced back at my queen, I saw her complete agreement.

'If anything, I should have you and the Fool hang back while we investigate,' she told me severely. 'You are the ones at risk here. If Carrod has been here, Burl and Will could be back there.'

In the end it was decided we would all approach, but with great caution. We spread out in a fan and moved forward across the quarry floor. I could not tell them specifically where I sensed the creature, and so we were all on edge. The quarry was like a nursery floor with some immense child's blocks and toys scattered across it. We passed one partially carved block of stone. It had none of the finesse of the carvings we had seen in the stone garden. It was lumpish and crude, and somehow obscene. It reminded me of the foetus of a miscarried foal. It repulsed me and I slipped past it as swiftly as I could to my next vantage point.

The others were doing likewise, moving from cover to cover, all of us endeavouring to keep at least one other of our party in sight. I had thought I could see nothing more disturbing than that crude stone carving, but the next one we passed wrenched at me. Someone had carved, in heart-breaking detail, a mired dragon. The thing's wings were half spread and its half-lidded eyes were rolled up in agony. A human rider, a young woman, bestrode it. She clutched the undulant neck and leaned her cheek against it. Her face was a mask of agony, her mouth open and the lines of her face taut, the muscles of her throat standing out like cords. Both the girl and the dragon had been worked in detailed colours and lines. I could see the woman's eyelashes, the individual hairs on her golden head, the fine green scales about the dragon's eyes, even the droplets of saliva that clung to its lips. But where the dragon's mighty feet and lashing tail should have been, there was only puddled black stone, as if the two had landed in a tar pit and been unable to escape it.

Just as a statue, it was wrenching. I saw Kettle turn her face aside from it, tears starting in her eyes. But what unnerved Night-eyes and me was the writhing of Wit-sense that it gave off. It was fainter than what we had sensed in the statues back in the garden, but all the more poignant for that. It was like the final death throes of a trapped creature. I wondered what talent had been used to infuse such a living nuance into a statue. Even as I appreciated the artistry of what had been done, I was not sure I approved it. But that was true of much that this ancient Skilled race had wrought. As I crept past the statue, I wondered if this was what the wolf and I had sensed. It prickled my skin to see the Fool turn and stare back at it, his brow furrowed in discomfort. Plainly he sensed it, though not as well. *Perhaps this is what we sensed, Nighteyes. Perhaps there is no living creature in the quarry after all, only this monument to slow death.*

No. I smell something.

I widened my nostrils, cleared them with a silent snort, then took in a deep slow breath of air. My nose was not as keen as Nighteyes', but the wolf's senses augmented my own. I smelled sweat and the faint tang of blood. Both were fresh. Suddenly the wolf pressed close to me and as one we slunk around the end of a block of stone the size of two huts.

I peered around the corner, then cautiously crept forth. Nighteyes slipped past me. I saw the Fool round the other end of the stone, and felt the others drawing near as well. No one spoke.

It was another dragon. This one was the size of a ship. It was all of black stone, and it sprawled sleeping upon the block of stone it was emerging from. Chips and chunks and grindings of rock dust surrounded the ground around the block. Even from a distance, it impressed me. Despite its sleep, every line of the creature spoke of both strength and nobility. The wings folded alongside it were like furled sails while the arch of the powerful neck put me in mind of a battle charger. I had looked at it for some moments before I saw the small grey figure that sprawled alongside it. I stared at him and tried to decide if the flickering life I sensed came from him or the stone dragon.

The discarded fragments of stone were almost a ramp up to the block the dragon was emerging from. I thought the figure would stir to my crunching footsteps, but he did not move. Nor could I detect any small motions of breath. The others hung back, watching my ascent. Only Nighteyes accompanied me, and he came hackles abristle. I was within arm's reach of the figure when he jerkily arose and faced me.

He was old and thin, grey of both hair and beard. His ragged garments were grey with stone dust, and a smear of grey coated one of his cheeks. The knees that showed through the legs of his trousers were scabbed and bloody from kneeling on broken stone. His feet were wrapped in rags. He gripped a much-notched sword in a grey-gauntleted hand, but he did not bring it up to the ready. I felt it taxed his strength to hold the blade at all. Some instinct made me lift my arms wide of my body, to show him I held no weapon. He looked at me dully for a bit; then he slowly lifted his eyes to my face. For a time we stared at one another. His peering, near-blind gaze reminded me of Harper Josh. Then his mouth gaped wide in his beard, baring surprisingly white teeth. 'Fitz?' he said hesitantly.

I knew his voice, despite the rust. He had to be Verity. But all I was cried out aghast that he could have come to this, this wreckage of a man. Behind me I heard the swift crunching of footsteps and turned in time to see Kettricken charging up the ramp of crumbling stone. Hope and dismay battled in her face, yet, 'Verity!' she cried, and there was only love in the word. She charged, arms reaching for him, and I was barely able to catch her as she hurtled past me.

'No!' I cried aloud to her. 'No, don't touch him!'

'Verity!' she cried again, and then struggled against my grip, crying out, 'Let me go, let me go to him.' It was all I could do to hold her back.

'No,' I told her quietly. As sometimes happens, the softness of my command made her stop struggling. She looked her question at me.

'His hands and arms are covered with magic. I do not know what would happen to you, were he to touch you.'

She turned her head in my rough embrace to stare at her husband. He stood watching us, a kindly, rather confused smile on his face. He tilted his head to one side as if considering us, then stooped carefully to set down his sword. Kettricken saw then what I had glimpsed before. The betraying shimmer of silver crawled over his forearms and fingers. Verity wore no gauntlets; the flesh of his arms and hands was impregnated with raw power. The smudge on his face was not dust, but a smear of power where he had touched himself.

I heard the others come up behind us, their footsteps crunching slowly over the stone. I did not need to turn to feel them staring. Finally the Fool said softly, 'Verity, my prince, we have come.'

I heard a sound between a gasp and a sob. That turned my head, and I saw Kettle slowly settling, going down like a holed ship. She clasped one hand to her chest and one to her mouth as she sank to her knees. Her eyes goggled as she stared at Verity's hands. Starling was instantly beside her. In my arms, I felt Kettricken calmly push against me. I looked at her stricken face, then let her go. She advanced to Verity a slow step at a time and he watched her come. His face was not impassive, but neither did he show any sign of special recognition. An arm's length away from him, she stopped. All was silence. She stared at him for a time, then slowly shook her head, as if to answer the question she voiced. 'My lord husband, do you not know me?'

'Husband,' he said faintly. His brow creased deeper, his demeanour that of a man who recalls something once learned by rote. 'Princess Kettricken of the Mountain Kingdom. She was given me to wife. Just a little slip of a girl, a wild little mountain cat, yellow-haired. That was all I could recall of her, until they brought her to me.' A faint smile eased his face. 'That night, I unbound golden hair like a flowing stream, finer than silk. So fine I durst not touch it, lest it snag in my callused hands.'

Kettricken's hands rose to her hair. When word had reached her of Verity's death, she had cut her hair to no more than a brush on her skull. It now reached almost to her shoulders, but the fine silk of it was gone, roughened by sun and rain and road-dust. But she freed it from the fat braid that confined it and shook it loose around her face. 'My lord,' she said softly. She glanced from me to Verity. 'May I not touch you?' she begged.

'Oh –' He seemed to consider the request. He glanced down at his arms and hands, flexing his silvery fingers. 'Oh, I think not, I'm afraid. No. No, it were better not.' He spoke regretfully, but I had the sense that it was only that he must refuse her request, not that he regretted being unable to touch her.

Kettricken drew a ragged breath. 'My lord,' she began, and then her voice broke. 'Verity, I lost our child. Our son died.'

I did not understand until then what a burden it had been for her, seeking for her husband, knowing she must tell him this news. She dropped her proud head as if expecting his wrath. What she got was worse.

'Oh,' he said. Then, 'Had we a son? I do not recall . . .'

I think that was what broke her, to discover that her earthshaking tidings did not anger nor sorrow him, but only confused him. She had to feel betrayed. Her desperate flight from Buckkeep Castle and all the hardships she had endured to protect her unborn child, the long lonely months of her pregnancy, culminating in the heart-rending stillbirth of her child, and her dread that she must tell her lord how she had failed him: that had been her reality for the past year. And now she stood before her husband

and her king, and he fumbled to recall her and of the dead child said only 'Oh.' I felt shamed for this doddering old man who peered at the Queen and smiled so wearily.

Kettricken did not scream or weep. She simply turned and walked slowly away. I sensed great control in that passage, and great anger. Starling, crouched by Kettle, looked up at the Queen as she passed. She started to rise and follow, but Kettricken made a tiny movement of her hand that forbade it. Alone she descended from the great stone dais and strode off.

Go with her?

Please. But do not bother her.

I am not stupid.

Nighteyes left me, to shadow off after Kettricken. Despite my caution to him, I knew he went straight to her, to come up beside her and press his great head against her leg. She dropped suddenly to one knee and hugged him, pushing her face against his coat, her tears falling into his rough fur. He turned and licked her hand. *Go away*, he chided me, and I pulled my awareness back from them. I blinked, realizing I had been staring at Verity all the while. His eyes met mine.

He cleared his throat. 'FitzChivalry,' he said, and drew a breath to speak. Then he let half of it out. 'I am so weary,' he said piteously. 'And there is still so much to do.' He gestured at the dragon behind him. Ponderously he sank, to sit beside the statue. 'I tried so hard,' he said to no one in particular.

The Fool recovered his senses before I did mine. 'My lord Prince Verity,' he began then paused. 'My king. It is I, the Fool. May I be of service to you?'

Verity looked up at the slender pale man who stood before him. 'I would be honoured,' he said after a moment. His head swayed on his neck. 'To accept the fealty and service of one who served both my father and my queen so well.' For an instant I glimpsed something of the old Verity. Then the certainty flickered out of his face again.

The Fool advanced and then knelt suddenly beside him. He patted Verity on the shoulder, sending up a small cloud of rock dust. 'I will take care of you,' he said. 'As I did your father.' He stood up suddenly and turned to me. 'I am going to fetch firewood, and find clean water,' he announced. He glanced past me to the women. 'Is Kettle all right?' he asked Starling.

'She nearly fainted,' Starling began. But Kettle cut in abruptly with, 'I was shocked to my core, Fool. And I am in no hurry to stand up. But Starling is free to go and do whatever must be done.'

'Ah. Good.' The Fool appeared to have taken complete control of the situation. He sounded as if he were organizing tea. 'Then, if you would be so kind, Mistress Starling, would you see to the setting up of the tent? Or two tents, if such a thing can be contrived. See what food we have left, and plan a meal. A generous meal, for I think we all need it. I shall return shortly with firewood, and water. And greens, if I am lucky.' He cast a quick look at me. 'See to the King,' he said in a low voice. Then he strode away. Starling was left gaping. Then she arose and went in search of the straying jeppas. Kettle followed her more slowly.

And so, after all that time and travel, I was left standing alone before my king. 'Come to me', he had told me, and I had. There was an instant of peace in realizing that that nagging voice was finally stilled. 'Well, I am here, my king,' I said quietly, to myself as much as to him.

Verity made no reply. He had turned his back to me and was busy digging at the statue with his sword. He knelt, clutching the sword by the pommel and by the blade and scraped the tip along the stone at the edge of the dragon's foreleg. I stepped close to watch him scratching at the black rock of the dais. His face was so intent, his movement so precise that I did not know what to make of it. 'Verity, what are you doing?' I asked softly.

He did not even glance up at me. 'Carving a dragon,' he replied.

Several hours later, he still toiled at the same task. The monotonous scrape, scrape, scrape of the blade against the stone set my teeth on edge and shredded every nerve in my body. I had remained on the dais with him. Starling and the Fool had set up our tent, and a second smaller one cobbled together from our now excess winter blankets. A fire was burning. Kettle presided over a bubbling pot. The Fool was sorting the greens and roots he had gathered while Starling arranged bedding in the tents. Kettricken had rejoined us briefly, but only to get her bow and quiver from the jeppas' packs. She had announced she was going hunting with Nighteyes. He had given me one lambent glance from his dark eyes, and I had held my tongue.

I knew but little more than I had when we had first found Verity. His Skill walls were high and tight. I received almost no sense of the Skill from him. What I discovered when I quested toward him was even more unnerving. I grasped the fluttering Wit-sense I had of him, but could not understand it. It was as if his life and awareness fluctuated between his body and the great statue of the dragon. I recalled the last time I had encountered such a thing. It had been between the Wit-man and his bear. They had shared the same flowing of life. I suspected that if anyone had quested toward the wolf and me, they would discover the same sort of pattern. We had shared minds for so long that in some ways we were one creature. But that did not explain to me how Verity could have bonded with a statue, nor why he persisted in scraping at it with his sword. I longed to grab hold of the sword and snatch it from his grasp, but I refrained. In truth, he seemed so obsessed with what he did that I almost feared to interrupt him.

Earlier I had tried asking him questions. When I asked him what had become of those who left with him, he had shaken his head slowly. 'They harried us as a flock of crows will haunt an eagle. Coming close, squawking and pecking, and fleeing when we turned to attack them.' 'Crows?' I had asked him, blankly.

He shook his head at my stupidity. 'Hired soldiers. They shot at us from cover. They came at us at night, sometimes. And some of my men were baffled by the coterie's Skill. I could not shield the minds of those who were susceptible. Night fears they sent to stalk them, and suspicion of one another. So I bid them go back; I pressed my own Skill-command into their minds, to save them from any other.' It was almost the only question he truly answered. Of the others I asked, he did not choose to answer many, and the answers he did give were either inappropriate or evasive. So I gave it up. Instead, I found myself reporting to him. It was a long accounting, for I began with the day I had watched him ride away. Much of what I told him, I was sure he already knew, but I repeated it anyway. If his mind was wandering, as I feared, it might anchor him to refresh his memory. And if my king's mind was as sharp as ever beneath this dusty demeanour, then it could not hurt for all the events to be put in perspective and order. I could think of no other way to reach him.

I had begun it, I think, to try to make him realize all we had gone through to be here. Also, I wished to awaken him to what was happening in his kingdom while he loitered here with his dragon. Perhaps I hoped to wake in him some sense of responsibility for his folk again. As I spoke, he seemed dispassionate, but occasionally he would nod gravely, as if I had confirmed some secret fear of his. And all the time the sword tip moved against the black stone, scrape, scrape, scrape.

It was verging on full dark when I heard the scuff of Kettle's footsteps behind me. I paused in recounting my adventures in the ruined city and turned to look at her. 'I've brought you both some hot tea,' she announced.

'Thank you,' I said, and took my mug from her, but Verity only glanced up from his perpetual scraping.

For a time, Kettle stood proffering the cup to Verity. When she spoke, it was not to remind him of tea. 'What are you doing?' she asked in a gentle voice.

The scraping stopped abruptly. He turned to stare at her, then glanced at me as if to see if I, too, had heard her ridiculous question. The querying look I wore seemed to amaze him. He cleared his throat. 'I am carving a dragon.'

'With your sword blade?' she asked. In her tone was curiosity, no more.

'Only the rough parts,' he told her. 'For the finer work, I use my knife. And then, for finest of all, my fingers and nails.' He turned his head slowly, surveying the immense statue. 'I would like to say it is nearly done,' he said falteringly. 'But how can I say that when there is still so much to do? So very much to do . . . and I fear it will all be too late. If it is not already too late.'

'Too late for what?' I asked him, my voice as gentle as Kettle's had been.

'Why . . . too late to save the folk of the Six Duchies.' He peered at me as if I were simple. 'Why else would I be doing it? Why else would I leave my land and my queen, to come here?'

I tried to grasp what he was telling me, but one overwhelming question popped out of my mouth. 'You believe you have carved this whole dragon?'

Verity considered. 'No. Of course not.' But just as I felt relief that he was not completely mad, he added, 'It isn't finished yet.' He looked again over his dragon with the fondly proud look he had once reserved for his best maps. 'But even this much has taken me a long time. A very long time.'

'Won't you drink your tea while it's hot, sir?' Kettle asked, once more proffering the cup.

Verity looked at it as if it were a foreign object. Then he took it gravely from her hand. 'Tea. I had almost forgotten about tea. Not elfbark, is it? Eda's mercy, how I hated that bitter brew!'

Kettle almost winced to hear him speak of it. 'No, sir, no elfbark, I promise you. It is made from wayside herbs, I'm afraid. Mostly nettle, and a bit of mint.'

'Nettle tea. My mother used to give us nettle tea as a spring tonic.' He smiled to himself. 'I will put that in my dragon. My mother's nettle tea.' He took a sip of it, and then looked startled. 'It's warm . . . it has been so long since I had time to eat anything warm.'

'How long?' Kettle asked him conversationally.

'A . . . long time,' Verity said. He took another sip of the tea. 'There are fish in a stream, outside the quarry. But it is hard enough to take time to catch them, let alone cook them. Actually, I forget. I have put so many things into the dragon . . . perhaps that was one of them.'

'And how long since you slept?' Kettle pressed him.

'I cannot both work and sleep,' he pointed out to her. 'And the work must be done.'

'And the work shall be done,' she promised him. 'But tonight you will pause, just for a bit, to eat and drink. And then to sleep. See? Look down there. Starling has made you a tent, and within it will be warm, soft bedding. And warmed water, to wash yourself. And such fresh clothing as we can manage.'

He looked down at his silvered hands. 'I do not know if I can wash myself,' he confided to her.

'Then FitzChivalry and the Fool will help you,' she promised him blithely.

'Thank you. That would be good. But . . .' His eyes went afar for a time. 'Kettricken. Was not she here, a while ago? Or did I dream her? So much of her was what was strongest, so I put it into the dragon. I think that is what I have missed the most, of all I have put there.' He paused and then added, 'At the times when I can recall what I miss.'

'Kettricken is here,' I assured him. 'She has gone hunting, but she will return soon. Would you like to be washed and freshly clothed when she returns?' I had privately resolved to respond to the parts of his conversation that made sense, and not upset him by questioning the other parts.

'That one sees past such things,' he told me, a shade of pride in his voice. 'Still, it would be nice . . . but there is so much work to do.'

'But it is getting too dark to work any more today. Wait until tomorrow. It will get done,' Kettle assured him. 'Tomorrow, I will help you.'

Verity shook his head slowly. He sipped more of the tea. Even that thin beverage seemed to be strengthening him. 'No,' he said quietly. 'I am afraid you cannot. I must do it myself, you see.'

'Tomorrow, you will see. I think, if you have strength enough by then, then it may be possible for me to help you. But we shall not worry about it until then.'

He sighed and offered the empty mug back to her. Instead, she quickly gripped his upper arm and drew him to his feet. She was strong for such an old woman. She did not seek to take the sword from his grasp, but he let it fall. I stooped to gather it up. He followed Kettle docilely, as if her simple act of taking his arm had deprived him of all will. As I followed, I ran my eyes down the blade that had been Hod's pride. I wondered what had possessed Verity to take such a kingly weapon and turn it into a rock-carving tool. The edges were turned and notched from the misuse, the tip no more pointed than a spoon. The sword was much like the man, I reflected, and followed them down to the camp.

When we got down to the fireside, I was almost shocked to

see that Kettricken had returned. She sat by the fire, staring dispassionately into it. Nighteyes lay almost across her feet. His ears pricked toward me as I approached the fire, but he made no move to leave the Queen.

Kettle guided Verity directly to the makeshift tent that had been pitched for him. She nodded to the Fool, and without a word he took up a steaming basin of water from beside the fire and followed her. When I ventured to enter the tiny tent also, the Fool shooed both me and Kettle away. 'He will not be the first king I have tended to,' he reminded us. 'Trust him to me.'

'Touch not his hands nor forearms!' Kettle warned him sternly. The Fool looked a bit taken aback by that, but after a moment he gave a bobbing nod of agreement. As I left he was untying the much-knotted thong that closed Verity's worn jerkin, speaking all the while of inconsequential things. I heard Verity observe, 'I have missed Charim so. I should never have let him come with me, but he had served me so long . . . He died slowly, with much pain. That was hard for me, watching him die. But, he, too, has gone into the dragon. It was necessary.'

I felt awkward when I returned to the fire. Starling was stirring the pot of stew that was bubbling merrily. A large chunk of meat on a spit was dripping fat into the fire, making the flames leap and hiss. The smell of it reminded me of my hunger so that my belly growled. Kettle was standing, her back to the fire, staring off into darkness. Kettricken's eyes flickered toward me.

'So,' I said suddenly, 'how was the hunting?'

'As you see,' Kettricken said softly. She gestured at the pot, and then tossed a hand casually to indicate a butchered out wood-sow. I stepped over to admire it. It was not a small animal.

'Dangerous prey,' I observed, trying to sound casual rather than horrified that my queen would take on such a beast alone.

'It was what I needed to hunt,' she said, her voice still soft. I understood her only too well.

It was very good hunting. Never have I taken so much meat with so little effort, Nighteyes told me. He rubbed the side of his head against her leg in true affection. She dropped a hand to pull gently at his ears. He groaned in pleasure and leaned heavily against her.

'You'll spoil him,' I mock-warned her. 'He tells me he has never taken so much meat with so little effort.'

'He is so intelligent. I swear, he drove the game toward me. And he has courage. When my first arrow did not drop her, he held her at bay while I nocked another one to my bow.' She spoke as if she had nothing else on her mind but this. I nodded to her words, content to let our conversation be thus. But she suddenly asked me, 'What is wrong with him?'

I knew she did not speak of the wolf. 'I am not sure,' I said gently. 'He has known a great deal of privation. Perhaps enough to . . . weaken his mind. And . . .'

'No.' Kettle's voice was brusque. 'That is not it at all. Though I will grant you he is weary. Any man would be, to do what he has done alone. But –'

'You cannot believe he has carved that whole dragon himself!' I interrupted her.

'I do,' the old woman replied with certainty. 'It is as he told you. He must do it himself, and so he has done it.' She shook her head slowly. 'Never have I heard such a thing. Even King Wisdom had the help of his coterie, or what was left of it when he reached here.'

'No one could have carved that statue with a sword,' I said stubbornly. What she was saying was nonsense.

For answer, she rose and stalked off into the darkness. When she returned, she dropped two objects at my feet. One had been a chisel, once. Its head was peened over into a lump, its blade gone to nothing. The other was an ancient iron mallet head, with a relatively new wooden handle set into it. 'There are others, scattered about. He probably found them in the city. Or discarded hereabouts,' she observed before I could ask the question.

I stared at the battered tools, and considered all the months that Verity had been gone. For this? For the carving of a stone dragon?

'I don't understand,' I said faintly.

Kettle spoke clearly, as if I were slow. 'He has been carving a dragon, and storing all his memories in it. That is part of why he seems so vague. But there is more. I believe he used the Skill to kill Carrod, and has taken grievous hurt in so doing.' She shook her head sadly. 'To have come so close to finishing, and then to be defeated. I wonder how sly Regal's coterie is. Did they send one against him, knowing that if Verity killed with the Skill, he might defeat himself?'

'I do not think any of that coterie would willingly sacrifice himself.'

Kettle smiled bitterly. 'I did not say he was willingly sent. Nor did I say he knew what his fellows intended. It is like the game of stones, FitzChivalry. One plays each stone to best advantage in the game. The object is to win, not to hoard one's stones.'

THIRTY-FOUR

Girl on a Dragon

Early in our resistance to the Red Ships, before anyone in the Six Duchies had begun to call it a war, King Shrewd and Prince Verity realized that the task facing them was overwhelming. No individual man, no matter how Skilled, could stand alone to fend the Red Ships from our coasts. King Shrewd summoned before him Galen, the Skillmaster, and directed him to create for Verity a coterie to aid the prince's efforts. Galen resisted this idea, especially when he found that one of those he must train was a royal bastard. The Skillmaster declared that none of the students presented to him were worthy of training. But King Shrewd insisted, telling him to make the best of them that he could. When Galen grudgingly gave in, he created the coterie that bore his name.

It soon became apparent to Prince Verity that the coterie, while internally cohesive, did not work well with the Prince at all. By then Galen had died, leaving Buckkeep with no successor to the post of Skillmaster. In desperation, Verity sought for others trained in the Skill who might come to his aid. Although there had been no coteries created in the peaceful years of King Shrewd's reign, Verity reasoned that there might still live men and women trained for coteries before that. Had not the longevity of coterie members always been legendary? Perhaps he could find one who would either help him, or be able to train others in the Skill.

But Prince Verity's efforts in this area availed him nothing. Those he could identify as Skill-users from records and word of mouth were all either dead, or mysteriously vanished. So Prince Verity was left to wage his war alone.

* * *

Before I could press Kettle to clarify her answers, there was a cry from Verity's tent. Every one of us jumped, but Kettle was the first to the tent flap. The Fool emerged, gripping his left wrist in his right hand. He went straight to the water bucket and plunged in his hand. His face was contorted with either pain or fear, perhaps both. Kettle stalked after him to peer at the hand he gripped.

She shook her head in disgust. 'I warned you! Here, take it out of the water, it won't do it any good. Nothing will do it any good. Stop. Think about it. It's not really pain, it's just a sensation you've never felt before. Take a breath. Relax. Accept it. Accept it. Breathe deep, breathe deep.'

All the while she spoke, she tugged at the Fool's arm until he reluctantly drew his hand from the water. Kettle immediately overset the bucket with her foot. She scuffed rock dust and gravel over the spilled water, all the while gripping the Fool's arm. I craned my neck to peer past her. His first three fingers on his left hand were now tipped with silver. He looked at them with a shudder. I had never seen the Fool so unnerved.

Kettle spoke firmly. 'It won't wash off. It won't wipe off. It's with you now, so accept it. Accept it.'

'Does it hurt?' I asked anxiously.

'Don't ask him that!' Kettle snapped at me. 'Don't ask him anything just now. See to the King, FitzChivalry, and leave the Fool to me.'

In my worry over the Fool, I had all but forgotten my king. I stooped to enter the tent. Verity sat on two folded blankets. He was struggling to lace up one of my shirts. I deduced that Starling had ransacked all the packs to find clean clothes for him. It smote me to see him so thin that one of my shirts fit him.

'Allow me, my king,' I suggested.

He not only dropped his hands away, he put them behind his back. 'Is the Fool much hurt?' he asked me as I fought with the knotted strings. He sounded almost like my old Verity.

'Just three fingertips are silvered,' I told him. I saw that the Fool had laid out a brush and thong. I stepped behind Verity, and began to brush his hair back. He hastily snatched his hands around in front of him. Some of the grey in his hair had been rock dust, but not all. His warrior's queue was now grey with black streaks in it and coarse as a horse's tail. I struggled to smooth it back. As I tied the thong I asked him, 'What does it feel like?'

'These?' he asked, holding up his hands and waggling the fingers. 'Oh. Like Skill. Only more so, and on my hands and arms.'

I saw he thought he had answered my question. 'Why did you do it?' I asked.

'Well, to work the stone, you know. When this power is on my hands, the stone must obey the Skill. Extraordinary stone. Like the Witness Stones in Buck, did you know that? Only they are not nearly as pure as what is here. Of course, hands are poor tools for working stone. But once you have cut away all the excess, down to where the dragon waits, then he can be awakened with your touch. I draw my hands over the stone, and I recall to it the dragon. And all that is not dragon shivers away in shards and chips. Very slowly, of course. It took a whole day just to reveal his eyes.'

'I see,' I murmured, at a loss. I did not know whether he was mad or if I believed him.

He stood up as far as he could in the low tent. 'Is Kettricken angry with me?' he asked abruptly.

'My lord king, it is not for me to say . . .'

'Verity,' he interrupted wearily. 'Call me Verity, and for Eda's sake, answer the question, Fitz.'

He sounded so like his old self I wanted to embrace him. Instead, I said, 'I do not know if she is angry. She is definitely hurt. She came a long and weary way to find you, bearing terrible news. And you did not seem to care.'

'I care, when I think of it,' he said gravely. 'When I think of it, I grieve. But there are so many things I must think of, and I cannot think of them all at once. I knew when the child died, Fitz. How could I not know? He, too, and all I felt, I have put into the dragon.'

He walked slowly away from me, and I followed him out of the tent. Outside, he stood up straight, but did not lose the stoop in his shoulders. Verity was an old man now, far older than Chade somehow. I did not understand that, but I knew it was true. Kettricken glanced up at his approach. She looked back into the fire, and then, almost unwillingly she stood, stepping clear of the sleeping wolf. Kettle and Starling were binding the Fool's fingers in strips of cloth. Verity went straight to Kettricken and stood beside her. 'My queen,' he said gravely. 'If I could, I would embrace you. But you have seen that my touch . . .' He gestured at the Fool and let his words trail away.

I had seen the look on her face when she had told Verity about the stillbirth. I expected her to turn aside from him, to hurt him as he had hurt her. But Kettricken's heart was larger than that. 'Oh, my husband,' she said, and her voice broke on the words. He held his silvered arms wide, and she came to him, taking him in her embrace. He bowed his grey head over the rough gold of her hair, but could not allow his hand to touch her. He turned his silvered cheek away from her. His voice was husky and broken as he asked her, 'Did you give him a name? Our son?'

'I named him according to the customs of your land.' She took a breath. The word was so soft I scarce heard it. 'Sacrifice,' she breathed. She clung to him tightly and I saw his thin shoulders convulse in a sob.

'Fitz!' Kettle hissed at me sharply. I turned to find her scowling at me. 'Leave them alone,' she whispered. 'Make yourself useful. Get a plate for the Fool.'

I had been staring at them. I turned away, shamed to have been gawking, but glad to see them embrace, even in sorrow. I did as Kettle had ordered, getting food for myself at the same time. I took the plate to the Fool. He sat cradling his injured hand in his lap.

He looked up as I sat beside him. 'It doesn't rub off on anything else,' he complained. 'Why did it cling to my fingers?'

'I don't know.'

'Because you're alive,' Kettle said succinctly. She sat down across from us as if we needed supervising.

'Verity told me he can shape rock with his fingers because of the Skill on them,' I told her.

'Is your tongue hinged in the middle so that it flaps at both ends? You talk too much!' Kettle rebuked me.

'Perhaps I would not talk too much if you spoke a bit more,' I replied. 'Rock is not alive.'

She looked at me. 'You know that, do you? Well, what is the point of my talking when you already know everything?' She attacked her food as if it had done her a personal wrong.

Starling joined us. She sat down beside me, her plate on her knees, and said, 'I don't understand about the silvery stuff on his hands. What is it?'

The Fool snickered into his plate like a naughty child when Kettle glared at her. But I was getting tired of Kettle's evasions. 'What does it feel like?' I asked the Fool.

He glanced down at his bandaged fingers. 'Not pain. Very sensitive. I can feel the weave of the threads in the bandages.' His eyes started to get distant. He smiled. 'I can see the man who wove it, and I know the woman who spun it. The sheep on the hillside, rain falling on their thick wool, and the grass they ate . . . wool is from grass, Fitz. A shirt woven from grass. No, there is more. The soil, black and rich and . . .'

'Stop it!' Kettle said harshly. And she turned to me angrily. 'And you stop asking him, Fitz. Unless you want him to follow it too far and be lost forever.' She gave the Fool a sharp poke. 'Eat your food.'

'How is it you know so much about the Skill?' Starling suddenly asked her.

'Not you, too!' Kettle angrily declared. 'Is there nothing private any more?'

'Among us? Not much,' the Fool replied, but he was not looking at her. He was watching Kettricken, her face still puffy from weeping, as she dished up food for herself and Verity. Her worn and stained clothing, her rough hair and chapped hands and the simple, homely task she performed for her husband should have made her seem like any woman. But I looked at her and saw perhaps the strongest queen that Buckkeep had ever known.

I watched Verity wince slightly as he took from her hand the simple wooden dish and spoon. He shut his eyes a moment, struggling against the pull of the implement's history. He composed his face and took a mouthful of food. Even across camp from him, I felt the sudden awakening of plain hunger. It was not just hot food he had been long without, it was solid sustenance

709

of any kind. He took a shuddering breath and began to eat like a starved wolf.

Kettle was watching him. A look of pity crossed her face. 'No. Very little privacy left for any of us,' she said sadly.

'The sooner we get him back to Jhaampe, the sooner he can get better,' Starling said soothingly. 'Should we start tomorrow, do you think? Or give him a few days of food and rest to rebuild his strength?'

'We shall not be taking him back to Jhaampe,' Kettle said, an undercurrent of sadness in her voice. 'He has begun a dragon. He cannot leave it.' She looked around at us levelly. 'The only thing we can do for him now is stay here and help him finish it.'

'With Red Ships torching the entire coastline of the Six Duchies and Farrow attacking the Mountains, we should stay here and help the King carve a dragon?' Starling was incredulous.

'Yes. If we want to save the Six Duchies and the Mountains, that is exactly what we should do. Now, you will excuse me. I think I shall put on more meat to cook. Our king looks as if he could use it.'

I set my empty plate aside. 'We should probably cook it all. In this weather, meat will sour fast,' I said unwisely.

I spent the next hour butchering the pig into portions that could dry-cook over the fire all night. Nighteyes awoke and helped dispose of scraps until his belly was distended. Kettricken and Verity sat talking quietly. I tried not to watch them, but even so, I was aware that his gaze frequently strayed from her to the dais where his dragon crouched over us. The low rumble of his voice was hesitant, and often died away altogether until prompted by another question from Kettricken.

The Fool was amusing himself by touching things with his Skill-fingers; a bowl, a knife, the cloth of his shirt. He met Kettle's scowls with a benign smile. 'I'm being careful,' he told her once.

'You have no idea of how to be careful,' she complained. 'You won't know you've lost your way until you're gone.' She got up from our butchery with a grunt and insisted on rebandaging his fingers. After that, she and Starling left together to get more firewood. The wolf got up with a groan and followed them.

Kettricken helped Verity into the tent. After a moment she

reappeared to go into the main tent. She emerged carrying her bedding. She caught my quick glance and abashed me by meeting my eyes squarely. 'I have taken your long mittens from your pack, Fitz,' she told me calmly. Then she joined Verity in the smaller tent. The Fool and I looked everywhere except at each other.

I went back to my cutting on the meat. I was tired of it. The smell of the pig was suddenly the smell of something dead rather than that of fresh meat and I had smears of sticky blood up to my elbows. The worn cuffs of my shirt were soaked with it. I continued doggedly with my task. The Fool came to crouch beside me.

'When my fingers brushed Verity's arm, I knew him,' he said suddenly. 'I knew he was a worthy king for me to follow, as worthy as his father before him. I know what he intends,' he added in a lower voice. 'It was too much for me to grasp at first, but I have been sitting and thinking. And it fits in with my dream about Realder.'

A shiver ran through me that had nothing to do with chill. 'What?' I demanded.

'The dragons are the Elderlings,' the Fool said softly. 'But Verity could not wake them. So he carves his own dragon, and when it is finished, he will waken it, and then he will go forth to fight the Red Ships. Alone.'

Alone. That word struck me. Once again, Verity expected to fight the Red Ships alone. But there was too much I didn't quite grasp. 'All the Elderlings were dragons?' I asked. My mind went back to all the fanciful drawings and weavings of Elderlings I had ever seen. Some had been dragon-like, but . . .

'No. The Elderlings *are* dragons. Those carved creatures back in the stone garden. Those are the Elderlings. King Wisdom was able to wake them in his time, to rouse them and recruit them to his cause. They came to life for him. But now they either sleep too deeply or they are dead. Verity spent much of his strength trying to rouse them in every way he could think of. And when he could not, he decided that he would have to make his own Elderling, and quicken it, and use it to fight the Red Ships.'

I sat stunned. I thought of the Wit-life both the wolf and I had sensed crawling through those stones. With a sudden pang,

711

I remembered the trapped anguish of the girl on a dragon statue in this very quarry. Living stone, trapped and flightless forever. I shuddered. It was a different kind of dungeon.

'How is it done?'

The Fool shook his head. 'I don't know. I don't think Verity himself knows. He blunders toward it, blind and groping. He shapes the stone, and gives it his memories. And when it is finished, it will come to life. I suppose.'

'Do you hear what you are saying?' I asked him. 'Stone is going to rise and defend the Six Duchies from the Red Ships. And what of Regal's troops and the border skirmishes with the Mountain Kingdom? Will this "dragon" drive them off as well?' Slow anger was building in me. 'This is what we have come all this way for? For a tale I would not expect a child to believe?'

The Fool looked mildly affronted. 'Believe it or not as you choose. I but know that Verity believes it. Unless I am much mistaken, Kettle believes it as well. Why else would she insist we must stay here, and help Verity complete the dragon?'

For a time, I pondered this. Then I asked him, 'Your dream about Realder's dragon. What do you recall of it?'

He gave a helpless shrug. 'The feelings of it, mostly. I was exuberant and joyful, for not only was I announcing Realder's dragon, but he was going to fly me on it. I felt I was a bit in love with him, you know. That sort of lift to the heart. But . . .' he faltered. 'I cannot recall if I loved Realder or his dragon. In my dream, they are mingled . . . I think. Recalling dreams is so hard. One must seize them as soon as one awakes, and quickly repeat them to oneself, to harden the details. Otherwise they fade so quickly.'

'But in your dream, did a stone dragon fly?'

'I was announcing the dragon in my dream, and knew I was to fly upon it. I had not yet seen it, in my dream.'

'Then maybe it has nothing to do at all with what Verity does. Perhaps, in the time from which your dream came, there were real dragons, of flesh and blood.'

He looked at me curiously. 'You do not believe there are real dragons, today?'

'I have never seen one.'

'In the city,' he pointed out quietly.

'That was a vision of a different time. You said today.'

He held one of his own pale hands up to the firelight. 'I think they are like my kind. Rare, but not mythical. Besides, if there were no dragons of flesh and blood and fire, whence would come the idea for these stone carvings?'

I shook my head wearily. 'This conversation goes in circles. I am tired of riddles and guesses and beliefs. I want to know what is real. I want to know why we came all this way, and what it is we must do.'

But the Fool had no answers to that. When Kettle and Starling got back with the wood, he helped me layer the fire and arrange the meat where the heat would drive the fat from it. What meat we could not set to cook, we bundled aside in the pigskin. There was a sizeable pile of bones and scraps. Despite how he had gorged earlier, Nighteyes settled down with a leg bone to gnaw. I surmised he had regurgitated part of his bellyful somewhere.

There is no such thing as having too much meat in reserve, he told me contentedly.

I made a few attempts to needle Kettle into talking to me, but somehow it evolved into a lecture on how much more aware of the Fool I must be now. He must be protected, not only from Regal's coterie, but from the Skill-pull of objects that might take his mind wandering. For that reason, she wished us to stand our watches together. She insisted the Fool must sleep on his back, his bared fingers upturned so they touched nothing. As the Fool usually slept huddled in a ball, he was not overly pleased. But at last we settled for the night.

I was not due to take my watch until the hours before dawn. But it was short of that when the wolf came to push his nose under my cheek and jog my head until I opened my eyes.

'What?' I demanded tiredly.

Kettricken walks alone, weeping.

I doubted she would want my company. I also doubted that she should be alone. I rose noiselessly and followed the wolf out of the tent. Outside, Kettle sat by the fire, poking disconsolately at the meat. I knew she must have seen the Queen leave, so I did not dissemble.

'I'm going to go find Kettricken.'

'Probably a good idea,' she said quietly. 'She told me she was going to look at his dragon, but she has been gone longer than that.'

We needed to say no more about it. I followed Nighteyes as he trotted purposefully away from the fire. But he led me, not toward Verity's dragon, but back through the quarry. There was little moonlight, and what there was the looming black blocks of stone seemed to drink away. Shadows seemed to fall in all different directions, altering perspective. The need for caution made the quarry vast as I picked my way along in the wolf's wake.

My skin prickled as I realized we were going in the direction of the pillar. But we found her before we reached there. She was standing, motionless as the stone itself, by the girl on the dragon. She had clambered up onto the block of stone that mired the dragon, and reached up to lay a hand on the girl's leg. A trick of the moonlight made it look as if the girl's stone eyes looked down at her. Light sparkled silver on a stone tear, and glistened on the tears on Kettricken's face. Nighteyes padded lightly up, leaped weightlessly upon the dais and leaned his head against Kettricken's leg with a tiny whine.

'Hush,' she told him softly. 'Listen. Can you hear her weeping? I can.'

I did not doubt it, for I could feel her questing out with the Wit, more strongly than I had ever sensed it from her before.

'My lady,' I said quietly.

She startled, her hand flying to her mouth as she turned to me.

'I beg your pardon. I did not mean to frighten you. But you should not be out here alone. Kettle fears there may still be danger from the coterie, and we are not so far from the pillar.'

She smiled bitterly. 'Wherever I am, I am alone. Nor can I think of anything they could do to me worse than what I have done to myself.'

'That is only because you do not know them as well as I do. Please, my queen, come back to the camp with me.'

She moved and I thought she would step down to me. Instead she sat down and leaned back against the dragon. My Wit-sense of the dragon-girl's misery was echoed by Kettricken's. 'I just wanted to lie beside him,' she said quietly. 'To hold him. And to be held. To be held, Fitz. To feel . . . not safe. I know none of us are safe. But to feel valued. Loved. I did not expect more than that. But he would not. He said he could not touch me. That he dared not touch anything live save his dragon.' She turned her head aside. 'Even with his hands and arms gloved, he would not touch me.'

I found myself clambering up the dais. I took her by the shoulders and drew her to her feet. 'He would if he could,' I told her. 'This I know. He would if he could.'

She lifted her hands to cover her face, and her silent sliding tears suddenly became sobs. She spoke through them. 'You . . . and your Skill. And him. You speak so easily of knowing what he feels. Of love. But I . . . I don't have that. I am only . . . I need to feel it, Fitz. I need to feel his arms about me, to be close to him. To believe he loves me. As I love him. After I have failed him in so many ways. How can I believe . . . when he refuses to even . . .' I put my arms about her and drew her head down on my shoulder, while Nighteyes leaned up against both of us and keened softly.

'He loves you,' I told her. 'He does. But fate has laid this burden upon both of you. It must be borne.'

'Sacrifice,' she breathed, and I did not know if she named her child or defined her life. She continued to weep, and I held her, soothing her hair and telling her it would get better, it had to be better someday, there would be a life for them when all this was over, and children, children growing up safe from Red Ships or Regal's evil ambitions. In time I felt her quiet, and realized it was Wit as much as words I had been giving her. The feeling I had for her had mingled with the wolf's and joined us. Gentler than a Skill-bond, more warm and natural, I held her in my heart as much as in my arms. Nighteyes pressed up against her, telling her he would guard her, that his meat would ever be her meat, that she need fear nothing that had teeth, for we were pack, and always would be.

It was she who finally broke the embrace. She gave a final shuddering sigh, and then stepped apart from me. Her hand rose to smear the wetness on her cheeks. 'Oh, Fitz,' she said, simply, sadly. And that was all. I stood still, feeling the chill apartness where for a time we had been together. A sudden pang of loss assailed me. And then a shiver of fear as I realized its source. The girl on the dragon had shared our embrace, her Wit-misery briefly consoled by our closeness. Now, as we drew apart, the far, chill wailing of the stone rose up again, louder and stronger. I tried to leap lightly down from the dais, but as I landed I staggered and nearly fell. Somehow that joining had drawn strength from me. It was frightening, but I masked my uneasiness as I silently accompanied Kettricken back to the camp.

I was just in time to relieve Kettle on watch. She and Kettricken went to sleep, promising to send the Fool out to stand watch with me. The wolf gave me an apologetic glance and then followed Kettricken into the tent. I assured him I approved. A moment later the Fool emerged, rubbing his eyes with his left hand and carrying his right lightly curled against his chest. He took a seat on a stone across from me as I looked over the meat to see which pieces needed turning. For a time he watched me silently. Then he stooped, and with his right hand, picked up a piece of firewood. I knew I should rebuke him, but instead I watched, as curious as he. After a moment, he tucked the wood into the fire and straightened. 'Quiet and lovely,' he told me. 'Some forty years of growing, winter and summer, storm and fair weather. And before that, it was borne as a nut by another tree. And so the thread goes back, over and over. I do not think I need fear much from natural things, only those that have been wrought by man. Then the threads go ravelling out. But trees, I think, will be pleasant to touch.'

'Kettle said you should touch no live things,' I reminded him like a tattling child.

'Kettle has not to live with this. I do. I must discover the limits it places on me. The sooner I find what I can and cannot do with my right hand, the better.' He grinned wickedly, and made a suggestive gesture toward himself.

I shook my head at him, but could not keep from laughing.

He joined my laughter with my own. 'Ah, Fitz,' he said quietly a moment later, 'you do not know how much it means to me that I can still make you laugh. If I can stir you to laughter, I can laugh myself.'

'It surprises me that you can still jest at all,' I replied.

'When you can either laugh or cry, you might as well laugh,' he replied. Abruptly he asked, 'I heard you leave the tent earlier. Then, while you were gone . . . I could feel something of what happened. Where did you go? There was much I did not understand.'

I was silent, thinking. 'The Skill-bond between us may be growing stronger instead of weaker. I do not think that is a good thing.'

'There is no elfbark left. I had the last of it two days ago. Good or bad, it is as it is. Now explain to me what happened.'

I saw little point in refusing. So I attempted to explain. He interrupted with a number of questions, few of which I could answer. When he decided he understood it as well as words could convey it, he quirked a smile at me. 'Let us go see this girl on a dragon,' he suggested.

'Why?' I asked warily.

He lifted his right hand and waggled his silver fingertips at me as he lifted one eyebrow.

'No,' I said firmly.

'Afraid?' he needled me.

'We are on watch here,' I told him severely.

'Then you will go with me tomorrow,' he suggested.

'It is not wise, Fool. Who knows what effect it might have on you?'

'Not I. And that is exactly why I wish to do it. Besides. What call has a Fool to be wise?'

'No.'

'Then I shall have to go alone,' he said with a mock sigh.

I refused to rise to the bait. After a moment, he asked me, 'What is it you know about Kettle that I do not?'

I looked at him uncomfortably. 'About as much as I know about you that she does not.'

'Ah. That was well spoken. Those words could have been stolen from me,' he conceded. 'Do you wonder why the coterie has not tried to attack us again?' he asked next.

'Is this your night to ask unfortunate questions?' I demanded.

'Of late, I have no other kind.'

'At the very least, I dare to hope that Carrod's death has weakened them. It must be a great shock to lose a member of your coterie. Almost as bad as losing a Wit-beast companion.'

'And what do you fear?' the Fool pressed.

It was a question I had been pushing away from myself. 'What do I fear? The worst, of course. What I fear is that they are somehow marshalling greater strength against us, to offset Verity's power. Or perhaps they are setting a trap for us. I fear they are turning their Skill to seeking out Molly.' I added the last with great reluctance. It seemed the greatest bad luck even to think about it, let alone speak it aloud.

'Cannot you Skill a warning to her somehow?'

As if it had never occurred to me. 'Not without betraying her. I have never been able to reach Burrich with the Skill. Sometimes, I am able to see them, but I cannot make them aware of me. I fear that even making the effort might be enough to expose her to the coterie. He may know of her, but not know where she is. You told me that not even Chade himself knew where she was. And Regal has many places to send his troops and attention. Buck is far from Farrow, and the Red Ships have kept it in turmoil. Surely he would not send troops into that for the sake of finding one girl.'

'One girl and a Farseer child,' the Fool reminded me gravely. 'Fitz. I do not speak to grieve you, but only to warn you. I have contained his anger at you. That night, when they held me . . .' He swallowed and his eyes went distant. 'I have tried so hard to forget it. If I touch those memories at all, they seethe and burn within me like a poison I cannot be rid of. I have felt Regal's very being inside my own. Hatred for you squirms through him like maggots through rotting meat.' He shook his head, sickened at recalling it. 'The man is mad. He ascribes to you every evil ambition he can imagine. Your Wit he regards with loathing, and terror. He cannot conceive that what you do, you do for Verity. In his mind, you have devoted your life to injuring him since you came to Buckkeep. He believes that both Verity and you have come to these Mountains not to wake the Elderlings to defend

Buck, but to find some Skill-treasure or power to use against him. He believes he has no choice but to act first, to find whatever it is you seek and turn it against you. To that, he bends all his resources and determination.'

I listened to the Fool in a sort of frozen horror. His eyes had taken on the stare of a man who recalls torture. 'Why have you not spoken of this to me before?' I asked him gently when he paused to catch his breath. The skin of his arms was standing up in gooseflesh.

He looked away from me. 'It is not a thing I enjoy recalling.' He was trembling very lightly. 'They were in my mind like evil, idle children, smashing what they could not grasp. I could keep nothing back from them. But they were not interested in me at all. They regarded me as less than a dog. Angry, in that moment of finding I was not you. They nearly destroyed me because I was not you. Then they considered how they might use me against you.' He coughed. 'If that Skill-wave had not come . . .'

I felt like Chade himself as I said quietly, 'Now I will turn that back upon them. They could not hold you in thrall like that without revealing much of themselves to you. As much as you can, I ask you to reach back to that time, and tell me all you can recall.'

'You would not ask that, if you knew what you were asking.'

I thought I did know, but I refrained from saying it. Instead, I let silence bid him think it through. Dawn was greying the sky, and I had just returned from walking a circuit of our camp when next he spoke.

'There were Skill books you know nothing about. Books and scrolls that Galen removed from Solicity's rooms as she was dying. The information they held was for a Skillmaster alone, and some were even fastened shut with clever locks. Galen had many years to tinker those locks loose. A lock does no more than keep an honest man honest, you know. Galen found there much he did not understand. But there were also scrolls listing those who had been Skill-trained. Galen sought out all he could find and questioned them. Then he did away with them, lest others should ask them the same questions he had. Galen found much in those scrolls. How a man might live long and enjoy good health. How to give pain with the Skill, without even touching a man. But in the oldest scrolls he found hints of great power awaiting a strongly Skilled man in the Mountains. If Regal could bring the Mountains under his sway, he could come into power no one could withstand. To that end did he seek the hand of Kettricken for Verity, with no intent that she would ever be his bride. He intended that when Verity was dead, he would take her in his brother's stead. And her inheritance.'

'I don't understand,' I said gently. 'The Mountains have amber and furs and . . .'

'No. No.' The Fool shook his head. 'It was nothing like that. Galen would not divulge the whole of his secret to Regal, for he then would have had no hold over his half-brother. But you can be sure that when Galen died, Regal immediately possessed those scrolls and books and set to studying them. He is no master of the older languages, but he feared to seek the help of others, lest they discover the secret first. But he puzzled it out at last, and when he did, he was horrified. For by then he had eagerly dispatched Verity into the Mountains to die on some foolish quest. He finally ciphered out that the power Galen had sought for him was power over the Elderlings. Immediately he decided Verity had conspired with you to seek that very power for himself. How dare he seek to steal the very treasure that Regal had worked so long to gain! How dare he try to make a fool of Regal in such a way!' The Fool smiled weakly. 'In his mind, his domination over the Elderlings is his birthright. You seek to steal it from him. He believes he upholds what is right and just by trying to kill you.'

I sat nodding to myself. The pieces all fit, every one of them. Holes in my understanding of Regal's motives were being closed up, to present me with a frightening picture. I had known the man was ambitious. I also knew he feared and suspected anyone or anything he could not control. I had been a double danger to him, a rival for his father's affection and with a strange Wit-talent he could neither understand nor destroy. To Regal, every other person in the world was a tool or a threat. All threats must be destroyed.

He had probably never considered that all I wanted from him was to be left alone.

THIRTY-FIVE

Kettle's Secrets

Nowhere is there mention of who raised the Witness Stones that stand on the hill near Buckkeep. They may very well pre-date the actual building of Buckkeep Castle itself. Their supposed power seems to have little to do with the worship of Eda or El, but folk believe in it with the same fierce religious fervour. Even those who profess to doubt the existence of any gods at all would still hesitate to give false oath before the Witness Stones. Black and weathered those tall stones stand. If ever they bore inscriptions of any kind, wind and water have erased them.

Verity was the first of the others to rise that morning. He came staggering from his tent as the first true light of day brought colour back to the world. 'My dragon!' he cried as he stood blinking in the light. 'My dragon!' For all the world as if he expected it to be gone.

Even when I assured him his dragon was fine, he was like a spoiled child. He wished to resume his work on it instantly. With the greatest difficulty, I persuaded him to drink a mug of nettle and mint tea, and eat some of the slow-cooked meat from the skewers. He would not wait for the porridge to boil, but left the fire with meat and sword in hand. He did not mention Kettricken at all. In time the scrape, scrape, scrape of the sword's point against the black stone resumed. The shadow I had seen of Verity last night had fled with the morning's coming.

It seemed strange to greet a new day and not immediately pack up all our belongings. No one was in a good humour. Kettricken was puffy-eyed and silent, Kettle sour and reserved. The wolf was still digesting all the meat he had consumed the day before and only wanted to sleep. Starling seemed annoyed with everyone, as if it were our fault that our quest had ended in such confusing disappointment. After we had eaten, Starling declared that she was going to check on the jeppas and do some washing in the stream the Fool had found. Kettle grumpily agreed to go with her for safety, though her eyes strayed often to Verity's dragon. Kettricken was up there also, gloomily watching her husband and king as he gouged away at the black stone. I busied myself in removing the fire-dried meat, wrapping it, refuelling the slow fire and putting the rest of the meat to dry over it.

'Let's go,' the Fool invited me as soon as I was finished.

'Where?' I asked, thinking longingly of a nap.

'The girl on a dragon,' he reminded me. He set off eagerly, not even looking back to see if I followed. He knew I must.

'I think this is a foolish idea,' I called after him.

'Exactly,' he replied with a grin, and would say no more until we approached the great statue.

The girl on a dragon seemed more quiescent this morning, but perhaps I was merely becoming more accustomed to the trapped Wit-unrest I sensed there. The Fool did not hesitate, but immediately clambered up on the dais beside the statue. I followed more slowly. 'She looks different to me today,' I said quietly.

'How?'

'I can't say.' I studied her bent head, the stone tears frozen on her cheeks. 'Does she look different to you?'

'I didn't really look at her that closely yesterday.'

Now that we were actually here, the Fool's banter seemed dampened. Very gingerly, I set a hand to the dragon's back. The individual scales were so cunningly worked, the curve of the beast's body so natural that I almost expected it to heave with breath. It was cold, hard stone. I held my breath, daring myself, then quested toward the stone. It felt unlike any questing I had ever done before. There was no beating heart, no rush of breath, nor any other physical sign of life to guide me. There was only my Wit-sense of life, trapped and desperate. For a moment it eluded me; then I brushed against it, and it quested back to me. It sought the feel of wind on skin, the warm pumping of blood, oh, the scents of the summer day, the sensation of my clothing against my skin, any and all that was part of the experience of living it hungered for. I snatched my hand back, frightened by the intensity of its reaching. Almost I thought it might draw me in to join it there.

'Strange,' whispered the Fool, for linked to me as he was, he felt the ripples of my experience. His eyes met mine and held for some time. Then he reached a single bare silver fingertip toward the girl.

'We should not do this,' I said, but there was no force in my words. The slender figure astride the dragon was dressed in a sleeveless jerkin, leggings and sandals. The Fool touched his finger to her upper arm.

A Skill-scream of pain and outrage filled the quarry. The Fool was flung backwards off the pedestal, to land hard on his back on the rock below. He sprawled there senseless. My knees buckled under me and I fell beside the dragon. From the torrent of Wit-anger I felt, I expected the creature to trample me underfoot like a maddened horse. Instinctively I curled up, my arms sheltering my head.

It was done in an instant, yet the echoes of that cry seemed to rebound endlessly from the slick black stone walls and blocks all around us. I was shakily clambering down to check on the Fool when Nighteyes came rushing up to us. *What was that? Who threatens us?* I knelt by the Fool. He had struck his head and blood was leaking onto the black stone, but I didn't think that was why he was unconscious. 'I knew we shouldn't have done it. Why did I let you do it?' I asked myself as I gathered him up to take him back to camp.

'Because you're a bigger fool than he is. And I am the biggest of all, to have left you alone and trusted you to act with sense. What did he do?' Kettle was still puffing from her hurry.

'He touched the girl on the dragon. With the Skill on his finger.'

I glanced up at the statue as I spoke. To my horror, there was a bright silver fingerprint on the girl's upper arm, outlined in scarlet against her bronze-toned flesh. Kettle followed my gaze and I heard her gasp. She spun on me and lifted her gnarled hand as if to strike me. Then she clenched her hand into a contorted fist that trembled and forced it down by her side. 'Is it not enough that she is trapped there in misery forever, alone and cut off from all she once loved? You two must come to give her pain on top of all that! How could you be so vicious?'

'We meant no harm. We did not know . . .'

'Ignorance is always the excuse used by the cruelly curious!' Kettle snarled.

My own temper suddenly rose to match hers. 'Don't rebuke me with my ignorance, woman, when all you have done is refuse to lift it for me. You hint and warn and give us ominous words, but you refuse to speak anything that might help us. And when we make mistakes, you rail at us, saying we should have known better. How? How can we know better when the one who does refuses to share her knowledge with us?'

In my arms, the Fool stirred faintly. The wolf had been prowling about my feet. Now he came back with a whine to sniff at the Fool's dangling hand.

Careful! Don't let his fingers touch you!

What bit him?

I don't know. 'I don't know anything,' I said aloud, bitterly. 'I'm blundering in the dark, hurting everyone I care about in the process.'

'I dare not interfere,' Kettle shouted at me. 'What if some word of mine set you on the wrong course? What of all the prophecies then? You must find your own way, Catalyst.'

The Fool opened his eyes to look at me blankly. Then he closed them again and leaned his head on my shoulder. He was starting to get heavy and I needed to find out what was wrong with him. I shrugged him up more firmly in my arms. I saw Starling coming up behind Kettle, her arms laden with wet laundry. I turned and walked away from them both. As I headed back to camp with the Fool, I said over my shoulder, 'Maybe that is why you are here. Maybe you were called here, with a part to play. Maybe it is lifting our ignorance so we can fulfil this bedamned prophecy of yours. And maybe keeping your silence is how you will thwart it. But,' and I halted to fling the words savagely over my shoulder, 'I think you keep silent for reasons of your own. Because you are ashamed!'

I turned away from the stricken look on her face. I covered my shame to have spoken to her so with my anger. It gave me new strength of purpose. I was suddenly determined that I was going to start making everyone behave as they should. It was the sort of childish resolution that often got me into trouble, but once my heart had seized hold of it, my anger gripped it tight.

I carried the Fool into the big tent and laid him out on his bedding. I took a ragged sleeve off what remained of a shirt, damped it in cool water, and applied it firmly to the back of his head. When the bleeding slowed, I checked it. It was not a large cut, but it was on top of a respectable lump. I still felt that was not why he had fainted. 'Fool?' I said to him quietly, then more insistently, 'Fool?' I patted his face with water. He came awake with a simple opening of his eyes. 'Fool?'

'I'll be all right, Fitz,' he said wanly. 'You were right. I should not have touched her. But I did. And I shall never be able to forget it.'

'What happened?' I demanded.

He shook his head. 'I can't talk about it just yet,' he said quietly.

I shot to my feet, head slapping against the tent roof and nearly bringing the whole structure down around me. 'No one in this whole company can talk about anything!' I declared furiously. 'Except me. And I intend to talk about everything.'

I left the Fool leaning up on one elbow and staring after me. I don't know if his expression was amused or aghast. I didn't care. I strode from the tent, scrabbled up the pile of tailings to the pedestal where Verity carved his dragon. The steady scrape, scrape, scrape of his sword point against the stone was like a rasp against my soul. Kettricken sat by him, hollow-eyed and silent. Neither paid me the slightest bit of attention.

I halted a moment and got my breathing under control. I swept my hair back from my face and tied my warrior's tail afresh, brushed off my leggings and tugged the stained remnants of my shirt straight. I took three steps forward. My formal bow included Kettricken.

'My lord, King Verity. My lady, Queen Kettricken. I have come to conclude my reporting to the King. If you would allow it.'

I had honestly expected both of them to ignore me. But King Verity's sword scraped twice more then ceased. He looked at me over his shoulder. 'Continue, FitzChivalry. I shall not cease my work, but I shall listen.'

There was grave courtesy in his voice. It heartened me. Kettricken suddenly sat up straighter. She brushed the straggling hair back from her eyes, then nodded her permission at me. I drew a deep breath and began, reporting as I had been taught, everything that I had seen or done since my visit to the ruined city. Sometime during that long telling, the scraping of the sword slowed, then ceased. Verity moved ponderously to take a seat beside Kettricken. Almost he started to take her hand in his, then stopped himself and folded his own hands before him. But Kettricken saw that small gesture, and moved a trifle closer to him. They sat side by side, my threadbare monarchs, throned on cold rock, a stone dragon at their backs, and listened to me.

By one and by two, the others came to join us. First the wolf, then the Fool and Starling, and finally old Kettle ranged themselves in a half circle behind me. When my throat began to grow dry and my voice to rasp, Kettricken lifted a hand and sent Starling for water. She returned with tea and meat for all of us. I took but a mouthful of the tea and went on while they picnicked around me.

I held to my resolution and spoke plainly of all, even that which shamed me. I did not leave out my fears nor foolishness. I told him how I had killed Regal's guard without warning, even giving him the name of the man I had recognized. Nor did I skirt about my Wit-experiences as I once would have. I spoke as bluntly as if it were only Verity and me, telling him of my fears for Molly and my child, including my fear that if Regal did not find and kill them, Chade would take the child for the throne. As I spoke, I reached for Verity in every way I could, not just my voice, but Wit and Skill, I tried to touch him and reawaken him to who he was. I know he felt that reaching, but try as I might, I could stir no response from him.

I finished by recounting what the Fool and I had done with the girl on a dragon. I watched Verity's face for any change of expression, but there was none I could see. When I had told him all, I stood silent before him, hoping he would question me. The old Verity would have taken me over my whole tale again, asking questions about every event, asking what I had thought, or suspected of anything I had observed. But this grey-headed old man only nodded several times. He made as if to rise.

'My king!' I begged him desperately.

'What is it, boy?'

'Have you nothing to ask me, nothing to tell me?'

He looked at me, but I was not sure he was really seeing me. He cleared his throat. 'I killed Carrod with the Skill. That is true. I have not felt the others since then, but I do not believe they are dead, but only that I have lost the Skill to sense them. You must be careful.'

I gaped at him. 'And that is all? I must be careful?' His words had chilled me to the bone.

'No. There is worse.' He glanced at the Fool. 'I fear that when you speak to the Fool, he listens with Regal's ears. I fear it was Regal who came to you that day, speaking with the Fool's tongue, to ask you where Molly was.'

My mouth went dry. I turned to look at the Fool. He looked stricken. 'I do not recall . . . I never said . . .' He took a half-breath, then suddenly toppled to one side in a faint.

Kettle scrabbled over to him. 'He breathes,' she told us.

Verity nodded. 'I suspect they have abandoned him then. Perhaps. Do not trust that is true.' His eyes came back to me. I was trying to remain standing. I had felt it as they fled the Fool. Felt it like a silk thread abruptly parting. They had not had a strong hold on him, but it had been enough. Enough to make me reveal all they needed to kill my wife and child. Enough to ransack his dreams each night since then, stealing whatever was of use to them.

I went to the Fool. I took his unSkilled hand and reached for him. Slowly his eyes opened and he sat up. For a time he stared at us all without comprehension. His eyes came back to mine, shame washing through their smoky depths. ' "And the one who loves him best shall betray him most foully." My own prophecy. I have known that since my eleventh year. Chade, I had told myself, when he was willing to take your child. Chade was your betrayer.' He shook his head sadly. 'But it was me. It was me.' He got slowly to his feet. 'I am sorry. So sorry.'

I saw the start of tears on his face. Then he turned and walked slowly away from us. I could not bring myself to go after him, but Nighteyes rose soundlessly and trailed at his heels.

'FitzChivalry.' Verity took a breath, then spoke quietly. 'Fitz. I will try to finish my dragon. It is really all I can do. I only hope it will be enough.'

Despair made me bold. 'My king, will not you do this for me? Will not you Skill a warning to Burrich and Molly, that they may flee Capelin Beach before they are found?'

'Oh, my boy,' he said pityingly. He took a step toward me. 'Even if I dared to, I fear I have not the strength any more.' He lifted his eyes and looked at each of us in turn. His gaze lingered longest on Kettricken. 'It all fails me. My body, my mind, and my Skill. I am so tired, and there is so little left of me. When I killed Carrod, my Skill fled me. My work has been greatly slowed since then. Even the raw power on my hands weakens, and the pillar is closed to me; I cannot pass through it to renew the magic. I fear I may have defeated myself. I fear I will not be able to complete my task. In the end, I may fail you all. All of you, and the entire Six Duchies.'

Kettricken bowed her face into her hands. I thought she would weep. But when she lifted her eyes again, I saw the strength of her love for the man shining through whatever else she felt. 'If this is what you believe you must do, then let me help you.' She gestured at the dragon. 'There must be something I can do to help you complete it. Show me where to cut stone away, and then you can work the details.'

He shook his head sadly. 'Would that you could. But I must do it myself. It all must be done by me.'

Kettle suddenly surged to her feet. She came to stand beside me, giving me a glare as if everything were all my fault. 'My lord, King Verity,' she began. She seemed to lose courage for a moment, then spoke again louder. 'My king, you are mistaken. Few dragons were created by a single person. At least, not the Six Duchies dragons. Whatever the others, the true Elderlings could do on their own, I do not know. But I know that those dragons that were made by Six Duchies hands were most often made by an entire coterie working together, not a single person.'

Verity stared at her mutely. Then, 'What are you saying?' he demanded in a shaking voice.

'I am saying what I know. Regardless of how others may come to think of me.' She gave one glance around at us, as if bidding us farewell. Then she put her back to us and addressed only the King. 'My lord king. I name myself Kestrel of Buck, once of Stanchion's Coterie. But by my Skill I did slay a member of my own coterie, for jealousy over a man. To do so was high treason, for we were the Queen's own strength. And I destroyed that. For this I was punished as the Queen's Justice saw fit. My Skill was burned out of me, leaving me as you see me: sealed into myself, unable to reach beyond the walls of my own body, unable to receive the touch of those I had held dear. That was done by my own coterie. For the murder itself, the Queen banished me from the Six Duchies, for all time. She sent me away so that no Skilled one would be tempted to take pity on me and try to free me. She said she could imagine no worse punishment, that one day in my isolation, I would long for death.' Kettle sank slowly to her old knees on the hard stone. 'My king, my queen, she was right. I ask your mercy now. Either put me to death. Or . . .' Very slowly she lifted her head. 'Or use your strength to reopen me to the Skill. And I will serve you as coterie in the carving of this dragon.'

All was silence for a time. When Verity spoke, it was in confusion. 'I know of no Stanchion's Coterie.'

Kettle's voice shook as she admitted, 'I destroyed it, my lord. There were but five of us. My act left only three alive to the Skill, and they had experienced the physical death of one member and the . . . burning of myself. They were greatly weakened. I heard that they were released from their service to the Queen, and sought the road that once began in Jhaampe town. They never returned, but I do not think they survived the rigours of this road. I do not think they ever made a dragon such as we once used to dream about.'

When Verity spoke, he did not seem to be replying to her words. 'Neither my father nor either of his wives had coteries sworn to them. Nor my grandmother.' His brow wrinkled. 'Which queen did you serve, woman?'

'Queen Diligence, my king,' Kettle said quietly. She was still kneeling on the hard stone.

'Queen Diligence reigned over two hundred years ago,' Verity observed.

'She died two hundred and twenty-three years ago,' Starling interposed.

'Thank you, minstrel,' Verity said drily. 'Two hundred and twenty-three years ago. And you would have me believe you were coterie to her.'

'I was, my lord. I had turned my Skill upon myself, for I wished to keep my youth and beauty. It was not regarded as an admirable thing to do, but most Skilled ones did it to some extent. It took me over a year to master my body. But what I had done, I did well. To this day, I heal swiftly. Most illnesses pass me by.' She could not keep a note of pride from her voice.

'The legendary longevity of the coterie members,' King Verity observed softly to himself. He sighed. 'There must have been much in Solicity's books that Chivalry and I were never made privy to.'

'A great deal.' Kettle spoke with more confidence now. 'It amazes me that, with as little training as you and FitzChivalry have, you have managed to come this far alone. And to carve a dragon alone? It is a feat for a song.'

Verity glanced back at her. 'Oh, come, woman, sit down. It pains me to see you kneel. Obviously there is much you can and should tell me.' He shifted restlessly and glanced back at his dragon. 'But while we are talking, I am not working.'

'Then I shall say to you only what needs most to be said,' Kettle offered. She clambered painfully to her feet. 'I was powerful in the Skill. Strong enough to kill with it, as few are.' Her voice halted, thickening. She took a breath and resumed. 'That power is still within me. One strongly Skilled enough could open me to it again. I believe you have that strength. Though right now, you may not be able to master it. You have killed with the Skill, and that is a heinous thing. Even though the coterie member was not true to you, still, you had worked together. In killing him, you killed a part of yourself. And that is why you feel you have no Skill left to you. Had I my Skill, I could help you heal yourself.'

Verity gave a small laugh. 'I have no Skill, you have no Skill, but if we did, we could heal one another. Woman, this is like a tangle of rope with no ends. How is the knot to be undone, save with a sword?'

'We have a sword, my king. FitzChivalry. The Catalyst.'

'Ah. That old legend. My father was fond of it.' He looked at me consideringly. 'Do you think he is strong enough? My nephew August was Skill-burned and never recovered. For him, I sometimes thought it a mercy. The Skill was leading him down a path ill-suited to him. I think I suspected then that Galen had done something to the coterie. But I had so much to do. Always so much to do.'

I sensed my king's mind wavering. I stepped forward resolutely. 'My lord, what is it you wish me to attempt?'

'I wish you to attempt nothing. I wish you to do. There. That is what Chade often said to me. Chade. Most of him is in the dragon now, but that is a bit I left out. I should put that in the dragon.'

Kettle stepped closer to him. 'My lord, help me to free my Skill. And I will help you to fill the dragon.'

There was something in the way she said those words. She spoke them aloud before us all, yet I felt that only Verity truly knew what she said. At last, very reluctantly, he nodded. 'I see no other way,' he said to himself. 'No other way at all.'

'How am I to do a thing, when I don't even know what that thing is?' I complained. 'My king,' I added, at a rebuking look from Kettricken.

'You know as much as we do,' Verity rebuked me quietly. 'Kestrel's mind was burned with the Skill, by her own coterie, to condemn her to isolation for the rest of her life. You must use what Skill you have in any way you can, to try to break through the scarring.'

'I have no idea how to begin,' I began. But then Kettle turned and looked at me. There was pleading in her old eyes. Loss, and loneliness. And Skill-hunger that had built to the point at which it was devouring her from within. Two hundred and twenty-three years, I thought to myself. It was a long time to be exiled from one's homeland. An impossible time to be confined to one's own body. 'But I will try,' I amended my words. I put out my hand to her.

Kettle hesitated, then set her hand in mine. We stood, clasping hands, looking at one another. I reached for her with the Skill, but felt no response. I looked at her and tried to tell myself I knew her, that it should be easy to reach Kettle. I ordered my mind and recalled all I knew of the irascible old woman. I thought of her uncomplaining perseverance, of her sharp tongue, and her clever hands. I recalled her teaching me the Skill game, and how often we had played it, heads bent together over the gamecloth. Kettle, I told myself sternly. Reach for Kettle. But my Skill found nothing there.

I did not know how much time had passed. I only knew that I was very thirsty. 'I need a cup of tea,' I told her, and let go of her hand. She nodded at me, keeping her disappointment well hidden. It was only when I let go her hand that I became aware of how the sun had moved above the mountaintops. I heard again the scrape, scrape, scrape of Verity's sword. Kettricken still sat, silently watching him. I did not know where the others had gone. Together we left the dragon and walked down to where our fire still smouldered. I broke wood into pieces as she filled the kettle. We said little as it heated. There were still herbs that Starling had gathered earlier for tea. They were wilted, but we used them, and then sat drinking our tea together. The scraping of Verity's sword against the stone was a background noise, not unlike an insect sound. I studied the old woman beside me.

My Wit-sense told me of a strong and lively life within her. I had felt her old woman's hand in my own, the flesh soft on the swollen, bony fingers save where work had callused her skin. I saw the lines in her face around her eyes and at the corners of her mouth. Old, her body said to me. Old. But my Wit-sense told me that there sat a woman of my own years, lively and wild-hearted, yearning for love and adventure and all that life might offer. Yearning, but trapped. I willed myself to see, not Kettle, but Kestrel. Who had she been before she had been buried alive? My eyes met hers. 'Kestrel?' I asked her suddenly.

'So I was,' she said quietly, and her grief was still fresh. 'But she is no more, and has not been for years.'

When I said her name, I had almost sensed her. I felt I held the key, but did not know where the lock was. There was a nudge at the edge of my wit. I looked up, annoyed at the interruption. It was Nighteyes and the Fool. The Fool looked tormented and I ached for him. But he could not have picked a worse time to come to speak to me. I think he knew it.

'I tried to stay away,' he said quietly. 'Starling told me what you were doing. She told me all that was said while I was gone. I know I should wait, that what you do is vital. But . . . I cannot.' He suddenly had trouble meeting my eyes. 'I betrayed you,' he whispered softly. 'I am the Betrayer.'

Linked as we were, I knew the depth of his feelings. I tried to reach through that, to make him feel what I felt. He had been used against me, yes, but it was no doing of his own. But I could not reach him. His shame, guilt and remorse stood between us, and blocked him from my forgiveness. Blocked him, too, from forgiving himself.

'Fool!' I suddenly exclaimed. I smiled at him. He looked horrified that I could smile at all, least of all at him. 'No, it is all right. You have given me the answer. You are the answer.' I took a breath and tried to think carefully. Go slowly, be careful, I cautioned myself, and then, no, I thought. Now. Now is the only time in which to do this. I bared my left wrist. I held it out to him, my palm up. 'Touch me,' I commanded him. 'Touch me with the Skill on your fingers, and see if I feel you have betrayed me.'

'No!' Kettle cried aghast, but the Fool was already reaching for me like a man in a dream. He took my hand in his right hand. Then he laid three silver fingertips against my upturned wrist. As I felt the cold burn of his fingers on my wrist, I reached over and grabbed Kettle's hand. 'KESTREL!' I cried aloud. I felt the stir of her, and I pulled her into us.

I was the Fool and the Fool was me. He was the Catalyst and so was I. We were two halves of a whole, sundered and come together again. For an instant I knew him in his entirety, complete and magical, and then he was pulling apart from me, laughing, a bubble inside me, separate and unknowable, yet joined of me. *You do love me!* I was incredulous. He had never truly believed it before. *Before, it was words. I always feared it was born of pity. But you are truly my friend. This is knowing. This is feeling what you feel for me. So this is the Skill.* For a moment he revelled in simple recognition.

Abruptly, another joined us. *Ah, little brother, you find your ears at last! My kill is ever your kill, and we shall be pack forever!*

The Fool recoiled at the wolf's friendly onslaught. I thought he would break the circle. Then suddenly he leaned into it. *This? This is Nighteyes? This mighty warrior, this great heart?*

How to describe that moment? I had known Nighteyes so completely for so long, it shocked me to see how little the Fool had known of him.

Hairy? That was how you saw me? Hairy and drooling?

Your pardon. This from the Fool, quite sincerely. *I am honoured to know you as you are. I had never suspected such nobility within you.* Their mutual approval was almost overwhelming.

Then the world settled around us. *We have a task,* I reminded them. The Fool lifted his touch from my wrist, leaving behind three silver prints on my skin. Even the air pressed too heavily against that mark. For a time, I had been somewhere else. Now I was once more within my own body. It all had taken but moments.

I turned back to Kettle. It was an effort to look only through my eyes. I still gripped her hand. 'Kestrel?' I said quietly. She lifted her gaze to mine. I looked at her and tried to see her as she had once been. I do not think she even knew then of that tiny hair of Skill between us. In the moment of her shock at the Fool touching me, I had pressed past her guard. It was too fine a line to be called a thread. But I now knew what choked it. 'All this guilt and shame and remorse you carry, Kestrel. Don't you see? That is what they burned you with. And you have added to it, all these years. The wall is of your own making. Take it down. Forgive yourself. Come out.'

I caught at the Fool's wrist and held him beside me. Somewhere I felt Nighteyes as well. They were back within their own minds, but I could reach them easily. I drew strength from them, carefully, slowly. I drew their strength and love and turned it against Kettle, trying to force it into her through that tiny chink in her armour.

Tears began to trickle down her seamed cheeks. 'I can't. That is the hardest part. I can't. They burned me to punish me. But it was not enough. It would never be enough. I can never forgive myself.'

Skill was starting to seep from her as she reached to me, trying to make me understand. She reached, to clasp my hand between both of hers. Her pain flowed through that clasp to me. 'Who could forgive you then?' I found myself asking.

'Gull. My sister Gull!' The name was torn from her, and I sensed she had refused to think of it, let alone utter it, for years. Her sister, not just her coterie-mate, but her sister. And she had killed her in a fury when she had found her with Stanchion. The leader of the coterie?

'Yes,' she whispered, though no words were needed between us now. I was past the burn wall. Strong, handsome Stanchion. Making love to him, body and Skill, an experience of oneness like no other. But then she had come upon them, him and Gull, together, and she had . . .

'He should have known better,' I cried out indignantly. 'You were sisters and members of his own coterie. How could he have done that to you? How could he?'

'Gull!' she cried out loud, and for an instant I saw her. She was behind a second wall. Both of them were. Kestrel and Gull. Two little girls, running barefoot down a sandy shore, just out of reach of the icy waves licking up the sand. Two little girls, as like as apple pips, their father's joy, twins, racing to meet the little boat coming in to shore, hurrying to see what Papa had caught in his nets today. I smelled the salt wind, the iodine of the tangled, squidgy kelp as they dashed through it squealing. Two little girls, Gull and Kestrel, locked and hidden behind a wall inside her. But I could see them even if she could not.

I see her, I know her. And she knew you, through and through. Lightning and thunder, your mother called you, for while your temper flashed and was gone, Gull could carry a grudge for week. But not against you, Kestrel. Never against you, and not for years. She loved you, more than either of you loved Stanchion. As you loved her. And she would have forgiven you. She would never have wished this on you.

I . . . don't know.

Yes, you do. Look at her. Look at you. Forgive yourself. And let the part of her within you live again. Let yourself live again.

She is within me?

Most certainly. I see her, I feel her. It must be so.

What do you feel? Cautiously.

Only love. See for yourself. I took her deep inside her mind, to the places and memories she had denied to herself. It was not the burn-walls her coterie had imposed on her that had hurt her most. It was the ones she had put up between herself and the memory of what she had lost in a moment of fury. Two girls, older now, wading out to seize the line their father threw to them, and helping to pull his laden boat up onto the beach. Two Buck girls, still as alike as apple pips, wanting to be the first ones to tell their Papa they had been chosen for Skill-training.

Papa said we were one soul in two bodies.

Open, then, and let her out. Let both of you out to live.

I fell silent, waiting. Kestrel was in a part of her memories she had denied for longer than other folk lived. A place of fresh wind and girlish laughter, and a sister so like yourself you scarcely needed to speak to one another. The Skill had been between them from the moment they were born.

I see what I must do now. I felt her overwhelming surge of joy and determination. *I must let her out, I must put her into the dragon. She will live forever in the dragon, just as we planned it. The two of us, together again.*

Kettle stood up, letting go of my hands so suddenly that I cried out at the shock. I found myself back in my body. I felt I had fallen there from a very great distance. The Fool and Nighteyes were still near me, but no longer a part of a circle. I could scarcely feel them for all else I felt. Skill. Racing through me like a riptide. Skill. Emanating from Kettle like heat from a smith's furnace. She glowed with it. She wrung her hands, smiled at the straightened fingers.

'You should go and rest now, Fitz,' she told me gently. 'Go on. Go to sleep.'

A gentle suggestion. She did not know her own Skill-strength. I lay back and knew no more.

When I awoke, it was full dark. The weight and warmth of the wolf's body were comfortable against me. The Fool had tucked a blanket around me and was sitting by me, staring raptly into the fire. When I stirred, he clutched at my shoulder with a sharp intake of breath.

'What?' I demanded. I could make no sense of anything I heard or saw. Fires had been kindled up on the stone dais beside the dragon. I heard the clash of metal against stone, and voices lifted in conversation. In the tent behind me, I heard Starling trying notes on her harp.

'The last time I saw you sleep like that, we had just taken an arrow out of your back and I thought you were dying of infection.'

'I must have been very tired,' I smiled at him, able to trust he understood. 'Are not you wearied? I took strength from you and Nighteyes.'

'Tired? No. I feel healed.' He did not hesitate, but added, 'I think it is as much that the false coterie has fled my body, as knowing that you do not hate me. And the wolf. Now, he is a wonder. Almost, I can still sense him.' A very strange smile touched his face. I felt him groping out for Nighteyes. He had not the strength to truly use the Skill or the Wit on his own. But it was unnerving to feel him try. Nighteyes let his tail rise and fall in one slow wag.

I'm sleepy.

Rest then, my brother. I set my hand to the thick fur of his shoulder. He was life and strength and friendship I could trust. He gave one more slow wag of his tail and lowered his head again; I looked back to the Fool and gave a nod toward Verity's dragon.

'What goes on, up there?'

'Madness. And joy. I think. Save for Kettricken. I think her heart eats itself hollow with jealousy, but she will not leave.'

'What goes on up there?' I repeated patiently.

'You know more of it than I do,' he retorted. 'You did something to Kettle. I could understand part of it, but not all. Then you fell asleep. And Kettle went up there and did something to Verity. I know not what, but Kettricken said it left them both weeping

737

and shaking. Then Verity did something to Kettle. And they both began to laugh and to shout and to cry out it would work. I stayed long enough to watch both of them start attacking the stone around the dragon with chisels and mallets and swords and anything else that was to hand. While Kettricken sits silent as a shadow and watches them mournfully. They will not let her help. Then I came down here and found you unconscious. Or asleep. Whichever you prefer. And I have sat here a long time, watching over you and making tea or taking meat to anyone who yells at me for some. And now you are awake.'

I recognized his parody of me reporting to Verity, and had to smile. I decided that Kettle had helped Verity unlock his Skill and that work was proceeding on the dragon. But Kettricken. 'What makes Kettricken sad?' I asked.

'She wishes she were Kettle,' the Fool explained, in a tone that said any moron would have known that. He handed me a plate of meat and a mug of tea. 'How would you feel, to have come this long and weary way, only to have your spouse choose another to help him in his work? He and Kettle chatter back and forth like magpies. All sorts of inconsequential talk. They work and chip, or sometimes, Verity just stands still, his hands pressed to the dragon. And he tells her of his mother's cat, Hisspit, and of thyme that grew in the garden on the tower. And all the while, Kettle speaks to him, with no break, of Gull who did this, and Gull who did that, and all she and Gull did together. I thought they would cease when the sun went down, but that was the only time that Verity seemed to recall Kettricken was alive. He asked her to bring firewood and make fires for light. Oh, and I think he has allowed her to sharpen a chisel or two for him.'

'And Starling,' I said stupidly. I did not like to think of what Kettricken must be feeling. I reined my thoughts away from it.

'She works on a song about Verity's dragon. I think she has given up on you and me ever doing anything of note.'

I smiled to myself. 'She is never about when I do anything of significance. What we wrought today, Fool, was better than any battle I have ever fought. But she will never understand all of that.' I cocked my head toward the yurt. 'Her harp sounds mellower than I recall it,' I said to myself.

In answer, he lifted his eyebrows and waggled his fingers at me.

My eyes widened. 'What have you been doing?' I demanded.

'Experimenting. I think that if I survive all this, my puppets shall be the stuff of legend. I have always been able to look at wood and see what I wished to call forth. These,' and again he waggled his fingers at me, 'make it so much easier.'

'Be cautious,' I pleaded with him.

'Me? I have no caution within me. I cannot be what I am not. Where are you going?'

'Up to see the dragon,' I replied. 'If Kettle can work on it, so can I. I may not be as strongly Skilled, but I've been linked with Verity for far longer.'

THIRTY-SIX

The Wit and the Sword

The Outislanders have always raided the coastline of the Six Duchies. The founder of the Farseer monarchy was, in fact, no more than a Raider grown weary of the sea life. Taker's crew overwhelmed the original builders of the wooden fort at the mouth of the Buck River and made it their own. Over a number of generations, the black stone walls of Buckkeep Castle replaced it, and the Outislander raiders became residents and monarch.

Trade and raiding and piracy have all existed simultaneously between the Six Duchies and the Out Islands. But the commencement of the Red Ship raids marked a change in this abrasive and profitable interchange. Both the savagery and destruction of the raids were unprecedented. Some attributed it to the rise to power in the Out Islands of a ferocious chieftain who espoused a bloody religion of vengeance. The most savage of his followers became Raiders and crew for his Red Ships. Other Outislanders, never before united under one leader, were coerced into swearing fealty to him, under threat of Forging for those and their families who refused him. He and his raiders brought their vicious hatred to the shores of the Six Duchies. If he ever had any intent beyond killing, raping, and destroying, he never made it known. His name was Kebal Rawbread.

'I don't understand why you deny me,' I said stiffly.

Verity stopped his endless chopping at the dragon. I had expected him to turn and face me, but instead he only crouched lower, to brush away rock chips and dust. I could scarcely believe the progress he had made. The entire clawed right foot of the dragon now rested upon the stone. True, it lacked the fine detail of the rest of the dragon, but the leg itself was now complete.

Verity wrapped a careful hand over the top of one of its toes. He sat motionless beside his creation, patient and still. I could not see any movement of his hand, but I could sense Skill at work. If I reached toward it at all, I could feel the tiny fissuring of stone as it flaked away. It truly seemed as if the dragon had been hidden in the stone, and that Verity's task was to reveal it, one gleaming scale at a time.

'Fitz. Stop it.' I could hear annoyance in his voice. Annoyance that I was Skill-sharing with him, and annoyance that I was distracting him from his work.

'Let me help you,' I begged again. Something about the work drew me. Before, when Verity had been scraping at the stone with his sword, the dragon had seemed an admirable work of stone-carving. But now there was a shimmering of Skill to him as both Verity and Kettle employed their powers. It was immensely attractive, in the way that a sparkling creek glimpsed through trees draws the eye, or the smell of fresh-baked bread wakes hunger. I longed to put hands on, and help shape this powerful creature. The sight of their working awakened a Skill-hunger in me such as I had never known. 'I have been Skill-linked with you more than anyone has. In the days when I pulled an oar on the *Rurisk*, you told me I was your coterie. Why do you turn me away now, when I could help, and you need help so badly?'

Verity sighed and rocked back on his heels. The toe was not done, but I could see the faint outline of scales upon it now, and the beginning of the sheath for the wickedly curved talon. I could feel how the claw would be, striated like a hawk's talon. I longed to reach down and draw forth those lines from the stone.

'Stop thinking about it,' Verity bade me firmly. 'Fitz. Fitz, look at me. Listen to me. Do you remember the first time I took strength from you?'

I did. I had fainted. 'I know my own strength better now,' I replied.

He ignored that. 'You didn't know what you were offering me, when you told me you were a King's Man. I took you at your word that you knew what you were doing. You didn't. I tell you plainly right now that you don't know what you are asking me for. I do know what I am refusing you. And that is all.'

'But Verity . . .'

'In this, King Verity will hear no "buts", FitzChivalry.' He drew that line with me as he had so seldom before.

I took a breath and refused to let my frustration become anger. He placed his hand carefully on the dragon's toe again. I listened a moment to the clack, clack, clack of Kettle's chisel working the dragon's tail free of the stone. She was singing as she worked, some old love ballad.

'My lord, King Verity, if you would tell me what it is I don't know about helping you, then I could decide for myself, perhaps, if . . .'

'It is not your decision, boy. If you truly wish to help, go get some boughs and make a broom. Sweep the rock chips and dust away. It is damnable stuff to kneel in.'

'I would rather be of real help to you,' I muttered disconsolately as I turned away.

'FitzChivalry!' There was a sharp note to Verity's voice, one I had not heard since I was a boy. I turned back to it with dread.

'You overstep yourself,' he told me bluntly. 'My queen keeps these fires going and sharpens my chisels for me. Do you put yourself above such work?'

At such times, a brief answer suffices best. 'No, sir.'

'Then you shall make me a broom. Tomorrow. For now, much as I hate to say it, we all should rest, at least for a time.' He stood slowly, swayed, then righted himself. He placed a silver hand affectionately on the dragon's immense shoulder. 'With the dawn,' he promised it.

I had expected him to call to Kettle, but she was already standing and stretching. Skill-linked, I thought to myself. Words were no longer necessary. But they were for his queen. He walked around his dragon to where Kettricken sat near one of the fires. She was grinding at a chisel's edge. The rough rasping of her work hid our soft footsteps from her. For a time, Verity looked down at his queen as she crouched at this chore. 'My lady, shall we sleep awhile?' he asked her quietly.

She turned. With a grey-dusted hand she wiped the straggling hair from her eyes. 'As you wish, my lord,' she replied. She was able to keep almost all her pain from her voice.

'I am not that tired, my lord king. I would continue working, if you will it.' Kettle's cheerful voice was almost jarring. I marked that Kettricken did not turn to look at her at all. Verity only said, 'Sometimes it is better to rest before you are tired. If we sleep while it is dark, we will work better by the day's light.'

Kettricken winced as if criticized. 'I could build the fires larger, my lord, if that is what you wish,' she said carefully.

'No. I wish to rest, with you beside me. If you would, my queen.'

It was no more than the bones of his affection, but she seized on it. 'I would, my lord.' It hurt me to see her content with so little.

She is not content, Fitz, nor am I unaware of her pain. I give her what I can. What it is safe for me to give her.

My king still read me so easily. Chastened, I bid them good night and went off to the tent. As we drew near, Nighteyes rose up, stretching and yawning.

Did you hunt?

With all this meat left, why would I hunt? I noticed then the tumble of pig bones all round him. He lay down amongst them again, nose to tail, rich as any wolf could ever be. I knew a moment's envy of his satisfaction.

Starling sat watch outside the tent by the fire, her harp nestled in her lap. I started to go past her with a nod, then halted to peer at her harp. With a delighted smile, she held it up for my inspection.

The Fool had outdone himself. There was no gilt or curlicues, no inlays of ivory or ebony such as some would say set a harp apart. Instead there was only the silken gleam of curving wood, and that subtle carving that highlighted the best of the wood's grain. I could not look at it without wanting to touch it and hold it. The wood drew the hand to it. The firelight danced upon it.

Kettle stopped to stare also. She folded her lips tightly. 'No caution. It will be the death of him someday,' she said ominously. She then preceded me into the tent.

Despite my long nap earlier, I sank into sleep almost as soon as I lay down. I do not think I had slept long before I became aware of a stealthy noise outside. I Wit-quested toward it. Men.

Four. No, five of them, moving softly up the hillside toward the hut. I could know little more about them than that they came in stealth, like hunters. Somewhere in a dim room, Burrich sat up soundlessly. He rose barefoot and crossed the hut to Molly's bed. He knelt by the side of it, then touched her arm softly.

'Burrich?' She caught her breath on his name, then waited in wonder.

'Make no sound,' he breathed. 'Get up. Put on your shoes and wrap Nettle well, but try not to wake her. Someone is outside, and I do not think they mean us well.'

I was proud of her. She asked no questions, but sat up immediately. She pulled her dress on over her nightgown and thrust her feet into her shoes. She folded up the bedding around Nettle until she looked like little more than a bundle of blankets. The baby did not wake.

Meanwhile Burrich had drawn on his own boots and taken up a short sword. He motioned Molly toward the shuttered window. 'If I tell you to, go out that window with Nettle. But not unless I say to. I think there are five of them.'

Molly nodded in the firelight. She drew her belt knife and stood between her child and danger.

Burrich stood to one side of the door. The entire night seemed to pass as they waited silently for their attackers to come.

The bar was in place, but it had little meaning on such an old door frame. Burrich let them slam into it twice, then, as it started to give, he kicked it out of its brackets, so that on their next onslaught the door was flung wide. Two men came staggering in, surprised at the sudden lack of resistance. One fell, the other fell over the first, and Burrich had put his sword in and out of both of them before the third man was in the door.

The third man was a big man, red-headed and red-bearded. He came in the door with a roar, trampling right over the two injured men who squirmed under his boots. He carried a long sword, a lovely weapon. His size and blade gave him almost twice Burrich's reach. Behind him, a stout man bellowed, 'In the name of the King, we've come for the Wit-Bastard's whore! Put down your weapon and stand aside.'

He'd have been wiser not to rouse Burrich's anger any brighter than it was. Almost casually, Burrich dropped his blade to finish one of the men on the floor, and then brought the blade back up inside Red-beard's guard. Red-beard retreated, trying to get space for the advantage of his blade. Burrich had no choice but to follow him, for if the man reached a place where he could swing freely, Burrich would have small chance. The stout man and a woman immediately surged into the door. Burrich spared a glance for them. 'Molly! As I told you!'

Molly was already by the window, clutching Nettle who had begun to wail in fear. She leaped to a chair, snatched the shutters open, and got one leg out the window. Burrich was busying Red-beard when the woman dashed behind him and sank her knife into his lower back. Burrich cried out hoarsely, and frantically parried the longer blade. As Molly got her other leg over the window sill and began to drop outside, the stout man leaped across the room and snatched Nettle from her arms. I heard Molly's shriek of terror and fury.

Then she ran away into the darkness.

Disbelief. I could feel Burrich's disbelief as plainly as my own. The woman pulled her knife from his back and lifted it to strike again. He banished his pain with anger, spun to cut her a slash across her chest and then turned back to Red-beard. But Red-beard had stepped back. His sword was still at the ready but he stood motionless as the stout man said, 'We've got the child. Drop your sword or the baby dies here and now.' He darted his eyes at the woman clutching at her chest. 'Get after the woman. Now!'

She glared at him, but went without a murmur. Burrich did not even watch her go. He had eyes only for the wailing babe in the stout man's arms. Red-beard grinned as the tip of Burrich's weapon slowly dropped toward the floor. 'Why?' Burrich asked in consternation. 'What have we ever done, that you attack us and threaten to kill my daughter?'

The stout man looked down at the red-faced baby screaming in his arms. 'She's not yours,' he sneered. 'She's the Wit-Bastard's bastard. We have it on the best authority.' He lifted Nettle high as if he would dash her against the floor. He stared at Burrich. Burrich made an incoherent sound, half-fury, half-plea. He dropped his sword. By the door, the injured man groaned and tried to sit up.

'She's only a tiny baby,' Burrich said hoarsely. As if it were my own, I knew the warmth of the blood running down Burrich's back and hip. 'Let us go. You are mistaken. She's my own blood, I tell you, and no threat to your king. Please. I have gold. I'll take you to it. But let us go.'

Burrich, who would have stood and spat and fought to the death, dropped his sword and pleaded for the sake of my child. Red-beard roared out his laughter, but Burrich did not even turn to it. Still laughing, the man stepped to the table and casually lit the branch of candles there. He lifted the light to survey the dishevelled room. Burrich could not take his eyes off Nettle. 'She's mine,' he said quietly, almost desperately.

'Stop your lies,' the stout man said disdainfully. 'She's the Wit-Bastard's get. As tainted as he was.'

'That's right. She is.'

All eyes turned to the door. Molly stood there, very pale, breathing hard. Her right hand was reddened with blood. She clutched to her chest a large wooden box. An ominous humming came from it. 'The bitch you sent after me is dead,' Molly said harshly. 'As you will soon be, if you don't put down your weapons and free my child and man.' The stout man grinned incredulously. Red-beard lifted his sword.

Her voice shook only slightly as she added, 'The child is Witted, of course. As am I. My bees will not harm us. But injure one of us, and they will rise up and follow you and give you no quarter. You shall die of a million burning stings. Think your swords will be of much use against my Wit-bees?' She looked from face to face, her eyes flashing with anger and her threat as she clutched the heavy wooden hive box to her. One bee escaped it, to buzz angrily about the room. Red-beard's eyes followed it, even as he exclaimed, 'I don't believe it!'

Burrich's eyes were measuring the distance to his sword as Molly asked softly, almost coyly, 'Don't you?' She smiled oddly as she lowered the hive to the floor. Her eyes met Red-beard's as she lifted the lid of the box. She reached in and even as the stout man gasped aloud, she drew out her hand, gloved with moving bees. She closed the lid of the hive and then stood. She looked down at the bees coating her hand and said quietly, 'The one with the red beard, little ones.' Then she held her hand out as if offering them as a gift.

It took a moment, but as each bee took flight, it unerringly sought out Red-beard. He flinched as first one and then another buzzed past him, and then came back, circling. 'Call them back or we kill the child!' he cried out suddenly. He batted at them ineffectually with the branch of candles he held.

Molly instead stooped suddenly and heaved up the whole hive as high as she could. 'You'll kill her anyway!' she cried out, her voice breaking on the words. She gave the hive a shake, and the agitated humming of the bees became a roar. 'Little ones, they would kill my child! When I set you free, avenge us!' She raised the hive higher yet in her arms, preparatory to smashing it to the floor. The injured man at her feet groaned loudly.

'Hold!' cried the stout man. 'I'll give you your child!'

Molly froze. All could see that she could not hold the weight of the hive box much longer. There was strain in her voice but she calmly directed, 'Give my baby to my man. Let them both come to me. Or you shall all die, most certainly and most horribly.' The stout man looked uncertainly at Red-beard. Candles in one hand and sword in the other, Red-beard had retreated from the table, but the bees still buzzed confusedly about him. His efforts to slap them away only seemed to make them more determined. 'King Regal will kill us do we fail!'

'Then die from my bees instead,' Molly suggested. 'There are hundreds of bees in here,' she added in a low voice. Her tone was almost seductive as she offered, 'They will get inside your shirts and the legs of your trousers. They will cling to your hair as they sting. They will crawl into your ears to sting, and up your noses. And when you scream, they will crowd into your mouth, dozens of humming, fuzzy bodies, to sting your tongue until it will not fit inside your mouth. You will die choking on them!'

Her description seemed to decide them. The stout man crossed the room to Burrich, thrust the still-screaming babe into his arms. Red-beard glared but said nothing. Burrich took Nettle, but did not neglect to stoop and seize up his sword as well. Molly glared at Red-beard. 'You. Get over there beside him. Burrich. Take Nettle outside. Take her to where we picked mint yesterday. If they force me to act, I do not wish her to see it. It might make her fear the very bees who are her servants.'

Burrich obeyed. Of all the things I had witnessed that night, that seemed to me the most amazing. Once he was outside, Molly backed slowly toward the door. 'Do not follow,' she warned them. 'My Wit-bees will be keeping watch for me, right outside the door.' She gave the hive a final shake. The roaring hum increased and several more bees escaped into the room, buzzing angrily. The stout man stood frozen, but Red-beard lifted his sword as if it would defend him. The man on the floor gave an incoherent cry and scrabbled away from her as Molly backed outside. She dragged the door shut behind her, then leaned the hive against it. She took the lid off the hive and then kicked it before she turned and ran off into the night. 'Burrich!' she called quietly. 'I'm coming.' She did not go toward the road, but off toward the woods. She did not look back.

'Come away, Fitz.' It was no Skilling, but Verity's soft voice close by me. 'You have seen them safe. Watch no more, lest others see with your eyes and know where they go. It is better if you do not know yourself. Come away.'

I opened my eyes to the dimness inside the tent. Not only Verity, but Kettle sat beside me. Kettle's mouth was set in a flat line of disapproval. Verity's face was stern, but understanding was also there. He spoke before I could. 'Did I believe you had sought that, I would be most angry with you. Now I say to you plainly. It is better if you know nothing of them. Nothing at all. Had you heeded me when I first advised you of that, none of them would have been threatened as they were tonight.'

'You both were watching?' I asked quietly. For an instant, I was touched. They both cared that much for my child.

'She is my heir, too,' Verity pointed out relentlessly. 'Do you think I could stand by and do nothing if they had injured her?' He shook his head at me. 'Stay away from them, Fitz. For all our sakes. Do you understand?'

I nodded my head. His words could not distress me. I had already decided I would choose not to know where Molly and

Burrich took Nettle. But not because she was Verity's heir. Kettle and Verity stood and left the tent. I flung myself back into my blankets. The Fool, who had been propped on one elbow, lay down also. 'I will tell you tomorrow,' I told him. He nodded mutely, his eyes huge in his pale face. Then he lay back down. I think he went to sleep. I stared up into darkness. Nighteyes came to lie beside me.

He would protect your cub as his own, he pointed out quietly. *That is pack.*

He meant the words for comfort. I did not need them. Instead I reached to rest a hand on his ruff. *Did you see how she stood and faced them down?* I demanded with pride.

A most excellent bitch, Nighteyes agreed.

I felt I had not slept at all when Starling woke the Fool and me for our watch. I came out of the tent stretching and yawning, and suspecting that keeping watch was not really a necessity. But the last shard of night was pleasantly mild and Starling had left meat broth simmering at the fire's edge. I was halfway through a mug when the Fool finally followed me out.

'Starling showed me her harp last night,' I said by way of greeting.

He smirked with satisfaction. ' "A crude bit of work. Ah, this was but one of his early efforts," they shall say of it some day,' he added with strained modesty.

'Kettle said you have no caution.'

'No, I have not. Fitz. What do we do here?'

'Me? What I'm told. When my watch is over, I'm off to the hills, to gather broom twigs. So that I can sweep the rock chips out of Verity's way.'

'Ah. Now there's lofty work for a Catalyst. And what shall a Prophet do, do you suppose?'

'You might prophesy when that dragon will be finished. I fear we shall think of nothing else until it is done.'

The Fool was shaking his head minutely.

'What?' I demanded.

'I do not feel we were called here to make brooms and harps. This feels like a lull to me, my friend. The lull before the storm.'

'Now there's a cheery thought,' I told him glumly. But privately I wondered if he might not be right.

'Are you going to tell me what went on last night?'

When my account was finished, the Fool sat grinning. 'A resourceful lass, that one,' he observed proudly. Then he cocked his head at me. 'Think you the baby will be Witted? Or be able to Skill?'

I had never stopped to consider it. 'I hope not,' I said immediately. And then wondered at my own words.

Dawn had scarcely broken before both Verity and Kettle arose. They each drank a mug of broth standing, and carried off dried meat as they headed back up to the dragon. Kettricken had also come out of Verity's tent. Her eyes were hollow and defeat was in the set of her mouth. She had but half a mug of broth before setting it aside. She went back into the tent and returned with a blanket fashioned into a carry-sack.

'Firewood,' she replied flatly to my raised eyebrow.

'Then Nighteyes and I may as well go with you. I need to gather broom twigs and a stick. And he needs to do something besides sleep and grow fat.'

And you fear to go off in the woods without me.

If sows like that abound in these woods, you are absolutely correct. Perhaps Kettricken would bring her bow?

But even as I turned to make the suggestion, she was ducking back into the tent to fetch it. 'In case we meet another pig,' she told me as she came out.

But it was an uneventful expedition. Outside the quarry, the countryside was hilly and pleasant. We stopped at the stream to drink and wash. I saw the flash of a tiny fingerling in the water, and the wolf immediately wanted to fish. I told him I would after I had finished gathering my broom. So he came at my heels, but reluctantly. I gathered my broom twigs and found a long straight branch for a handle. Then we filled Kettricken's carry-sack with wood, which I insisted on bearing so her hands could be free for her bow. On the way back to camp, we stopped at the stream. I looked for a place where plants overhung the bank, and it did not take us long to find one. We then spent far longer than I had intended in tickling for fish. Kettricken had never seen it done before, but after some impatience, she caught the trick of it. They were a kind of trout I had not seen before, tinged with pink along their bellies. We caught ten, and I cleaned them there, with Nighteyes snapping up the entrails as quickly as I gutted them. Kettricken threaded them onto a willow stick, and we returned to camp.

I had not realized how much the quiet interlude had soothed my spirits until we came in sight of the black pillar guarding the mouth of the quarry. It seemed more ominous than ever, like some dark scolding finger lifted to warn me that, indeed, this might be the lull but the storm was coming. I gave a small shudder as I passed it. My Skill-sensitivity seemed to be growing again. The pillar radiated controlled power alluringly. Almost against my will, I stopped to study the characters incised on it.

'Fitz? Are you coming?' Kettricken called back to me, and only then did I realize how long I had been gawking. I hastened to catch up with them, and rejoined them just as they were passing the girl on a dragon.

I had deliberately avoided that spot since the Fool had touched her. Now I glanced up guiltily to where the silver fingerprint still shone against her flawless skin. 'Who were you, and why did you make such a sad carving?' I asked her. But her stone eyes only looked at me pleadingly above her tear-specked cheeks.

'Maybe she could not finish her dragon,' Kettricken speculated. 'See how its hind feet and tail are still trapped in the stone? Maybe that's why it's so sad.'

'She must have carved it sad to begin with, don't you see? Whether or not she finished it, the upper portion would be the same.'

Kettricken looked at me in amusement. 'You still don't believe that Verity's dragon will fly when it is finished? I do. Of course, I have very little else to believe in any more. Very little.'

I had been going to tell her I thought it a minstrel's tale for a child, but her final words shut my mouth.

Back at the dragon, I bound my broom together and went at my sweeping with a vengeance. The sun was high in a bright blue sky with a light and pleasant breeze. It was altogether a lovely day and for a time I forgot all else in my simple chore.

Kettricken unloaded her firewood and soon left to get more. Nighteyes followed at her heels, and I noticed with approval that Starling and the Fool hastened after her with carry-sacks of their own. With the rock chips and dust cleared away from the dragon, I could see more of the progress Verity and Kettle had made. The black stone of the dragon's back was so shiny it almost reflected the blue of the sky. I observed as much to Verity, not really expecting an answer. His mind and heart were focused entirely on the dragon. On all other topics his mind seemed vague and wandering, but when he spoke to me of his dragon and the fashioning of it he was very much King Verity.

A few moments later, he rocked back on his heels from his crouch beside the dragon's foot. He stood and ran a silver hand tentatively over the dragon's back. I caught my breath, for in the wake of his hand there was suddenly colour. A rich turquoise, with every scale edged in silver, followed the sweep of Verity's finger. The hue shimmered there for an instant, then faded. Verity made a small sound of satisfaction. 'When the dragon is full, the colour will stay,' he told me. Without thinking, I reached a hand toward the dragon, but Verity abruptly shouldered me aside. 'Don't touch him,' he warned me, almost jealously. He must have seen the shock on my face, for he looked rueful. 'It's not safe for you to touch him any more, Fitz. He is too . . .' His voice trailed off, and his eyes went afar in search of a word. Then he apparently forgot all about me, for he crouched back to his work on the creature's foot.

There is nothing like being treated like a child to provoke one to act that way. I finished the last of my sweeping, set my broom aside, and wandered off. I was not overly surprised when I found myself staring up at the girl on a dragon again. I had come to think of the statue as 'Girl-on-a-Dragon', for they did not seem like separate entities to me. Once more I climbed up on the dais beside her, once more I felt the swirling of her Wit-life. It lifted like fog and reached toward me hungrily. So much entrapped misery. 'There is nothing I can do for you,' I told her sadly, and almost felt that she responded to my words. It was too saddening to remain close to her for long. But as I clambered down, I noticed that which alarmed me. Around one of the dragon's hind feet, someone had been chiselling at the miring stone. I stooped down for a closer inspection. The chips and dust had been cleared from the cut, but the edges of it were new and sharp. The Fool, I told myself, was truly without caution. I stood with the intention of seeking him out immediately.

FitzChivalry. Return to me at once, please.

I sighed to myself. Probably more stone chips to sweep. For this I must be away from Molly, while she fended for herself. As I walked back to the dragon, I indulged myself in forbidden thoughts of her. I wondered if they had found a place to shelter, and how badly Burrich was hurt. They had fled with little more than the clothes on their backs. How would they survive? Or had Regal's men attacked them again? Had they dragged her and the baby off to Tradeford? Did Burrich lie dead in the dirt somewhere?

Do you truly believe that could happen and you not know of it? Besides. She seemed more than capable of caring for herself and the child. And Burrich for that matter. Stop thinking of them. And stop indulging in self-pity. I have a task for you.

I returned to the dragon and picked up my broom. I had been sweeping for some minutes before Verity seemed to notice me. 'Ah, Fitz, there you are.' He stood, stretched, arching his back to take the ache out of it. 'Come with me.'

I followed him down to the campfire where he busied himself for a moment by putting water to heat. He picked up a piece of the dry-cooked meat, looked at it, and said sadly, 'What I would not give for one piece of Sara's fresh bread. Oh, well.' He turned to me. 'Sit down, Fitz, I want to talk to you. I've been giving much thought to all you told me, and I've an errand for you.'

I sat down slowly on a stone by the fire, shaking my head to myself. One moment he made no sense at all to me; the next he sounded just like the man who had been my mentor for so long. He gave me no time to mull my thoughts.

'Fitz, you visited the place of the dragons, on your way here. You told me that you and the wolf sensed life in them. Wit-life, you called it. And that one, Realder's dragon, seemed almost to awaken when you called him by name.'

'I get the same sense of life from the girl on the dragon, in the quarry,' I agreed with him.

Verity shook his head sadly. 'Poor thing, nothing can be done for her, I fear. She persisted in trying to keep her human shape, and thus she held back from filling her dragon. There she is and likely to remain for all time. I have taken to heart her warning; at least her error has done that much good. When I fill the dragon, I shall hold nothing back. It would be a poor ending, would it not, to have come so far and sacrificed so much, to end only with a mired dragon? That mistake, at least, I shall not make.' He bit off a chunk of the dry meat and chewed it thoughtfully.

I kept silent. He had lost me again. Sometimes all I could do was wait until his own thoughts brought him back to some topic where he made sense. I noticed he had a new smudge of silver at the top of his brow, as if he had unthinkingly wiped sweat away. He swallowed. 'Are there any tea-herbs left?' he asked, and then added, 'I want you to return to the dragons. I want you to see if you can use your Wit with your Skill to awaken them. When I was there, try as I might, I could detect no life in any of them. I feared they had slumbered too long, and starved themselves to death, feeding only on their own dreams until nothing was left.'

Starling had left a handful of wilted nettles and mint. I gingerly coaxed them into a pot then spilled the heated water over them. While they steeped, I sorted my thoughts.

'You want me to use the Wit and Skill to awake the dragon statues. How?'

Verity shrugged. 'I don't know. Despite all Kestrel has told me, there are still great gaps in my knowledge of the Skill. When Galen stole Solicity's books, and ceased all training for Chivalry and me, it was a master stroke against us. I still keep coming back to that. Did he even then plot to secure the throne for his half-brother, or was he merely greedy for power? We will never know.'

I spoke then of a thing I had never before voiced. 'There is something I do not understand. Kettle says that your killing Carrod with the Skill left you injured yourself. Yet you drained Galen, and seemed to suffer nothing from it. Nor did Serene and Justin seem to take ill from draining the King.'

'Draining off another's Skill is not the same as killing one with a blast of Skill.' He gave a brief snort of bitter laughter. 'Having done both, I well know the difference. In the end, Galen chose to die rather than surrender all his power to me. I suspect that my father made the same choice. I also suspect that he did so to keep from them the knowledge of where I was. What secrets Galen died protecting, we now have an inkling.' He looked at the meat in his hand, set it aside. 'But what concerns us now is waking the Elderings. You look about us and see a lovely day, Fitz. I see fair seas and a clean wind to bring Red Ships to our shores. While I chip and scrape and labour, Six Duchies folk die or are Forged. Not to mention that Regal's troops harry and burn the Mountain villages along the border. My own queen's father rides to battle to protect his folk from my brother's armies. How that rankles within me! Could you rouse the dragons to their defence, they could take flight now.'

'I am reluctant to undertake a task when I do not know just what it demands,' I began, but Verity stopped me with a grin.

'It seems to me that just yesterday that was what you were begging to do, FitzChivalry.'

He had me. 'Nighteyes and I will set out tomorrow morning,' I offered.

He frowned at me. 'I see no reason to delay. It is no long journey for you, but merely a step through the pillar. But the wolf cannot pass through the stone. He will have to stay here. And I would that you went now.'

He told me so calmly to go without my wolf. I would sooner have gone stark naked. 'Now? As in *immediately?*'

'Why not? You can be there in a matter of minutes. See what you can do. If you are successful, I shall know it. If not, come back to us tonight, through the pillar. We will have lost nothing by trying.'

'Do you think the coterie is no longer a danger?'

'They are no greater a danger to you there than here. Now go.'

'Should I wait for the others to return and let them know where I have gone?'

'I will tell them myself. FitzChivalry. Will you do this thing for me?'

There could be only one answer to such a question. 'I will. I go now.' I hesitated a final time. 'I am not sure how to use the pillar.'

'It is no more complicated than a door, Fitz. Place your hand on it, and it draws on the Skill within you. Here, this symbol.' He sketched with a finger in the dust. 'That is the one for the place of the dragons. Simply put your hand on it and walk through. This,' another sketch in the dust, 'is the sign for the quarry. It will bring you back here.' He lifted his dark eyes to regard me steadily. Was there a test in those eyes?

'I shall be back this evening,' I promised him.

'Good. Luck ride with you,' he told me.

And that was it. I rose and left the fire behind me, walking toward the pillar. I passed Girl-on-a-Dragon and tried not to be distracted by her. Somewhere off in the woods, the others were gathering firewood while Nighteyes ranged all around them.

Are you really going without me?

I shall not be gone long, my brother.

Shall I come back and wait for you by the pillar?

No, watch over the Queen for me, if you would.

With pleasure. She shot a bird for me today.

I sensed his admiration and sincerity. What finer thing than a bitch who kills efficiently?

A bitch who shares well.

See that you save some for me, as well.

You can have the fish, he assured me magnanimously.

I looked up at the black pillar that now loomed before me. There was the symbol. As simple as a door, Verity had said. Touch the symbol and pass through. Perhaps. But my stomach was full of butterflies and it was all I could do to lift my hand and press it to the shining black stone. My palm met the symbol and I felt a cold tug of Skill. I stepped through.

I went from bright sunlight to cool dappling shade. I stepped away from the tall black pillar and onto deeply grassed earth. The air was heavy with moisture and plant smells. Branches that had been beaded with leaf buds the last time I had been here were now lush with foliage. A chorus of insects and frogs greeted me. The forest around me swarmed with life. After the empty silence of the quarry, it was almost overwhelming. I stood for a time, just adjusting to it.

Cautiously I lowered my Skill walls and reached warily out. Save for the pillar behind me, I had no sense of Skill in use. I relaxed a bit. Perhaps Verity's blasting of Carrod had done more than he realized. Perhaps they feared to challenge him directly now. I warmed myself with that thought as I set off through the luxuriant growth.

I was soon soaked to the knee. It was not that there was water underfoot, but that the riotous growth of grasses and reeds that I waded through were laden with moisture. Overhead twining vines and hanging leaves dripped. I did not mind. It seemed refreshing after the bare stone and dust of the quarry. What had been a rudimentary pathway the last time we were here was now a narrow corridor through leaning, sprawling plant-life. I came to a shallow gurgling stream, and took a handful of peppery cress from it to nibble as I walked. I promised I would take some back to camp with me come nightfall, and then recalled myself to my mission. Dragons. Where were the dragons?

They had not moved, though greenery grew taller around them than it had been. I spotted a lightning-blasted stump I remembered, and from there found Realder's dragon. I had already decided he might be the most promising one to start with, for I had definitely felt a strong Wit-life in him. As if it could make some difference, I took a few minutes to clear him of vines and wet, clinging grasses. As I did so, one thing struck me. The way the sleeping creature was sprawled upon the earth followed the contour of the ground beneath him. It did not look like a statue carved and then set in place here. It looked like a living creature that had flung itself down to rest and never moved again.

I tried to force belief on myself. These were the very Elderlings that rose to King Wisdom's call. They flew like great birds to the coast and there they defeated the Raiders and drove them from our shores. From the skies they fell on the ships, driving the crews mad with terror or oversetting the ships with the great wind from their wings. And they would again, could we but wake them.

'I shall try,' I said aloud, and then repeated, 'I shall wake them,' and sought to have no doubt in my voice. I walked slowly about

Realder's dragon, trying to decide how to begin. From the wedge-shaped reptilian head to the barbed tail, this was one stone dragon that was all of the stuff of legend. I reached an admiring hand to run it over the gleaming scales. I could sense the Wit curling lazily through it like smoke. I willed myself to believe in the life in it. Could any artist have contrived so perfect a rendering? There were knobs of bone at the apex of its wings, similar to those on a gander. I did not doubt that it could clout a man down with it. The barbs of its tail were still sharp and nasty. I could imagine it lashing through rigging or rowers, shearing, slicing, snagging. 'Realder,' I cried aloud to it. 'Realder!'

I felt no response. Not a stirring of Skill, not even much difference in its Wit. Well, I told myself I had not expected it to be that easy. In the next few hours, I tried every way I could imagine to wake that beast. I pressed my face to its scaly cheek, and quested into that stone as deeply as I could probe. I got less response from it than an earthworm would have given me. I stretched my body out beside that cold stone lizard, and willed myself to oneness with it. I sought to bond with that lazy stirring of Wit within it. I radiated affection toward it. I commanded it strenuously. Eda help me, I even sought to threaten it with dire consequences if it did not arise to obey my command. It all availed me nothing. I began to clutch at straws. I recalled the Fool to it. Nothing. I reached back for the Skill-dream the Fool and I had shared. I brought into my mind every detail of the woman in the rooster crown that I could recall. I offered her to the dragon. There was no response. I tried basic things. Verity said perhaps they had starved. I visualized pools of cool, sweet water, fat, silvery fish there for the devouring. I Skill-visualized Realder's dragon being devoured by a greater one, and offered it that picture. No response.

I ventured to reach for my king. *If there is life in these stones, it is too small and sunken for me to reach.*

It troubled me a little that Verity did not even bother to reply. But perhaps he too had seen this as a desperation measure, with small chance of success. I left Realder's dragon and wandered for a time, from stone beast to stone beast. I quested amongst them, looking for any that might have a stronger flicker of Wit-life to them. Once, I thought I had found one, but a closer check showed me that a fieldmouse had made its home under the dragon's chest.

I chose a dragon antlered like a buck and tried again every tactic I had tried on Realder's dragon, with as little result. By then, the daylight was waning. As I picked my way through the trees back to the pillar, I wondered if Verity had truly expected any sort of success. Doggedly, I moved from dragon to dragon on my way back to the pillar, giving each one a last effort. It was probably what saved me. I straightened from one, thinking I felt a strong Wit-life coming from the next one. But when I got to him, the hulking winged boar with his curving razor tusks, I perceived the Wit was coming from beyond him. I lifted my eyes and peered through the trees, rather expecting to see a deer or wild pig. Instead I saw a man with a drawn sword standing with his back to me.

I folded up behind the boar. My mouth was suddenly dry, my heart hammering. He was neither Verity nor the Fool. That much I knew in an instant's glance. He was someone shorter than I, sandy-haired, and holding a sword as if he knew how to wield it. Someone dressed in gold and brown. Not bulky Burl, nor slender dark Will. Someone else, but Regal's.

In a moment all became clear to me. How stupid could I have been? I had destroyed Will and Burl's men, horses and supplies. What else would they do, but Skill to Regal that they needed more? With the constant skirmishing along the Mountain borders it would be no trick for another raiding party to slip through, bypass Jhaampe and travel up the Skill road. The slide area we had crossed was a formidable barrier but not an insurmountable one. Risking his men's lives was something Regal was proficient at. I wondered how many had attempted the crossing and how many had survived. I was sure now that Will and Burl were once more comfortably provisioned.

Then a more chilling thought struck me. He might be Skilled. There was nothing to stop Will from training others. He had all Solicity's books and scrolls to draw on, and while Skill-potential was not common, it was not excessively rare. In moments my imagination had multiplied the man to an army, all at least marginally Skilled, all fanatically loyal to Regal. I leaned against the stone boar, trying to breathe softly despite the fear coursing through me. For a moment, despair had me in thrall. I had finally realized the immensity of the resources that Regal could turn against us. This was no private vendetta between us; this was a king, with a king's armies and powers, out to exterminate those he had branded as traitors. The only thing that had bound Regal's hands before was the possible embarrassment if it were discovered that Verity had not died. Now, back in this remote area, he had nothing to fear. He could use his soldiers to do away with his brother and nephew, his sister-in-law, with all witnesses. Then his coterie could dispose of the soldiers.

These thoughts passed through my mind the way lightning illuminates the blackest night. In one flash, I suddenly saw all details. In the next moment, I knew I must get to the pillar and back to the quarry to warn Verity. If it were not already too late.

I felt myself calm as soon as I had a goal in mind. I considered Skilling to Verity, and quickly rejected the idea. Until I knew my enemy better, I would not risk exposing myself to him. I found myself seeing it as if it were Kettle's game. Stones to capture or destroy. The man was between me and the pillar. That was to be expected. What I now had to discover was if there were others as well. I drew my own belt knife; a sword was no weapon to use in dense brush. I took a deep steadying breath, and slipped away from the boar.

I had a rough familiarity with the area. It served me in good stead as I moved from dragon to tree trunk to old stump. Before darkness was complete, I knew there were three men and that they seemed to be guarding the pillar. I did not think they had come here to hunt me, but rather to keep anyone save Regal's coterie from using the pillar. I had found the tracks of their passage from the Skill road; they were fresh, the men newly arrived. I could then rely that I knew the lay of the land better than they did. I decided I would believe them unSkilled, as they had come by the trail rather than by the pillar. But they were probably very able soldiers. I also decided I should believe Will and Burl might be very close by. Able to come through the pillar at a moment's notice. For that reason I kept my Skill walls high and tight. And I waited. When I did not return, Verity would know something was wrong. I did not think he would be so unwary as to come through the pillar in search of me. In truth, I did not think he would leave his dragon for that long. This was my own fix to get myself out of.

As darkness fell, insects came out. Stinging, biting, swarming insects by the hundreds, and always the one who insisted on humming right by my ear. Ground mists began to rise, damping my clothes to my body. The guards had made a small fire. I smelled hearth-cakes cooking and found myself wondering if I could kill them before they had eaten them all. I grinned hard to myself and ghosted closer. Night and a fire and food usually meant talk. These men spoke little and most of it was in low tones. They did not care for this duty. The long black road had driven some men mad. But tonight it was not the long way they had come, but the stone dragons themselves that bothered them. I also heard enough to confirm what I had guessed. There were three men guarding this pillar. There were a full dozen guarding the one at the plaza where the Fool had had his vision. The main body of soldiers had pushed on toward the quarry. The coterie was seeking to close off escape routes for Verity.

I felt a bit of relief that it would take them fully as long to get there as it had taken our party. For tonight, at least, Verity and the others were in no danger of attack. But it was only a matter of time. My resolution to get back through the pillar as swiftly as possible hardened. I had no intention of fighting them. That left killing them by ambush, one by one, a feat I doubted even Chade could have accomplished. Or creating enough of a diversion to draw them off long enough for me to make a dash for the pillar.

I slipped well away from the men, to where I judged I was out of earshot and proceeded to gather dry firewood. It was not an easy task in such a lush and verdant place, but I finally had a respectable armful. My plan was simple. I told myself it would either work or it wouldn't. I doubted I would get a second chance; they would be too cautious for that.

I considered where the symbol for the quarry was on the pillar and worked my way around to the dragons that were on the opposite side of it. Of the dragons, I chose the fierce-looking fellow with ear tufts that I had remarked upon on my first visit here. He would cast a fine shadow. I cleared a space behind him of wet grass and leaves and set my fire there. I had only enough fuel for a small fire, but I hoped I would not need more than that. I wanted enough light and smoke to be mysterious without enlightening. I got the fire going well, then slipped away from it in the darkness. Belly in the grass, I worked my way as close to the pillar as I dared. Now I only need wait until the guards noticed my fire. I hoped at least one man would go to investigate it, and that the other two would watch where he had gone. Then a noiseless dash, a slap to the pillar, and I'd be gone.

Save that the guards did not notice my fire. From my vantage, it seemed glaringly obvious. There was rising smoke and a rosy glow through the trees, partially outlining the dragon's silhouette. I had hoped that would pique their interest. Instead it was blocking my fire too well. I decided a few well-placed rocks would draw their attention to my fire. My groping hands found only lush plant life growing in thick loam. After an interminable wait, I realized my fire was going out, and the guards had noticed it not at all. Once more I slipped out of earshot. Once more I gathered dry sticks in the dark. Then my nose as much as my eyes guided me back to my smouldering fire.

My brother, you are long gone. Is all well? There was anxiety in Nighteyes' faint thought.

I am hunted. Be still. I shall come as soon as I can. I pushed the wolf gently from my thoughts and stole through the dark toward my dwindling fire.

I refuelled it and waited for it to catch. I was just slipping away from it when I heard their voices raised in speculation. I do not think I was careless. It was but an ill twist of luck that as I moved from the cover of a dragon to that of a tree, one guard lifted his torch high, throwing my shadow into stark relief. 'There! A man!' one shouted, and two of them charged out at me. I eeled away through the wet underbrush.

I heard one trip and fall, cursing, in a patch of vines, but the second was a swift and agile fellow. He was on my heels in an instant, and I swear I felt the wind from the first sweep of his sword. I lunged away from it, and found myself half leaping, half falling over the stone boar. I clipped a knee painfully on his rocky back and fell to the earth on the other side of him. Instantly I scrabbled to my feet. My pursuer leaped forward, swinging a mighty blow that surely would have cloven me in two if he had not caught his leg on one curving, razor tusk. He tripped and fell squarely, impaling himself on the second tusk where it thrust up like a scimitar from the boar's red maw. The sound the man made was not a large one. I saw him begin to struggle to rise, but the curve of the tusk was hooked inside him. I leaped to my feet, mindful of the second man who had been pursuing me, and fled into the dark. Behind me rose a long cry of pain.

I kept my wits enough to circle. I had nearly reached the pillar when I felt a questing twist of Skill. I recalled the last time I had felt such a thing. Was Verity himself under attack, back at the quarry? One man still guarded the pillar, but I decided to risk his sword to get back to my king. I emerged from the trees, racing toward the pillar while the guard stared off toward my fire and the cries of the fallen man. Another tendril of Skill brushed me.

'No!' I cried out, 'Don't risk yourself!' as my king came through the pillar, notched grey sword clutched in his gleaming silver grip. He emerged behind the guard who had remained on post. My foolish cry had turned him toward the pillar, and he came at my king, sword lifted, even as his face betrayed his terror.

Verity in their firelight looked like a demon out of a tale. His face was splashed with silver from the careless touching of his hands, while his hands and arms gleamed as if made of polished silver. His gaunt face and ragged clothes, the utter blackness of his eyes would have terrified any man. I will have to give Regal's guard this: he stood his post, and caught the King's first blow and turned it. Or so he thought. It was an old trick of Verity's. Instead his blade wrapped the other. His cut should have severed the hand from the arm, but the dulled blade stopped at the bone. Nonetheless the man dropped his sword. As the man fell to his knees clutching at the gouting wound, Verity's sword swept in again, across his throat. I felt a second tremoring of Skill. The lone remaining guard came racing toward us from the trees. His eyes fixed on Verity and he cried out in terror. He halted where he stood. Verity took a step toward him.

'My king, enough! Let us leave!' I cried out. I did not want him to risk himself for me again.

Instead Verity glanced down at his sword. He frowned. Suddenly he grasped the blade in his left hand just below the hilt and drew it through his shining grip. I gasped at what I saw. The sword he brandished now gleamed and came to a perfect point. Even by torchlight, I could see the wavering ripples of the many-folded metal of the blade. The King glanced at me. 'I should have known I could do that.' He almost smiled. Then Verity lifted it to the other man's eyes. 'When you are ready,' he said quietly.

What happened next stunned me.

The soldier fell to his knees, casting his sword into the grass before him. 'My king. I know you, even if you do not know me.' Buck accent spoke plainly in his tumbling words. 'My lord, we were told that you were dead. Dead because your queen and the Bastard had conspired against you. Those were who we were told might be found here. It was half for that revenge that I came. I served you well at Buck my lord, and if you live, I serve my king still.'

Verity peered at him in the flickering torchlight. 'You're Tig, aren't you? Reaver's boy?'

The soldier's eyes widened that Verity recalled him. 'Tag my lord. Serving my king as my father did before me.' His voice shook a bit. His dark eyes never left the point of the sword Verity had levelled at him.

Verity lowered his blade. 'Do you speak truth, lad? Or simply seek to save your skin?'

The young soldier looked up at Verity and dared to smile. 'I have no need to fear. The prince I served would not strike down a kneeling, unarmed man. I dare say the King will not either.'

Perhaps no other words would have convinced Verity. Despite his weariness, he smiled. 'Go then, Tag. Go as swift as you may and as silent as you may, for those who have used you will kill you if they know you are true to me. Return to Buck. And on the way there, and when you get there, tell everyone that I shall be returning. That I shall bring my good and true queen with me, to sit the throne, and that my heir will claim it after me. And when you get to Buckkeep Castle, present yourself to my brother's wife. Tell the Lady Patience that I commend you to her service.'

'Yes, my king. King Verity?'

'What is it?'

'More troops are coming. We are but the vanguard . . .' He paused. He swallowed. 'I accuse no one of treachery, least of all your own brother. But . . .'

'Let it not concern you, Tag. What I have asked you to do is important to me. Go quickly and challenge no one on your way. But carry back those tidings as I have asked you.'

'Yes, my king.'

'Now,' Verity suggested.

And Tag rose, took up his sword and sheathed it, and strode off into the darkness.

Verity turned and his eyes shone with triumph. 'We can do it!' he told me quietly. He gestured me fiercely toward the pillar. I reached to palm the symbol and tumbled through as the Skill clutched at me. Verity came on my heels.

THIRTY-SEVEN

Feeding the Dragon

By midsummer of that final year, the Six Duchies situation had become desperate. Buckkeep Castle, so long avoided by the Raiders, came under sudden siege from them. They had possessed Antler Island and its watchtowers since midwinter. Forge, the first village to fall victim to the scourge that took its name, had long since become a watering stop for Red Ships. There had been for some time rumours of Outisland sailing ships anchoring off Scrim Island, including several sightings of the elusive 'White Ship'. For most of the spring, no ships had made passage either into or out of Buck harbour. This strangle of trade was felt not just in Buck, but in every trade village on the Buck, Bear and Vin Rivers. The Red Ships had become a sudden reality to the merchants and lords of Tilth and Farrow.

But at the high point of summer, the Red Ships came to Buckkeep Town. The Red Ships came in the dead of night after several weeks of deceptive quiet. The fighting was the savage defence of a cornered folk, but they were also a starved and beggared folk. Almost every wooden structure of the town was burned to the ground. It is estimated that only one quarter of the town's residents were able to flee up the steep hills to Buckkeep Castle. Although Lord Bright had endeavoured to refortify and supply the castle, the weeks of strangulation had taken their toll. The deep wells of Buckkeep Castle assured them a good supply of fresh water, but all other things were in scarce supply.

Catapults and other engines of war had been in place for decades to defend the mouth of the Buck River, but Lord Bright diverted them to the defence of Buckkeep Castle itself. Unchallenged, the Red Ships beat their way up the Buck River, carrying their war and Forging deep into the Six Duchies like a spreading poison following a vein to the heart.

At a time when Red Ships threatened Tradeford itself, the lords of

Farrow and Tilth were to discover that a great part of the Six Duchies armies had been sent far inland, to Blue Lake, and beyond, to the very borders of the Mountain Kingdom. The nobles of these duchies suddenly discovered that their own guardsmen were all that stood between them and death and ruin.

I emerged from the pillar into a circle of frantic people. The first thing to happen was that a wolf hit me full force in the chest, driving me backwards, so that as Verity emerged he all but fell over me.

I made her understand me, I made her know you were in danger and she made him go after you. I made her understand me, I made her understand me! Nighteyes was in a puppyish frenzy. He thrust his nose into my face, nipped at my nose, then flung himself to the ground beside me and half in my lap.

'He stirred a dragon! Not quite to wakening, but I felt one stir! We may yet wake them all!' This was Verity, laughing and shouting to the others these good tidings as he calmly stepped over us. He flourished his shining sword aloft as if to challenge the moon. I had no idea what he was talking about. I sat flat on the earth, staring around at them. The Fool looked wan and weary, Kettricken, ever a mirror to her king, smiled at his exultation. Starling looked at all of us with greedy minstrel eyes, memorizing every detail. And Kettle, her hands and arms silver to the elbow, knelt carefully beside me to ask, 'Are you all right, FitzChivalry?'

I looked at her magic-coated arms and hands. 'What have you done?' I asked her.

'Only what was necessary. Verity took me to the river in the city. Now our work will proceed more swiftly. What happened to you?'

I did not answer her. Instead I pinned Verity with a glare. 'You sent me off so I would not follow you! You knew I could not wake the dragons, but you wanted me out of the way!' I could not conceal the outrage and betrayal I felt.

Verity gave me one of his old grins, denying all regrets. 'We know one another very well, don't we?' was all he offered by way of apology. Then his grin grew wider. 'Yes, it was a fool's errand

I sent you on. But I was the fool, for you did it. You woke one, or stirred him at least.'

I shook my head at him.

'Yes, you did. You must have felt it, that rippling of Skill, just before I reached you. What did you do, how did you stir him?'

'A man died on the stone boar's tusks,' I said flatly. 'Perhaps that is how you rouse these dragons. With death.' I cannot explain the hurt I felt. He had taken what should have been mine and given it to Kettle. He owed that Skill-closeness to me, no other. Who else had come so far, given up so much for him? How could he deny me the carving of his dragon?

It was Skill-hunger, pure and simple, but I did not know it then. At that time, all I could feel was how perfectly linked he was with Kettle, and how firmly he repulsed me from joining that link. He walled me out as tightly as if I were Regal. I had forsaken my wife and child and crossed all of the Six Duchies to be of service to him, and now he turned me away. He should have taken me to the river, been beside me as I had that experience. I had never known myself capable of such jealousy. Nighteyes came back from frisking about Kettricken to push his head under my arm. I rubbed his throat and hugged him. He, at least, was mine.

She understood me, he repeated anxiously. *I made her understand, and she told him he must go.*

Kettricken, coming to stand beside me, said, 'I had the strongest feeling you needed help. It took much urging, but finally Verity left the dragon and went for you. Are you much hurt?'

I got to my feet slowly, dusting myself off. 'Only my pride, that my king would treat me as a child. He might have let me know he preferred Kettle's company.'

A flash of something in Kettricken's eyes made me recall to whom I spoke. But she hid her twin hurt well, saying only, 'A man was killed, you say?'

'Not by me. He fell on the stone boar's tusks in the dark and gutted himself. But I saw no stirring of dragons.'

'Not the death, but the spilled life,' Kettle said to Verity. 'That might be it. Like the scent of fresh meat rousing a dog starved near to death. They are hungry, my king, but not past rousing. Not if you find a way to feed them.'

'I like not the sound of that!' I exclaimed.

'It is not for us to like or dislike,' Verity said heavily. 'It is the nature of dragons. They must be filled, and life is what fills them. It must be given willingly to create one. But dragons will take what they need to sustain them, once they rise in flight. What had you supposed that King Wisdom offered them in return for defeating the Red Ships?'

Kettle pointed a scolding finger at the Fool. 'Pay heed to that, Fool and understand now why you are so weary. When you touched her with Skill, you linked with her. She draws you to her now, and you think you go out of pity. But she will take from you whatever she needs to rise. Even if it is your whole life.'

'No one is making any sense,' I declared. Then, as my own scattered wits returned to me, I exclaimed, 'Regal has sent soldiers. They are on the march here. They are no more than a few days away at most. I suspect they push themselves and travel swiftly. The men guarding the pillars are placed there to prevent Verity's escape.'

It was much later that night before I had it all sorted out. Kettle and Verity had indeed gone to the river, almost as soon as I left. They had used the pillar to get down to the city, and there they had laved Kettle's arms in the stuff and renewed the power in Verity's. Every glimpse of that silvering of her arms woke in me a Skill-hunger that was almost a lust. It was something I masked myself and attempted to hide from Verity. I do not believe he was deceived, but he did not force me to confront it. I masked my jealousy with other excuses. I told them both hotly it was only the purest luck they had not encountered the coterie there. Verity had calmly replied that he had known the risk and taken it. Somehow it hurt me all the more that even my anger left him so unmoved.

It had been on their return that they had discovered the Fool chipping at the stone that mired Girl-on-a-Dragon. He had cleared an area around one foot, and begun on the other. The foot itself remained a shapeless chunk of stone but the Fool insisted that he could feel the foot, intact inside it. He felt certain that all she wished from him was that he chop the dragon free of that which mired it. He had been shaking with exhaustion when they found him. Kettle had insisted he go right to bed. She had taken the last piece of often-boiled elfbark and ground it down fine, to make one last dose of tea for him. Despite the drug, he remained detached and weary, scarcely even asking a question as to what had happened to me. I felt deep uneasiness for him.

The news I had brought of Regal's men stirred everyone to action. After food, Verity sent Starling, the Fool, and the wolf to the mouth of the quarry, to keep watch there. I sat by the fire for a time, with a cold wet rag wrapped around my swollen and discoloured knee. Up on the dragon dais, Kettricken kept her fires burning, and Verity and Kettle worked the stone. Starling, in helping Kettle search for more elfbark, had discovered the carris seeds that Chade had give me. Kettle had appropriated them and brewed them up into a stimulant drink she and Verity were sharing. The noise of their work had taken on a frightening tempo.

They had also found the sunskirt seeds I had bought so long ago as a possible substitute for elfbark. With a sly grin, Starling asked me why I was carrying those. When I explained, she had snorted with laughter, and finally managed to explain they were regarded as an aphrodisiac. I recalled the herb-seller's words to me and shook my head to myself. A part of me saw the humour, but I could not find a smile.

After a time of sitting alone by the cook fire, I quested toward Nighteyes. *How goes it?*

A sigh. *The minstrel would rather be playing with her harp. The Scentless One would rather be chipping at that statue. And I would rather be hunting. If there is danger coming, it is a long way away.*

Let us hope it stays there. Keep watch, my friend.

I left the camp and gimped up the scree of stone to the dragon dais. Three of its feet were free now, and Verity worked on the final front foot. I stood for a time beside him, but he did not deign to notice me. Instead he went on chipping and scraping, and all the while muttered old nursery rhymes or drinking songs to himself. I limped past Kettricken listlessly tending her fires back to where Kettle was smoothing her hands over the dragon's tail. Her eyes were distant as she called for the scales, and then deepened their detail and added texture to them. Part of the tail also remained hidden in the stone. I started to lean on the thick portion of the tail to take weight off my bruised knee, but she immediately sat up and hissed at me. 'Don't do that! Don't touch him!'

I straightened away from him. 'I touched him before,' I said indignantly. 'And it did no harm.'

'That was before. He is much closer to completion now.' She lifted her eyes to mine. Even in the firelight, I could mark how thickly rock dust coated her features and clung to her eyelashes. She looked dreadfully tired and yet animated by some fierce energy. 'As close as you are to Verity, the dragon would reach for you. And you are not strong enough to say no. He would pull you in completely. That's how strong he is, how magnificently strong.' She all but crooned the last words as she stroked her hands again down the tail. For an instant, I saw a sheen of colour right behind their passage.

'Is anyone ever going to explain any of this to me?' I asked petulantly.

She gave me a bemused look. 'I try. Verity tries. But you of all people should know how wearisome words are. We try and try and try to tell you, and still your mind does not grasp it. It is not your fault. Words are not big enough. And it is too dangerous to include you in our Skilling now.'

'Will you be able to make me understand after the dragon is finished?'

She looked at me and something like pity crossed her face. 'FitzChivalry. My dear friend. When the dragon is finished? Rather say that when Verity and I are finished, the dragon will be begun.'

'I don't understand!' I snarled in frustration.

'But he told you. I said it again when I warned the Fool. Dragons feed on life. A whole life, willingly given. That is what it takes to make a dragon rise. And usually not just one. In olden times, when wise men sought out Jhaampe town, they came as a coterie, as a whole that was more than the sum of its parts, and gave that all over into a dragon. The dragon must be filled. Verity and I must put all of ourselves, every part of our lives, into it. It is easier for me. Eda knows I have lived more than my share of years, and I have no desire to go on in this body. It is harder, much harder, for Verity. He leaves behind his throne, his pretty, loving wife, his love of doing things with his hands. He leaves behind riding a fine horse, hunting stags, walking amongst his own people. Oh, I feel them all within the dragon already. The careful inking of colour onto a map, the feel of a clean piece of vellum under his hands. I even know the smells of his inks, now. He has put them all into the dragon. It is hard for him. But he does it, and the pain it costs him is one more thing he puts into the dragon. It will fuel his fury toward the Red Ships when he rises. In fact, there is only one thing he has held back from his dragon. Only one thing that may make him fall short of his goal.'

'What is that?' I asked her unwillingly.

Her old eyes met mine. 'You. He has refused to allow you to be put into the dragon. He could do it, you know, whether you willed it or not. He could simply reach out and pull you into him. But he refuses. He says you love your life too much, he will not take it from you. That you have already laid down too much of it for a king who has returned you only pain and hardship.'

Did she know that with her words she gave Verity back to me? I suspect she did. I had seen much of her past during our Skill-sharing. I knew the experience had to have flowed both ways. She knew how I had loved him, and how hurt I had been to find him so distant when I got here. I stood up immediately to go speak with him.

'Fitz!' she called me back. I turned to her. 'Two things I would have you know, painful as you may find them.'

I braced myself. 'Your mother loved you,' she said quietly. 'You say you cannot recall her. Actually, you cannot forgive her. But she is there, with you, in your memories. She was tall and fair, a Mountain woman. And she loved you. It was not her choice to part from you.'

Her words angered me and dizzied me. I pushed away the knowledge she offered me. I knew I had no memories of the woman who had borne me. Time and again, I had searched myself, and found no trace of her. None at all. 'And the second thing,' I asked her coldly.

She did not react to my anger, save with pity. 'It is as bad, or perhaps worse. Again, it is a thing you already know. It is sad, that the only gifts I can offer you, the Catalyst who has changed my living death to dying life, are things you already possess. But there it is, and so I will say it. You will live to love again. You know you have lost your springtime girl, your Molly on the beach with the wind in her brown hair and red cloak. You have been gone too long from her, and too much has befallen you both. And what you loved, what both of you truly loved, was not each other. It was the time of your life. It was the spring of your years, and life running strong in you, and war on your doorstep and your strong, perfect bodies. Look back, in truth. You will find you recall fully as many quarrels and tears as you do love-making and kisses. Fitz. Be wise. Let her go, and keep those memories intact. Save what you can of her, and let her keep what she can of the wild and daring boy she loved. Because both he and that merry little miss are no more than memories any more.' She shook her head. 'No more than memories.'

'You are wrong!' I shouted furiously. 'You are wrong!'

The force of my cries had brought Kettricken to her feet. She stared at me, in fear and worry. I could not look at her. Tall and fair. My mother had been tall and fair. No. I recalled nothing of her. I strode past her, heedless of the wrench of pain my knee gave me at every step. I walked around the dragon, damning it with every step I took, and defying it to sense what I felt. When I reached Verity working on the left fore-foot, I crouched down beside him and spoke in a savage whisper.

'Kettle says you are going to die when this dragon is done. That you will put all of yourself into it. Or so, with my feeble understanding of her words, I take it. Tell me I am wrong.'

He leaned back on his heels and swiped at the chips he had loosened. 'You are wrong,' he said mildly. 'Fetch your broom, would you, and clear this?'

I fetched my broom and came up beside him, almost of a mind to break it over his head more than use it. I knew he sensed my simmering fury, but he still gestured for me to clear his work-space. I did so with one furious brush. 'Now,' he said gently. 'That is a fine anger you have. Potent and strong. That, I think, I shall take for him.'

Soft as the brush of a butterfly's wing, I felt the kiss of his Skill. My anger was snatched from me, flayed whole from my soul and swept away to . . .

'No. Don't follow it.' A gentle Skill-push from Verity, and I snapped back to my body. An instant later, I found myself sitting flat on the stone while the whole universe swung dizzyingly around my head. I curled forward slowly, bringing up my knees to lean my head against them. I felt wretchedly ill. My anger was gone, replaced by a weary numbness.

'There,' Verity continued. 'As you asked for, I have done. I think you understand better now, what it is to put something into the dragon. Would you care to feed it more of yourself?'

I shook my head mutely. I feared to open my mouth.

'I will not die when the dragon is finished, Fitz. I will be consumed, that is true. Quite literally. But I will go on. As the dragon.'

I found my voice. 'And Kettle?'

'Kestrel will be a part of me. And her sister Gull. But I shall be the dragon.' He had gone back to his wretched stone chipping.

'How can you do that?' My voice was filled with accusation. 'How can you do that to Kettricken? She's given up everything to come here to you. And you will simply leave her, alone and childless?'

He leaned forward so that his forehead rested against the dragon. His endless chipping stopped. After a time, he spoke in a thick voice. 'I should have you stand here and talk to me while I work, Fitz. Just when I think I am past any great feelings at all, you stir them in me.' He lifted his face to regard me. His tears had cut two paths through the grey rock dust. 'What choice do I have?'

'Simply leave the dragon. Let us go back to the Six Duchies, and rally the folk, and fight the Red Ships with sword and Skill, as we did before. Perhaps . . .'

'Perhaps we would all be dead before we even reached Jhaampe. Is that a better end for my queen? No. I shall carry her back to

Buckkeep, and clean the coasts, and she shall reign long and well as Queen. There. That is what I choose to give her.'

'And an heir?' I asked bitterly.

He shrugged wearily and took up his chisel again. 'You know what must be. Your daughter will be raised as heir.'

'NO! Threaten me with that again, and regardless of the risk, I will Skill to Burrich to flee with her.'

'You cannot Skill to Burrich,' Verity observed mildly. He appeared to be measuring for the dragon's toe. 'Chivalry closed his mind to the Skill years ago, to keep Burrich from being used against him. As the Fool was used against you.'

Another small mystery laid to rest. For all the good it did me. 'Verity, please. I beg you. Do not do this thing to me. Far better I should be consumed in the dragon as well. I offer you that. Take my life and feed it to the dragon. I will give you anything you ask of me. But promise me that my daughter will not be sacrificed to the Farseer throne.'

'I cannot make you that promise,' he said heavily.

'If you bore any feelings at all for me any more,' I began, but he interrupted me.

'Cannot you understand, no matter how often you are told? I have feelings. But I have put them into the dragon.'

I managed to stand up. I limped away. There was nothing more to say to him. King or man, uncle or friend, I seemed to have lost all knowledge of who he was. When I Skilled toward him, I found only his walls. When I quested toward him with the Wit, I found his life flickering between himself and the stone dragon. And of late, it seemed to burn brighter within the dragon, not Verity.

There was no one else in camp and the fire was nearly out. I flung more wood on it, and then sat eating dried meat beside it. The pig was nearly gone. We'd have to hunt again soon. Or rather, Nighteyes and Kettricken should hunt again. She seemed to bring meat down easily for him. My self-pity was losing its savour, but I could think of no better solution than to wish I had some brandy to drown it in. At last, with few other interesting alternatives, I went to bed.

I slept, after a fashion. Dragons plagued my dreams and Kettle's game took on odd meanings as I tried to decide if a red stone were powerful enough to capture Molly. My dreams were rambling and incoherent, and I broke often to the surface of my sleep, to stare at the dark inside the tent. I quested out once to where Nighteyes prowled near a small fire while Starling and the Fool slept turn and turn about. They had moved their sentry post to the brow of a hill where they could command a good view of the winding Skill road below them. I should have walked out and joined them. Instead I rolled over and dipped into my dreams again. I dreamed of Regal's troops coming, not by dozens or scores, but hundreds of gold and brown troops pouring into the quarry, to corner us against the vertical black walls and kill us all.

I awoke in the morning to the cold poke of a wolf's nose. *You need to hunt*, he told me seriously, and I agreed with him. As I emerged from my tent, I saw Kettricken just coming down from the dais. Dawn was breaking, her fires were needed no longer. She could sleep, but up by the dragon, the endless clinking and scraping went on. Our eyes met as I stood up. She glanced at Nighteyes.

'Going hunting?' she asked us both. The wolf gave a slow wag to his tail. 'I'll fetch my bow,' she announced, and vanished into her tent. We waited. She came out wearing a cleaner jerkin and carrying her bow. I refused to look at Girl on a Dragon as we passed her. As we walked by the pillar, I observed, 'Had we the folk to do it, we should put two on guard here, and two overlooking the road.'

Kettricken nodded to that. 'It is odd. I know they are coming to kill us, and I see small way for us to escape that fate. Yet we still go out to hunt for meat, as if eating were the most important thing.'

It is. Eating is living.

'Still, to live, one must eat,' Kettricken echoed Nighteyes' thought.

We saw no game truly worthy of her bow. The wolf ran down a rabbit, and she brought down one brightly coloured fowl. We ended up tickling for trout and by midday had more than enough fish to feed us, at least for that day. I cleaned them on the bank of the stream, and then asked Kettricken if she would mind if I stayed to wash myself.

'In truth, it might be a kindness to us all,' she replied, and I smiled, not at her teasing, but that she was still able to do so. In a short time I heard her splashing upstream from me, while Night-eyes dozed on the creek bank, his belly full of fish guts.

As we passed Girl on a Dragon on the way back to camp, we found the Fool curled up on the dais beside her, sound asleep. Kettricken woke him, and scolded him for the fresh chisel marks about the dragon's tail. He professed no regrets, but only stated that Starling had said she would keep watch until evening, and he would really prefer to sleep here. We insisted he return to camp with us.

We were talking amongst ourselves as we returned to the tent. Kettricken it was who stopped us suddenly. 'Hush!' she cried out. And then, 'Listen!'

We froze where we were. I half expected to hear Starling crying a warning to us. I strained my ears, but heard nothing save the wind in the quarry and distant bird sounds. It took a moment for me to grasp the importance of that. 'Verity!' I exclaimed. I shoved our fish into the Fool's hands and began to run. Kettricken passed me.

I had feared to find them both dead, attacked by Regal's coterie in our absence. What I found was almost as strange. Verity and Kettle stood, side by side, staring at their dragon. He shone black and glistening as good flint in the afternoon sunlight. The great beast was complete. Every scale, every wrinkle, every claw was impeccable in its detail. 'He surpasses every dragon we saw in the stone garden,' I declared. I had walked about him twice, and with every step I took, the wonder of him increased. Wit-life burned powerfully in him now, stronger than it did in either Verity or Kettle. It was almost shocking that his sides did not bellow with breath, that he did not twitch in his sleep. I glanced to Verity, and despite the anger I still harboured, I had to smile.

'He is perfect,' I said quietly.

'I have failed,' he said without hope. Beside him, Kettle nodded miserably. The lines in her face had gone deeper. She looked every bit of two hundred years old. So did Verity.

'But he is finished, my lord,' Kettricken said quietly. 'Is not this what you said you must do? Finish the dragon?'

Verity shook his head slowly. 'The carving is finished. But the dragon is not completed.' He looked around at us, watching him, and I could see how he struggled to make the words hold his meaning. 'I have put all I am into him. Everything save enough to keep my heart beating and the breath flowing in my body. As has Kettle. That, too, we could give. But it would still not be enough.'

He walked forward slowly, to lean against his dragon. He pillowed his face on his thin arms. All about him, where his body rested against the stone, an aura of colour rippled on the dragon's skin. Turquoise, edged with silver, the scales flashed uncertainly in the sunlight. I could feel the ebbing of his Skill into the dragon. It seeped from Verity into the stone as ink soaks into a page.

'King Verity,' I said softly, warningly.

With a groan, he stood free of his creation. 'Do not fear, Fitz. I will not let him take too much. I will not give up my life to him without reason.' He lifted his head and looked around at us all. 'Strange,' he said softly. 'I wonder if this is what it feels like to be Forged. To be able to recall what one once felt, but unable to feel it anymore. My loves, my fears, my sorrows. All have gone into the dragon. Nothing have I held back. Yet it is not enough. Not enough.'

'My lord Verity.' Kettle's old voice was cracked. All hope had run out of it. 'You will have to take FitzChivalry. There is no other way.' Her eyes, once so shiny, looked like dry black pebbles as she looked at me. 'You offered it,' she reminded me. 'All your life.'

I nodded my head. 'If you would not take my child,' I added quietly. I drew a breath deep into my lungs. Life. Now. Now was all the life I had, all the time I could truly give up. 'My king. I no longer seek any bargain of any kind. If you must have my life so that the dragon may fly, I offer it.'

Verity swayed slightly where he stood. He stared at me. 'Almost, you make me feel again. But . . .' He lifted a silver finger and pointed it accusingly. Not at me, but at Kettle. His command was as solid as the stone of his dragon as he said, 'No. I have told you that. No. You will not speak of it to him again. I forbid it.' Slowly he sank down to his knees, then sat flat beside his dragon. 'Damn this carris seed,' he said in a low voice. 'It always leaves you, just when you need its strength most. Damn stuff.'

'You should rest now,' I said stupidly. In reality, there was nothing else he could do. That was how carris seed left one. Empty and exhausted. I knew that only too well.

'Rest,' he said bitterly, his voice failing on the word. 'Yes. Rest. I shall be well rested when my brother's soldiers find me and cut my throat. Well rested when his coterie comes and tries to claim my dragon as their own. Make no mistake, Fitz. That is what they seek. It won't work, of course. At least, I don't think it will . . .' His mind was wandering now. 'Though it might,' he said in the faintest of breaths. 'They were Skill-linked to me, for a time. It might be enough that they could kill me and take him.' He smiled a ghastly smile. 'Regal as dragon. Do you think he will leave two stones of Buckkeep Castle upon each other?'

Behind him, Kettle had folded herself up, her face against her knees. I thought she wept, but when she slowly fell over onto her side, her face was lax and still, her eyes closed. Dead, or sleeping the exhausted sleep of the carris seed. After what Verity had said to me, it scarcely seemed to matter. My king stretched himself out on the bare gritty pedestal. He slept beside his dragon.

Kettricken went and sat down beside him. She bowed her head to her knees and wept. Not quietly. The rending sobs that shook her should have roused even the dragon of stone. They did not. I looked at her. I did not go to her, I did not touch her. I knew it would have been of no use. Instead I looked to the Fool. 'We should bring blankets and make them more comfortable,' I said helplessly.

'Ah. Of course. What better task for the White Prophet and his Catalyst?' He linked arms with me. His touch renewed the thread of Skill-bond between us. Bitterness. Bitterness flowed through him with his blood. The Six Duchies would fall. The world would end.

We went to fetch blankets.

THIRTY-EIGHT

Verity's Bargain

When all the records are compared, it becomes plain that no more than twenty Red Ships actually ventured inland as far as Turlake, and only twelve proceeded past Turlake to menace the villages adjoining Tradeford. The minstrels would have us believe there were scores of ships, and literally hundreds of Raiders upon their decks. In song, the banks of the Buck and Vin Rivers were red with flames and blood that summer. They are not to be faulted for this. The misery and terror of those days should never be forgotten. If a minstrel must embroider the truth to help us recall it fully, then let her, and let no one say she has lied. Truth is often much larger than facts.

Starling came back with the Fool that evening. No one asked her why she no longer kept watch. No one even suggested that perhaps we should flee the quarry before Regal's troops cornered us there. We would stay and we would stand, and we would fight. To defend a stone dragon.

And we would die. That went without saying. Quite literally, it was knowledge that none of us uttered.

When Kettricken had fallen asleep, exhausted, I carried her down to the tent she had shared with Verity. I lay her down on her blankets, and covered her well. I stooped and kissed her lined forehead as if I were kissing my sleeping child. It was a farewell, of sorts. Better to do things now, I had decided. Now was all I had for certain.

As dusk fell, Starling and the Fool sat by the fire. She played her harp softly, wordlessly, and looked into the flames. A bared knife lay on the ground beside her. I stood a time and watched how the firelight touched her face. Starling Birdsong, the last minstrel to the last true Farseer King and Queen. She would write no song that anyone would recall.

The Fool sat still and listened. They had found a friendship, of sorts. I thought to myself, if this is the last night she can play, he can give her no finer thing than that. To listen well, and let her music lull him with her skill.

I left them sitting there and took up a full waterskin. Slowly I climbed the ramp up to the dragon. Nighteyes followed me. Earlier, I had built a fire on the dais. Now I fed it from what remained of Kettricken's firewood, and then sat down beside it. Verity and Kettle slept on. Once Chade had used carris seed for two days straight. When he collapsed, he had taken most of a week to recover. All he had wanted to do was sleep and drink water. I doubted that either would awaken soon. It was all right. There was nothing left to say to them anyway. So I simply sat beside Verity and kept watch over my king.

I was a poor watchman. I came awake to his whispering my name. I sat up instantly and reached for the waterskin I had brought with me. 'My king,' I said quietly.

But Verity was not sprawled on the stone, weak and helpless. He stood over me. He made a sign to me to rise and follow him. I did, moving as quietly as he did. At the base of the dragon's dais, he turned to me. Without a word, I offered him the waterskin. He drank half of what it held, paused a bit, and then drank the rest. When he was finished, he handed it back to me. He cleared his throat. 'There is a way, FitzChivalry.' His dark eyes, so like my own, met mine squarely. 'You are the way. So full of life and hungers. So torn with passions.'

'I know,' I said. The words came out bravely. I was more frightened than I had ever been in my life. Regal had scared me badly in his dungeon. But that had been pain. This was death. I suddenly knew the difference. My traitorous hands twisted the front hem of my tunic.

'You will not like it,' he warned me. 'I do not like it. But I see no other way.'

'I am ready,' I lied. 'Only . . . I should like to see Molly once more. To know that she and Nettle are safe. And Burrich.'

He peered at me. 'I recall the bargain you offered. That I would not take Nettle for the throne.' He glanced away from me. 'What I ask of you will be worse. Your actual life. All the life and energy of your body. I have spent all my passions, you see. I have nothing left. If I could but kindle in myself one more night of feelings . . . if I could recall what it was to desire a woman, to hold the woman I loved in my arms . . .' His voice dwindled away from me. 'It shames me to ask it of you. Shames me more than when I drew strength from you, when you were no more than an unsuspecting boy.' He met my eyes again and I knew how he struggled to use words. Imperfect words. 'But you see, even that. The shame I feel, the pain that I do this to you . . . even that is what you give me. Even that I can put into the dragon.' He looked away from me. 'The dragon must fly, Fitz. He must.'

'Verity. My king.' He stared away from me. 'My friend.' His eyes came back to mine. 'It is all right. But . . . I should like to see Molly again. Even briefly.'

'It is dangerous. I think what I did to Carrod woke true fear in them. They have not tried their strength against us since then, only their cunning. But . . .'

'Please.' I said the small word quietly.

Verity sighed. 'Very well, boy. But my heart misgives me.'

Not a touch. He didn't even take a breath. Even as Verity dwindled, that was the power of his Skill. We were there, with them. I sensed Verity retreating, giving me the illusion I was there alone.

It was an inn room. Clean and well furnished. A branch of candles burned beside a loaf of bread and a bowl of apples on a table. Burrich lay shirtless on his side on the bed. Blood had clotted thickly about the knife-wound and soaked the waist of his breeches. His chest moved in the slow, deep rhythms of sleep. He was curled around Nettle. She was snugged against him, deeply asleep, his right arm over her protectively. As I watched, Molly leaned over them and deftly slid the babe from under Burrich's arm. Nettle did not stir as she was carried over to a basket in the corner and tucked into the blankets that lined it. Her small pink mouth worked with memories of warm milk. Her brow was smooth beneath her sleek black hair. She seemed none the worse for everything she had endured.

Molly moved efficiently about the room. She poured water into a basin, and took up a folded cloth. She returned to crouch beside Burrich's bed. She set the basin of water on the floor beside the bed and dipped the rag into it. She wrung it out well. As she set it to his back he jerked awake with a gasp. Fast as a striking snake, he had caught her wrist.

'Burrich! Let go, this has to be cleaned.' Molly was annoyed with him.

'Oh. It's you.' His voice was thick with relief. He released her.

'Of course it's me. Who else would you expect?' She sponged at the knife-wound gently, then dipped the rag in the water again. Both the rag in her hand and the basin of water beside her were tinged with blood.

His hand groped carefully over the bed beside him. 'What have you done with my baby?' he asked.

'Your baby is fine. She's asleep in a basket. Right there.' She wiped his back again, then nodded to herself. 'The bleeding has stopped. And it looks clean. I think the leather of your tunic stopped most of her thrust. If you sit up, I can bandage it.'

Slowly Burrich moved to sit up. He gave one tiny gasp, but when he was sitting up, he grinned at her. He pushed a straggle of hair back from his face. 'Wit-bees,' he said admiringly. He shook his head at her. I could tell it was not the first time he had said it.

'It was all I could think of,' Molly pointed out. She could not keep from smiling back. 'It worked, did it not?'

'Wondrously,' he conceded. 'But how did you know they'd go after the red-bearded one? That was what persuaded them. And damn near persuaded me as well!'

She shook her head to herself. 'It was luck. And the light. He had the candles and stood before the hearth. The hut was dim. Bees are drawn to light. Almost like moths are.'

'I wonder if they are still inside the hut.' He grinned as he watched her rise to take away the bloody rag and water.

'I lost my bees,' she reminded him sadly.

'We will go burning for more,' Burrich comforted her.

She shook her head sadly. 'A hive that has worked the whole summer makes the most honey.' At a table in the corner, she took up a roll of clean linen bandaging and a pot of unguent. She sniffed at it thoughtfully. 'It doesn't smell like what you make,' she observed.

'It will probably work all the same,' he said. A frown creased his brow as he looked slowly around the room. 'Molly. How are we to pay for all this?'

'I've taken care of it.' She kept her back to him.

'How?' he asked suspiciously.

When she looked back at him, her mouth was flat. I'd known better than to argue with that face. 'Fitz's pin. I showed it to the innkeeper to get this room. And while you both slept this afternoon, I took it to a jeweller and sold it.' He had opened his mouth, but she gave him no chance to speak. 'I know how to bargain and I got its full worth.'

'Its worth was more than coins. Nettle should have had that pin,' Burrich said. His mouth was as flat as hers.

'Nettle needed a warm bed and porridge far more than she needed a silver pin with a ruby in it. Even Fitz would have had the wisdom to know that.'

Oddly enough, I did. But Burrich only said, 'I shall have to work many days to earn it back for her.'

Molly took up the bandages. She did not meet his eyes. 'You are a stubborn man, and I am sure you will do as you please about that,' she said.

Burrich was silent. I could almost see him trying to decide if that meant he had won the argument. She came back to the bed. She sat beside him on the bed to smear the ointment on his back. He clenched his jaws, but made no sound. Then she came to crouch in front of him. 'Lift your arms so I can wrap this,' she commanded him. He took a breath and lifted his arms up and away from his body. She worked efficiently, unrolling the bandaging as she wrapped it around him. She tied it over his belly. 'Better?' she asked.

'Much.' He started to stretch, then thought better of it.

'There's food,' she offered as she went to the table.

'In a moment.' I saw his look darken. So did Molly. She turned back to him, her mouth gone small. 'Molly.' He sighed. He tried again. 'Nettle is King Shrewd's great-grandchild. A Farseer. Regal sees her as a threat to him. He may try to kill you again. Both of you. In fact, I am sure he will.' He scratched at his beard. Into her silence, he suggested, 'Perhaps the only way to protect you both is to put you under the true king's protection. There is a man I know . . . perhaps Fitz told you of him. Chade?'

She shook her head mutely. Her eyes were going blacker and blacker.

'He could take Nettle to a safe place. And see you were well provided for.' The words came out of him slowly, reluctantly.

Molly's reply was swift. 'No. She is not a Farseer. She is mine. And I will not sell her, not for coin or safety.' She glared at him and practically spat the words. 'How could you think I would!'

He smiled at her anger. I saw guilty relief on his face. 'I did not think you would. But I felt obliged to offer it.' His next words came even more hesitantly. 'I had thought of another way. I do not know what you will think of it. We will still have to travel away from here, find a town where we are not known.' He looked at the floor abruptly. 'If we were wed before we got there, folk would never question that she was mine . . .'

Molly stood as still as if turned to stone. The silence stretched. Burrich lifted his eyes and met hers pleadingly. 'Do not take this wrong. I expect nothing of you . . . that way. But . . . even so, you need not wed me. There are Witness Stones in Kevdor. We could go there, with a minstrel. I could stand before them, and swear she was mine. No one would ever question it.'

'You'd lie before a Witness Stone?' Molly asked incredulously. 'You'd do that? To keep Nettle safe?'

He nodded slowly. His eyes never left her face.

She shook her head. 'No, Burrich, I will not have it. It is the worst of luck, to do such a thing. All know the tales of what becomes of those who profane the Witness Stones with a lie.'

'I will chance it.' He spoke grimly. I had never known the man to lie before Nettle had come into his life. Now he offered to give a false oath. I wondered if Molly knew what he was offering her.

She did. 'No. You will not lie.' She spoke with certainty.

'Molly. Please.'

'Be quiet!' she said with great finality. She cocked her head and looked at him, puzzling something out. 'Burrich?' she asked with a tentative note to her voice. 'I have heard it told . . . Lacey said that once you loved Patience.' She took a breath. 'Do you love her still?' she asked.

Burrich looked almost angry. Molly met his stare with a pleading look until Burrich looked away from her. She could barely hear his words. 'I love my memories of her. As she was then, as I was then. Probably much as you still love Fitz.'

It was Molly's turn to wince. 'Some of the things I remember . . . yes.' She nodded as if reminding herself of something. Then she looked up and met Burrich's eyes. 'But he is dead.' So oddly final, those words coming from her. Then, with a plea in her voice, she added, 'Listen to me. Just listen. All my life it's been . . . First my father. He always told me he loved me. But when he struck me and cursed me, it never felt like love to me. Then Fitz. He swore he loved me and touched me gently. But his lies never sounded like love to me. Now you . . . Burrich, you never speak to me of love. You have never touched me, not in anger nor desire. But both your silence and your look speak more of love to me than ever their words or touches did.' She waited. He did not speak. 'Burrich?' she asked desperately.

'You are young,' he said softly. 'And lovely. So full of spirit. You deserve better.'

'Burrich. Do you love me?' A simple question, timidly asked.

He folded his work-scarred hands in his lap. 'Yes.' He gripped his hands together. To stop their trembling?

Molly's smile broke forth like the sun from a cloud. 'Then you shall marry me. And afterwards, if you wish, I shall stand before the Witness Stones. And I will admit to all that I was with you before we were wed. And I will show them the child.'

He finally lifted his eyes to hers. His look was incredulous. 'You'd marry me? As I am? Old? Poor? Scarred?'

'You are none of those things to me. To me, you are the man I love.'

He shook his head. Her answer had only baffled him more. 'And after what you just said about bad luck? You would stand before a Witness Stone and lie?'

She smiled a different sort of smile at him. One I had not seen in a long time. One that broke my heart. 'It need not be a lie,' she pointed out quietly.

His nostrils flared like a stallion's as he surged to his feet. The breath he drew swelled his chest.

'Wait,' she commanded him softly, and he did. She licked her thumb and forefinger. She swiftly pinched out all but one candle. Then she crossed the darkened room to his arms.

I fled.

'Oh, my boy. I am so sorry.'

I shook my head silently. My eyes were squeezed tight shut, but tears leaked from them anyway. I found my voice. 'He will be good to her. And Nettle. He is the sort of man she deserves. No, Verity. I should take comfort in it. To know he will be with her, caring for them both.'

Comfort. I could find no comfort in it. Only pain.

'It seems a very poor bargain I have made you.' Verity sounded genuinely grieved for me.

'No. It's all right.' I caught my breath. 'Now, Verity. I would it were done quickly.'

'Are you sure?'

'As you will.'

He took my life from me.

It was a dream I had had before. I knew the feel of an old man's body. The other time, I had been King Shrewd, in a soft nightshirt, in a clean bed. This time was harsher. I ached in every joint of my body. My gut burned inside me. And I had scalded myself, on my face and hands. There was more pain than life left in this body. Like a candle almost burned to the socket. I opened my eyes stickily. I sprawled on cold, gritty stone. A wolf sat watching me.

This is wrong, he told me.

I could think of nothing to say to that. It certainly did not feel right. After a time, I pushed myself up to my hands and knees. My hands hurt. My knees hurt. Every joint in my body creaked and complained as I drew myself up and looked around. The night was warm, but I still shivered. Above me, on a dais, an incomplete dragon slumbered.

I do not understand. Nighteyes pleaded for an explanation.

I do not wish to understand. I do not want to know.

But whether I wished it or not, I did know. I walked slowly and the wolf came at my heels. We walked past a dying fire between two tents. No one kept watch. From Kettricken's tent, there were small noises. Verity's face was what she saw in the dimness. Verity's dark eyes, looking into hers. She believed her husband had finally come to her.

In truth, he had.

I did not want to hear, I did not want to know. I walked on with my old man's careful pacing. Great black blocks of stone loomed around us. Ahead of us, something clicked and chinked softly. I walked through the sharp-edged stone shadows and into moonlight again.

Once you shared my body. Is this like that?

'No.' I spoke the word aloud, and in the wake of my voice, I heard a small scrabbling. *What's that?*

I'll go and see. The wolf melted into the shadows. He returned instantly. *It's only the Scentless One. He hides from you. He does not know you.*

I knew where I would find him. I took my time. This body had all it could do to move, let alone move swiftly. When I came to Girl on a Dragon, it was horribly hard to clamber up on her dais. Once I was up, I could see the fresh rock chips everywhere. I sat down by the dragon's feet, a cautious lowering of my body to cold stone. I looked at his work. He had almost cut her free. 'Fool?' I called out softly in the night.

He came slowly, from the shadows, to stand eyes down before me. 'My king,' he said softly. 'I tried. But I cannot help myself. I cannot just leave her here . . .'

I nodded slowly, wordlessly. At the base of the dais, Nighteyes whined. The Fool glanced down at him, then back up at me. Puzzlement crossed his face. 'My lord?' he asked.

I reached for the thread of Skill-bond between us and found it. The Fool's face grew very still as he struggled to understand.

He came to sit beside me. He stared at me, as if he could see through Verity's skin. 'I like this not,' he said at last.

'Nor I,' I agreed.

'Why have you . . .'

'Better not to know,' I said briefly.

For a time we sat in silence. Then the Fool reached back to brush a handful of fresh stone chips from about the dragon's foot. He met my eyes, but there was still furtiveness as he drew a chisel from his shirt. His hammer was a stone.

'That's Verity's chisel.'

'I know. He doesn't need it any more, and my knife broke.' He set the edge carefully to the rock. 'It works much better anyway.' I watched him tap another small chip free. I aligned my thoughts with his.

'She draws on your strength,' I observed quietly.

'I know.' Another chip came free. 'I was curious. And my touch hurt her.' He placed his chisel again. 'I feel I owe her something.'

'Fool. She could take all you offer her and it would still not be enough.'

'How do you know?'

I shrugged. 'This body knows.'

Then I stared as he laid his Skill-fingers to the place where he had chiselled. I winced, but sensed no pain from her. She took something from him. But he had not the Skill to shape her with his hands. What he gave her was only enough to torment her.

'She reminds me of my older sister,' he said into the night. 'She had golden hair.'

I sat in stunned silence. He did not look at me as he added, 'I should have liked to see her again. She used to spoil me outrageously. I would have liked to have seen all my family again.' His tone was no more than wistful as he moved his fingers idly against the chiselled stone.

'Fool? Let me try?'

He gave me a look that was almost jealous. 'She may not accept you,' he warned me.

I smiled at him. Verity's smile, through his beard. 'There is a link between us. Fine as thread and neither the elfbark nor your weariness aid it. But it is there. Put your hand to my shoulder.'

I did not know why I did it. Perhaps because he had never before spoken to me of a sister or a home he missed. I refused to stop and wonder. Not thinking was so much easier, and not feeling was easiest of all. He put his unSkilled hand, not to my shoulder, but to the side of my neck. Instinctively, he was right. Skin to skin, I knew him better. I held Verity's silver hands up before my eyes and marvelled at them. Silver to the eye, scalded and raw to the senses. Then, before I could change my mind, I reached down and grasped the dragon's shapeless forefoot between my two hands.

Instantly, I could feel the dragon. Almost it squirmed within the stone. I knew the edge of each scale, the tip of each wicked claw. And I knew the woman who had carved it. The women. A coterie, so long ago. Salt's Coterie. But Salt had been too proud. Her features were on the carven face, and she had sought to remain in her own form, carving herself upon the dragon that her coterie shaped around her. They had been too loyal to object. And almost she had succeeded. The dragon had been finished, and almost filled. The dragon had quickened and began to rise as the coterie was absorbed into it. But Salt had striven to remain only within the carved girl. She had held back from the dragon. And the dragon had fallen before it could even rise, sinking back into the stone, miring down forever. Leaving the coterie trapped in the dragon and Salt trapped in the girl.

All this I knew, swifter than lightning. I felt, too, the hunger of the dragon. It pulled at me, pleading for sustenance. Much had it taken from the Fool. I sensed what he had given, light and dark. The jeering taunts of gardeners and chamberlains when he was young at Buckkeep. A branch of apple blossoms outside a window in spring. An image of me, my jerkin flapping as I hurried across the yard at Burrich's heels, trying to make my shorter legs match his long stride. A silver fish leaping above a silent pond at dawn.

The dragon tugged at me insistently. I suddenly knew what had really drawn me here. *Take my memories of my mother, and the feelings that went with them. I do not want to know them at all. Take the ache in my throat when I think of Molly, take all the sharp-edged, bright-coloured days I recall with her. Take their brilliance and* leave me but the shadows of what I saw and felt. Let me recall them without cutting myself on their sharpness. Take my days and nights in Regal's dungeons. It is enough to know what was done to me. Take it to keep, and let me stop feeling my face against that stone floor, hearing the sound of my nose breaking, smelling and tasting my own blood. Take my hurt that I never knew my father, take my hours of staring up at his portrait when the great hall was empty and I could do so alone. Take my –

Fitz. Stop. You give her too much, there will be nothing left of you. The Fool's voice inside me was horror-stricken at what he had encouraged.

– *memories of that tower-top, of the bare windswept Queen's Garden and Galen standing over me. Take that image of Molly going so willingly to Burrich's arms. Take it and quench it and seal it away where it can never sear me again. Take –*

My brother. Enough.

Nighteyes was suddenly between me and the dragon. I knew I still gripped that scaly foreleg, but he snarled at it, defying it to take more of me.

I do not care if it all is taken, I told Nighteyes.

But I do. I would sooner not be bonded with a Forged one. Get back, Cold One. He snarled in spirit as well as beside me.

To my surprise the dragon yielded. My companion nipped at my shoulder. *Let go. Get away from that!*

I let go of the dragon's foreleg. I opened my eyes, surprised to find it was still night all around me.

The Fool had his arm around Nighteyes. 'Fitz,' he said quietly. He spoke into the wolf's ruff, but I heard him clearly. 'Fitz, I am sorry. But you cannot throw away all your pain. If you stop feeling pain . . .'

I did not listen to the rest of what he said. I stared at the dragon's foreleg. Where my two hands had rested against the lumpy stone there were two handprints now. Within those shapes, each scale stood fine and perfect. All of that, I thought. All of that, and this is how much dragon it brought me. Then I thought of Verity's dragon. It was immense. How had he done it? What had he held inside him, all those years, to have enough for the shaping of such a dragon?

'He feels much, your uncle. Great loves. Vast loyalty. Sometimes I think that my two hundred odd years pale beside what he has felt in his forty some.'

All three of us turned to Kettle. I felt no surprise. I had known she was coming and I had not cared. She leaned heavily on a stick and her face seemed to hang from the bones of her skull. She met my eyes and I knew that she knew everything. Skill-linked as she was to Verity, she knew it all. 'Get down from there. All of you, before you hurt yourselves.'

We obeyed slowly and I slowest of all. Verity's joints ached and his body was weary. Kettle looked at me balefully when I finally stood beside her. 'If you were going to do that, you might have put it in Verity's dragon instead,' she pointed out.

'He wouldn't let me. You wouldn't let me.'

'No. We wouldn't have. Let me tell you something, Fitz. You are going to miss what you gave away. You will recover some of the feelings in time, of course. All memories are connected, and like a man's skin, they can heal. In time, left to themselves, those memories would have stopped hurting you. You may someday wish you could call up that pain.'

'I do not think so,' I said calmly, to cover my own doubt. 'I still have plenty of pain left.'

Kettle lifted her old face to the night. She drew a long breath in through her nose. 'Dawn comes,' she said, as if she had scented it. 'You must return to the dragon. To Verity's dragon. And you two,' her head swivelled to regard the Fool and Nighteyes, 'you two should go up to that look-out point and see if Regal's troops are in sight yet. Nighteyes, you let Fitz know what you see. Go on, both of you. And Fool. You leave Girl on a Dragon alone after this. You would have to give her your entire life. And even then, it might not be enough. That being so, stop torturing yourself. And her. Go on, now!'

They went, but not without some backward looks. 'Come on,' Kettle ordered me tersely. She began to hobble back the way she had come. I followed, walking as stiffly as she, through the black and silver shadows of the blocks that littered the quarry. She looked every bit of her two hundred odd years. I felt even older. Aching body, joints that caught and creaked. I lifted my hand

and scratched my ear. Then I snatched it down, chagrined. Verity would have a silver ear now. Already the skin of it burned, and it seemed the distant night insects chirred more loudly now.

'I am sorry, by the way. About your Molly girl and all. I did try to tell you.'

Kettle did not sound sorry. But I understood that now. Almost all of her feelings were in the dragon. She spoke of what she knew she would have felt, once. She still had pain for me, but she no longer recalled any pain of her own to compare it with. I only asked, quietly, 'Is there nothing private any more?'

'Only the things we keep from ourselves,' she replied sadly. She looked over at me. 'It is a good thing you do this night. A kind thing.' Her lips started to smile but her eyes teared. 'To give him one last night of youth and passion.' She studied me, the set look on my face. 'I shall say no more of it, then.'

I walked the rest of the way beside her in silence.

I sat by the warm embers of last night's fire and watched the dawn come. The shrilling of night insects changed gradually to the morning challenges of distant birds. I could hear them very well now. It was strange, I thought, to sit and wait for myself. Kettle said nothing. She breathed deep of the changing scent of the air as night turned to dawn and watched the lightening of the sky with avid eyes. Storing it all up to put into the dragon.

I heard the grate of boot against stone and looked up. I watched myself coming. My stride was confident and brisk, my head up. My face was freshly washed, my wet hair slicked back from my brow into a warrior's tail. Verity wore my body well.

Our eyes met in the early light. I saw my eyes narrow as Verity appraised his own body. I stood up and without thinking, began to brush my clothes off. Then I realized what I was doing. This was not a *shirt* I had borrowed. My laugh boomed out, louder than I used it. Verity shook my head at me.

'Leave it, boy. There's no making it better. And I'm almost finished with it anyway.' He slapped my chest with the palm of my hand. 'Once I had a body like this,' he told me, as if I hadn't known. 'I had forgotten so much of how that felt. So much.' The smile faded from his face as he regarded me peering at him from his own eyes. 'Take care of it, Fitz. You only get one. To keep, anyway.'

A wave of giddiness. Black closed from the edges of my vision, and I folded up my knees and sank down to keep from falling.

'Sorry,' Verity said quietly, and it was in his own voice.

I looked up to find him looking down on me. I stared up at him mutely. I could smell Kettricken's scent on my skin. My body was very tired. I knew a moment of total outrage. Then it crested and fell away as if the emotion were too much effort. Verity's eyes met mine and accepted all I felt.

'I will neither apologize to you nor thank you. Neither would be adequate.' He shook his head to himself. 'And in truth, how could I say I am sorry? I am not.' He looked away from me, out over my head. 'My dragon will rise. My queen will bear a child. I will drive the Red Ships from our shore.' He took a deep breath. 'No. I am not sorry for our bargain.' His eyes came back to me. 'FitzChivalry. Are you sorry?'

Slowly I stood up. 'I don't know.' I tried to decide. 'The roots of it go too deep,' I said at last. 'Where would I start to undo my past? How far back would I have to reach, how much would I have to change in order to change this, or to say I was not sorry now?'

The road is empty below us. Nighteyes spoke in my mind.

I know. Kettle knows, too. She but looked for something to busy the Fool and sent you along to keep him safe. You can come back now.

Oh. Are you all right?

'FitzChivalry. Are you all right?' There was concern in Verity's voice. But it could not completely mask the triumph there as well.

'Of course not,' I told them both. 'Of course not.' I walked away from the dragon.

Behind me, I heard Kettle ask eagerly, 'Are we ready to quicken him?'

Verity's soft voice carried to my ears. 'No. Not just yet. For a little while longer, I would have these memories to myself. For a short time more, I would remain a man.'

As I passed through the camp, Kettricken emerged from her

tent. She wore the same travel-wearied tunic and leggings she had the day before. Her hair was caught back from her face in a short, thick braid. There were still lines in her brow and at the corners of her mouth. But her face had the warm luminescence of the finest pearls. Renewed faith shone in her. She took a deep breath of the morning air and smiled at me radiantly.

I hurried past her.

The stream water was very cold. Coarse horsetail grasses grew along one bank. I used handfuls of them to scrub myself. My wet clothes were draped on the bushes on the other side of the stream. The heat of the day promised they would soon be dry. Nighteyes sat on the bank and watched me with a pucker between his eyes.

I do not understand. You do not smell bad.

Nighteyes. Go hunting. Please.

You wish to be alone?

As much as that is possible any more.

He stood up and stretched, curtseying low to me as he did so. *Someday, it will be only you and I. We shall hunt and eat and sleep. And you will heal.*

May we both live to see that, I agreed wholeheartedly.

The wolf slipped off through the trees. Experimentally, I scrubbed at the Fool's fingerprints on my wrist. They did not come off, but I learned a great deal about the life cycle of a horsetail fern. I gave it up. I decided I could take my entire skin off and still not feel free of what had happened. I waded out of the stream, dashing the water off myself as I went. My clothing was dry enough to put back on. I sat down on the bank to put my boots on. I nearly thought of Molly and Burrich but I quickly pushed the image away. Instead I wondered how soon Regal's soldiers would arrive and if Verity would have his dragon finished before then. Perhaps it was even now finished. I should want to see it.

I wanted more to be alone.

I lay back on the grass and looked up into the blue sky overhead. I tried to feel something. Dread, excitement, anger. Hate. Love. Instead I felt only confused. And tired. Weary of flesh and spirit. I closed my eyes against the brightness of the sky.

The harp notes walked alongside the sounds of the stream

flowing. They blended with it, then danced apart. I opened my eyes to it and squinted at Starling. She sat on the stream bank beside me and played. Her hair was down, drying in ripples down her back in the sun. She had a stem of green grass in her mouth and her bare feet nestled against the soft grass. She met my eyes but said nothing. I watched her hands play on the strings. Her left hand worked harder, compensating for the stiffness in the last two fingers. I should have felt something about that. I didn't know what.

'What good are feelings?' I didn't know I had the question until I spoke it aloud.

Her fingers poised over the strings. She furrowed her brow at me. 'I don't think there's an answer to that question.'

'I'm not finding answers to much of anything lately. Why aren't you back in the quarry, watching them complete the dragon? Surely that is the stuff for a song to spring from.'

'Because I am here with you,' she said simply. Then she grinned. 'And because everyone else seems busy. Kettle sleeps. Kettricken and Verity ... she was combing his hair when I left. I do not think I had seen King Verity smile before. When he does, he looks a great deal like you, about the eyes. Anyway. I do not think they will miss me.'

'And the Fool?'

She shook her head. 'He chips at the stone around Girl on a Dragon. I know he should not, but I do not think he can stop. Nor do I know any way to force him.'

'I don't think he can help her. But I don't think he can resist trying. For all his quick tongue, he has a soft nature.'

'I know that. Now. In some ways I've come to know him very well. In others, he will always be unknowable to me.'

I nodded silently to that. The silence lasted a time. Then, subtly, it became a different kind of silence. 'Actually,' Starling said uncomfortably. 'The Fool suggested I should find you.'

I groaned. I wondered just how much he had told her.

'I'm sorry to hear about Molly ...' she began.

'But not surprised,' I filled in for her. I lifted my arm and put it across my eyes to block the sunlight.

'No.' She spoke quietly. 'Not surprised.' She cast about for something to say. 'At least you know she is safe and cared for,' she offered.

I knew that. It shamed me that I could find so little comfort in it. Putting it into the dragon had helped in the same way that cutting off an infected limb helped. Being rid of it was not the same as being healed of it. The empty place inside me itched. Perhaps I wanted to hurt. I watched her from the shade of my arm.

'Fitz,' she said quietly. 'I asked you once, for yourself. In gentleness and friendship. To chase a memory away.' She looked away from me, at the sunlight glinting on the stream. 'Now I offer that,' she said humbly.

'But I don't love you,' I said honestly. And instantly knew that it was the worst thing I could have said just then.

Starling sighed and set her harp aside. 'I know that. You know that. But it was not a thing that had to be said just now.'

'And I know that. Now. It is just that I don't want any lies, spoken or unspoken . . .'

She leaned over me and stopped my mouth with hers. After a time she lifted her face a little. 'I am a minstrel. I know more about lying than you will ever discover. And minstrels know that sometimes lies are what a man needs most. In order to make a new truth of them.'

'Starling,' I began.

'You know you will just say the wrong thing,' she told me. 'So why don't you be quiet for a time? Don't make this complicated. Stop thinking, just for a while.'

Actually, it was quite a while.

When I awoke, she still lay warm against my side. Nighteyes stood over us, looking down at me, panting with the heat of the day. When I opened my eyes, he folded his ears back and gave his tail a slow wag. A drop of warm saliva fell on my arm.

'Go away.'

The others are calling you. And looking for you. He cocked his head at me and offered, *I could show Kettricken where to find you.*

I sat up and squashed three mosquitoes on my chest. They left bloody smears. I reached for my shirt. *Is something wrong?*

No. They are ready to wake the dragon. Verity wishes to tell you goodbye.

I shook Starling gently. 'Wake up. Or you will miss Verity waking the dragon.'

She stirred lazily. 'For that, I shall get up. I can think of nothing else that would stir me. Besides, it may be my last chance at a song. Fate has ruled that I always be elsewhere whenever you do something interesting.'

I had to smile at that. 'So. You will make no songs about Chivalry's Bastard after all?' I teased her.

'One, perhaps. A love song.' She gave me a last secret smile. 'That part, at least, was interesting.'

I stood up and drew her to her feet. I kissed her. Nighteyes whined his impatience, and she turned quickly in my arms. Nighteyes stretched and bowed low to her. When she turned back to me, her eyes were wide.

'I warned you,' I told her.

She only laughed and stooped to gather up our clothes.

THIRTY-NINE

Verity's Dragon

Six Duchies troops poured into Blue Lake and took ship for the farther side and the Mountain Kingdom on the very days that the Red Ships were beating their way up the Vin River to Tradeford. Tradeford had never been a fortified city. Although word of the ships' coming preceded them by fast messenger, the news was greeted with general disdain. What menace were twelve ships of barbarians to such a great city as Tradeford? The city guard was alerted, and some of the dockside merchants took steps to remove their goods from warehouses close to the water, but the general attitude was that if they did manage to get as far up the river as Tradeford, archers would easily pick off the Raiders before they could do any real damage. The general consensus was that the ships must be bringing some offer of treaty to the King of the Six Duchies. There was much discussion as to how much of the Coastal Duchies they would ask ceded to them, and the possible value of reopening trade with the Out Islands themselves, not to mention restoring the trade flow down the Buck River.

This is but one more example of the errors that can be made when one thinks one knows what the enemy desires, and acts upon it. The folk of Tradeford ascribed to the Red Ships the same desire for prosperity and plenty that they themselves felt. To base their estimation of the Red Ships on that motive was a grievous mistake.

I don't think Kettricken had accepted the idea that Verity must die for the dragon to quicken until the actual moment he kissed her goodbye. He kissed her so carefully, his hands and arms held wide of her, his head cocked so that no silver smear would touch her face. For all that, it was a tender kiss, a hungry and lingering one. A moment longer she clung to him. Then he said something softly to her. She immediately put her hands to her lower belly. 'How can you be so sure?' she asked him, even as the tears began to course down her cheeks.

'I know,' he said firmly. 'And so my first task must be to return you to Jhaampe. You must be kept safe this time.'

'My place is in Buckkeep Castle,' she protested.

I had thought he would argue. But, 'You are right. It is. And thither I shall bear you. Farewell, my love.'

Kettricken did not reply. She stood watching him walk away from her, an intense look of incomprehension on her face.

For all the days we had spent striving for this very thing, at the end it seemed rushed and untidy. Kettle paced stiffly by the dragon. She had bid us all farewell with a distracted air. Now she hovered beside the dragon, breathing as if she had just run a race. At every moment, she was touching the dragon, a fingertip caress, a dragging hand. Colour rippled in the wake of her touch and lingered, fading slowly.

Verity took more care with his goodbyes. To Starling, he admonished, 'Care for my lady. Sing your songs well and true, and let no man ever doubt the child she carries is mine. With that truth I charge you, minstrel.'

'I shall do my best, my king,' Starling replied gravely. She went to stand beside Kettricken. She was to accompany the queen on the dragon's broad back. She kept wiping her damp palms down the front of her tunic and checking to make sure the pack that carried her harp was secure to her back. She gave me a nervous smile. Neither of us needed more farewell than that.

There had been some furore about my decision to stay. 'Regal's troops draw nearer with every passing moment,' Verity reminded me yet again.

'Then you should hurry, so I will not be in this quarry when they arrive,' I reminded him.

He frowned at that. 'If I see any of Regal's troops upon the road, I shall see they do not get this far,' he offered me.

'Take no risks with my queen,' I reminded him.

Nighteyes was my excuse to stay. He had no wish to ride upon a dragon. I would not leave him. I am sure Verity knew the real reasons. I did not think I should return to Buck. I had already made Starling promise me that there would be no mention of me in song. It had not been an easy promise to wring from a minstrel. But I had insisted. I never wanted either Burrich or Molly to know that I yet lived. 'In this, dear friend, you have been Sacrifice,' Kettricken had told me quietly. She could offer me no greater compliment. I knew no word of me would ever pass her lips.

The Fool was the one who was being difficult. All of us urged him to go with the Queen and the minstrel. He consistently refused. 'The White Prophet will stay with the Catalyst,' was all he would say. I privately believed it was more a case of the Fool staying with Girl on a Dragon. He had become obsessed with her and it frightened me. He would have to leave her before Regal's troops arrived at the quarry. I had privately told him that, and he had nodded easily, but with a distracted look. I doubted not that he had plans of his own. We had run out of time to argue with him.

There came a time when there was no reason left for Verity to linger. We had said little to one another, but I felt there was little we could say. Everything that had happened now seemed inevitable to me. It was as the Fool said. Looking back, I could see where his prophecies had long ago swept us into this channel. No one could be blamed. No one could be blameless.

He gave me a nod, before he turned and walked toward the dragon. Then he halted suddenly. As he turned back, he was unbuckling his battered sword belt. He came toward me, wrapping the belt loosely about the sheath as he came. 'Take my sword,' he said abruptly. 'I won't need it. And you seem to have lost the last one I gave you.' He halted suddenly in mid-stride, as if reconsidering. He hastily drew the sword from the sheath. One last time he ran a silver hand down the blade, leaving it gleaming behind his touch. His voice was gruff as he said, 'It would be a poor courtesy to Hod's skill to pass this on with a blunted blade. Take better care of it than I did, Fitz.' He resheathed it and handed it to me. His eyes met mine as I took it. 'And better care of yourself than I did. I did love you, you know,' he said brusquely. 'Despite all I've done to you, I loved you.'

At first I could think of no answer to that. Then, as he reached his dragon and placed his hands on its brow, I told him, *I never doubted it. Never doubt I loved you.*

I don't think I shall ever forget that final smile over his shoulder. His eyes went a last time to his queen. He pressed his hands firmly to the dragon's chiselled head. He watched her as he went. For an instant, I could smell Kettricken's skin, recall the taste of her mouth on mine, the smooth warmth of her bare shoulders gripped in my hands. Then the faint memory was gone and Verity was gone and Kettle was gone. To my Wit and my Skill they disappeared as completely as if they had been Forged. For an unnerving instant, I saw Verity's empty body. Then he flowed into the dragon. Kettle had been leaning on the statue's shoulder. She was gone faster than Verity, spreading out across the scales as turquoise and silver. Colour flooded the creature and suffused him. No one breathed, save that Nighteyes keened softly. A great stillness held under the summer sun. I heard Kettricken give a single, choked sob.

Then, like a sudden wind, the great scaled body drew air into its lungs. His eyes, when he opened them, were black and shining, the eyes of a Farseer, and I knew Verity looked out of them. He lifted his great head upon his sinuous neck. He stretched like a cat, bowing and rolling reptilian shoulders and spreading claws. As he drew his clawed feet back, his talons scored the black stone deeply. Suddenly, like a sail catching the wind, his immense wings unfurled. He rattled them, a hawk settling his plumage, and refolded them sleek to his body. His tail gave a single lash, stirring rock dust and grit into the air. The great head turned, his eyes demanding we be as pleased with this new self as he was.

Verity-as-Dragon strode forward to present himself to his queen. The head he bent to her dwarfed her. I saw her whole reflection in one gleaming black eye. Then he dipped a shoulder to her, bidding her mount.

For one instant, grief controlled her face. Then Kettricken drew a breath and became Queen. Fearlessly she strode forward. She placed her hand on Verity's shining blue shoulder. His scales were slick and she slipped a trifle as she clambered to his back and then crawled forward to where she could straddle his neck. Starling gave me a look, of terror and amazement, and followed the

Queen more slowly. I saw her take her place behind Kettricken, and check once more that her harp-pack was secured to her back.

Kettricken lifted an arm in farewell to us. She shouted something, but the words were lost to me in the wind of the dragon's opening wings. Once, twice, thrice he flapped them, as if getting the feel of them. Rock dust and grit flew stingingly against my face and Nighteyes pressed close against my leg. The dragon crouched as he gathered his great legs under him. The wide turquoise wings beat again and he sprang up suddenly. It was not a graceful launch, and he wobbled a bit as he took flight. I saw Starling clutch desperately at Kettricken, but Kettricken leaned forward against his neck, shouting her encouragement. In four beats, his wings carried him half the length of the quarry. He lifted, circling over the hills and trees that surrounded the quarry. I saw him dip his wings and turn to inspect the Skill road that led to the quarry. Then his wings began to beat steadily, carrying him higher and higher. His belly was a bluish white, like a lizard's. I squinted to see him against the summer sky. Then, like a blue and silver arrow, he was gone, speeding toward Buck. Long after he was gone from sight, I stared after him.

I let out my breath finally. I was trembling. I wiped my eyes on my sleeve and turned toward the Fool. Who was gone.

'Nighteyes! Where is the Fool?'

We both know where he is gone. There is no need to shout.

I knew he was right. Yet I could not deny the urgency I felt. I ran down the ramp of stone, leaving the empty dais behind me. 'Fool?' I cried as I reached the tent. I even paused to look inside, hoping that he might be packing up what we'd need to take with us. I don't know why I indulged such a foolish hope.

Nighteyes had not waited. When I reached Girl on a Dragon, he was already there. He was sitting patiently, tail neatly coiled about his feet, looking up at the Fool. I slowed when I saw him. My premonition of danger faded. He was sitting on the edge of the dais, feet dangling, head leaned back against the dragon's leg. The surface of the dais was littered with fresh chips from this day's efforts. I walked toward him. His eyes were lifted to the sky and the expression on his face was wistful. Contrasted against the dragon's rich green hide, the Fool was white no longer, but the palest of golds. There was even a tawny edge to his silky fine hair. The eyes he turned to me were pale topaz. He very slowly shook his head at me, but he did not speak until I leaned against her pedestal.

'I had been hoping. I could not help hoping. But I have seen today what must be put into a dragon so it can fly.' He shook his head more forcefully. 'And even if I had the Skill to give it, I do not have it to give. Even were she to consume all of me, it would not be enough.'

I did not say that I knew that. I did not even say that I had suspected it all along. I had finally learned something from Starling Birdsong. I let him have a silence for a time. Then I said, 'Nighteyes and I are going to go get two jeppas. When I come back, we had better pack swiftly and be gone. I did not see Verity give chase to anything. Perhaps that means Regal's troops are still far away. But I don't want to take any chances.'

He drew a deep breath. 'That is wise. It is time for this Fool to be wise. When you come back, I shall help you pack.'

I realized then I was still gripping Verity's sword in its sheath. I took off the plain short sword and replaced it with the blade Hod had made for Verity. It weighed strangely against me. I offered the short sword to the Fool. 'Want this?'

He glanced at me, a puzzled look. 'What for? I'm a Fool, not a killer. I've never even learned to use one.'

I left him there, to say his farewells. As we wended our way out of the quarry and toward the woods where we had been pasturing the jeppas, the wolf lifted his nose and snuffed.

Nothing left of Carrod but a bad smell, he noted as we passed the vicinity of the body.

'I suppose I should have buried him,' I said as much to myself as him.

No sense in burying meat that is already rotten, he noted with puzzlement.

I passed the black pillar, but not without a small shudder. I found our straying jeppas on a hillside meadow. They were more reluctant to be caught than I had expected. Nighteyes enjoyed rounding them up considerably more than they or I did. I chose the lead jeppa and one other, but as I led them away, the others

decided to trail along after us as well. I should have expected it.
I had rather hoped the rest would stay and go wild. I did not
relish the idea of six jeppas at my heels all the way back to
Jhaampe. A new thought came to me as I led them past the pillar
and into the quarry.

I did not have to return to Jhaampe.

The hunting here is as good as any we've found.

We've the Fool to think of, as well as ourselves.

I would not let him go hungry!

And when winter comes?

When winter comes, then . . . He is attacked!

Nighteyes did not wait for me. He streaked past me, grey and
low, claws scratching against the black stone of the quarry floor
as he ran. I let go of my jeppas and ran after him. The wolf's
nose told me of human scent in the air. An instant later, he had
identified Burl, even as he hurtled toward them.

The Fool had not left Girl on a Dragon. That was where Burl
had found him. He must have come quietly, for the Fool was
never easy to take unawares. Perhaps his obsession had betrayed
him. Whatever the case, Burl had got the first cut in. Blood ran
down the Fool's arm and dripped from his fingertips. He had left
smears of it all up the dragon as he climbed her. Now he clung,
feet braced against the girl's shoulders and one hand gripping the
dragon's gaping lower jaw. In his free hand he gripped his knife.
He stared down at Burl balefully, waiting. Skill boiled from Burl,
angry and frustrated.

Burl had climbed up onto the dais and was seeking to clamber
up the dragon itself now as he strove to reach up and impose a
Skill-touch on the Fool. The smoothly-scaled hide was defying
him. Only one as agile as the Fool could have shinnied up to the
perch where he clung just out of Burl's reach. Burl drew his sword
in frustration and swung it at the Fool's braced feet. Its tip missed,
but not by much, and its blade rang against the girl's back. The
Fool cried out as loudly as if the blade had bit truly, and sought
to scrabble higher. I saw his hand slip where his own blood had
greased the dragon's hide. Then he was sliding down, scrabbling
frantically as he came down hard right behind the girl's seat on
the dragon's back. I saw his head bounce glancingly against her

shoulder. He looked half stunned, and clung where he was.

Burl lifted his sword for a second swing, one that could easily separate the Fool's leg from his body. Instead, soundless as hate could be, the wolf surged up onto the dais and took Burl from behind. I was still running toward them as I saw Nighteyes' impact drive Burl forward to smack against Girl on a Dragon. He sank to his knees against the statue. His sword blow missed the Fool and rang again against the dragon's gleaming green hide. Ripples of colour raced away from that clash of metal against stone, like the ripples made when one tosses a pebble in a still pond.

I reached the dais as Nighteyes darted his head in. His jaws closed, gripping Burl from behind, between his shoulder and neck. Burl screamed, his voice going amazingly shrill. He dropped his sword and lifted his hands to clutch at the wolf's ravening jaws. Nighteyes worried him like a rabbit. Then the wolf braced his front feet on Burl's wide back and made more sure of his grip.

Some things happen too swiftly to tell well. I felt Will behind me at the same moment that the wild spattering of Burl's blood became a sudden gushing. Nighteyes had severed the great vein in his throat, and Burl's life was pumping out in jumping gouts of scarlet. *For you, my brother!* Nighteyes told the Fool. *This kill for you!* Nighteyes still did not let go, but shook him again. The blood leaped like a fountain as Burl struggled, not knowing he was already dead. The blood struck the dragon's gleaming hide and ran down it, to puddle in the chiselled troughs the Fool had made attempting to free his feet and tail. And there the blood bubbled and steamed, eating into the stone as scalding water would have eaten into a chunk of ice. The scales and claws of the dragon's hind feet were unveiled, the detail of the whiplike tail exposed. And as Nighteyes finally flung down Burl's lifeless body, the dragon's wings opened.

Girl on a Dragon soared up into the sky as she had strained to do for so long. It seemed an effortless lifting, almost as if she floated away. The Fool was borne away with her. I saw him lean forward, clutching instinctively at the supple waist of the girl before him. His face was turned away from me. I glimpsed the bland eyes and still mouth of the girl's face. Perhaps her eyes saw, but she was no more separate from the dragon than its tail or wing; merely another appendage, one to which the Fool clung as they rose higher and higher.

I saw all these things, but not because I stood and stared. I saw them in glimpses, and through the wolf's eyes. My own gaze I turned on Will as he ran up behind me. He carried a bared blade in his hand and ran easily. I drew Verity's sword as I turned, and found it took longer coming out of its sheath than the short sword I had become accustomed to.

The strength of Will's Skill hit me in a buffeting wave just as the tip of Verity's blade came free of the scabbard. I staggered back a step and threw up my walls against him. He knew me well. That first wave had been compounded not just of fear, but of specific pains. They had been prepared especially for me. I knew again the shock of my broken nose, I felt the burn of my split face even if it did not stream hot blood down my chest as it once had. For a frozen heartbeat, all I could do was hold my walls against that crippling pain. The sword I gripped seemed suddenly made of lead. It sagged in my hand, its tip drooping toward the earth.

Burl's death saved me. In the moment that Nighteyes flung his lifeless body down, I saw that death lap against Will. His eyes sagged almost shut with the impact of it. The last member of his coterie was gone. I felt Will diminish abruptly, not just as Burl's Skill no longer supplemented his own, but as grief washed over him. I found in my mind an image of Carrod's rotting body and flung that at him for good measure. He staggered back.

'You've failed, Will!' I spat the words. 'Verity's dragon has already risen. Even now it wings toward Buck. His queen rides with him, and she bears within her his heir. The rightful king will reclaim his throne and crown, he will scourge his coasts of Red Ships and scour Regal's troops from the Mountains. No matter what you do here now, you are defeated.' A strange smile twisted my mouth. 'I win.' Snarling, Nighteyes advanced to stand at my side.

Then Will's face changed. Regal looked at me out of his eyes. He was as unmoved by Burl's death as he would be by Will's. I sensed no grief, only anger at a lessening of his power. 'Perhaps,' he said with Will's voice, 'perhaps then, all I should care for is killing you, Bastard. At whatever the cost.' He smiled at me, the smile of a man who knows how the tumbling dice will fall before they land. I knew a moment of uncertainty and fear. I flung my walls up tighter against Will's insidious tactics.

'Do you really think a one-eyed swordsman has a fighting chance against my blade and my wolf, Regal? Or do you plan to throw his life away as casually as you have the rest of the coterie?' I flung the question in a faint hope of stirring discord between them.

'Why not?' Regal asked me calmly with Will's voice. 'Or did you think I was truly as stupid as my brother, to be content with only one coterie?'

A wave of Skill struck me with the force of a wall of water. I staggered back before it, then regained myself and charged at Will. I'd have to kill him quickly. Regal had control of Will's Skill. He little cared what it would do to Will, how it might scorch him if he killed me with a Skill-blast. I could feel him drawing up Skill-power into himself. Yet even as I put all my heart into killing Will, Regal's words ate at me. Another coterie?

One-eyed or not, Will was fast. His blade was a part of him as he met my first thrust and turned it. I wished for an instant for the familiarity of my battered short sword. Then I threw such thoughts aside as useless and thought only of breaking past his guard. The wolf moved swiftly past me, belly low, as he sought to close on Regal from Will's blind side.

'Three new coteries!' Will's voice gasped with effort as he parried my blade again. I slipped away from his thrust and tried to wrap his blade. He was too fast for that.

'Young, strong Skill-users. To carve dragons of my own.' A swiping slash whose breeze I felt. 'Dragons at my beck, loyal to me. Dragons to bring down Verity, in blood and scales.' He spun and darted a thrust at Nighteyes. The wolf leapt wildly away. I sprang in, but his blade was already back to meet mine. He fought with incredible speed. Another use of the Skill? Or a Skill-illusion he forced on me?

'Then they shall clear the Red Ships. For me. And open the Mountain passes. The Mountains will be mine as well. I shall be a hero. No one will oppose me then.' His blade struck mine hard, a jolt I felt in my shoulder. His words jolted me as well. They rang with truth and determination. Skill-imbued, they pounded against me with the solid force of hopelessness. 'I shall master the Skill road. The ancient city will be my new capital. All my Skill-users shall be drenched in the river's magic.'

Another swipe at Nighteyes. It shaved a wisp of hair from his shoulder. And again that opening passed too swiftly for my own clumsy blade. I felt I stood shoulder-deep in water and fought a man whose blade was light as a straw. 'Stupid Bastard! Did you truly think I cared about one pregnant whore, one dragon a-wing? The quarry itself is the true prize, the one you have left unguarded for me. The stuff from which a score, no, a hundred dragons shall rise!'

How had we been so stupid? How had we not seen what Regal truly sought? We had thought with our hearts, of Six Duchies folk, of farmers and fishermen who needed their king's arm to defend them. But Regal? He had thought only of what the Skill could win for him. I knew his next words before he flung them. 'In Bingtown and Chalced they will bend their knees to me. And in the Out Islands, they will cower at my name.'

Others come! And above us!

Nighteyes' warning nearly killed me. For in the instant I lifted my eyes, Will sprang at me. I gave ground, all but running backwards to avoid his blade. Far behind him, from the mouth of the quarry, a dozen men ran toward us, brandishing blades. They moved, not in step, but with a oneness to them far more cohesive than any mere troops could have mastered. A coterie. I sensed their Skill as they approached like the storm winds that precede a squall. Will suddenly halted his advance. My wolf raced to meet them, teeth bared, snarling.

Nighteyes! Stop! You cannot fight twelve blades wielded by one mind!

Will lowered his blade, then casually sheathed it. He called to the coterie over his shoulder, 'Don't bother with them. Let the archers finish them.'

A glance at the towering walls of the quarry showed me this was no bluff. Gold-and-brown-clad soldiers were coming into position. I grasped this was what the troops were about. Not to defeat Verity, but to take and hold this quarry. Another wave of humiliation and despair washed over me. Then I lifted my blade and charged at Will. Him, at least, I would kill.

An arrow clattered across the stone where I had stood, another skittered right between Nighteyes' legs. A scream rose from the walls of the quarry to the west of us. Girl on a Dragon swept low over me, the Fool on her back, a gold and brown archer writhing in the dragon's jaws. The man was gone suddenly, a puff of smoke or steam swept away by the wind of her passage. She banked her wings, came in low again, snatching up another archer and sending one leaping into the quarry to avoid her. Another puff of smoke.

On the floor of the quarry, all of us were frozen, gaping up. Will recovered more quickly than I did. An angry shout to his archers, ringing with Skill. 'Fire upon her! Bring her down!'

Almost instantly a phalanx of arrows went singing toward her. Some arched and fell before they even reached her. The rest she deflected with a single powerful beat of her wings. The arrows suddenly wobbled in the gust of her wind, and fell tumbling like straws to shatter on the quarry floor. Girl on a Dragon abruptly stooped and came diving directly at Will.

He fled. I believe Regal abandoned him for at least as long as it took him to make that decision. He ran, and for an instant it appeared that he chased the wolf who had nearly closed the distance between him and the coterie. Save at the moment the coterie realized that Will was fleeing toward them with a dragon sheering through the air behind him, the coterie turned on their heels and fled as well. I caught a brief flash of Nighteyes' delighted triumph that twelve swordsmen would not stand to meet his charge. Then he cowered to the earth as Girl on a Dragon swept low over all of us.

It was not only the harsh wind of her passage that I felt, but also a dizzying sweep of Skill, that in an instant snatched from my mind every thought I had been holding. It was as if the world had been plunged briefly into absolute darkness and then handed back to me in full brightness. I stumbled as I ran, and for an instant could not recall why I carried a bared sword or whom I chased. Ahead of me Will faltered as her shadow swept him, and then the coterie staggered in their turn.

Her claws snatched fruitlessly at Will as she passed. The scattered blocks of black stone were his salvation, for such was her wing span that he could elude her in the narrowness of their maze. She shrieked her frustration, the high wild cry of a hawk thwarted. She rose and banked to make a second sweep at him. I gasped as she flew right into a singing flight of arrows. They rattled uselessly off her hide as if the archers had targeted the black stone of the quarry itself. Only the Fool cowered away from them. Girl on a Dragon changed course abruptly, to fly low over the archers and snatch another from their midst and consume him in an instant.

Again her shadow swept over me, and again a moment of my life was snatched from me. I opened my eyes to find Will gone. Then I caught a brief glimpse of him, veering as he ran dodging between the standing blocks of stone much as a hare breaks his trail as he flees from a hawk. I could no longer see the coterie, but suddenly Nighteyes sprang from the shadow of a stone block to race by my side.

Oh, my brother, the Scentless One hunts well! he exulted. *We were wise to take him into our pack!*

Will is my kill! I declared to him.

Your kill is my kill, he pointed out, quite seriously. *That is pack. And he shall be no one's kill unless we spread out to find him.*

He was right. Ahead of us, I heard shouts and occasionally saw a gold and brown flash as a man dashed across a wide space between the blocks of stone. But most of them had rapidly understood that the way to remain sheltered from the dragon was to cling closely to the edges of the immense stone blocks.

They are running for the pillar. If we get to where we can see it, we can wait for him there.

It seemed logical. To flee through the pillar would be the only way they could hope to escape the dragon for any length of time. I still heard the occasional clatter as arrows rained down in the dragon's wake, but a good portion of the archers who had ringed the quarry walls had retreated to the shelter of the surrounding forest.

Nighteyes and I abandoned all efforts to find Will and simply went directly to the pillar. I had to admire the discipline of some of Regal's archers. Despite all else, if the wolf and I broke cover for more than a few strides, we would hear a cry of 'There they are!' and moments later arrows would be hailing down where we had been.

We reached the pillar in time to see two of Regal's new coterie dash across the open, hands reaching, to plunge into the dark pillar itself the moment they touched it. The rune for the stone garden was the one they chose, but perhaps it was only because it was the side of the pillar closest to cover. We did not move from the angle of a great block that sheltered us from arrows.

Did he go through already?

Perhaps. Wait.

Several eternities passed. I became certain that Will had eluded us. Above us Girl on a Dragon swept her shadow over the quarry walls. The cries of her victims were less frequent. The archers were using the cover of trees to hide themselves. Briefly I watched her rise, circling high above the quarry. She hung shining green high against the blue sky, rocking on her wings. I wondered what it was like for the Fool to ride so. At least he had the girl part of the dragon to cling to. Abruptly Girl on a Dragon tipped, side-slipped in the sky, and then folded her wings, plummeting down toward us. At the moment she did, Will broke cover and ran for the pillar.

Nighteyes and I leaped after him. We were agonizingly close behind him. I ran fast, but the wolf ran faster, and Will fled the fastest of all. At the moment when his reaching fingertips brushed the pillar, the wolf made a final spring. His front paws slammed into Will's back, sending him head first toward the pillar. As I saw him melting into it, I cried out a warning to Nighteyes and gripped his fur to drag him back. He seized one of Will's calves as Will was snatched away from us. At the moment that his jaws closed on Will's flesh, the dragon's shadow swept over us. I lost my grip on the world and fell into blackness.

Tales abound of heroes who have wrestled dark foes in the underworld. There are a few told of those who have willingly entered the dark unknown to rescue friends or lovers. In a timeless moment, I was offered quite clearly a choice. I could seize Will and choke the life out of him. Or clasp Nighteyes to me and hold him together against all the forces that tore at his wolf's mind and being. It was, really, no decision at all.

We emerged into cool shade and trampled grass. One moment there was only darkness and passage; in the next we breathed, and felt again. And feared. I scrabbled to my feet, amazed to find I still gripped Verity's sword. Nighteyes heaved himself up, staggered two steps and fell over. *Sick. Poisoned. The whole world sways.*

Lie still and breathe. I stood before him and lifted my eyes to glare around us. My gaze was returned, not only by Will but by most of Regal's new coterie. Most of them were still breathing hard, and one gave a shout of alarm at the sight of us. When Will shouted, a number of Farrow guards came running as well. They fanned out to surround us.

We must go back through the pillar. It's our only chance.

I cannot. You go. Nighteyes' head drooped toward his paws and his eyes closed.

That is not pack! I told him sternly. I lifted Verity's sword. So this was how I was going to die. I was glad the Fool had not told me. I probably would have killed myself first.

'Just kill him,' Will ordered them. 'We've wasted enough time on him. Kill him and the wolf. And then find me an archer who can shoot a man off a dragon's back for me.' Regal turned Will's back to me and strode away, still issuing orders. 'You, Third Coterie. You told me a finished dragon could not be wakened and made to serve. Well, I have just seen an unSkilled Fool do that very thing. You will find out how it was done. You will begin now. Let the Bastard test his Skill against swords.'

I lifted my sword and Nighteyes pulled himself to his feet. His queasiness lapped against my fear as the circle of soldiers closed around us. Well, if I must die now, there was no more to fear. Perhaps I would try my Skill against their swords. I discarded my walls, flinging them aside disdainfully. The Skill was a river that raged all around me, a river that in this place was always in flood. As easily as drawing a breath it was to fill myself with it. A second breath banished my body's weariness and pains. I reached out with strength to my wolf. Beside me, Nighteyes gave himself a shake. The rising of his hackles and the baring of his teeth made him twice as large. My eyes circled the swords that surrounded us. Then we no longer waited, but sprang to meet them. As swords lifted to meet mine, Nighteyes raced forward and under them, then spun to slash a man's leg from behind.

Nighteyes became a creature of speed, teeth and fur. He did not try to bite and hold. Instead he used his weight to knock men off balance, sending them stumbling into one another, hamstringing them when he could, slashing with his teeth rather than biting. For me the challenge became not to strike at him as he dashed thither and yon. He never tried to challenge their swords. The moment a man turned to him and advanced, he fled, to shoulder past the legs of those who sought to confront me.

As for me I wielded Verity's sword with a grace and a skill I had never before known with such a weapon. Hod's lessons and Hod's work finally came together for me, and if such a thing were possible, I would say that the spirit of the swordmaster was in the weapon and that she sang to me as I wielded it. I could not break out of the circle they pinned me in, but neither could they get past my guard to do more than minor damage.

In that first flurry of battle, we fought well and did well, but the odds were impossible. I could force men back from my sword and step toward them, but in the next moment I must turn to fight those who had closed behind me. I could move the circle of battle, but not escape it. Still, I blessed the greater reach of Verity's sword that kept me alive. Other men were coming at a run to the din and shouts of fighting. Those who came drove a wedge between Nighteyes and me, forcing him ever further away.

Get clear of them all and run. Run. Live, my brother.

For answer he raced away from them all, then suddenly came looping back, charging right through their midst. Regal's men hacked at each other in a futile effort to stop him. They were not used to an opponent less than half the height of a man and with twice the speed of one. Most aimed chopping blows at him that did no more than cleave the earth in his wake. In an instant, he was past them and had vanished once more into the lush forest. Men glared about wildly, wondering where next he would come from.

But even at the hottest of the fight, I knew the hopelessness of what we did. Regal would win. Even were I to kill every man here, Will included, Regal would win. Had already won for that matter. And had I not known he always would? Had not I known, from the very beginning, that Regal was destined to rule?

I took a sudden step forward, took off a man's arm at the elbow, and used the momentum of that blow to call the sword's blade back in an arc that took the tip across the face of another man. As the two fell, tangling together, there was a tiny opening in the circle. I took a step into the brief space, focused my Skill and seized Will's insidious grip upon my mind. I felt a blade lick against my left shoulder as I did so. I spun to engage my attacker's sword, then bade my body think for itself for a moment and made good my grip on Will. Wound through Will's consciousness I found Regal, twisted into him like a drill-worm in a deer's heart. Will could not have broken free of him even if he had been able to think of doing it. And it seemed to me that there was not enough left of Will to even form a thought for himself. Will was a body, a vessel of meat and blood, holding Skill for Regal to wield. Bereft of the coterie that had strengthened him, he was not all that formidable a weapon any more. Less valuable. One that might be used and cast aside with little remorse.

I could not fight in both directions at once. I kept my grip on Will's mind, forced his thoughts away from mine, and strove to direct my body as well. In the next instant, I took two cuts, one to my left calf and one to my right forearm. I knew I could not sustain it. I could not see Nighteyes. He at least had a chance. *Get clear of this, Nighteyes. It's all over.*

It but begins! he contradicted me. He surged through me like a flash of heat. From some other part of the camp, I heard a cry in Will's voice. Somewhere, a Wit-wolf ravaged his body. I could sense Regal trying to unwind his mind from Will's. I clamped my hold tighter on them both. *Stay and face it, Regal!*

The point of a sword found my hip. I jerked away from it and stumbled against stone, leaving a bloody handprint as I pushed myself upright again. It was Realder's dragon; I had dragged the battle that far. I put my back to him thankfully and turned to face my attackers. Nighteyes and Will still fought; plainly Regal had learned something from his tortures of Witted ones. He was not as vulnerable to the wolf as he once would have been. He could not hurt the wolf with Skill, but he could wrap him with layer upon layer of fear. Nighteyes' heart was suddenly thundering in my ears. I opened myself once more to the Skill, filled myself and did what I had never attempted before. I fed Skill-strength as Wit to Nighteyes. *For you, my brother.* I felt Nighteyes *repel* at Will, breaking free of him for an instant. Will used that instant to flee us both. I longed to give chase, but behind me, I felt an answering stir of the Wit in Realder's dragon. In a brief stench, my bloody handprint on his hide smoked away. He stirred. He was awakening. And he was hungry.

There was a sudden crackling of branches and a storm of torn leaves as a great wind broke into the still heart of the forest. Girl on a Dragon landed abruptly in the small cleared space by the pillar. Her lashing tail cleared the area around her of men. 'Over there!' the Fool shouted to her, and in a moment her head snaked out, to seize one of my attackers in her fearsome jaws. He vanished in a puff of smoke, and I felt her Skill swell with the life she had consumed.

Behind me, a wedge-shaped reptilian head lifted suddenly. For a moment all was blackness as that shadow passed over me. Then the head darted out, swifter than a striking snake, to seize the man nearest us. He vanished, the steam of what he had been stinking briefly past me. The roar the dragon gave near deafened me.

My brother?

I live, Nighteyes.

As do I, brother.

AS DO I, BROTHER. AND I HUNGER!

The Wit-voice of a very large carnivore. Old Blood indeed. The strength of it shivered through my bones. Nighteyes had the wit to reply.

Feed, then, large brother. Make our kill yours, and welcome. That is pack.

Realder's dragon did not have to be invited twice. Whoever

Realder had been, he had put a healthy appetite into his dragon. Great clawed feet tore clear of the moss and earth, a tail lashed free, felling a small tree as it passed. I was barely able to scramble out of his path as he lunged to engulf another Farrowman in his jaws.

Blood and the Wit! That is what it takes. Blood and the Wit. We can wake the dragons.

Blood and the Wit? At the moment, we are drenched in both. He understood me instantly.

In the midst of slaughter, Nighteyes and I played an insane child's game. It was almost a contest to see who could wake the most, a contest the wolf easily won. He would dart to a dragon, shake blood from his coat onto it, then bid it, *Wake, brother, and feed. We have brought you meat.* And as each great body smoked with wolf-blood and then stirred, he would remind it, *We are pack!*

I found King Wisdom. His was the antlered dragon, and he roused from his sleep shouting *Buck! For Buckkeep! Eda and El, but I am hungry!*

There are Red Ships aplenty off the coast of Buck, my lord. They but await your jaws, I told him. For all his words, there was little human left about him. Stone and souls had merged, to become dragons in truth. We understood one another as carnivores do. They had hunted as a pack before, and that they recalled well. Most of the other dragons had nothing at all human about them. They had been shaped by Elderlings, not men, and we understood little more of one another than that we were brothers and had brought them meat. Those who had been formed by coteries had dim recollections of Buck and Farseer kings. It was not those memories that bound them to me, but my promise of food. I counted it as the greatest blessing that I could imprint that much on those strange minds.

There came a time when I could find no more dragons in the underbrush. Behind me, where Regal's soldiers had camped, I heard the cries of hunted men and the roaring of dragons as they competed for, not meat, but life. Trees gave way before their charges and their lashing tails sliced brush as a scythe cuts grain stalks. I had paused to breathe, one hand braced on my knee, the other still gripping Verity's sword. Breath came harsh and dry to me. Pain was beginning to break through the Skill I had imposed on my body. Blood was dripping from my fingers. Lacking a dragon to give it to, I wiped my hand down my jerkin.

'Fitz?'

I turned as the Fool ran up to me. He caught me in his arms, hugged me hard.

'You still live! Thank all gods everywhere. She flies like the wind itself, and she knew where to find you. Somehow she felt this battle, from all that distance.' He paused for breath, and added, 'Her hunger is insatiable. Fitz, you must come with me, now. They are running out of prey. You must mount her with me, and lead them to where they can feed, or I do not know what they will do.'

Nighteyes joined us. *This is a large and hungry pack. It will take much game to fill them.*

Shall we go with them, to their hunting?

Nighteyes hesitated. *On the back of one? Through the air?*

That is how they hunt.

That is not this wolf's way. But if you must leave me, I will understand.

I do not leave you, my brother. I do not leave you.

I think the Fool sensed something of what passed between us, for he was already shaking his head before I spoke. 'You must lead them. On Girl on a Dragon. Take them back to Buck and Verity. They will hearken to you, for you are pack with us. It is something they understand.'

'Fitz, I cannot. I was not made for this, this slaughter! This taking of life is not why I came. I have never seen this, not in any dream, nor read of it in any scroll. I fear I may lead time awry.'

'No. This is right. I feel it. I am the Catalyst, and I came to change all things. Prophets become warriors, dragons hunt as wolves.' I hardly knew my own voice as I spoke. I had no idea where such words came from. I met the Fool's unbelieving eyes. 'It is as it must be. Go.'

'Fitz, I . . .'

Girl on a Dragon came lumbering toward us. On the ground,

her airy grace deserted her. Instead she walked with power, as a hulking bear or a great horned bull does. The green of her scales shone like dark emeralds in sunlight. The girl on her back was a breathtaking beauty, for all her empty expression. The dragon head lifted and she opened her mouth and darted her tongue out to taste the air. *More?*

'Hurry,' I bid him.

He embraced me almost convulsively, and shocked me when he kissed my mouth. He spun and ran toward Girl on a Dragon. The girl part of her leaned down, to offer him a hand as she drew him up to sit behind her. The expression on her face never changed. Just another part of the dragon.

'To me!' he cried to the dragons that were already gathering around us. The last look he gave me was a mocking smile.

Follow the Scentless One! Nighteyes commanded them before I could think. *He is a mighty hunter and will lead you to much meat. Hearken to him, for he is pack with us.*

Girl on a Dragon leaped up, her wings opened, and with powerful beats they carried her steadily upwards. The Fool clung behind her. He lifted a hand in farewell, then quickly put it back to clutch at her waist. It was my last sight of him. The others followed, giving cry in a way that reminded me of hounds on a trail, save they sounded more like the shrilling of raptor birds. Even the winged boar rose, ungainly as was his leap into the air. The beating of their wings was such that I covered my ears and Nighteyes shrank belly-down to the earth beside me. Trees swayed in that great passage of dragons, and dropped branches both dead and green. For a time the sky was filled with jewelled creatures, green and red and blue and yellow. Whenever the shadow of one passed over me, I knew a blackness, but my eyes were opened and watching as Realder's dragon lifted, last of them all, to follow that great pack into the sky. In a short time, the canopy of the trees hid them from my view. Gradually their cries faded.

'Your dragons are coming, Verity,' I told the man I had once known. 'The Elderlings have risen to Buck's defence. Just as you said they would.'

FORTY

Regal

The Catalyst comes to change all things.

In the wake of the dragons' departure, there was a great silence, broken only by the whispers of leaves as a few sifted down to the forest floor. Not a frog croaked, not a bird sang. The dragons had broken the roof of the forest in their departure. Great shafts of sunlight shone down on soil that had been shaded since before I was born. Trees had been uprooted or snapped off and great troughs had been gouged in the forest floor by the passage of their immense bodies. Scaly shoulders had gashed the bark from ancient trees, baring the secret white cambium beneath. The slashed earth and trees and trampled grasses gave up their rich odours to the warm afternoon. I stood in the midst of the destruction, Nighteyes at my side, and looked about slowly. Then we went to look for water.

Our passage took us through the camp. It was an odd battle scene. There were scattered weapons and occasional helms, trampled tents and scattered gear, but little more than that. The only bodies that remained were those of soldiers that Nighteyes and I had killed. The dragons had no interest in dead meat; they fed on the life that fled such tissue.

I found the stream I had recalled and threw myself flat by it to drink as if my thirst had no bottom. Nighteyes lapped beside me, then flung himself to the cool grass by the stream. He began a slow, careful licking of a slash on his forepaw. It had parted his hide, and he pressed his tongue into that gap, cleaning it carefully. It would heal as a fusing of dark hairless skin. *Just another scar*, he dismissed my thought. *What shall we do now?*

I was carefully peeling my shirt off. Drying blood made it cling to my injuries. I set my teeth and jerked it loose. I leaned over the stream, to splash cold water up onto the sword cuts I had taken. Just a few more scars, I told myself glumly. And what shall we do now? *Sleep.*

The only thing that would sound better than that would be eating.

'I've no stomach to kill anything else right now,' I told him.

That's the trouble with killing humans. All that work, and nothing to eat for it.

I heaved myself wearily to my feet. 'Let's go look through their tents. I need something to use for bandaging. And they must have some food stores.'

I left my old shirt where it had fallen. I'd find another. Right now, even its weight seemed too much to bother carrying. I probably would have dropped Verity's sword, except that I had already sheathed it. Drawing it again would have been too much trouble. I was suddenly that tired.

The tents had been trampled flat in the dragons' hunting. One had collapsed into a cook fire and was smouldering. I dragged it away and trampled it out. Then the wolf and I began systematically to salvage what we would need. His nose quickly found their food supplies. There was some dried meat, but it was mostly travel bread. We were too famished to be fussy. I had gone so long without bread of any kind that it tasted almost good. I even found a skin of wine, but one taste persuaded me to use it to wash my injuries instead. I bound my wounds in brown cambric from a Farrowman's shirt. I still had some wine left. I tasted it again. Then I tried to persuade Nighteyes to let me wash his injuries, but he refused, saying they already hurt enough.

I was starting to stiffen, but I forced myself to my feet. I found a soldier's pack and discarded from it all things useless to me. I rolled up two blankets and tied them snugly, and found a gold and brown cloak to wear against chilly evenings. I rummaged up more bread and put it in the pack.

What are you doing? Nighteyes was drowsing, nearly asleep.

I don't want to sleep here tonight. So I gather what I will need for our journey.

Journey? Where are we going?

I stood still for a moment. Back to Molly and Buck? No. Never again. Jhaampe? Why? Why travel that long and wearisome black road again? I could think of no good reasons. *Well, I still don't want to sleep here tonight. I'd like to be well away from that pillar before I rest again.*

Very well. Then, What was that?

We froze as we stood, every sense prickling. 'Let's go and find out,' I suggested quietly.

Afternoon was venturing into evening, and the shadows under the trees were deepening. What we had heard was a sound that didn't belong amongst the creakings of the frogs and insects and the fading calls of the day birds. It had come from the place of battle.

We found Will on his belly, dragging himself toward the pillar. Rather, he had been dragging himself. When we found him, he was still. One of his legs was gone, severed away jaggedly. Bone thrust out of the torn flesh. He had bound a sleeve about the stump, but not tightly enough. Blood still leaked from it. Night-eyes bared his teeth as I stooped to touch him. He lived, but barely. No doubt he had hoped to reach the pillar and slip through to find others of Regal's men to aid him. Regal must have known he still lived, but he had sent no one back for him. He had not even the decency to be loyal to a man who had served him that long.

I loosed the sleeve, and bound it more tightly. Then I lifted his head, and dribbled a little water into his mouth.

Why do you bother? Nighteyes asked. *We hate him, and he's nearly dead. Let him die.*

Not yet. Not just yet.

'Will? Can you hear me, Will?'

The only sign was a change in his breathing. I gave him a bit more water. He breathed some in, gasped, then swallowed the next mouthful. He took a deeper breath, and sighed it out.

I opened myself and gathered Skill.

My brother, leave this. Let him die. This is the doing of carrion birds, to peck at a dying thing.

'It's not Will I'm after, Nighteyes. This may be the last chance I'll ever get at Regal. I'm going to take it.'

He made no reply, but lay down on the ground beside me. He watched as I drew still more Skill into myself. How much, I wondered, did it take to kill? Could I summon enough?

Will was so weak I almost felt shamed. I thrust past his defences as easily as one would push aside a sick child's hands. It was not just the loss of blood and the pain. It was Burl's death, following so close on Carrod's. And it was the shock of Regal's abandonment. His own loyalty to Regal had been Skill-imprinted on him. He could not grasp that Regal had felt no real bond with him. It shamed him that I could see that in him. *Kill me now, Bastard. Go ahead. I'm dying anyway.*

It's not about you, Will. It was never about you. I saw that clearly now. I groped inside him as if I were probing a wound for an arrowhead. He struggled feebly against my invasion, but I ignored that. I shuffled through his memories, but found little that was useful. Yes, Regal had coteries, but they were young and green, little more than groups of men with potential for the Skill. Even the ones I had seen at the quarry were uncertain. Regal wanted him to make large coteries, so they could pool more power. Regal did not understand that closeness could not be forced, nor shared by that many. He had lost four young Skill-users on the Skill road. They were not dead, but vacant-eyed and vague. Another two had come through the pillars with him, but had lost all ability to Skill afterwards. Coteries were not so easily made.

I went deeper and Will threatened to die on me but I linked with him, and forced strength into him. *You won't die. Not yet,* I told him fiercely. And there, deep within him, my probing finally found what I sought. A Skill-link to Regal. It was tenuous and faint; Regal had abandoned him, done all he could to leave Will behind. But it was as I had suspected. They had been linked too strongly for too long for the bond to be easily dissolved.

I gathered my Skill, centred myself and sealed myself. I poised myself, and then I leaped. As when a sudden rain gathers and fills a stream bed that has been dry all summer, so I flowed through that Skill-link between Will and Regal. At the last possible moment, I held myself back. I seeped into Regal's mind like slow poison, listening with his ears, seeing with his eyes. I knew him.

He slept. No. He almost slept, his lungs thick with Smoke, his mouth numb from brandy. I drifted into his dreams. The bed was soft beneath him, the coverlets warm over him. This last falling fit had been a bad one, a very bad one. It was disgusting, to fall and twitch like the Bastard Fitz. Not proper for this to happen to a king. Stupid healers. They could not even say what had brought these fits on. What would people think of him? The tailor and his apprentice had seen, now he would have to kill them. No one must know. They would laugh at him. The healer had said he was better, last week. Well, he would find a new healer, and hang the old healer tomorrow. No. He would give him to the Forged ones in the King's Circle, they were very hungry now. And then let the big cats out with the Forged ones. And the bull, the big white one with the sweeping horns and the hump.

He tried to smile and tell himself it would be amusing, to tell himself that tomorrow would bring him pleasure. The room was thick with the cloying odour of Smoke, but even it could scarcely soothe him. All had been going so well, so very very well. And then the Bastard had ruined it all. He had killed Burl, and wakened the dragons and sent them to Verity.

Verity, Verity, it was always Verity. Ever since he'd been born. Verity and Chivalry got tall horses, while he was kept to a pony. Verity and Chivalry got real swords, but he must practise with wood. Verity and Chivalry, always together, always older, always bigger. Always thinking they were better, even though he came of finer blood than they, and by right should have inherited the throne. His mother had warned him of their jealousy of him. His mother had bid him always be careful, and more than careful. They would kill him if they could, they would, they would. Mother had done her best, she had seen them sent away as much as she could. But even sent away, they might come back. No. There was only one way to be safe, only one way.

Well, he would win tomorrow. He had coteries, did he not? Coteries of fine strong young men, coteries to make dragons for him, and him alone. The coteries were bound to him and the dragons would be bound to him. And he would make more coteries and more dragons, and more, until he had far more than Verity. Except Will had been teaching the coteries for him, and now Will was useless. Broken like a toy, the dragon bit his leg off when he flung him in the air, and Will had landed in a tree like a kite with no wind. It was disgusting. A man with one leg. He couldn't stand broken things. His blind eye had been bad enough, but to lose a leg, too? What would men think of a king who kept a crippled servant? His mother had never trusted cripples. They are jealous, she had warned him, always jealous, and they will turn on you. But Will he had needed for the coteries. Stupid Will. It was all Will's fault. But Will was the one who knew how to wake Skill in people and form them into coteries. So maybe he should send someone back for Will. If Will still lived.

Will? Regal Skilled tentatively toward us.

Not exactly. I closed my Skill around him. It was ridiculously easy, like picking up a sleeping hen from its perch.

Let me go! Let me go!

I felt him reaching for his other coteries. I slapped them away from him, closed him off from their Skilling. He had no strength, he had never had any real Skill-strength. It had all been the coterie's power that he had puppeteered. It shocked me. All the fear I had borne inside me, over a year's time now. Of what? Of a whining, spoiled child who schemed to take his older brothers' toys. The crown and the throne were no more to him than their horses and swords had been. He had no concept of governing a kingdom; only of wearing a crown and doing what he wished. First his mother and then Galen had done his scheming for him. He had learned from them only a sly cunning as to how to get his way. If Galen had not bound the coterie to him, he would never have wielded any true power. Stripped of his coterie, I saw him as he was: a cosseted child with a penchant for cruelty that had never been denied.

This is what we have feared and fled? This?

Nighteyes, what do you here?

Your kill is my kill, my brother. I would see what meat we have come so far to take.

Regal squirmed and thrashed, literally sickened by the Wit-touch of the wolf against his mind. It was unclean and disgusting, a dirty doggy thing, nasty and smelly, as bad as that rat creature that scuttled in his rooms at night and could not be caught.

Nighteyes leaned closer, pressed the Wit against him as if he could smell him all that way away. Regal retched and shuddered.

Enough, I told Nighteyes, and the wolf relented.

If you are going to kill him, do it soon, Nighteyes advised. *The other one weakens and will die if you do not hurry.*

He was right. Will's breath had gone shallow and rapid. I gripped Regal firmly, then fed more strength into Will. He tried not to take it, but his self-mastery was not that strong. Given a chance, the body will always choose to live. And so his lungs steadied and his heart beat more strongly. Once more I drew Skill into myself. I centred myself in it and honed its purpose. I turned my attention back to Regal.

If you kill me, you will burn yourself. You will lose your own Skill if you kill me with it.

I had thought of that. I had never much enjoyed being Skilled. I would rather far be Witted than Skilled. It would be no loss.

I forced myself to recall Galen. I called to mind the fanatical coterie he had created for Regal. It gave shape to my purpose.

As I had longed to do for so long, I loosed my Skill upon him.

Afterwards, there was little left of Will. But I sat by him, and gave him water when he asked for it. I even covered him when he complained faintly of cold. It puzzled the wolf, my death-watch. A knife across his throat would have been so much faster for both of us. Kinder, perhaps. But I had decided I was no longer an assassin. So I waited for his last breath, and when he sighed it out, I stood up and walked away.

It is a long way from the Mountain Kingdom to the coast of Buck. Even as the dragon flies, tirelessly and swift, it is a long, long way. For a few days, Nighteyes and I knew peace. We travelled far from the empty Stone Garden, far from the black Skill road. We were both too stiff to hunt well, but we had found a good trout stream and we followed it. The days were almost too warm, the nights clear and kind. We fished, we ate, we slept. I thought only of things that did not hurt. Not of Molly in Burrich's embrace, but of Nettle sheltered by his good right arm. He would be a good father to her. He had had practice. I even found it in me to hope that she might have younger brothers and sisters in years to come. I thought of peace returning to the Mountain Kingdom, of Red Ships driven from the coast of the Six Duchies. I healed. Not completely. A scar is never the same as good flesh, but it stops the bleeding.

I was there on the summer afternoon when Verity-as-Dragon appeared in the skies over Buckkeep. With him, I saw the shining black towers and turrets of Buckkeep Castle far below us. Beyond the castle, where Buckkeep Town had been, were the blackened shells of buildings and warehouses. Forged ones ambled through the streets, pushed aside by swaggering Raiders. Masts with tatters of canvas dangling from them thrust up through the calm waters. A dozen Red Ships rocked peacefully in the harbour. I felt the heart of Verity-as-Dragon swell with anger. I swear I heard Kettricken's cry of anguish at the sight.

Then the great turquoise and silver dragon was alighting in the centre grounds of Buckkeep Castle. He ignored the flight of arrows that rose to meet him, ignored, too, the cries of the soldiers who cowered before him, senseless as his shadow spread over them and his great wings beat to lower his bulk to the ground. It was a wonder he did not crush them. Even as he was alighting, Kettricken was trying to stand up upon his shoulders, crying to the guard to lower their pikes and stand away.

On the ground, he dipped his shoulder to let a dishevelled Queen Kettricken dismount. Starling Birdsong slid down behind her and distinguished herself by bowing to the line of pikes that were pointed at them. I saw not a few faces I recognized, and shared Verity's pain at how privation had transformed them. Then Patience came forth, pike gripped tightly, helm askew upon her bundled hair. She pushed through the awe-stricken guards, her hazel eyes flinty in a pinched face. At the sight of the dragon, she halted. Her gaze went from the Queen to the dragon's dark eyes. She took a breath, caught it, then breathed the word. 'Elderling.' Then she threw both helm and pike into the air with a whoop, and rushed forward to embrace Kettricken, crying, 'An Elderling! I knew it, I knew it, I knew they would come back!'

She spun on her heel, issuing a flurry of orders that included everything from a hot bath for the Queen to readying a charge from the gates of Buckkeep Castle. But what I will always hold in my heart is the moment when she turned back, to stamp her foot at Verity-as-Dragon and tell him to hurry up and get those damned ships out of her harbour.

The Lady Patience of Buckkeep had become used to being obeyed swiftly.

Verity rose and went to the battle as he always had. Alone. Finally, he had his wish, to confront his enemies, not with the Skill, but in the flesh. On his very first pass, a slash of his tail shattered two of their ships. He intended that none should escape him. It was but hours later that the Fool and Girl on a Dragon and their followers arrived to join him, but by then not a Red Ship remained in Buck Harbour. They joined him in his hunting through the steep streets of what had been Buckkeep Town. It was not yet evening when the streets were empty of Raiders. Those who had sheltered in the castle poured back into the town, to weep at the wreckage, it is true, but also to come near and wonder at the Elderlings who had returned to save them. Despite the number of dragons who came, Verity was the dragon that the folk of Buck would remember clearest. Not that folk remember anything too clearly when dragons are flying overhead, casting their shadows below. Still, he is the dragon one sees on all the tapestries of the Cleansing of Buck.

It was a summer of dragons for the Coastal Duchies. I saw it all, or as much as would fit into my sleeping hours. Even awake, I was aware of it, like thunder more felt than heard from the distance. I knew when Verity led the dragons northward, to purge all Buck and Bearns and even the Near Islands of Red Ships and Raiders. I saw the scouring of Ripple Keep, and the return of Faith, Duchess of Bearns, to her proper keep. Girl on a Dragon and the Fool flew south along the coast of Rippon and Shoaks, rooting Raiders out from their strongholds on the islands as well. How Verity conveyed to them that they must feed only on the Raiders, I do not know, but that line was held. The folk of the Six Duchies feared them not. Children ran out from huts and cottages, to point overhead at the jewelled passing of the creatures. When the dragons slept, temporarily satiated, on the beaches and in the pastures, the people came out to walk among them fearlessly, to touch with their own hands these jewel-glittering creatures. And everywhere the Raiders had established strongholds, the dragons fed well.

The summer died slowly, and autumn came to shorten the days and promise storms to come. As the wolf and I gave thought to shelter for the winter, I had dreams of dragons flying over shores I had never seen before. Water churned cold against those harsh shores, and ice encroached on the edges of their narrow bays. The Out Islands, I surmised. Verity had always longed to bring the war to their shores, and did so with a vengeance. And that, too, was as it had been in King Wisdom's time.

It was winter and snows had come to the higher reaches of the Mountains but not to the valley where the hot springs steamed in the chill air when the dragons last passed over my head. I came to the door of my hut to watch them pass, flying in great formations like migrating geese. Nighteyes turned his head to their strange calls, and sent up a howl of his own in answer. As they swept over me, the world blinked around me and I lost all but the vaguest memory of it. I could not tell you if Verity led their flight, or even if Girl on a Dragon was among them. I only knew that peace had been restored to the Six Duchies and that no Red Ships would venture near our shores again. I hoped they would all sleep well in the Stone Garden as they had before. I went back into the hut to turn the rabbit on the cooking spit. I looked forward to a long quiet winter.

So the promised aid of the Elderlings was brought to the Six Duchies. They came, just as they had in King Wisdom's time, and drove the Red Ships from the shores of the Six Duchies. Two great sailed White Ships were sunk as well in that great cleansing. And just as in King Wisdom's time, their outstretched shadows on the folk below stole moments of life and memory as they passed. All the myriad shapes and colours of the dragons made their way into the scrolls and tapestries of that time, just as they had before. And folk filled in what they could not remember of the battles when dragons filled the sky overhead, with guesses and fancies. Minstrels made songs of it. All the songs say that Verity came home himself upon the turquoise dragon, and rode the beast into the battle against the Red Ships. And the best songs say that when the fighting was over, Verity was carried off by the Elderlings, to feast with them in great honour and then sleep beside them in their magic castle until such time as Buck shall need to call on him again. So the truth became, as Starling had told me, something bigger than the facts. It was, after all, a time for heroes and all sorts of marvellous things to occur.

As when Regal himself came riding, at the head of a column of six thousand Farrow men, to bring aid and supplies, not just to Buck, but to all the Coastal Duchies. The news of his return had preceded him, as had the barges of livestock, grain and treasures from Tradeford Hall itself that came in a steady stream down the Buck River. All spoke in wonder, of how the prince had started up from a dream, and run half-dressed through the halls of Tradeford, miraculously foretelling the return of King Verity to Buckkeep and the summoning of the Elderlings to save the Six Duchies. Birds were sent, withdrawing all troops from the Mountains and offering his most humble apologies and generous monetary reparation to King Eyod. He summoned his nobles, to foretell to them that Queen Kettricken would bear Verity's child, and that he, Regal, wished to be first to pledge fealty to the next Farseer monarch. In honour of the day, he had ordered all gallows pulled down and burned, all prisoners pardoned and freed, and the King's Circle was to be renamed the Queen's Garden, and planted with trees and flowers from all six of the duchies as a symbol of new unity. When, later that day, the Red Ships attacked the outskirts of Tradeford, Regal himself called for his horse and armour, and rode to lead the defence of his folk. Side by side he fought, next to merchants and longshoremen, nobles and beggars. He gained in that battle the love of the common folk of Tradeford. When he announced his allegiance must always be to the child Queen Kettricken carried, they joined their vows to his.

When he reached Buckkeep, it is said he remained on his knees and robed only in sackcloth at the gate of Buckkeep Castle for some days until the Queen herself deigned to come forth and accept his most abject apologies for ever doubting her honour. Into her hands he returned both the crown of the Six Duchies, and the simpler band of the King-in-Waiting. He no longer wished, he told her, to hold any higher title than uncle to his monarch. The Queen's paleness and silence at his words were put down to the uneasy stomach her pregnancy gave her. To Lord Chade, the Queen's advisor, he returned all the scrolls and books of Skillmaster Solicity, with the plea that he guard them well, for there was much in them that could be turned to evil in the wrong hands. He had lands and a title he wished to confer on the Fool, as soon as he returned from his warrioring to Buckkeep. And to his dear, dear sister-in-law Lady Patience, he returned the rubies that Chivalry had given her, for they could never grace any neck as finely as they did her own.

I had considered having him erect a statue in my memory, but had decided that would be going too far. The fanatical loyalty I had imprinted on him would be my best memorial. While Regal lived, Queen Kettricken and her child would have no more loyal subject.

Ultimately, of course, that was not long. All have heard of the tragic and bizarre death of Prince Regal. The rabid creature that savaged him in his bed one night left bloody tracks, not just on his bed-clothes, but all about the bedchamber, as if it had exulted in its deed. Gossip had it that it was an extremely large river rat that had somehow journeyed with him all the way from Tradeford. It was most disturbing to all the folk in the Keep. The Queen had the rat-dogs brought in, to scour every chamber, but to no avail. The beast was never captured or killed, though rumours of sightings of the immense rat were rampant among the keep servants. Some say that that was why, for months afterwards, Lord Chade was seldom seen without his pet ferret.

FORTY-ONE

The Scribe

*If the truth be known, Forging was not an invention of the Red Ships.
We had taught it well to them, back in the days of King Wisdom. The
Elderlings that took our revenge on the Out Islands soared many
times over that country of islands. Many Outislanders were devoured
outright, but many others were overflown by dragons so often that
they were stripped of their memories and feelings. They became callous
strangers to their own kin. That was the grievance that had rankled
so amongst that long-memoried folk. When the Red Ships sailed, it
was not to claim Six Duchies territory or wealth. It was for revenge.
To do to us as so long ago we had done to them, in the days of their
great, great grandmothers.*

*What one folk know, another may discover. They had scholars and
wise folk of their own, despite Six Duchies disdain of them as barbarians. So it was that mention of dragons was studied by them, in
every ancient scroll they could find. While it would be difficult to find
absolute proof, it seems to me that some copies of scrolls collected by
the Skillmasters of Buck might actually have been sold, in the days
before the Red Ships menaced our coasts, to Outislander traders who
paid well for such things. And when the slow movement of glaciers
bared, on their own shores, a dragon carved of black stone and outcrop-
pings of more of that black stone, their wise men combined their
knowledge with the insatiable lust for vengeance of one Kebal Rawbread. They resolved to create dragons of their own, and visit upon
the Six Duchies the same savage destruction we had once served upon
them.*

*Only one White Ship was driven ashore by the Elderlings when they
cleansed Buck. The dragons devoured all her crew, down to the last
man. In her hold were found only great blocks of shining black stone.
Locked within them, I believe, were the stolen lives and feelings of the*

832

*folk of the Six Duchies who had been Forged. Their studies had led
the Outislander scholars to believe that stone sufficiently imbued with
life-force could be fashioned into dragons to serve the Outislanders. It
is chilling to think how close they came to discovering the complete
truth of creating a dragon.*

*Circles and circles, as the Fool once told me. The Outislanders
raided our shore, so King Wisdom brought the Elderlings to drive them
back. And the Elderlings Forged the Outislanders with Skill when
they flew over their huts so frequently. Generations later, they came
to raid our shores and Forge our folk. So King Verity went to
wake the Elderlings, and the Elderlings drove them back. And
Forged them in the process. I wonder if once more the hate will fester
until . . .*

I sigh and set my quill aside. I have written too much. Not all
things need to be told. Not all things should be told. I take up
the scroll and make my slow way to the hearth. My legs are
cramped from sitting on them. It is a cold damp day, and the fog
off the ocean has found every old injury on my body and awakened
it. The arrow wound is still worst. When cold tightens that scar,
I feel its pull on every part of my body. I throw the vellum onto
the coals. I have to step over Nighteyes to do it. His muzzle is
greying now and his bones do not like this weather any more
than mine do.

*You are getting fat. All you do any more is lie by the hearth and
bake your brains. Why don't you go hunting?*

He stretches and sighs. *Go bother the boy instead of me. The fire
needs more wood.*

But before I can call him, my boy comes into the room. He
wrinkles his nose at the smell of burning vellum and gives me a
scathing look. 'You should have just asked me to bring more
wood. Do you know how much good vellum costs?'

I make no reply, and he just sighs and shakes his head over
me. He goes out to replenish the wood supply.

He is a gift from Starling. I have had him for two years now,
and I am still not used to him. I do not believe I was ever a boy
such as he is. I recall the day she brought him to me, and I have

to smile. She had come, as she does, some twice or thrice a year, to visit me and chide me for my hermit ways. But that time she had brought the boy to me. He had sat outside on a skinny pony while she pounded on my door. When I opened to her, she had immediately turned and called to him, 'Get down and come inside. It's warm here.'

He had slid from the pony's bare back and then stood by him, shivering, as he stared at me. His black hair blew across his face. He clutched an old cloak of Starling's about his narrow shoulders.

'I've brought you a boy,' Starling announced, and grinned at me.

I met her gaze incredulously. 'Do you mean . . . he is mine?'

She shrugged at me. 'If you'll have him. I thought he might do you good.' She paused. 'Actually, I thought you might do him good. With clothing and regular meals and such. I've cared for him as long as I can, but a minstrel's life . . .' She let her words trail off.

'Then he is . . . Did you, did we . . .' I floundered my way through the words, denying my hope. 'He is your son? Mine?'

Her grin had widened at that, even as her eyes had softened in sympathy. She shook her head. 'Mine? No. Yours? I suppose it's possible. Did you pass through Flounder Cove about eight years ago? That's where I found him six months ago. He was eating rotten vegetables from a village midden heap. His mother is dead, and his eyes don't match, so her sister wouldn't have him. She says he's a demon-gotten bastard.' She cocked her head at me and smiled as she added, 'So I suppose he might be yours.' She turned back to him again and raised her voice. 'Come inside, I tell you. It's warm. And a real wolf lives with him. You'll like Nighteyes.'

Hap is a strange boy, one brown eye and one blue. His mother had not been merciful, and his early memories are not gentle ones. She had named him Mishap. Perhaps, to her, he was. I find I call him 'boy' as often as not. He does not seem to mind. I have taught him his letters and his numbers and the growing and harvesting of herbs. He was seven when she brought him to me.

Now he is nearly ten. He is good with a bow. Nighteyes approves of him. He hunts well for the old wolf.

When Starling comes, she brings me news. I do not know that I always welcome it. Too many things have changed, too much is strange. Lady Patience rules at Tradeford. Their hemp fields yield fully as much paper now as they do fine rope. The size of the gardens there has doubled. The structure that would have been the King's Circle is now a botanical garden of plants gathered from every corner of the Six Duchies and beyond.

Burrich and Molly and their children are well. They have Nettle and little Chivalry and another on the way. Molly tends her hives and candle shop, while Burrich has used stud fees from Reddy and Reddy's colt to begin to breed horses again. Starling knows these things, for it was she who tracked them down and saw to it that Reddy, and Sooty's colt were given over to him. Poor old Sooty was too old to survive the journey home from the Mountains. Molly and Burrich both believe I am many years dead. Sometimes I believe that, too. I have never asked her where they live. I have never seen any of the children. In that, I am truly my father's son.

Kettricken bore a son, Prince Dutiful. Starling told me he has his father's colouring, but looks as if he will be a tall slender man, like Kettricken's brother Rurisk, perhaps. She thinks he is more serious than a boy should be, but all of his tutors are fond of him. His grandfather journeyed all the way from the Mountain Kingdom to see the lad who will someday rule both lands. He was well pleased with the child. I wondered what his other grandfather would have thought of all that had come to pass from his treaty-making.

Chade no longer lives in the shadows, but is the honoured advisor to the Queen. According to Starling, he is a foppish old man who is entirely too fond of the company of young women. But she smiles as she says it, and 'Chade Fallstar's Reckoning' will be the song she is remembered for when she is gone. I am sure he knows where I am, but he has never sought me out. It is as well. Sometimes, when Starling comes, she brings me curious old scrolls, and seeds and roots for strange herbs. At other times she brings me fine paper and clear vellum. I do not need to ask the source. Occasionally, I give her in return scrolls of my own writing; drawings of herbs, with their virtues and dangers; an account of my time in that ancient city; records of my journeys through Chalced and the lands beyond. She bears them dutifully away.

Once it was a map of the Six Duchies that she brought to me from him. It was carefully begun in Verity's hand and inks, but never completed. Sometimes I look at it and think of the places I could fill in upon it. But I have hung it as it is upon my wall. I do not think I will ever change it.

As for the Fool, he returned to Buckkeep Castle. Briefly. Girl on a Dragon left him there, and he wept as she rose without him. He was immediately acclaimed as a hero and a great warrior. I am sure that is why he fled. He accepted neither title nor land from Regal. No one is quite sure where the Fool went or what became of him after that. Starling believes he returned to his homeland. Perhaps. Perhaps, somewhere there is a toymaker who makes puppets that are a delight and a marvel. I hope he wears an earring of silver and blue. The fingerprints he left on my wrist have faded to a dusky grey.

I think I will always miss him.

I was six years in finding my way back to Buck. One we spent in the Mountains. One was spent with Black Rolf. Nighteyes and I learned much of our own kind in our seasons there, but discovered we like our own company best. Despite Holly's best effort, Ollie's girl looked at me and decided I would most definitely not do. My feelings were not injured in the least and it provided an excuse to move on again.

We have been north to the Near Islands, where the wolves are as white as the bears. We have been south to Chalced, and even beyond Bingtown. We have walked up the banks of the Rain River and ridden a raft back down. We have discovered that Nighteyes does not like travelling by ship, and I do not like lands that have no winters. We have walked beyond the edges of Verity's maps.

I had thought I would never return to Buck again. But we did. The autumn winds brought us here one year, and we have not left since. The cottage we claimed as ours once belonged to a charcoal burner. It is not far from Forge, or rather where Forge used to be. The sea and the winters have devoured that town and drowned the evil memories of it. Someday, perhaps, men will come again to seek the rich iron ore. But not soon.

When Starling comes, she chides me, and tells me I am a young man yet. What, she demands of me, became of all my insistence that one day I would have a life of my own? I tell her I have found it. Here, in my cottage, with my writing and my wolf and my boy. Sometimes, when she beds with me and I lie awake afterwards listening to her slow breathing, I think I will rise on the morrow and find some new meaning to my life. But most mornings, when I awake aching and stiff, I think I am not a young man at all. I am an old man, trapped in a young man's scarred body.

The Skill does not sleep easily in me. In summers especially, when I walk along the sea-cliffs and look out over the water, I am tempted to reach forth as Verity once did. And sometimes I do, and I know for a time, of the fisherwoman's catch, or the domestic worries of the mate of the passing merchant ship. The torment of it, as Verity once told me, is that no one ever reaches back. Once, when the Skill-hunger was on me to the point of madness, I even reached for Verity-as-Dragon, imploring him to hear me and answer.

He did not.

Regal's coteries long ago disbanded for lack of a Skillmaster to teach them. Even on the nights when I Skill out in despair as lonely as a wolf's howling, begging anyone, anyone to respond, I feel nothing. Not even an echo. Then I sit by my window and look out through the mists past the tip of Antler Island. I grip my hands to keep them from trembling and I refuse to plunge myself whole into the Skill river that is waiting, always waiting to sweep me away. It would be so easy. Sometimes all that holds me back is the touch of a wolf's mind against mine.

My boy has learned what that look means, and he measures the elfbark carefully to deaden me. Carryme he adds that I may sleep, and ginger to mask the elfbark's bitterness. Then he brings me paper and quill and ink and leaves me to my writing. He knows that when morning comes, he will find me, head on my desk, sleeping amidst my scattered papers, Nighteyes sprawled at my feet.

We dream of carving our dragon.